THE SPHINX'S HEART

THE SPHINX'S HEART

RISE OF THE GRIGORI BOOK 2

TALENA WINTERS

MY SECRET WISH
PUBLISHING

Published by My Secret Wish Publishing
www.mysecretwishpublishing.com

The Sphinx's Heart

Contact the author at www.talenawinters.com.

Summary: Calandra has failed, and her island nation of the undines has been plunged into chaos and rebellion. Humanity's oldest enemy is loose and trying to free the rest of his kind from Tartarus, assisted by an evil, power-hungry Order. And Calandra's brother, Zale, has inexplicably turned against her. With the threat of Madness growing ever stronger, can Calandra undo a mistake that has plagued the undines for millennia . . . before the entire world pays the price?

ISBN (hardcover): 978-1-989800-05-8
ISBN (paperback): 978-1-989800-04-1
ISBN (ebook): 978-1-989800-03-4

Cover design by Patrick Knowles www.patrickknowlesdesign.com
Edited by Ellen Forget www.ellenmichelle.com; Denise Willson https://beop.ca/
Author Photo © Amanda Monette. Used by permission.
Printed in the United States of America, or the country of purchase.

This volume contains excerpts of lyrics from "Amazing Grace" by John Newton and "A Mighty Fortress is Our God" by Martin Luther, translated by Frederick H. Hedge. Both songs are in the public domain.

To Jason.
You are the wind beneath my wings.

Sirenia
Trinity
Silkie Lake
Pearl Bay
Perrynea Ridge
Shield of Atargatis
Margaret's House
Dragontooth Mountains
Elpida
Perrynea
Light Lake
Mermaid Rock
Light River
Opal Palace

N
To Atlantis
Greenside
Serenity
Nixie Lake
Hope
River
Haven
Katica
Clearbridge
Fire
Mountains
Fire River
Persephone's
Cauldron
Dolphin
Cove
Nadia's
Ruin
Mistwood
Mistolt
Potnia
Mitera
Mist Lake
Melissa
Valerian
Opal Lake
dise
ley
apolis
Irene Plains
Irene River

PROLOGUE

CALANDRA DISTINCTLY REMEMBERED THE DAY she'd learned she was most likely destined for Madness. She'd been seven, a second-year novice, and she and her classmates at the Royal Academy were sitting in a circle on the flagstones in the Grotto atrium of the Opal Palace for history class. Calandra wanted to go sit on the edge of the fountain of Atargatis and change to *ichthys* state, like the erect statue of the Mother in its centre, letting her banded blue-green fish-like tail dangle in the cool water— but she'd already asked, and Daskala Medea had said no. That didn't stop Calandra from daydreaming about it.

The *daskala*—a young woman with bright green eyes and a bright smile in her round brown face who'd just recently graduated from the Academy herself—leaned forward, trying to meet the eyes of each pupil in turn as she told them the story of Nadia kor'Hera, the Mad Queen who'd sunk Atlantis.

"Panaceas are extremely rare," Daskala Medea said, "and Nadia was the most powerful one of all. They say she could move the earth without even touching it. She could make water dance like no one had ever seen. She could even control the wind. Unfortunately, when she went Mad, her great power was her downfall, and everyone on Atlantis, especially the humans, paid the price."

Calandra's hand shot up in the air.

"Yes, Calandra?" the *daskala* said with a long-suffering air. Calandra had already asked quite a few questions that day.

"Panaceas use all the elements, right?"

Daskala Medea shook her head. "No, not fire. No one can use that.

Some of them use air, though. Really powerful ones like Nadia." She grinned and winked at Calandra. "You might be that powerful someday."

Calandra pondered this, wrapping her hand in one of her long wavy honey-coloured pigtails. She hadn't managed to use air yet, though she kept trying and she thought she was close. But Daskala Thea had told her several times how she would most likely be as powerful a panacea as her mother, and even more powerful than she herself was. Already, while most of her classmates wouldn't specialize into healers or sirens for another four years, Calandra's stone healing came as naturally as breathing, her plant healing ability surpassed many adepts', and she'd made significant progress as a physic.

She raised her hand again.

The *daskala*'s smile became a bit forced.

"Yes, Calandra?"

"Why didn't everyone just leave Atlantis and move over to Sirenia? The undines could have helped the humans, and—"

"I'm sure they tried, dear, and obviously some succeeded, or we wouldn't be here."

The *daskala* looked around the circle for other hands, but Calandra raised her hand again, jabbing it toward the arched marble ceiling until the *daskala* pursed her lips and acknowledged her once more.

"But *why* did Nadia go Mad?" she asked.

The *daskala* sighed, the cowrie shells woven into her long black braids clicking with the movement. "No one knows. But after the Sinking, she was condemned to the Abyss, and her consort, Alessandro, was never heard from again. Her daughter Melissa was left to carry the Atargasian undines through the greatest tragedy in our history. Under her guidance, we thrived and grew strong once more. Now, does anyone *else* have a question?"

Calandra's cousin Narcissa, who sat several girls over in the circle from Calandra, raised her hand. Her pale blond hair was arranged in neat braids pinned up on her head, and her short sapphire-coloured chiton was made of the finest silk, the hems embroidered with gold thread and pearls. Her icy green eyes were narrowed and calculating, and a pit formed in Calandra's stomach.

Tiny bubbles of surprise at the princess's atypical participation floated from Daskala Medea into Calandra's spirit. "Yes, your highness?"

Narcissa gave Calandra a sly look before asking, "Isn't it true that *all* panaceas go Mad?"

The *daskala* drew in a breath, her discomfort hitting Calandra like sprayed sand. She glanced at Calandra and slowly nodded her head.

"Unfortunately, most of them have, yes. Daskala Thea is the only exception I know of."

Narcissa smiled smugly, and Calandra shrank into herself. Her mother had gone Mad—everyone said so. That's why Mother had left, so her powers wouldn't hurt anyone. But it wasn't until that moment Calandra realized the same thing was likely to happen to her.

That was eleven years ago, and much had changed since then—she'd become a panacea to rival Nadia in strength, or so everyone kept saying. She'd tried—and failed—to heal the Heartstone, the Light of Atargatis, and it had nearly been snuffed out as a result. She'd been trained by a dream spirit named Damon who claimed to also be Alessandro, Nadia's long-dead consort, and he'd almost ruined her. She had started a revolution, exiled the man she loved, and discovered she had a brother—the first undine male to be born in over three thousand years.

She'd even found the reason why healers like her went Mad. But she had no way to stop it.

And her Madness had already begun.

1

SHIPWRECKED

Bridgetown, Barbados
July 11, AD 1799/8 Dumuzid 4155 EK

ROBERT COX PULLED HIS WIDE-BRIMMED straw hat low over his eyes and kept his chin low, trying to remain unnoticed as he loped along the crowded, dusty street. Avoiding notice was something he was quite used to; since the accident five years before that had left half his face puckered with scars, he'd become an expert at becoming invisible. Back in England, it had been easier—the cooler weather had allowed for collars and coats that the sweltering heat of Barbados in July made unfathomable. Still, seeing gentlemen walk the narrow streets of Bridgetown in the tall collars and long sideburns that were so in fashion was not uncommon, so most of the passersby barely gave him a second glance, even if the hair combed low over his scars was the colour of flame.

Ahead of him, his quarry rounded a corner, and he sped his pace to catch up before he lost her. The street was crowded with black slaves and white workers driving donkey carts loaded with enormous rum puncheons, bags of sugar, or bales of cotton on the way to the wharf. Dodging gentlemen and ladies about their business at the shops that crowded the edges of the street, he reached the corner just in time to see the gold-tipped dark brown spiral curls of the object of his pursuit disappear into a coffee shop with a purr of tawny silk.

Robert stopped and waited, crossing his arms when she did not immediately re-emerge. He frowned. That shop didn't allow coloureds. How had she not been thrown out immediately?

He sighed. Why was he still surprised at anything Miss Abela Bethel could accomplish?

This morning when he'd gone down to breakfast in the common room of the Port House Inn, he'd insisted to his companions once more that he was fully ready to take a stroll down to the quay alone. However, it had been to his utter shock that both Reverend Berian and Miss Bethel had agreed, letting him go on his solemn oath that he was feeling in quite good spirits and would attempt nothing untoward. As irritating as it was to have self-appointed guardians shadowing his every move since they'd arrived here, given the physical and emotional malaise he'd been plagued with, he could hardly blame them. But after three weeks, nearly half of them bed-ridden, he was ready to stretch his legs on his own—and do a little investigating as to the potential fates of the crew and cargo of the *Atlanta*. He couldn't believe that the three of them had been the only survivors out of several hundred. He *daren't* believe it, or the black pit that had nearly swallowed him while on board and several times since would be impossible to resist.

Please, God, if you have any mercy, grant me some small absolution.

But his queries of both the harbour master and at the local slave agencies had availed nothing. He'd been returning to the inn, fighting the gravity of the pit, when he'd seen Miss Bethel hurrying away from their residence along the covered sidewalk on the other side of the narrow street.

Where is she going?

He wrestled with himself for only a moment before he started trailing after her. For her own protection, of course. A young gentlewoman, especially one of her lineage on Barbados, should never be without protection.

Now, he strolled forward, pretending interest in some shop window displays, but keeping an eye on the door of the London Coffeehouse in case Miss Bethel's powers of persuasion failed her after all. Eventually, he reached the window of the coffee shop itself. Inside, the beautiful bronze-skinned woman he'd been pursuing sat at a small round table immediately beyond the painted glass. Her back was to him, and she was not alone.

A man Robert had never seen before sat across from her. A despicably handsome gentleman with flawless tan skin and short dark hair left wild and deliberately oiled and tousled. He wore fine clothes and had fine teeth, which he displayed often with a charming smile that made Robert want to punch them right out of that smug face, though he wasn't usually the violent sort. The man looked like an utter dandy. A Spanish dandy. The nerve of a Spaniard showing up on one of the English islands. The nerve of him wooing Miss Bethel!

The Spaniard and Miss Bethel were engaged in intense conversation, their eyes locked on each other.

Robert's gut clenched. Is this what Miss Bethel had been doing when she'd been slipping away from the inn for her *important appointments*? Was this man why she'd travelled to Barbados in the first place? Is this why she continually spurned his affections? He'd thought her rejection was because of Zale Teague, the handsome young man she'd been travelling with when he'd met her. After all, she'd barely left the lad's side on the *Atlanta*, despite the tension between them, and Zale's perfect face was much less repulsive than Robert's own disfigured one. Almost as perfect as this interloper's.

Robert touched his scars, sliding his fingers over the ridges around his eye. His heart caved in. If Miss Bethel preferred the company of someone less repulsive than himself, such as Zale or this dandy in the coffee shop, it was another thing he couldn't blame her for. Especially as he had no right to be jealous of Zale for anything—not when the lad had come back from the dead, relieving Robert's personal load of guilt a smidgen.

Despite the four-year gap in their ages, Zale had been Robert's childhood playmate until the accident that had left Robert scarred, after which Zale had disappeared. Robert had thought his friend dead and blamed himself. If he'd only stood up to his brother Gryffyn's bullying, the events of that terrible day five years ago at Chyandour Brook would have gone very differently. Talwyn Penrose, the pretty girl with skin like cream who had followed Zale around like a puppy, might still be alive. At fifteen, it had been up to Robert to protect both the younger children from Gryffyn and his friends—and his failure would haunt him all his days.

That, and so many others. The slave hold of the *Atlanta* filled his vision, and the pit clawed at his stomach. How many times had he imagined the dark bodies of the men and women floating on the waves since the ship had sunk—a ship that had made their final days a misery? *My fault . . .*

Desperately, he blinked away the gruesome images and stared through the painted letters on the shop window, studying the man who had won the heart of the woman he loved.

Miss Bethel began to turn toward the window, and Robert ducked away before she could see him.

I should go. This is none of my business.

But instead of walking back the way he had come, he sat at a table on the wooden boardwalk near the propped-open door and quietly ordered a black coffee from the thin mustachioed waiter.

While he waited for his coffee, he watched the people passing by. White men in fine clothes engaged in indolent conversation in the shade while they watched dark-skinned men load wagons with food and other supplies. The working poor plied their trades among the shops, calling out to passersby to see if they needed shoes or barrels mended. Sailors on shore leave loitered on the corners and watched the women with rum jugs in hand. There was even the occasional group of fair-skinned ladies under frothy parasols and bonnets out for a lark at the shops with their friends—often trailed by black women in the clothing of domestics with loaded shallow wicker baskets on their heads holding their mistresses' purchases.

Robert realized he was searching the faces of the slaves and sailors as they passed. Not one of them was a face he recognized. He frowned, but the disappointment had been expected. If God didn't think him worthy of forgiveness, who was Robert to argue?

The waiter brought his coffee, and he took a sip. Just then, he overheard the throaty voice he loved best say something about Tartarus, the place where Zale's mother, Delphine, had been taken, and he stopped, the cup halfway to his lips. He didn't mean to eavesdrop, but could he help it if the sound from the table just inside the door carried particularly well to this spot?

"Do you think he could be looking for a way in on his own?" asked the man. His voice was a rich baritone with a slight accent, the kind women swooned over. Of course.

"Zale?" Miss Bethel replied. "I'm sure of it. He's very determined when he wants to be, and even though he's under house arrest, so my sources tell me, he's probably looking for escape at every opportunity. It is only by the grace of Elyon his circumstances aren't much worse, considering what we've discovered of the place." She paused. "I ask you to reconsider allowing me to go after him."

Zale was alive and captive somewhere on Barbados? Why had Miss Bethel not told him? And what did she think she could do to save the lad? He could call lightning and kill with a touch—Robert shuddered at the memory of Mr. Crow's convulsing body hitting the floor of the *Atlanta's* orlop deck—and, more than that, Zale wasn't even human. No, the boy hadn't meant to kill the first mate. He hadn't meant to call the lightning that had left Robert blind on the bank of Chyandour Brook either. He'd only been trying to defend someone helpless to defend themselves—something Robert should have been doing both times. And, both times, Zale had manifested as a merman, with a silvery green tail and frilly neck gills that finally explained those weird, luminescent green eyes of his.

For five years, Gryffyn had told Robert the water demon he'd seen at Chyandour Brook was a figment of his imagination. But when Robert saw Zale dive off the deck of the *Atlanta* with his legs fused into an enormous fish tail after Mr. Crow's untimely demise, he'd understood the truth. Whenever he'd brought up the event with Miss Bethel, however, she'd acted like she didn't know what he was talking about. But Robert knew what he'd seen—or did he? A lump formed in his throat, and he swallowed. Wherever Zale was, he didn't need help protecting himself, house arrest or not. Certainly not from a young mulatto gentlewoman of uncertain ancestry, no matter how capable and charming she might be.

Who will help him then? Me?

The spot between his shoulder blades itched, and he shrugged to ease the sensation away.

"I'm sorry," said the Spaniard to Miss Bethel with such tenderness, it took all Robert's willpower not to look around to see if he had taken her hand as he said it. "You know how important it is to guard your heart. We cannot risk it, not when he is so well protected."

Even if Robert applauded the man's response, how presumptuous was he to talk about guarding her heart, and in that tone!

Not knowing what the man was doing was maddening. Robert glanced over his shoulder, but he could barely see the edge of the man's chair through the open shop door. He frowned and turned back to his coffee, straining to listen while his conscience strained against the urge. He ignored it.

"Berian, then?"

"It's even riskier for him, uh? Your previous visits can't have gone unnoticed, and—"

"We were very careful," Miss Bethel said. "The only ones who know our true appearance are the allies we contacted."

When Robert had first seen Zale swindling passersby on the street six months ago in Bristol, the boy's features had been distorted beyond recognition. It was only later, when Zale and Miss Bethel fled the scene, that his disguise must have fallen away so Robert could identify him. Had the disguise been Miss Bethel's doing? What was she, some kind of spy? But that would be ridiculous.

The Spaniard's next words were so quiet, Robert couldn't make them out.

Miss Bethel sighed. "Of course. But if we can't go to him, how will he get to us?"

"You have told him what he needs to know to find his mother. Now it is up to him, uh? And once he's outside the middle ground, you can rejoin him."

He said *middle ground* with special emphasis, like it was a specific place. The Middle Ground. Maybe there was a new plantation called the Middle Ground somewhere in the centre of Barbados. But even if the Spaniard justifiably didn't want Miss Bethel anywhere near a plantation, why wouldn't he approve of Reverend Berian going to find Zale? And who gave him the right to decide?

Robert frowned. This was the most confusing lovers' conversation he'd ever heard. Even with this man, Zale was all Miss Bethel could talk about.

"You're certain Delphine is still alive?" Miss Bethel said. "Berian has been trying to locate her, but . . ." Her voice faded beneath Robert's hearing.

Robert drew in a sharp breath. It was thanks to Delphine Teague's healing touch that Robert had only ended up scarred, not blinded. As far as he was concerned, he owed her his life.

In fact, it was to bring news to Zale about Delphine that Robert had abandoned—definitely not fled—his brother and their shipping partnership in Bristol. He'd caught up to Zale off the coast of Africa, transferring to the ill-fated *Atlanta*, and finally shared what he'd overheard Gryffyn say about Delphine's kidnapping and location with Zale and his companions, Miss Bethel and Reverend Berian.

He shuddered as he remembered the strange ceremony he'd witnessed. Gryffyn and the other hooded figures had been addressing—no, worshipping—a glowing dragon-like face with red eyes who had appeared in a strange black mirror. They'd said Delphine had been taken to Tartarus. He didn't know where on Earth that was, but Miss Bethel and Mr. Berian had seemed to. Not that they'd illuminated him. Those two had more secrets than the Catholic Church.

The man cleared his throat. "It's difficult to get information on Delphine from her current location, but we know she is little use to them dead."

"I'm afraid Zale will fall into their clutches. Can you imagine how disastrous that would be? Especially now that his sister is dead . . ." Her voice quivered. "I can't believe we were too late to save her. I don't want Zale to suffer the same fate."

"I understand," said the Spaniard. "But you must not give in to fear."

"I know." She sighed. "But the island is in a much worse state than I would have thought possible. If they could manage that with their limited resources, what would happen if they get their claws on Zale, with Delphine already in their grasp?"

Robert frowned. Zale had never had a sister. He was an only child. But that wasn't the reason for the tightening grip of dread in his heart. He'd been jesting before, but *was* Miss Bethel a spy? Perish the thought!

"What if Zale takes too long to break free and the Soulstone fails?" Miss Bethel's voice became pleading. "You know what's at stake. Not just for the world, but for me."

The man blew out a long stream of air. Finally, he said, "I was going to wait to give you this, but, circumstances being what they are, I think you should have it now."

Whatever he handed to Miss Bethel caused a sharp intake of breath. "Solomon's Ring? It's more beautiful than I'd even imagined."

"You and Zale will need it to retrieve Delphine. Protect it with your existence. It cannot fall into enemy hands."

"Thank you. This means so much."

Enemy hands? What's at stake? The lump was back in Robert's throat. Miss Bethel sounded emotional, as most young ladies did when presented with a ring. If it had been a romantic gesture, though, why was the conversation still all about Zale? The seed of doubt that had been planted moments ago grew, and Robert's heart raced.

"Don't worry," the man said. "You'll find Delphine and Zale. Elyon will protect them."

"Like he protected Calandra?"

Robert couldn't hear the Spaniard's murmured reply. But from what he *had* heard, they were hardly discussing picnics or parties or walks in the park.

Robert had been wrong about Miss Bethel yet again—she wasn't here for a lovers' rendezvous. This dandy, whomever he was, sounded like he was merely an informant of some kind, someone Miss Bethel conducted business with. *Spy business?* He shook his head. Whatever was going on here, Miss Bethel was *not* a spy. Though Robert had yet to determine why she was so invested in Zale's welfare. This conversation was the most nefarious activity he'd seen Miss Bethel engage in—and it had been all about locating Zale and Delphine. Wasn't that the reason Robert himself was here in Barbados?

But if the Spaniard were a simple informant, why did he speak to

Miss Bethel with such affection in his voice? And why was she the one having this conversation instead of the dumpy reverend? Women, especially coloured women, didn't conduct business on Barbados. It simply wasn't done.

It seemed clear the sect that had kidnapped Delphine was also after Zale, who was being held captive by someone else, somewhere on the island. But who? Someone who was afraid of Zale's abilities perhaps, or trying to use him as leverage? Perhaps Robert could make enquiries and surprise Miss Bethel with answers. Prove to her and Mr. Berian that he was more fit than they believed him to be . . . and try to make up for the sins of his past.

It would help if he knew a bit more about where Zale was being kept. He would have to find a way to bring the topic up with Miss Bethel later—not in such a way that she'd know he'd overheard her, of course. Just casually, as if he'd heard a rumour that some of the people from the *Atlanta* had survived and he wondered if Zale was among them. If he could find out where Zale was being kept, he might even be able to negotiate the boy's release. Robert was the son of a lord, after all. He had connections, or he could use his position to make them.

Maybe that would prove how earnest his intentions were to Miss Bethel. If only he could get her to trust him with her secrets, maybe she would eventually trust him with her heart.

The tinkle of bangles drew his attention. He glanced up the street, then grew cold, despite the growing heat of the day. For just a moment, he thought he'd seen the young gypsy woman who had come looking for Zale and Miss Bethel back in Bristol—the one who had summoned the face in the mirror—standing in a shop door, watching him. But when he looked again, the door was empty.

He shook his head. It would make no sense for the gypsy woman to be in Barbados. His guilty conscience was playing tricks with his eyes. *Perhaps I'm not fully recovered after all.*

"Excuse, you help?" said a woman's smooth voice nearby.

Robert glanced toward the woman, who stood on the sidewalk in front of the jeweller's shop next to the London Coffeehouse addressing a young lady in the flock of gadabouts Robert had seen earlier. The woman was stocky, middle-aged, and black, with a cap of short curly hair and an erect bearing. She wore an unusual flowing mustard-yellow linen dress with a high waist gathered only by a woven hemp girdle, a Greek style that would be the envy of many a young lady in London if it weren't for how grubby it was. Behind the woman stood a tall muscular black man in a rough cotton shirt that looked about three sizes too small. He had the casual grace of a soldier. Despite their regal postures, both of them looked like they had seen better days—their garments were torn and dirty and they bore a desperate look of hunger in their coal-black eyes.

The beribboned young lady wrinkled her freckled nose at the woman in disdain. "Begone, slave. Help yourself."

"Please, I only want ask—"

The girl's blue eyes narrowed. "Are you deaf?"

The older woman closed her mouth, her face blank.

The young lady shied around the woman with a fearful glance at her tall young companion, and the group walked on in a cloud of girlish titters.

The woman turned to her companion. "Do not worry, my son. We will find someone."

Robert stared. The accent was unusual, but the woman had spoken in perfect Classical Greek, better than Robert himself could manage. How would a slave have learned to speak like that?

He glanced over his shoulder. Miss Bethel and the Spaniard were still deep in conversation. Robert stood and stepped toward the unusual duo on the sidewalk.

"What is the trouble?" he asked in Greek.

The woman glanced up at him in surprise and blinked—a common reaction when someone first saw him—then gave him a broad smile. The young man said nothing, but his eyes filled with cautious hope.

"Good sir, God bless you. We need someone to help us trade our gems for coins with the jeweller. He would not help us. He treated us with the utmost animosity and threw us out. I did not understand his words. I only speak a little English." She stopped and looked up at Robert. "You understand me, do you not?"

Robert gave a small smile. "Yes, madam, I understand you. How did you come to learn such fluent Greek?"

The two of them exchanged glances. "We . . . worked in a place where it was spoken much."

Robert frowned. "In Greece? How did you come here?"

"No, not Greece. Our mistresses spoke it."

The woman looked prepared to say no more on the subject, and Robert nodded. How odd that the woman should specify *mistresses* instead of masters as their owners, though. Perhaps the lady of the household was a widow. He knew of several landholding widows on the island—perhaps one of them was Greek. But with Barbados being a British colony, it seemed unlikely. His gut tightened.

"Why do your mistresses not help you with changing the gems? Are they unable to do it themselves?"

It was odd for someone to entrust such a task to their slave, who would get a far worse price than if the mistress had come to make the bargain herself. But if she had, the trust she placed in this woman far exceeded the norm. Again, an unlikely circumstance. Something about this woman's story was starting to smell.

"No, sir," the woman explained. "We do not work for them any longer. They set us free, and we wish to return to Africa, so we must have coin to buy our passage."

Robert raised his brows, the expression pulling uncomfortably at his scars. He pursed his lips, trying to decide if he should believe them.

There were several things about their story that didn't add up. The last thing he wanted was to be charged for abetting escaping slaves. And the longer he stood there, the more tension coiled into the two people before him, until they looked as tight as two springs ready to loose. It was all very suspicious.

"Do you have your papers of manumission? I would very much like to see them." He held out his hand expectantly.

The man spoke for the first time, also in Greek. "Perhaps this would suffice?"

He placed a cool angular stone in Robert's hand. When Robert examined it, a perfectly formed amethyst crystal the size of a pebble rested on his palm, with a deep violet pointed terminal that faded to clear quartz on the rough end. He stared at it in astonishment. If this was what they offered him in bribe to help them, how many more did they have to exchange?

He glared at the man. "You have no papers, but you have a queen's ransom in jewels. Where did you get this? Did you steal it? Who are your mistresses?"

The man's face darkened. "We didn't—"

"There they are!" came a man's shout from behind them. "Those are the two I told you about."

The jeweller, a paunchy balding man with a ruddy complexion, stood in front of his shop talking to the leader of a group of rough-looking men, pointing toward the man and the woman. Before they could even take two steps, they were surrounded. One of the thugs grabbed the woman's arms from behind, and two others attempted to grab the man. He evaded several lunges, but the street was too crowded for him to get far, and the attackers eventually caught him. He struggled valiantly until he was subdued by several blows to the head and kidneys and sagged.

"What is this? Why you do this?" the woman cried. "We free blacks. Let us go."

The leader of the group, a slaving agent named Marcel Kaminski whom Robert had met only that morning while making enquiries, swaggered to stand before the two of them, giving Robert a nod of acknowledgement.

"Thank you for keeping these runaways occupied until we could nab 'em, Mr. Cox. You saved us a great deal of trouble chasing after 'em."

The woman stared at him in astonishment, and the man glared at him.

Robert swallowed, his hand wrapped around the gem. He didn't know whom to believe. If they were truly free, could he allow them to be returned to their enslaved state after what he had witnessed on board his own slaving ship?

Then again, what free black would ever be without their papers, the only proof of their freedom? He couldn't, in good conscience, aid a couple of runaways either, who had more than likely robbed their mistresses, to boot.

"Of course, Mr. Kaminski. What will be done with them?"

Kaminski smiled. "We'll see if someone claims 'em. If not, they'll go back on the block."

At this, the woman gave a cry of alarm and began shouting in a language that Robert didn't recognize. The men put iron manacles on her and her son's wrists and urged them away.

Eventually, she turned to Robert and cried in Greek, "Help us, please! We are not runaways. We are not even from Barbados, and know no one here who can vouch for us. We will be sold into slavery if you do not help us."

"Hush, you," growled the man who held the woman's arm. He pushed her ahead of him down the street.

Robert stared after her. Had he made the wrong choice? He looked at the amethyst. This certainly did not come from Barbados, and what were the chances a lady would keep unset, uncut gems in her jewellery box? But where would two blacks, even free ones, come by such riches?

But what if they had been telling the truth?

"If you're not from here, where are you from?" he shouted after her.

The woman closed her mouth and glanced at her son uncertainly. The young man glared at his mother. They were nearly lost in the crowd.

"I can't help you if I don't know where you're from," Robert called after them.

The woman glanced at her captor, then shouted over her shoulder. "Sirenia. We are from Sirenia."

The man who held her growled at her to be quiet and pushed her in front of him into the crowd.

Robert stared after them in consternation. While his Greek was shaky, his geography was not. He'd spent months poring over maps as part of his job with the shipping company, and he knew every charted island in the West Indies like the back of his hand. But he'd never heard of a place called Sirenia.

Something tickled the back of his mind, and he frowned.

"What is happening?" asked Miss Bethel's voice from beside Robert, and the thought faded to nothing.

Robert glanced at her guiltily. Her companion was nowhere to be seen, and all of her fingers were still bare. Where had she concealed the ring?

"Miss Bethel, what are you doing here? I was, er, getting some fresh air and a change of scenery. I had no idea you were—"

"Never mind that," she said, glancing up at him, her brows furrowed in irritation. "What happened with them?" She flicked her hand at the backs of Kaminski's men and the two people they held captive.

"Those two blacks wanted help trading some jewels, but it appears they were runaways. They tried to bribe me with this." He held up the amethyst for Miss Bethel to see.

She took it and examined it closely. "There are no amethysts like this on Barbados. How did they come by the jewels?"

Robert shook his head. "I wondered the same thing. They said they were from a place called Sirenia."

The word had the most startling effect on Miss Bethel. Her gaze snapped to meet his, her golden eyes wide and intense.

"Sirenia? You're certain?" She scanned the street, but there was no sign of Kaminski, his men, or their charges. They'd been lost amongst the crowd.

He nodded. "Yes. You know it?"

"Yes." She grasped his arm above the elbow. "I must speak to them as soon as possible. Do you know where they were being taken?"

"I suspect to the merchants' yard. But it is not fit for a lady, Miss Bethel."

She grew very still, cocking her head at him in that maddening way that made him want to reach out and stroke her lovely neck. "After I spent four months on a slave ship, you think the merchants' yard will upset me? We must go there at once."

Robert debated the wisdom of such a thing. "I could go by myself and bring you word."

Miss Bethel's jaw set. "Robbie Cox, take me there *at once*."

Robert sighed. "Yes, Miss Bethel." He didn't know where she had learned of his childhood nickname, but it somehow sounded completely natural falling from her lips. And when she used it, he knew she would not be swayed.

She smiled, and it was as though the sun shone for him alone. "Thank you."

He paid for his coffee, then offered his arm to Miss Bethel so they could make their way along the crowded boardwalk.

"What happened to your companion?" The words slipped out before he considered them properly, and he cursed himself.

She looked at him sideways. "He has gone about his business."

She said nothing else, though her mouth was set in a bemused line. Robert did not press her further.

They turned the corner of the street and the Careenage came into view. The shallow sliver of water that served as a harbour for the small craft used to aid in loading and unloading the ships anchored out in the bay bounded the far side of Trafalgar Square, the green where slaves were auctioned off. The square was empty now but for the few slaves erecting rope pens for tomorrow's auction of the shipment that had come in that morning. At the sight, he was once more thrust into the stench and close-ness of the hold of the *Atlanta*, with hundreds of slaves forced to lay in the heat and dark in their own filth, and the weight of his conviction heavier than the smell. All of them were probably now dead.

My fault.

He closed his eyes and shuddered. The black pit that had pursued him for weeks clawed at him with sticky molasses tentacles once more, and his gut felt lined with lead.

"What is the matter, Mr. Cox?"

He opened his eyes to see Miss Bethel gazing up at him in concern. "'Tis nothing. The wind, it gave me a chill."

She nodded. "Winds can do that. They can also push us to our destinations. Might this be such a wind, Mr. Cox?" She looked at him with that steady gaze that pierced to his very soul.

He glanced away, afraid of the truth she might see there. "One can only hope," he muttered.

2

HOUSE ARREST

Opal Palace, Sireniapolis, Island of Sirenia

ZALE TEAGUE LUNGED AT THE girl posed in defensive position opposite him, his bamboo deiktis staff clutched in slippery, sweaty hands. His shoulder-length blond hair flopped in his face and he tossed his head to clear his vision. Around the semicircular courtyard, the clacks of staves reverberated off the marble walls of the stone palace on one side and echoed into the empty blue sky on the other, fading beneath the occasional roar of pounding surf far below.

"Remember to flow with your opponent," said Daskala Stamatia. The siren instructor, dressed in a short blue practice peplos with a wide woven hemp belt with her black hair pulled back in a braided bun, strolled between the sparring students with her hands clasped behind her back, watching them with an appraising gaze. "Be stable like earth and fluid like water."

Sweat dripped into Zale's eye. He'd been practising the *Tropos Hydor Zon*—the Way of Water—with the class of fifth-year siren cadets for the last hour, and he was starting to flag. He was taller than most of them, and he'd definitely become more fit in the last few months while scampering over the decks and the rigging of the *Atlanta*. But that was not enough to compensate for the fact that the girls who surrounded him had been training in the art since they were seven, whereas he'd spent most of the last five years in a water tank, being gawked at for money. He'd been assigned to this class because they were all approximately the same age, not the same skill level.

Scratch that. His age mates were in sixth year. He couldn't imagine trying to keep up with them.

"Hah!" Damaris, his sparring partner, a girl of about fifteen with a ponytail taming long wild curls the colour of wet sand and luminescent eyes several shades paler than his own emerald-green ones, lunged at him in a ferocious attack. "Stay on task, Wonder Boy. It's easy enough to beat you when you're paying attention. At least give me a challenge."

Daskala Stamatia stopped near them, observing them with interest. "Keep your stance wider, Zale. Let the energy flow through you like water. Remember to use your own energy sparingly, and direct your opponent's energy against them."

Zale tightened his gut. The *daskalas* were always on his case about using the water element, no matter what he was doing. After spirit, water and earth seemed to be the most common elements among the women of his kind. Since he was the first male to have been born for three thousand years, he tried to be patient as he explained to them over and over that he could barely even sense water, let alone use it. Fire and air, on the other hand . . .

"Like this, *tapeinos*." Damaris, who looked like she was barely exerting herself, feinted around him. With a jab as fast as the flick of an eel's tail, she caught him in the back of the knees with her staff and sent him hurtling to the sanded tiles of the practice courtyard.

Zale stared up at her, heat gathering in his veins and a breeze rustling the leaves of the fruit trees surrounding the terrace courtyard. In the three weeks he'd been on Sirenia, he hadn't lost control of his powers and hurt anyone once. Well, that wasn't true—he had once, on the second day, but not since. But there were times he'd come close, like now. Normally, he kept the feldspar bracelet that would dampen his powers and prevent disaster near him in his waistcoat pocket—the waistcoat that lay in a bright yellow patchwork heap next to the far wall of the courtyard. Zale closed his eyes and took a breath, and the heat cooled. With a single, fluid motion, he pushed himself off the floor of the courtyard with his back, leapt to his feet, and swung his *deiktis* staff in the move that Daskala Stamatia had taught them only that morning. When Damaris moved to block it, he twisted his staff around hers until her staff went flying away, clattering to the sandy stone. She glanced at her fallen weapon, which was her undoing. By the time she looked at him again, Zale had the butt end of his staff pressed against her throat.

"Do you yield?"

Damaris, her open hands in the air, glared at him with a tense jaw. "I yield."

Zale stepped away and lowered his staff, then looked around. The other students had stopped their own sparring to watch the ferocious match between him and Damaris, but none of them looked impressed by his surprise win. The expressions on their faces ranged from stunned disbelief to annoyance to outright anger. Even Daskala Stamatia looked less than pleased. As Damaris bent to pick up her stave, the *daskala* pressed her lips into a thin line, then turned to face the rest of the class.

"Sparring practise is over for this afternoon. We'll resume tomorrow morning, as usual." With a final unreadable glance in Zale's direction, she turned toward the open archway that lead to the Royal Academy wing of the Opal Palace.

Zale ran the back of his hand over his eyebrows to divert some of the sweat as he waited for his turn to put his practice stave in the wooden stand along the wall. The girls in the class shrank away from him when he came near, subtly avoiding his touch. He stared at the smooth white marble wall behind the stand and took a deep breath to hide how much it bothered him. The girls put their staves in the stand, then headed to the refreshment table, the occasional comment and giggle disturbing the after-exercise tranquility. No one bothered speaking to him.

He was used to people not touching him. In the human world, it had been understandable. After all, he was a freak as far as humans were concerned, and besides, it's hard to touch someone separated from you by glass. But when he finally came home, to the land of the undines, he'd expected it to be different. After all, he was like *them*.

Except he wasn't. The very fact that he was a male set him apart in a way he'd never experienced before. He glanced at the pairs of human *tapeinos* guards posted at each entrance to the courtyard. He was certain the class of sparring siren cadets did not usually require such heavy security, or any at all. Not even Narcissa, his cousin and the acting queen, trusted him.

He moved to the refreshment table and poured himself a bowl of water from a flask with lemon slices floating in it. After taking a few swallows to quench his thirst, he moved away from the others to the far side of the courtyard near the rail. Settling himself on the grass beneath an orange tree with his back to the trunk, he surreptitiously studied the human men that stood guard around the courtyard—their blank faces testimony to their equally blank minds. He suppressed a shudder. What the undines did to these men—a practice they called Redemption, but as far as Zale could see, was turning the men *into* slaves, not redeeming them from anything—was one of the most horrific things he'd ever seen. And he'd spent five years as a freak show in a tank and had travelled on a slave ship to get here.

"I hate how quickly you pick everything up. It's annoying."

Zale looked up to see who had spoken. Damaris glared down at him, her brows furrowed and her lips twisted, but she didn't seem hostile. She held a bowl of water in one hand and two barley cakes in the other.

"You mean you weren't just letting me win to be nice?" Zale gave her what he hoped was a disarming smile, but after three weeks of being ignored by his classmates, he'd lost faith in the charm that had always served him so well while hustling *gorgios* with his friend Gio. The best he could hope for was to annoy her enough that she'd leave him alone.

"I'm not that nice."

She surprised him by joining him beneath the orange tree. After sitting on the grass, she handed him a barley cake, then took a bite of her own. Resting her arm on her knee, she stared over the curved white marble railing that separated them from a steep drop and the view of the turquoise-blue ocean beyond. Light, puffy clouds scudded across the cerulean blue sky, and far below, the Atlantic pounded against the black basalt cliffs. From this terrace, the city of Sireniapolis was completely concealed from view, and the verdant spike of Green Mountain was just barely visible beyond the pointed tip of the royal quarters wing, already starting to cast shadows into the yard. Across another low marble railing defining the convex opposite boundary of the yard, the kitchen gardens lay nestled between the two southern wings of the triquetra-shaped palace. Bright pink bougainvillea and other colourful flowers Zale didn't recognize clambered over the barrier, leaving their sweet, heavy scent in the air.

Zale quirked his mouth, wondering if the conversation were over. He shrugged and took a bite of the barley cake, expecting to be met, once again, with a new flavour experience. Most of the food here was unfamiliar to him. Having grown up in Cornwall, England, he was used to honey cakes and pasties. His mother hadn't often made him the food of her homeland. Possibly because she never learned to cook until she left here, what with being a princess of the realm and all—not that she'd ever let that slip.

However, as soon as Zale took a bite of the barley cake, bittersweet sadness exploded in his mouth. He closed his eyes, back on a rocky cliff in Cornwall, eating the packed lunch his mother had made him to enjoy while playing with his childhood friends, Robert Cox and Talwyn Penrose.

The memory was quickly followed by a wave of frustration and anger. The whole reason he was even here was because his mother had been kidnapped and somehow taken to the Underworld, and he was on a mission to rescue her. Finding Sirenia had only been meant to be one step on his way so he could be reunited with his older sister, Calandra. But that hadn't worked out at all. His chest tightened. *I didn't mean to kill her. It was an accident.*

He'd had so many accidents. His breath hitched and the breeze picked up again, rustling the leaves of the lemon and orange trees surrounding the terrace. He glanced at his waistcoat once more, the security of the bracelet calling to him. Narcissa had forbidden him to wear it during practice—to decrease his dependence on it, she said. But practice was over . . .

"So, how do you like living here?" Damaris asked.

Zale shrugged, taking another bite of barley cake. "The food's good."

She barked a short laugh, then sobered. "Oh, you were serious?" She eyed her barley cake. "This isn't bad, I guess. But you should try the ones Cook Stephanie makes at my mother's house. And her Panselinos bread. Mm." She stuffed another bite in her mouth and chased it with a gulp of water.

"My mother made the best barley cakes I've ever tasted," Zale said wistfully.

"Your mother cooked?"

Zale blew out a breath. "Yeah, she made all kinds of things."

Damaris laughed. "I'm just trying to picture Queen Adonia cooking. Or Narcissa or Calandra or Hebe. Can't do it. How did the queen's sister pick it up?"

"I don't know. She just did."

"Like you, huh?" Damaris eyed him.

Zale ignored her, picking a few crumbs off his cake and placing them in his mouth to savour the flavour. He hadn't really known his aunt, Queen Adonia, but he'd known enough. She'd been killed less than a day after he'd met her by Thea, one of her own advisers, and he'd spent most of that time under a *sklavia* bond she'd subjected him to. *Redemption, Saint Peter's knees.* He clenched his fists to suppress the sudden panic the memory evoked.

All he'd wanted was to find his sister and his home and go save his mother. How had it all gone so terribly wrong? He'd asked Narcissa about helping him get to Tartarus a few times to find his mother—he'd heard a rumour there was a gate near here—but she kept putting him off by saying . . . by saying . . .

What *had* she been saying? Actually, why was he so upset? Narcissa was taking care of everything. She'd promised she would. A dreamy feeling of peace washed over him, and he smiled. He took another bite of barley cake, enjoying the sound of birdsong.

Something's wrong with me, he thought lazily, but the thought faded as soon as it had come. He struggled against the lethargy that weighed his limbs down. *I need to find Mother. I need to—*

"Hey, Damaris!" shouted one of the girls from under a tree across the courtyard. "Are you going fishing later? Oh, wait. You're doing it now."

The girl and her three friends exploded in a chorus of giggling.

Damaris shook her head and rolled her eyes. "Ignore them. They're just mad they didn't get the nerve to come over here and talk to you first."

Zale barely heard her. *Mother. I need to . . . why can't I remember?*

He took another bite of his cake, but it tasted like paste in his dry mouth.

Damaris glanced at him. "For someone who just bested the top siren cadet in the class, you seem awfully upset."

That caught his attention. He still wasn't used to the fact that many of the undines could sense emotions, or your very presence, without ever looking at you. When he'd realized it was one of their most common abilities, he finally understood why his own intuition had always been so strong. However, it was quite another thing to be surrounded by others with the same ability at all times. It was difficult to put on a stoic mask of nonchalance when everyone in the room could tell your mood with a single glance.

"You don't want to talk about it?" Damaris studied him, sunlight glittering from her seafoam-green eyes.

"Do you want to hear about it?"

Damaris cocked her head in challenge, but then relented, her posture softening.

"Look, I know I haven't exactly been welcoming. Having a boy in the class is taking some getting used to. But you know what? You're pretty good. And I thought maybe you were getting tired of sitting by yourself all the time. But hey, I can go back to my friends." She glanced at the girls in the shade of a tree against the wall, who were staring at the two of them. She snorted and muttered, "I don't want to stay where I'm not wanted."

Damaris began to rise, but Zale put out a hand. "I'd like you to stay."

Damaris glanced at him over her shoulder, and her eyebrow arched in surprise. "You sure?"

Zale nodded. Damaris sat back down, leaning against the trunk of the orange tree, but she still didn't touch him. Zale wondered if it were intentional or not. The small cluster of girls on the far side of the courtyard kept glancing at them and giggling behind their hands. Suddenly, Zale regretted asking Damaris to stay. She was probably here on some kind of dare, gathering information about the freak that the girls could laugh about in their dorm rooms later. He'd experienced something similar a time or two with girls from other Roma families at gatherings.

Zale sighed. He was so lonely, he didn't even care.

He took a sip of his water, studying Damaris's profile. Her sandy hair was pulled back into a long ponytail of unruly curls, and her round, olive-toned face was still slightly flushed from the exercise. She was nearly as beautiful as Abela.

He swallowed, feeling slightly guilty at the comparison. Not that there was anything going on between him and Abela, the sphinx-lamassu guardian who'd accompanied him from England. The one time he'd tried to kiss her, she'd ducked away so fast, he'd almost banged his nose on a door instead.

But still. He couldn't help but wonder if, somewhere in her cherub heart, she carried a candle for him. After all, she'd been looking out for him his entire life—her previous iteration in flesh had been his friend, Talwyn, who had been around as long as he could remember. She had been pretty as Talwyn Penrose, but as Abela Bethel—the brown-skinned, golden-eyed African girl she'd become when she returned from wherever lumasi went when they weren't here "on the Ground," as Abela called it— she was breathtaking. Zale's heart sped up and his veins started to warm again. He gulped the last swallow of cool water from his bowl to hide his discomfiture.

Damaris glanced sideways at him, her head cocked. "Watcha thinkin'?"

By all the saints! There's no privacy in this place at all, is there?

Zale cleared his throat. "I was thinking of my friend I was travelling with. I haven't seen her since I got here, and I'm worried about her." Abela wouldn't have been affected by the sirensong, which only worked on men, and she'd probably used her chariot to blink herself away from the ship before the undines scuttled it. But if she was okay, why hadn't she come and found him yet? "Not that Narcissa would let me look for her, anyway."

"You have friends?" Damaris looked at him innocently.

He gave her a tight smile. "Hilarious."

She grinned. "Aw, lighten up, Icarus. I'm just teasing you."

"Icarus?"

"You know, the idiot child of the brilliant inventor Daedalus who got cocky, flew too close to the sun, and died trying to escape the labyrinth?"

Zale scowled and said nothing. He hadn't heard that story, but he was certain he was *not* an Icarus. He could breathe underwater, not fly. Abela and Berian could, though, or so he assumed—he'd never actually seen them do it, but the wings of their lumasi forms implied as much.

Damaris raised an askance eyebrow at his silence. "Besides, I know being restricted to the palace grounds probably seems severe, but Narcissa is being cautious for your own good. It's not safe out there for you. With the city guard under orders to Redeem any Wild male on sight, you wouldn't get five steps down the Street of Pearls before you were turned into a mind-melted moron like them." She jerked her thumb toward the *taps* at the nearest entrance. "And, call me sentimental, but I just started getting used to you like this."

Zale felt a grin trying to creep out of the corner of his mouth and squelched it. She didn't get to call him an idiot child and make him laugh in the same breath. Baked offerings notwithstanding, she was right—she wasn't that nice. He didn't want to encourage whatever little game she and her friends were playing.

She batted her eyelashes at him in mock coyness. "So, is this *friend* you were thinking about pretty?"

Zale gave a barely there shrug. "Why do you care?"

Damaris's glib manner slipped, and Zale sensed her hurt. Which meant she was much more hurt than she was letting on, because he couldn't usually do that.

"Well, if you must know, I thought I could look for her, or send a message to my mother or sister Eudora to do so."

Zale sat up straighter and frowned. "Why would you do that?"

Damaris looked uncomfortable, all her breezy superiority gone. She fidgeted with a pebble on the grass. "I guess I just thought it must get pretty lonely with no one to talk to, and no one who wants to talk to you . . . or even touch you."

"So that's intentional, then."

Damaris's face flushed slightly. "Touch is a powerful way of sharing emotions for sirens, since all of us have the gift of spirit. I think everyone might be, um, *scared* to find out what you're feeling." She glanced down. "I guess, what I mean to say is, I decided it was stupid to be scared. I mean, how different can you be?"

Zale studied her, trying to decide if she was being sincere. Her thick dark eyelashes hid her beautiful eyes and her curls tumbled around her bare shoulders and down the back of her turquoise sparring bodice. She was at least putting on a good act of penitence—but he'd lived with the Roma, who made a living out of duping unsuspecting *gorgios* out of every available pence. After five years with them, he knew how convincing an act someone could put on.

But then, he also knew that if she would touch him, he'd see exactly how sincere she was.

He held his hand palm-up in her line of sight. She glanced up, following the line of his arm until she met his eyes.

He pulled out the disarming grin again. "Do you want to find out if you were right about me?"

She said nothing, looking like a rabbit caught in a snare. She glanced over her shoulder at her friends. The girls were watching her and Zale's every move with rabid intensity.

He didn't even care. He looked back at Damaris, his hand still outstretched.

Slowly, she reached out and clasped his hand in her own.

The instant they touched, a flood of her emotions surged through him—fascination, revulsion, and another emotion he couldn't quite place. Attraction? Surely not.

She stared into his face, obviously processing what she was feeling from him too. Her delicate nostrils flared slightly, and from this close, he noticed that she had a little mole on her cheekbone that accentuated her beauty instead of diminished it. She really was stunning. He stared at her soft, pink lips, which slowly curved into a smile.

Realizing what he was feeling, and that she would know exactly what it was, he let go of her hand and jammed his back against the tree trunk, his face burning. She leaned against it next to him, chuckling. This time, their bare arms touched, putting the awareness of those same emotions front and centre in his mind. He thought about Reverend Berian, the fat ungainly human form of the bull-lamassu who had made the journey with him and Abela, to douse the fire rushing through his veins. Lidded lizard eyes. Frog mouth. Crow legs.

No use. The physical touch on its own was distracting enough, let alone the amusement that rippled through him. *Her* amusement, at *his* emotions.

He'd never felt so exposed.

She giggled. "It's okay, you know. I don't mind."

"Mind what?" Zale tried to sound casual, but his breath still came in shallow gasps and made his voice crack.

Which only made her laugh again.

"You're not half-bad-looking yourself. Certainly more attractive than the options we're usually presented with for mates from the Redemption Harvest. Most of those men are old, or missing teeth, or way too skinny." She made a face.

Zale laughed nervously. "You . . . you want to be my mate?"

"What?" Damaris sat bolt upright, turning to glare at him. "No. That's not what I meant. I mean, we're too young for that, and besides, sirens don't usually have consorts, and besides, Narcissa would never let her cousin marry a siren, and besides . . ."

She ran out of points to add to her list and stared up at him with wide eyes. It was her turn to blush.

Zale decided the best thing was to just move past it.

"Er, speaking of the Redemption Harvest—"

He swallowed, remembering the night the *Atlanta* had been captured by sirens and he and every other soul on board—the men mesmerized by sirensong and then Redeemed—had been brought to this island with the intention of auctioning them off as consorts and *douloi* to the highest bidders. It had been the night he'd met his sister, Calandra, who'd Freed him and told him he was different, even here. It had also been the day before he'd lost her. *Killed her, you mean.*

He swallowed again, trying to move the lump lodged in his throat. Damaris once again placed her hand on his in the grass, but this time, only soothing peace flowed from it. Calandra had done that to him once, helping him get a grip on his out-of-control powers. He glanced up and smiled. "Thanks."

Damaris nodded. "I miss Calandra too. She was a friend of Eudora's. It wasn't your fault, you know."

Zale looked away, out at the flawless blue sky. "Whose was it, then?"

After a moment of awkward silence, Damaris cleared her throat. "What were you going to ask me?"

Zale drew in a deep breath, then pulled his hand away, bent his knees, and wrapped his arms around his legs.

"I did have friends on that ship. Abela, but other friends too. Men. Would it be possible for your mother to . . . to see if she can find them? Could she tell me if they are, um, safe?"

He wanted to ask if their minds were Free, but with the way Narcissa's siren pods had been roaming the city looking for strays, he didn't hold out much hope of that. But just knowing that Berian and Kofi had at least made it to the island safe and unharmed would be a great relief. The last time he'd seen Kofi, the sailor had been lashed to the capstan on the gun deck, his back a bloody mess from the unjust beating he'd just taken for defending Abela's honour—an enslaved sailor attacking a white crewman had deserved such punishment, apparently. Never mind that the crewman—the first mate, no less—had attacked Abela and another slave woman first.

That was one thing about this place, Zale noted, glancing at the group of girls against the wall as evidence. Nobody here cared what colour your skin was. Since arriving at the island, he'd seen women of every shade mingling as equals. They didn't even care much if your eyes were the luminescent green of an undine or not. Human women, such as there were, held many positions of importance within the palace and, he'd been told, society in general.

They only cared whether or not you were male.

Damaris smiled. "I'd be happy to ask her to try. After how I've been behaving—after how all of us have been behaving—it's the least I can do." She pulled her lips to the side and chucked him on the shoulder. "Hey, we're not all stuck-up peacocks all the time. Just most of us most of the time." Her eyes sparkled.

He restrained a smile. "You're wrong, you know."

She frowned. "It's a joke. I know it must seem like we're all snobs, but most of us aren't like that. You just represent something we haven't had to think about for a very long—"

"That's not what I meant."

She frowned, waiting for him to explain.

He grinned at her, thankful for what little contact she'd offered him today, and thankful he hadn't turned her away.

"You *are* pretty nice."

She gave an embarrassed chuckle, ducked her head, and looked at him out of the corner of her eye. "Don't tell anyone."

Zale smiled and turned to the cadets gossiping across the courtyard. He gave a little wave. So did Damaris. Then she leaned against his shoulder, curling her fingers through his. He stiffened, then relaxed, putting his arm around her shoulders like he used to do with Talwyn.

The girls' eyes widened so much that Zale wondered if they might lose them onto the stone tiles.

He grinned. He didn't care. For the first time in weeks, he didn't feel completely alone.

He ate the final bite of his barley cake and smiled.

It was delicious.

3

THE CADET

After the other girls left for afternoon task duty, Damaris sat up and looked at Zale, breaking contact. She rubbed her arm where a deep purple bruise had begun to blossom.

He frowned at it. "Did I do that? Sorry."

Damaris waved the comment away. "Happens all the time. No big deal. This one won't even require healing."

"Why not?"

Damaris looked down at her arm, examining the bruise. "Not worth the bother. It'll go away in a few days."

Zale reached toward it, and she looked up at him in confusion.

"May I?"

She hesitated, but since she didn't tell him no, he laid his hand on the bruise and closed his eyes.

With the inner vision he'd had so much practice developing while on the *Atlanta*, he sensed the ruptured blood vessels, swelling tissue, and tender nerves. The last thing she needed was more heat. Carefully, he channelled cool energy from the air into her flesh and even managed to add a little earth to reduce the swelling and repair the damaged tissue. In moments, her arm had returned to its normal unmarred perfection.

Damaris gaped. "You can heal?"

Zale gave an embarrassed smile. "Yeah, but I hear it's a little different for me."

When Zale had first arrived on Sirenia, he'd been surprised to discover that not all undines could heal. While most of them had some ability with spirit, only those with exceptional talent could become sirens. If they had skills with the other elements in addition to spirit, they often became healers—either physics, plant healers, or the stone healers who created the crystal devices the undines used to store and transfer information, among other things. His sister, Calandra, had been a panacea, able to work in all three disciplines, as had Thea and, apparently, his mother, Delphine. Not that his mother had ever revealed her supernatural healing ability to him. He'd just thought she was good with herbs, much like the Romani *shuvani* women of his later experience.

Delphine had never spoken of his undine heritage. Then his powers had manifested in the most disastrous way possible, killing his father and blinding his friend. Scared and confused and trying to protect his mother from the same fate, he'd run away from home at the age of eleven—so there was a lot he didn't know.

When I get out of here and find her, I'll ask her why . . . The thought faded away into silver mist and he gave his head a shake. *What was I thinking about?*

"How did you learn to do it?" Damaris propped her elbow on her knee and her chin in her hand, staring at him with rapt attention.

He stared at her blankly. He couldn't even remember what she was talking about. "Do what?"

She frowned in annoyance. "Heal. Remember?" She pointed at her arm.

Right. Zale's face warmed.

"On the *Atlanta*, my friend, Kofi, he, er . . . well, he got really sick. Him and some other crewmen. One of the other men died, and it looked like Kofi might die too. Reverend Berian kept telling me that undines were healers and that I might be able to save him, and I had to just try, you know? And then I did. And then Kofi called me an angel and kept having me heal other slaves when they got sick. The crewmen never figured out why the slaves all treated me with such respect."

Damaris looked like a startled doe. "You mean you're the reason why no one on that ship was sick? I heard my sister Zoe talking about it. They'd never seen anything like it before. And you figured it out on your own?"

Zale shrugged, embarrassed. "Yeah, I guess."

Damaris shook her head. "You're not just a Wonder Boy, you're a living, breathing miracle, Zale bet'Delphine. What else can you do?"

Zale wanted to keep that look of amazement on her face. He pointed at the fluffy white clouds above the sparkling sea, and she followed the direction of his finger with her gaze. Closing his eyes, he concentrated.

Within moments, the clouds that had been floating lightly along above them zoomed across the sky as though they were seeds a giant had just blown from an enormous dandelion. He glanced back at Damaris and was gratified by the look of wonder on her face.

"A miracle," she breathed, shaking her head and staring at the rushing clouds.

Zale played with some blades of grass. "I guess. But I can't *see* people like you all can. I almost always have to touch them first. And even that only started a few months ago."

Damaris shook her head curtly. "No way. If you can heal, and you have that much power with other elements, then there's no reason you can't use spirit without touching someone too. It's just a different way of using your emotions."

Zale blinked, suddenly uncertain if he wanted to learn how to do what they did. "You know, it's overwhelming enough when I touch someone, let alone being able to sense folks all the time. I think I'm good."

Damaris frowned. "It can come in handy, you know."

Zale swallowed. "Are you sure? Even when everyone isn't actively avoiding touching me, I've kind of been avoiding them, because it can be pretty disconcerting to suddenly see exactly what someone is feeling. Not to mention, I don't necessarily want them to feel *me* either."

Damaris looked sympathetic. "Yes, it can take some getting used to. However, sirens and other undines with training use an emotional shield to prevent others from feeling everything they feel. Like yours. Funny you can't sense others when you've already mastered shielding your own emotions so well." She frowned.

Zale straightened a little. "What do you mean?"

"I can't sense you at all unless we're touching. Now *that* is disconcerting."

"You can't?" He shook his head. "Then how did you know what I was feeling earlier?"

She gave him a sardonic look. "You wear your emotions on your face, Wonder Boy. An infant would know how you feel most of the time."

Oh. Maybe Zale wasn't as great at hiding his emotions as he thought. But how could he hide himself from their sensate abilities without even trying?

He rubbed the smooth striped brown river stone in the hemp bracelet on his wrist. It had been a gift from his mother, one he'd always kept for sentimental reasons, not realizing until Berian told him so that it had served another purpose—to hide him from the devices known as finders used by lumasi and others like them and to protect him from the same people who had . . . had what?

He shook his head to clear the fog again. *Why does this keep happening to me?*

"What's that?" Damaris pointed at the stone in his bracelet.

He gazed at it stupidly, trying to remember what the stone was for. Finally, his brain latched on to the answer, but it was like catching a frog in a swamp. "It's . . . something my mother gave me. Apparently, it acts as some kind of invisibility shield. Maybe it shields my emotions too."

"Really?" She quirked her mouth. "That would explain a lot. May I see it?"

Zale extended his wrist toward her, and she took his hand again. He thrilled once more as her warm curiosity surged through him, although with much less intensity than the first time. "Why can't I feel you as strongly now?"

"I told you," she said, focusing on the stone, "I'm using a shield."

"Weren't you doing that before?"

She rubbed the smooth surface one last time, then sighed and dropped his wrist, shrugging.

"I'm no stone healer. I have no idea how your mother did it. I can sense spirit woven into the stone, but I can't see how." She met his eyes. "And no, I wasn't. I didn't know how much you'd be able to sense through your shield, and I wanted to make sure you saw how sincere I was. I guess I needn't have worried, Wonder Boy."

Zale smiled. "You know, *Wonder Boy* isn't that bad. I far prefer that to Waterboy, which is what they used to call me when I was, um, putting on a show."

"Yeah? Well, Wonder Boy, if you can do all that other stuff, can you sense me without looking at me?"

Zale closed his eyes and concentrated. He could hear her gentle breathing between the loud chirps of the birds in the fruit trees, but he couldn't sense her in any other way. He opened his eyes and shook his head.

"Nope. Nothing."

"Here, let's try this." She moved to sit cross-legged in front of him so their knees almost touched, then took both his hands in hers. "You can sense me now, right?"

Her frank curiosity and earnest intention flowed through him.

"Yes."

She studied him, her brow furrowed slightly. "You don't have your own emotional shield at all, do you? It was all the bracelet."

He shook his head. "I wouldn't have the faintest idea how to make one."

"Huh. So bizarre."

The expression on her face reminded him a bit too much of the wonder-filled gazes he'd seen for years from his tank when he'd been a curiosity on display, and he shifted uncomfortably.

The shift in his mood wasn't lost on her. She straightened, all business now. "First, I'm going to teach you how to shield yourself from others' emotions. Close your eyes."

Zale hesitated before he complied. He felt a little silly and awkward to be sitting cross-legged and holding hands with a beautiful girl, especially with his eyes closed.

"Now what?"

"Now I want you to picture me in your mind. Picture that we're both standing in the middle of the terrace. Feel my emotions as coming from the image of me in your head. Can you see it?"

"Yes."

"Great. Now imagine a wall between us with an open door. You can still see me, but I'm on the other side of the door."

Zale did as she said, placing Damaris and her emotions on the other side of the wall in his mind.

"Now close the door. Walk over to it in your imagination and close it, with me and my emotions on the other side of it."

Zale opened his eyes in surprise.

"It worked! I mean, I can still feel you, but it's not nearly as intense. It's more like hearing someone talking in another room but having no idea what they're saying." The sudden stem of the flow of her presence brought back his feelings of loneliness. "Um, thank you."

He tried to hide his disappointment, knowing she'd be able to sense it, but he had no idea how to shield himself without letting go of her hands— and he wasn't willing to lose that final thread of connection just yet. He snorted and looked away.

"You must think I'm pretty stupid, asking you to teach me to do something, and then being upset when it works."

"Is that what happened? I thought you were thinking about something else again. Your emotions have been all over the place while we've talked."

"You couldn't tell?"

"I'm empathic, Zale. I can't read your mind. No one can." She looked thoughtful. "That's probably a good thing."

Zale laughed. "Thank God—I mean, Elyon—for that," he muttered, looking at their hands. "You know, I've been taking daily lessons from Narcissa for three weeks on how to use my powers, and she never once mentioned this emotional shield thing. All she ever talks about is taking control of the fire within me. When are you usually taught how to do this?"

Damaris tapped her chin. "Hmm. Usually as soon as our abilities start to manifest, I suppose. Maybe earlier, as most undines have some ability with spirit, and it's not polite to walk around with your own private feelings on display or snooping into the feelings of others. But Narcissa hasn't ever really had much power to speak of. Not until she started taking the *sklavia* bonds this summer, anyway. Maybe she doesn't know about it, or it just didn't occur to her as an issue—especially since your personal shield seemed to work just fine." She glanced meaningfully at the bracelet.

"Maybe," Zale said, but something about that seemed off.

Damaris gave him a sidelong glance. "I'm surprised she's been able to teach you much, considering."

"Me, too, I guess." He lowered his voice. "Honestly, she hasn't taught me a lot. I mean, she seems to know how to channel fire—she does it easily enough herself—but the way she tells me to do it doesn't make sense at all. I feel like I learned more in the last twenty minutes with you than I have in three weeks with her." Guilt pricked him at the admission, as though he were being disloyal, and he closed his mouth.

"Really?" Damaris smiled shyly, then deflated. "That sucks. Why do you keep going then?"

"Why do you keep coming to sparring practice when you're already the best in your year?"

"To improve."

"Yeah. That. Also, I don't have a choice."

Damaris gave a wry smile. "Also that."

There was another reason, though—during Zale's tutoring session, he was the centre of Narcissa's attention. But the moment he left, she barely seemed to care if he existed. He couldn't explain why, but he lived for the two hours every morning when he knew she'd be doting on him—her pale blond hair tickling his cheek as her slim arms guided his movements, every move punctuated by an athlete's grace. Even now at the thought of her, an overwhelming desire to be by her side and do everything she said flowed over him like honey, seeping into his pores. *Ah, Narcissa.* He'd do anything to please her. Narcissa was so wonderful and beautiful. Like Venus. Or Aphrodite. Or—

Damaris adjusted her posture. "Next, I'm going to show you how to—Zale, why are you smiling?"

Zale started, soupy golden fog sifting through his thoughts. "I'm smiling?" He straightened his face and focused on her hands with effort. "Sorry. What were you saying?"

Damaris smiled uncertainly, then continued. "Now for part two of the lesson." Damaris pulled her hands from his. "Close your eyes again and look at that closed door between me and you. Do you see it?"

Zale closed his eyes, conjuring the imagined courtyard from before. "Yes."

"Now open the door and look at me. Picture yourself walking through the door, or the part of yourself that usually senses emotions in others. Can you feel anything?"

Zale breathed deep, concentrating. Nothing. He opened his eyes. "I can see you, but it's only because I've imagined you there. I can't feel anything."

Damaris frowned. "Hmm. Try again. This time, picture the courtyard with only you in it. Then just turn around and *look* at everything in it, but look with your heart. Don't picture anything unless you can feel it."

Zale closed his eyes and pictured himself back in the courtyard. On impulse, he imagined him holding his arms out wide and spinning slowly around in a circle. And then he felt it—Damaris's presence. He snapped his attention toward it, and there she was. She stood there in the courtyard in a beautiful white dress, the sun glowing on her hair, which flowed down her shoulders in a curly cascade, and a beatific smile on her face. She looked like an angel he'd seen in a painting in the squire's house once, perfect and with hardly any clothes on. He walked closer to her in his mind, mesmerized by the image. As he concentrated, Damaris's emotions changed from expectation to amusement and then discomfort. He opened his eyes.

"It worked. I could sense you."

Amusement and embarrassment played on Damaris's face. "I gathered as much."

Zale's face grew hot. He coughed to clear his husky throat. "Sorry about that."

She rolled her eyes. "That's nothing. If you knew what the girls in my dorm were like . . ." She seemed to think better of continuing and gave her head a shake. "Anyway, that door trick works both ways. If you want to shield your own emotions—you know, *without* your bracelet—you can also close them behind a door, or gather them in a ball and put them in a basket, or whatever works for you. Those are all different ways to use the same technique. Even though you weren't trying to do that during our exercise, it did have some effect when you closed the door in your mind."

"Let me try." He took her hands again so she would be able to feel him, then conjured up the wicker pack basket he used to use to take pasties and vegetables to the market for his mother. He pictured his own emotions as a burlap bag of onions, put them in the basket, and closed the lid.

Damaris wrinkled her nose. "I see that, in your typical annoying fashion, you picked up a new technique on the very first try. You're making it hard for me to like you, Wonder Boy."

Damaris's voice was deadpan, but, cracking open that door in his head, he could feel the amusement leaking through.

"You're not annoyed. You're pleased."

"See? Super annoying. Wonder Boy."

He dropped her hands and leaned back. "And you're a real rum kiddy."

"What does that mean?"

Zale's heart skipped. "It's what we used to call the one who brought in the best haul in a day when I was with the Roma, because they'd been the most clever thief."

"You're calling me a thief?"

He could sense her now. She was not happy. Why on earth had he said that?

"I only meant to say you're the best fighter in fifth year. And the best teacher I've had so far." Zale chuckled to cover his embarrassment. "Sal used to call Gio a rum kiddy."

Thinking of Gio and Sylvie and Lucius and all his other Roma family, Zale was struck with a wave of homesickness. When he'd run away from home, the Chapman clan had taken him in as one of their own. He'd been happy there, even if his long days in the tank earning his keep had been excruciatingly boring. But Eric, the man who had become like a father to him, had been lying all along. His throat tightened. Had everyone else been in on the ruse too? Were they just playing him for a sap? How gullible he'd been.

"That was a different life, though. Whatever I thought about them, I was wrong. My mother is the only family I have left, and I have to get to her."

He clenched his fists. He needed to accept that his Roma family was gone. Eric and his daughter, Josefine, the people who had welcomed Zale for the past five years, were now pursuing him on behalf of the Order they served. All that time, they'd only been guarding him until the plans of some unknown mastermind had been ready to put into place. If it weren't for Abela, he'd probably be in Tartarus right now, chained and in torment, like his . . . the thought disappeared into mist.

"Where is she?" Damaris asked.

"Where is who?" Zale asked, gazing through her.

"Your mom. You said you had to get to her?" She looked annoyed. "Chains of Prometheus, your mind is as focused as a sea slug's. Are you always like this?"

He shook his head, trying to remember what he'd been thinking about.

"My mom is . . . Abela's gone. Did I tell you that? She should have found me by now. She has a chariot, and Berian has a chariot, and they could find me whenever they . . ." That thought slipped away into golden mist too.

Damaris looked at him, brow furrowed in worry. "You're really not with it right now. Maybe we should go see Healer Evadne. You might be coming down with something."

He shook his head. "No. No. I'm fine."

"You're as fine as Icarus's wings. May I try something?" She raised her hand toward his forehead and paused, waiting for permission.

He nodded, and she put a palm on his forehead and closed her eyes. After several seconds, she dropped her hand, frowning, and opened her eyes.

"Maybe you just need more water. Stay here."

She jumped up, took his bowl over to the water fountain and refilled it, then brought it back to him. He guzzled it down.

The cool water did clear his head a little, enough to know that Damaris was right. Something weird was happening to him. Something he couldn't control and couldn't see.

He didn't like it.

In the distance, dark clouds gathered on the horizon, and the low rumble of thunder reached them. Damaris glanced at the storm that had seemingly formed out of nowhere, then at Zale.

"Is that because of you?"

Zale closed his eyes, took a deep breath, and cooled his anxiety to a low simmer. When he opened them, the clouds had dissipated into friendly white puffballs.

"Nothing I can't handle."

She looked worried, though, and kept glancing at him sideways and then at the archway, like she might be thinking about possible ways of escape. Just like every other undine woman on this bloody island had done since he'd arrived. Zale had had enough of being distrusted just for being a boy. If Damaris couldn't trust him, then he wanted to know it now.

He glared at her. "Why did you come over and talk to me? Was it just so you could brag to the other girls later how you touched the scary boy?" He hadn't meant to sound so harsh, but he wasn't sorry.

Damaris jerked her face toward him. "Is that what you think? I just wanted to use you to gain some kind of popularity points?"

Zale shrugged noncommittally. "Why not? You don't seem to trust me. No one does. Not even my own cousin."

Narcissa. He started feeling all floaty again, but he was too angry to daydream, and he wasn't done.

"They lock me in an enormous empty dorm room at night and keep *taps* on me at all times. I can't even go to the latrines alone. And they never let me go anywhere to swim. I'm a merman in a city of mermaids, and I'm not allowed to swim! They're probably afraid I'll swim away or something, and they might be right, the way I've been treated. And now here you are, acting like you want to be my friend, but at the first hint that I might be a little upset, you start acting all cagey. So what's your deal? Do you want to be here or not? Because if not, I don't need you. I'm better off alone."

He jumped to his feet and strode away from her, needing some space. The storm clawed at his gut once more.

She gripped his arm and spun him around to face her. He crossed his arms and scowled at the tiles.

"Look, Zale. I'm sorry, okay? You have to understand, though, that until you showed up here three weeks ago and Calandra made her big announcement about why we can't have boys, none of us had ever imagined that someone like you could exist. You are . . . well, you're different. You're a brand-new thing. And no one knows if what Calandra said is true."

Zale threw his hands in the air in exasperation. "Everyone keeps saying that, but it doesn't make sense. You have men here. They can't all be imbecilic automatons. Don't you have a father? Aren't there human boys around here somewhere? Surely there are a few."

Damaris stopped, her jaw working. "All human boys are Redeemed and trained as *douloi* or *tapeinoi* from the age of twelve. The only one I knew at all as a freeman was Redeemed when I was still very young. He is now my sister Eudora's consort. And my father was the same. Redeemed. He was my whole life, since before he arrived on the island until the day he died, just like the men you were brought here with. You really are different."

At the news of her father's death, Zale paused. "I'm sorry about your father."

She shrugged. "Don't worry about it. He died years ago. An accident."

Zale's throat went dry. "Mine died in an accident too."

He missed his own father so much, sometimes it was still a physical pain, the loss compounded by guilt at the part Zale played in his death. Kenver Teague was the best man Zale had ever known, his hero. He couldn't imagine having never known him at all. Yet Damaris hardly seemed bothered by her father's loss. Her reaction only added fuel to his fire.

"But I *am* sorry. I'm sorry you missed out on knowing your father, and he missed out on knowing you. What if he was the most wonderful person who ever lived?" He gestured around. "Isn't it high time things started to change on this island? Most men are absolutely harmless, just like most women. Aren't you sad you aren't more sad?"

Harmless? Zale hadn't exactly proved harmless—but his intentions had always been good. Not like his childhood friend Robert Cox, or Robbie's older brother Gryffyn and his friends. While Gryffyn's gang had been trying to hurt Talwyn and Zale, Robbie had stood by and done nothing, which is when Zale had lost control and the lightning had responded. He hadn't known Talwyn was his guardian back then—she'd just been the girl who had always been there.

They'd all been younger then, just kids, and people could change. Or at least, he desperately hoped they could, or how could he ever redeem himself for his own past mistakes? Though lately Robert had been trying to turn over a new leaf, Gryffyn seemed to be getting worse. Zale had to admit, it was pretty great that Robert had followed him across the ocean to warn him about Gryffyn and the Order taking Zale's mother.

But men like Gryffyn Cox were the exception, not the rule. Surely Damaris and all the other women in this whole crazy society could see that? If she could only understand, maybe he could get her to help him find Robert and Kofi and his other friends from the *Atlanta* and Release them, since they must all be *douloi* now themselves.

Damaris did not appear to see it. "Whether it is time for things to change or not is not for me to say. Narcissa has decreed to uphold the law in all cases except yours, and a household caught harbouring Freemen is subject to imprisonment and death. Even if I knew Calandra's trick for Releasing a man whose bond I don't hold—and, frankly, my instructors won't even teach me how to *make* the *sklavia* bond for two more years—it would be treason to do so. Besides, my father was not like you. He was human. Who's to say that human men aren't every bit as dangerous as we've been taught to believe? You heard what Cain did at the Bonding Ceremony. Why, that one man alone killed two dozen sirens in seconds—"

"I thought it was four, total."

Damaris scowled. "You may be right. Even undines are prone to exaggeration. But whether four or twenty-four, he killed several women before he got away. And in case you've forgotten, when all the men in Sireniapolis for whom Adonia had been bondmistress were suddenly Free, it was chaos. There were at least five other deaths around the city and plenty more injured before order was restored. And the Wildmen keep picking people off. I heard another girl went missing yesterday, someone who worked right here in the palace. That hardly seems harmless."

"How can the Freed men be responsible for that? There are no Freemen in the palace, are there?"

"Except you." She arched a taunting brow, then relented and peered at the refreshment stand across the lawn, which had been emptied by servants while they sat chatting. "I never said she lived in the palace, Icarus, only worked here."

Zale wanted to argue further, tell her about how torturous it had been to have his emotions and will stolen by someone else when *he* had been Redeemed, and how disorienting it was to be Freed from that state—all his emotions swirling in a big, confusing jumble—but she didn't seem to be in a listening mood. Besides, every time he thought about what it had been like to be Redeemed, he went cold.

He crossed his arms again. "Well, if you're afraid of me, perhaps we'd be better off going back to acting the same as before. It's hard enough with the others jumping every time I sneeze. Maybe you'd better go. Thanks for the water and the barley cake."

Damaris scowled. "So you're going to do that, are you?"

Zale said nothing, just concentrated on keeping the door closed in his mind. He didn't want to know what she was feeling right now.

In the distance, a gong sounded.

Zale glanced at the shadows falling long across the courtyard. "It's time for the evening meal. Best go find your pod before they wonder what's become of you."

"*My* pod? Won't you be joining us?"

Zale crossed his arms and stood his ground. "I've lost my appetite. Besides, prisoners have no pods."

When he showed no signs of moving, Damaris turned and strode away, eventually disappearing through the archway that would take her through the royal quarters wing to the Great Hall for supper.

Once her footsteps faded away, he went to the wall and picked up his waistcoat, dusted it off, and put it on. Narcissa didn't like him wearing it over the fitted linen *tapeinos* shirt she'd provided him, but he wore it anyway. In this land where nothing fit, it reminded him of the familiar world he'd left behind.

He hiked to the far end of the courtyard and stepped through the same archway Damaris had used, hoping he could sneak into the Great Hall without her noticing. Despite what he'd said, he'd worked up a healthy appetite. And he had no intention of returning to his empty dorm room a moment sooner than necessary.

The *tapeinoi* near the door fell into place behind him, and Zale glanced uneasily over his shoulder. The faces of the men remained as blank as always, staring straight ahead as though seeing nothing, yet somehow seeing everything. He'd seen them sparring in the courtyard in the mornings, and their dispassionate movements had made him think of the sparring dummies along the wall—while the men moved with intention and skill, they did it without emotion. Their blank presence was yet another reminder that although this was the land of his own kind, he didn't really belong.

How long until Narcissa decided to lift the reprieve she'd given to him alone among all the men on this island to remain Free? And how long until the novelty of Damaris's new male undine friend wore off, and she abandoned him? He'd made the right decision, blowing her off. He had to make sure he stayed focused on his mission to save . . .

Narcissa. He had to trust Narcissa. She was the one who would do the saving of . . . whomever it was that needed it.

Floating on a dreamy golden cloud, he turned and wandered toward his dorm room, smiling when the lock clicked shut behind him.

4
THE REBEL

Calandra kor'Delphine glided through the dark green water of the narrow drainage tunnel, propelling herself toward the centre of the lowest level of the Opal Palace with a flick of her tail, using her hands to keep herself away from the rough-hewn, algae-covered stone walls. In the soft glow of the lightstone laced onto the left shoulder of her bodice, she could make out the aubergine fluke-like tail fins of Kynthia in front of her. Ahead of Kynthia, a defected siren singer named Airlea led the way, and Nelly kor'Nyx followed Calandra. The antiques merchant's salty pilot of a sister, Nicandra—or Nick, as she insisted on being called—had stayed behind with the submersible, waiting for the rest of them to return.

Other than Nick and Kynthia, every member of this team had joined the Free Will Society in the last three weeks, and most of their skills lay far outside the territory of stealth and rescue. But when one incites a rebellion, one must take what one can get.

Rebel. There's a word I never thought I'd claim.

Then again, three weeks ago, Calandra wasn't sure she'd even live this long.

Calandra's Tear bumped against the bare pale flesh of her décolletage as she swam. The dark green opal pendant had been bequeathed to her by her mother, Delphine. Normally, Calandra would take the Tear off in the water, but for this mission she needed the emotional field dampening abilities that her mother had imbued it with. Last week, she'd finally figured out how Delphine had created the emotional shield, and now the other three members of the stealth team wore their own dampening shield-stones—multi-coloured red, orange, yellow, green, and black oval fire agate stones from the mines at Fire Lake, not teardrop opals, on woven hemp bands around their upper arms. If Atargatis smiled and Narcissa hadn't increased the guard at the lower levels of the palace, they would get all the way to their goal undetected. Calandra closed her eyes and sent up a silent prayer for insurance.

The tunnel went on forever, and she was glad she'd brought lightstones. Even though she hadn't had a nightmare for weeks, it was dark enough in the passage that even her and her companions' sharp night vision wouldn't have been able to see much, and the last thing she needed was to feel trapped in the darkness of a vast, empty ocean. Not that a tunnel would have felt like that anyway, she supposed. Still, she kept peering past Kynthia's and Airlea's fluttering swimming skirts, hoping for a hint they were nearing the grates that would let them into the pool at the base of the Mother's Heart chamber, the home of the Heartstone.

The enormous spherical fire opal encased in rock quartz suspended five stories above the waterline in the Mother's Heart chamber was the most precious object on Sirenia—Atargatis's gift to protect her children from the bloodthirsty humans who would prey on them. Despite its long, slow decline over the millennia, the Heartstone was still Sirenia's primary source of power. At least it used to be, until three weeks ago when Calandra and her brother, Zale, had attempted what no undine in three millennia had been able to do—use conjoined male and female powers to heal it. But instead of renewing the hope of the Atargasian undines, she and Zale had damaged it further, and the barrier that protected their island had vanished. *Some Saviour of the Heartstone I turned out to be.*

She still got a shiver up her spine every time she thought of the bolts of lightning and the booming crack that had signalled the Stone's further devastation. Never in all their history had their island been so defenseless and exposed. It was what kept Calandra up at night.

Well, one of the things. There were so many others—how to feed the rebels and Freed human men sheltering at Margaret House. How to help those in the city who were cowering in fear of the feral Freemen roaming the streets and bring those men under the FWS's protection. How to protect the island from outside ships until the barrier could be restored—*if* it could be restored. And what to do about her cousin Narcissa's complete lack of concern for any of it.

Ironic—I finally get rid of my nightmares and there are four other even bigger problems to take their place. Or more like four dozen.

The bundle of stinging nettle-like *sklavia* bonds she carried in the back of her mind—tethers to the minds of men around the island—flared red and bright in her vision, and a dull, throbbing ache in her temples threatened a seizure. *Not now. Please!*

She hummed under her breath, reaching for the peaceful centre that had been her refuge since she'd become one with the Spirit of the Heartstone three weeks ago. That Spirit, which she'd felt so keenly at first, had been harder and harder to sense ever since—and so had the peace she needed to prevent the seizures. Which was why Airlea had come on this mission, though Calandra would have preferred to leave the clingy volunteer at home—she seemed to have a knack for soothing Calandra's headaches, something that had eluded every physic who'd tried.

The throbbing pain signalled the biggest problem causing her to lose sleep—the eventual insanity that would surely mean the destruction of the entire island and beyond. With the way her power had been growing lately, probably *far* beyond. Unless, of course, she did the right thing, following in the wake of the Mad healers before her, and exiled herself to the Abyss.

She shivered and flexed the hand her mentor, Thea kor'Aglaia, had had to regrow after she'd lost it to the Voidstone. She'd had a brush with the Abyss and the creatures who lived there already, and she didn't care to repeat the experience.

Still, if it's between me or the destruction of the island . . .

She knew which she would choose. It was what she always chose. She just hoped it wouldn't come to that.

Airlea peered through the grate into the darkness beyond. When she looked back at Calandra, her emerald-green eyes glowed faintly in her pale, heart-shaped face.

"Feels clear."

Calandra moved forward and placed her hands against the edges of the copper grate. Copper was not as easy to manipulate as stone or crystal—most stone healers wouldn't even attempt what Calandra was about to do. To Calandra, though, breaking the bonds that held the metal in place was as simple as tying her bodice or combing her hair. But she felt no pride in the fact. Why should she? She had failed in her duty, the one thing she'd been raised to succeed in—healing the Heartstone. No other accomplishment could ever shine brightly enough to make her forget that.

She moved the grate aside and slipped into the Mother's Pool. Moonlight from the open tower above the pool didn't penetrate this deep, but the water was a slightly lighter shade of night.

Her empathic sense on high alert, she reached out with spirit to see who was in proximity and if there were any danger from within the palace. She sensed only one presence in the vicinity of the antechamber above—someone with an emotional aura of waiting about her. That would be Zoe kor'Dione, the siren singer who'd been working with them from the inside. Zoe had been with Calandra when she'd finally learned the truth about the Madness and had helped her in many ways since. Calandra felt a sliver of gratitude that not everyone in the palace who trusted her had suffered for it. Without Zoe's continued loyalty, Calandra could never have gotten this far.

She hummed the all-clear signal to her teammates over her shoulder. When Airlea—the only other team member fully trained with spirit—hummed back confirmation that she also sensed no danger, Calandra used her powerful tail to propel herself to the surface of the pool. The water brightened with every thrust, until she broke the surface into one of her favourite places in the Opal Palace—the tricorn-shaped tower at its core.

Moonlight streamed through the glass ceiling over seven storeys above them, refracted and amplified by the thousands of rock crystals that lined the walls of the vast chamber, making her feel as though she were floating in a cavern of silver fire. Far above her head, connected to the wall by six golden spokes, loomed the Heartstone, its centre pulsing with a dull red glow like the last embers of a dying fire. Calandra stared at the Stone. The beating heart of their island should be blazing with brilliant red fire. Instead, its rock quartz surface was marred with a jagged fissure on one side, and the fire opal at its heart would barely outshine a candle.

Still, the Stone was not as damaged as she'd expected. There was the crack in the surface, yes, but the Heartstone was otherwise completely intact, the rest of the surface smooth and whole, and no other fissures pierced the heart. She stared at it in curiosity. If the Heartstone was still working, why had the barrier gone down? Tentatively, she reached out with spirit to see if she could touch the presence she knew resided in the Stone.

Nelly broke the surface beside her. "Is that it?" She frowned at the Heartstone, sounding more disappointed than incredulous.

Calandra ignored the question and opened her heart a little further. The Spirit was definitely there, warm and welcoming, like sun on the salt sea with clear blue sky above. She took a breath that smelled of tangy summer rain on an easterly wind, despite the still air of the chamber. She drank in the promise and comfort of it. For a moment, everything seemed less hopeless.

Beside her, Nelly and the others floated in the dazzling water, staring around the Mother's Heart chamber in wonder. It was the first time any of them besides Airlea had seen it.

"It's stronger than I expected," Airlea murmured, staring at the sphere above them. The Heartstone's dim pulse reflected in her big eyes. She turned her earnest, heart-shaped face on Calandra as though waiting for a response.

Calandra sucked in her lips and studied the Heartstone. So it wasn't just her imagination.

"I agree." She retracted her empathic sense to return to the task at hand. They didn't have time to solve the mystery of the Heartstone right now. She jerked her finger at the small ledge about ten feet above their heads. "Zoe's waiting above."

She began swimming toward the ladder, making soft swooshing noises as she pulled herself through the water, her long, honey-blond braid trailing behind her.

As though on cue, a woman with a dark brown braided ponytail hanging over her shoulder stuck her head over the ledge. When she saw them, a spike of alarm shot from her and she whispered, "Took you long enough."

Calandra smirked. So the shieldstones had worked. It was rare for Zoe's emotional shield to be rattled by anything.

"We had to avoid the siren pods patrolling the cove." Calandra reached for the ladder notches cut into the smooth stone of the wall. When she looked up again, Zoe had disappeared into the room beyond.

Calandra changed to *podia* state, her banded blue-green tail dividing into slender legs, the scales fading, the slick protective layer of gel absorbing into her skin, and her ruffled leathery gills flattening against her neck. She ascended to the small ledge protruding from the wall at the top of the ladder and clambered into the small arched marble antechamber beyond, standing near the edge of the black marble triquetra inlaid on the white floor. On the wall, torches burned in sconces next to lightstone fixtures that hadn't been used for years—not since Calandra's aunt, Queen Adonia, had declared a blackout as a preventative measure against the further degradation of the Heartstone when Calandra had been thirteen.

The five-year blackout had probably helped the Stone to survive until Calandra came of age last month, which is exactly what Adonia had intended. Just as she'd intended for Calandra to take the *sklavia* bonds of all the unmarried men on the island—which Calandra had been doing when she'd lost her hand and had to return to Sireniapolis midway through the island tour—and bond a consort in order to enhance her power as much as possible before attempting to heal the Heartstone with the help of a circle of stone healers. She'd also intended for Calandra to eventually take the throne, naming her the Opal Princess, much to Narcissa's outrage.

Then again, there were a lot of things Adonia hadn't intended—for Calandra to learn that the *sklavia* bonds were not only the reason why powerful healers like herself went Mad, but also why no boys had been born on the island for three millennia. For Calandra to Free her intended consort, Osaze, proving to herself and the rest of the island that not all men were the violent monsters she'd been raised to believe. And for the son Adonia's sister had fled the island to raise to return right before the Heartstone healing ceremony by a stroke of divine grace, proving that a woman who conceived with a free-minded consort could, indeed, bear a son—and that son could be gifted with fire, an element no female undine had ever had access to.

Delphine hadn't been Mad. She'd been convicted with glorious purpose. And she'd given Calandra the burden of following in her footsteps.

For Releasing Osaze, Adonia had intended to have Calandra executed, as was the law. Except, instead, she'd gone Mad and died, and the niece she'd raised to be the Saviour of the Heartstone had fled the city in defeat—her mentor dead, her consort-elect exiled by her own volition, her brother abandoned, several of her allies imprisoned, and the Heartstone darker than ever.

So many mistakes. Tonight, she intended to right two of those wrongs.

Calandra and her companions stood in a loose circle on the marble floor, water dripping from their dark green hemp swimming skirts and scoop-necked bodices, with small oiled-canvas dry pouches tied to their swimming belts. Working quickly, they withdrew small towels from their pouches and dried off as best they could, then tied short linen sarongs around their hips over the wet thigh-length skirts, covering them to the knees.

Zoe descended the stairs just beyond the antechamber's back arched entrance and reentered the room. The siren was in full land-duty uniform, the communication stone and silver triquetra pin set with a single pearl denoting her rank as a singer laced onto the left shoulder of her leather-belted turquoise-blue fitted bodice. She laid her bamboo *deiktis* staff against her shoulder and flicked her regulation braid behind her.

"We're still clear. How did you get this far without me sensing any of you?"

Zoe's tone was casual, but her unease at their stealthy entrance seeped from her pores and into Calandra's empathic soul, and the throbbing behind Calandra's eyes increased.

Calandra pointed to her Tear, which still glistened with drops of water. "I finally figured out how my mother made this. Should make it easier for us to get to the dungeons this way."

Zoe eyed the teardrop-shaped cabochon-cut opal pendant hanging from the silver chain around Calandra's neck, then glanced at the fire agates the others wore. "Did you bring one for me?"

"We don't have that many yet. I'll add you to the list."

Zoe nodded once, then indicated the hallway receding into the dark depths beneath the Opal Palace next to the stairwell that ascended to the upper levels.

"Everything's looked after. No one suspects a thing." Zoe glanced around the circle of women. "Are you going to introduce me?"

Calandra swallowed. "Sorry. This is Kynthia, a woman who joined us from Fire Lake. You remember, we met her that day at Elpida. She has a little boy named Xander."

"Yes, I remember." Zoe nodded toward Kynthia but did not salute.

Kynthia bunched the fingers and thumb of her right hand together and pressed them to the centre of her slightly bowed forehead. "Nice to see you again, Singer kor'Dione."

Calandra indicated the elegant middle-aged woman with her light brown hair in thin rows of long braids gathered in a ponytail.

"This is Penelope —"

"Nelly," she interjected, bunching the fingers of her right hand and pressing them against her forehead in salute. "I believe you've met my sister, Nick. You're doing good work here, Singer kor'Dione."

Zoe nodded, hesitantly returning the salute.

"And you probably know Singer kor'Phile." Calandra indicated the slim young woman next to her.

Airlea gave a crisp salute, pressing her fingers to her forehead as though they'd been pulled there by magnetic force. "Singer kor'Dione."

Zoe's expression did not change, but Calandra sensed a coolness come over her.

"You still use your designation?"

Airlea's face turned red. "I do not. Calandra insists. Please call me Airlea."

She dropped her gaze in shame, and Calandra realized she should have felt bad for embarrassing her. But, like the rest of her emotions lately, the place in her heart that should have held shame for hurting another was as dead as the Heartstone in the chamber behind them.

"I apologize," Calandra said woodenly. "I still call her by the rank she held when she served with Rhapsodist kor'Zelia."

While Calandra and Zale had been trying to heal the Heartstone, Calandra's insane aunt had been trying to kill them from inside the Mother's Heart Observation Chamber using spirit—something Calandra hadn't thought possible until she'd seen Adonia do it in Fire Lake. If Calandra's best friend, Tanni kor'Zelia, hadn't attacked, Adonia probably would have succeeded. Tanni had diverted Adonia's attention but had been killed seconds later with a single blast of spirit from the queen's hands.

Calandra's hands shook at the memory. She pressed them against her legs to still them. "I have so few ways to honour her sacrifice, or the sacrifice that Airlea has made in joining our cause so publicly. Not that I want you to do that," she added quickly. "We need you on the inside, and I appreciate the risk you take in remaining where you are."

Zoe nodded. "Your appreciation is appreciated. It's not easy, as I'm sure you can imagine, while surrounded by so many powerful healers and sirens."

Calandra nodded. The Opal Palace was populated by humans and undines alike in various roles, but it was also the home of the Royal Academy, where the most gifted girls on the island were sent to train to become sirens, stone healers, plant healers, and physics. And since the events of three weeks ago, Zoe had been in danger every moment from either her siren podmates or any other undine with sufficient power who happened to notice something off about her. Fortunately, Zoe had the most emotional discipline of anyone Calandra knew—she rarely let her own emotions show, even without a shieldstone.

"I know. Thank you." Calandra laid a hand on Zoe's arm, hoping to convey gratitude, but found her well dry. She said the words, but that's all they were.

Startlement and something else—guilt?—seeped through the touch before Zoe stiffened and turned away. Was Zoe hiding something?

But of course she was. She was aiding and abetting a wanted criminal, a defector, and two other rebels in getting into the palace to break other criminals out of prison. Calandra hadn't realized how much the siren's subterfuge bothered her, but, if anything, Zoe's inner struggle put Calandra's mind at ease. It wasn't easy standing against tradition for what one knew was right—Calandra knew that better than anyone. If Zoe weren't questioning herself, that would be of greater concern.

Zoe frowned and gestured down the hallway. "Let's get to this, shall we? The longer we stand here, the greater the risk of discovery."

"Yes, let's. After you, Singer kor'Dione."

With a look around the circle of women, Zoe turned and padded down the hall in bare feet.

Calandra swallowed. No turning back now. Their fate was in Zoe's hands.

She beckoned to the others and followed Zoe into the bowels of the Opal Palace.

5

JAILBREAK

As soon as the silvery moonlight diffusing from the Mother's Heart faded behind Calandra and the others, Zoe pressed her thumb against a lightstone on her wrist and held it aloft. Calandra glanced high up on the wall—yes, even the lightstone that had stayed dimly alight during the blackout had gone dark. Calandra lit her own lightstone, and the others did the same. *If the barrier is down and not even the guide lights remain, how long until the Voidstone fails too?*

A charging red-gold dragon with its mouth open to consume her filled her vision, and she blinked it away. Cold sweat trickled down her back.

How long until Damon comes for me?

Zoe led them up a level on a staircase that had been hewn directly out of the black basalt of the mountain, then set off along the curving stone passage toward the dungeons. Calandra could have guided the group herself—while growing up in the palace, she'd spent many nights wandering the hallways, plagued by sleeplessness. The lower corridors carved from black stone by long-dead stone healers—passages others had forgotten— had been her refuge. When she'd been caught, which wasn't often, she'd paid for it. But that had been better than enduring the nightmares of an ocean devoid of life and light—every living creature dead by her failure.

Damon had taken the nightmares away . . . for a time. But then he'd proven to be the worst nightmare of all. What had happened to the dragon spirit who'd attacked her and Zale in the Heartstone? Had he escaped as she feared, or was he still trapped in the Void?

And why hadn't Adonia replaced the guide lights with self-powered lightstones years ago? Perhaps torches were more readily available.

52

The more crowded Sirenia had become, the further resources had had to stretch. Calandra may not have always agreed with Adonia's tactics, but until she'd gone Mad, the queen had been a good leader of her people. If only her daughter could have taken the best, instead of the worst, from her mother.

In the darkness ahead of them, she saw Tanni fall once more, the siren's throat crushed by Adonia's outstretched hand from across the Observation Chamber. Something about being here again, where it had all happened, was bringing everything back. Calandra's heart sped up and the throbbing in her temples increased.

A light touch on her shoulder made her open her eyes.

Airlea looked at her in concern. "Are you okay?"

Calandra nodded. "Splashy," she muttered, and shrugged off Airlea's hand. She might be wearing an emotional damper, but Airlea would be able to sense her emotions through touch, regardless, and she didn't want to share them with anyone. Not right now. Her pain was all she had left of Tanni. And it was *hers*.

If Tanni were here, she'd call me a lump fish.

She clamped her jaw and clenched her fists.

If Tanni were here, she'd be calling me a lot of things right now. But at least she'd be here.

She had shared everything with Tanni from the age of seven when they became bunkmates at the Academy, right down to an empathic bond no one else had known about—a technique Calandra had discovered by accident. Well, no one except her consort-elect, Osaze, with whom she had shared one much like it. At the thought of the man she loved, a man who was now thousands of miles away, never to return, tears threatened at last, and she blinked them away. Where those two emotional links used to be in her brain, comforting her and connecting her to her loved ones, all that remained was a vacuum to remind her of all she had lost.

Zoe motioned for them to stop, and they melted against the wall. To their right, a short stairwell descended to dungeon level. If they continued along the hallway, they would eventually reach the stairwell that would lead them down to the other underwater entrance Calandra had discovered long ago, which she, Nick, and Thea's consort Gerrick had used to escape after their plans had gone so awry. Calandra had originally planned to use that as the entrance for this rescue mission, thinking it would have been simpler and less dangerous to come back that way, but Zoe had warned them that Narcissa had posted guards at the entrance to the passage, and no one was allowed in or out. Entering through the Mother's Heart had been the only other option besides coming in the front door. And her cousin would not have given her a warm reception.

A quick check with spirit revealed four presences in various stages of alertness in the otherwise-empty dungeons below. Calandra leaned toward Zoe.

"I thought you said you cleared the way for us." She jerked her head toward the stairs. "There are four people down there. I don't want to give anyone a story to tell. We can't afford for you to blow your cover."

Zoe arched an eyebrow. "Don't you trust me?"

Calandra, chagrined, nodded. "If I didn't, we wouldn't be here."

Zoe gave a perfunctory nod. "Good."

She walked over to a nearby alcove and fetched two copper flasks from behind an antique Phrygian vase depicting Melissa stalking the white hart. It was chipped and dusty and the paint had faded—Calandra could see why it had been stashed out of the way down here.

"Now, to take care of my duty-mate." Zoe turned toward the stairwell.

Calandra eyed the flasks, wondering what she planned to do with the other siren who had been posted on guard duty for the night. "But—"

Zoe halted next to Calandra. "I forgot to mention, they brought in a new prisoner last night, a young human woman they caught trafficking Freemen out of the city. I assume you'll want to take her with you."

A human woman helping the Freemen? Intriguing. Trying to sneak Freemen past the royal guard now patrolling every road out of Sirenia-polis was either incredibly foolish or incredibly brave. Or both. Calandra wondered where she'd been taking them. At least that explained the fourth person. She supposed the Freemen had already been re-enslaved and re-turned to their mistresses, and her heart pinched. *But Osaze is safe.*

"What are you planning to do about your podmate?" Calandra asked.

From the back of the line, Kynthia strained to hear the answer.

Zoe smiled. "Don't worry. As I said, I've got you covered. Just stay out of sight until I signal."

"How will we know what your signal is?" Kynthia asked.

Zoe gave her a look of disdain. "You'll know."

Kynthia, chastened, took a step back and said nothing more.

Zoe gestured for them to stay out of sight, and Calandra and the others pressed themselves into the wall of the hallway. Then Zoe turned and strutted down the stairs and along the passageway, hailing her fellow guard.

"What took you so long?" came the other woman's voice. "Was there a lineup at the lavs in the middle of the night?"

"I really had to go," Zoe said, and laughed. "And I stopped at the kitchen on the way back. Here. Courtesy of Maria. Mulled spiced wine, fresh from the cauldron."

"I thought you were going to the lavs, not to flirt with that scullery maid who fancies you."

"Too bad I don't like women. She's a pretty one." Zoe's tone was jovial. "Besides, it was on the way, and I thought we could use a little nightcap. It's not like anything ever happens down here."

"That's the truth," the woman said. "But drinking on duty? I don't know . . ."

Zoe guffawed. "What do you think will happen? Someone will come check on us? Like anyone ever comes down here unless they absolutely have to. We won't see another soul until duty change at dawn."

"What if Narcissa goes on one of her rampages and starts stalking about again?"

"Don't you mean *her majesty?*"

The other guard harrumphed. "Such a pity that Calandra died before she could claim the throne. But until there's a formal ceremony, I'll call Narcissa what I want. Her name's a lot better than some of the choice words I had in mind."

Calandra's throat closed and she exchanged glances with her companions. *They think I'm dead? Why would they think that?*

"Your funeral," said Zoe. "And as for her majesty, she won't be stalking any time soon. I just saw her, let's say, *holding court* in the Great Hall."

The other woman gave a dry, barking laugh. "If you can call drinking herself into a stupor and being fawned on by *douloi* 'holding court.'"

"Yes, that is what I meant." Zoe's voice was tight, but when she continued, it had returned to joviality. "So, are you going to make me drink alone, or what?"

"Well, I hate to see good mulled wine go to waste."

Calandra could feel the woman's desire to give in washing up the stairs in little ripples. But even Kynthia, who had almost no talent with spirit, could probably discern Zoe's victory in the woman's voice. Zoe was an exceptional actress. She never let a hint of her duplicity shine through her emotions. No wonder she had remained undetected in the palace for so long.

"Thank you," the woman said at last, followed by a quiet space which must have meant she'd taken a long swig from the flask. "If only all of my podmates were as relaxed as you. This duty is the worst, isn't it? Give me barrier duty any day over—"

The soft *whump* of a body being eased onto the stone floor signalled the success of Zoe's plan. In moments, Zoe called softly up the stairwell.

"All clear!"

Calandra and the others crept down the stairs and joined her. There were far more cells on this level than ever got used, so the only torchlit space was the small guards' common room near the bottom of the stairs. Zoe's wine flask sat on a small table along with a small cloth-covered basket that likely contained a snack for later. On the wall, a broom and some feldspar cuffs hung from pegs. Anxious to see her friends, Calandra jogged past the unconscious siren slumped against the wall and stopped at the entrance to the hallway beyond, where Zoe was opening the last of the cells, and the others followed. Three women cautiously moved into the corridor and stared at them with shocked expressions. With a muttered comment, Zoe returned to the common room for the key to unlock Meg's feldspar cuffs, pushing past Kynthia and Airlea, who stepped backward into the common room to give her space.

"Calandra!" Judith ran to her and threw her arms around her, and Calandra returned her former lady's maid's embrace. "You're alive!"

Calandra gave a short laugh. "Of course I'm alive. It's good to see you."

Judith stepped back and looked down at her filthy indigo chiton, one of her palace livery outfits she'd received when she'd signed up as Calandra's lady's maid. She'd been wearing it when she was arrested for helping to Free as many of the *douloi* at Calandra's failed wedding as she could manage before being captured. Her dusky skin was smudged with dirt and her long curly black hair was snarled and greasy, but she had obviously tried to keep it braided.

"Are you sure? I feel as fit as last month's Panselinos bread."

Judith had been Calandra's first contact with the Free Will Society, the rebel organization started by Calandra's mother, before Calandra even knew they existed. Though she and Judith had gotten off to a rocky start, the girl had become a loyal friend, risking her life to help Calandra multiple times—as had Judith's mother, Ignatia, when she'd brought Judith's little brother, Zeke, to face Adonia at the Court of the Redeemed three weeks ago, showing all of Sirenia that Delphine's theories about the bonds and androsterility were true—Zale's existence was not an isolated incident. Calandra would trust Judith with her life.

"You have no idea how good, no matter how you look. Or smell."

Calandra gave a teasing smile, and Judith chuckled. "I take the blame. If it hadn't taken me so long to rescue you, you might have looked less a fright."

"I'll go guard the entrance," Airlea said, and moved away.

Calandra barely glanced at her in acknowledgement, caught up in the elation of the moment. She turned to the other familiar face, a tall, willowy girl with long, straight black hair, a round face, and long, narrow green eyes beneath perfect black eyebrows. She rubbed her wrists where the cuffs that had dampened her powers had been chafing them.

"Meg." Calandra clasped the other girl's hands, noting that her stone healer ring was still in place. At least they hadn't stripped her of that.

"Calandra." Meg dropped her hands and gave her an awkward hug instead. "I have so many questions, but I assume they will have to wait." She stepped aside. "This is Tafrara. She came in last night for . . . harbouring Freemen, was it?"

She turned to the slim young woman behind her for confirmation. The girl had pretty round black eyes, her thick, shiny black hair spilled down her shoulders to her waist, and she wore a natural-coloured linen chiton belted at the waist. Bisecting her golden-brown face on the forehead and chin were intricate dark blue tattoos made of hatched geometric lines. She looked slightly younger than Calandra's and Meg's eighteen years.

"Yes, that's right," Tafrara replied in a timid voice. She darted her bunched fingers to her puckered forehead in a nervous salute, then clasped her hands in front of her and wrung them. "Are you sure this is a good idea?" She looked back and forth around the group. "Won't we be in worse trouble if we're caught?"

"Don't worry," Kynthia said soothingly. "We'll be away from the city before anyone's the wiser."

This trembling sea urchin was harbouring Freemen?

Then again, Calandra had been surprised by people before. The girl must have more gumption than met the eye. She glanced at the inert body of the woman in a turquoise siren uniform slumped against the wall—Zoe's duty mate.

"What did you use?" she asked Zoe.

Zoe was busy locking the doors and glanced over her shoulder to see what Calandra was talking about. "Daphne's Bane. She'll sleep it off in a few hours."

"Won't she be suspicious? Especially when the prisoners all escaped during this time?"

"Not if I threaten to report her for drinking on duty. I'll tell her that after she passed out, you came in and put me to sleep using your physic-sedation trick and she should say the same thing happened to her. I'll take these women to the exit point and be back long before she wakes up, trust me. Everyone will assume you broke them out of prison with your abilities. You've certainly proved your adeptness at getting through locked doors before."

Calandra nodded. She'd been opening locks since she was a child, which was why her aunt had insisted on posting guards outside her door at night from the age of thirteen. She had gotten into trouble one too many times for her guardian's liking. She and Tanni.

It had always been her and Tanni.

"Why did she think I was dead?" She looked at the prisoners. "Why did you all think I was dead?"

Zoe looked uncomfortable. "That's what Narcissa has told everyone. I could hardly correct her without exposing myself."

Nelly growled. "She probably thinks it will bring her more support for claiming the throne if everyone thinks you're no longer an option. Then her only real competition will be Hebe, and she's so young, she's not much competition at all. Chains of Prometheus, that girl has some nerve."

Calandra turned back to Zoe. "Do you think she believes it? That I'm dead, I mean?"

Zoe shrugged. "Who knows. She's been acting strange lately. But then, some odd behaviour is to be expected after the death of her mother and her, um, best friend."

"Best friend?" Meg looked blankly between them.

"Mari," Zoe replied. "When Cain's bond was loosed, he killed everyone on the platform with him before running off, including her. Did you hear Narcissa's blaming Thea for Adonia's death?"

Calandra frowned and nodded. She'd heard, but she didn't know whether or not to believe it. The last time she'd seen either woman, they had joined battle in the Observation Chamber while Calandra and Zale had been engaged in healing the Heartstone, and in the end, both were dead. It didn't seem likely that Thea would kill the queen, but who knew what could happen in the heat of battle? And as for Mari, the girl that had been Narcissa's lover . . . well, both sides had suffered losses. She thought of Tanni again, then pushed the thought away.

"Wait." Judith looked at Calandra. "Exit point? Are you not taking us out of here?"

Calandra shook her head. "Nelly and Kynthia will lead you to the submersible once Zoe gets you out of the palace. Airlea and I need to go find Zale. We'll join you once we've rescued him."

Judith nodded, biting her nail.

Meg laid a hand on Calandra's arm. "Be careful. Soldier gossip says Narcissa is worse than ever."

Calandra glanced at Zoe, whose face remained unchanged. She turned back to Meg. "We will."

Meg nodded, then she and the others turned to follow Zoe back the way they'd come. Calandra wondered what Zoe would do if any of Narcissa's sirens showed up, then shrugged. Zoe would handle it. She had never let them down so far.

She turned to Airlea. "Ready?"

Airlea pulled her demi-*deiktis* staff from its holster on her back and gave a curt nod. "Lead on, your majesty."

Calandra sobered. "Don't call me that."

Airlea's brows drew together, but she nodded. "Sorry, I forgot."

Calandra turned toward the stairs and gave a grim smile. "All right, then. Let's go save my brother. From the sounds of it, he should be happy to see me."

6

RATTLING CHAINS

ZALE STARED AT THE CEILING of the empty dorm. A soft breeze blew through the scrolled-iron grates covering the windows and carried in the salty smell of ocean and blooming flowers. He tossed and turned, first on one side, and then the other. No matter which way he faced, rows of empty beds were all he could see.

He sat up, swung his legs over the side of the bed, and made his way to the window. The grate was locked, and from what he'd heard of his sister's nighttime escapades, he suspected Calandra was to blame for even this infringement on his freedom. He pressed his forehead against the bars and strained to see the ocean meeting the base of the cliff below, but all he could see was the glint of moonlight far out to sea. His sister must've been quite the daredevil to require the locking of window grills seventy feet high in a sheer drop to the ocean. He wasn't sure even he would attempt such a feat.

His earlier conversation with Damaris bothered him. With the exception of Narcissa, every undine on this island had acted on edge around him—even Calandra, though that may have been due to the politically charged atmosphere under which they had met. But what if it hadn't been? Was this what he had to look forward to here? A lifetime of imprisonment and being regarded with nervous suspicion? Maybe he'd been better off in a tank among the Roma.

He shook his head. No. Better to be among people who openly distrusted him than those who pretended to love him while stabbing him in the back.

His stomach growled. Had he eaten supper? He couldn't remember.

Why couldn't he remember? His stomach declared he hadn't, though. Maybe he could convince his guards to take him to the kitchen for a midnight snack. He went to the wooden door and knocked, and stood waiting impatiently until the siren singer on duty opened it.

"What do you want? You're supposed to be sleeping."

"I'm hungry. I would like to get a snack."

The woman rolled her eyes. "I'm not sending a servant down to the kitchens in the middle of the night because you skipped supper. You'll have to wait until morning."

That answered that question. At least he hadn't forgot about consuming a whole meal.

"I thought I might go. No need to wake a servant. I'm sure I could find my way there on my own."

The woman put her hands on her hips. "And you honestly expect me to let you wander around the palace all by yourself?"

"You could come with me." Zale wasn't interested in company, but he wanted food more than he wanted to be alone. "I'm sure we could find something for the both of us." He gave her his best charming smile.

The siren crossed her arms. "Hmph." She regarded him steadily, then shook her head. "Go back to bed, boy. You'll survive until morning."

She slammed the door in his face, and the slide-lock rattled and clicked into place on the other side.

He turned and looked at the unoccupied room in dissatisfaction. Squares of moonlight stretched along the floor, crosshatched with shadows from the window grills. He supposed that Calandra had escaped even locked windows like these using the same trick she'd used to get inside the crystal cavern the night he'd met her. Did he have enough talent with earth to do what she had done?

He went over to the nearest window and placed his hand on the lock. Closing his eyes, he extended his spirit into the essence of the metal through his hand. He hadn't done anything like this before, and it felt strange to move his mind along the rigid links that bound the metal together. It was like wandering around blindfolded in an unfamiliar room. He couldn't make enough sense of what he was seeing to affect it.

Frustrated, he opened his eyes. The breeze coming in the window picked up his shaggy blond bangs and tickled his face with them, cooling the heat of his frustration. He ran his hands through his hair and tucked the errant locks behind his ears, looking out at the moonlit sea. If only he could go for a swim. For the residence of a race of water creatures, this palace on a mountain was surprisingly devoid of water—even the Pool of Atargatis near the Grotto was only for the sacred koi, so he'd been told. Most of the palace residents would go swimming in the Light Canal or down in the bay—both off-limits for him. Fire simmered in his gut with nowhere to go.

He looked at the lock. Placing his hand on it again, he called on the element that always came most easily to him. His hand warmed, and the box beneath it grew red, then white with heat. He sensed the warmth, but it didn't burn him. In a few minutes, the metal softened enough that he could pull the grate wide open.

He stood there in triumph for a moment, enjoying the unobstructed view. Then he stuck his head out the window to determine his options. There was a narrow ledge of marble not far below it that ringed the gently bowed wall of the palace, eventually joining the barrier of the sparring courtyard beyond. He looked at the ledge skeptically. It would certainly not be an easy journey, nor without risk. Maybe he should just go back to bed after all.

His stomach gave a loud rumble. *By all the saints. Calandra did this, and so can I.*

He pressed his lips together in grim determination, clambered over the window frame, and eased himself down onto the ledge. He clutched the frame and leaned back as far as he could, then peered over his shoulder at the ocean below. White frothy waves batted playfully at the base of the black cliffs that formed the foundation of the palace. It reminded him of being in the crow's nest of the *Atlanta*—higher, yes, but without the constant swaying of the ship. His fear drained out of him. This wouldn't be much harder than scrambling over the rigging.

He pulled himself upright and, keeping his weight on the balls of his feet, shuffle-stepped sideways toward the courtyard. After a few steps, he gained confidence and soon travelled the whole distance.

He stepped down into the courtyard beyond the railing and smiled. He was still a prisoner, to be sure. And what freedom he did have could be removed from him at any time. However, standing in the moonlight on that terrace with no guards and the ocean stretching out to the horizon before him, he revelled in his small victory and crept along the wall. When he reached the railing separating the sparring courtyard from the gardens, he glanced carefully at the archway leading into the Academy wing behind him. Seeing no one in the curving corridor beyond, he struck out toward the archway on the far side of the terrace that would take him toward the kitchen.

He couldn't help but think how proud Gio would be of him right now. He wondered if his mother or Calandra would be too.

For one of them, he'd never know.

Guilt at Calandra's death clenched his heart. He'd already let his sister down. He would not do the same for his mother. He was determined to find Delphine if it was the last thing he did, even if he had to do it without Abela and Berian. He just had to figure out how to get to her. Calandra had told him the gateway to the Underworld was in Atlantis, the Sunken City. But where was that? And how could he find out? Narcissa had ignored him every time he'd asked, and none of the students he'd talked to seemed to know—or they'd been playing dumb to avoid talking to him. Maybe he could ask Damaris, except she was mad at him—justifiably, he supposed. Besides, he wanted answers now, he didn't want to wait until tomorrow.

He stopped outside the archway in the shadow of a lemon tree, pondering. If he was going to help his mother, he'd obviously have to do some searching on his own. And there was one place where he was sure he'd find the answers . . . eventually. That's where he should go.

A strange golden fog closed in on his thoughts, and a wave of fatigue overwhelmed him. What had he been about to do? He looked around the terrace blankly, then looked back the way he'd come, his movements slow and heavy. The ledge that would lead him back to his room called to him. Maybe that's what he should do—just go back to bed. He was so tired.

His stomach growled, loud and long, and he snapped to alertness, focused once more on his goal. He stepped inside, sneaking through rooms and corridors until he'd almost reached the Great Hall—but instead of heading down the stairs that would take him to the kitchens, he veered toward the corridor opposite.

That singer was right. His stomach could wait until morning. What he really needed to do was find out how to get to Tartarus—to his mother.

With a determined step, he headed toward the Archive.

7

THE LITTLE REBELS

Calandra and Airlea crept silently up the rarely used triangular stairwell in the tip of the Academy wing. The servants tended to avoid this stairwell because of its inconvenient location, and students rarely needed to descend this far. They were still several levels below ground—almost to the siren quarters—when Calandra sensed people in a nearby chamber. She waved her hand at Airlea, but the girl had already halted. They doused their lightstones and pressed their backs against the tower wall a few steps above the landing.

By the dim moonlight filtering into the stairwell from the glass ceiling four stories above, Airlea used diving sign language to ask what Calandra would like to do now. Calandra replied to wait. It felt as though the group of presences was dispersing. She peeked around the corner to see who was there just as two young girls crept into the hall. Calandra recognized the smaller of the two as Melany, who would now be in her third year as a novice. The other girl could not have been much older, maybe eleven or twelve. In the dim light of the small lightstone Melany carried, her saffron hair was a dark smudge.

What are they doing out after curfew? And all the way down here?

That wasn't their biggest problem, though. If the girls discovered them, would they betray their position?

Calandra gestured for Airlea to start back down the stairwell, then froze as flickering light from an approaching torch threw the girls' silhouettes and long shadows against the landing.

"Quick!" one of them whispered.

Seconds later, the two girls ran right into Calandra and Airlea.

Calandra caught Melany and clapped her hand over the little girl's mouth to cut off her scream. Airlea did the same with the other girl.

Melany struggled in Calandra's arms, but Calandra poured calm and peace through their physical connection until Melany's brain could register what Calandra was saying.

"Quiet. Melany, it's me. Calandra."

Melany stopped struggling and, after Calandra released her, slowly turned to face her attacker.

"Calandra?" she said in disbelief. Then, bouncing on her toes, "Calandra!" in a high-pitched squeak.

Calandra clapped her hand over Melany's mouth again. "Ssh! Do you want the whole palace to hear you?"

The other girl stared at Calandra, speechless and a little awestruck.

Melany's gaze travelled to the flickering light on the landing and she doused her lightstone. Calandra released her again, and at her gesture, the four of them padded silently up the shadowy stairwell and turned the corner—or, rather, Calandra and Airlea padded silently. The other girls made so much noise that as soon as they reached the corner landing, Calandra grabbed Melany's shoulder to extend her own emotional dampener field, pulling the girl against the wall out of sight of the entrance below. Airlea did the same with the other girl. As they waited, barely breathing, Calandra watched the flickering light on the entrance landing and prayed whomever it was hadn't heard anything.

The golden light faded to black.

"Whew!" Melany whispered loudly. "She must not have sensed us. Or maybe she mistook us for some very excited rats."

Calandra rolled her eyes. Only a child could think a siren would mistake a person for a rat.

The other girl swatted Melany's shoulder. "It was probably a *taps*, not a siren."

Melany's face fell. "Oh. Right. I guess I can't tell the difference yet."

It had been a siren—the sense of alertness had given her away—but Calandra didn't have time to give a lesson in empathic sensory discernment. She turned on her shoulder lightstone, crossed her arms, and stared at the two truant girls in the soft white light it emanated. "What are you two doing out of bed so late? You would've been in big trouble if that siren would have found you."

Melany brightened. "So it was a siren?"

Calandra glared, trying to look intimidating. Time to scare these girls straight. "Lucky for you, we were here to shield you. You would have earned at least three demerits for being out past curfew."

"Oh, pshaw. It's nothing compared to what you used to do. But how can you be alive?"

Calandra's heart quickened, thinking of her many midnight escapades, particularly the one when Tanni had accidentally Released Osaze over five years ago. Releasing a man without permission was a capital offense for adults, but what Tanni had done at fourteen should have been impossible—and she'd had no idea how she'd done it. As punishment, Thea had forbade Calandra and Tanni to spend time together until they'd both graduated the Academy, which meant Calandra and Tanni's friendship had been conducted in careful secrecy for five years, cemented by the *pisti* bond they shared. While good things had come of it—not least of which was Calandra eventually solving the puzzle of how to Release a man whose bond she didn't hold—the pleasure of sneaking out that night so long ago had not been worth the price.

"It's quite easy, when one has never died. And I paid dearly for my disobedience. Stop sidestepping the question."

Melany grinned up at Calandra and crossed her arms. "We're resisting."

The other girl, who had finally seemed to catch up to what was happening, matched Melany's smile and nodded enthusiastically. "We're standing up to the Madness of Narcissa."

"Narcissa isn't Mad," said Airlea, looking concerned and amused at the same time.

"You don't know. You haven't been here." Melany looked back and forth between them. She started ticking off items on her fingers as she listed her evidence. "She stalks the halls at night and spends half her time looking through dusty old storage rooms. She tore up half the Grotto for no reason at all. She never sleeps anymore. She drinks all the time. She throws fireballs at the servants who displease her. And she has more *douloi* coming through her room than an Athanasian wench."

Calandra choked on a snort of surprise. "Where did you hear that expression?"

"Cook Madeleine said it last week."

Calandra rolled her eyes. The palace's English cook certainly had a way with words. She'd learned a few colourful turns of phrase from the woman herself.

"Do you even know what that means, young lady?"

Melany's face clouded, and Calandra could tell she didn't, but the impertinent little girl would admit to no such thing. "She doesn't like eating alone?"

Airlea chuckled.

The other girl swatted Melany's arm again. "No, you ninny. It means she's taken to sparring in her room, since she never does it in the practice courts anymore."

Airlea snorted and covered her mouth as though she had to sneeze. The girl looked at her suspiciously, then turned to Calandra.

"It's not true, anyway," she said. "Melany's just repeating silly palace gossip."

"What isn't?" Calandra frowned. "Which part? The fireballs? The drinking? The Grotto? The men?"

The part about stalking the halls they'd already overheard from the siren guard in the dungeons. Why Narcissa would be digging up the Garden of the Mother's Delight, Calandra had no idea. If Narcissa were drunk all the time and drowning her grief in another's arms, though, Calandra would not have expected her to find refuge with a single *doulos*, let alone multiple men.

Narcissa had always been wildly jealous of Calandra. As such, she had manipulated her mother into giving her Osaze as a personal bodyguard for years, just because she knew Calandra wanted him. Narcissa hadn't known the only reason Calandra had been interested at the time was because of her childhood promise, made the same fateful night Tanni had accidentally Released him, to free him from the *sklavia* bond again as soon as she had the chance. All Narcissa had cared about was taking what Calandra desired.

When Calandra had finally succeeded in fulfilling her promise to Osaze a couple months ago, he'd been haunted by the things Narcissa had had him do while he was in her service. He would never speak of them, but he did say she had not once been intimate with him. Later, Calandra found out that Narcissa preferred the company of her childhood friend Mari. They may have even been in love. The rumour about Narcissa finding comfort in the arms of men was the most far-fetched she had heard yet.

"No, those are all true," said the older girl. "Well, except the last one."

"Is too true," Melany insisted.

"No, it's not." The girl frowned at Melany, then looked back at Calandra. "There is only one boy, that new *doulos*, Matthew. She never lets him leave her side." The girl smiled as though she had just delivered the most important information in the world.

Calandra blinked at Airlea. So Matthew had survived the massacre at Calandra's bonding ceremony.

"You know him?" Airlea asked.

Calandra nodded. "I healed him from deafness at Fire Lake. Then Narcissa demanded him for her consort-elect." Right after Adonia had killed his mother with a flick of her wrist for allowing her grown son to be Unredeemed.

A twinge of pity, muted by more recent losses, pinched Calandra's chest. Judith and the others from Elpida, where Matthew had grown up, had been sorely grieved at the loss of Elizabeth and at Matthew's enslavement. Especially Judith. If it were possible to rescue Matthew as well as Zale on this mission, Calandra had to try.

Still, that wasn't the only surprising bit of news the girls had shared.

"But surely the fireballs are an exaggeration? Narcissa doesn't have much power in anything, but definitely not fire. No undine I know of can use fire. Well, except Zale. Is he the one throwing fireballs?"

Both girls shook their heads adamantly.

"No," said Melany. "That's as true as my tail is blue. Ever since she came back from the tour, she's been able to use fire. Everyone in the palace is terrified of her. *I* think she's just doing it to show off."

Calandra clenched her jaw. When she'd been sent home from Haven in disgrace so Thea could regrow her hand, Adonia had had Narcissa collect the bonds of the men from the last third of the island, a chance for her daughter to prove her worth, she'd said. But Narcissa's only talent with the elements had been a meagre helping of spirit. How could the bonds of a couple thousand men have let her use fire, when Calandra, who was much more naturally gifted, still could not? It didn't make sense.

"That doesn't explain why you two girls are down here in the middle of the night instead of tucked into your bunks in the Royal Academy dorm."

Melany's eyes grew wide. "Someone has to stop her. The councillors aren't doing anything, and our mothers think we're exaggerating, but we're not. We couldn't just let her keep rampaging around and domineering us as though we are all *douloi*. Besides, Hebe has just as much right to the throne as she does."

Airlea frowned. "Hebe's too young to rule."

The older girl shook her head and set her jaw. "She's not too young. She's a year older than me, and *I'd* do a better job than Narcissa. Hebe's younger, but she's still Adonia's daughter."

A slow smile spread across Melany's face and she beamed at Calandra.

"But since you're alive, it doesn't matter. Adonia named you heir."

Calandra's chest constricted. She didn't want to get into the succession debate with an eight-year-old, nor explain why she had no intention of taking the throne. She agreed that Narcissa was a poor choice of ruler, but that didn't mean Calandra would be a better one. Not after her catastrophic failure to fulfill the one destiny she'd been raised to achieve. And not with Madness creeping closer by the day. At her current rate of mental decline, by the time she got rid of the *sklavia* bonds, it would be too late for her anyway.

As though in agreement, piercing agony sliced through her temples. She drew a deep breath to control the pain. At Airlea's worried frown, she gave her head a slight shake to prevent the ex-siren from intervening in front of the girls. *Let them hope. Better that than giving up in defeat.*

Instead she asked, "Who's 'we'?"

Melany bounced on her toes again. "The student resistance. I told you. We're resisting!"

"There's someone coming," Airlea whispered.

Calandra doused her lightstone and they resumed their previous positions pressed against the wall of the landing. Someone carrying a lightstone stepped into the stairwell from below, and Calandra's gut clenched. Keeping one hand on Melany, she hunched down on the stairs just above the sharp inside corner of the landing, prepared to sedate whomever was coming toward them. Airlea stood on the other side with her staff at the ready.

The light source grew nearer, and she tensed. When the light tread reached the top step, Calandra leapt forward and then froze.

A girl of about fifteen with long unruly sandy blonde curls pulled back in a ponytail stared back at her.

"C-Calandra? Is that really you?"

Calandra recognized the younger sister of her friend Eudora, who had been a year ahead of Calandra at the Academy as a siren until she'd withdrawn several years ago to attend to household affairs.

"Hello, Damaris." Calandra pressed her bunched fingers to her forehead and inclined her head in salute. "Surprise."

Overcoming her shock, Damaris hastily pressed her fingers to her forehead. "Hello, Calandra. I mean, your majesty. Where have you been? Everyone thinks you're dead. Zale—he thinks he killed you."

Calandra drew in a sharp breath. That's why everyone thought she was dead? She'd been unconscious for several minutes after Damon's attack, but why would Zale think he'd killed her? That lie would have added to the torment she'd sensed in her brother during their brief interaction, the torment that had hinted at a tumultuous history with his gifts.

"I'm sorry, Damaris. I don't have time to explain. I—"

"Melany! Charis! What are you still doing here?"

Charis looked guilty, but Melany grinned. "We found Calandra."

Damaris crossed her arms and smirked. "I see that. All by yourselves."

Calandra repressed a smile. "Do you happen to know where I might find Zale?"

Oddly, a hint of guilt leaked through Damaris's shield and she glanced upward toward the dorm levels. "It's past curfew, so he's probably closed into his quarters."

"As you all should be?" Calandra cocked her head at the younger girls with a stern expression.

Charis looked abashed, but Melany's attempt to look sheepish failed miserably.

Calandra turned to Damaris. "I suppose this means you're part of the student resistance too."

Damaris hesitated, as though she wasn't sure how Calandra would react. Then she straightened and held her head proudly. "Yes, I am. We believe in a free Sirenia. We believe in the true queen. We will not abide by tyranny."

That sounded like a slogan if Calandra had ever heard one. Maybe Damaris's talents would be wasted as a siren. She should become a merchant with that kind of marketing savvy.

Calandra sighed. If there were students being foolish, she should probably try to nip it in the bud. "Tell me about this resistance. How many are there, and what have you been doing?"

Damaris relaxed slightly. "There are only about a dozen of us right now, but more will come. We heard about what you said that night at the Court of the Redeemed, and we believe you. We don't want to grow up in a place where boys like Zale aren't free to make their own choices."

At the mention of Zale's name, Charis blushed and giggled. "I hope there are more boys like Zale. He tells the best jokes." She seemed to remember to whom she was speaking, and her blush deepened. She looked at the floor.

Damaris eyed the girl, her mouth quirked to the side. "And you talk to Zale all the time, do you?"

"Well, no, but, uh, I heard you talking about the joke he told the other day in practice, and . . ." She trailed off and studied the wall.

Calandra rolled her eyes and turned back to Damaris. "I don't want you to do anything foolish. I won't have any more deaths on my conscience."

Damaris took a deep breath. "Truth is, we haven't done much yet except meet and voice our grievances. We don't know what we *can* do. And we didn't know if there was anyone outside the palace that we could connect with. We thought we were on our own."

Calandra studied her. No matter what she said, a headstrong girl like Damaris would do exactly what she wanted, and Melany and the others would follow her.

"Is Zale part of your secret resistance, by chance?"

Damaris shook her head, a wave of embarrassment rolling off her. "No. He's, uh, been *resistant* to being approached."

There was definitely more to that story, but Calandra didn't have time to hear it.

"Tell you what. You promise to follow the rules from now on so you don't attract unnecessary notice, and I'll give you a mission to help us out."

The eyes of all three students lit up. The two younger girls leaned forward, excitement on their faces. Damaris cocked her head in curiosity. Airlea hid a smile, amusement in her eyes.

"Promise?" Calandra prompted. "No more running around the palace at night?"

The younger two looked at Damaris, and Calandra got the distinct feeling that the whole student resistance may have been her idea. Zoe would be proud of her little sister when she found out. Either that or infuriated.

Damaris gave them both a searching stare, then looked at Calandra. "We promise."

Calandra smiled. "Good. First, keep your eyes and ears and hearts open for anything . . . suspicious. Anything that seems out of the ordinary."

Calandra paused. She didn't want to scare the girls, but she wanted to be alerted to any sign that Damon may still be at large in the general vicinity. But what would a disembodied dragon spirit do to cause trouble that might look suspicious to a bunch of students? If he'd escaped the Void, could he even manifest in physical form? If so, which one—a dragon, an undine man, or something else altogether?

Melany's eyebrows bunched. "Like Narcissa's fireballs?"

Calandra resisted the urge to roll her eyes. That *had* to be a rumour.

"No, more like—like, say, someone talking about ruling the world or acting violent. Or things you can't explain, like objects moving on their own, or other unexplained phenomenon."

Damaris tilted her head. "So you want us to look for someone who can use air. Can't you use air, Calandra?"

Calandra threw her hands up in the air. "Yes. No. I don't know. Just watch for strange stuff, okay?"

She looked at each of the girls, who nodded in turn.

"Great. Also, if you ever need to get a message to us, go see Singer kor'Dione. She'll make sure we get it."

Damaris's eyes widened, but then her expression pinched in annoyance. "Zoe is part of the resistance? She didn't say anything."

Airlea smirked at her. "She probably didn't want her little sister to get ideas in her head and cause trouble. I'm sure she'll be thrilled when we tell her you found trouble all on your own."

Damaris had the good grace to look sheepish.

Calandra held back a smile. "How do you all intend to sneak back into bed without being noticed?"

Melany smiled mischievously. "The same way we got out."

Charis grinned. "If you come with us, we'll show you where Zale's dorm is. Then you can see for yourself."

Calandra looked at Airlea, who raised her eyebrows as though to say *Might as well.*

"Okay." Calandra indicated the stairwell. "Lead on."

Melany gave a small squeal and clapped her hands. "Oh, goody!"

Damaris shushed her.

Calandra covered a smile with a stern look. "*Quietly*, Melany. If we're to free Zale, we can't have the whole palace knowing about it."

Charis raised an eyebrow. "Free him? But Zale is already Free."

Calandra blinked. "You mean, he's been able to leave anytime he wishes?" Zoe hadn't said anything about that.

Damaris put a hand on Charis's arm to stop her speaking. "No, Charis. He is Unredeemed, but he is not free. And I think it's best for all of us if he doesn't remain in the palace any longer."

Calandra looked sideways at Damaris, wondering what had been going on between her and Zale. But before she could ask, Damaris crept between them up the stairs and beckoned for them to follow.

"Nuh-uh, we can't go that way," Melany said. "The guards will know I was up to something for sure."

"Okay," Damaris said. "But be careful."

"We will," Charis assured her.

With a final warning glance, Damaris continued up the stairs without them.

"We have to use the other stairs that go up by the lavs. C'mon," Melany said. She crept back down to the landing, peeked into the hall, and gestured for them to follow.

Calandra glanced at Airlea—those stairs had much heavier traffic. But, seeing little other choice, she set off after the precocious young rebels with Airlea a step behind.

As Calandra trailed the younger girls through the halls of the mostly abandoned storage level, her empathic senses on high alert, she wondered if Damaris's embarrassment and discomfort when she talked about Zale were simply because he was a Free boy—a Free *undine* boy—and she was still getting used to him, or if there was something more. If even the student resistance was uncomfortable with a Freeman, how long would it take for her entire island to break the bonds that held them to tradition and change their way of thinking about men?

And would she even be there to see it?

*

THE students' methods of espionage were not nearly so exciting as they had hinted earlier.

When they reached the novice floor, they slunk along the corridors to the dorm hall, avoiding several *douloi* walking the halls on missions for their mistresses and avoiding some stoic human *tapeinoi* on night guard duty by ducking behind archways or into alcoves. Calandra stifled a twinge of regret. As much as she wished she could take every *doulos* she met with her, the men would only slow her down and might even cause a scene once they were Released. They had a close call when one of the *taps* started walking toward their hiding spot. Calandra laid her hand on the wall and directed earth energy to a nearby door, giving it a rattle that turned him in that direction until they could hurry away—an old trick she'd been using for years.

"Can you teach me to do that?" Charis said wistfully.

"You're a stone healer?" Airlea asked.

"Second-year apprentice," Charis said proudly.

"No." Calandra tried to look stern, gripped with consternation at the bad ideas she was giving these girls. But when Charis's shoulders fell, she relented. "Not tonight. When we have more time, maybe."

The girl brightened, and as Calandra walked on, she hid a smile.

There were sirens walking the halls too, but they were easier to avoid because they expected to sense someone before they saw them. Thanks to the shieldstones, the four of them may as well have been invisible.

When they reached the novice corridor, they hunkered out of sight of the night guards in front of the dorms behind an enormous potted tree.

"Zale's dorm is across the hall from ours at the other end, but they always keep it locked at night," said Charis. She frowned, as though realizing the implications of such treatment for the first time.

"The other end?" Airlea shook her head. "You mean, by the other stairs?"

Charis's face flushed red, and she gave a sheepish nod. "Oops."

"Do you want us to help you get in there?" Melany asked.

Calandra resisted the urge to roll her eyes again. This child had that effect on her.

"No, thanks. I think we can manage. Now, show me your super-secret method for sneaking in and out of your dorm at night."

Melany grinned, her eyes twinkling. "Watch this."

They moved around the plant in the shadows so Calandra and Airlea could see the novice hallway. Adopting her most innocent expression, Melany walked straight up to the sirens on duty, making as though to slip inside her dorm. The siren standing guard halted her, and the other woman, probably bored out of her girdle, came over to watch with her hand on her hip while the first siren grilled Melany about why she took so long to use the lavs.

In a sweet tone, Melany told her how, after she'd gone to the lavs, she needed a drink, so then she'd gone to the kitchen, and then after that she had to use the lavs again. While Calandra could sense that she was not telling the whole truth, everything she said held the air of sincerity. She wouldn't have been surprised if Melany had done all that before going to their little secret meeting, just to make sure her story checked out. While Melany kept the sirens distracted, Charis sneaked down the corridor and through the unlocked door of the dorm across the hall. When Melany finally made her own escape, her night guard turned around and rolled her eyes, and her companion laughed.

"Better keep an eye on that one," she said, returning to her post.

"Don't I know it," said the other siren, chuckling.

Calandra shook her head, then glanced down the hall where a third siren stood at bored ease. The two smaller dorms at the far end had been abandoned since Calandra was a child. There were simply not enough girls to fill the space. It was only logical they would put Zale there, apart from the others. As Charis had said, the door on his room was bolted shut.

His mind may be free, but Narcissa and Despoina Cleo, the siren mistress-at-arms, obviously didn't trust him at all. If Calandra hadn't received her mother's startling message, she might feel the same.

I learned better, and so can they.

Airlea leaned close to Calandra's ear. "Should we go back around?"

Calandra held up a finger to signal for Airlea to be patient. She closed her eyes and reached out with spirit along the long hallway, questing into the room beyond. She wanted to know if Zale were even awake so she could make a plan about what to do once they got in there.

After several moments, she opened her eyes and looked at Airlea, confused. "He's not there. I searched the whole room, and there's nothing alive in there."

"Do you think the girls got it wrong?"

Calandra shook her head. "They're far too clever for that. And look at those sirens. *They* think they're guarding someone. No, my guess is that, like our little student resistance friends, Zale has found some way to fly the coop. The question now is, how do we find him?"

Airlea looked at the sirens walking up and down the corridor, completely unaware that all their vigilance had failed—but without enough vigilance to check for his presence inside the dorm with spirit once in a while. That's what came of living in such a peaceful society for so long. Not nearly enough suspicion amongst the soldiers—a fact for which Calandra was currently grateful.

Airlea must have been thinking much the same thing. "If we live through this and I ever have kids of my own, help me remember they are so much smarter than I think they are. I should start learning to sleep with one eye open now."

Calandra pressed her lips together. What made Airlea think she and Calandra would be spending time together that far in the future? Either Calandra would be free of the bonds and no longer need Airlea's abilities . . . or she'd be exiled to the Abyss for the protection of everyone.

She muttered under her breath, "If we live through this and you have kids, I'll probably be the one teaching them to outsmart you."

Airlea must have heard, because she gave Calandra a confused, startled look.

Ignoring her, Calandra jerked her head to signal they should move away from the sirens. "Let's try the kitchens next."

They'd almost reached the stairs when Calandra stopped short. A humming electricity vibrated through her. She'd felt this sensation before, but only when she was in close proximity to her brother. It was as though their bodies created harmonic resonance with each other, the same way plucking a single string on the lyre caused other strings to vibrate, but amplified.

Airlea turned to see why Calandra had stopped. "What is it?"

Calandra smiled. "I found him."

8

THE ARCHIVE

Calandra followed the buzzing under her skin along the corridor, moving closer and closer to the source. Sensing someone coming, she and Airlea ducked behind another tree. A blank-faced brown-skinned man with dark eyes and high cheekbones emerged from the arched double wooden doors of the Archive with a datastone in his hands. *Healer Evadne's consort. I don't even know his name.* She felt a brief urge to Release him, but let him pass. She would never rob a woman of her consort. Even if she did think he should be Freed from the *sklavia* bond, the *syzagos* bond a couple shared was not nearly as constricting—nor as easily broken. She hoped she could help the women of this island see that slavery and matrimony were not requisites for each other.

When he was gone, she looked across the hall at the closed doors of the Archive, the treasury of knowledge accumulated in hundreds, maybe thousands, of datastones acquired throughout her people's long history. She laid a hand on Airlea's arm to catch her attention.

"He's in there," she whispered, pointing.

Airlea nodded and signalled for Calandra to wait in the shadows. She glanced up and down the hall to make sure it was empty and then dashed toward the Archive door. When Calandra joined her, Airlea held up a hand to stop her.

"He's not alone. Should we wait?"

Calandra closed her eyes and concentrated. She sensed two people in the room—one with the blank emotional profile that could only mean a *doulos*, accompanied by a determined, slightly desperate person. Could that be Zale? More likely it was the *doulos's* mistress. She could sense no one else in the room, but the bees under her skin insisted her brother was in there. Had Damaris and the girls been wrong about him being Unredeemed? Maybe it was a new development. But if so, who had done it?

If Narcissa had decreed that Zale remain exempt, she'd be the only one with the authority to reverse it. Whether she had legal claim to the throne or not, as Adonia's eldest daughter, Calandra could certainly understand why everyone was treating her as though she did, especially if they thought Calandra dead. *I'm going to have to do something about that.* But what would Narcissa be doing in the Archive? She'd never been much for book learning, being more a woman of action. That and petty manipulation.

The two presences were near the far end of the vast room, which meant the entrance was probably hidden from their view by the stacks.

Calandra whispered over her shoulder, "I think we can get closer without being detected. Follow me."

Airlea nodded.

Calandra eased open one large brass-worked wooden door, thankful the hinges were kept well-oiled and didn't squeak. They tiptoed inside, moving steadily toward the two people near the back wall. Beneath the high arched ceilings, rows of shelves holding tagged datastones of all types and colours surrounded them. Calandra was familiar with every aisle and topic—history, science, stories of the Mother. She had spent many hours in this room, searching for answers to the mystery of the Madness and how she might prevent that from becoming her own fate. She'd even read datastones of transcribed human documents—though not the originals, which were kept in a locked room. Only the archivists were allowed to see the human books brought in from ships, scanning them to determine if they contained useful knowledge to be added to the collection. Not many did. The transcribed books had been little help to Calandra either.

All that time, she hadn't known the answer lay in the broken stone around her neck.

Now I know the answer, but there's nothing I can do about it except let the Madness slowly overtake me.

Or was there? If Narcissa thought her dead, maybe she *could* sneak into the communities around the island to Release the men. But then what? Go door to door, asking if there were any men inside for whom she was bondmistress? Release them and insist they not be re-enslaved? Leave more women with confused, frightened Freemen on their hands in her wake? And how long would it take for Narcissa to hear of what she was doing and have her brought in?

Her head pulsed and she winced, glad Airlea couldn't see her face. Too bad the stone her mother found in the Atlantean Archive hadn't explained how to Release a man without touching him along with the dangers of the *sklavia* bonds. Not that such a thing was possible, but she could dream. And, thanks to her mother and the Free Will Society, at least she finally had the answers she'd sought for so long. *Cognitive dissonance. Such a complicated term for something that causes such excruciating pain.*

Lost in her thoughts, Calandra didn't notice how close they were getting to their quarry until Airlea pulled her by the arm between two rows of shelves.

Calandra glanced toward the presences, which were several rows away at a desk on the back wall of the room. She could see glimpses of their colourful clothing between the shelves.

Airlea pointed at a figure Calandra could just make out in the flickering light of an oil lamp. "I think that's Narcissa."

Calandra dared a peek around the end of the shelf to get a better look. The young woman was stooped over a stone reader on a desk near the back wall, swiping through information at an alarming speed and muttering to herself. Her pale blond hair fell around her shoulders in a dishevelled mess. The hems of her knee-length peplos were uneven and looked hastily arranged, and the gold chain belt didn't match the aquamarine fabric. It was most definitely Narcissa, but something about her was off. For one thing, she would normally never appear such a wreck.

"And look there."

Airlea pointed again at a stiff figure standing directly in their line of sight several paces behind Narcissa, staring blankly at the wall above Narcissa's head—Matthew. He held a *deiktis* staff in his hand, and he wore a belted red-trimmed white linen tunic that fell to his thighs over loose black trousers and a fine red silk cloak trimmed with gold embroidery which was pinned at the shoulders of his tunic. Despite his finery, he did not look healthy. Bags under his brilliant blue eyes indicated that Narcissa expected him to keep the same sleepless hours she did. Calandra wondered if she even used another bodyguard these days or if she put the entire load on poor Matthew's shoulders.

Calandra looked at him sadly, thinking of the brave, undaunted man whose hearing she had healed at Fire Lake—right before Adonia had killed his mother before his eyes and had forced Calandra to Redeem him.

Enslave, not Redeem.

Some habits were hard to break.

Calandra no longer held Matthew's bond, but he was definitely enslaved. Probably by Narcissa. Creating a *sklavia* bond required very little talent—even Narcissa had enough power to do that, which was why Adonia had had her nearly discordant daughter carry on Calandra's unfinished task during the tour in an attempt to increase Narcissa's power. Calandra was disappointed, though unsurprised, that Narcissa's acceptance of Zale's value as a Freeman had not extended in Narcissa's mind to the other men of the island.

Calandra looked around. She could still sense the crackling electricity of her brother's presence, but she couldn't see him anywhere. Neither could she sense his emotions. The proximity resonance she felt was strong enough that she should be standing beside him, but all she could see were the rows of shelves, Narcissa's back, and Matthew's blank profile.

She tugged on Airlea's arm and signed, *Let's go.*

As much as she hated to admit it, she must've been wrong about Zale being here. It wouldn't be the first time her powers had gone astray recently.

She and Airlea crept out of the stacks and moved back the way they had come, Airlea in the lead and Calandra casting furtive glances at Narcissa over her shoulder. They were halfway to the door when Narcissa shouted her name.

"Calandra kor'Delphine!"

Calandra's heart chilled to ice. She gestured for Airlea to remain in the shadows between two shelves, where she'd been when Narcissa had spoken, then spun slowly to face her cousin.

Narcissa crossed her arms and planted her feet wide. "You've got a lot of nerve showing your face here."

If possible, Narcissa sounded more arrogant than ever.

Calandra pulled herself to her full, diminutive height, refusing to be intimidated by her taller cousin. She took a few steps toward Narcissa to distract her gaze from Airlea's location. "Of the two of us, I'm not sure who would win a contest for nerve. Claiming I'm dead? All the better to take the throne, I assume. I'm surprised you haven't already made your claim official. The archons are objecting, I take it?"

Narcissa narrowed her icy green eyes. "Not so much as you might think. They'll come around. Especially when I take the only living undine man as my consort. How can they deny my right to the throne when they see they'd be putting not one but two members of the royal line into power, ensuring the stability of the throne for generations to come?"

Calandra swallowed. So Narcissa intended to bond Zale as consort.

Politically, she supposed it made sense. Still, she couldn't imagine Zale being thrilled about the idea.

"And how does my brother feel about his engagement?"

"He'll come around too. One way or another."

Narcissa smiled, revealing perfect, white teeth. Her smile was predatory, like a shark. Adonia had smiled like that toward the end, when the Madness had begun to take her.

Doubt stirred in Calandra's chest. Could it be possible that Narcissa *was* going Mad?

No. For one, she didn't have enough natural talent with spirit to be affected by the abrasion of the bonds. Besides, she'd only held *sklavia* bonds for a few weeks. While that had been enough to inflict symptoms on Calandra, for someone like Narcissa, she should be able to endure for years before she noticed the effects. As near as Calandra could figure, Adonia had held the bonds of thousands of men in the city for at least fifteen years before she had finally succumbed, and she had had much more innate power than Narcissa.

"What are you doing here?" Narcissa demanded. "Surely you don't intend to take over the throne by sneaking around the Archive in the middle of the night?"

Calandra regarded her cousin with a level gaze. "You've never had a very good idea of what I intend, have you, Narcissa?"

"Oh, little lark, I know you much better than you imagine." Her smile sharpened. "You, with your grandiose delusions and inflated sense of self-importance."

Calandra's breath caught in her throat. There had only been one other person who had ever called her *little lark*. Damon.

Calandra had only been thirteen years old when Damon had first appeared in her dreams as a beautiful undine man with unusual golden eyes. He'd told her he knew how to prevent the Madness and offered to train her so she could heal the Heartstone, and she had jumped at the chance. But the more time she'd spent with him, the more he had encroached on her mind and manipulated her will. When she started getting wise to his ways, he tricked her into believing he'd taken her Tear, and when she reached into the Voidstone to retrieve it, he tried to take over her body. Judith and Zoe had had to cut her hand off to free her. She later discovered he'd never had her Tear. It had all been in her mind.

It wasn't until he attacked while she and Zale were healing the Heartstone that she saw his true face—the face of a fiery red-gold dragon, an ancient race that had been imprisoned in the Abyss. He hadn't wanted to help her heal the Heartstone at all—he'd wanted her to destroy it so he could escape, and she'd nearly fallen for the ploy. If the Spirit of the Heartstone hadn't helped her repel him, he probably would have consumed her will completely.

What happened to him next, she had no idea. She was just glad she was finally free of him.

Calandra watched her cousin warily. Could Damon possess another person? He'd never possessed Calandra, not completely, but she'd thought he'd tried. She'd never heard of an undine being possessed, but who knew what was possible? After all, didn't she now carry the Spirit of the Mother in her?

She studied Narcissa, trying to detect any hint of Damon in her cousin's behaviour. Her cousin had an emotional shield erected—another odd thing for her—and delving it would require an invasion of privacy that would not go unnoticed. But was it so unreasonable for Narcissa to use the same nickname as Damon? After all, that was what Calandra's name meant. Perhaps it was just a coincidence.

That must be it. Narcissa was spoiled and vain enough on her own—there was no need to read more into it than that.

Calandra crossed her arms, refusing to let her cousin intimidate her. The odds between them were balanced in Calandra's favour—she had her abilities and a trained siren, and all Narcissa had was her skill in *Tropos Hydor Zon*, considerable as it was, and a barely trained *doulos*.

"To answer your question, I came for my brother. You didn't think I'd let him suffer under your charms forever, did you?"

Narcissa's lips curved wickedly. "Did you now? And are you sure you'll find him anxious to leave?"

Calandra frowned. "What have you done to him, Narcissa?"

"Done? Why, I've done nothing except keep my promises. He remains free to do what he wishes, as long as it's within the safety of the palace walls. And he's been making a great deal of progress with his abilities. I've seen to that."

"You?" Calandra frowned in confusion. "Who has been teaching him?"

In the brief time Calandra had known Zale, his powers had been almost completely out of control, raging through him like a storm. If she hadn't been so desperate, she never would have asked him to help her heal the Heartstone in that condition. He'd been so afraid of his gifts that he'd actually chosen to wear a feldspar dampening cuff. She could only imagine what had led him to take that drastic step.

Narcissa's voice grew smug. "I have."

Calandra must have reacted more dramatically than she supposed, because Narcissa laughed and extended her closed fist toward Calandra, then turned her hand palm up.

Calandra stared.

Floating in the air above Narcissa's palm was a little ball of fire.

9

THE GRIGORI

CALANDRA STARED AT THE FLOATING ball of flame in disbelief. Melany's ludicrous rumours about the fireballs had been true? How was it even possible? Surely the *sklavia* bonds could not have enhanced Narcissa's powers so much?

Narcissa gave a gloating laugh. "Now you're not the only special one. I bet *you* can't even do that. Can you, dear cousin?"

Calandra ignored the question. She decided to change the subject and affected a casual tone.

"Do you know where Zale is? He's not in his assigned quarters."

This was obviously news to Narcissa. Her gloating expression melted to frustration and she began cursing under her breath, muttering something about the foolish boy and how was she supposed to keep him safe if he kept defying her.

"I'm going to take that as a no," Calandra said.

"That boy is as headstrong and difficult to manage as you," Narcissa growled. "Sometimes, I wonder if his freedom is worth the trouble. If he weren't so gifted, I'm not sure I'd even bother."

A soft gasp came from somewhere in the empty aisle to Calandra's right. Without moving her head, she reached out with spirit to find the location of whomever was hiding there, but still sensed no one besides Narcissa, Matthew, and Airlea. Calandra glanced to the right and spotted a low cupboard along the wall between two shelves, its door slightly ajar. An iridescent green eye peeked through the crack, then disappeared.

Calandra swallowed, her heart thumping. Why could she not sense the person the eye belonged to? She almost strolled over and exposed them, but they had obviously been hiding from Narcissa, and Calandra would not be so cruel. Perhaps it was another of the student resistance, spying on the would-be queen. She would really have to have a stern word with Damaris about the risks they had been taking.

Unless . . .

If her mother had put an emotional dampener field in her Tear, had she given Zale something similar? She thought of the striped brown agate bracelet he'd worn. She'd known it had been processed by a stone healer, but not in what way. The resonance vibrating through her made her want to run to the cupboard and fling it open to see if her guess was right, but she couldn't expose Zale any more than anyone else. She had to distract Narcissa so Airlea could get Zale—or whoever it was—out of here.

Coughing over her shoulder as though her throat were dry to mask her intent, Calandra caught Airlea's eye, then flicked her gaze toward the row with the cupboard before turning around to face Narcissa again. She took a few more steps toward her cousin and moved across the aisle, diverting Narcissa's gaze away from her companion.

"I'd be happy to take my brother off your hands, if he's that much trouble. It sounds like you've got plenty to occupy you, what with stealing the throne and rounding up all the men in the city that disappeared when Adonia di—"

She cut herself off, realizing that it might not be wise to bring up her aunt's death, but it was too late. Narcissa's eyes narrowed, and her anger filled the space between them.

"What do you want with him?"

Calandra stopped a few paces away from her cousin, planting her feet. "The same thing I want for every man on this island—freedom. When will you see that what we've been doing to them is wrong?"

Narcissa crossed her arms, her jaw working. "Is it wrong to confine a beast for their own and others' protection?"

"Is that how you see them? Is that how you see Zale? Or Gerrick, who was free in this very palace for forty-five years? Or Osaze, who protected me more loyally as a Freeman than he ever had as a *doulos*?"

Her voice caught on the last sentence, and Narcissa smiled.

"Where is your dearly beloved, anyway? Would his keeper not let him out to play?"

Her words were meant to point out Calandra's hypocrisy, and Calandra knew it. Worse, her words cut deeper than Narcissa knew. She swallowed her shame and grief and focused on the woman in front of her. Freeing

Zale mattered more than her feelings.

"Osaze's location is none of your concern."

Narcissa arched a brow. "Well, Zale's is none of yours. Don't worry, I'm taking good care of him."

Behind Narcissa, Matthew had shifted to face the room, still standing at attention. He looked at Calandra and through her at the same time. Could she rescue him too? Her cousin would never let him go if she thought Calandra wanted him. But if she simply Freed him, he would be disoriented and they would never be able to make a clean escape. And how would she get to him with Narcissa here? She doubted she could subdue Narcissa by herself—her cousin's fighting skill surpassed her own. Still, she had to try. It was the only way to get both Matthew and Zale out of here before Narcissa brought the entire palace guard on their heads.

She glanced at Airlea, who had reached the row of shelves with the cupboard at the back and was standing just beyond Narcissa's line of sight, watching the exchange. Whoever was in the cupboard would have to come out to the corridor to reach the door, which was at least twenty-five paces behind Calandra's back.

A plan formed in Calandra's mind. She gestured with her eyes toward the cupboard she could no longer see and then the door. Airlea looked down the aisle toward the cupboard, gave Calandra a curt nod, and disappeared from view between the stacks. Calandra pressed her lips together. The woman might be an unwanted shadow most of the time, but she was a quick-minded one, and she certainly knew how to make herself useful.

Narcissa narrowed her eyes at Calandra and glanced toward the row of shelves, taking a step toward it. "What are you looking at?"

Calandra's heart skipped. She charged toward Narcissa, intending to knock her cousin off-balance and put her to sleep using the same physic technique she'd used to her advantage before, but Narcissa was too well trained for that. She avoided Calandra's attack with a simple side-step, deflecting her with a basic block. Calandra swung around to avoid a counter-attack from her cousin and ran straight into Matthew's *deiktis*. The blow landed in her gut and knocked her backward off her feet. He raised his staff above his head to strike again.

"Hold, *doulos*," said Narcissa, and Matthew froze. "Stand down."

Matthew stepped back to his place near the stacks obediently.

Narcissa gloated down at Calandra. "So now you intend to fight me? You amuse me, cousin. Come, get up. Let's see where this sport leads, shall we?"

Calandra rose slowly to her feet, watching Narcissa warily. Her opponent planted her feet, ready for another attack. Calandra's feint had put her between Narcissa and Matthew, who now stood only a few paces behind her.

With lightning speed, she spun around and dashed over to Matthew, her forefinger already extended toward his forehead. As Narcissa reached for the jewelled knife hilt on her belt and lunged toward her, Calandra Released him, then re-bonded him to her with a short trill of notes. She knew Rhea would not be happy when she reported this later, but she saw little other choice.

"What are you doing?" shrieked Narcissa. She swung her gilt-handled diving knife at Calandra, slicing her upper arm. "He's mine! You can't have him!"

Calandra cried out and stepped back, clasping her hand over the wound and cursing again that healers could not heal themselves. "Matthew, help me!"

In a fluid motion, Matthew swung his *deiktis* around to block Narcissa's attack on Calandra, his new mistress. Unfortunately, he was not very skilled in the use of the staff yet, especially compared to Narcissa's exemplary ability. In moments, she had disarmed him and pinned him to the ground. Keeping her knee in the centre of his back and his arm pinned behind him with one hand, she held her knife to his throat with the other and glared at Calandra.

"Tell him to yield, or I'll slice him open right here."

Calandra tensed, relieved that Narcissa didn't yet appear to know the trick to free a man whose bond was held by someone else. It was hardly a secret Judith and Meg would have kept if they'd been asked, but Narcissa's lack of curiosity on the matter worked in Calandra's favour now.

Matthew was squirming like a trapped eel, roaring in defiance. A trickle of blood dripped from his neck.

"Matthew, be still," Calandra said, still gripping her own wound.

Matthew went limp, panting into the tile floor.

Narcissa smiled. "Now tell him he must obey me and no one else, not even you. No matter what I say, he must do it."

Calandra swallowed, and Narcissa pressed her blade harder against Matthew's throat. She would never be able to rescue him if he were dead. His bond pulsed in her brain and the rest of the bonds flared in response. She pressed her fingers to her temples and closed her eyes, taking deep breaths. Blood from her hand left a trail of warm drops down her cheek.

She didn't want his bond. Didn't need it. She could free him again at any time, no matter who held it, as long as she could touch him. And until she could get him away from here, it was one more straw added to her already overwhelming burden.

"How about I Release him instead and—"

"No!" Narcissa barked.

Calandra's eyes snapped open. Narcissa schooled her expression to something less desperate.

"No," Narcissa said, her voice strained. "Just adjust his permissions like I said."

Calandra blinked. Why would Narcissa prefer that? Not once in her life had her cousin wanted Calandra to keep an advantage over her in anything. Why would she allow this?

Narcissa dug in the blade, and Matthew lay unflinching. But Calandra couldn't allow her to continue.

The buzzing sensation was diminishing. She hoped that meant Airlea had found Zale in the cupboard and the two of them were moving toward the door. She didn't dare move her head to check in case it attracted Narcissa's attention. She almost wished that Airlea and Zale were not wearing shielding devices, which was foolish, but she didn't like not being able to feel the others around her. It was like she was missing an eye.

There were several drops of Matthew's blood on the floor now. Closing her eyes, she gave him the instructions Narcissa had commanded.

"Good." Narcissa grinned smugly at Calandra, then released Matthew's arm and got off his back. "Stand up, *doulos*."

Matthew scrambled to his feet, his blood darkening the embroidery on the collar of his tunic. Unless Narcissa commanded him to, he wouldn't wipe it away. Of course, she said nothing to him.

Narcissa let the hand holding her knife drop to her side, then advanced on Calandra. "Now I think it's time for you to die. It would be terribly inconvenient for you to come back from the dead and disrupt all my plans to take the throne."

Calandra took a step back and bumped against the end of one of the shelves of datastones. Narcissa had just proved her superior fighting ability. It was time for Calandra to play to her own strengths.

Laying her hand on the shelf, she reached out with earth and spirit, latching on to the many small stones that lined the shelves, preparing to hurl them at her opponent. She winced at the chaos that would cause in the library's order, but she had to distract Narcissa long enough for Airlea and Zale to get out the door. Taking a deep breath, she let fly.

Teardrop crystals of all kinds flew through the air toward her cousin. Narcissa flicked her knife blade through the air, deflecting them with ease. When had she gotten so fast? The first volley didn't even touch her.

"Is that all you've got?" Narcissa crowed.

Calandra growled in determination. "You have no idea." She tightened her gut and stepped away from the shelf, extending her splayed hands and her awareness to the stones that surrounded her, holding them with her mind.

Narcissa scoffed. "Now what? You can't use earth without touching them or something else that touches them." She hesitated. "Can you?"

What she said barely registered. Calandra glared at her, ready to hurl every stone in this room so the others could escape. She looked at Matthew regretfully. Except him.

"Calandra?" came a young man's voice, the syllables slurred as though he were intoxicated or waking up.

Calandra and Narcissa both turned toward him. Zale stood near the door of the Archive with Airlea, staring at them both.

"Run, Zale," Calandra hissed, her arms still held wide. "Go with Airlea!"

Narcissa appeared unalarmed. "Zale, your sister betrayed you and abandoned you, and she is about to do it again. She came to kill you."

Zale's expression was clouded with confusion. He began walking toward them. Airlea grabbed Zale's arm, then snatched her hand back as though burned.

"What in the name of the Mother?" she muttered, holding her hand with the other one.

Zale was getting dangerously close to the battlefield between Narcissa and Calandra. Calandra still held the stones of the Archive in her mind, but she didn't want to hurt Zale or Matthew. She didn't want to hurt Narcissa either, only distract her, but the delicacy of the work required to do so was getting more complicated with every step Zale took.

"Zale, get out of here!" She flicked one wrist at him to go back.

Airlea looked over Calandra's shoulder, her eyes widening. "Calandra, look out!"

Calandra spun her head around to see Narcissa spinning backward, swinging her foot into Calandra's sternum. Calandra hit the ground with a *whoof* of expelled air. Narcissa chopped toward her head with the knife. Calandra rolled away, glancing at her brother. Airlea was trying to use her *deiktis* to redirect Zale, who stubbornly ignored her, though he'd stopped walking. He was blinking in confusion, almost as though he had been recently Released. Airlea must have found him enslaved and had had to Release him to make him come with her.

Narcissa lunged with the knife again, and Calandra barely had time to harden a block of air between them. Narcissa's arm bounced from it and the knife went flying. She stepped back, surprised, and Calandra scrambled to her feet.

"Zale!" shouted Narcissa. "Go to your room. We'll talk in the morning."

"Yes, Narcissa," said Zale, nodding and shuffling toward the door.

"No, Zale," Airlea said, reaching for him again. This time, Calandra saw the spark that made Airlea cry out and snatch her hand away.

She turned back to Narcissa in confusion. Zale was not enslaved, not like Matthew or other *douloi*, but there was something wrong.

"What have you done to him?" she demanded.

"Done?" Narcissa smiled innocently. "Nothing. I told you, I'm merely helping him realize his potential, and he has been completely complicit in the entire process. He'll need to have full use of his abilities if he ever wants to free your mother from the Abyss, as he keeps demanding."

Mother! When Zale had arrived on Sirenia, he'd claimed he was on a quest to free their mother from Tartarus, where he believed she'd been taken by some evil people trying to free the Grigori. *Grigori! I know where I heard that before. Mother's Tear.*

Her heart thumped. Damon had been one of the Grigori—not a race, but a group of supernatural beings who'd been imprisoned for horrific crimes against the world, rebels in an ancient war.

Is that who captured Mother?

Narcissa watched Calandra's face with a gloating smile. "I see you knew nothing of this. Poor Zale doesn't know the Abyss is where all the Mad healers end up. Ssh. Don't tell him. His goals keep him motivated."

"Mother wasn't Mad," Calandra growled. "She was kidnapped and taken to the Abyss by some human order."

Narcissa's expression grew pitying. "Keep telling yourself that. But you know, sooner or later, you'll end up there, just like the panaceas before you." She clucked her tongue. "Such a terrible fate for someone so gifted. But I know you, little lark. I know you'd rather exile yourself to the Abyss than sink our beloved home."

Calandra froze, staring at her cousin. For a moment, she'd thought she saw gold flashing from Narcissa's eyes. *Just like Damon's eyes.*

When she looked again, her cousin's eyes were her typical glacial green. *I must be seeing things.*

"Wait!" Calandra yelled over her shoulder, then turned to Narcissa. "Don't you want to restore the barrier? Let Zale and I try again. If he's been learning to control his powers as you say, then perhaps we can do it, even though it's not solstice. I'm certain the significance of the Summer Solstice for the annual Healing Ceremony is only because of the concentration of fire energy from the sun that floods the tower that day. We've never had a fire wielder, so we've always needed the sun. But Zale is powerful enough to generate that on his own."

"Now, why would I want that? I quite like the idea of declaring the undines' presence to the world. First, we subdue the humans on this island. Then we take over the lesser races of the Earth. Why should we cower in fear behind a barrier when we could rule them all?" Narcissa laughed, and her irises swirled with gold. "Besides, I must keep my promise to young Zale to help him free his mother—and if the Heartstone is restored, dear Aunt Delphine will be trapped in the Soulstone forever. That would be a shame."

"Damon!" Calandra hissed. There was a shift in Narcissa's emotional shield, and Calandra was suddenly aware of the strange activity within the woman before her, like a spiritual double vision.

But Narcissa frowned, her eyes going green. "Who's that?"

Calandra shook her head. Whatever was going on, she still had to get her and Zale and Airlea to safety. She turned to run toward Zale but paused when Narcissa raised her hands, her fingers curved and pointed outward as though she intended to focus power.

Out of nowhere, a massive wall of flame appeared from Narcissa's hands, rolling toward Calandra and the others.

Calandra ran.

10

THE ESCAPE

C ALANDRA RACED TOWARD THE DOOR, yelling at Zale and Airlea to get away. Zale stared at the oncoming wall of flame as though he didn't understand what it was, not budging despite Airlea's shouts. Calandra bowled into his chest and pushed him over, covering him with her body.

Zale shrieked and clawed at her like a howler monkey. "Get off, you traitor, get off! Leave me alone, you . . . you betrayer! Leave me alone!"

Why is he so hot? Her chest, arms, and hands screamed in agony at the heat from her brother's body. But she didn't move until the wall of flame rolled over them and died out.

She hadn't even felt the heat from above. Lifting her head, she saw Airlea hunched nearby, but neither she nor anything else in the library appeared to be scorched.

Gritting her teeth in pain, Calandra tried to pour calm into her brother, raising her body on one arm and placing her other hand on his searing hot shoulder. He wriggled away from her touch and sat up, then scuttled backward like a crab, staring at her with wild eyes.

Calandra stared at him in bewilderment. He was Unredeemed, that much was obvious. But what had Narcissa done to him? Or what had *Damon* done?

She turned toward the sound of running footsteps and saw Matthew bearing down on her, his staff raised. She thought about standing her ground, but using her powers to incapacitate him would only hurt him. Zale was still staring at her in outright terror. The door hung open only a pace behind her. Airlea had already regained her feet.

"Go!" she said to Airlea, pointing at the door.

They fled as another wall of flame blasted the door behind them. The image of Narcissa's dragon-like smile burned into Calandra's brain.

In the hall, palace guards and *tapeinoi* pounded toward them from both sides, shouting. Calandra extended both arms, one facing each direction in the hall, and extended her awareness toward the giant planters of trees that lined the corridor. Pulling with the elements, she toppled several on each side. Sirens and *tapenoi* stopped and covered their heads in fear.

"Whoa," Airlea said, staring wide-eyed at Calandra's outstretched hands and the fallen trees. She raised her *deiktis* staff. "Now what?"

Calandra looked around. The soldiers were already scrambling over the trees and would be here in seconds.

Matthew charged through the Archive door hollering, and Narcissa's maniacal laughter followed him.

If you're there, Spirit, I could really use your help now.

As soon as she'd prayed, Calandra's senses flared to life. The Matrix of Creation flowed around her in a pattern she could manipulate in ways normally unavailable to her. Closing her eyes, she sensed the oncoming people, felt Airlea's heartbeat, tingled with the resonance from Zale's proximity, and, with a sidestep, avoided Matthew's clumsy attack. She opened her eyes.

Airlea disarmed Matthew with a single strike.

Maybe I can bring him after all.

She took a step toward him as her cousin appeared in the open doorway of the Archive.

"Matthew, return," Narcissa ordered.

Matthew obediently dashed to her side, and Narcissa gathered another fireball in her hand.

Only this time, tuned in to the Matrix, Calandra could see why it hadn't burned. Narcissa wasn't using fire at all.

She was using something else, something that looked like fire. But not fire. Normally, with Calandra's lack of sensitivity to fire, she wouldn't be able to tell. But right now, she could.

The first siren was upon them, and Airlea engaged her in battle. "Calandra, what should we do?"

The siren made a connecting blow with her staff, and Airlea cried out. Others were pouring over the downed trees—three sirens and two *taps* on one side, and one of each on the other.

Calandra closed her eyes and concentrated, hardening the air like blocks of cement around the legs of the siren and *tapeinos* guard on the less-defended side, as well as the woman fighting Airlea. They stopped, crying out when they realized they couldn't move.

"Run! I won't be able to hold them for long." Calandra bolted that direction, and Airlea followed.

They dashed through the halls and burst into the Great Hall near the front platform, then sprinted between the dining tables toward the floor-to-ceiling glass doors beyond the vestibule. When the sirens on duty at the doors saw them, they instinctively raised their staves to face the threat—and froze when they saw who it was.

"Calandra," said one of them in surprise—a singer named Sandra whom Calandra had known since childhood.

"Stop her!" came Narcissa's distant shout from behind them.

The women advanced on Calandra and Airlea. Calandra glanced over her shoulder. She didn't want to hurt any of these women—all of them loyal soldiers only doing their duty. But these doors were the only way out.

Can I bind them in air too? Her concentration was already stretched thin. In desperation, she released the air fetters on the sirens in the corridor behind them and bound the legs of the guards in front of them with the same trick. They stared at their unmoving legs, their arms windmilling to keep their balance. Quickly, she touched her palm to their foreheads and put them to sleep. Airlea helped her lay them gently on the floor. Hurrying across the main courtyard as quietly as they could, they surprised the guards on duty at the front gate and did the same to them.

They burst onto the wide pavement that terminated the upper tier of the Street of Pearls. Fine walled estates fronted by lines of graceful trees stood like sentinels of the mountain on the left, and on the right, the Light Canal flowed smoothly toward them along its stone channel before tumbling down the open locks to the tier below. The curving street was empty except for a few street sweepers and rag pickers doing their work by moonlight or, if they were human, a small oil lamp for illumination.

"We should find a place to hide until the furor dies down. It's a long hike to the ocean from here," Airlea said, panting. "We should swim—it would be faster, and they'd be less likely to see us."

Calandra shook her head. The cool water would be heavenly on her burns, but that would be the first place the sirens would look. "We'll keep to the back of the street and make for the stairs. If we can get down a level, there'll be more places to hide."

She turned and looked back at the building that had been her home. Another failure for her list. What had Narcissa done to Zale?

And what had Damon done to Narcissa?

As though Airlea were reading her mind, she said, "We'll come back for Zale."

Calandra nodded. "Soon."

No sooner had she said it than every sense exploded with white agony. She fell to the cobblestone pavement on hands and knees, trembling from the exertion of maintaining control—or was the pavement trembling? She was dimly aware of Airlea swaying beside her, yelling something in her ear, but she had no room in her mind for anything but the pain.

She curled into a ball, wrapping her arms around her head as though that could shield her from the torment within. The earth heaved beneath her, and the sound of cracking stone split the air.

A cool hand on her forehead transferred calm into her, and gentle humming lulled the pain into a distant throbbing. The ground stopped shaking and all became still again.

Calandra lifted her head and looked at Airlea's frightened face.

"That was a bad one." Airlea dropped her hand and helped Calandra to her feet. "The whole palace would have felt that one."

Calandra looked around. There were cracks in the pavement that hadn't been there moments ago, and one of the barred bronze gates of the palace was hanging askew on a single hinge. From the courtyard beyond came shouts and screams of terror.

Calandra got unsteadily to her feet, holding Airlea's arm, her scalded palms stinging from the fall. "Do you think anyone was hurt?"

Airlea sucked in her lips in thought and shook her head. "No, it wasn't that strong. They'll just be a bit shaken up. Hurry, we need to get out of here."

Shouting women burst into the courtyard and drew nearer. The sirens she'd incapacitated near the gate were awake and picking themselves off the pavement.

"Right behind you." Calandra took one last look at the palace, hardening a wall of air through the gate that would hold long enough to slow her pursuers down, then took off running after Airlea down the street. They kept to the shadows next to the buildings and trees, scanning ahead for the city guard.

Perhaps it would be better if someone else came back for Zale. She was becoming more dangerous by the day, and the way he'd reacted to her . . . Someone else might have more luck. How did everything get so topsy-turvy that her own brother didn't trust her?

A wave of longing to run into Osaze's arms and feel safe and protected washed over her, but she shook it off. Between the increasing magnitude of her seizures, the mayhem in the city, and the possibility that Damon might be possessing Narcissa, she was even more thankful he was far, far from her, safe among his own people in Africa.

They'd almost reached the stairs when movement at the edge of the street caught her eye. She glanced toward the shadows between two buildings a short distance ahead of them and froze.

Cain stood there, watching them. The muscular man had several days' beard stubble on his tanned cheeks, wore the same dark breeches he'd had on at her bonding ceremony, and held a long siren's diving knife with cautious readiness. He stared at her, his dark eyes gleaming like a feral wolf's—a far cry from the passive *doulos* Adonia had kept as her latest plaything for the several months before her death.

"Cain," Calandra called softly, focusing her voice so he would be the only one to hear her. "I mean you no harm. Come with us. We can help you."

The man blinked, tense.

"Someone's causing trouble at the palace," came a woman's shout from further up the street.

Two women in the dark blue bodices and skirts of the city guard ran toward them. Cain gave Calandra one more glance, then bolted across the street and down the stairs, not looking back.

"There!" The guard pointed after him, and the two women darted toward the landing.

Calandra gestured at a recessed alley next to them, and she and Airlea ducked inside, pressing themselves against the wall behind the lip of a stone facade.

Footsteps pounded down the stairs. The sirens must not have noticed their quarry was a man, or they would already have been singing by now. *Run, Cain.* Even if he had killed those sirens in the confusion of Release, he didn't deserve to be Redeemed again. Still, mild relief that he hadn't taken her up on her offer trickled down her sweaty back.

"Your highness, is that you?"

Calandra whirled, her heart thundering, and Airlea raised her staff.

A fair-skinned girl with eyes shining like dark green embers in the night stood in the shadows some distance behind them, staring at them. "You're alive!"

The girl's dark brown hair had been plaited and wrapped around the back of her head like a crown behind a blue fabric headband, and she wore the calf-length livery of a household servant. Calandra recognized the sky blue-and-red striped hem that signalled the house of Dione, which was only three estates over from here.

The girl hurried toward Calandra with a rushed salute. "Where have you been? Everyone says you're dead."

"I, uh . . ."

Calandra glanced around the corner toward the palace, now a small silhouette against the moonlight at the other end of the street. The wall of air had dissipated. Sirens poured through the broken gate, fanning out along the pavement and into the canal.

Calandra looked back at the girl, who oozed earnestness. "Are you with Steadfast House?"

The girl nodded. "Her ladyship hired me only last week. It was a lucky break, it was, for a discordant like me. I was just on my way home when that earthquake happened, and then I saw that Wildman, so I hid here." She noticed Calandra's arm. "You're hurt."

Calandra glanced at the cut. Although it had scabbed over, her arm was still smeared with blood. "It's nothing."

The servant girl glanced up the street toward the palace. "Is the guard after you?"

Calandra had rarely met a discordant—an undine without any sensitivity to the elements, not even spirit, the most common gifting of all. While it was expected that humans lacked such sensitivity, an undine without even the ability to use spirit made Calandra, and everyone else she knew, cringe as though she were a *wrong* thing, like an ugly kitten or a black tooth. It was like being born deformed—except a physical deformity could usually be healed. No one had ever found a way to heal discordance.

Still, the girl's lack of sensitivity to the elements didn't mean she had no insight, as she'd just proved.

"Yes. My cousin wasn't happy to see me."

Her face lit up. "I know a way you can escape that the sirens won't suspect. It will take you right to the ocean, it will. Come with me."

At Calandra's nod, the girl peered in both directions along the street, then gestured for them to follow her. Staying close to the building, she made for the alley next to Steadfast House.

"You go next, your highness," Airlea whispered. "I'll stay in the rear and watch for the guard."

Calandra followed the girl's careful steps. She seemed nervous, but that was to be expected, given the circumstances. Once they slipped into the alley, Calandra expected to see some secret path leading up the mountain, but all she saw was a sheer wall of black rock covered in ferns and moss, the mountainous backdrop for every estate on this tier.

Calandra put a hand on the girl's arm. "Wait. Where are you taking us?"

"There's a passageway just there, through the house." The servant pointed at a door near the back of the alley. "I will show you where to go."

"In Kyria Dione kor'Eirene's house?"

"Begging your pardon, but 'tis Kyria Eudora kor'Dione's house now. The lady mother passed on the inheritance when her young ladyship took a consort."

Eudora was already lady of the house? She was only nineteen, at best. Despite Kyria Dione's past friendship with Delphine and Calandra's familiarity with her daughters Eudora and Zoe, it was a long shot that the widowed Dione or even Eudora would be sympathetic to their cause. Dione had her reputation as a city archon to consider, and an allegiance with the rebels could cause problems for her family. Eudora was a possibility, depending on her feelings toward her consort. Still, for Calandra to impose on them would require them to choose between turning her in or committing treason—or that's how Narcissa would see it.

However, if neither woman ever knew they were there, they could hardly be accused of collaboration and treason. The sirens working their way down the street knocking on gates were growing ever closer. Right now, Calandra was willing to take the risk.

"All right," she said. "Show me your secret passage. But you must not tell your mistress we were here. If you do, you put the entire household at risk, and I'm sure you don't want that."

The girl's eyes widened. "Yes, your highness."

She led them to the servant's door. Calandra thought the girl would have to knock and have the gatekeeper let her in, but she pushed on the door and it swung open.

"Come." She beckoned and stepped into the dark room beyond.

Sensing it was empty of other people, Calandra and Airlea cautiously followed, their eyes quickly adjusting to the dim light. They were in a larder, with clay jars of food and baskets and bags of fruits and vegetables lining the shelves and walls. The girl bolted the door behind them, then led them to the door on the other side of the room. She was just about to open it when Calandra sensed the person on the other side.

"Wait," Calandra said, but it was too late.

The door opened and the flickering light of an oil lamp spilled into the darkness, revealing its bearer—a brown-eyed woman with long, curly grey hair framing a tanned face creased with stories. She stood erect, her thin shoulders wrapped in a knitted shawl, though the air was warm.

Calandra and Airlea eased as far away from the ring of light as they could. The small room offered no hiding place, but Calandra hoped the dim light would be enough to hide them from her aging human eyes.

"Kelaino, why are you out so late? The mistress is beside herself with worry. We couldn't find you after the earthquake, and I was about to go looking for you."

"I'm sorry, Wilhelmina. I left my mother's later than I meant to."

The woman saw Calandra and Airlea standing behind the girl. She narrowed her eyes at the servant.

"For shame, Kelaino! You are not to bring guests this way. Ever! The outrage to our lady's good name . . ."

So much for sneaking into the house.

Calandra stepped forward to stop the tirade. "It's quite all right, Mistress Wilhelmina. I asked her to do it. We had need of secrecy."

The woman stared at her in shock. "Y—your highness? You're alive?" She dropped the lamp and it went out, leaving them in almost perfect darkness.

Calandra sighed. She was becoming dreadfully tired of people reacting that way to seeing her.

11

STEADFAST HOUSE

"Caught out in that earthquake, were you?" Wilhelmina said over her shoulder. She led Calandra and Airlea out of the larder of Steadfast House and through a room with a cooking brazier in the centre. The discordant servant girl followed behind. "That one was a tooth-rattler."

Calandra's face warmed. "Yes, it was. Was anyone here hurt?"

"No, just a bit shaken up, if you'll pardon the pun."

The woman chuckled and led them through a side door that took them to a portico surrounding an open tiled courtyard. In the centre of the rectangular yard, a white marble bathing fountain with a statue of a nude undine in *ichthys* state, her hands raised to the Mother, gleamed in the light of the waxing quarter-moon. Streams of water flowed out of the woman's hands and splashed into the pool. Near the gatekeeper's booth stood a middle-aged woman wearing a half-*deiktis* on her back. She wore the leather girdle and long diving knife of a siren, but her bodice and skirt were red and sky blue instead of the turquoise or green of the siren corps—a household guard. Many households on this tier employed them, but few saw the need for them to remain at their posts all night long. Were men like Cain the reason for the change? She shivered.

The guard gave Calandra a long look of recognition and a salute, then cast a curious glance at the servants. Calandra returned an appropriately stiff salute. That made three servants aware she'd come. How many more people would find out about her visit? This had been a terrible idea.

"Wait here," said Wilhelmina, pointing to the shadows of the colonnaded porch. She turned to the guard at the gate. "Fedra, Kelaino's been found. Please go inform her ladyship and tell her she has guests."

The guard gave a curt nod of acknowledgement and set off across the yard toward the door to the second level at the far end of the portico.

Wilhelmina turned to the servant girl. "Kelaino, go prepare the receiving room next to the kitchen."

"Mistress Wilhelmina, please," said Calandra, halting the young servant with an upheld hand. "The fewer people who know we were here, the better. We'll just be on our way."

"Nonsense, your highness. Both Kyria Dione and Kyria Eudora will want to see you. Kelaino?"

Kelaino nodded and was about to turn to go when Wilhelmina held up a warning finger.

"Tell no one else, mind you."

"Yes, mistress." Kelaino hurried to the next door along the portico and went inside.

Calandra exchanged glances with Airlea, who looked as uneasy as Calandra felt. As a city archon, it was unlikely Dione would sympathize with the rebel cause. If they left now, perhaps they could evade the sirens outside before Dione had her guards detain them.

Wilhelmina gave her an appraising look. "Now, your highness, let me see about those burns. I can send for Healer Niobe—"

"No. Thank you, mistress," Calandra said. "The burns can wait."

Wilhelmina pressed her lips together. "They're starting to blister. But, as you wish, your highness. I think Cook Stephanie keeps some lavender ointment in the kitchen. Let me see if I can find it. Wait here."

She moved back the way they'd come. Calandra caught Airlea's eye and signalled toward the gate, signing that they should make their escape through the unguarded door.

"Hail, gatekeeper of Steadfast House!" shouted a woman's voice from beyond the wooden gate. "Open for Rhapsodist kor'Valeria of the palace guard!"

Calandra froze.

Wilhelmina turned and frowned. "Is this the trouble you were expecting, your highness?"

"Please don't tell them we're here," Calandra whispered. "Trust me, they will not discover us if you say nothing."

Wilhelmina raised her eyebrows, but patted Calandra's shoulder. "Anything for you, your highness. Best hide there."

She indicated a place behind a large potted shrubbery next to a column at the edge of the portico a short distance beyond.

Calandra breathed a sigh of relief. That the woman trusted her with so little explanation, and still afforded her the styling she'd acquired when named the Opal Princess by Adonia, set her at ease somewhat. Once she and Airlea had assumed their hiding place, the fountain was directly between them and the entrance as well. *Clever woman.*

"Hail, gatekeeper!" rang the woman's sharp voice. The rap of bamboo on wood rattled through the courtyard as the siren knocked a *deiktis* against the gate.

Wilhelmina shuffled across the courtyard to the front gate at an exaggeratedly slow pace.

"I'm coming, I'm coming," she said, a quake in her voice that hadn't been there before.

Calandra smiled to herself. Wilhelmina had always been a sly one, but she had to appreciate the woman's use of sympathy for their benefit. A few seconds later, Calandra heard the sliding of the gatekeeper's hatch.

"Ah, greetings to you, Rhapsodist kor'Valeria, on behalf of Kyria Eudora of Steadfast House," Wilhelmina croaked.

Calandra peeked over the rim of the pot. Through the fronds of the tree and the water falling from the fountain, she glimpsed the back of Wilhelmina's head, and nothing else—the gatekeeper had completely obstructed the siren's view. Calandra smiled and ducked behind the pot once more, squatting on the cold tiles next to Airlea.

"Where is your gatekeeper?" the siren asked.

"That's none of your concern. What brings you to our door?"

"Have you seen or heard anything unusual this night, old woman?"

"Do you take me for a fool?" Wilhelmina said sharply. "I am old, not infirm. I doubt anyone on the upper tier did not feel that earthquake. When was the last time we had one such as that? I remember not."

"That is not what I was referring to. Have you heard or seen anyone suspicious on the street?"

"Ah, I see your intention. How excellent that her highness, Princess Narcissa, is so concerned about her citizens as to check that the Wildmen are not taking advantage of the disturbance by pillaging or looting fine, upstanding citizens. Rest assured, rhapsodist, that this house remains unmolested. I'm sure her ladyship will be pleased to know how concerned Princess Narcissa is with the welfare of her people. Unless you wish me to summon Kyria Eudora so you may discuss it with her yourself. She and the household have just begun to settle after the earthquake, but she may yet be awake . . ."

"No need to disturb your mistress, *anthropos*."

The suspicion had left the siren's voice. Probably because every word Wilhelmina said was true—she'd concealed the truth without telling a single lie. Just as Melany had done.

Well done.

"Rest assured," the guard continued, "we will take care of the instigators of the problem. Send word to the royal guard if anything changes."

Wilhelmina's smile infused her tone. "I will indeed. Thank you for your faithful service, good woman."

"Goodnight, housekeeper."

Calandra peeked over the pot once more. Wilhelmina peered through the hatch, watching the siren leave, then slid it closed and returned to Calandra and Airlea, all pretense of frailty gone.

"Thank you, mistress," Calandra said as she and Airlea rose to their feet. "We owe you a debt."

"Nonsense." Wilhelmina waved a hand. "You owe me nothing."

"Princess Calandra?" came a voice from the darkness of the stairwell behind her.

Calandra turned to see a lovely middle-aged woman with olive-toned skin and a face artfully made up in colours to complement her sea-foam-green eyes. Her long indigo cloak looked as though it had been wrapped around her shoulders in haste. Fedra stood behind her.

Calandra smiled and pressed her fingers to her forehead, inclining her head slightly as was proper for a princess to a city councillor and a lady of the nation. "Kyria kor'Eirene. I request temporary sanctuary in your home for myself and my companion, Airlea kor'Phile. I'm afraid my cousin was not best pleased to discover my current state of well-being this night and is combing the city for me." She was about to mention the secret passage, but thought Kelaino may have disclosed a household secret out of turn. Not wanting to get the girl in trouble, she refrained.

Dione rushed forward and threw her arms lightly around Calandra's shoulders, avoiding Calandra's burns. The tension around her eyes belied the warmth in her smile.

"Calandra, you are always welcome here. I am so glad you came to me. Come, I have so many questions. Fedra, alert us if there are any further disturbances."

"Yes, *kyria*." The guard saluted and returned to her post by the door.

Wilhelmina spoke up. "I was about to get lavender oil for her highness's burns. She didn't want a healer."

Dione raised a surprised eyebrow at Calandra, then nodded to the housekeeper. "Excellent. Thank you, Wilhelmina."

The old woman hurried toward the kitchen.

"Come," Dione said.

She led them into the room Kelaino had gone to prepare. Lit oil lamps hung from hooks on the walls, and Kelaino and another servant girl were setting cushion-covered stools around a clay brazier that was giving off a gentle heat. *So much for not telling anyone else.* There was a light panel next to the door, but no lightstone sconces remained on the walls—Dione must have had them removed. Calandra looked away.

Dione gestured to the stools. "I'm sorry for not receiving you in the courtyard, but it seems best to not appear too active at this late hour."

"I agree completely, *kyria*. I appreciate your discret—"

"Princess Calandra?" came an incredulous voice.

Calandra turned to see Eudora, her abdomen bulging beneath her gown in the late stages of pregnancy. Behind her stood a tall, dark-skinned *doulos* Calandra recognized from her few previous visits to the household. Was this Eudora's consort?

Eudora's face reflected the same disbelief Calandra had seen repeatedly today.

Calandra smiled. "Yes, Kyria kor'Dione, I'm alive."

Eudora rushed forward and gave her a careful hug. "You are a sight for sore eyes, and that's the truth. But where did your burns come from?"

"It's a long story."

Wilhelmina returned and proffered a small clay jar and a damp rag. "The cloth is for your arm," she said. "Would you like me to apply the ointment, your highness?"

"I will." Airlea held out her hand.

Calandra glanced at the ex-siren, her jaw tight, then nodded. "Thank you, singer."

Wilhelmina handed the supplies over. "Kelaino will take them when you're finished. I must go see to the refreshments."

"Come, sit down, sit down. We have much to discuss." Dione indicated the cushioned stools once more and sat in one facing the door to the courtyard.

Calandra took a seat across from her, facing Airlea's stool. The young woman wasted no time washing the dried blood from Calandra's arm, then began dabbing ointment onto the blisters on her face, chest, shoulders, arms, and hands. While she worked, Calandra eyed Eudora, who sat with her hands resting on her belly. Though the young lady's emotions were warm and open, there was a tension to her shoulders and tightness around her eyes. At her stage of pregnancy, lack of sleep was likely to blame. Or was there more behind Eudora's worry?

"Congratulations, Kyria kor'Dione." Calandra indicated her hostess's belly.

Eudora smiled and rubbed her bulging abdomen. "Please, your highness, in private, just call me Eudora. I'm getting used to my new title, but it sounds strange coming from my childhood acquaintances."

Calandra knew exactly what that was like. "And, in private, you may call me Calandra."

Eudora gave her a warm smile, but Calandra's nervousness eased only slightly.

Eudora had studied at the Academy in the same year as Tanni. She'd been in her third year as a siren cadet when Zoe, the eldest daughter of the family, had declared her perpetual dedication to Atargatis in service to the siren corps and had abdicated her role as heir of the household, which meant Eudora would inherit. Four years ago, at age fifteen, Eudora had withdrawn from the Academy to begin learning the running of the household and other responsibilities of the noble class under the tutelage of her mother. Calandra had seen her at feasts and functions since then. Though they'd never been close, they had at least been friendly. But with the current unrest in the city, *friendly* was not the same as *friends*. While she'd felt no animosity from any of the household so far, tension crackled around the room. Calandra was putting this household in danger, and she couldn't relax because of it. A trickle of Airlea's anxiety flowed through her touch—her companion was as eager to leave as she was.

"And welcome, Singer kor'Phile." Eudora gave a brief salute to Airlea, who'd been in the same year as her and Tanni.

"It's just Kore kor'Phile now, your ladyship." Airlea returned the salute with a deep, respectful one of her own, then returned to her work on Calandra's burns.

Eudora shook her head. "We are all making choices of loyalty these days. Just because you're no longer with the palace guard doesn't mean you're no longer a singer."

Airlea flicked an embarrassed glance at Calandra, then nodded. "Thank you. It's good to see you, *kyria*."

"Again, just Eudora. I know it's been some time since the Academy, but please, consider me a friend."

Calandra's heart skipped. Could they trust Eudora? She dared hope.

Airlea gave a cautious smile. "All right then. Eudora."

She finished with the ointment and Kelaino took the jar and cloth from her. Calandra murmured her thanks and then turned in her seat to face their hosts.

Kyria Dione clasped her hands on her lap, beaming at them proudly. "Look at you young ladies. The three of you give me hope for this city. Delphine would be so proud."

Eudora gave a smile that was both pleased and long-suffering. Calandra tried to smile, but her lips wouldn't obey. *Mother would be proud of me? For destroying the Heartstone and plunging the island into chaos? For allowing Narcissa to turn my own brother against me?* Or had it even been Narcissa's doing? Her chest tightened, and she clenched her hands together to keep from fidgeting.

A servant brought a tray of wine and offered it to all those seated, as well as to Eudora's *doulos*, which surprised Calandra. She watched him closely, and he looked directly back at her, his agitation prickling against her.

She stared, her breath catching in her throat. He was not a *doulos* at all. This man was Free.

12

THE CONSORT

CALANDRA'S HEART THUMPED AGAINST HER ribs in excitement and relief. The man's bright gaze could only mean one thing—Eudora and her household were allies to the Free Will Society.

Eudora smiled. "I see you have already discerned our secret. Calandra, allow me to introduce my consort, Ewelike."

The man stepped forward, bowed, and saluted with stilted formality. "Pleased to make your acquaintance, Princess Calandra. I understand I have you to thank for recent . . . events."

He stepped back and lowered his gaze to watch his consort. His emotions were mixed, but there was a definite undertone of affection toward the woman he shared a *syzagos* bond with.

Calandra's heart twinged. His height, his glittering up-slanted black eyes and obsidian skin, his gentle strength—all of them reminded her so much of Osaze. The bundle of bonds in her mind throbbed. She pushed aside the thought of her one-time consort-elect, and the many *sklavia* bonds she carried along with it.

She inclined her head in acknowledgement. "The honour is mine, K— Kyrios Ewelike." She glanced at Eudora to see if the title was warranted and breathed easier at Eudora's slight nod. "I am pleased to see my words did not fall on completely deaf ears."

Dione took a sip of wine. "Indeed, your highness. In fact, it must be the grace of the Mother that brought you to us tonight. We have a request to make of you."

The grace of the Mother, indeed. Who else could have orchestrated such a divine coincidence?

"I will do what I can to help you, of course," Calandra said. "It is the least I can do to repay your kindness."

Dione glanced at her daughter.

Eudora cleared her throat. "I want you to take Ewelike with you."

Calandra choked on her mouthful of wine. "Pardon?"

"Since I Freed him, it has been more difficult to protect our secret than I expected," Eudora said, her voice strained. "We believe in what you said, about how it isn't right that we enslave the minds of any man. Ewelike has been a member of our household since he was a child, and I took him as consort last year. After what happened on the Redemption Moon, I couldn't get what you said out of my mind. Despite my uncertainty about whether he'd want to remain here with me, I had to Free him. I had to let him decide for himself. But there are not many in the city who feel as we do. Or, if they do, they are prevented from taking this step by fear of the law."

Eudora glanced up at her consort, who returned the look with a difficult-to-read expression. The parallels to Calandra's own situation with Osaze were stark. She remembered Osaze's confusion and pain when she Released him at last, fulfilling a promise she'd made to him when they were children. She'd been terrified he would be nothing like the boy she remembered. And he *had* been different—but his friendship and loyalty to her had remained unchanged. More than friendship—it hadn't been long before she'd realized he was in love with her. And, like she was caught in one of the human love stories his mother, Urbi, used to tell, she with him, though she'd had no idea how someone in love with a Freeman should behave. She recognized the same love and uncertainty between Eudora and Ewelike now. Based on her own poor choice in sending Osaze away, she refused to let Eudora make the same mistake.

"Eudora, may I have a word with you privately?" Calandra indicated the door to the room next door, the one that had the cooking brazier in it.

Eudora's face grew firm. "Whatever you have to say can be said here. I keep nothing from Ewelike, or my mother."

Calandra's throat closed. She looked at the handsome man, then around the circle at Dione, Eudora, and Airlea. Kelaino and another servant girl waited near the edges of the room.

"Fine. We are happy to take another man to Margaret House. There is a great deal to do there and the extra set of hands would be welcome. But I will not take him if he doesn't choose to go on his own. So, Ewelike, what is your choice?"

"We have already decided that he should go," Eudora said firmly.

Ewelike cleared his throat and laid a gentle hand on his consort's shoulder. "Actually, I did not say I would."

Eudora turned to him in surprise. "We discussed it just this morning, that we would find a way to the safe house of the resistance and join the cause. You said you agreed. It is the blessing of the Mother that Calandra has arrived to take you before you had to leave on your own."

"I agreed to us both going. Not for me to go alone. I will not leave you when you are to give birth so soon. You and the child may need me. Will you not come also?"

"If I may interject," Calandra said, "the journey will require a great deal of walking. I suspect it would be quite uncomfortable for Eudora."

"See?" Eudora rubbed her bulging belly. "Besides, if I also go, who will bring change among those who remain? Mother cannot do it alone. As a city archon, she has to be very careful. It would seem too suspicious if we both left. Better we put out the story that we sent you to work on the family property up the valley with the other *douloi* until the chaos in the city dies down. That should avert suspicion."

Ewelike set his jaw. "I will not leave you."

Eudora drew herself up, looking about to object, then the iron in her posture softened. She took Ewelike's hand.

"I love that you want to be here to protect us. But we are quite safe here, I assure you. The only real danger we face is from roving Freemen trying to survive, and we can handle them." She gave a sly grin. "I've even bested you once or twice during our household training bouts, if you'll recall."

"I do recall." Ewelike's doubt tickled Calandra's cheeks, but he gave his consort a small smile.

"Indeed," added Dione, setting her wine goblet on a table next to her stool. "Though my insistence that everyone in Steadfast House be versed in the *Tropos Hydor Zon* was for exercise more than anything else, such skills come in useful during times such as these. I was a formidable siren myself once, and I assure you, I will let my daughter come to no harm. I am far more concerned for you in this current climate, Ewelike. What would happen if Narcissa's guards did another surprise inspection of our home, and this time, we were unable to hide you from them? Not only would you be Redeemed, but Eudora and I would both be sentenced to death, and what would become of the babe then? Far safer for all of us if you go into hiding."

Ewelike looked like he was wavering. "And what of the other *douloi?* What do you intend to do with them?"

"They are to go, as well," said Eudora. She turned to the waiting servants. "Melina, go fetch Kofi and Cogger."

The girl saluted and hurried away to obey.

Calandra frowned. "The more people we take with us, the more likely we will be apprehended. I don't think this is a good idea."

Eudora stood and her expression hardened. "Surely you wouldn't deny my consort the same freedom you gave yours? Zoe told us how you had her take him back to his home so he could have a different life. I was also willing to make such a sacrifice when we Released Ewelike. If he'd no longer wanted to stay, we would have found somewhere safe for him to live his life. Eventually. I'm just glad he . . . I'm glad that wasn't necessary."

She flushed and fell into an awkward silence, glancing away. Calandra wondered if they assumed Osaze had preferred to return to his homeland than stay with her, unlike Ewelike, who obviously didn't want to leave his consort's side.

Neither did Osaze. I didn't give him the choice.

Her heart sped up and the bonds throbbed behind her temples. She gripped the front of her stool. She had to talk about something else.

Airlea looked at Calandra with a furrowed brow, then turned to Eudora. "Of course we wouldn't deny your consort his freedom. But he must be the one to choose, or it's not freedom at all. Ewelike, what say you?"

Ewelike looked into Eudora's eyes and took her hand, smoothing a lock of her curly light brown hair behind her ear. "I do not want to leave you, but your mother is correct about the dangers if I stay. If you refuse to leave, you will be much safer if I am either Redeemed or far away from here. Of the two options, I will take the latter."

Eudora nodded, sad but satisfied. "Thank you. I will hold you in my heart, and I'll come to you as soon as it is safe. These are uncertain times, and we will continue to fight for the justice that will allow us to live together—as husband and wife."

She stretched up on tiptoes and pecked him on the lips, and he wrapped his arms around her.

Calandra turned away, avoiding the painful reminder of what she'd given up. Taking long, deep breaths, she managed to tamp down the throbbing bonds once more.

Melina returned with two men walking mechanically in tow—one wiry, slight, and dark-skinned with short coarse curls, and one barrel-shaped, tall, and ruddy with strawberry-blond hair. Both had the unfocused gaze of the Redeemed.

"The *douloi*, m'lady," Melina said.

The men stood near the entrance of the room and saluted.

Calandra recognized these men. Both of them had been in the same recent harvest as Zale. The big blond man had the weathered face that came from years on the sea. The African was the only man whom she'd had to heal when she'd been processing the intake of *douloi* during the Redemption Harvest. He had recently been flogged, his back oozing blood and pus from shredded skin. Every other person on the ship had been in remarkable good health—a fact that had alerted her to her brother's healing abilities.

The same brother who'd been thrashing and wailing on the floor of the Archive less than an hour ago. He hadn't been under the *sklavia* bond like these two—but he'd been a far cry from the clear-minded, intelligent young man she'd met at the Harbour Physic Bay three weeks ago. What had been done to him?

Dione gestured toward them. "You are bondmistress for both of these men, yes?"

Calandra stood and took a step toward the men, two of the tethers in her mind tugging at her awareness. She held their bonds. That meant she could finally be rid of them. Only two, but better than none.

She nodded. "And would be only too happy to change that, if you would permit it. If you intend to send them to Margaret House, they must be Freed. If not, I would transfer the bond to your household bondmistress."

The men's unseeing eyes made her skin crawl. It was amazing how quickly it had begun to rankle to see a man in this state. However, she and Airlea were at the mercy of their hostess themselves, and she dared not presume she had the authority to simply Release these men without permission. As Narcissa had proved, seeing the value of one Freeman didn't automatically mean they wanted all their *douloi* Freed.

Dione smiled, and her voice was motherly. "Rest assured, Calandra. Unlike many of my sisters in the nobility, I have been fully convinced of the error of our ways—thanks in part to my strong-willed daughter and her consort." She gave Eudora a kind smile, and Eudora returned it.

Dione turned back to Calandra. "As such, we have decided to give the men in our care the freedom to choose their own path—within the bounds of keeping our island safe—beginning with these two."

She beckoned toward the servant girl. "Some rope, please, Melina. And ask Fedra to join us."

The girl flitted out of the room again, returning a moment later with rope coiled over her arm and the guard from the gate only a step behind. She and Fedra began binding the men's wrists.

Calandra frowned. "What are you doing?"

Eudora set down her drink on the small table between her and her mother—tea instead of wine. "We learned from freeing Ewelike—and from your memorable bonding ceremony three weeks ago—that the process of Releasing can be quite disorienting, so we will temporarily restrain these men until they get their bearings. Then they, too, will have the choice to remain here or go with you until the city has been made safer for their presence."

Calandra noted that returning to their own peoples had not been listed, just as it had not for Ewelike earlier. Not that she was surprised. The undine fear of humans was deeply founded in the persecution they'd endured thousands of years before at human hands that had resulted in the near-extinction of their people. *Is that why Eudora was uncomfortable when she talked about Osaze leaving? Because she didn't want to accuse me of violating one of our deepest taboos?* Calandra's gut clenched. She couldn't see either Osaze or Urbi giving away the undines' secret, but she *had* committed a crime by sending them back to Africa. After earning the death sentence by Releasing him in the first place, the further infraction had seemed trivial. However, exposing the existence of their island to the outside world was so forbidden, doing so was usually never considered—which was why Narcissa's attitude toward raising the barrier made no sense. If she truly wanted the archons' support in her claim to the throne, restoring the Heartstone and the barrier should be her highest priority.

Airlea regarded the men doubtfully. "One is fine, but three?"

Calandra smiled graciously at Dione. "What Airlea means to say is that while Airlea and I bear devices that prevent us from being discovered by those using spirit, these men do not. We can much more easily extend the protection around Ewelike alone than all three men. Unless . . ." She glanced at Kelaino, deciding it was safe to bring up the passage the girl had mentioned. "Your servant suggested you had a more secure route to the ocean than simply taking the street or canal. Is that true?"

Eudora gave Kelaino a surprised glance. "Yes. Through the back gardens. Well done for remembering it to her highness, Kelaino."

"The back gardens?" Calandra had no idea what she meant. She'd thought the passage Kelaino had mentioned would lead to a lower tier of the city or perhaps be a secret tunnel to another alley farther along the street. But with the back rooms of Steadfast House abutting the cliff behind the house, what gardens could Eudora mean?

Dione looked from Airlea to Calandra. "I assume you have a means of transportation?"

Calandra nodded. "We have a submersible, though not a large one. Fortunately, we don't have far to go, so we can fit quite a few if everyone is willing to stand like fish in a jar of oil for an hour. However, it is getting to the sub that is the biggest problem."

Dione smiled reassuringly. "Like many of the old houses on this street, we have a garden plot on the west side of the mountain, accessible from here in the house. We have been devising a plan to take Ewelike and the others out of the city to a hiding place in the Light Valley until we could find a way to contact the resistance. Now, we can use that same plan to whisk you all to safety."

She turned and beckoned Kelaino forward.

"I believe you've already met Kelaino. Despite being discordant, she has many useful talents. Not least of which is that she is quite familiar with the pathways down the back side of the mountain. She will lead you to the ocean safely from here, and the guard will be none the wiser."

There were pathways down the back of the mountain? Calandra's heart leapt, and she glanced at Kelaino with grateful curiosity. *Thank you*, she prayed, and her chest warmed in response.

"That is . . . wonderful. Thank you. I don't know what to say."

Dione smiled. "Your mother once spoke to me of her strange ideas about men and the bonds and the Heartstone. I had always dismissed them, until that day I saw you standing with your brother and that other woman with her young son in the Court of the Redeemed. While we will love this little girl with all our hearts," she said, gesturing toward Eudora's belly, "I hope to one day bounce a grandson on my knees. You are right, your highness. It is time for our nation to change. And I believe you are the one who will bring that change. Narcissa is following too closely in her mother's wake."

"You risk death for this," Calandra said.

"As have you," Eudora answered gravely.

Calandra's chest tightened. The chaos on the island wasn't Narcissa's fault—it was Calandra's. And if her cousin had somehow got mixed up with Damon, who had unleashed him on her? The memory of the booming crack as the Heartstone split and the dragon spirit fled answered her—Damon had said he couldn't have got there without her. She'd carried him there, though she knew not how. If Damon had been released on the island, Calandra had to find a way to stop him—even if it meant carrying him back to the Abyss herself.

She shuddered. Why did all paths lead to the Voidstone, no matter which way she turned? And how could she ensure the lasting change she sought for her people if she had to flee to the Abyss to protect them from her own Madness and past mistakes?

Mother. That was how. Mother was trapped in the Abyss—and she wasn't Mad. Never had been. If Calandra could free her and return her to Sirenia, she could be the leader Sirenia needed. The revolution had been started by Delphine when she'd given up everything to prove the truth. It only made sense that she should be the one to see it to completion since her daughter could not.

The band of tension around Calandra's heart relaxed slightly. The Voidstone terrified her, but she wouldn't wait until the Madness took her past the point of no return to see what lay beyond it. She would find a way to get through to Zale, and then the two of them would heal the Heartstone, raise the barrier, capture Damon if he were at large, and go rescue their mother from the Abyss so Delphine could take the throne in Calandra's place. But first, Calandra had to ensure there was still an island left to rule when her mother returned, and that meant ensuring the risk these women were taking didn't lead to more heartache.

"Fine. Thank you. Tell me your plan, and let us proceed. I want to be away from this place before daylight makes it even more difficult to hide from the guard."

Eudora relaxed, grasping Ewelike's hand in relief.

Dione smiled warmly. "Excellent. The first step is to give these men their freedom. Please show Eudora your technique for freeing another bondmistress's *douloi* as you do so."

Calandra smiled. If Kyria Dione, an archon from one of Sireniapolis's oldest families, could be swayed from tradition, then perhaps more could be persuaded to join their cause. And if the cause could continue without her, she could face her fate. Thank the Mother she'd taken the risk to trust Zoe that day at Elpida—the loyalty of the siren's entire family had been the reward.

Calandra felt lighter already. "Gladly."

13

THE SLAVE MARKET

Osaze stood bare-backed in the hot sun, sweat trickling down his oily skin in beads. It was only midmorning and the barren dirt square was already blanketed in stagnant, moist heat punctuated by the constant whine of mosquitoes. He stared longingly at the palm trees bunched in the distance near a cluster of boats, but none were remotely close enough to offer relief. Once in a while, a slight breeze from the ocean wended its way between the press of dark-skinned bodies around him like a small boon from Oya, the Orisha of winds. And change.

That was likely the only boon he'd be granted today.

He stood in one of several roped-off areas of the square with a couple dozen other strong young black men, all of whom had their hands and feet manacled, and all of whom were awaiting the fate apportioned to them. His captors had taken his shirt and knife—and the small pouch full of amethysts, which had put a greedy smile on the face of the one named McCoy—but left him his breeches. The rest of the men wore only a piece of plain blue cloth wrapped around their hips and between their legs. Hanging from the rope of each enclosure was a sign with symbols Osaze couldn't read.

Thank Olokun the purse hadn't contained all the gems—his mother had buried most of them in a gully outside the city in case something should go wrong. If they could find a way to escape, they could retrieve them and . . .

And what? What good were riches when everyone thought you'd stolen them and saw you as something to possess?

"Is that your mother?" asked the man next to him, pointing at Urbi in the enclosure of women across the square. Bayowa spoke Yoruba, which had been a small comfort while they'd been jammed together in the merchants' yard last night. So few of the others did.

A man with ragged yellow hair holding a lash against his shoulder looked up at the comment, glaring at the group in the enclosure. Osaze kept his lips sealed until the overseer resumed his pacing, then gave Bayowa a brief nod.

Urbi's yellow gown was even worse for wear after a night in the merchants' yard, and the woven girdle she belted it with had started to fray. But her dirty dress still offered more dignity than the short skirts of blue cloth worn by the young women who surrounded her. Whenever the man with the yellow hair passed by, he openly leered at the women, making Osaze's gut clench with rage and revulsion.

Urbi gave him an anxious glance, and he looked away, his jaw working. If it weren't for her, neither of them would be in this situation. He had not found it in himself to forgive her yet.

He knew it wasn't entirely fair of him to blame all their current woes on her. If that siren, Zoe, hadn't betrayed them and brought them here, they'd be in Africa now, on their way to finding the family Urbi had been stolen from so many years ago while he'd still been a babe at the breast. And if Calandra hadn't sent him away in the first place, he'd still be with her on Sirenia. Perhaps he wouldn't even need to hide the fact that his mind was free now that Calandra had revealed the truth to her people.

Either that, or Adonia would have killed Calandra and re-enslaved him. But he had no way of knowing one way or the other what would have happened—or what had actually happened. Maybe it was for the best. If Calandra didn't want him there, he didn't want to be there. But he would like to know if she'd survived.

He ground his teeth, ignoring a trickle of sweat that ran down his temple. Mosquitoes nipped at his bare flesh, and he ignored them too. Rage, his constant companion of late, boiled in his belly—all the harder for him being helpless to do anything about the unfairness of his circumstances.

At the edge of the square, a group of white men and women, some accompanied by African slaves in pale blue cotton or striped clothing, stood waiting. For what, he didn't know, but the whole scenario was so similar to the scene he'd witnessed at the Court of the Redeemed a few weeks ago that he suspected it was for some kind of signal.

He studied the group. Never had he seen such a starkly dichotomous mix—so many pale faces, so many dark ones, with so few shades in between.

What particularly interested him was the men—he'd never seen so many Freemen in his life. Every face was alive with emotion—annoyance, amusement, boredom, fear.

That wasn't true. Many of the men and women inside the enclosures had blank expressions—not vacant, as the *douloi* on Sirenia had been, but neutral, not revealing any emotion. As though by not showing their fear or despair, they could prevent more from occurring.

Osaze knew better—it didn't matter how well you hid your emotions. More bad luck could always find you. Still, he'd grown quite skilled at pretending to be a *douloi*, and he put that talent to use now. The yellow-haired man seemed to enjoy preying on those who showed fear, and Osaze didn't intend to give him an excuse to use his lash.

So far, his experience with free human men had been less than positive. Between the men who had captured them, the red-haired man who wouldn't help them, and Yellow Hair, no one had shown him and his mother the least bit of kindness—no one except the old man in a slave village who'd given Osaze a little food when he'd gone and begged for it. No wonder the undines feared humans. But no—when Osaze was a child, his mother had often talked about his father and grandfather. Those stories had grown dim in his memory, but she'd always made them out to be noble, taking their duty as husbands and fathers seriously—unlike the local oba who'd stolen her from her husband to make her his own wife, then later sold her into slavery.

Duty is everything, Urbi had often told him. *And your first duty is to your family.*

The only family Osaze knew was his mother and Calandra. The latter had exiled him and the former had been complicit. Is that what duty was meant to look like?

Osaze looked toward the ocean and licked his parched lips. They'd been fed and given water before being marched out to the square, but not nearly enough. Even though he'd been sorted into a group of the healthiest and strongest, all the other slaves were in terrible condition—nearly all of them were infested with lice, despite having been washed before being confined for the night and rubbed with oil this morning. Many of them were ill and pale. Osaze couldn't understand how humans could do this to their own kind. What kind of monsters would allow someone to reach such a pitiful state? The undines would never have allowed their *douloi* to live in this misery.

Of course, a *doulos* couldn't feel anything, even misery.

For a brief flicker of a moment, Osaze wished he could return to that numb, stupefied state to have a reprieve from terror and anger. Then he shook his head.

No. Never. He'd give up his pain if he could, but not his mind. Never again.

While he waited, he assessed the situation. There were several boats in a marina nearby, but they were wooden and slow, just like the human ships the undines could easily overtake with their submersibles. He didn't put much stock in being able to escape in one. He wasn't sure he could even sail one on his own—there seemed to be a great deal more contraptions to manage than the console of a submersible.

"Bayowa," he whispered. "Do you know how to sail?"

Bayowa looked at him with wide eyes. "I never saw the big water until the white devils took me on their ship. No, I don't know how to sail."

The man with the yellow hair came and snapped his lash menacingly in front of them, and they quieted. When the man had walked a little beyond hearing range, Osaze whispered from the corner of his mouth, "We will find a way to escape, Bayowa. Be ready."

Bayowa shook his head, his shoulders slumped. "You cannot escape the white devils. They will catch you. The only escape is death, when you can return to our good country, but they don't even let you die. If you refuse to eat, they beat you. If you try to drown yourself, they save you and then beat you. I heard they will fatten us up and eat us in their pots."

Osaze glanced at him in astonishment, but said nothing. Yellow Hair was coming toward them with an expression of mean boredom.

After he passed, Osaze whispered, "They are not devils, they're only men." He scowled. Not even Adonia and Narcissa, with all their faults, were actual devils. He was fairly certain the golden-eyed dragon Calandra had encountered was, though. "And they don't intend to eat us."

He hoped. That thought had never occurred to him. How barbaric were these people, anyway? From Bayowa's askance expression, the answer was *fairly*.

Urbi watched him from across the yard where she stood with the women. A small ball of panic settled in his belly. They intended to sell her separately. No matter how angry he was with her, he didn't want to be separated from her—his duty now was to her. She needed him to get them off this island and back to Africa—he could not think of the place as *home*. That was why she had allowed Calandra to ship them off with Zoe in the first place while he was unconscious and had no chance to prevent it. If they were separated now, how would he find her again?

Fortunately, from their trek from the southeast corner of the island to here, he knew the island was not that big. He was also aware of many of the dangers it presented. As long as he could escape his bondage, he could find her eventually. But what if whomever bought them put one of them on a ship while the other went elsewhere?

He wriggled his wrists against the iron shackles he wore, but there would be no breaking out of those. He would have to watch for an opportunity to overpower someone and then run for it, though that would have to wait—there were too many people here for that already.

A disturbance among the people waiting at the entrance to the square caught his attention. He glimpsed a flash of hair the colour of flame and a handsome freckled face marred by scars around one eye and his heart leapt—the man from the street! Had he come to help them, as he promised?

Standing with the man was the source of the disturbance—a stunningly beautiful woman with deep bronze skin and a halo of dark brown corkscrew curls dressed in deep green silk. She was arguing with the man guarding the gate while the red-haired man tried to placate her.

She looked around the square. Her gaze fell on Osaze and stopped.

He froze. Her eyes . . . her eyes seemed to hold the light of the sun captive in their depths. That was exactly what Calandra had said Damon's eyes had looked like. And Zale had mentioned a lumasi woman named Abela with golden eyes who'd been helping him.

Could this be her? How many golden-eyed people could be walking around the Caribbean?

The red-haired man bent close to the guard and handed him something—something small that quickly disappeared into the man's breast pocket. Then the guard unhooked the rope and allowed the two to enter, much to the consternation of the other waiting people.

The red-haired man and the golden-eyed woman made straight for Osaze.

14

TRAFALGAR SQUARE

Robert allowed himself to be dragged over to the slave enclosure by the arm. "This is most irregular, Miss Bethel. We should wait with the others until the market opens."

Miss Bethel arched her brow. "And let someone buy them before we have a chance to talk to them? I think not."

"We're already inside. Do we need to be in such a blasted hurry?"

"'Out of the same mouth proceedeth blessing and cursing,'" Miss Bethel quoted to him, but she stopped tugging at his arm and adopted a more reasonable stride.

His face grew hot. How could he have let himself slip and curse in front of Miss Bethel? If he wanted her to admire him, he would need to be perfect. "'But the tongue is a fire, a world of iniquity.' I apologize, Miss Bethel. That language was inexcusable."

She flashed him a distracted smile. "Maybe, but everything is forgivable. 'Tis forgiven."

Robert's face still flamed. He swallowed. "You know your Bible well."

"As do you, it would seem," she said, squeezing his arm.

A spot of warmth formed in his chest. Perhaps he'd managed to redeem himself.

She turned to face the group of men, homing in on the young man they'd seen in the street yesterday. He was not hard to spot, standing half a head taller than any other man in the enclosure, with broad shoulders and a lean, muscular frame—in stark contrast to the wasted, thin men surrounding him. Robert thought the man was close to his own age.

"You there." Miss Bethel pointed at the young man and beckoned him nearer with a finger.

The young man blinked, looking behind him, then, when Miss Bethel caught his eye and nodded, edged nearer the rope.

The overseer, a lanky man wearing only suspenders over his shirtsleeves and a dirty straw hat covering his choppy blond hair, saw what was happening and hurried over to them, a buggy whip resting over his shoulder. A cloud of body odour came with him, and Robert forced himself not to flinch away.

"'Ere now, what's this?" He scowled at the young man, who watched him and his lash with a guarded expression.

Miss Bethel turned to him and smiled. "Yes, Mr. Jones, is it? Mr. McCoy at the gate said we would need to speak to you. We only need a word with this man and a woman over yonder and we'll be on our way." She indicated the women's enclosure, where the young man's mother stood.

"Did 'e now?" Mr. Jones scowled, leering at Miss Bethel, though he cast a cautious glance at Robert.

Robert could almost see the gears turning in the man's head. A young gentleman with a coloured woman on his arm in the West Indies was not so uncommon—inside a brothel or the privacy of his own home. But out on the street in public? It was simply not done. In London, people would be amused by the diversion of a scandal but leave him to his own devices. Here, they tended to draw harsher conclusions.

Robert could see the exact moment the man decided what his conclusions would be. The overseer frowned, his poorly concealed derision turning on Robert as well.

"I don't think so. Go wait in line with the others. The market opens at ten. First come, first served then."

Heat flared in Robert's chest. Miss Bethel's smile became strained, and she nudged Robert in the ribs with the hand laced around his elbow.

Robert cleared his throat and slipped his hand inside his breast pocket to retrieve a piece of eight. While fishing it out, his fingers brushed the gem the young black man had given him the day before. He ignored the prick of his conscience. *I have to learn the truth first.*

"Mr. Jones, I don't think you understand," Robert said with a polite smile. "We only need a few minutes with each of them. Surely you can give us that?" He extended his hand to Jones as though to shake, but with the silver dollar visible between his fingers.

When Jones saw the coin, his eyes filled with greed. He glanced over at the watching crowd, then shook Robert's hand. The cold metal slid from between his fingers.

"We got about fifteen minutes or so. I suppose you can chat for a few of 'em." Jones slipped the coin in his pocket and turned away, eyeing Miss Bethel in suspicion. "But no funny business. I'll be watching."

"We wouldn't dream of it, Mr. Jones," said Miss Bethel in a voice like silk.

Once the pungent man had retreated a few paces, the smile dropped from her face and she turned back to the young man in the enclosure. He had been watching the whole exchange with the same guarded expression as before. She spoke to him in Greek.

"Don't be afraid. We're friends. What is your name?"

Robert blinked at her. Of course she also knew Greek. She knew every other language they had encountered thus far. Once again, he wondered where this woman had come from and how she had acquired her considerable list of talents.

The young man's face relaxed slightly. "I am Osaze. My mother is Urbi. Did you come to free us?" He turned a hopeful gaze on Robert, and Miss Bethel turned a similar expression toward him.

Robert's resolve wavered. She'd tried to convince him to purchase the two already, and he'd refused. He had no money with him but what the bank had loaned him, his belongings having sunk with the *Atlanta*. He was running on the credit and good name of Cox Bros Shipping until more could be sent to him, though it would take months for his letter to reach Gryffyn in Bristol and help to be sent back. He knew slaves were often purchased on credit here, but he had enough explaining to do to his brother already without purchasing at full retail what they had meant to sell for profit. Besides, he never wanted to own a slave again. And he definitely couldn't afford to buy one only to set him free.

That is, if the man was truly a runaway with stolen jewels. If not, the value of the one amethyst in his breast pocket alone would purchase the man and his mother with some left over, according to the figure the jeweller had quoted Robert when he'd had it appraised yesterday. That much money would also go a fair way toward repaying the loss of the *Atlanta*. But the jeweller had had no idea where the gems might have originated—no other customers had asked for such jewels to be set. And Robert couldn't in good conscience trade it in until he'd discovered if it had been stolen.

But if it hadn't, that would mean he'd let two innocent people who had asked him for help be put on the auction bock, and he couldn't live with that either. He hadn't needed Miss Bethel's reminder that the window of opportunity to help the pair was very narrow. She hadn't thought much of his runaway slave theory, but she'd offered no proof to the contrary, so what else could they be? Since no one he'd asked in the past day had heard of Sirenia, he hoped Miss Bethel's questions might illuminate the truth so he would know the best way to proceed.

Why must everything be so complicated?

"Er, no, I am sorry, O—Osah . . ." He stumbled over the unfamiliar name. "Miss Bethel only has a few questions to ask you about where you are from. About Sirenia."

At this, the man's expression closed. "I don't know what you're talking about."

Miss Bethel smiled warmly. "Come now, Osaze. I recognize the Greek of the Atargasian undines when I hear it. I am well acquainted with one myself. Zale bet'Delphine. Do you know him?"

Osaze's eyelids flickered, but he gave no other indication the words meant anything to him. Robert, on the other hand, felt like a fish out of water. Miss Bethel had only wanted to ask this man about Zale? What about Sirenia? The word *undine* tickled a memory from his study of classical history. Is that what Zale was—one of the Greek mythological water spirits? He stared at Miss Bethel—so she *had* seen Zale's transformation. Why had she pretended otherwise?

Robert turned to the man. "If you could tell me about this island you said you're from. Sirenia. In which direction is it from here?"

Miss Bethel frowned at him. Osaze continued looking straight ahead, his jaw set and his face blank.

Robert leaned closer. "Look, I want to help you, but I must verify your story first. So if you want my help, you're going to have to give me something to work with. Where can I find your former mistresses, the ones who gave you the gems?"

"I told you, Mr. Cox," Miss Bethel whispered, "the only possible way for Osaze to have been freed from his mistress would be for her to set him free. He couldn't be here otherwise. They don't use papers of manumission where he's from."

"But how do you know that?" Robert asked in English. He had yet to hear of a place so secure the slaves couldn't escape, nor an island in the Caribbean, no matter who'd colonized it, where freed slaves weren't given papers. "Did your Spanish friend tell you that?"

She narrowed her eyes at him. "I can't tell you," she replied in Greek.

"You're going to have to trust me."

That was all the confirmation Robert needed. Jealousy clutched his throat. What if the Spaniard had been lying? As much as he adored the divine creature on his arm, she was a woman. A clever one—but even clever women could be deceived.

Osaze cast a look of curiosity at Miss Bethel, then turned a hard gaze toward Robert. Robert got the sensation he was being weighed and measured . . . and found wanting.

Osaze met Robert's gaze with a brazen glare. "You must free us."

Robert drew in a breath of frustration. Miss Bethel's grip on Robert's elbow tightened.

"What time is it, Mr. Cox?" she asked in English.

Robert tugged on the gold chain of his pocket watch and flipped it open to check the time. "Nine fifty-two."

"Thank you . . ." She glanced at his watch and froze, dropping her hand from his arm to bend closer. "Where did you get that?"

"You like it? Gryffyn gave it to me."

It had been quite a nice gift. The face of the clock was made from a polished stone with a pattern of concentric blue and green circles that reminded him of an eye. He rubbed his thumb over the glass, admiring the beauty of it. "He has one too. Said he got them from a little shop in France a few years ago."

Miss Bethel's eyes widened, and she stared at him in alarm.

"I say, Miss Bethel, is everything all right?"

She snapped from her reverie.

"Quite all right." She gave her head a shake, then glanced back at Osaze and switched to Greek. "Speaking of time, it is running short. Mr. Cox, given the narrowing window of opportunity," she said pointedly, "I ask you to reconsider my request to purchase—"

She stopped at his firm head shake and sighed.

"Then perhaps his mother would be of more use to us." She replaced her hand in the crook of Robert's elbow. "Come, Mr. Cox, let us see if she is more talkative."

She turned to walk away, bringing Robert with her.

"Is your name Abela?" the young man called after her.

Miss Bethel glanced at Robert, then turned them around. "Yes. Miss Abela Bethel."

"Zale mentioned you."

Miss Bethel's face split open in a grin. Letting go of Robert, she hurried back to the enclosure. Robert drew near in time to hear her whisper to the young slave, "If we free you, will you tell us what you know about Zale and Sirenia?"

Osaze gave the merest of nods. "Yes."

Miss Bethel straightened, beaming. "Come, Mr. Cox, let us speak to Mr. Jones."

Robert glanced at her in alarm. He hadn't agreed to anything yet—and he felt no closer to unravelling the mystery of the boy, his mother, and the gems. "Erm, Miss Bethel, may I have a word?"

But Miss Bethel wasn't listening. She was watching Mr. Jones speak to a man with hard grey eyes, thin legs, and a corpulent belly in a finely cut pale blue cotton suit that had been fashionable a good twenty years earlier. The man was actually wearing a wig—rolled and powdered, its length tied at his neck with a black ribbon. He held himself as though he were going to court instead of a day at the market. The man looked like one of those caricatures in the *London Times*.

Beside him stood another man in a light grey jacket. Sweat trickled down the second man's red face.

The man in the blue jacket seemed very accustomed to getting what he wanted, and Mr. Jones seemed annoyed by whatever that was at the moment.

"That's John, Lord Middleton," Miss Bethel whispered to Robert. "Around here, they just call him The Baron, but that's Caribbean manners for you. Not someone you want to cross. I wonder what he wants."

"Miss Bethel, I'm not entirely comfortable—"

"Mr. Cox." She pursed her lips. "You had every chance to do the right thing. I'm afraid the choice is no longer yours."

Robert gaped at her.

She glanced at the chain of Robert's pocket watch, which he'd returned to its place in his waistcoat, as though it had committed some heinous crime. She shifted her attention to the baron, drew an elegantly carved folding wooden fan from her reticule, and fanned herself while she waited. The rotund gentleman was obviously negotiating something with Jones, and he kept glancing at Osaze and Urbi.

Miss Bethel looked at Urbi and Osaze, then snapped the fan closed in alarm. "Oh, no. He can't."

She clasped her free hand to her chest, covering a pendant that Robert knew resided there beneath her gown but which he had never seen. She closed her eyes as though deciding against something.

"Too many people here," she murmured, and looked at the baron with determination. "It appears you are to be given another chance after all, Mr. Cox."

Robert followed her glance in confusion. "What is the matter?"

She tucked her fan into her reticule and grasped his arm. "The Baron must not be allowed to speak to either Osaze or Urbi. You must buy them. Now." She caught his expression, and hastily added, "Not to keep. You must free them after."

"Miss Bethel . . ."

She drew a deep breath, then laid her hand on his chest. "Mr. Cox," she said in a low voice, "if you will not do it for the sake of your soul, then do it for me."

He studied her angelic face, his resolve weakening. Aside from his affection for her, he was fairly certain he owed her and Mr. Berian his life. He didn't remember how he got from the *Atlanta* to his room in Barbados, and didn't quite believe Miss Bethel's claim that he swam on a piece of debris until a passing vessel had picked them up. His enquiries at the dock had revealed no such vessel had come into port—a discovery he had not yet mentioned to Miss Bethel. Besides, he wasn't that strong a swimmer.

However his life had been saved, this was something he could do to repay her. He had to admit, the likelihood of him ever finding the truth about the gems was slim, and he wouldn't learn more from the young black man unless he took a leap of faith and did what Miss Bethel wanted. He could just imagine Gryffyn's reaction if he ever found out—but, thanks to the gem the young man had given him, Gryffyn never needed to know.

Besides, after what Robert had seen in Bristol, he wasn't so sure he cared what Gryffyn thought anymore.

He nodded. "Anything for you, Miss Bethel."

She smiled like the sun, and any remaining reluctance faded beneath her warmth.

He turned to face the baron.

15

THE BARON

Robert strode over to Lord Middleton with Miss Bethel the picture of charm on his arm. Jones was stuttering something to the baron about waiting until ten like the others, and he'd have to speak to McCoy, when Robert broke in.

"Lord Middleton, I presume." Robert bowed politely. "Forgive my appalling boldness. Mr. Robert Cox, at your service. This is Miss Abela Bethel."

Miss Bethel curtsied.

Lord Middleton did a double take at Robert's scars and Miss Bethel's eyes. He glanced coolly back at Robert. "To what do I owe the pleasure?"

"Pardon me, but we actually need to speak to Mr. Jones." Robert turned to the surprised overseer. "We would like to purchase the two slaves we spoke of."

Mr. Jones frowned. "Like I was telling my lord Baron here, it's first come, first served. You don't think all those other fine ladies and gents want first crack at it, just like you?"

He indicated the gate, where Mr. McCoy was in a heated discussion with a gentleman who was waving his arms and pointing at Robert and the others. His shouts could be heard from here.

"Besides," said Lord Middleton with a smug smile, "if you're referring to that tall piece of flesh you were just speaking to, it's too late. I've already bought him. Him and the woman."

Miss Bethel's smile didn't change, but her hand tightened around Robert's arm. From across the yard, Urbi was watching the entire exchange with an anxious expression.

127

"Actually, sir," Jones said, "you only made an offer . . ."

The baron turned such a glare on the overseer, Robert almost felt sorry for him.

"I'll have to speak to McCoy," Jones mumbled, frowning.

Robert fixed a polite smile on his face. "I'm sure Mr. McCoy wouldn't object to turning a higher profit. I'll pay double what they're worth."

He winced internally. The scrawled price on the sign hanging on the rope of Osaze's enclosure was already the highest in the yard. So much for using some of the gem money to pay off his debts.

Lord Middleton gave him a measuring stare.

"What's going on here?" came a huffy new voice. McCoy had found someone else to guard the gate and was striding in their direction. "You all said you only wanted to check out the merchandise in advance. It's almost ten o'clock, so if you would kindly make your way to the gate with the others." He gestured toward the waiting crowd with a flourish as though to soften the demand he was making of two gentleman so far above his station.

"It's what I was saying," said Jones smugly. "If you want to buy the slaves, you'll have to—"

"I'll see your bid and add ten quid," said Middleton to Robert, as though the agent and overseer hadn't even spoken.

"Ten more from me," replied Robert.

McCoy paused. "What's this now?" He glanced back and forth between the two men.

Robert replied before the baron had a chance. "Mr. McCoy, I would like to buy that man"—he pointed at Osaze— "and that woman"—he pointed at Urbi— "for double plus twenty. What say you?"

"I'll pay triple for both." The baron flicked his steady gaze from Robert to McCoy. Behind Middleton, his companion's jaw worked, but the man said nothing.

The same greed that had gotten Robert and Miss Bethel into the yard in the first place flickered in McCoy's eyes.

He turned to Robert. "Will you beat that?"

The rules of the sale seemed to be much less important *now*.

Robert kept his breath slow and measured. If he bid any higher, he'd be dipping into his own pocket to purchase the two slaves, all to set them free.

Miss Bethel glanced up at him. "Come, Mr. Cox. Why do you hesitate?" she whispered.

He bent to speak to her. "It is a dear price to pay for information.

You're certain it's worth it?"

"You still think this is only about a little information?"

She arched her brow, and hot shame melted down his ribcage. *What are a few quid for two people's lives? Especially with so many others' marked against my balance already?*

But what about my life? If Miss Bethel is wrong about them being free blacks, I'm risking gaol. Is it right to risk my own reputation on a hunch? And if her information came from the Spaniard, how could he trust it?

"I don't have quite enough to cover the full price." It was a half-truth—he could find the money. But perhaps it would help her see reason . . . and prevent a very awkward conversation with the bank manager later.

She gazed at the woman across the yard and fidgeted with one of her curls. "Perhaps there is another way. It's not ideal, but sometimes we have to do what's right, not what is easy. Wouldn't you agree, Mr. Cox?"

"Er, I suppose." Though he rarely did so. The shame poured through his gut like hot oil.

Miss Bethel smiled as though that was all the agreement she needed. Her hand squeezed Robert's arm even tighter, and she looped her fingers around her necklace chain. "Get ready . . ." she said beneath her breath.

Get ready? Ready for what?

Lord Middleton eyed her hand as though the gesture meant something to him and tensed. "Wait—"

Miss Bethel paused her motion and arched a brow. "Wait for what, m'lord?"

Tension creased Lord Middleton's brow. He flicked his gaze from Miss Bethel's hand to the two slaves.

"Mr. Cox, may I speak with you alone for a moment?"

Robert exchanged glances with Miss Bethel, but she released his arm and stepped aside. Robert followed Middleton a few steps away from the others. McCoy rolled his eyes.

Middleton turned his back to the others and whispered to Robert. "I know who you are, Mr. Cox. Your brother, Mr. Gryffyn Cox, is an associate of mine. After our business here this morning, I was going to come find you. He wanted me to give you this."

He pulled a letter from his breast pocket with Robert's name scrawled on it in Gryffyn's stiff hand. Robert accepted it, his mouth dry. Questions swirled in his head, but what came out of his mouth was probably the one that mattered least.

"How . . . how did you get this so soon? I only arrived a few weeks ago."

Gryffyn would have had to send the letter almost immediately after Robert had left England for it to have gotten here so quickly.

Middleton smiled coldly. "My associates have abilities that defy the ordinary. As does yours." He tipped his head in Miss Bethel's direction.

Robert stared at him, unsure how to respond. He glanced at Miss Bethel, who was squinting against the glaring sun and fanning herself with a Japanese pocket fan.

"Miss Bethel? Yes, she is an amazing woman, but—"

Middleton barked a laugh. "A woman? You think she's only a woman? Ha!"

Robert floundered. What was Middleton on about?

"Anyway, there is no sense in us continuing this foolish bidding war when we should ultimately be on the same side. I know why your companion wants the slaves, and though I am unwilling to give her even an inch of ground, I also fear that if I refuse to negotiate, she will do something rash."

Middleton patted his chest as though that explained his meaning, but it only confused Robert more. He glanced at the chain around Miss Bethel's neck and back to the baron. What did she have concealed beneath her neckline? It must be something more than an average pendant. But how did the baron know about it?

"I propose this solution: what if we were to take one each? I'll take the boy. You take the woman. We both get what we want. Perhaps we'll have better luck with them if they're separated, anyway."

Robert gave his head a shake. "Better luck with what?"

"There is a war coming, Mr. Cox. Best make sure you choose the right side." Middleton gestured at the letter. "Once you've read that, you will know the information we seek. Come find me when you have it. Huntley Hall, St. Michael's parish."

With that, he strode back to the others, and Robert had no choice but to follow. When she saw them coming, Miss Bethel closed her fan and once more reached for the chain around her neck. What *did* she have concealed there?

"Mr. Cox and I have come to an accord," said Middleton. "We will each buy one of the slaves. I will take the boy to work my fields. The woman seems a better choice for a lady's maid, and I already have more domestics than I need. That is, if you agree, Miss Bethel." He bowed to Miss Bethel in deference, though it had a hint of mockery about it.

Miss Bethel looked at Robert, a plaintive look on her face. "You agreed to this?"

He leaned in to whisper in her ear. "I'm afraid I have no choice. It's either this or I relinquish them both. The Baron's pockets are deeper than mine."

Miss Bethel locked gazes with the baron, then nodded, releasing her grip on the chain. "As you say, m'lord. Agreed."

McCoy crossed his arms. "For triple the price?"

Robert frowned at the man. "Triple?"

McCoy returned the look with a smug smile. "The market's opening. Could be someone else wants them more than you do."

Lord Middleton frowned, but nodded. "Aye. Triple." He turned to his red-faced companion. "Thatcher, please see to the paperwork and take the new one with you to fetch supplies. I'll meet you at the Drunken Mermaid later."

"Yes, sir." Thatcher nodded and made his way to the clerk's table, mopping his flushed, sweaty brow with a smudged white handkerchief and slapping at mosquitoes.

Robert glanced at Miss Bethel as they turned to follow suit. "I hope this is worth it."

She gave him a lingering gaze. "Helping another is always worth it, Mr. Cox."

He swallowed, mesmerized by her beautiful eyes. Middleton's words swam in his brain. *There's a war coming. You think she's only a woman?*

Doubts plagued him as she slipped her hand from his arm and walked over to Osaze. Could Miss Bethel really be more than she seemed? He thought of her strange conversation with the Spaniard. Had she been playing him for a fool all along? And what war did Middleton mean?

Britain was already at war, trying to avert the threat of the little French general who was conquering Europe one country at a time. Is that what Middleton meant—that Miss Bethel was some kind of French agent? Was Sirenia one of the French colonies, then? It didn't sound French, but that was no indication. She exchanged a few words with the tall black man before returning to Robert. Suspicion hardened his gut.

"What was that about?" he asked, indicating the enclosure where Osaze stood. He hated the note of distrust in his voice. From her sharp glance, she heard it too.

"I told him what happened, and that we will come for him soon."

Robert's throat closed. "You did? How are we supposed to convince Lord Middleton to give him up now?"

Her face darkened in a determined scowl. "We'll find a way. Trust me. We must."

Robert stopped and turned to her. "Why?" He couldn't keep the exasperation from his voice. "What is so important about these two slaves? And what is this place, Sirenia, that you keep speaking of?"

Perhaps, if she volunteered the information that proved her innocence, he could banish the doubt that now threatened to strangle him.

She looked up at him, her expression softening. "Mr. Cox, how often you look without really seeing."

He frowned. He'd seen plenty that others, including her, had denied, and she dared accuse him of being wantonly blind? He was the only one who ever acknowledged the truth!

She placed a bare hand on his cheek and stroked his scars with her thumb. Even though her skin was cool, her touch burned.

"There are things I wish I could tell you, but, for now, I must ask that you trust me. Can you do that?"

He blinked at the unexpected prick of tears in his sinuses. He hadn't cried in five years, and he had no intention of starting now. He'd left that blubbering boy behind him on the day his eyes had been seared by lightning. But a single touch from this woman made him want to break down weeping.

Not trusting his voice, he only nodded. She smiled and he basked in the warmth, even while he wondered if he could truly do as she asked with the cloud of misgivings that had just come between them.

"Thank you," she said.

He glanced over the crowd streaming through the now-open gate of the square and froze. Beyond the heads of the plantation owners and managers coming to shop for new labourers, he thought he saw the gypsy girl again. This time, her mustachioed companion from Bristol was with her. But when he looked again, they were gone.

He stared after them for a moment more, scanning the surrounding buildings, but couldn't see them anywhere.

"Mr. Cox, what is it?" She followed his glance.

He shook his head. He didn't need her to tell him he'd imagined this too. "Nothing. I thought I saw something, but it was nothing."

She turned back to him and tilted her head. "Shall we, then?"

He focused on her once more. "Of course."

She slipped her hand back through the crook of his elbow, and they went to buy a slave.

16

THE SLAVE VILLAGE

IT WAS LATE IN THE day when the wagon carrying Osaze and another man in the box finally pulled into the lane of a grand estate. It reminded him somewhat of Elpida, Calandra's family *latifundium* near Fire Lake. The memory was prompted not by the similarities, but by the stark differences between the two properties. Instead of laughing children playing among the buildings and labourers happy with their work, he was met with the silent, haunted stares of men and women in rags. The wagon bumped up the lane between rows of palm trees toward a cluster of stone buildings, which included a long barn with a thatch roof, a windmill, and several other buildings.

The wagon stopped in front of the pale stone barn, and a tawny-skinned man wearing a straw hat, ankle-length blue pants, and a loose white shirt greeted them. The man had a timid walk and kept his head slightly bowed, despite the short-tailed lash he had tucked in his belt, as he accepted the instructions the red-faced man who had been driving the wagon snapped at him. Then he came to the rear of the wagon and his timid manner fell away.

"Twi?" he barked.

Osaze and the other slave stared at him blankly. The overseer snapped a question he didn't understand, but the other man nodded understanding and responded in the same tongue. Then the tawny-skinned man turned to Osaze and asked again. When Osaze shook his head, he spoke again, this time in Yoruba.

"Where are you from, Winslow?"

Osaze frowned. "I am from Ife-Oke," he said, giving the name of the village in Africa his mother had often told him about. "And my name is Osaze."

The man gave a mocking half-smile and shook his head. "Not anymore. Thatcher says you are called Winslow now. Better get used to it. Now off you get."

He gestured with the lash to punctuate his command. Other dark-skinned men and women were already unloading the wagon contents and taking them into the barn or toward the back of the sprawling house surrounded by carefully tended trees a short distance away.

Osaze eased off the wagon bed, thankful for a chance to stretch his aching muscles.

"I'm David," the man said. He produced a key and unbound the shackles around Osaze's wrists, but not his ankles. "I'll show you what's what, and then the master wants to see you up in the big house."

He removed the other man's wrist irons, speaking in his language—presumably repeating what he'd just told Osaze.

"Follow." David took off toward the collection of thatch-roofed huts just visible beyond the lush gardens and a large pond some distance away. His timid veneer had disappeared beneath a cocky swagger. Along the way, he shared gruesome stories of what happened to slaves who broke the rules or tried to escape.

"And don't even bother trying, anyway," David said. "There's nowhere to hide on this island. You'll be caught or killed before you get two miles."

Osaze knew the truth of his words all too well. It had been a wonder that he and his mother had evaded detection so long on this flat piece of rock.

"How did you learn to speak my language?" he ventured, rubbing his wrists where the iron had chafed them.

David gave him a cocky grin. "Yoruba is my mother tongue."

Osaze narrowed his eyes. There was something about the man he did not trust. However, it was a relief that there was at least one person here with whom he could communicate. Maybe he could convince David to help him escape.

But based on the way the man kept one hand on the lash in his waistband, that didn't seem likely.

David showed them around the slave village, pointing out the small thatch-roofed hut they would be sharing with two other men. Though it was late in the day, the only visible inhabitants of the village were several young children—two boys and a girl—who leaned against a palm tree and stared at them until David shouted at them in yet another tongue. The imps ran into a nearby hut and peeked out the small window.

Osaze stared at the children. He was unused to seeing small boys—there had been very few on Sirenia. He realized he'd fallen behind and hurried to catch up to David as best he could with the ankle fetters on.

"How is it you speak so many tongues?" Osaze persisted.

"I was born here, in this very village." David gestured around them. "I grew up learning to speak the words around me." He cocked his mouth in a wry grin. "Effin wunna waun, I use de Bajan instead."

At the pronouncement, the other slave's eyes widened, and he rattled off some words in his language. David responded using a mix of English and African words, though none in Yoruba. Osaze recognized the syllables of both, having heard the undines speak nearly every language imaginable with their *douloi*, but the mishmash made little sense to him. He shook his head, confused.

David smiled and slapped his shoulder. "You'll learn, tall man," he said in Yoruba. "Bussa here, he's Igbo. Many, many slaves here are from that place."

They had reached a hut near the entrance of the village. A wiry, handsome woman with a face lined by labour and years stood in front of a small fire stirring mush in a pot with a long, flat wooden stick. Her hair was pulled into a thick knot at the back of her neck and wrapped with a blue scarf, and she wore a long cotton skirt and a short-sleeved long tunic tied in at the waist with a cord.

"Good evening, Mama," David said in Yoruba.

The woman looked up. "Good evening, son. Who has the master brought us today?"

David introduced Osaze and Bussa to his mother, Ifeoluwa.

At a loss for the proper way to address her, Osaze pressed his fingers to his forehead and hunched his shoulders in the undine greeting of respect. "Greetings, Kyria Ifeoluwa."

The woman gave him an unreadable look and kept stirring her mush.

"What are you doing?" David asked, frowning.

Osaze's throat tightened. "How should I greet her?"

"She is *Iya*—Mother—to you. You don't use her name, hear? Show proper respect." David shook his head in disgust.

Osaze's shoulders tensed, and he nodded. "My apologies."

A girl of about thirteen, with the same glittering brown eyes as Ifeoluwa and dressed in much the same manner as her mother, came out of the house, her hair hidden by a bright red scarf.

"This is my sister, Olubunmi," said David in Yoruba and Twi.

The girl greeted the two men with downcast eyes, a dip of her head, and no words at all.

"Come here, Bunmi," said Ifeoluwa, eyeing the men suspiciously.

The girl went to help her mother, pouring hot water from a pot into a hollowed gourd and adding a handful of leaves. She was on the verge of womanhood and quite comely, with high cheekbones and up-slanted eyes like Osaze's. Bussa stared at her and David frowned. Osaze watched the powerfully built Bussa, trying to ascertain if he would be an ally or enemy.

"Yorubaland?" Ifeoluwa asked Osaze.

"Yes, Iya."

"He said he is from Ife-Oke," David added.

She gave a satisfied nod. "I am from Akure in Ondo. My father served as *Babalawo* to the Deji there. You may have heard of him. Ademola?"

Osaze blinked. How had the daughter of the king's priest ended up here?

"Perhaps my mother has. I . . ." He decided to risk a little more of the truth. "I was very young when we were taken. I don't remember anything about it."

"And where have you been since?"

Osaze regretted his rashness. He could think of no other African place names to give her, and what if she recognized those too? "I am sorry, Iya, I do not know the name."

She studied him for a moment. "You are from here now. Come. Eat."

She ladled some of the thick mush—a kind of yellow porridge with bits of green vegetable in it—into wooden bowls, and Olubunmi handed them to the men along with a wooden spoon. The older woman clucked something in the Bajan creole which Osaze didn't understand. He was ravenous. Settling himself on the ground cross-legged, he arranged the chains on his legs as comfortably as he could and began shovelling food in his mouth. Ifeoluwa put a cautioning hand on his arm.

"Do not eat too quickly," she said in Yoruba this time. "You will make yourself vomit."

She was right, of course. Weeks with barely enough food had made his body weak, including his stomach. He proceeded at a slower, steadier pace, interspersing his bites with sips of the hot green tea she provided in a small hollow gourd.

As Osaze ate, he studied his companions. Bunmi sat on the far side of the fire with her bowl, eating silently. The woman sat next to her daughter and watched the three men as they ate, glaring at Osaze and Bussa if their gaze lingered on her daughter for more than a moment. She reminded him of his mother in some ways—proud, doting, protective, and making the best of the situation she was in.

Bussa also seemed to be taking the measure of this place, his shoulders bunched and tense. He looked to be in worse shape than Osaze, who could have counted the man's ribs if he'd wanted. And David . . .

David was healthy and well-fed and in his element. He carried on a one-sided conversation with Osaze, Bussa, and even his sister and mother, telling them about the weather and the livestock and ways he'd had to keep the other slaves in line that day. Those same slaves started wandering back into the village as Osaze and his companions ate, some of them eyeing up the newcomers, some coming to say hello, but most looking at David and passing by in silence. As Bussa's belly filled, his tongue loosened, and he and David began talking in Igbo. Osaze didn't understand a word.

Osaze should feel kinship with these people. After all, Ifeoluwa was from a village near where he was born. They were all enslaved on the same plantation, far from their homes. But he only felt lost. There was a deep, hollow ache where the *pisti* bond with Calandra used to be—the one that had connected their minds even when they were apart. Pulsing anger throbbed in his belly. He kept his eyes on his meal and schooled his face to blankness to mask his thoughts.

When they had nearly finished eating, David looked at Osaze and laughed. "You don't say much, do you, Winslow?"

"My name is Osaze."

David shook his head. "Not anymore. Thatcher says you're Winslow, so you're Winslow."

Osaze frowned and shovelled his last bite in his mouth, then growled, "I already have a name. I will answer to no other."

Before Osaze could blink, David had leapt to his feet, pulled the lash out of his belt, and whipped Osaze across his back in a single motion. Osaze scrambled to his feet, his bowl and spoon clattering to the ground. His shackles kept his feet from spreading too wide, but he found his balance and caught David's wrist in his hand on the shorter man's second swing. With the ease of years of training in the sparring ring, Osaze twisted David's arm behind his back and pinned it there, disarmed him, and wrapped his elbow around David's throat from behind. Bussa jumped to his feet and took a step back, watching them warily. Bunmi sat still, like a frightened rabbit trying to avoid notice. Ifeoluwa made a sucking noise with her lips against her teeth, but said nothing else as she bent to pick up the dropped dishes.

David squirmed and pulled at the arm pressing against his windpipe. "Get off me, you son of a mongrel! Is this how you repay our hospitality?"

"Is this"—Osaze brandished the lash in David's face—"how you treat one of your own?"

But David did not seem intimidated. A slow smile spread across his face. "*My own?* I am not like you, though. Tell him, Mama."

Ifeoluwa did not look impressed. "You forget yourself, son."

"Do I?" David turned his head, straining to see Osaze's face behind him. "My mother was quite beautiful when she was younger, and Lord John noticed. He has promised that when I turn twenty-one, he will free me, since I am his son."

Osaze's grip loosened slightly in surprise. The plantation owner had enslaved his own son?

Then again, Adonia had enslaved her own nephew. Was it really so different?

David laughed.

"That's right. That's the difference between you and me. One day, I'll be free. But you will be here for the rest of your miserable life . . . unless Lord John sells you first."

Osaze snarled, released David, and threw the lash in the fire. Ifeoluwa clucked her teeth again—whether at him or her son, Osaze did not know.

"No!" David lunged after the lash, snatching it to the ground and stomping the flames out with feet as bare as the rest of the men and wom-en in the village—something Osaze had already learned was a defining mark of a slave on this island. David may claim superior status, but he was in the same pond as the rest of them.

David waved a hand wildly from Bussa to Osaze and shouted some-thing in Igbo. Osaze gathered the meaning when Bussa hesitated, then came and held his arms from behind while David finished stamping the coals out of his lash. Osaze could have freed himself in seconds, but he didn't see the sense in it. He was still hobbled, and he'd made his point—David would think twice before using the lash against him again.

"We shall see which of us will be free first," he muttered under his breath.

David didn't hear him, but sharp-eared Ifeoluwa's head snapped toward him, and Bunmi watched him with a measuring gaze.

Osaze pressed his lips together and said nothing more.

17
THE BIG HOUSE

Osaze shifted his weight, uncomfortable in the loose cotton clothes he'd been given by Ifeoluwa. They were much the same as he'd seen on the other slaves, only newer. He'd never worn anything like it, and even though they made him look like everyone else, he felt conspicuous.

David and Bussa stood on either side of him in the centre of a long, many-windowed room nearly as grand as any in the Opal Palace. In some ways, it was grander. Polished wooden pillars with intricately carved details accented plaster walls, which were painted in some kind of floral design, and the frescoed ceiling depicted a story Osaze was not familiar with. He thought it strange that all the characters had skin as pale as the marble of the Opal Palace walls, as though the painter only knew how to create a single complexion type. Potted plants and ornate furniture crowded the room, making it feel cluttered, but the overall effect was still pleasant.

Open windows along one wall faced the darkening eastern sky. A young woman with skin the colour of night in a long, plain white dress came and closed them. She sneaked curious glances in their direction as she worked.

"Hello, Mary," said David in English, nodding to her.

She acknowledged the tawny-skinned man with downcast eyes and a dip of her head before bustling away.

David held his lash in one hand and his straw hat in the other. He had once again assumed the falsely timid posture he had used with Thatcher when Osaze had first seen him, but his tight grip on the handle of the lash was a warning.

The chains on Osaze's wrists clinked. After the incident at supper,

David had revoked his privileges of free movement for bad behaviour and now kept a wary eye on him at all times. Bussa, having proven himself trustworthy, had had his hobbles removed.

Osaze scowled and looked away from his companions, cursing the lapse of temper that had further hampered his freedom. He couldn't afford foolish mistakes like that. From now on, he intended to follow the rules as meekly as possible. If he had managed to pretend to be a blank-minded idiot for a month on Sirenia with no one discovering him, he could suffer the indignities here until he found a way to get out of this place, find his mother, and get off this chained island.

"You be good now, you hear?" David tapped his lash handle on Osaze's tense shoulders. "Don't make me look bad in front of The Baron. *Winslow.*"

Osaze clenched his jaw and said nothing. *Calm. I need to appear calm.* He stared at a spot on the far wall and focused on his breathing, creating an emotional shield as Calandra had taught him. At the memory, his composure slipped, and he tensed again. But a few moments more and he had managed to school his face and relax his muscles into the familiar mask of blank readiness he had maintained for so long—both unwillingly and willingly—while a *tapeinos* in the Opal Palace.

He would lull them into trusting him. No more mistakes.

They'd only been standing there for a few minutes when a man as straight as a *deiktis* staff entered the room. He wore a red jacket trimmed with gold, and his precisely trimmed sandy blond moustache and goatee accentuated his thin face. Everything about this man was disciplined and succinct.

Osaze recognized a fellow soldier when he saw one.

Behind the soldier came the man from the marketplace—not the red-faced Thatcher, but the pot-bellied man in the ridiculous wig who had been arguing with Abela and the young man with the scarred face about purchasing him and his mother. *Lord John.*

The baron had also freshened up, having changed into a green waistcoat with no jacket. Two others entered the room and stayed near the fireplace on the far side—a man who was nearly as tall as Osaze, with wavy black hair, a bushy moustache, and swarthy skin clad in a bright blue waistcoat and white linen shirt. Behind him walked a petite young woman who bore a striking resemblance to the man, except her long curly black hair was pulled back by a crimson scarf. A dozen or so gold bangles on the woman's wrists tinkled as she walked, and a bright yellow skirt swished around her ankles. He'd never seen clothing so designed to attract attention.

Lord John rubbed his hands together, looking Osaze up and down. The soldier stood to the side, his piercing grey gaze less voracious, but just as observant.

"Ah, the undines' slave," said Lord John, his powdered curls framing a face flushed in anticipation.

Osaze wasn't sure of the meaning behind his words. David's expression was no help—he looked as confused as Osaze felt.

Lord John turned to his overseer and said something else using that same English word, *undine*. David asked a question, and Lord John replied. An incredulous expression flitted across David's face, but he buried it and turned to Osaze, frowning.

"The Baron wants to know if you were the property of the *fish* women."

Osaze's heart quickened. Fish women? Did that English word, *undine*, mean the same as the Greek word *neraida*, the name of Calandra's race? How did he know about the undines?

The man in the red jacket stood with his hands clasped in front of him, watching him with narrowed eyes.

Osaze stood tall and said nothing.

"Speak!" David barked, shifting the lash nearer.

Osaze flicked his glance at the overseer, then back to meet the gaze of the two white men, unflinching. One advantage he had that they did not—he'd lived his life among beings who could sense when you were being deceptive, and he'd successfully deceived them. Surely he could mislead a few mere humans.

"I don't know of any fish women."

David translated, and Lord John frowned. He stepped nearer, looking up the several inches required to meet Osaze's gaze. He asked something else, and this time Osaze recognized the name of his home.

"Why did your mother say you were from Sirenia?" David translated.

"She did not. We are from Ife-Oke, like I told you."

"Yes, she did," said the young woman by the fireplace in Greek, and Osaze met her black-eyed gaze. "I heard her yesterday, on the street in Bridgetown. She said you were from Sirenia, the island of the undines."

She stepped toward him, her big eyes searching his. He didn't remember seeing her on the street, but it had been crowded, and he had been a little preoccupied with being arrested.

He said nothing. If this woman knew he understood her and he responded, she might recognize his accent as Abela had, and he may as well admit he knew exactly what they were asking him. He set his jaw and looked straight ahead as the fat man asked the girl a question and she replied in English.

He never saw the lash coming. The sting across the back of his thighs made him jump, and he grunted involuntarily. Another breath, and he controlled his reaction to the pain.

David's face was implacable, his hand falling to his side with the lash. "You speak when you are spoken to, Winslow." There was a vindictive gleam in his eyes, but when he turned to face his master, his expression became neutral once more.

Lord John nodded approvingly and asked David something in English, indicating Osaze's shackles. David relayed something, and Osaze suspected he was explaining the incident at supper.

Then the baron looked Bussa up and down and, after some more exchanged words, summoned a male servant wearing colours similar to Mary's dress to escort Bussa back to the slave village. Once they had left, he turned back to Osaze.

"Josefine insists you speak Greek." The baron glanced toward the young woman and back at Osaze, watching his reaction.

Despite himself, Osaze's eyes widened. The accent was unusual, but he did not expect to find yet another person here that spoke the language of the undines. Did everyone speak Greek in this place? He glanced at David, whose brow was furrowed. Perhaps *he* did not, despite his claims to speak *all* the languages.

The man chuckled dryly. "I see she is correct. You certainly understand it. And David tells me you are quite the fighter, which would make sense for someone of your stature on that island. Trained you as a soldier, did they? It would seem that, whether you want to admit it or not, your mother's claim holds true. That striking woman Mr. Cox and Miss Bethel purchased was your mother, was she not?"

Osaze kept his face blank, still saying nothing. This time, he was ready for the lash, and didn't even flinch as it cut into the backs of his legs. He ground his teeth and kept his knees straight, lowering his gaze to the carpet as David had instructed him on their way to the house. It made it easier to hide the moisture in them.

"Oh, ho!" the baron exclaimed, turning to face the man in the red jacket. "This one has spirit, does he not?" He glanced at the overseer. "You will have your work cut out for you, David."

"Yes, sir," said David, clasping his hands in front of him around the lash handle, a satisfied, smug set to his shoulders.

The baron's eyes glittered as though he were examining a new toy. The man in the red jacket said something Osaze didn't understand. He did not look nearly as pleased as Lord John.

"Now," said the baron, rubbing his palms together once more in excitement. "You are to tell us all about Sirenia and the undines."

The young woman took a few steps forward and regarded him with frank curiosity. Her companion came to stand next to her, his massive forearms crossed in front of his chest. Something about the way they looked at him made his skin crawl. It was just like being in the market, on display for others to judge and purchase.

I am not *a* doulos *anymore. No matter what they think. They will not break me.*

The baron was looking at him expectantly, waiting for an answer. He could wait all night, as far as Osaze was concerned.

In Yoruba, Osaze said to David, "I do not know what he is saying to me."

David's eyelid twitched as he translated.

Lord John's face was impassive. "You're lying."

He nodded at David, and another stinging lash against the back of Osaze's calves made his knees want to buckle, but he tensed and remained upright. His only acknowledgement of the pain was a sharp intake of breath.

"Again," said Lord John.

Snap.

Osaze's eyes watered.

Lord John glared at him through narrowed eyes. "Again."

Snap.

Osaze started panting, trying to control the pain, but his flesh burned. It took all his willpower to remain standing.

The baron stepped closer. His smile had become decidedly unpleasant. "Now let us try again, shall we?" he continued in Greek. "Tell me what you know about the undines."

It took several deep breaths before Osaze could control the pain enough to speak.

"I no speak English," he said, nearly exhausting his entire English vocabulary.

The lash fell once more, deeper, this time against his back. His skin burned, worse than the time Narcissa had told him to put his hands in the fire for her amusement. She'd had a friend of hers heal him before anyone else found out. At the time, he'd been under the *sklavia* bond and could no more resist her demand than stop breathing. But he'd still felt the pain, which had only been fully realized once his mind was Free once more. Once Calandra had Freed him.

Calandra. He closed his eyes and pictured her beautiful face, her luminescent, determined green eyes, her gentle voice telling him to hold on, that he was stronger than they were. He could almost smell the sweet lotus scent of her ivory skin and taste her soft lips.

He opened his eyes, rage filling him. Calandra had sent him away. He was doing this for himself now.

And this time, there was no *sklavia* bond to compel him to obey. Which meant he could hold out forever.

The man with the white hair scrutinized him. "I see you need some convincing to make you pliable. Fortunately, David here is quite good at that language too."

He flicked his gaze to David and spoke in English. Whatever he said caused the soldier's face to grow harder and the young woman's eyes to widen and glance at Osaze in dismay. The tall mustachioed man beside her stepped forward, frowning.

"I say, Lord Middleton, surely there is another way to find out what we need to know," he said in a gruff voice.

Osaze heard the English words, but did not understand most of them. He supposed the man must have been objecting on his behalf, though, for the baron went over to look the man in the eyes, much as he'd done to Osaze only moments before, and glared him down.

"It will be a cold day in hell before I let a gypsy tell me how to handle my slaves, even one as useful as you. Is that understood, Eric?"

The tall man's jaw worked, but then he nodded once.

The baron turned back to David and flicked his wrist in dismissal. Then he exchanged a few more words with Eric that made the man tense further. However, when David escorted Osaze out, Eric followed. And after Osaze's bound hands had been hung from a peg on a post in the centre of the slave village and his shirt pulled over his head to expose his back, it was the tall man with the moustache, not the grinning David, who administered the lash.

All during the flogging that followed, Osaze held onto his calm.

If he could hold onto that, he had won. They might own his body—for now—but they could not control his mind.

With every blow of the lash, he focused on a single thought.

I.
Am.
Not.
Your.
Doulos*!*

18

THE HEALER

Osaze lay on his stomach on a woven straw mat on the floor of the thatch hut, the flesh of his back on fire. Blood oozed in thick, sticky rivulets down his sides and crusted in scabs over the wounds left by the lash.

It hurt to move. Each indrawn breath broke open the scabs that had begun to form. He was too tired and in too much pain to even slap away the mosquitoes that swarmed around him in the warm night air, or the flies drawn by the smell of blood.

Nearby, Bussa and two other men lay on mats, breathing deeply in sleep. One of the others, Chidindu, had helped Osaze into the hut after the flogging. Ifeoluwa had wanted to wash and tend to his wounds, but David wouldn't let her. Instead, the overseer told Chidindu to wash Osaze's back and leave him be. Ifeoluwa tried to protest, but when David threatened her with the back of his hand, she acquiesced.

David threatened his own mother. Through his pain, Osaze was still flabbergasted. David was not the sort of man who would help Osaze escape. He was not the sort of man who would help his own kind at all. What little power he had, he was drunk on.

Osaze tried to sleep, hoping for temporary relief from the pain in his back, but it wouldn't come. His brain floated in and out of a string of surreal images and memories. He'd had a fever once, when he was seven. His dreams had terrified him and he'd ached all over. His mother had brought a palace healer to tend to him, and almost as soon as the sickness had begun, he'd been back on his feet and playing with the other children.

This was like that, only so much worse.

Outside, the plaintive song of whistling frogs echoed the anger, loneliness, and despair in his heart and permeated his fever-born dreams.

How had his world turned so upside down? Three weeks ago, he was consort-elect to the heir of a nation, a beautiful woman whom he had loved and wanted to protect with all his heart. Granted, he'd had to hide his true nature from the world, but Calandra had had plans to change that world, and he was going to help her do it. Thanks to the *pisti* bond they had shared, he *knew* she felt the same way about him as he felt about her. Why would she have broken it? What made her lose faith? The space in his heart that had once held the awareness of her emotions had hardened like a callous created from repeated rubbing. He barely felt it anymore, unless he thought about it directly, like now.

He wondered if Calandra and Zale had succeeded in healing the Heartstone. He wondered if Adonia had already assigned her a new consort-elect, or if the queen had sentenced her niece to death, the way she had done to Thea when her treasonous act of daring to free her consort from the *sklavia* bond had been discovered. Was Calandra even alive anymore? He wanted to believe he would know if she had died, but the truth was, without the *pisti* bond or the *syzagos* bond the undines shared with their consorts, he would have no idea. Circumstances being what they were, he wasn't sure if he was even upset Adonia had interfered with their bonding ceremony.

Osaze clenched his sweaty fists, one of a few gestures he could make that was not excruciating. His whole life, he'd been at the mercy of the will of women. Malicious women, women who hated and feared men. Even Calandra, who claimed to love him, had still treated him like a *doulos*, even right up to the end when she had decided his fate for him.

He wanted to punch something, but he didn't dare move.

The door of the hut creaked open, and a quiet shadow stepped inside. The intruder paused, probably getting used to the dim light. Osaze turned his head that direction, but he could see little except the outline of a woman. Straining to look was painful. He let his head fall back to the mat.

"Winslow?" a woman whispered.

Bangles tinkled softly as she moved. It was the young woman with the long black hair from the baron's hall. Following his soft moan of pain, she skirted the sleeping figures of the other men and crouched between him and Bussa, placing her cool hand on his forehead.

"You're burning up," she said in Greek. "I'm sorry I could not come earlier. I had to wait until everyone in the house was asleep."

Osaze could not see her with his face pressed against the floor, but he heard the catch in her voice.

"By the wisdom of the ancients, what has he done to you?" she muttered. She unrolled a small bundle beside him on the floor.

"Lie still," she said. "I will not hurt you, but this may sting a little."

Osaze lay there as she administered some cold, lumpy poultices to the wounds on his back and shoulders. He had endured far worse. Adonia had once cut off his hand, and Calandra had had to reattach it. At the time, he had been Redeemed and had been dissociated from the pain. Even still, he could remember every moment of it. That, and the many cruel tortures Narcissa had administered during his two years in her service.

Still, as excruciating as that pain had been, it had always been short-lived. The undines were healers, and if they had found him in this condition, they wouldn't have left him in it. Even Narcissa had quickly grown bored of watching him bleed and had her healer friend, Zenobia, repair him soon after he'd been injured. She'd been fascinated by blood. But under Redemption, he'd given her no reaction to further fuel her cruelty.

Thank Olodumare.

"Still pretending you don't understand me, are you?" she said as she worked. "You are a stubborn one. But I know you do. However, if you wish to maintain the pretense, I won't give you away to the others again."

He pondered that for a moment. It could be a trick—but he didn't think it was. Something about her said she was as good as her word.

"My name isn't Winslow. It's Osaze," he croaked.

She continued with her work in silence for a few more moments. Then, "I'm Josefine."

It seemed Josefine was a healer too. But, as grateful as he was for the muck taking the sting out of his back, he refused to be duped into revealing information that could be used to further harm his island.

No, not his island. Not anymore. But still, the undines had enough problems on their own, without him adding to them.

"Why are you doing this?" His words were muffled against the mat, but Josefine seemed to understand.

"Do you know much about my people, the Roma?"

Osaze was ashamed that he knew nothing about them, but that was true of most peoples on Earth.

"Not much. Why do you ask?"

"For as long as there have been people, there have been Roma. We are travellers, sentenced into exile after our ancestor was commissioned to make the nails for the crucifixion. Now, we are bound to wander the world as penance for our sins."

Osaze frowned. "And who decided that?"

Josefine smiled. He could hear it in her voice.

"Actually, that is the story we tell the *gorgios* so they let us pass through their lands or live in them. The *gorgios* do not like us, because they do not understand our ways. Yet for hundreds of years, we have found a way to survive. We have kept our own language and our own traditions alive. We are scattered, but we are strong." Her voice became pensive. "It is too bad my father does not see that."

"What do you mean?"

"Let's just say I no longer have much faith in the cause my father professes. Not when it can make a man turn against the ways of his own people like this."

Her father must be the mustachioed man who had administered Osaze's beating with so much vigour. He hadn't looked like he'd enjoyed it, not like David had as he'd looked on with his smug smile, but he hadn't held back either.

"I suppose you're telling me the Roma are not typically violent." He didn't try to keep the derision out of his voice.

"Yes, that is exactly what I'm saying," she said sadly. "But my father has changed. He has been blinded by the promise of peace for our people. If this is how we must achieve it, I'm not sure it's worth the cost."

"And yet you didn't try to stop it."

Josefine didn't reply for a moment, busying herself with rolling her herbs and medicines back into her bundle. When she spoke, her voice trembled.

"There is much going on here you don't understand. You do not know the power you are up against. Please, Osaze, for your own sake, tell The Baron and the colonel what they want to know. If you don't, they *will* kill you. But even that will not let you escape from the clutches of those they serve."

Osaze pondered her words. How could the power of these men extend beyond the grave? No one on Earth had that power, not even the undines. Could it be possible Josefine was playing him for a fool after all?

But no. Josefine was afraid, that was obvious. What was going on beneath the surface? Who were the baron and those other men working for? *Who is Josefine working for?*

She sat next to him. "Can you at least tell me if you met my foster brother, Zale? Is he all right?"

He blinked. She knew Zale? How much would he give for news of Calandra and those he had been forced to leave behind? He heard that same ache in her voice.

"I don't know," he said truthfully. "I met him. But I was forced to leave before I found out what happened to him."

"What do you mean? What was going on? Did he find his sister?"

Osaze turned his face away, regretting that he'd spoken. "Thank you for your kindness. I think it's best you leave."

Josefine sighed softly. A few moments later, she tiptoed out of the hut and gently closed the door behind her.

And Osaze was left with only the ghosts of all the people he cared about.

Eventually, with the pain in his back eased somewhat, he fell into a fitful sleep.

*

Eric sat in the dark, watching the shadow of the palm leaves sway across the floor of the baron's main hall in the moonlight. He'd been unable to sleep since the flogging. He'd never seen a man so unresponsive under pain. Something told him it would take a long time to break Winslow—more time than they likely had—and he didn't relish having to be part of the process of doing so. He ground his teeth. It irked him that in his pursuit of freedom for his people, he was forced to work with people like the colonel and the baron—the very class of men who kept the Romani under heel. But if it served his purpose in the end, he had certainly endured worse. All Roma had.

Restless, he had gone to find Josefine to have her help him consult with their otherworldly masters about how to proceed should this Winslow prove uncooperative. However, she hadn't been in her room. He'd looked all over the house, and when he hadn't found her, he'd consulted his finder—the smooth watch-like stone device bequeathed to him by the Master. She was on the property, he could ascertain that much, and he breathed easier. It was too dark outside, and the grounds too unfamiliar, to search for her there, especially when he could easily miss her. Instead, he'd planted himself here at the baron's dining room table with a view of several of the doors, hoping she'd only taken a walk and would soon return.

He was pondering the palm tree shadows, trying to decide what to do next, when he heard the quiet sliding of the patio door in the Great Room beyond the archway and the gentle padding of slippered feet across the hardwood. Glancing up, he saw his daughter's silhouette and leapt to his feet.

"Josefine Chapman."

She jumped and whirled to face him.

"Oh, it's you, Papa." She put her hand to her heart. "You scared me half to death."

"I'm sorry, daughter," he said in Romani. He went over to her and put his hands on her arms. "Are you all right? Where have you been?"

Her eyes grew accusatory, and she adjusted the small bundle in her arms—her healing roll.

"I was tending the back of the man you flogged."

She said nothing more, but she didn't need to. Her eyes said it all—eyes that were so like her mother's.

He dropped his hands and rubbed his chin.

"It was not pleasant, but it had to be done. We are in a very delicate place here, Josefine. Lord Middleton is not the easiest of bedfellows, but he has the power to get us what we want. He also has the power to destroy our hopes if we were to get on his bad side."

She narrowed her eyes, her confusion and suspicion plain.

"Oh, my girl, do not look at me that way. In the end, it will all be worth it. Don't you see that? When we succeed, your mother can finally be at peace."

"Really, Papa? Mother? You think what happened to her justifies what you're doing now? What do you think she would say if she knew what you did today?"

He frowned, trying to find the words to convince her. She had to understand what was at stake. "She would say what I'm telling you now. The way of our people has never been easy, but we always find a way to survive. If we're to survive in the coming New World Order, this is what we must do."

Josefine's eyes grew hard. "You're wrong. If there is anyone who's not letting Mother rest, it is not the *gorgios* who caused her death. Good night."

She hurried out of the room, ascending the stairs to her bedroom in the servants' quarters.

Eric sat back down in the chair and stared at the swaying trees.

He couldn't tell Josefine what he truly feared.

Their masters had promised them immunity and wealth beyond measure when their power was established.

But if he and Josefine were to turn their backs now, instead of protecting the Romani, those masters would annihilate them—every single one. Of all the powers throughout history who had tried to do so, these might have the ability to succeed.

And no matter what Josefine thought, her mother would want him to protect her.

No matter the cost.

<h1 style="text-align:center">19</h1>

<h1 style="text-align:center">THE FREEMEN</h1>

CALANDRA AND EUDORA STEPPED AWAY from the two constrained men they had just Released from the *sklavia* bond in the receiving room of Steadfast House, then waited while the stupor of Redemption fell away from their minds.

The men blinked, trying to focus. The one named Kofi came around first. He looked at his bound hands, then up at Calandra, and his expression transformed into confusion and alarm.

"You . . ." he said in heavily accented English. "I know you. You heal my back. Jus' like my *obroni* heal de sickness. Are you an angel too?"

Calandra smiled. Taking a cue from the Twi word, she replied in that language, "No, no angel. The angel you speak of is my brother, Zale, yes?"

His coal-black eyes widened, and he replied in the same language. "He is your brother?" He squinted. "Yes, I can see the resemblance. You have the same eyes. And he also spoke Twi."

Another piece of the fog drifted away and he glanced around the room in alarm. "You all have the same eyes. And I—I remember now. The ship. The strange boats that took us under the water. The strange women." He took a step backward. "You're all *mami wata*—mermaids!"

"Stay back, witches!"

The cry came from the other man, Cogger, who had come around from the confusion and was backing away from them with his bound hands raised in front of him as though he could ward them off.

Calandra had anticipated this possible reaction, however. Airlea and Fedra stood behind him and grabbed his arms, halting his progress. Airlea began humming—not to stupefy, merely to calm. It seemed to be working,

154

but then the man wrenched free of their grasp and made a break for the door to the courtyard.

Airlea switched to sirensong and Cogger stopped just before the slack of the rope tied to Kofi's wrists ran out, standing with a look of wonder on his face as though he had just seen the most beautiful thing in the world.

Eudora glanced at Ewelike's face, which bore the same stunned, blissful expression, then looked at Calandra in dismay. "That's what happened with most of the others too—the ones who were Freed when Adonia died. As soon as they could, they ran away. We are only fortunate no one was hurt in the process. Not like what Cain did at your bonding ceremony." Eudora wrung her hands. "That man and his band certainly don't make decisions like this easier."

Calandra frowned. "What band?"

"You haven't heard?" Eudora asked. "Ever since the Summer Solstice, he has become a terror in this city, leading a band of rebel Freemen seeking revenge for their enslavement."

Dione frowned. "Every few days, someone else has been reported missing."

Calandra's throat went dry. She knew Cain had killed when he'd been unexpectedly Released at her ceremony, but she'd been able to excuse it to a certain degree as an act of desperation by a man not in his right mind. But what was she to make of this? And what would have happened if he'd responded to her invitation earlier?

Eudora's comment explained why Dione and her daughters didn't seem to have any other *douloi* in the house. The archon's consort died many years ago, so Ewelike, whose bond would have been held by Eudora, and the two *douloi* whose bonds had just been loosed would have been all that remained.

Calandra stood in front of Cogger with her arms crossed. What would she do with him now? She couldn't force him to come with her. Well, she could, but she had sworn never to Redeem—make that *enslave*—anyone ever again. However, she supposed there were other ways to subdue a person until they could be made to see reason.

She took the rope that bound Cogger's and Kofi's hands and led the docile men outside to the portico. The others followed, watching in curiosity, and Airlea and Fedra came to stand nearby. Calandra had Kofi stand still while Cogger walked around the pillar several times, lifting his hands over the shorter man's head, anchoring both men with a short lead. Then she signalled Airlea to stop singing.

The fog cleared much faster this time—a few blinks and Cogger's face twisted from blissful peace to suspicious anger. And fear. The fear rolled off him like tidal waves, making Calandra a little nauseous.

Kofi silently took everything in. Cogger struggled against his bonds, grunting in frustration. Finally, he gave up.

Calandra crossed her arms. "Are you finished?"

The panting man looked around at Airlea and the other women, his eyes wild.

"What do ye want with me? What have ye done to me?" Cogger demanded in English.

Calandra's jaw tensed. This explanation was never easy. In fact, she did not have time to give it all. But she had to get these men to trust her, and quickly, so they could use the secret path Dione had mentioned and leave before the guard heard the disturbance and came back for another sweep.

"You two are known as Kofi and Cogger, correct?" Calandra said in English.

Kofi nodded, and Cogger narrowed his eyes.

Good enough.

She launched into an explanation of why they were here, why they'd been enslaved, and why they'd been Freed—so they could choose whether to join the revolution and fight for their freedom and the freedom of all men on their island. When she explained they wouldn't be permitted to leave, Eudora's sharp glance confirmed her suspicion—the young *kyria's* earlier awkwardness *had* been about Osaze leaving.

While Kofi silently took in her words, Cogger was less than agreeable.

"Are ye saying ye've made a slave out of me, just like that darkie there?" Cogger gestured at Kofi with his bound hands. "Ye can't do that! I'm not the same as *him.*"

"That's the truth," Airlea muttered under her breath.

Kofi's jaw tightened, but he said nothing. Ewelike looked between the men, a storm brewing behind his eyes.

Cogger stared at Dione and Eudora, whose mixed ethnic heritage was evident in their sharp cheekbones, thick black hair, and olive-toned skin. When he saw Ewelike's hand on Eudora's elbow, he made a face but said nothing, turning his sneer on the flagstones.

Calandra shook her head. Cogger's hate was as overwhelming as his fear, and for what? What had Kofi ever done to him? The undines' gender-based prejudices were no more excusable than the humans' pigment-based ones, but she didn't have the energy—or the time—to battle against so much prejudice at once. Especially as every second spent discussing this increased the chance that either they or their team at the submersible would be discovered by the guard. But if she didn't calm Cogger down, his distress would be a beacon to any siren in the neighbourhood.

She cleared her throat. "I'm saying that here, we are fighting to make all people equal, regardless of gender. Or race. We have no races here except undines and humans. And on Sirenia, human men have the least rights of anyone. We'd like to change that."

Cogger focused on Calandra as though finally seeing her for the first time. "I remember you. You were the one who . . ." He trailed off as though unable to find the words for what he was trying to describe.

Calandra glanced down. "Yes, I enslaved you. I'm sorry. But now, I'm giving you a chance at freedom."

Kofi spoke at last. "Freedom? You already said we may not leave."

Calandra turned to face him. "The island. You can't leave this island. But you can come with me to a safer place than this, one where you will find other Freemen like yourselves and be able to fight for the rights of your brethren."

Cogger sneered at Kofi. "He will never be my brethren. Nor none like him." He looked at Ewelike and the women in disdain. Then he resumed struggling against the bonds, his panic hitting Calandra like sharp rocks, despite her emotional shield. "Let me go! You can't do this to me! I'm an Englishman!"

"Hush him up! He'll bring the whole palace down upon us," said Dione in distress.

Airlea began the ethereal strains of sirensong again, and Cogger's, Kofi's, and Ewelike's faces all relaxed to wondrous bliss once more.

Calandra shook her head. "That's no good. We'll never get anywhere with him now."

Eudora rubbed her belly in agitation, glancing at her besotted consort in concern. "What should we do? He's being so unreasonable!"

While continuing her song, Airlea signed that they should Redeem him again.

"No. No way." Calandra shook her head, adamant. "Rhea made it clear we're not to use the *sklavia* bond for any reason."

Dione inspected the stunned men. "I'm not sure what other choice we have in this situation. You can hardly take him with you like this. Nor leave him."

Calandra stared at the men. Dione was right. Cogger was built like an ox—there was no way for them to manage him with physical strength alone. She could keep him in line using her abilities, but she would have to be constantly vigilant in case he tried to lash out or run away again, endangering them all. Besides, doing so would likely involve hurting him to show what she could do, and the very idea of using her powers in that way made her want to throw up.

Eudora frowned. "I'm sorry, Calandra. Mother is right. We must either Redeem him again and keep him here, or Redeem him again so he can go with you. But I don't want my Ewelike stupefied for a moment longer!"

Dione nodded confirmation. "You could Free him again the instant you are out of danger. Instead of letting him choose between the safe house and our service, perhaps he could take his chances with the sea. You could leave him on Nadia's Ruin or something similar. There is enough food on that little heap of rock to give him time to rethink his choice."

Calandra scowled at Cogger. Here was a man whose violence and lack of self-control epitomized everything she'd been taught to fear about human men. But she'd come to realize that undine women were just as capable of the same behaviour. And, thanks to Osaze and Gerrick, she knew not all men were like Cogger. Ewelike and this Kofi, what little she knew of them, were both prime examples. And how did the humans deal with men who would not be reasoned with?

They restrained them.

For the undines, the most convenient form of restraint was the *sklavia* bond.

She wavered. Would the cost really be so great?

To her, it might. Releasing two men out of the thousands of burning bonds in her head had not made any sort of noticeable impact on the pain, but still, she was not willing to add to it again.

"Fine," she said at last. "But I won't do it. I have far too many bonds already. Airlea?"

Airlea signalled that she'd heard by stepping toward Cogger, placing her forefinger on his forehead, and changing from sirensong to the short trill that subverted a man's will and emotions beneath the will of his new bondmistress.

Calandra cringed as she swatched Cogger's eyes become unfocused once again. At the same time, Ewelike and Kofi returned to full awareness.

Kofi had tears at the corners of his eyes as he looked at Cogger. "How can a song that is so beautiful be so horrible too?"

Calandra went over to Kofi, looking in his troubled eyes. She sensed none of the volatility in this man that had pervaded Cogger's being, but she still had to be sure before untying his bonds.

"What say you, Kofi? Will you stay here in service to Kyria kor'Dione and her household, risking discovery and death, or come fight for the freedom of the men of this island, risking the same, though with more personal freedom and opportunity to institute change?" She wanted to let him know what was at stake.

Kofi eyed Cogger's slack face. Airlea had untied the big sailor, and he now stood placidly awaiting instructions. Calandra wondered if Kofi were weighing what kind of freedom he would be fighting for.

"You will not do that to me again?" He pointed at the other man.

Calandra winced at the evidence of what she'd done. How could she espouse freedom when she so willingly took it away for the sake of convenience?

Another bolt of blinding pain stabbed through her forehead, and she put her hands to her temples. *Not again!* The pain passed in moments, but it had dissolved her compassion into irritation.

"As long as you don't give me a reason to, you should be fine," she snapped.

Kofi blinked at her, frowning as he contemplated his response. "I have been a slave for many years now, but I have never before had my mind taken from me. I would not do it again. And, though these mistresses have been kind"—he indicated Kyria kor'Eirene and the rest of the household—"I think my skills would be put to better use fighting with you and your cause, whatever that may be."

"So be it." Calandra untied his wrists.

As soon as he was free, he fell to his knees, his hands clasped in front of him. "I will serve you, Lady Mami Wata."

Calandra grunted in both irritation and amusement. "I am only a woman, not a goddess. But I accept your service, Kofi."

She turned and looked at the group of them, whose expressions and emotions ranged from satisfaction to distress to heartbreak. Eudora and Ewelike went to share a quiet moment in the corner of the courtyard. Dione began directing servants to pack some food for the travellers, which Calandra didn't object to—they should be at Margaret House in hours, but finding food in their remote location was a constant chore. She would take whatever they could get.

Since all seemed to be settled, she placed her thumb on the communication stone on her wrist, then raised it to her mouth. "Nick, are you there?"

Moments later, the matter-of-fact voice of their pilot vibrated tinnily from the stone. "Good to hear from you, your highness. Been wondering if we should go back for you."

"No, we're safe, but still in the city. We'll be bringing a few extras with us, but we should all fit. Meet us at Sibyl's Cove. We'll be there in about . . ." She glanced at Dione for confirmation.

"An hour, maybe a little longer," said the matriarch.

Calandra repeated the time, then ended the call and turned to the assembled travellers. The men now carried packs of food and supplies on their backs, and Dione had given Airlea, Kelaino, and Fedra, who would travel to the ocean and back with the servant, flasks of water for the journey. Calandra gave instructions for the human men, who had poorer night vision, to be interspersed between the women at all times. Cogger, of course, obeyed without any question at all, but the other two also arranged themselves in order with no trouble.

Calandra turned to Eudora, who stood to the side with her mother. "A word, please?"

Eudora followed her a few paces away, out of earshot of the others. "What is it?"

Calandra cleared her throat. "I saw Zale tonight. He was . . . not himself."

Eudora's brow furrowed. "How do you know?"

"He gave me these burns." Calandra held up her blistered palms, which had been significantly soothed by the ointment.

Eudora's eyes widened. "Maybe that's why he's been put under constant care. Zoe didn't give us details."

Care. That was one word for his unrelieved siren guard.

"I have reason to believe Narcissa may be the cause of his behaviour, though I can't explain why or how. I intend to return for him as soon as possible. However, if you or your mother can extend your protection to him in any way, would you please?"

Eudora clasped Calandra's arm. "Of course."

A throb of pain surged through her, but this time it wasn't her own. Eudora's face contorted and she grabbed her belly with both hands. Calandra took Eudora's elbow to support her and quickly delved the young *kyria*.

"Eudora, the baby is coming. You should lie down. And Ewelike should stay with you."

Eudora clutched Calandra's shoulder. "No. He must go. Don't tell him until you're at the safe house. I'll send word about the child as soon as I can."

Calandra hesitated, then nodded. "As you wish."

"I'm hardly alone," Eudora added.

That was the truth. For a moment, Calandra envied Eudora's beautiful family, so perfect and supportive compared to Calandra's own ruined and scattered one.

Eudora's face became strained, and she turned away from her consort, taking short, panting breaths. "Now go. Please. I must call the physic."

Calandra laid a hand on Eudora's back. "Be safe, my friend."

Eudora nodded and smiled with effort, and Calandra hurried back to the queue of people, heading off Ewelike's concerned look with, "Eudora's going to rest. It's late, and she's been on her feet a while."

He nodded, casting a long look after his retreating wife.

Calandra turned to Kelaino, who would show them the way to Daphne's Ladder, the name of the path down the back side of the mountain, before she and Fedra returned to Steadfast House. Calandra was anxious to see the path. What else about the city she'd been raised in did she not know?

"Lead on, please, Kelaino."

Kelaino smiled. "With pleasure, your highness."

20

THE BURDEN OF CHOICE

THE ODD PARTY SET OUT through a door in one of the back rooms in Steadfast House that led into a narrow, upward-sloping tunnel carved through the black rock of the mountain. There were locked doors set in the stone walls on either side, and Calandra wondered if this were a family crypt, or maybe a vault. After a brief ascent, which included two flights of stairs in the steepest sections, they emerged through a locked iron gate into a meadow nestled between two moss-covered black rock spires at least twenty feet above the house. A well-tended plot of vegetables and fruit trees filled the space, and several goats bleated in a small pen near the wall. By the light of the setting moon, the graceful arches of the Light River Aqueduct were visible in the distance, following the line of the mountain ridge. She turned toward the city, but Sireniapolis was hidden from view by the ridge of black stone. At the far edge of the meadow, worn, irregular stone steps led up to another garden plot on a higher tier, with a low fence covered in vines visible along its edge. The path continued lower, where the tops of fruit trees from a garden on the tier below were just visible.

Airlea raised her staff and whirled toward the path leading upward. "Who goes there?"

Calandra's heart leapt in her throat. Fedra grabbed the *deiktis* protruding from her back holster in readiness.

A plump woman with her face hidden by a fine embroidered shawl draped over her head like a hood stepped out from behind an orange tree. A tall, slender young woman followed a few steps behind carrying two bulging satchels.

Airlea leapt between Calandra and the woman, her staff at the ready.

162

The woman threw out her hands. "Wait, I mean you no harm!" She pulled her shawl off her head, and brown curls threaded with tiny pearls spilled onto her shoulders, framing a pretty, tawny-skinned face with slightly protruding green eyes. "I want to join your cause." She stared at Calandra in awe. "Oh, your highness! I can't believe it's really you."

"Who are you?" Calandra asked.

The young woman cautiously lowered her hands. "I am Polyxo kor'Theano. This is my lady-in-waiting, Bryce."

Bryce gave a courteous but shallow bow with no salute, since her hands were holding the satchel straps.

Calandra frowned, but gestured for Fedra and Airlea to stand down. "I know of no Theano in the city. What house are you with?"

Polyxo folded her hands in front of her, the picture of earnestness. "I am from Anemone House in Haven. I came to Sireniapolis as soon as I heard what happened at the Redemption Moon and have been looking for a way to connect with you ever since. And now you're here!" Her gaze roved along their party, lingering on Kofi, Ewelike, and Cogger.

Anemone House. Calandra had never heard of it, but it could belong to one of the minor merchant families. The names of the households she'd met during her tour had blurred together after a while, and Haven, Sirenia's only other city, had been her last stop. "How did you know where to find us?"

"It was the Mother's own luck. I have been staying at Summerside Court with Kyria kor'Damiani. I am friends with her younger sister, Adela. When the sirens came looking for suspicious activity, I discovered they were searching for you, not roving Wildmen. Since they'd had no luck finding you on the street, I hazarded a guess you might have found the back way through the gardens. I was just making my way to the lowest garden, there, when you appeared."

The Mother's own luck, indeed, that this visitor to the city even knew of the gardens when Calandra hadn't. Something about Polyxo's story didn't sit right. Then again, the Spirit of Atargatis had been guiding her. Was it so hard to believe the Mother would also be guiding others?

Calandra sighed. She supposed they could find room for two more in the sub, even if someone stood in the moon pool room the whole way. "Fine. Walk up there behind Kelaino. Try not to make any noise."

Polyxo broke into a wide grin. "Yes, your highness. Thank you, your highness. Oh, I can't believe I've actually found you. And I'll be fighting with the rebels! How exciting!"

Fedra gave Polyxo a sharp look. "If you keep yammering like that, you'll get us all caught before we move ten paces."

Polyxo, chastened, closed her mouth.

"Please take your place behind Kelaino, Kore kor'Theano." Calandra indicated the space near the front of the line.

"Oh, please, your highness, call me Polyxo," she gushed. "I mean, we're all on the same side here, and . . ."

At Fedra's glare, she stopped talking again. Calandra stifled an amused smile.

Calandra and Airlea stepped to the side of the path to let the two women pass. Polyxo saluted on the way by, looking like a child who could hardly contain her feast-day excitement. She barely acknowledged the blank-faced Cogger, then tiptoed warily around Ewelike, who returned her alarm at his lucid salute with a bemused expression. Bryce followed quietly in her mistress's footsteps.

Once they were all in order, Calandra gave the signal to Kelaino to continue, falling into place behind Cogger's retreating back, whom she had placed in front of her so she could keep an eye on him in case he needed specific direction.

Kofi moved within a pace behind her. "Mistress?"

Calandra should probably correct his address, but not right now. Instead, she just replied, "Yes?" in Twi, glancing over her shoulder.

His expression was troubled. "What you did to Cogger—I don't like it. But that man is a bad man. Maybe he's better off that way."

Calandra didn't know what to say at first. She glanced at Cogger's stiff, obedient posture. Was Kofi right? Were there some men who were beyond actual redemption, who truly deserved to lose the right to choose? She thought about the deep, fresh lacerations that had marked Kofi's back when she first met him and wondered if Cogger was responsible for them. If so, she supposed she could understand his dislike. There were legitimate reasons why her kind had feared human men for so long. In the few years she'd been helping with the Redemption Harvests, she had seen far worse than Kofi's ragged back. What humans could do to each other was sickening.

"But then," Kofi continued thoughtfully, "I am not God. If God did not take away our choice, perhaps I should not wish to do so either. Maybe I am no better than Mr. Cogger or Mr. Crow." He sounded disturbed. "Please forget I said anything, mistress."

"As you wish." She smiled kindly, and he fell back a pace, lost in his own thoughts.

But she wasn't sure she could forget. Kofi's words struck a chord deep inside her.

After all, as she'd told Kofi earlier, she wasn't a goddess either—yet she'd decided to remove Cogger's choice, albeit temporarily. Just as she'd removed Osaze's choice when she'd sent him away. Adonia had once reprimanded her for not being willing to make the hard choices, but she'd been making plenty of them lately. This time, it hadn't even been that difficult. Was that because of the Madness? Was she already becoming like Adonia? She hoped not. Yet she'd sacrificed Cogger's freedom with barely a qualm, all for the sake of convenience and their safety.

Were there times, such as right now, when the good of one ought to be sacrificed for the benefit of many? And what made her think she had the right to choose who suffered such a fate?

Calandra stared at Cogger's back while the question ate at her soul.

*

THE *Luz de Paz* glided through the midnight blue ocean only a length above the sea floor. Calandra stood behind Nick in the cockpit, watching the scenery slip by the semi-spherical window. The moon had set, and the sub's guide lights illuminated the coral and seaweed around them, making it look like they were in some kind of eerie underwater forest.

As a safety measure to avoid the siren patrols that would be on the lookout for them, Nick had piloted the recovery team, their new recruits, and the rescued prisoners to a small islet a few hundred yards off-shore from the mouth of the Barren River that had a sheltered grotto they could sleep in. Rather than risk discovery in the dark with their extra human companions, who would not be as sure-footed as the undines, they would begin the last leg of their journey to the safe house in the early morning hours.

"Is that it? The safe house?" came Polyxo's voice at Calandra's elbow. She had come up to stand behind Nick and Nelly, craning to look through the window at the natural stone pillars they were approaching.

Nelly, who was helping her sister navigate, cast Polyxo an irritated glance, but the young woman didn't notice.

Calandra answered before Nelly could snap out a sarcastic reply. "No, it's not the safe house. But it's safe enough for tonight."

Nelly glanced at Calandra, and Calandra could sense the woman's mounting irritation. Her patience with Polyxo was even shorter than Fedra's had been. Polyxo's constant chatter had long since exhausted Calandra, too, but they couldn't afford a scene while they were all pressed into such cramped quarters. Once they got on the trail in the morning, it would be better, and the safe house was spacious and populated enough to give Polyxo other outlets for her nervous energy.

In the meantime, Calandra tried to bear it patiently. The young woman had taken a risk in joining them and was probably anxious. Still, by the time they had reached the submersible, Calandra was trying to remember physic tricks she could use to make Polyxo be quiet without slowing them down. So far, she hadn't thought of any—though if Polyxo didn't go to sleep quickly in the cave, Calandra might be tempted.

Nick navigated the sub between the stony roots of the island, bringing it to the surface in the protected inner cove of the islet to allow the humans to disembark onto the small spit of sandy rock inside without having to swim.

As the passengers took their turns ascending the ladder, Tafrara stood in the walkway near the front cabin. She watched Cogger compliantly climb the ladder to the upper deck with a tight jaw, but she said nothing.

Polyxo's face creased in an anxious frown. "Isn't this near Mermaid Rock?"

Behind her, Nick shook her head and flipped a few switches on the control panel to shut the sub down. "Not that near. No one posted at the fortress will sense us here, and they're more worried about what's happening out at the barrier these days anyway. It's the guard we have to worry about most, but it will take them hours to start looking this far away from the city. By then, we should be long gone."

Polyxo cast Nick a worried look. "But—"

"Just keep quiet and don't make a fuss and we'll be fine," Nelly snapped, her dark hair bouncing as she jerked around and pushed past Polyxo to climb the ladder with decisive steps.

"Don't worry," Calandra said, "there's only a single siren pod stationed at Mermaid Rock, and we've been avoiding them for weeks."

Polyxo stood wringing her dimpled hands, not looking at all mollified.

From behind Polyxo, Kynthia scowled at the girl. "What did you think it would be like living as a rebel? Parties and pampering?"

"No, of course not." But Polyxo cast another anxious look at the ladder.

Nick cast a glance behind her with her good eye while she flipped a few switches. "If you can't handle a night sleeping rough, you're not going to fit in very well at Margaret House."

Polyxo's brow creased even more, but she set her jaw, hiked up her skirt with one hand, and climbed up the ladder. Bryce followed behind, and Calandra thought she caught a small smile on the lady-in-waiting's face.

There was no food or vegetation in the small grotto, and they didn't dare light a fire. While the starlight filtering in from the split in the rocks above was enough for the undines to see with ease, the human men stared blankly into the dark, unable to make out details in the dim light. Airlea and Kynthia helped them find places to claim for the night.

Calandra gave Judith, Meg, and Tafrara most of the food they'd brought with them from Eudora. When Polyxo saw it, she looked so pathetic that Calandra sighed and gave her the rest. Calandra didn't begrudge the rescued prisoners the food—their gaunt faces were testimony to the lack of nutrition they'd recently received. Calandra scowled. *Even Narcissa should do better than that.* However, Polyxo had come of her own accord and had likely eaten a plentiful supper at Archon Damiani's abode. Why should she need a bedtime snack?

Ewelike and Kofi said little, even when Calandra tried to break the ice with them by asking about their pasts. She turned to Tafrara next, who revealed she was the daughter of Baya Damya, the woman who owned and ran the Irene Human Cooperative—the *latifundium* where many human women lived and worked. Tafrara asked how soon she could go home, and after Calandra assured her they'd get her home as soon as possible, the girl said nothing else. Perhaps it was the chill and dark, but the night would have passed in near silence were it not for Polyxo's constant chatter. Eventually, Polyxo wound down enough to sleep, and Calandra breathed a sigh of relief.

She thought she'd fall asleep immediately, but, as often happened, she tossed and turned on the sandy floor of the grotto, staring at the stars twinkling above them. She wondered if Osaze were looking at those same stars, which was ridiculous—he was on the other side of the world.

After half an hour, she sat up, frustrated.

Meg's dark green eyes glowed softly in the dark. "You can't sleep either?"

Calandra shook her head. "I used to think it was my nightmares that gave me insomnia. Now I'm not so sure. Maybe my body is just out of the habit of sleeping."

Meg nodded. "If I were a physic, I could help."

Calandra swallowed. "Well, I could do that for you, at least. I was tempted to put Polyxo to sleep earlier."

Meg chuckled and shook her head. "No, I'm tired enough. I'll sleep soon. I've just been enjoying having my powers returned to me and have been feeling the resonance of the stones."

Calandra nodded. She'd worn feldspar cuffs for a single night when Adonia had arrested her for treason, and she had never felt so helpless. She could only imagine how the newly raised stone healer had felt with her own abilities suppressed for three weeks.

"What you did, at the bonding ceremony . . ." Calandra stopped, uncertain what to say next.

Meg had been the one to broadcast Delphine's message from Calandra's Tear publicly as a distraction while Calandra, Zale, and Osaze fled Adonia's perverted wedding, which was what had gotten her captured. It was probably only the uncertain state of the throne that had kept her and Judith, who had Freed every man at the wedding with the help of the other FWS rebels, alive until they could be rescued.

She glanced at Meg and opened her mouth, but words seemed inadequate to express both her gratitude and her regret.

"It's all right, I know. And I'd do it again." Meg smiled.

Calandra nodded and gave Meg a tight smile. She wrapped her arms around her knees. "All that effort, and we ended up worse off than before. I *have* to find a way to raise the barrier again."

"So having Zale there didn't help, huh?"

"No, it did. I think. It's just . . . I don't know what went wrong. I thought we must have damaged the Heartstone beyond repair, but when I saw it tonight, it didn't seem that bad. Other than a deep crack marring one side that's never been there before, the Heartstone looked better than I've ever seen it."

Meg frowned. "That's strange. Did the crack reach all the way to the inner core?"

Calandra shook her head. In her memory, the fire opal had been completely intact. "I don't think so, it was only the casing that was cracked. And the Spirit of the Heartstone—"

"The what?" Meg blinked.

"The, um, Spirit of the Stone. I met it. When I was healing the Stone. It's not just the normal spirit that's imbued in a stone's structure. It was more than that. This spirit is . . . alive."

Meg nodded slowly. "Huh. Okay. You were saying?"

Calandra smiled. Only another stone healer would accept her

explanation so easily.

"Anyway, the Spirit was as strong as it was before too. I'd wondered if it had been injured when the Stone was injured, but it was the same."

So why am I having such a hard time sensing it now? When she'd fled the Mother's Heart three weeks ago, the presence of that Spirit had remained with her, a constant boon to soothe her pain. But lately, she'd only felt it sporadically—like earlier today, when she'd been in close proximity to the Stone.

Maybe that was the problem. The Heartstone was damaged, so she could only feel the Spirit when she was close to it.

Meg's expression was pensive. "Maybe there's something else wrong with it. Like it's not the Stone itself that's broken, but something preventing the Stone's power from getting out."

Calandra thought about it. Could that be true? It would also explain why the Spirit was so difficult to access. "Maybe. But what would it be?"

"I don't know. I'd have to see it to figure it out. What are the chances Narcissa would let me and some other stone healers in for a quick checkup?" Meg's mouth twisted in sardonic humour.

Calandra snorted. "Based on what she said today, not good."

Narcissa's eyes flashed gold in the dark, and Calandra's heart skipped. What had her cousin meant that if the Heartstone were restored, Calandra's mother would be trapped in the Soulstone forever? *What's a soulstone?*

Delphine's Tear had included her theory that the Heartstone powered more than just the barrier around Sirenia, but also kept the Grigori trapped in the Abyss. Calandra had assumed that meant it powered the Voidstone, the gateway to the Abyss. But what if it were something else? And how did Narcissa know about a stone Calandra had never heard of . . . unless it hadn't been Narcissa speaking at all? She shuddered and blinked her cousin's unsettling golden-eyed image away.

She yawned, exhaustion creeping up on her. "We'll talk to the council about it when we get back to the safe house. Maybe they'll have some ideas about how to check it. Another stealth mission or something. I hope they've come up with some ideas for protecting the island in the meantime too. With the barrier down, it's only a matter of time before the royal guard misses a ship and we're exposed to the world. We can't keep adding to our population indiscriminately like this. There's a reason we usually only bring in ships bi-annually."

Meg nodded. "If I think of anything else, I'll let you know."

"If too many humans come," said another voice, "will you finally let some of us leave?"

Calandra rolled over and saw Tafrara watching them.

"Let you leave?" Calandra sighed. "I'm sorry. You know that's not possible. Hasn't your family been on Sirenia for generations?"

Tafrara's eyes gleamed. "Not by choice."

The girl rolled over to face the men laid out next to her. Cogger was snoring gently.

Calandra lay back down. Despite leading a rebellion about the right for men to choose, she'd spared little thought to the human women who had joined their population over the years. Though they retained their will, the very fact they weren't permitted to leave the island made them prisoners of a different kind. How would she feel if she were captured and taken somewhere far from home and told she could never return?

Her pounding head reminded her that may soon be her fate. But in her case, it would be the fate she chose out of duty to her people. But what about the human women? What fealty did they have to their undine neighbours?

Who had the right to choose for them?

*

Wilhelmina had just gotten settled in her room, the one nearest the gate, hoping for a couple hours sleep before sunrise, when a soft voice calling in the courtyard made her sit up. She thought about letting Selina, the guard who'd taken over for Fedra, deal with it—but what if Kyria Eudora needed something? The baby and mistress had been sleeping when Wilhelmina had left them, but with newborns, that could change by the moment. And Melina and the other girls were too inexperienced with little ones to know what to do.

"My old bones aren't cut out for this anymore," she muttered.

Heaving a sigh, she sat up, wrapped her shawl around her shoulders, lit an oil lamp, and shuffled out of her room. She took a sharp turn toward the stairs at the back of the courtyard, her eyes bleary with exhaustion. The moon had long since set, and her lamp cast flickering shadows on the walls.

"Excuse me," said a voice in the middle of the courtyard.

Wilhelmina whirled and froze.

Before her stood a lovely woman with golden-brown skin, curly hair, and an unusual ankle-length green dress. The golden lamplight seemed to pool in her eyes.

Selina rushed out of her booth, fumbling her knife out of its sheath and pointing it at the young woman. "Hold!"

The woman smiled graciously, releasing a silver pendant of nested rings, which fell against her chest with a metallic tinkle. She took a step toward them. "You don't happen to know Zale bet'Delphine by any chance, do you?"

For the second time that night, Wilhelmina dropped her lamp.

21

MEMORY SHIFT

Zale woke to someone shaking him, hard. He cracked open eyes still bleary with sleep. Singer kor'Renata stood beside the bed with her hands on her hips and annoyance painted on her ochre-brown face.

"Mmm . . . Leave me alone."

"Zale. Time to get up. You'll miss breakfast," she said in her typical no-nonsense voice.

"I don't care. Let me sleep."

She grabbed his big toe, and a crackle of energy jolted through him. He sat bolt upright and put his hands on his head to stop the room from spinning.

"I'm up, I'm up."

"Mm-hmm. Sure you are." She grabbed the corner of his blanket and whipped it off, throwing it on the floor.

He jerked his knees toward his naked chest and scowled. "Hey! That was uncalled for."

People of Sirenia seemed to have absolutely no discomfort with nudity, but he certainly did. Being on display in his tank as a merman—or in *ichthys* state, as these people called it—was one thing, but he didn't think he'd ever get used to being on full display for others to see while in *podia* state. Despite the fact the Roma were no prudes, he'd spent too many years among humans for that.

And all the undines knew it.

Singer kor'Renata smiled, looking satisfied with herself.

"*Now* you're up." She gave his leg a swat for good measure on the way by. "If you're not outside this door in two minutes, I'm going to drag you

172

into the dining hall in whatever state of dress—or undress—you may be. I'm not missing breakfast for you."

When she shut the door, Zale scrambled out of bed and pulled on his trousers and shirt. He eyed his bright waistcoat and the bracelet it concealed, but he decided to leave it behind. The day was already promising to be hot and humid, and he certainly didn't need any extra layers. Besides, he hadn't lost control of his powers for weeks. He just wished he knew why his head was pounding.

By the time he and Singer kor'Renata got to the triangular dining hall, most of the students had cleared their dishes and were heading off to after-breakfast work duty before their first class. Narcissa and the palace's other noble inhabitants took their food in their rooms, but students and guards ate in the Great Hall—the same one used for assemblies and other gatherings when the occasion called for it.

Several sirens sat at a table near the raised dais at the narrow front of the grand auditorium-like room, with a few *tapeinoi* eating woodenly at a table next to them. Near the main entrance at the wide end of the room, Damaris ate alone with her back toward him, watching a work crew mend some broken window panes in the floor-to-ceiling windows of the vestibule.

Zale frowned. *How did that happen?*

"I'll be over there." Singer kor'Renata pointed toward the siren table. "Come and get me before you leave."

She glared the promised consequences if he didn't. When he gave a nod, she went over to greet her fellow guards.

He made his way to the food table near the pillars along one side of the room—a fine spread of pulses, cheese, and fruit. Two girls passed him on their way to deposit their dishes in the collection carts, jabbering excitedly about an earthquake. Some kind of history lesson? Who got that excited about history?

Then he remembered, the images like shapes through fog—Calandra had been here. Right here in the palace.

She had tried to kill him, but Narcissa had rescued him.

The memory was fuzzy, like it had happened a long time ago. He'd been in the Archive. Narcissa had used her powers to fend Calandra off. There was a huge earthquake.

The next thing he remembered, Singer kor'Renata had been waking him up.

He gave his head a shake. Why was it so hard to remember something like that, when he could still remember every detail of the day he'd struck the explosives shed his father had been standing beside with lightning, and that was over six years ago?

"You all right, lad?"

Zale glanced at the plump elderly woman supervising the food table—human, from her brown eyes. Her expression was a mix of concern and fear, unlike the undines, who were simply afraid. Judging from her motherly expression, she was more afraid *for* him than *of* him—which most of the humans seemed to be.

"Uh, yeah. Thanks."

She gave him an askance look but said nothing, going back to her task of refilling a trencher with fresh cut pineapple.

After filling up his bowl with porridge and snagging a few delicious-looking pieces of pineapple, he turned and surveyed the tables to decide where to sit. He felt bad for how he'd ended it with Damaris yesterday and thought now might be as good a time as any to patch things up. But as soon as he started walking toward her, she stood, picked up her bowl and spoon, and headed toward the collection bins.

"Damaris!"

She glanced at him, and her expression brightened slightly. Then her eyes darkened beneath the thundercloud of her bunched eyebrows. He thought she might keep walking and ignore him, but she stood as though waiting for him.

I guess that's a good sign.

As he walked toward her, he tried to think of a good line to preemptively deflect the sarcastic comment he was sure she had ready.

He put on his most charming grin. "So, are you ready for another demonstration of my superior combat skills in the ring this afternoon?"

Damaris did not react how he expected. Her eyebrows rose and she stared at him.

"What are you doing here?" she hissed.

"What do you mean, what am I doing here? I live here."

"But you shouldn't be here anymore. Calandra came to rescue you."

Zale barked a laugh. "*Rescue* me? Is that what they call attempted murder around here?"

He set his food on the table—a little too hard—and sat down. *My own sister tried to kill me. Go figure.* He shrugged, then started shovelling porridge into his mouth with his spoon.

Damaris straddled the bench and sat down beside him, placing her empty dishes on the table. "What are you talking about? Calandra wouldn't try to kill you. She was trying to get you out of here."

When he ignored her, her face pinched in exasperation.

"Can't you see you're trapped, Zale? Narcissa hasn't Redeemed you, but you're still her prisoner."

Zale scoffed and dipped some bread in his porridge. "Yeah. Okay." He took a bite. With his mouth still full, he said, "I get to live in the most beautiful place in the world with my own kind, being trained by my cousin to use my powers, and you call it imprisonment. And when my traitorous sister comes to kill me, you call it rescuing. I'm beginning to wonder how smart you really are."

Damaris frowned, looking at him sideways in confusion. "That's not what you said yesterday. When we thought Calandra was *dead*. I thought you'd be more excited that she's not."

Zale shook his head. He hadn't thought she was dead. Had he? She was a traitor to the crown living on the lam with the other rebels. Why would he think she was dead?

Something else occurred to him, and he turned to Damaris. "Wait. When did you see her?"

Damaris's cheeks flushed pink. "I—I was out using the lavs and ran into her in the hallway. She had come with Airlea kor'Phile—to rescue you, she said. I made sure she knew where your dorm was. Is that where she found you?"

"No, I, uh . . ." No, not in his dorm. But where had he been? He'd remembered this just a few minutes ago. He grasped at the shiny, slippery memory. "I was in the Archive?"

Damaris made a face. "The Archive? How did you end up there?"

Zale took a few more bites without answering. How *had* he gotten to the Archive? He walked through the events of the previous evening in his mind.

He'd gone to his dorm room without supper—rather, had been escorted to his dorm room, whether he'd been ready for bed or not.

That's right, he'd snuck out by melting through the window grate. He probably would've noticed the broken lock this morning if Singer kor'Renata hadn't rushed him out the door so quickly. He'd been hungry and wanted a snack. Did he go to the kitchen?

No, wait. He didn't go there. He'd meant to, but then he decided he needed to look for something. A way to find his mother and Tartarus. Now he remembered. He'd gone to the Archive, and then . . . then . . .

Then Calandra and her friend had come and tried to kill him. But that was the strangest memory of all. It was suddenly crystal clear, but had an air of unreality about it, like a layer of paint applied to a wooden chest to hide damage. There was no way he was going to explain that to Damaris, though. She'd only make him feel small.

He shook his head. "Just trust me. I was."

"Fine."

Damaris sat back and crossed her arms, scowling at the workers fixing the windows.

Zale pressed his lips together, watching her sulk. This wasn't exactly how he'd planned to make up with her.

Damaris turned back toward him. "What were you doing in the Archive, anyway?"

Zale squirmed under her scrutiny. "If you must know, I went to do research."

Damaris raised her eyebrows skeptically. "Research? What for?"

Zale frowned and thought better of telling her. Even though she was talking to him now, he still wasn't sure how much he trusted her. "My business, not yours."

She blinked, but didn't press the matter. "So what makes you think Calandra was trying to kill you?"

Zale looked at her, annoyed. "Look, you don't have to believe me, okay? But I know what I saw. I was there. Calandra and this siren, probably that Airlea you mentioned, both came into the Archive while I was there. Calandra tried to do that mind-enslavement thing on me, and when Narcissa stepped in, she tried to kill me with her diving knife. If it weren't for Narcissa, I'd be dead right now."

Zale stopped. He'd been betrayed again. This time, by his own sister.

There were so few people he could trust. Thank Elyon he had Narcissa.

"Well, I wasn't there, so maybe you're right and Calandra acted completely out of character." Damaris tapped the table with the tip of her pointing finger. "But answer me this, Icarus—why would Calandra risk her own life and that of her friend to sneak into the palace and find you just to kill you when you posed absolutely no threat to her? And why would someone powerful enough to cause that"—she pointed at the cracked wall and the freshly repaired windowpanes—"need to use a diving knife if she wanted to kill you? Who would benefit from you believing that's what happened?"

She stood and picked up her dishes. Zale opened his mouth to answer, and she held up a hand to stop him.

"I don't need to know those answers. But you do." She gave him a meaningful glare, then walked away.

Zale scooped another spoonful of porridge, then dropped it back in the bowl, no longer hungry. Instead, he glanced up at the workers, considering Damaris's question. A stone healer with short grey curls laid her hands on an enormous crack in the wall next to the window nearest them and began binding it together.

He thought about that bright, shiny memory floating in the clinging fog of last night's events. There was something very unusual about all this. And this wasn't the first time he'd felt this way recently, he was sure of it—where some memories seemed polished to a high gloss and others were smothered in oil.

But if Damaris were right and Calandra had come to rescue him, why had she left without him? At the thought, he suddenly realized he didn't really want to go. But that made no sense. All he wanted was to get out of this place and find his mother.

No, he didn't.

Yes, he did.

Sweat beaded on his forehead.

What is happening to me?

Zale closed his eyes, clenching his spoon and taking deep breaths to calm himself down like his mother had taught him to do when he was young and feeling anxious about his father going into the mine. He thought of his mother's sweet face, her gentle green eyes, and his heart slowed. *I'm coming for you, Mother. Somehow, I'll find you. I promise.*

The image of her face was drowned in syrupy apathy and he sighed, content in the morning sunshine and the beautiful room filled with the low murmur of voices and softly clinking dishes.

He finished his breakfast in silence, put his dishes in the cart, and went to find Singer kor'Renata to accompany him to his morning lesson with Narcissa. Maybe this would be the day she'd agree to let him go after his mother.

Not that he wanted to.

Yes, he *did*.

But not as much as he wanted to see Narcissa.

For the first time that morning, he felt a tingle of excitement.

22
REPORTS

NARCISSA BLINKED AND focused on the woman before her. Her mind must have wandered. She had no idea what Letitia, the palace steward, had been saying. Retreating through the archway of her receiving room was the athletic back of her cousin, Zale. When had he even arrived?

The angular steward looked down her nose at Narcissa like a testy heron. She wore her salt-and-pepper hair in a severe bun at the nape of her neck, and her palace livery, an indigo peplos with intricate silvery embroidery at the hem and cuffs to indicate her rank, was impeccable. Letitia was always impeccable. That's why she was so good at her job. Still, Narcissa wondered briefly how much better the steward would be at her job, and how many fewer tedious conversations like this Narcissa would have to endure, if human women could be Redeemed as well as men.

She frowned. Where had that idea come from?

Letitia was still waiting for a response.

"Pardon?" Narcissa raised a hand to her mouth to cover a yawn.

Letitia frowned at the sheaf of papers in her arms. "What would you like to do about Kyria Patricia's wine losses? If we pay her the damages she's asking for, every other merchant who suffered losses from Wildmen looting the city will be coming to ask for their share. I'm not sure the treasury can support it."

Narcissa glanced at Letitia in annoyance. The woman was always perfectly respectful, but Narcissa couldn't help but feel the steward was prompting Narcissa toward her own predetermined ends—as though she were the servant, and Letitia the superior! But it was obvious the steward actually *enjoyed* numbers and the running of the day-to-day trivialities of the palace. The woman might as well be Redeemed already, for how much personality she had.

Narcissa would rather have someone bash her over the head with a *deiktis* staff, repeatedly, than listen to one more moment of this drivel.

She waved her hand dismissively and stood. "Do whatever you think best. I'm going to train."

Fatigue dragged at her bones. She glanced at the *taps* who stood behind her—not Matthew, whom she'd sent to have a bath when they'd awoken this morning, but one of her other favourites, Ali. His brown eyes looked stoically ahead without flickering. Perhaps a nap would be in order instead of an hour in the sparring ring. What time was it, anyway? Had she even had breakfast? The empty tray near the door waiting for servants to pick it up said she did, though she didn't remember eating it.

Letitia looked up, her mouth a firm line. "So I should deny her request? If we pay her nothing, she will likely extract the cost tenfold in her contract next season."

"As I said, do what you want." Narcissa glanced toward the door. "Do you know why Zale was here?"

"I believe he was here for his morning training session, just as he's come every morning for three weeks, your majesty." Letitia's frown deepened.

Narcissa shook her head, trying to clear the fog that surrounded her memories. Suddenly, as though it had been dropped into her brain, she clearly remembered spending an hour with him, working with him and his ability to use fire and air, his two strongest elements. Her doubt faded, and she smiled.

"Of course. Thank you, Letitia. That will be all."

Letitia's expression smoothed. She bent slightly at the waist and touched her forehead in a perfectly executed salute. "Yes, your majesty." She spun on her heel and walked out of the room.

An older siren in dress blue with her glossy black hair pulled back in a braided ponytail entered and saluted.

"Despoina Cleo kor'Andromachi and Singer Zoe kor'Dione are both here to see you, your majesty."

Narcissa sat down again before replying, trying to remember if she had summoned the two women or not. Like shutters opening to reveal a landscape, the events of the previous night filled her mind.

Of course. Calandra's attack on Narcissa and Matthew. Her attempt to take Matthew's bond and kill Zale. How she'd run in shame when Narcissa had defeated her.

But why was I even in the Archive? I went to bed early . . . didn't I?

She was so tired all the time recently, no matter how late she slept. The fight with Calandra sprang to her mind, and her gut tightened. Her cousin was always turning up where she wasn't wanted and taking things that didn't belong to her. Like Osaze. And Matthew. But Narcissa had gotten Matthew back. Creating a *sklavia* bond was something she *could* do. She smiled to herself, then yawned again. She really *would* have to get more sleep tonight.

To the siren, she said, "Send Singer kor'Dione in and have Despoina kor'Andromachi wait in the hall until I send for her."

Narcissa thought of Cleo's expression when a subordinate got an audience while she was kept waiting and smirked.

The siren saluted. "Yes, your majesty."

"And have a servant bring me some coffee."

"Yes, your majesty."

The woman exited.

Narcissa leaned back in her mother's chair. *Her* chair now, no matter how her mother's cronies—like Despoina Cleo and Letitia the Steward—might disapprove. They didn't have to approve. They only had to obey and remain loyal.

Zoe entered, saluted, and stood at attention. "Good morning, your majesty. I trust you slept well?"

There was an undertone of something in Zoe's question, but Narcissa was still not sensitive enough in spirit to ascertain what it was. How was it that she could teach Zale how to use fire and air, but she still couldn't sense the most basic emotions of the woman standing right in front of her? It didn't make sense.

And then her perspective shifted and it made perfect sense. Why had she thought the two incongruous?

She arched a brow at the woman in front of her.

"So, singer. Was our plan a success? Did the traitors take the mole with them?"

"Yes, your majesty. She is supposed to report in every evening using the communication stone frequency you designated." She frowned. "I received word from my mother that Calandra and the deserter Airlea kor'Phile kidnapped two *douloi* from my family home last night. My mother and sister are quite distraught that their household was implicated in this unfortunate situation." She clenched her jaw. "They had already lost all their other *douloi* during the, er, attack three weeks ago. As a precaution against further losses, they have sent my sister Eudora's consort to reside at our family estate up-valley."

Narcissa pursed her lips, trying to look sympathetic.

"Thank you, Singer kor'Dione, for your part in this. I know it is difficult to conceal your true loyalties when it affects your loved ones so. Don't worry, we will retrieve what has been lost soon enough, and then your loyalty will be rewarded. In the meantime, I will send two of the palace *douloi* to serve in your mother's household to make up for what was lost."

Narcissa already had a mole in Steadfast House, but it never hurt to have more. *Douloi* would report everything to her without question, though their lack of discernment over what was an important detail could be quite tiresome. Besides, with the recent influx of men due to the downed barrier, there were *douloi* to spare, despite those who'd been freed after her mother's death who remained unaccounted for. The newcomers were not yet trained, to be sure—but she'd let Dione worry about that. Narcissa had enough on her plate just now.

"Thank you, your majesty," said Zoe, inclining her head respectfully. "I'm sure she will be extremely grateful for the gesture. If there is nothing else . . . ?"

"No, I will call you again if I have need of you. Good day, singer. Please send in Despoina Cleo on your way out."

Zoe saluted again, backed away, and left the room.

Narcissa drummed her fingers on the arm of the chair, plotting how she would word her command to Cleo. While she did not yet have reason to suspect either Cleo or Zoe of treason, it never hurt to be constantly on guard. Her mother had taught her that.

Her Mistress of Sirens entered, the *despoina*'s every movement full of grace and power. Cleo bowed and saluted, her tightly cropped silver curls impeccably shaped around her dark brown face. Narcissa frowned, the old feeling of inferiority surfacing again. Sure, until Adonia's death, Cleo had been second only to her mother in authority. But now, Narcissa was not only Opal Princess but waited only for accord from the archons to be crowned queen. By all qualifications that mattered, she already was.

So why did Cleo still intimidate her?

Narcissa stood so she would be eye-to-eye with the tall woman.

"*Despoina*, report."

Cleo inclined her head respectfully. "I regret to inform you, your highness, that there is no sign of Princess Calandra and the rebels who attacked the palace last night anywhere in or around the city of Sireniapolis, or in the bay and surrounding waters. I will continue to have my sirens search the area, but if they escaped by water using submersibles, which seems likely, they could have reached any point along the coast by now. Or even another land mass, though I doubt any among them are so foolhardy."

"Send me news the moment you hear anything, *despoina*," Narcissa said. "In the meantime, Singer kor'Dione just brought me news that her family was also attacked by the rebels last night. Pay Kyria kor'Eirene a visit and assure her we are doing everything in our power to restore order in the city."

Cleo gave a slight nod, her hands behind her back. "I have already done so, your highness. I went as soon as I heard the unfortunate news. By then, Kyria kor'Dione had already sent her consort to their family estate for his own safety. However, the report is not all bad—her baby was born late this morning."

Narcissa smiled thinly. "Well done for your prompt attention to the matter, and for sharing the happy news. I'll be sure to have a gift sent for the child."

Cleo inclined her head. "Thank you, your highness."

"And how are the siren corps reacting to news of my cousin's resurrection from the dead?"

"Reactions are mixed." Cleo's face was stoic. "But they are good soldiers, all of them. They will serve the queen as they have always done."

Narcissa couldn't help notice Cleo gave no indication that said queen would be her.

"And the citizens? I assume the news of Calandra's return has already spread?"

"Indeed, your highness. The citizens are restless. Some of them see news of Calandra's survival as hope the Heartstone could still be restored. Others blame her for loosing the Wildmen on them. So again, reactions are mixed. If you could find a way to restore the barrier—"

"And how am I supposed to do that?"

"Have you sent stone healers to check the underwater anchor points?"

Narcissa scowled. "Of course I have. Do you think I'm an idiot?" The archons had insisted. "The anchor points aren't the problem. Whatever caused this happened on Summer Solstice while Calandra and Zale were playing hero with the Heartstone."

Narcissa stomped to the window overlooking the valley. Calandra's appearance in the palace last night had been a setback to her plans to claim the throne. If she'd only waited another week . . . But Cleo was right—the vulnerability of their island was a problem. She'd woken up in a cold sweat more than once from nightmares of their island being ravaged by humans. It was little wonder the people were making rumblings about Calandra, when, for years, they'd been led to believe she would save the Heartstone. Ha! The only thing Calandra had saved was herself. And Zale . . . Zale had his uses. But healing the Heartstone wouldn't be one of them. In fact, she was determined he'd never get near it again.

She whirled to face the *despoina*. "As for the Wildmen, why do they continue to elude you?"

Cleo cleared her throat. "My forces are spread thin at the barrier, your highness. I believe the Wildmen have established a camp in the mountains, but we have not yet been able to determine where. Rest assured, restoring complete order to the island is of the highest priority."

"Not high enough," she retorted.

Cleo placidly met Narcissa's glare. "Which threat would you prefer I prioritize, your highness? The humans at the barrier or the humans on the island?"

"Both." Narcissa drew in a frustrated breath. She had no reason to doubt Cleo was already doing her best on both fronts. *None of this is Cleo's fault.*

She turned toward the window again, staring at her beleaguered island.

"You see what Calandra has done—turned our own people against each other and made upstanding citizens fear for their safety? I've heard that some still view Calandra as some kind of saviour, even though she's the one responsible for this mess." She paused, considering. "We must show the nobles we're working in their best interests, whether to return their *douloi* or to ensure the safety of their entire household, especially consorts."

"Yes, your highness."

"Panselinos is in less than a week, and I want the celebration to continue as usual. That means we'll need to have the Wildmen in the city contained beforehand. Can you see to that?"

"Certainly, your highness."

Narcissa studied Cleo and stifled another yawn. She couldn't deal with palace politics when she was so exhausted. Where was her coffee?

Cleo's gaze flicked from Narcissa's indecorous yawn to the archway leading to the bedchamber beyond. Narcissa thought she detected a hint of disdain in the woman's posture, but she couldn't be sure. Curse her limited empathy! What she wouldn't give to have a better idea what the woman was thinking.

"Have you something to add, *despoina*?"

Cleo shook her head. "Not at all, your highness."

Narcissa narrowed her eyes, but let it go.

"Good. Report to me if you find anything unusual or out of order. And be sure to keep an eye on Steadfast House. Kyria Dione kor'Eirene is an old friend of my mother's, and I'd hate to see their household come to harm."

"Of course, your highness. Will there by anything else?"

Narcissa frowned. "Yes, one other thing." She gave the *despoina* her coldest glare. "It's *your majesty*, not *your highness*."

Cleo saluted. "I mean no disrespect. I am merely according you the most correct styling for your current station. When that station changes in a legal sense, I will change your address. One must be particular about such things, wouldn't you agree?"

Narcissa ground her teeth. Cleo had her wedged into a clamshell with that argument. The *despoina* knew Narcissa was trying to win over the remaining archons to her claim, and forcing the issue would not do her any favours in their eyes. Narcissa could do nothing but agree with her.

"Of course, *despoina*. May the Mother be with you."

Cleo gave her a crisp salute. "And with you, your highness."

Cleo left as the servant brought Narcissa's coffee. Wanting to be alone, she dismissed the servant and sent Ali to wait in the hall. She went to the window while she drank, surveying the city her mother had bequeathed her and Calandra had destroyed.

No, not destroyed. Her cousin had marred it, to be sure, trying to take the loyalty that should rightfully be hers, but Narcissa knew how to fight fire with fire. She had to show the archons that the crown should be hers, not Calandra's. She needed to find a way to prove her superiority to Calandra.

But how? The halfway houses were already stretched to their limits with the new humans who had been brought in, and more were added to their numbers every day. If this kept up, she'd have to issue orders to start drowning the men instead of Redeeming them to protect their island's location and waning resources—but even the archons who supported her would rebel at that. That would have to wait until she'd taken the throne. And she'd never take the throne as long as some of them remained loyal to Calandra.

Even Shinara, the high priestess of Atargatis, seemed to be wavering in her loyalty. The woman had had the audacity to ask Narcissa what had happened to one of her acolytes who disappeared, a pretty little thing Narcissa knew only in passing. Oh, Shinara hadn't come right out and accused her of murder, but she'd certainly hinted at the accusation, claiming Narcissa was the last one to see her alive after her final sojourn to the temple to pray—as though Wildmen couldn't have found the girl at the temple as easily as they'd been ravaging other areas of the city. Ridiculous.

There was nothing for it. Even subduing the Wildman threat wasn't likely to win councillors who'd been friends of Thea kor'Aglaia's, though her spies assured her the dissenting archons' *douloi* were still Redeemed. For now. Thea had had too many friends in this palace. Trusting that insidious traitor had been her mother's first mistake. Her second one had been waiting so long to kill her. And now Thea's protegé was trying to finish what the old hag had started—the destruction of three thousand years of tradition, and the throne along with it.

Narcissa ground her teeth, remembering Thea's and her mother's bodies lying at awkward angles among the vines in the Grotto where they'd fallen—Thea at Adonia's hand, and Adonia at Narcissa's. Narcissa had stopped the Madness of her mother. Could she do the same for her cousin's?

If she could find her mother's quaternaria, that would help, but so far, her search had been in vain. If only she'd had the presence of mind to grab it then and there. When she found out who'd stolen it . . .

Narcissa sighed and took another sip of coffee, walking across the room to the window facing the bay. In the sparring courtyard below, the *tapeinoi* were putting their staves away to go have the midday meal. Maybe she should go train—her mind was always clearer after a good workout. Too bad the archons didn't respect her ability with *Tropos Hydor Zon*. No. Just like her mother, all they cared about was Calandra's talent with the elements. Even gaining powers of her own hadn't changed their minds.

Narcissa paused with her cup nearly to her lips, staring across the turquoise bay.

That's it! If she restored the barrier, if *she* healed the Heartstone and succeeded where Calandra had failed, she could silence the doubters who thought Calandra the traitor still deserved the throne.

Narcissa held up her free hand, a small flame flickering above her forefinger. Calandra had said the Heartstone needed all the elements, including fire, to be restored. Fire was something Narcissa could now produce.

All she needed was to gather the circle of stone healers.

She grinned in glee. She wanted to see her cousin's face when she realized Narcissa had won. What better way to do that than to bring her to the palace to enjoy the show? Have her watch Narcissa heal the Heartstone, then, with the archons finally silenced, arrest her for treason to the crown.

She had little doubt she could lure Calandra into her trap—there were so many things her *dear* cousin wanted that Narcissa could promise her. Promise, even if what she gave instead was only what Calandra deserved.

She smiled in victory and set down her cup on the silver tray.

"Mesi," she called.

When her lady-in-waiting did not instantly appear, she aimed her face at the archway leading to the bedchamber and shouted the name again.

Instead of the girl entering the room, however, the air in the middle of the floor shimmered with oily black mist. Then the mist solidified into the form of a beautiful, terrifying man. A man with thick black hair, too-white skin that stretched over exquisite cheekbones, and narrow, upturned eyes as black as the bottom of the deepest trench of the sea.

"Playing with fire again, Semyaza?" the man said in a voice that reverberated inside Narcissa's skull.

She opened her mouth, speechless with surprise.

Then she knew no more.

23

THE LETTER

ROBERT SAT NEAR A WINDOW in the common room of the Port House Inn, staring at the letter on the wooden table before him. Late afternoon sunlight seeped between the slats of the shutters in brilliant golden lines, but the room had not yet begun to fill with dinner guests, which was perfect for the peace and quiet Robert had been seeking to consider the madness of his brother. He'd read the letter five times since Middleton had given it to him yesterday, and each time, he became more convinced his brother had joined an esoteric cult and become a traitor to the crown.

Gryffyn, what have you got yourself into now?

When he'd first read the letter, he'd been severely rattled, retreating to a tavern for a fortifying drink or two to think. Fortunately, Miss Bethel had spent most of yesterday afternoon out and about finding clothes and some personal items for the exhausted Urbi, who'd slept in Miss Bethel's room most of the day. And Mr. Berian had been paying a visit to a local minister he'd befriended.

These are the people Gryffyn accuses of being evil spirits and spies.

Robert wanted to write the entire letter off as lunacy, except everything in it had been written in the cold, factual manner his brother always employed—these were not the ramblings of a madman. Even the disturbing truth that Gryffyn had known all along Zale was the so-called demon at Chyandour Brook and had tried to make Robert think he'd been hallucinating to keep him quiet and protect their family reputation was relayed in his typical arrogant tone.

In addition, the claim that Robert's two companions were spies revived his own doubts from when he'd overheard Miss Bethel talking to the

Spaniard the other day. Hadn't he wondered the same thing? Foreboding created a little lump of ice in his belly.

Miss Bethel a spy? No. The idea was ludicrous. But most disturbing was Gryffyn's other claim about Miss Abela Bethel. With trepidation, Robert reread the pertinent paragraph.

Remember, Rob, "a person with golden eyes is a spirit in disguise." I have reason to believe the golden-eyed woman who accompanied Zale Teague onto the Atlanta *is the same spirit who was responsible for the death of Talwyn Penrose. Do not trust her.*

Gryffyn didn't include anything to support the claim. What had Gryffyn seen after Robert had been blinded?

The next line was even more alarming. It was the clincher that convinced him Gryffyn must be out of his mind: *Seek out the blood-red heartstone jewel she bears, but be wary of the power it holds—its value is beyond price. Don't tell her you know of its existence. When you retrieve it, take it to Lord Middleton. He'll know what to do.*

A magical jewel? What could Gryffyn be referring to? Robert had never seen Miss Bethel wear one, and she packed extremely light—he had no idea where she might conceal such a gem. And, of all people, why did Gryffyn want Robert to take the jewel to Middleton? According to Gryffyn, he and Middleton were both part of some secret order—but what could be so special about this one gemstone that they'd need to steal it?

"A letter from home, Mr. Cox?" came Miss Bethel's voice from behind him.

Robert nearly jumped out of his skin. Grabbing the letter, he stuffed it in his breast pocket and turned to see Miss Bethel coming toward him. Urbi and Reverend Berian walked behind her. He stood and gave a small bow.

"'Tis only a letter from the bank manager, reviewing my accounts. With care, I should be fine until I receive a further advance from my brother."

He smiled, trying to look casual, but it felt strained. The bank manager's letter sat on his desk in his room, and what he'd said about its contents was true. The truth about *this* letter would draw too many questions.

He helped Miss Bethel seat herself on the chair to one side of the small table, her back to the door from the street. Urbi, now bathed and groomed and in a new, dark blue dress, sat across from him with Mr. Berian's assistance—after her initial confusion about why the reverend was pulling out her chair for her had been allayed. As Robert sat down again, Berian seated his bulky frame with surprising grace in the remaining chair with his back to the stairs leading to their rooms, his hooded golden eyes making him appear half asleep. The chair didn't even squeak.

Miss Bethel looked elegant in a bottle green muslin gown with short sleeves that highlighted her lustrous warm brown décolletage—bare but for the fine silver chain she always wore, its pendant hidden beneath the bodice of her dress. Was that where the stone Gryffyn sought was kept? Middleton's wary reaction to her necklace still confused him—a reaction hardly warranted by a simple gem. But a magical one? Maybe. Still, Robert had never seen Miss Bethel with a jewel of any kind. He stared at the chain, wondering if he dared ask to see the pendant.

"Ahem." Berian cleared his throat very pointedly in Robert's direction.

Robert startled, realizing he'd been staring at Miss Bethel's fine chest for far too long. His face burned, but Miss Bethel didn't seem to notice. She had been answering a question Urbi had asked in that unfathomable language of hers.

Robert leaned back in his chair and turned toward the reverend, who looked the same as he always did—respectable in a minister's black tail-coat that made his pale skin seem pasty, his heavy jowls and bulky frame a testament to his lifestyle spent as a man of letters and study. Hardly spy material.

Nor spirit material.

And the kind-hearted Miss Bethel didn't have a violent bone in her body, he'd swear to it. Gryffyn had her all wrong.

So why could he not banish the seed of doubt completely?

Miss Bethel said something that made Urbi laugh, and Mr. Berian's resonant chuckle joined theirs. Robert hadn't understood the words, but he understood the joy on their faces well enough.

Bah. I'm letting Gryffyn get in my head again. Miss Bethel and Mr. Berian are as flesh-and-blood as I am.

He gave his head a shake, determining to write Gryffyn a scathing reply once he returned to his room.

"So, is everyone ready for dinner?" Miss Bethel asked in Greek.

"That sounds delightful," said Berian.

Urbi smiled. "Please."

The black woman looked much better than she had yesterday morning, but a single day's recovery hadn't been enough to take the gauntness from her cheeks or the haunted look from her eyes. Still, she'd looked a fair sight healthier than anyone else in the women's pen yesterday morning, the others worn down by months in a hold at sea—just like the slaves on the

Atlanta had been when he'd finally dared to visit.

The pit tugged at him, and he saw his face in the blade of the knife he'd nearly used to go there. He blinked the image away.

"Mr. Cox, shall I order for you?" Miss Bethel smiled at him expectantly.

He gave a brief nod in reply, not trusting his voice.

Miss Bethel hailed Mildred Varley, the innkeeper's brown-haired thirteen-year-old daughter, who was passing by on her way to the kitchen. The girl looked around and cast a curious glance at Urbi, but when she saw Miss Bethel, she smiled. Wiping her hands on the clean but threadbare apron she wore over a shapeless blue frock, she came over to the table.

"Yes, miss?"

"Good evening, Mildred. Where's Anne-Marie?" Miss Bethel asked, referring to the server who usually worked the evening meal.

The girl looked around and shrugged. The only other staff member in the room was Barnum, who was polishing glasses behind the bar.

"She must be doing something for father. Can I help you with something?"

"I believe so. What is the kitchen serving tonight?"

The girl tilted her head and looked upward, remembering. "I think Cook said it was stewed pork with buttered yams."

"Sounds delicious," Miss Bethel said with a warm smile. "We'll have one for each of us, and please have Barnum bring us some tea."

"Yes'm," the girl said. She skipped toward the bar to pass the tea order to the bartender before disappearing into the kitchen.

Urbi, who had probably barely understood the English conversation, had been looking around the room in wonder, as though she had never seen a place quite like it before. Perhaps she hadn't. The louvred bamboo shutters on the tall, narrow windows, the thick painted plaster walls, and the lofty ceilings were unusual, even by English standards. An obvious effort had been made to make the decor feel like a British inn, with wooden shelves lining the bar and some pastoral paintings of the English countryside on the walls, but the concessions made for the tropical climate still added a uniquely foreign flavour.

"This place is so unusual. What do you call it?" Urbi asked in Greek.

"This is an inn, a type of lodging house," Mr. Berian answered.

Robert frowned. Seeing this woman, who had so recently been on the auction block, sit at the table with him made his arms grow itchy. He restrained the urge to scratch them. "Do you not have inns where you come from?"

Urbi took in the wooden beams, the whitewashed walls, and the rows of bottles lining the wall behind the bar. "There are lodging houses, but they are not like this."

So Sirenia most likely wasn't a British colony. Interesting.

Miss Bethel turned her earnest eyes on Robert.

"Thank you for what you did yesterday for Urbi. I know it was a sacrifice, but you will be rewarded for it, surely—if not in this life, then the next."

Robert swallowed, doubt needling him. "Is that something about which you have particular knowledge, Miss Bethel?"

She squinted at him and cocked her head. "To what are you referring, Mr. Cox?"

Pinned by her steady gaze, he lost his nerve. He couldn't come right out and ask her if she was a spirit. Then he would sound as raving mad as Gryffyn. "The merits of sacrifice and reward. You seem a woman of strong faith."

She sighed and looked toward an open window, through which no breeze stirred. Her curls, tight from the humidity, bobbed next to her chin as she moved. "Sometimes I wonder if I have any faith at all."

Mr. Berian chuckled. "Faith is confidence that what we hope for will come to pass, my child. In these uncertain times, you have more faith than most, certainly. Otherwise, you would not even be here, risking so much."

She gave him a grateful smile. "Thank you, Mr. Berian. It can often be easy to lose sight of our hope in times such as these."

Robert watched the exchange in curiosity. What was Miss Bethel risking by being here that she would not be risking anywhere else? The conversation reminded him of what she'd told the Spaniard—*what's at stake, not just for the world, but for me.*

Could she be a spy, after all? Not for the forces of darkness, of course, but for something less supernatural—like the French?

When he'd probed her for more information about Sirenia on the way home from the market yesterday, the only thing she'd revealed was that it was the homeland of Zale and his mother, Delphine. After fortifying himself with a glass or two of rum at the tavern, he'd decided it was time to learn more on his own about Zale, Sirenia, and the inimitable Lord Middleton. Fortunately, a rather chatty barmaid had happily answered his questions for a few bits—though she'd looked a tad disappointed he hadn't intended to hire her for more. He'd never get used to the depraved morals of the colonies, he was certain of it.

He'd found out a fair amount about the baron, all of which explained Miss Bethel's wariness of him. The man had owned Huntley Hall for over twenty-five years and was one of the few landholders who spent nearly all his time on the island instead of home in England. His influence among the governing class was not to be underestimated—he'd held a seat in the Barbadian House of Assembly for over fifteen years, and there were few on the island who didn't owe him a favour of some sort. Exactly the type of man Robert preferred to avoid.

However, about Sirenia, or Zale's location, he'd discovered nothing. Nor had the barmaid nor any of the patrons he questioned heard of the Order of the Ascension of the Grigori.

The Cox family had never been big on fraternal organizations and secret societies, but Gryffyn claimed their father, James, Lord Alverton the First, had joined the Order when his eldest son, the current Lord Alverton, had still been wearing dresses. The squire had introduced his two eldest sons to the Order when they turned eighteen—but by the time Robert had reached that age, the elder James Cox had already passed. Gryffyn derided their brother James as short-sighted for declining to get involved, adamant that allying with the Order was the only way to assure a place in the regime that was coming—a political coup that could not be stopped, and against which Berian and Miss Bethel were agents of subterfuge.

The Order of the Ascension, working toward a New World Order. Most definitely a cult.

It appeared if he wanted to find out more, though, he'd have to pay Lord Middleton a visit, and he rebelled at the thought. The man was so pompous and overbearing—Robert would be quite happy to never cross paths with him again. For Zale and Miss Bethel, though, he'd do what he must.

His gaze fell on Miss Bethel's chain. He could solve one mystery, at least.

"Miss Bethel, I have often wondered what that pendant you wear looks like. It is always hidden beneath your dress. Would you mind letting me admire it?"

Miss Bethel opened her mouth and exchanged glances with Berian, whose expression was unreadable. Then she cocked her head. "I don't see any harm. 'Tis simply a trinket, not much more."

She pulled on the chain and withdrew an intricate design of nested silver rings. When she first pulled it out, the rings lay flat, but as soon as they were free of their constraints, they began spinning gently, each ring turning on a different axis. In the very centre of the group was a small reddish-gold stone the size of a water droplet. Could this be the heartstone Gryffyn wanted him to find?

Urbi studied it in astonishment. "This is wonderful," she said. "What do you call it?"

"It is a gyroscope," Miss Bethel replied.

Robert stared at the design in fascination. He had never seen such fine metalwork. It was hardly a trinket—though it seemed a bit underwhelming to be the jewel Gryffyn sought.

"Where did you get such a lovely piece?" he asked.

She hesitated, and before she could answer, movement beyond her shoulder caught his eye.

Robert pressed his lips together in dismay.

"What is he doing here?" he said before he could stop himself.

Coming in the door was the Spaniard.

24

THE SPANIARD

MISS BETHEL, URBI, AND MR. Berian turned to follow Robert's gaze in time to see the rakish rogue whom Miss Bethel had met at the London Coffeehouse the other morning enter the common room. The man saw them sitting there and made a beeline straight for them.

Miss Bethel dropped the pendant beneath her neckline, smiling widely as the man approached, obviously delighted to see him. "I asked Eduardo to come, as we have important business to discuss. If you'll excuse us, we will be right over there." She pointed at an empty table near the far wall.

Robert cleared his throat. "Are you not going to introduce us?"

Before Miss Bethel could do the honours, the man stopped at the table, gave a charming smile, and bowed.

"Señor Eduardo Romero, at your service," he said. "Miss Bethel, wonderful to see you again."

Ugh. Even his voice sounded charming. Though his manners left much to be desired—the nerve, to introduce himself as though he were Robert's equal or better!

"And this is Mr. Robert Cox," Miss Bethel said with a gesture, apparently oblivious to the man's indiscretion. "Of course, you know Mr. Berian. And this is . . ."

She trailed off, an expression of consternation on her face. She turned to Urbi and asked her something. After a brief discussion, she looked back at Romero, but took in the group in the same glance.

"She says to call her 'Mrs. Urbi.'"

Mr. Romero took off his hat and greeted the women, then grinned at Robert and managed a proper bow of respect. "I've heard so much about

194

you, Mr. Cox."

Robert gave a tight smile. "And I've heard so little about you."

Robert wouldn't humiliate Miss Bethel with a pointed stare, but it may not have mattered. She seemed oblivious to both his discomfort and the appalling manners of their visitor.

Romero pulled out Miss Bethel's chair. "Shall we, my dear?"

My dear?

Robert's stomach clenched into a knot so tight, it was a wonder he could still breathe.

Then, with a start, he realized this Eduardo Romero also had golden eyes. What were the chances of three people with such an unusual feature congregating in the same small inn in Barbados?

"Mr. Berian. Mrs. Urbi," Romero said in succession, bowing to Berian and lifting his hat to Urbi—which surprised Robert no end. Then Miss Bethel and the rogue strolled to the table across the room.

Blood rushed in hot pulses through Robert's ears. He didn't realize he was staring until Berian spoke.

"She's not for you, lad."

Robert straightened, taken aback. Were his feelings so transparent? And how presumptuous of the reverend to think he had a right to say whom Robert could or could not pursue.

Then again, if there were a future where he and Miss Bethel were together, he knew what they would be risking. A lifetime on the fringes of society. A lifetime of whispers when others saw them arrive. Their story would be one long scandal that would never go away. Any path that lay ahead for him and Miss Bethel would not be an easy one. Could he truly handle the scorn of everyone he knew? This time, he scratched his itchy arms.

The letter in his breast pocket crinkled with the movement, and he frowned. Perhaps the scandal wasn't the reason for Berian's objection at all.

"And you approve of them, then, do you?"

Robert gestured toward Miss Bethel and the despicable Eduardo Romero, who were deep in conversation. Despite the relative emptiness of the room and the hard, echo-inducing surfaces, Robert couldn't hear the faintest whisper of a sound coming from their direction. He frowned. That was odd. Miss Bethel held a thin silver rod upright on the table in front of her. That was odd too.

Maybe there was something to Gryffyn's wild claims.

He shook his head. No. He wouldn't believe it. He *couldn't* believe it.

Mr. Berian glanced at the two of them with an unreadable expression. "That is not what you think it is."

Barnum brought tea for their table, setting the service down in front of them with the soft clink of porcelain. Then he proceeded to take a second pot with two cups to Miss Bethel and Mr. Romero at her new location.

"Then what is it, pray? There are not many reasons for a young lady to have an unchaperoned conversation with a stranger."

Berian arched an eyebrow. "There are probably more than you realize. And what makes you think they are strangers?"

My dear. No, obviously not strangers. But if Romero and Miss Bethel were not lovers, they could be . . . compatriots?

Stop letting Gryffyn into your head. They were probably childhood friends or something. It was a perfectly reasonable explanation for their familiarity with each other.

But if that were the case, why didn't Miss Bethel introduce him that way? And why has she never mentioned his name to me before?

"Enough about them," said Berian, pouring some tea for the three of them. "What are your plans, Mr. Cox, now that you're feeling better and back on your feet?"

Urbi picked up the sugar bowl and inspected the golden crystals closely.

"Please," Urbi said in cautious English, "what this?"

Mr. Berian gave her an amused smile. "It's sugar, child. You put it in your tea, like this. See?" He took the tiny ornate silver spoon and measured two spoonfuls into his own cup, then stirred it in. "You might even add a bit of milk, if you're so inclined."

"You've never seen sugar before?" Robert asked.

Urbi glanced at him, then touched the tip of her finger to her tongue and dabbed it in the bowl, licking off the crystals that had clung to the damp spot. Her eyes widened in surprise and delight. "It taste like honey, but more sweet."

"*Sweeter*, we say," said Berian.

She put a spoonful in her cup and stirred it in, then took a sip and smiled. "Very nice."

Robert shook his head as the reverend poured a little milk into Urbi's cup also. Where in the West Indies could this woman have lived and be unfamiliar with sugar? Wherever Sirenia was, it was obviously not one of the sugar islands, which might explain why no one had heard of it.

Mr. Berian's question about his plans still hung in the air, and he was not yet certain how to answer it. Logically, he should go home—go back to Bristol, hide in his maps and charts at Cox Bros Shipping, and try to put all the unsettling events of the last few months behind him. He could pretend he'd never received Gryffyn's letter, and he could try to pretend he had never seen him talk to a dragon or his childhood friend turn into a merman and dive into the ocean. He could pretend he believed his companions' story that he was saved from a watery death by a passing vessel for which there was no evidence, and that Sirenia was only another colonized island in the West Indies that had yet to find its way onto a map. That he'd never heard of a magical stone or golden eyes or whispers of treason.

But he knew there was no way he could pretend any of that. His whole life had been buffeted by the unexplained. What if golden eyes did indicate spirits in camouflage? Did that automatically mean they were evil spirits? Looking at Berian gently explaining the English names of the different items in the room to the woman Miss Bethel had insisted he free from slavery, he thought not. There was no way the kind, ebullient woman he'd come to know could have killed Talwyn Penrose or that this corpulent, warm-hearted reverend he'd known since childhood could be a traitor. On the other hand, while Gryffyn had always had a very one-sided way of looking at the world, that didn't mean his information was completely false. It was time Robert stopped ignoring what was going on around him and started understanding it, so he would not be at its whim any longer.

And maybe, just maybe, once he understood it, he would know how to earn redemption for the ways he had failed as a child of God. He could be at peace.

He didn't believe Miss Bethel was evil—but she was definitely not ordinary. However, if his brother and Middleton wanted something from her, he couldn't abandon her. He would write to Gryffyn and Middleton and tell them he'd look into the matter of the stone to buy some time—time to decipher why they wanted it, and to find answers to his questions about his two golden-eyed companions. Which would, of course, require him to stay in Barbados . . . and spend more time with Miss Bethel.

Robert smiled, glad to have reached a decision. "I want to help you find Zale and Mrs. Teague."

At the mention of Zale's name, Urbi's gaze snapped to his face. She drank her tea but kept watching him with an inscrutable expression.

Berian blinked at him in confusion.

"You asked about my plans. I intend to stay here and join your search." Despite his preference to avoid Middleton, maybe he should call on the man instead of write. The irritating baron might have some answers to his questions—and Robert already had a ready-made excuse to see him again. "And I need to help free Mrs. Urbi's son."

Berian nodded. "Aye, well, your help will be appreciated."

Urbi asked him a question in her language, and Berian responded in the same one.

How was it that Miss Bethel and Mr. Berian both spoke so many languages? The obvious answer made his throat dry. *Lots of people speak multiple languages, including me. That doesn't make them spirits. Or spies.*

Urbi smiled at the reverend. "Yes," she said to Robert in English. "Free Osaze. Thank you."

Miss Bethel called Berian over.

"Excuse me," he said, gracefully standing and departing to the other table.

Robert frowned after him. Once again, not even the low murmur of voices could be detected from across the room.

He turned back to Urbi and switched to Greek. "This place you are from, Sirenia. How far is it from here?"

She took another sip of tea, draining the cup. "Not far."

"Do you know a young man named Zale? You seemed to recognize his name."

"I already told Miss Abela. Yes, I know him. He arrived just before Osaze and I left."

So Zale had made it to Sirenia. Things Robert had overheard Miss Bethel say fell into place—but if he'd made it home, why was he a captive there?

"Left how? What ship did you take?"

Urbi regarded him with a face as blank as a mask. It was as though she knew how to hide her thoughts behind nothingness. "The *Bendita Madre*," she said at last.

The *Blessed Mother* in Spanish. Sirenia was one of the Spanish colonies? There were Spanish ships all over the Caribbean, so her story seemed plausible. *Sirenia* even sounded a bit Spanish. If it was a Spanish colony, Miss Bethel's interaction with the Spaniard would suddenly make a lot more sense.

A thought occurred to him—Urbi and Miss Bethel were sharing a room.

He swallowed his embarrassment. "Mrs. Urbi, I was wondering . . . did you happen to notice if Miss Bethel has some kind of stone or jewel about her person? I am told it will be red, but I do not know what kind it may be."

She gave him a withering stare, and he felt ashamed for asking.

"No," was all she said, then she looked away.

He supposed he deserved that.

He turned to check on the activity between his beloved and his rival. Whatever Romero was saying to Miss Bethel, she looked thoroughly chastened, as though he were taking her to task for something. She put a hand over her heart, covering the hidden location of the pendant beneath her neckline and nodded. Romero took her hand and squeezed it comfortingly. Like any other somewhat infatuated girl would, she gave him a warm smile in return.

Not a spy. Not a spirit. If Robert wasn't careful, Mr. Romero would steal any chance he might have of winning Miss Bethel's heart. Let Berian and the rest of the world think what they wanted. He was determined to have Miss Bethel for his own. He would show them all he was not the same as his brother. Nor was he that cowardly boy by Chyandour Brook any longer. Let society do its worst. If an uncouth Spaniard was willing to risk mockery and ridicule for Miss Bethel's sake, Robert would go to the stake for her.

Just then, all three of the others returned to their table, and Robert jumped to his feet and pulled out Miss Bethel's seat. Romero dragged a chair over from a nearby table, wedging it between Miss Bethel and Urbi, much to Robert's chagrin. At Romero's gesture to be seated, Robert ground his teeth, but returned to his own seat.

"We have decided," said Romero with a wide grin. "Miss Bethel has discovered the whereabouts of young Zale, so she and I will go to Sirenia to seek him out, while you and Mr. Berian go to purchase Mrs. Urbi's son from Lord Middleton."

"No!" Robert said involuntarily. He clamped his mouth shut, embarrassed.

"I beg your pardon, Mr. Cox?" Miss Bethel regarded him in astonishment. "Mr. Berian said you wanted to help."

Robert took a deep breath and swallowed his pounding heartbeat. His face probably matched his hair.

"I simply meant," he began, breathing slowly to keep his voice steady, "that I would prefer to accompany you. Why not wait until we have finished our mission to see Middleton, and we can go together? I feel responsible for Zale, and you may need my help to pay for—"

"Never mind that," said Romero with a dismissive wave. "I've given

Miss Bethel and Mr. Berian enough to cover their expenses and more. In fact, here." He tossed a small, heavy-sounding purse on the table. "I'm sure that will tempt the *honourable* Lord Middleton to part with his new man. Keep the rest to cover your expenses here."

Robert regarded the purse as though it might bite him. The last thing he wanted was to be indebted to this man in any way. But he hadn't the cash to give him any real buying power with the baron either. He glanced at Urbi. What had happened to the rest of the gems she and Osaze had hoped to trade? Those ought to tempt the baron to—

"Oh, come, sir, take it." Romero gave him a half-grin and picked up the purse again, tossing it into Robert's lap so he was forced to catch it.

He glanced up to see Miss Bethel's eyebrows raised expectantly and Mr. Berian frowning in consternation.

"Er, thank you." He sighed and slipped the purse into his breast pocket with the letter. It weighed down his coat and created an unsightly bulge, so he withdrew it and set it on his lap until he could take it to his room. Who walked around with that kind of money on their person?

Romero stood partway and gave a sloppy half-bow. "It's my pleasure to do the Lord's work. And if it will make you feel better about our lady's honour, Berian may take my place to find Zale. I shall accompany you."

Robert nearly choked. Still, if it meant that Miss Bethel would not be in this man's clutches for a second longer than necessary . . .

"Agreed. We shall go first thing in the morning," said Robert. It was high time he started taking charge of the situation here.

The serving girl brought their food, and they spent the next few moments preparing to eat. Mr. Berian said grace and they sorted out napkins and cutlery. Romero, to Robert's great relief, excused himself for the evening.

While the others were occupied, Robert leaned over to speak to Miss Bethel in a low voice.

"I'd still prefer to accompany you on your voyage to Sirenia. Could it not wait a day until matters are settled with Middleton?"

Miss Bethel arched a brow at him in amusement. "Let me assure you, Mr. Cox, I will be back before you know it, and we can each discuss our day's adventures over supper tomorrow night."

Tomorrow night? How could she possibly make this voyage, find Zale, and be here in time for supper tomorrow night? Unless . . .

No. Absolutely not.

At the expression on his face, her golden eyes only twinkled, and she put a piece of roast pork in her mouth.

Robert began eating, but as he did, all the other questions swirling in his mind finally solidified into one:

Who was Miss Abela Bethel?

25

THE RETURN

Calandra awoke to Nelly calling for everyone to get up before sunrise the next morning. By the time Airlea returned from a scouting mission to check for siren patrols, everyone in the small grotto had been loaded into the submersible. Within minutes, the hot, close quarters had started to reek of body odour.

After about twenty minutes in the sub, Calandra made an excuse about checking their progress in order to escape the crowded rear passenger room and went to stand in the front cabin with Nick and Nelly. In the predawn light, the water beyond the window had lightened from deep blue to crystal clear, revealing the multi-coloured life festooning the reef below.

Nick glanced at Calandra, her lazy eye fixed on the window. "Almost there."

Calandra nodded and crossed her arms to watch.

Nick rotated her hand on the dome-shaped steering crystal, concentrating on the seascape beyond the glass. She manoeuvred the sub as close to shore as possible while remaining underwater. The sub stopped moving.

Nick turned to Calandra. "This is as close as we can get without chopping the reef."

Calandra peered out the window. The surface danced about ten metres above them in fiery pink sunrise hues. Tropical fish darted between reef formations. It was breathtaking, but she had no time to admire it. The higher the sun rose, the harder it would be to hide from any roving siren pod.

"Great work, Nick. I'll prepare everyone to disembark."

Calandra strode to the small passenger bay at the rear of the submersible.

The two facing red slubbed-silk benches held Tafrara, Polyxo, Bryce, Kynthia, and Meg, their knees practically touching. Airlea stood near the door, and the men and Judith stood at the far end. Ewelike and Cogger both had to hunch in the small cabin. Polyxo kept darting nervous glances their direction, and Bryce openly stared at the men. Calandra sighed. There was definitely a good deal of work to do.

"We have arrived at the disembarkation point," Calandra announced.

Polyxo perked up. "We're there?" She twisted and blinked through a porthole as though she expected an undine habitation to appear from clear water.

Nelly came up behind Calandra and snorted. "Yep. Only three hours of walking and we're *there*." She smirked. "Mind your silk slippers."

Polyxo looked deflated. Tafrara turned away to hide a smile. The girl didn't seem to like Polyxo much either, but at least she wasn't making a scene of it.

Calandra cleared her throat. "We'll be leaving the sub through the moon pool and remaining underwater for as long as possible before surfacing to lower the chances of siren detection. Airlea and I can sense no one nearby, but emotional sensate abilities have a more limited range than visual acuity."

"But—my dress will be ruined." Polyxo smoothed the thin silk of her ankle-length peplos, which was already a little worse for wear after her trek down the mountainside and night on the sand.

Nelly clucked. "Sorry to spoil your grand entrance, m'lady. Guess you'll have to stash it in your dry satchel and go naked."

Polyxo's mouth twisted and she crossed her arms, glancing at Kofi and Ewelike. "No, thanks. It will dry."

Calandra drew in a breath. *Mother, have mercy.* She addressed the group. "The trees come close to the water here, so once you break surface, make for the nearest cover as soon as possible. Airlea?"

Airlea nodded and produced two breathing masks—cone-like copper muzzles that fit over the nose and mouth with a felt strip as a buffer, held onto the head with a rubber strap.

Calandra continued. "We'll pair each person who has a shield crystal"—she touched her Tear—"with someone without. If you stay in physical contact, the field will extend around you. We don't have enough masks for all four humans, so Airlea and I will make two trips for the humans. Nelly and Kynthia, take two undines each. Three bodies might stretch the shields a little thin, but—"

"Forgive me, your highness," interjected Ewelike, which drew dark looks from Bryce and Nelly.

Polyxo jumped to her feet, glaring at him. "How dare you interrupt the princess! Apologize at once, *dou . . .*" She trailed off, noticing the eyes on her. "*Anthropos,*" she said in a smaller voice.

Calandra clenched her jaw. This woman had been sent by the Mother to test her patience, she was sure. "Peace, Kore kor'Theano. We accord respect to all here. If you cannot abide by that rule, we shall return you whence you came."

Polyxo flushed. "I—I can abide, your highness. My apologies."

She didn't turn to Ewelike as she apologized, but Calandra didn't feel this was the time or place to make a further scene. She drew in a breath and returned her attention to the tall man. Tension and shame rolled from him.

"You were saying, Kyrios Ewelike?" She accentuated *kyrios*—master—for Polyxo's benefit.

Ewelike dipped his chin in acknowledgement. "Thank you, your highness. I wanted to say that I can swim. 'Tis very shallow here. I think I could hold my breath until we reach the surface."

"As can I," added Tafrara. "Then you won't need to return for anyone."

Calandra smiled appreciatively. "Excellent. Cogger and Kofi, can either of you swim?"

Kofi shook his head, looking a little alarmed at the idea.

"No," said Cogger mechanically.

Calandra sighed. She expected as much. "Fine. Since Nick is coming after she parks the sub, the rest of the rescue team will take one undine and one human."

"Tafrara can come with me," Polyxo said quickly, drawing dark looks from several of the others.

Calandra ignored her and continued. "Bryce, go with Airlea and Cogger so you can help tow him. Kofi and Polyxo, you're with me."

If the two non-swimmers proved difficult to tow, at least the burden of assisting wouldn't fall on Meg and Judith, who both looked like they needed a week of nothing but eating and sleeping to restore them. Polyxo's expression grew tight, but, blissfully, she didn't object.

Nick, who leaned against the side of the passageway entrance behind Calandra, eyed the longer skirts most of the women wore. "You'll want to strip those, I'd wager."

"No, I will not," Polyxo said indignantly with a sideways glance at the

Freemen.

"Do you have something to hide under there, *kore*?" Nick quirked an eyebrow. "Or are you just shy?"

Polyxo glared at the skipper, then glanced at Judith, Meg, and Tafrara, who had opted to tuck their skirts into their belts, not having a way to carry their clothes with them. Looking relieved, Polyxo followed suit. But Bryce began unbuckling her girdle, stuffing it into one of the satchels before starting on the pins of her peplos. Neither Kofi nor Ewelike gave her more than a cursory glance before offering to carry her satchels, as they had on the way down the mountain. After a moment's hesitation, Bryce accepted Kofi's offer, insisting on taking one herself.

"You've already got one," she said to Ewelike, "and it will be harder to swim with two."

Ewelike gave her a brief salute and she smiled. Kofi slung the extra bag over his shoulder along with the bag Dione had sent from Steadfast House. Polyxo might not have thought her wardrobe through well, but Calandra was gratified to note that both pieces of luggage were dry satchels, at least.

Calandra assigned the other groups, then helped Kofi put on his breathing mask. While the tractable Cogger had quickly donned his and jumped in the water, Kofi looked askance at the tongue depressor holding the breathing crystal that would allow him to remain underwater without running out of air.

"How can a stone give me air?" He examined the stone closely.

Calandra smiled patiently. "It is difficult to explain. This is a special crystal, one that can absorb air and release it slowly. I repaired it myself. Trust me, it works. You just have to get used to breathing through your mouth."

Despite Kofi's hesitation, he was a quick study. He put on the mask and descended into the moon pool, Calandra beside him. Experimentally, he put his face under the water, and Calandra submerged to help him in case he panicked. However, his expression soon changed from alarm to surprised delight. Then he looked at Calandra, who had transformed to *ichthys* state and was tucking her thigh-length swimming skirt into her belt to keep it out of the way, and his eyes widened more.

She smiled reassuringly. Polyxo joined them, and Calandra signed they should each hook Kofi under one arm to tow him to shore. Airlea, Cogger, and Bryce were well ahead of them, and were running across the beach to the trees by the time Calandra's group reached the shallows.

After everyone had been concealed in the jungle without incident, they adjusted their clothes while they waited for Nick to park the submersible in a nearby underwater grotto. After she joined them, they began the steep three-mile hike upstream beside the Weeping River to the safe house.

They had been walking on the trail for some time when Judith came and walked beside Calandra.

Calandra eyed her friend, who'd been unusually quiet since they'd retrieved her from the palace. Judith wasn't as air-headed as Polyxo, but she was usually nearly as talkative.

"Do you need a break? I'm sure three weeks in the dungeon didn't do any wonders for your stamina. Sorry we didn't have more food for breakfast."

Judith grinned and shook her head. "For certain, the dungeon was not great, but I am doing all right. No, I wanted to talk to you about something I think you should be aware of." Her low voice and furtive glances at the group ahead made it clear this was not something she wanted overheard.

Calandra adjusted her satchel as a cover for glancing ahead to see how close the others were. Airlea walked in the lead, chatting with Polyxo, who had given up on peppering Calandra with questions and had moved on to someone who seemed more willing to discuss what she should expect at the safe house. Bryce followed closely on her mistress's heels. Then came Kynthia and Tafrara, who both walked in silence for the most part, admiring the beauty of the jungle and expending their energy on the climb. Cogger—who now carried Bryce's second satchel—Kofi, and Ewelike came next, followed by Nick and Nelly, then Calandra and Judith, with Meg a few paces behind.

Calandra slowed her pace some to put distance between them and the group ahead. She indicated Meg with a subtle hand gesture and raised her eyebrows questioningly at Judith. Meg's attention was on her footing.

Judith glanced behind her. "Meg already knows."

Calandra nodded. "Okay, what is it?"

Judith shared rumours she'd heard about Narcissa from the guards' gossip—her late-night rampages, wandering the halls and digging through cupboards and storerooms, and how she had all the servants and many of the sirens and councillors terrified of her.

Calandra nodded. She'd heard most of it already from Melany, Charis, and Damaris, and relayed her discovery of the young rebels to Judith and Meg, as well as the additional information they'd shared about Narcissa's use of fire and her razing of the Garden of the Mother's Delight.

"I didn't believe Melany's claims about Narcissa's ability with fire, but she was dead on." Calandra frowned. "Kind of. It looks like fire, but it's not."

Judith frowned. "How do you know?"

"I, uh . . ." Calandra searched for the words to explain. "Sometimes, I become so in tune with the Matrix of Creation that I can see it. It happened while I was fighting Narcissa. What she was throwing looked like fire, but it didn't use the fire element. She threw a blazing wall of it at me and I didn't even feel it."

"Where did those blisters come from then?"

Calandra sighed. "Zale. I'll explain later."

"I see." Judith examined Calandra's wounds, concern leaking through her shield. "I assume Xeni's at the safe house?" she said, referring to her cousin, a skilled physic.

"Yes, but it's not as bad as it looks. I'm fine." That was a stretch. Calandra's blisters had begun to pop that morning, and the raw flesh burned from the salt of the ocean and her sweat. But she would definitely survive until Xeni could heal her. The sting was nothing compared to the throbbing behind her temples.

Judith stepped over a root, and Calandra spied the quaternaria tattoo on her ankle—the secret symbol of the Free Will Society.

"I wonder how Narcissa could have so suddenly acquired her fire ability?" Judith said.

Calandra thought of the flash of gold she thought she'd seen in Narcissa's eyes. Had she really seen it? She decided not to burden her exhausted friend with the news just yet.

"I agree that it is odd. Another odd thing was that when I found Narcissa, she was in the Archive, obviously looking for something. Do you happen to know what that might be?"

Judith shook her head. "Sorry, no." They walked for a few minutes in silence. Then Judith said in a strained voice, "Was Matthew with her?"

At the mention of his name, the young man's bond pricked Calandra's mind, and she winced.

"Yes." She flicked her gaze at Judith, and continued in a quiet voice. "If I had to guess, she has taken him as her personal bodyguard and *doulos*. He looks like he's been training as a *tapeinos* too."

Judith nodded and watched the ground in front of her. "Not just that. Apparently, she has also taken him as her lover."

At the pain in Judith's voice, Calandra glanced at her friend, something she hadn't understood before coming clear.

"You love him, don't you?"

Judith glanced up, biting her lip. "Growing up together at Elpida, we didn't understand the obstacles that would keep us apart. Once we were old enough to comprehend them, we both knew we'd have to fight to be together. Neither of us expected the price to be so high." She dropped her gaze, her eyes gleaming with moisture.

Calandra studied Judith's profile, a little jealous that she'd grown up with her love while he was Free—unlike Osaze, who'd been Redeemed and under Narcissa's tender loving care for far too long. But now Matthew's mother, Elizabeth, was dead, and Matthew had been Redeemed and had taken Osaze's place as Narcissa's toy. Calandra's heart broke.

"We'll get him back. I promise."

A tear tracked down one of Judith's cheeks. "Thanks."

"You heard about Mari, I presume?" Calandra said to change the subject.

"Yes. I saw it, actually. I could not prevent it, though." Judith pursed her lips. "She was a jelly, but she didn't deserve that." Judith walked a few steps in silent contemplation, then smiled. "I can't believe Damaris and the others have started their own Student Free Will Society. Who would have expected it?"

Calandra chuckled, but couldn't quench her worry. She hoped the assignment she'd given the girls helped keep them out of trouble, not get them into it. The idea had seemed innocuous enough when she'd come up with it—but that was before she'd seen that flash of gold in Narcissa's eyes. The sweat dripping down her back went cold on her skin.

"Judith, have you ever heard of a connection between the Heartstone and the Abyss?"

Judith shook her head.

"Or something called a Soulstone?"

Judith frowned. "No. Why do you ask?"

Calandra pursed her lips. Ever since Narcissa had taunted her last night, she'd been searching her memory for anything that referred to the Heartstone's connection to the Abyss, but had come up dry. If the Heartstone powered the Voidstone, the barrier between their plane and the Underworld, it must be drawing all available power or they would have been inundated by escaping Grigori the moment the barrier had gone down. And why had these spirits captured their mother in the first place? As bait? Given what she'd discovered about how combined male and female undine powers were necessary to heal the Heartstone, and what her mother's Tear and Damon had both said about the Heartstone keeping the Grigori's abyssal prison intact, she had assumed that meant the Heartstone was connected to the Voidstone. But maybe she'd got it wrong. If the Soulstone was the name of their prison, destroying the Heartstone might unlock its doors, and healing it might fortify them, which would explain Narcissa's—or Damon's—comment about their mother, if that's where she was. But why go to the effort of capturing their mother and taking her to the Underworld if they wanted the Heartstone destroyed? There must be more to it. Even Zale's lumasi companions had thought it necessary for Zale, and possibly Calandra, since he'd been coming to find her, to go to Tartarus to free their mother. But why? And why did they care about Delphine so much?

Unless they were part of the plot.

That disturbing thought settled in her belly like a rock.

"Just something Narcissa said. The night Zale arrived, he told me our mother has been captured and is being held in Tartarus. Narcissa seems to know about it, and claims that if the Heartstone is restored, Mother will be trapped in the Soulstone forever. Does that mean anything to you?"

Judith frowned in thought. "No, but I will see what I can find. Besides me, Mama and Xeni have spent the most time studying the Atlantis stones. I will ask them."

"Thanks." Calandra gave her friend a tight smile.

Ahead of them, Airlea stopped before the corner of a cliff covered in climbing vines and called over her shoulder. "We're here."

26

THE SAFE HOUSE

AT AIRLEA'S ANNOUNCEMENT, THE GROUP glanced around expectantly as though the house might pop out of the jungle at any moment. The terrain hadn't changed in some time. On one side, the jungle pressed in to the trail, and the Weeping River flowed placidly on the other. The river was significantly reduced this close to the headwaters, its bubbling surface nearly at a level with the bank. The distant roar of falling water filtered toward them.

"We're where?" Judith looked questioningly at Calandra, who smiled back.

"You'll see." She pointed to a sharp turn in the river where it disappeared around the cliff a few paces ahead.

The path narrowed, skirting the moss-covered cliff next to the water. Calandra indicated that Judith should walk ahead. Meg followed only a step behind. The closer they got to the other end of the narrow pass, the louder the water got.

"I'm so glad the house is by the river," Polyxo said, raising her voice to be heard above the noise. "Such a shame we couldn't swim part of the way. I know, humans and all that, but my feet are—"

Polyxo's words stopped as soon as she turned the corner and the path opened up again. Calandra and the rest of the group at the back caught up, pressing in close to the first arrivals, who had all stopped to admire the view with gasps of wonder.

A waterfall fell from far above them, plunging over rocks and crags and spreading over several overhanging rocks into a wide curtain at the bottom. The edges of the falls and pool were lush with verdant greenery and tall trees, almost hiding a set of stairs carved into the rock that ascended the full height of the waterfall. You couldn't see the cleverly concealed lookout tower at the top of the cliff from here, but Calandra suspected someone would already be running to alert everyone of their arrival.

Calandra smiled, mist from the churning water moistening her face. The beauty of this place still took her breath away. She saw the same wonder on the faces of the others—everyone's but Cogger's, who stared straight ahead, waiting for whatever would happen next. Calandra looked away. She'd deal with him soon enough.

"Do . . . do we have to climb all the way up there?" Polyxo stared at the stone steps, looking as though she might cry.

Calandra felt a twinge of sympathy for the girl. It had been a gruelling hike from the ocean. Even Judith looked a little sorry for her. Of all of them, the walk had been hardest on Polyxo.

Calandra placed a reassuring hand on Polyxo's arm. "Never fear. The entrance to the safe house is hidden, but not at the top. You'll see."

Relief flooded the young woman's face.

Instead of continuing on the path toward the stairs, Airlea led them all down the rocky bank to the edge of the pool, then turned around. The wide curtain of water splashing down the cliff was only a few feet away.

"The safe house is beyond the falls," Airlea shouted, pointing to the dark space behind the streaming water.

The newcomers craned their necks to look for the building they were expecting.

"But, where is it?" asked Polyxo. "I still see nothing but the path there." She pointed at the stairs to the top.

Nick wore a smug smirk, and Nelly rolled her eyes. Nick, always dressed to swim, stuffed her sarong in her dry satchel, slung it across her shoulders, and jumped in the water, her legs fusing into a shimmering coppery-green scaled tail as she disappeared beneath the surface. Nelly, who'd stayed on the path, gestured to Calandra that she was going to continue on. At Calandra's nod, she headed toward the falls, seemingly toward the stairs.

Ewelike squinted at a narrow ledge running behind the falls from one side. "Is that the way there?"

Calandra smiled appreciatively. "You are a keen observer. That is the foot entrance, but pains have been taken to ensure it does not have a trod-upon look."

Nelly bypassed the stairs to follow the ledge, and disappeared behind the watery curtain.

Meg blinked. "Amazing. I would have walked right by it if I hadn't known."

Airlea addressed the group. "Undines, you may swim through the falls, if you wish. Humans, follow me."

"You don't have to tell me twice," said Meg.

She hiked her ragged ankle-length tunic up by the hem, tied it around her waist so it ballooned over her thighs, and dove off a rock into the deep blue pool, changing to *ichthys* state in the air. Judith followed her lead. Kynthia, who had slipped into the water immediately, breaststroked around the pool, smiling in pleasure.

Tafrara gazed at the water, fingering her salt-crusted hair. "May I swim too?"

"Of course, if you wish," said Airlea. "The falls are not difficult to pass through."

Tafrara smiled for the first time since Calandra had met her. Tying up her peplos as she'd done at the ocean, she slipped into the water, submerging her head so it could wash her clean.

"It feels *so* good to swim!" Judith backstroked around the pool, sunlight glinting from her deep emerald-green tail.

"Follow me, I'll show you the way in," said Kynthia to the swimmers, then dove beneath the surface.

Polyxo glanced down at her long gown.

"The silk just dried." She gave a long-suffering sigh. "I suppose Bryce and I will walk," she said like a true martyr.

Calandra rolled her eyes and flicked her gaze at Bryce, who looked longingly at the water.

"I can take your bag, miss," Kofi offered in Twi with his hand extended to the lady-in-waiting. "It will be easier to swim without it."

She glanced at her mistress, then his hand. Without another word, she handed him the strap of her satchel, tucked up her skirt, and ran into the water.

"Bryce!" Polyxo cried in dismay, but the girl barely glanced back before she followed the others through the waterfall.

Polyxo looked after her lady's maid forlornly. Calandra thought about reminding Polyxo of her yearning to swim a few moments ago, but thought better of it. It would do nothing to improve the atmosphere. The young woman was probably doing her best to deal with her uncertainty. After all, as far as most people on the island would see it, including Polyxo's own family, she was a traitor to the crown now. That couldn't be easy to accept.

Calandra watched the others disappear behind the falls in resignation. She would have dearly loved to get rid of the sweat of the morning and the ocean salt that still crusted her clumped hair, but she and Airlea had to guide the others. At the thought of the humans, a sharp throb of pain pulsed through her brain, and she put her hand on the rock wall beside them to steady herself.

When she looked up, Polyxo was still staring at the undines in the water with mournful eyes. Calandra tapped her on the shoulder and pointed above their heads at the falls.

"You're getting wet either way, I'm afraid," she said peevishly, thinking it might inspire the irritating girl to take the water entrance after all and stop slowing them down. "Your silks already got wet once today. What's one more?"

Polyxo glanced up at the streams of water forming a curtain over the path with a look of dismay. Calandra had a brief fantasy of pushing Polyxo into the pool to see the look on her—

Horrified at herself, Calandra stopped. Just because the red pulse drumming at the back of her skull was making her miserable didn't mean she had to spread that misery to others.

She closed her eyes and took a deep breath, willing the image away.

"Wait," she said.

Polyxo turned.

"There's another way in, and you can stay dry . . . but you'll have to climb the stairs." Calandra pointed to the base of the steps where they emerged from behind the mats of concealing vines.

Polyxo looked at the steps, then her gaze travelled up the three storeys to the top of the cliff. Resolutely, she turned back to the ledge and hiked up her hems, then crept forward, picking her way over the slippery rocks in her bare feet. At least she'd had the good sense to remove her flimsy silk slippers hours ago. Calandra wasn't sure if it had been out of vanity or practicality, but she thought it was the latter. Maybe the girl had a shot at making it here after all. Polyxo would have to get used to a lot worse than wet silks at the safe house, with its cramped living quarters and everyone pitching in to make the place run. It was a far cry from the estates on the Street of Pearls or Nob Hill in Haven. Calandra's head throbbed again, and she put her hand to her temple.

Airlea led the remaining group along the path beneath the falls, with Calandra bringing up the rear. Behind the falls, the entrance opened into an arching cavern. Clear blue water, dark in the gloom, filled the basin in a deep pool punctuated and edged with rounded sandstone boulders.

The path became wider and more structured here. It had obviously been levelled by stone workers and healers, and copper hand rails had even been installed in the more precarious sections, now coated in verdigris from long disuse. Stone steps that had been cut into some of the boulders made the climb easier to manage on the slippery rocks. Sunlight streamed in the depths of the airy cave somewhere beyond a turn in the wall, bathing the smooth shapes of the rocks and pool in gentle light.

Airlea paused at the edge of a short stone bridge and told the others to continue on along the path. She waited until Calandra caught up with her.

Calandra tensed. The way the ex-siren constantly checked up on her drove her crazy.

"Are you all right?" Airlea said in a low voice. "You seem—"

"I'm fine," Calandra snapped. "Let's get in there. I'm starving."

She kept walking, but caught the flash of Airlea's hurt on her face. Shame flooded Calandra.

"Wait," she said, turning. "I'm sorry. It's the pain. I'm . . . I'm trying to manage it, but sometimes it gets the better of me."

Airlea gave her an understanding, tight-lipped smile. "I know. Here."

She extended her palm, and Calandra let the siren lay it on her forehead. Cool relief washed through her—but although the pain subsided somewhat, her irritation remained. She couldn't wait to have a good meal and retreat to her small cell to rest.

She let Airlea walk ahead once more and watched her retreating back. It seemed whenever Calandra lashed out, Airlea received the brunt of it. Part of the problem was that the young woman had been Calandra's shadow for weeks, so she was always around when Calandra had an episode. Calandra thought Rhea must have assigned the former siren to some kind of guard duty without telling her.

What do they think I'll do?

But she knew what they were worried about—the Madness. Her escalating seizures and resulting episodes of irritability had not gone unnoticed, and Calandra could hardly blame her fellow fugitives for wanting to know when the most dangerous cannon among them was about to go off.

However, it wasn't just Airlea's constant presence that got under her skin.

Airlea had served with Tanni. They had been cadets together, then podmates. She knew Airlea must be grieving Tanni too, but she selfishly didn't want to share the memory of her dead friend. The pain was too raw, and it was hers. Every time she looked at Airlea, she was reminded that Tanni—loyal, steady Tanni—had died because of Calandra, because she'd tried to protect her. How could Calandra also let Tanni's friend put herself in harm's way for her sake?

Not that she'd been able to do much about it. No matter what she'd tried to do to have Airlea assigned elsewhere, the ex-siren always ended up in Calandra's general vicinity.

She sighed and adjusted her pack, rounding the corner that would reveal the face of Margaret House. None of what had happened with Tanni was Airlea's fault, and the young siren singer was probably just following orders. Calandra really needed to grow up.

The stone receiving platform at the edge of the pool in front of the main structure came into view. Rhea, the steward of Elpida, and Hammad, her consort, stood peering anxiously at the undines who were clambering up the stairs from the water to greet them. The sunlight glinted from Rhea's chestnut curls and highlighted her youthful face. Hammad saw the men approaching along the path and smiled warmly, waving in greeting.

The walking path descended a few feet at the end to the receiving platform. Kofi and Ewelike took the final steps slowly, staring slack-jawed at the three-storey face of Margaret House.

"Of all the wonders," muttered Kofi in Twi.

Polyxo, who had also been staring, glanced at Kofi in annoyance and edged toward the docile, unresponsive Cogger.

"That's not a safe house, that's a palace," breathed Bryce, water dripping from the fabric clinging to her legs.

Behind the receiving platform, wide stone steps led up to a large patio that fronted a magnificent structure—three storeys of carved columns, arches, and balconies that practically glowed in the sunlight streaming through the opening in the cavern above. The central column was carved in a thirty-foot figure of Atargatis in dual *ichthys* and *podia* state—standing on feet extending from a skirt fashioned like the tail of a fish—holding a dove in one hand and a sheaf of grain on the other, the mural crown on her head.

Nick watched the amazement on the faces of the newcomers with delight. "Yep, this is one of the purtiest places I've seen too. Reminds me of Atlantis."

Meg stared appreciatively at the intricate stone work. "By Ichthys's tail, this place is fantastic! I didn't even know it existed. How did you find it?"

Calandra gazed at the idol and flexed her regrown hand, thinking of the cost of discovering this forgotten temple. "Rhea kor'Eudoxia found a reference to it on one of the stones I brought back from Atlantis. I can hardly believe it had been lost to time. Like so many other things." Like why Nadia had sunk Atlantis in the first place, for instance.

"Are you done gawking yet, Judith?" Rhea's wide smile belied her caustic tone.

Judith recovered herself and practically ran up the stairs, her wet, bunched tunic flopping around her thighs and her dark curls plastered to her shoulders. "Aunt Rhea! Uncle Hammad!"

"Judith! You are a sight for sad eyes," said Hammad, wrapping an arm around his niece's shoulders.

When he released her, Rhea put her hands on both of Judith's cheeks and kissed her forehead. "What a relief to see you again!"

"But where are Mama, Papa, and Zeke?" said Judith, craning her neck toward the entrance of the building behind them and glancing around the bustling cavern.

Women, men, and children peppered the stone terraces of the cavern and the vast common room beyond the entrance, grinding grain for meals, weaving cloth or baskets, washing clothes in the pool, and hauling clean water captured from the falls in large jugs to cooking fires or other uses inside. With over two hundred people living at Margaret House, the cavern contained a small village, and took as much effort to run and feed. Calandra recognized most of the faces in the open area, but didn't see Judith's family anywhere.

"They're on their way," said Hammad, his gaze now including the rest of the group in the conversation. "Ignatia is working in the gardens fruiting plants to ensure enough food for the next several weeks, but we sent a messenger as soon as the lookout saw you coming. Jacob's out hunting, but he should be here soon too."

"Judy!" A little boy of about four with wavy black hair and the dark green luminescent eyes of an undine exploded from the entrance of Margaret House, barrelling toward the group. Zeke held his arms open wide until he reached Judith and wrapped them fiercely around her legs. "You're back!" He stretched his head back to look at her face. "You've been missing all the fun," he said accusingly.

Ignatia was not far behind her son. Her chestnut curls matched Rhea's, though she had fewer lines on her face. Her hands were stained and grubby from working with the plants, and she had a dirt smudge on her cheek.

"Zeke, careful. You don't want to knock your sister over."

Zeke didn't let go, clutching Judith's legs until she bent down and picked him up. Doing so was obviously not as easy as it used to be.

Ignatia kissed her daughter on the cheek and greeted her warmly, relief on her face, then reached to take Zeke from her arms.

"It is all right, Mama. I've got him."

Ignatia touched Judith's jaw, taking in her gaunt face with a frown. "You've spent three weeks in a dungeon. You don't have to pretend it didn't affect you."

Judith looked about to object, but she nodded and handed Zeke over.

"But, *Mama*—" Zeke whined.

"You can play with her once she's had a chance to settle in," Ignatia said.

Rhea gestured at the others, who had been standing awkwardly as they watched the happy family reunion. "Calandra, are you going to introduce us to our new members?"

"Of course."

Calandra began with Tafrara, Polyxo, and Bryce, then Meg, who had helped with the rescue effort at the wedding but whom Rhea had never met, and then explained how Ewelike, Kofi, and Cogger had come to join them. Kynthia, Nick, and Nelly had disappeared into the temple.

Rhea stared at Cogger's vacant face with hard eyes and turned to Calandra.

"What is the meaning of this?"

Calandra drew herself up, returning the glare. "He wasn't being cooperative. I made an executive decision."

Calandra was intensely aware of the stares of the others, and her gut tightened. The tension that suddenly filled the grotto pressed in on her, and she forced herself to maintain eye contact with Rhea.

Ever since Calandra's failure to heal the Heartstone, she'd been quite happy to hand over much of the responsibility of leadership to Rhea and the council the rebels had formed here at Margaret House. But that didn't mean she was willing to accept a rebuke for a decision she'd made in the field, especially in front of everyone else—even if she'd been questioning herself ever since they'd left Eudora's.

Especially because of that.

"Calandra, we've been over this," said Rhea.

"Healer kor'Eudoxia, there were extenuating circumstances," Calandra said, an edge to her tone. "Do you not believe I would have avoided this if it all possible?"

"What extenuating circumstances could possibly have justified enslaving this man's mind?" Rhea indicated Cogger. "And with you already carrying more bonds than is safe."

Calandra glanced at Airlea. She didn't hold Cogger's bond, but she'd managed to add Matthew's to her burden, so the fact seemed hardly worth mentioning. "I freed Kofi. That's something."

Rhea glared at her.

Ewelike shifted his weight.

"Mistress—" Kofi began in Twi.

"What?" Rhea whirled to pin him with a hard glare. At his startled expression, she immediately softened. "My apologies, Kofi," she said in Twi. "Please, continue."

Kofi cleared his throat. They had been speaking Greek, but the man seemed to have understood the gist. He must have an uncanny ability to understand languages, for a human. Nothing that compared to how quickly an undine could learn, but impressive, none the less. That could come in handy.

Kofi indicated the husky white man. "Mr. Cogger is a troublemaker and a bully," he said cautiously. "He would have been a problem during the whole journey. He would not have come on his own and would have cost all of us our freedom."

Rhea measured his words, then turned back to Calandra. "But still, to enslave him—"

"Narcissa is possessed," Calandra blurted out. "By Damon. She wants to enslave not only the men of the island, but all the human women too, and then she wants to enslave the whole world. If we'd been caught, there would have been no reasoning with her. I did what I had to do to get us away from there safely."

The shock that rolled from the listeners who understood what she was talking about hit Calandra like a wave. She rocked on her feet and steadied herself against the responding pulse of pain. She clenched her hands into fists at her sides to keep from putting them to her head.

Ignatia looked stunned. "No. It's not possible . . ."

Hammad stepped toward Rhea and put his hand on his wife's elbow. "Perhaps we should discuss this later."

Rhea glared at Calandra for a moment or two longer, then relented. "You're right, of course, husband." She turned to the group. "You must all be famished and exhausted. Let us get the newcomers settled, and then we will hear Calandra's report. Messengers have already been sent to the council to assemble after the evening meal."

Calandra nodded. "Good. There is much to discuss. Until then."

She strode away, ignoring the stares of the others.

Maybe she should have stayed to help the newcomers get settled, but right now she just wanted to be alone so she could think about all that had happened since yesterday—about Zale's strange behaviour, and Narcissa's wild new ambitions and golden eyes. About the thousands of humans imprisoned on their island, both Redeemed and not, and how they could never be truly free. About the barrier and the mystery of the mostly healed Heartstone.

About the decision she'd reached to trade places with her mother so Delphine could lead their island into the brave new world she'd envisioned, and she could prevent the untold destruction she might wreak when the Madness took her completely.

Calandra's head throbbed, and her chest collapsed. When the time came, could she go through with it? Could she condemn herself into exile in the Abyss?

The safe house thrummed with life around her, a microcosm of the dozens of other communities on the island, full of people who lived, and loved, and were looking to her to protect them, despite the many ways she'd failed them already.

She squared her shoulders and stepped into the cavernous common room of Margaret House.

Even though she hadn't always succeeded, she'd never once shirked her duty to her people. And she had no intention of starting now.

A spear of pain impaled her brain, and she halted, breathing with her fists clenched and her eyes closed until it passed. She moved on along the portico until she reached the stone corridor leading to her room, glad no one had taken notice of her.

The time to face the void again was coming sooner than she'd like. She just had to take care of a few things first.

27

THE REBEL COUNCIL

"POSSESSION ISN'T REAL." NELLY KOR'NYX placed her hands on the round stone table in front of her and stared at Calandra with steely green eyes, a look of skepticism on her face. She'd changed from her swimming hemp to a comfortable fine blue linen peplos with a silver chain-link girdle. "One race can't possess another. There has to be another explanation."

"I'm telling you, I know what I saw. She tried to kill me! Does that sound like something an undine would do?" Calandra stood, too agitated to sit any longer. She glared at Nelly, then glanced around the circle of women and men who made up the rest of the rebel council. On her right, her foster father, Gerrick, looked up at her with calm blue eyes as though to say *soft words do more to convince than loud ones*. Calandra drew a breath and tried to calm down, drawing on his gentle presence to soothe her like an anchor in the storm.

"Adonia tried to kill you too," Rhea said calmly from across the table.

"But she was Mad. Narcissa is not. My cousin has many faults, but I don't believe she'd try to murder me." Calandra sat down again. Losing control of her emotions wouldn't help her cause—and it was too dangerous to allow.

They were in a large stone room with a vaulted ceiling that was annexed to the Great Hall of Margaret House. The large horseshoe-shaped table, elaborately carved from the same stone as the walls, had been here when they'd found the place. Torches in wall sconces and oil lamps on the table lit the space, supplementing what moonlight filtered through a glass skylight above them—one so well-hidden by foliage that someone on the surface would likely never even notice. The skylight had been filthy when they'd found it, but once it had been cleaned up, there was barely a scratch on it. Through clever use of gravity and physics, water diverted from the river above streamed down one wall into a stone gutter at about waist height. The gutter guided the flow around the room and out to the pool in the Great Hall, then into the grotto pool.

However, the sound of flowing water did nothing to soothe Calandra's irritation. She glanced at Airlea, who sat on her left. The ex-siren had taken Cogger to a make-shift detention cell, where she'd Released him and he now sat under the guard of two men. He'd been as unwilling to see reason here as he had at Steadfast House. When the council had discussed his situation at the beginning of the meeting, they hadn't been able to agree on a course of action for what to do with him next. He looked destined to remain in custody until they could do so—and Calandra was sure this wouldn't be the last such dilemma they'd face as their cause progressed. They'd have to come up with a better solution than to put every man on Sirenia who wouldn't accept his lot under guard.

Cain's feral eyes shone in her memory, and she shivered. If ever there was a man who wouldn't be reasoned with, it would be Cain. It was disheartening to think that the very men they were fighting so hard to Free would abuse their freedom by endangering them, but Cogger and Cain were the proof this was so. Maybe that was why she couldn't shake her foul mood.

Hammad, who sat next to his wife, spoke up. "With respect, humans can be possessed by a jinn or a demon. This dragon-who-isn't sounds a great deal like a jinn."

Rhea smiled at her husband, but many of the women at the table new to the cause looked uncomfortable—not at what he said, Calandra knew, but that he'd spoken at all.

Nelly was one of them. Her nostrils flared, and she didn't look at Hammad. "Well, if it is real, it doesn't happen to undines. It can't."

"Why not?" Calandra crossed her arms, thankful for the new skin that had covered her healed burns.

Nelly arched a handsome brow. "Name me one time in history that an undine has been possessed."

The answer came to her almost immediately. "Alessandro."

"Nadia's consort?" interjected Amaryllis kor'Yianna, who had, until recently, been one of Adonia's closest advisers. She had somehow managed to bring silks and linens as fine as Polyxo's when she fled the city, and her brown hair was bound in an intricate golden snood. "What in the name of the Mother makes you say that?"

Calandra looked to Rhea, Hammad, Ignatia, and the other council members from Elpida for support, who had already heard what she was about to say next.

"Damon told me he was Alessandro, that his body had died but his spirit could not be killed. That was before I knew what he really was. But if he was truly Alessandro, how could my ancestors have descended from him—a dragon spirit with no material form—and Nadia? And how could she have Redee—er, *enslaved* him?"

"We don't know that the mind-taking doesn't work on these Grigori," Rhea said.

"True," Calandra said. "But I think the Grigori must require something that tethers them to the material plane, that they can't just manifest here themselves. That's why Damon attached himself to me."

It was the only thing that made sense. Otherwise, surely someone would have noticed an enormous dragon emerging from the Heartstone or flying around the island after the Spirit had freed her from his soul ties. Until now, she'd hoped he hadn't escaped from the Stone—that he'd somehow remained trapped there, or even gone back to where he was from. But after seeing Narcissa's eyes and hearing about her strange behaviour, she could no longer deceive herself.

If only she could convince everyone else so they could take necessary precautions. Maybe more of the Grigori had escaped—but if they had, how would her people recognize them unless they were prepared for such a threat?

"I think he might have tried to possess me and Zale in the Mother's Heart, but failed. Narcissa appeared in the antechamber moments later. It would make sense that—"

"This is nonsense," Nelly interjected. "You didn't see it happen, you're just guessing. If he was trying to possess you, why would he be unable to succeed?" She leaned toward Calandra. "Could it be that undines can't be possessed? In that case, assuming that's what he was trying to do, wouldn't he have failed with Narcissa too? There are plenty of humans in the palace. Maybe we should be more worried about them."

Calandra clenched her jaw, staring at Nelly. The woman would be a hard merchant to negotiate with, which was probably how she'd become so wealthy.

"I don't know." Calandra sighed and sat down. "But there is so little we know about these Grigori, what makes you so sure that Narcissa isn't possessed? She's certainly in the most powerful position in the palace—exactly the kind of person Damon would want to control. And when was the last time you saw an undine with golden eyes?"

She glared defiantly around the circle, daring anyone to challenge her further.

Rhea, who sat directly opposite Calandra, frowned. "We can't be sure, of course. But Calandra, you have to admit that lately, you've been a little . . . on edge. We know you've been struggling with the burden of the bonds. Dealing with that much pain on a constant basis can cause our minds to play tricks on us. Not to mention—"

Calandra opened her mouth to object, but Rhea held up a hand to silence her and continued, her voice kind.

"Not to mention your recent losses. You are under a lot of stress right now. It would be easy to misinterpret the situation."

Xeni, who sat next to Rhea, spoke softly. "Remember last week when you thought you saw Damon in the grotto and it was just Alexander? Are you sure this couldn't have been something like that?"

Calandra ground her teeth. Alexander was Kynthia's eight-year-old son by her Freeman consort, one of the boys born at Elpida. Whenever Damon had appeared as an undine man in Calandra's dreams, his tail had been a warm gold—just like young Alexander's. On the occasion in question, she'd been fighting off a pounding headache and had seen the sun glinting off golden scales in the grotto pool. When she dove into the water to confront Damon, solidifying the water around him to immobilize him, she'd scared the poor boy half to death. He'd swum home to his mother in tears and wouldn't come near her ever since.

"No," she said, knowing she sounded sulky. "It wasn't. This was different."

She took a deep breath, trying to regain her equilibrium—something that had been increasingly hard to find of late. Xeni looked at Calandra with troubled eyes. As a physic, she might not be able to sense Calandra's pain, but she could sense her distress. So could most of the women in this room. Calandra fortified her emotional shield to block out the expectations bearing down on her. She wished she hadn't left her salt-crusted Tear in her room until she could clean it.

Rhea looked around at the assembled council members. "Regardless, it doesn't change the fact that we are no closer to raising the barrier. Since Narcissa is obviously so hostile to the idea, it's unlikely she'll allow any stone healer, let alone Calandra, to investigate the cause of the Heartstone's current ineffectiveness."

Gerrick, who sat on Calandra's right, raised his hand slightly. "If I may, Kyria kor'Eudoxia?"

Rhea nodded at him. "You don't need to request permission to speak here, Kyrios Gerrick."

Gerrick hesitated, absorbing the words, then continued.

"I have known Narcissa since she was born. She fears human men. I think she even fears enslaved men. I didn't have to be an empath to ascertain her discomfort around me or the other palace *douloi*."

Gerrick's voice caught, and Calandra wondered if he were thinking about Thea, his dead consort. He had lived as her free consort for forty-five years, and no one had been the wiser until almost two months ago. Calandra's throat closed. Thea had been like a mother to her. How much more must Gerrick miss her?

Gerrick continued. "Narcissa's declaration that it is time for Sireniapolis to be made known to the world seems out of character for her. Why would she want to risk that kind of exposure?"

Heads around the table nodded at this.

Nelly tossed her hand dismissively. "What if Narcissa is right?"

"Huh?" Nick frowned at her sister.

"We have superior abilities to humans. And we have cowered from them for a long time. What if Narcissa is right? It's time to take our place in the world and stop hiding under the table like whipped dogs!"

Rhea's eyes were round. "You can't be serious!"

"As a hammerhead shark," Nelly replied, her expression stoic.

Ignatia shook her head. "If we do that, then we'll be no better than the humans who forced us to retreat to the West in the first place. Besides, the Atargasians are a peaceful people. Those who see the world as Narcissa does are rare. Most of us just want to live our lives and be left alone, free from the fear of exploitation and abuse that was rained on us in the past. Or have you forgotten our history?"

She stared at each person in turn, and many of them glanced away. There was a reason why Atargatis had instructed their ancestors to flee as far west from civilization as they could, ensconcing them on the islands of Atlantis and Sirenia with the protection of the Heartstone. Despite humans' inferior abilities and technology, they had always found a way to overcome the undines, murdering them by the thousands, so the stories went. Since then, they had only gained in technology and numbers—and their capacity for cruelty remained, as Calandra had seen ample evidence to prove during every Redemption Harvest. Every person here knew the fate that would likely befall them were they to be discovered by the human world. No, she no longer believed all men were monsters or that women didn't have the capacity to be monsters too. But there were enough monsters on Sirenia already.

Ignatia turned to Rhea. "Megara kor'Sibylle suggested that the Heartstone might be able to be repaired completely, or at least enough to raise the barrier again, but she'd need a better look at it to see what was wrong. If Narcissa will not address the issue, perhaps we could arrange another mission to get Calandra, Erigone, and Meg back into the Mother's Heart to take a closer look—"

"Why bother?" Calandra blurted.

"Excuse me?" Ignatia said, blinking.

"Why bother if you won't accept the result?"

"Calandra, I—" Rhea began, but Calandra cut her off.

"What I don't understand," she said, glaring at Rhea and then looking around the circle at each one there, "is that you push me for weeks to put aside my pain and take on leadership of the rebels . . . and when I finally do lead a mission, you question the report I bring back. You can't have it both ways. You either trust me, or you don't."

Her voice had gotten louder as she'd spoken, and she closed her eyes, trying to find the calm she used to retreat to in moments like these, but it refused to be found. All that was left was the anger, and the throbbing pain that reminded her she was slowly becoming a greater threat to everyone on this island than all the other problems they faced put together. No wonder the council was nervous. She would be, too, in their position. But she had to make them listen to her. She couldn't go after her mother knowing that Damon was wreaking havoc on her island and no one even believed he was there. She had to know her people were prepared and safe.

Her head gave a sharp throb, and she drew a breath to avoid letting the pain show. She hoped convincing them wouldn't take too long. She might not have much time left.

Ignatia took a breath and folded her hands on the table, casting a hard glance at Nelly. "No one thinks you unfit, your highness, or we wouldn't have supported you going on this mission. It's just . . . Narcissa possessed by a dragon spirit and wielding fire? Zale Free, but treating you as a threat and Narcissa as his ally? You don't think it sounds a bit far-fetched?"

Calandra stood, no longer able to contain her exasperation. "Of course I do! I know how ludicrous it all sounds. But Narcissa's and Zale's strange behaviour would be a lot more explainable if Damon—who, I'll remind you all, deceived me for five years before I got wise to him, only by the grace of the Mother—were possessing Narcissa, wouldn't it?"

Rhea's expression tightened. She turned to Airlea. "What did you see, Singer kor'Phile? Do you think Narcissa kor'Adonia is . . . possessed?" She made a face as though the word left a bitter taste in her mouth.

Airlea glanced at Calandra and back at the table. "If Calandra believes she is, I support her."

Calandra glanced at the siren, a stab of annoyance piercing her. Why was Airlea always jumping on Calandra's bandwagon? Not that she couldn't use the help right now, but why was Airlea, who barely knew her, the only one to give it?

A sharp pang of longing for Tanni and Thea pierced her. She glanced at Gerrick, who sat quietly on her other side. She wondered if the reason her foster father didn't speak up again in her defense was because he was doubting her too—but his encouraging smile and the pride and love he exuded contradicted her doubts. She sighed. After forty-five years of holding his tongue in the Opal Palace, speaking out was not Gerrick's way. He'd already said his piece. That would have to be enough.

Nelly arched a brow at Airlea. "As commendable as your loyalty is, singer, what we're looking for here is evidence, not mere belief."

"Well . . ." Airlea swallowed. "Narcissa was behaving strangely, as Calandra said, and the rumours shared by Judith and Megara as well as the students we met in the palace indicate that the odd behaviour doesn't stop there."

"But . . . ?" Rhea prompted gently.

"But," Airlea said, glancing guiltily at Calandra, "I didn't see any gold in her eyes. And from what I've often seen of Narcissa's temper and behaviour through the years, I don't think her behaviour is so unlikely, given the recent loss of her mother and her sudden rise to power. So, no. I don't believe she is possessed."

Calandra clenched her jaw. Remorse rolled from Airlea, who no longer wore her shieldstone. Calandra knew the siren had only answered according to her conscience, and felt a grudging mote of respect, but it made Calandra's position here more difficult.

"Maybe there's an explanation for why Airlea couldn't see it." Calandra straightened, keeping her voice calm. "I had some kind of special connection to Damon before. Maybe I'm the only one who can see him. And it was only a flash. Airlea may have missed it."

Her suggestions were met with varying degrees of acceptance and belief in the expressions of the council members.

"And if she is possessed, as you claim, what would you have us do about it?" asked Stella kor'Panorea. Her sharp voice and the black curls cascading over her shoulders reminded Calandra of the young woman's grandmother, Archon Iris of Fire Lake, who had secretly joined their cause.

Calandra let out a frustrated sigh. "I don't know. I don't know what we *can* do. It's one of the many things I would like to know, but the stones have been maddeningly silent on the subject."

That, and so many other things, like details about the Grigori, their abilities, and their crimes. Or how Damon had managed to haunt her dreams while still imprisoned in the Abyss. Or why her people had started using the *sklavia* bond in the first place—and whether there was a way to break it without touching the bondsman himself. If only she could decipher the strange stuttering script many of the stones were written in, perhaps the secrets would be revealed. Meg had a special interest in written languages. Perhaps she could make something of it.

Nelly tapped her fingers on the table. "Calandra brings up a fair point. We *don't* know much about the Grigori, or even the Heartstone itself and how the barrier is connected to it. If we could go back to Atlantis and retrieve more of the datastones she and the others had to leave behind—"

"No," said Rhea firmly. "We've been over this many times. Atlantis isn't safe, not with the guard using it as a staging point for their boundary patrols now that the barrier is down."

Nick, who'd been the one to take Calandra and the others to Atlantis on her sub the last time, waved her hand dismissively, one eye looking at Rhea and the other at her sister so Calandra wasn't sure whom she was addressing. Probably both.

"Atlantis is huge," Nick said, pushing away a short piece of salt-and-pepper hair that had fallen in front of her eyes. "Have you ever been there? I took a pass out there about a week ago."

Rhea sat straighter. "You did? Weren't you worried about being seen?"

"Nicandra, you foolish, headstrong daughter of a . . ." Nelly's tirade fell below audible levels and she glared at her hands.

Nick glared at her sister. "Yes, *Penelope?* You have something to say?"

Nelly's elegant eyebrows drew a line on her forehead, but she shook her head without looking up. Calandra smothered a smile. The two women could hardly be more opposite from each other.

Nick shrugged and turned back to Rhea. "I'm a salvage operator. Have been for years. No siren has reason to believe I'm doing anything else out there than what I always do—look for items valuable enough to sell."

Nelly scowled and crossed her arms with a harrumph. Calandra didn't know either woman well, but there seemed to be some unresolved tension between them that came out in moments like these. And as far as stubbornness went, the sisters were exactly the same.

Rhea frowned. "Fine. And?"

"The sirens are using one old tower on the north side, but the old Archive is in the centre of the city. If we use the shieldstones and go in at night from the south, we should be fine. They don't expect anyone to approach it from the island—in fact, I don't think any of them are likely to head into the city either. Too worried about the ghosts." She gave a wry grin.

Nelly looked up at her sister at last, begrudging respect in her eyes. "Old superstitions, but they might work in our favour. It would be much less dangerous than the mission we just undertook."

Nick gave her head a small shake. "After all these years, you still doubt me?"

Nelly quirked her mouth to the side. "Not that you've never given me reason to."

Nick winced, and Nelly's expression softened.

"That was uncalled for. I'm sorry."

Nick gave a curt nod of acknowledgement, but clasped her hands on the table before her and looked away.

Rhea pressed her mouth into a thin line. She had been dead-set against anyone returning to Atlantis ever since Calandra had nearly disappeared into the Voidstone, no matter who brought it up. Calandra wondered what her objection would be now.

But instead of objecting, she addressed the assembled council. "This should be Calandra's decision. She, more than anyone, knows what the risks are." She turned to Calandra. "What do you think, your highness? Would you find it advisable to send an expedition to the Sunken City?"

The memory of the last time Calandra had been to Atlantis—Damon's spirit in the Voidstone, the way he'd tricked her and nearly trapped her there, losing her arm to his deception and then Osaze to Narcissa's machinations, however temporary both losses had been—all flashed through her mind, and she shuddered. She knew the reason for the rumours of the city being haunted, and she feared them.

Rhea smiled pleasantly, knowing she'd won.

Calandra opened her mouth to answer, but at that moment, Xeni's dark-haired twelve-year-old son, Jason, ran into the room, panting as he scanned the assembled faces for the one he was looking for. A sliver of satisfaction ran through Calandra—Jason had been the oldest undine boy at Elpida. Had he been raised in the traditional way, he would have been Redeemed this year. Instead, he was a vital and active part of their community, able to interrupt important meetings whenever he wanted. Calandra smirked at her own annoyance.

Xeni turned to him in alarm. "Jason, what's the matter? Has something happened?"

Jason ran to stand between his mother and grandmother. "Papa said to come find you and tell you there's been a message on the commstone."

Rhea stood and placed a hand on Jason's shoulder. "Is it Elpida? Has something happened there?"

Jason shook his head. "No, Yaya. It's not for you. It's for Princess Calandra."

Calandra snapped to attention. "For me? Who is it?"

He found her and met her gaze. "It's a message from the Opal Palace. Princess Narcissa broadcast it to the whole island, and we picked it up. She wants you to come and heal the Heartstone."

All eyes turned to Calandra. Calandra stared at the boy, speechless.

What could Damon be up to now?

28

NIGHT CAPERS

ZALE CREPT DOWN THE MOONLIT corridor, keeping to the shadows, following the silent figure some distance ahead of him. So far, Damaris hadn't detected him, and he silently thanked his mother once again for whatever ability she'd put in his river stone bracelet—Tiger's Eye, Daskala Amaltheia had called the stone his mother had used—that hid him from the sensate abilities of the undines. And his Romani friend Gio for teaching him how to be completely unremarkable when he wanted.

Further up the corridor, Damaris moved behind a broad pillar. Zale frowned, waiting to see what she did next. When she did not reappear, he crept forward. But when he got there, she was nowhere to be seen.

He rubbed his hands all over the pillar and wall behind it, hoping they might reveal something his sharp eyesight had not.

Idiot. He shook his head at himself.

Damaris had disappeared. However, he knew invisibility was not a power the undines possessed—he'd already excitedly asked Daskala Lida when the question occurred to him and had shrivelled beneath the incredulous look she'd given him as an answer—so Damaris had to have gone somewhere. But where?

Hiding in the shadow between the pillar and the wall, he stood still and closed his eyes, picturing the sparring terrace with the closed door he'd used to shield himself from Damaris's emotions. Slowly, he placed his hand on the latch and opened it—just a crack at first, then, when he sensed nothing, he threw it wide open.

She wasn't standing on the other side like she had been that day on the terrace, and he sagged against the pillar. But something caught his

230

attention—something in the distance that shouldn't be there, because it was beyond the wall that bounded his mindscape courtyard. But, squinting at it, he could see Damaris's form faintly through the mist and dimly sense her alertness and anxiety filtering toward him.

He reached toward her, and his hand contacted cold stone.

He opened his eyes. He was staring at the smooth marble wall, and his hand had connected with a bevelled geometric figure sculpted into the trim at about shoulder height. It was of a little triquetra, the curved three-pointed knot symbol so precious to the people here—something to do with the Mother the undines worshipped. He frowned.

That was a bust.

But he could still sense Damaris somewhere beyond the wall, her emotions fading by the second as though she were walking away from him. But how?

He scanned the area again, once more running his hands over the wall and the molded trim, then returned to the triquetra, which had a spherical bulge in the centre, painted purple to represent a set stone.

Of course!

He pressed on the convex bump, and it gave beneath the pressure. At the same time, a rectangular portion of the wall beneath the section of trim silently swung away from him.

Zale bent and peered into the dark space beyond. *How very clever.*

Glancing up and down the corridor to confirm it was still clear, he ducked through the small doorway and closed the thick slab of stone behind him. It swung shut as silently and effortlessly as it had opened, plunging him into utter darkness.

Zale held his palm before him and concentrated, and a small golden ball of light appeared above it, no brighter than a shielded candle flame. He didn't want to draw undue attention to himself, but it was too dark for even him to see without it.

He needn't have worried about drawing attention though. The low, narrow passage he found himself in was completely empty but for himself. Damaris was already far enough away that he could barely sense her. He set off down the passageway at a quick trot.

All day, the questions Damaris had asked him at breakfast had been burning a hole in his mind, and he wanted to give her a piece of it. But when he'd snuck out of his dorm tonight to fetch her and have a good talk, he'd noticed her sneaking down the hallway in the shadows. He hadn't doubted her story about running into Calandra while on the way to the lavs until right then. Now, he wondered what else she'd lied to him about.

He turned a corner in the passageway and found himself at the top of a long, narrow flight of stone stairs. Damaris was still somewhere ahead of him, so he tiptoed on. Several flights deeper into the palace, the passage joined a wider corridor, and he pressed himself against the wall of the narrow one, peering out to get his bearings and extending the ball of light to see better.

He thought it was one of the many passageways beneath the palace, some of which he'd seen on his wild flight with Calandra and Osaze when he'd first arrived. After everything had gone wrong in the Mother's Heart, he had been supposed to flee back to the Crystal Cave through one of them and escape with the others, but Narcissa had found him first and promised to help him find his mother.

Narcissa—a warm, golden-caramel sweetness oozed over him as soon as he thought of her, and he closed his eyes, picturing her. She was so . . . he didn't know, exactly. Perfect. She made him feel . . . She always . . .

His mother's gentle face popped back into his mind, and he shook his head. It was like he'd been smothered in sticky-sweet, choking molasses and Delphine's image had banished it from whence it came. He frowned. That wasn't the first time that had happened, he was sure of it. What made his mind go fuzzy like that? What had he been thinking of? He couldn't remember.

A hand clasped the wrist of his extended palm and another clapped over his mouth. He yelped, to his utter embarrassment.

"Hush, Icarus," Damaris hissed. "And put that light out."

Zale's heart pounded in his chest. He nodded and clenched his hand, extinguishing the soft glow. After a few moments, his eyes adjusted and he could make out the vague outline of Damaris's face and the softly glowing green of her eyes in the faint blue light of an oval stone she wore on her wrist.

Damaris released him. "What are you doing here?"

"Following you," he whispered back. "What are *you* doing here?"

Just then, a plain wooden door beside them opened slightly, flooding the empty hall with flickering golden light from the room beyond. The slim opening was obstructed by a silhouetted figure that only came to Zale's chest.

"Password?" came a young girl's voice.

Damaris drew in a sharp breath, then turned to Zale, her eyes wide. She was alarmed—why would she be? Unless . . .

Realization washed over Zale.

Damaris definitely hadn't been sneaking out to the lavs. She was secretly meeting with some kind of group—maybe even a resistance. That was why she'd been talking to Calandra. She was a traitor, just like his murderous sister.

"Damaris, is that you?" said the girl.

"Hush, Melany!" Damaris waved at her impatiently. She turned back to Zale and put a threatening finger on his chest. "If you whisper one word of this to Narcissa, I'll . . . I'll . . ."

She didn't seem able to think of a consequence dire enough. However, at the mention of Narcissa's name, the syrupy golden sweetness oozed into his brain once more and the whole world felt better, like the air was made of sweets.

"Narcissa . . ." He looked at Damaris, then the small girl with shining green eyes who peered at him from the doorway, and backed away. "I must tell Nar—"

"Oh, no, you don't," came a voice behind him.

A sharp blow of pain exploded through the back of his skull. Then the darkness seeped into his eyes.

The last thing he saw was Damaris's worried expression as she caught him.

29

CAPTIVE

"Well, we can't just let him go!" said a shrill voice. "He'll tell her, and then we're all done for!"

The girl's voice penetrated the fog surrounding Zale's brain, and he slowly became aware of his surroundings. *I'm tied in a chair.* His head hung forward, and his long hair fell around his face. He opened his eyes but didn't move, trying to figure out where he was and who was there with him.

"But you can't keep him here forever either," came a much calmer voice from not far away. That was Damaris. He could see her muscular legs next to him through his hanging blond fringe. "So what are we going to do?"

A pair of sandalled feet came into view directly in front of him—tan skin, thigh-length skirt. Another student. "We could Redeem him."

"No," came a sharp chorus of voices, which surprised him.

"Not forever," the same girl said plaintively. "Just long enough to get him out of here and away from that witch."

Witch? Who were they talking about? By the standards Zale had grown up with, every girl in this room was a witch, albeit of a very different kind than the Romani *shuvanis* and *shuvanos*. Romani Wise Ones were respected and sought out for their ability to help with matters from healing to love potions to protection. *Witch* was only a pejorative term to the *gorgios*, not to the Roma. But whomever the girl spoke of, she didn't mean the word with respect.

"If we Redeem him, we betray Calandra and all that she sacrificed for him and the others," said Damaris. "Not to mention, we'd be in deep trouble. We're not even supposed to know how to do it yet. If it weren't for Zoe, we wouldn't."

234

Calandra. An irrational anger swept through Zale. *How could Damaris do this to me? Why would she side with that murdering traitor?* Betrayal, sharp and bitter, pierced the anger. *Narcissa is the only one who truly cares for me here, isn't she?*

Narcissa's porcelain-skinned visage floated in front of him, and warm lethargy seeped through him. Happy golden thoughts oozed through the anger, but the voice intruded on them once again.

"Well, what do you suggest?" said Legs peevishly. "Knock him on the head every time he comes to? Honestly, that isn't something I want to repeat."

"It's not something you should have done the first time, Talia," said Damaris with a dark note in her voice.

Another voice he didn't recognize interjected. "There are much more civilized ways to render someone unconscious. Why do sirens think the answer to everything is to stun a man's brain in one way or the other?"

"We aren't all physics like you, Geronimi," Talia said defensively. "We use the tools we have, and our Society has banned sirensong for that purpose, so . . ."

Zale stared at Talia's legs, rage swirling in his gut. *This* was the girl who'd knocked him out? How dare she? A familiar trembling ran through him, and he reached for the energy that would call fire from the air—but the way was barred. He couldn't access his powers. He wiggled his wrists against the scratchy ropes and the cold, hard stone encircling them. *Feldspar bracelets.* They were dampening his abilities.

For the first time, he began to feel afraid.

What did they intend to do to him? He couldn't access his powers, and no one knew he was here except these girls. He couldn't tell exactly how many there were, but he could sense at least a dozen people in the room. Some of them seemed quite young, but he'd bet anything that this Talia was a siren cadet he'd sparred with a time or two—she was nearly as good as Damaris and taller than he was.

And whatever they'd used to bind his arms behind him seemed unlikely to give. Hemp rope, probably.

Whatever he was going to do, though, he had to do it fast, before they realized he was awake and knocked him out again—sirensong or no, they'd proved capable and willing to do so.

His attention was caught by something one of the arguing voices was saying—the same girl who'd opened the door. Melany. He remembered her. A young novice with saffron braids and a precocious attitude.

"If we could only get him to Calandra, she'd know what to do."

"No!" he shouted before he could stop himself. His head snapped up, and the girls standing nearest him jumped back a little. "I don't *want* to see my sister. She'll try to kill me! She'll try to—"

"Zale!" Damaris stepped forward, a placating hand extended toward him. "It's all right. We're not going to hurt you. If you'll just listen—"

"No! I want to see Narcissa. Take me to Narcissa!" He wiggled his body back and forth, succeeding in getting the chair to rock a little on its legs. The younger girls in the circle took another step back, their eyes wide, but Damaris stepped closer and laid her hand on his head, humming a soft tune.

Calm poured through him, and he stopped thrashing. After a few moments more, his panting stopped. His heart rate slowed, and he exhaled a long breath. Only then did Damaris stop her soothing melody and take away her hand.

He raised his head to look at her, wishing he could sit higher and look more intimidating, but his tied hands prevented him from doing so. "What are you going to do to me?"

Talia stepped forward and crossed her arms, her dark hair curling into her green eyes in wild flyaways. "That depends on you, *anthropos*."

"I'm not human," Zale snarled.

Talia's lip curled, and she bent toward his face, placing her hands on her knees. "No. But you're not quite one of us either, are you?" She indicated the others with her head.

Zale glanced around. As he'd estimated, there were about a dozen students in the room—several siren cadets like Talia and Damaris, and the rest from all three healing disciplines at the Academy, judging by their belt colours. There was a range of ages, but Melany and another girl with glossy dark brown hair falling in a single braid down her back were the only novices—their belts were still the undyed hemp of the unraised. The other girls were all older, but Zale could never remember which belt colour meant what.

One thing they all had in common was how they were looking at him—like he was some kind of untamed beast who might lash out at them without warning. Their fear washed over him—no emotional shields now.

Could they really hate him so much?

He looked at the circle of wide eyes. When his gaze met Melany's, she tensed and put her hands to her mouth. She reminded him of Gio's little sister Marsha, who was about the same age—not in looks, which were completely different, but in her wide-eyed vulnerability.

"I wouldn't hurt you," he said gently.

She just stared at him, her freckles sharp on her pale upturned nose.

Damaris pushed Talia aside with an irritated look and crouched in front of Zale so he wouldn't have to strain to meet her eye. "Zale, I know you must be frightened, but we really don't intend to hurt you. We only tied you up until we could be sure you wouldn't hurt us."

He gazed at her incredulously. "Why would you think I'd hurt you?"

Her brow furrowed. "Under normal circumstances, I don't think you would. But lately, you've been . . . different."

Zale scoffed. "How would you know? Our first real conversation was yesterday."

"True, but this is a difference we would see in anyone. We've all seen it, but after what happened at the Archive last night . . . and then our conversation this morning . . ."

Zale scowled. "I have no idea what you're talking about."

Geronimi clasped her hands in front of her and stepped up beside Talia, whose hands were on her hips. "That's just it. You wouldn't. Not with this."

Zale glanced between Geronimi and Damaris, wishing he didn't feel so much like he'd just fallen down a well in the dead of night. "Are you going to illuminate me?"

Damaris glanced at Geronimi.

The older girl cleared her throat and licked her lips. "There are times when you don't seem to be quite, er, present. Or you say things happened that didn't happen, but you believe them, so you're not lying. It's like you have memories that aren't real."

Zale shook his head. A golden fog swirled at the edge of his mind. "That's ridiculous. And how would you even know? I never met you until a few minutes ago."

Geronimi dipped her chin in acknowledgement. "True, we have never met. But as the oldest physic apprentice in the Academy, I was asked by Healer Evadne to observe you. After Damaris told us about your conversation this morning . . ."

He whipped his head to look at Damaris. "The one where you lectured me and called me an imbecile?"

Damaris frowned and crossed her arms. "I didn't call you an imbecile."

"Imbecile, Icarus. Same thing, isn't it?" He glared at her, trying to look as intimidating as possible from his position, but he was afraid it wasn't working.

Geronimi cleared her throat to get their attention.

Zale glared at her. "So you've been watching me. Not creepy at all."

Geronimi blushed a little, but she continued. "The behaviours you are displaying, I've heard of them before. They are consistent with someone who has been conditioned to accept false memories—memories implanted in their brain by someone else."

Geronimi's words only added to the questions that had spurred him to seek out Damaris tonight. Why *would* Calandra need a diving knife to kill him? It didn't make sense. There was so much about his visit to the Archive that didn't make sense. And there were other places in his memory that were a little fuzzy, or *too* clear—almost like memories that weren't his own.

"I suppose this is another one of the lovely tricks you people do to pass the time," he snapped.

"No, it's not something that is a common practice." Geronimi's brow furrowed. "I only know of it because I saw it mentioned in one of my study Tears. I believe the technique is normally used to help overcome anxiety or heal emotional trauma, not to create new memories altogether. But after what Damaris said about your behaviour this morning—"

"What behaviour?" He shifted in his seat to glare at Damaris again. "I'm perfectly fine. It's you people who are the threat. You're in league with my sister, aren't you? Are you going to kill me now, or are you going to call her to come and do it?"

Damaris exchanged glances with Geronimi and Talia, her rosebud lips pressed firmly together. Then she turned back to Zale.

"Zale, Calandra doesn't want to kill you. That's one of the false memories. You're the only person who believes that."

Zale shook his head. These undines could do all kinds of things to the mind with their magic—he had no doubt that one of those would be to put false memories in someone's head. But surely he would have some kind of indication if that had happened to him?

"No. You weren't there. None of you were. How do you know?"

"Because I asked Matthew," said Damaris. "And he can't lie."

"Unless his mistress orders him to," Geronimi pointed out.

Talia nodded. "True. But it would seem his mistress was too busy duping Zale to worry about her *doulos*."

Horror and denial rose in Zale, starting at the ends of his toes and climbing up every nerve in his body. Matthew's mistress was Narcissa. Narcissa wouldn't hurt him. She was helping him. But Calandra had attacked Matthew too. Why hadn't he told Talia that?

"No, that's not true."

Damaris frowned at Zale. "Calandra tried to help you escape, like I told you. Narcissa told you she was there to murder you, and you freaked out. She had to run to escape with her own life." Damaris's voice lost its sharp edge. "Zale, Narcissa has been tricking you. Only it's so clever, you don't even know what's happening."

Every fibre of Zale's body rebelled.

"No!"

Rage swirled through him and the ropes on his wrists caught fire. He yanked his hands free, even as the ropes burned out and fell to the floor in pungent smoking threads.

"You're lying! You're all liars! Narcissa wouldn't do that to me. She loves me!"

He leapt to his feet. The girls gasped and took a step back.

Talia stared at the green feldspar bracelets on his wrists. "How—"

Zale shouted in rage and anger as he barrelled through them toward the door. He would show them. He'd go to Narcissa right now and find out the truth.

He jerked open the door. Ignoring Damaris's cries for him to stop, he ran through the corridors back the way he'd come, heedless of whose notice he attracted. When he reached the lush main corridor, he turned and started running toward the wing of the palace with the royal quarters. He kept to the shadows, though, not wanting to be stopped by a vigilant siren who would keep him from finding the truth he needed to know.

As he approached Narcissa's door, he slowed. A siren and a *tapeinos* he didn't recognize stood on guard outside the brass-worked wooden door. He hunkered behind one of the ubiquitous tree planters, pondering his options.

"You're not just going to ask to be let in?" came Damaris's whisper from behind him.

He stiffened, his heart climbing into his throat. He whirled to face her. "Leave me alone."

She shrugged. "I'd like to, but here's the thing. If you tell Narcissa about us, we could all be executed. I'm not sure she'd actually lay the death penalty on a bunch of students, but I'm not sure she wouldn't either."

"Narcissa wouldn't kill anyone."

Damaris scoffed. "Are you certain? Tell that to her mother and Daskala Thea kor'Aglaia."

"Thea and Adonia killed each other. Everyone knows that."

"Not everyone," said Damaris in a dry voice, "and my source is very reliable. At any rate, I can't let you talk to Narcissa right now. Not until we've finished our chat."

"I've got nothing more to say to you." Zale held up his hands palm-up, and a menacing ball of hot flame formed above them. Using fire was harder with the feldspar cuffs on, but he could still do it. That thought should have terrified him. Right now, he was too angry to care.

Damaris eyed the swirling fireball, then flicked her gaze back up to his, her stance loose and ready.

"Look, Zale, I—" She stared past him down the hall toward Narcissa's door. "What the . . . ?"

Zale glanced over his shoulder to see what she was looking at and saw a handsome man with black hair, a neatly-trimmed beard, and rich-looking gold-trimmed black clothes solidify in the hallway in front of the two guards. They reacted with swiftly raised *deiktes* and the siren shouted, but he smiled calmly back at them.

"Come now, I am only to here to deliver a message to my master. Surely you're not going to make this difficult for me?" He held his closed hands to the sides as though to show he meant no harm.

The siren paused. "Who are you?"

Her hesitation was her undoing. The man raised his open palms to his chin and blew a white powder into her face, then the *taps*'s face. They blinked and coughed. Within seconds, their faces went slack and they crumpled to the floor.

"It doesn't matter," said the man, smiling as he stepped over the bodies. "You won't remember me anyway. But, for the record," he said, staring down at their inert forms as he raised his hand to knock, "I'm Dagiel."

Just as he was about to rap on the door, it opened, and there stood Narcissa. She did not look pleased.

"Dagiel, I've told you to come directly into my room." She glanced disapprovingly at the incapacitated guards. "This way is far too much work. I'll have to varnish their memories now."

"Oh, will you?" said Dagiel innocently. "I'm sorry, Semyaza. Next time, I'll be sure to take the hidden back entrance like a common servant."

Narcissa scowled—except Zale wasn't so sure it *was* Narcissa. There was something different about her—her stance, her expression, and even her voice were a little different. As she swept her gaze up and down the hallway, he thought he saw a flash of gold in her eyes. And why had that man called her by a different name?

What in the name of all that was holy was going on?

Despite himself, he exchanged glances with Damaris and saw the same agog uncertainty reflected there.

The stranger entered Narcissa's room, and with a final sweep of the hallway and an annoyed look at her guards, Narcissa retreated and flattened the folding door closed behind her. Their muffled voices could barely be heard on the other side.

Damaris crept over to the still bodies, and Zale tiptoed toward the door. Damaris examined the *taps*, then the siren, checking for a pulse. Their eyes were wide and staring and they lay curled in the positions in which they'd fallen.

"They're alive," Damaris whispered.

Zale nodded and held up his hand for her to be quiet, straining to hear what was being said on the other side of the door. Damaris came to listen too.

As they listened to the two talk of keys and a Soulstone and Zale's training, three things became clear. One, Narcissa kor'Adonia was not the person speaking on the other side of that door. Two, she—or whomever that was—*had* been changing his memories somehow, just as she intended to change the memories of the guards on the floor. For what purpose, he couldn't imagine.

And three, she had no intention of helping him rescue his mother from Tartarus.

He was truly on his own.

When he looked at Damaris, all he saw reflected in her luminescent seafoam-green eyes was pity.

Shrivelling under shame and the weight of yet another betrayal, he fled.

*

NARCISSA struggled against the dream that bound her, a captive in her own mind. She felt as though she'd woken up from a deep sleep, but still had the weight of it on her limbs—she couldn't move anything, nor could she feel them moving. But she could see herself doing things—things she would never choose to do in her waking life. That's how she knew this must be a dream.

There was that man again, the one with skin the colour of coconut milk, hair as black as night, and eyes as black as the bottom of the deepest ocean trench. She watched herself talking to him, saying things she'd never say. What was this about sending Calandra and Zale to Tartarus? Calandra, fine—she deserved the Abyss for what she'd done to Mari and herself and this whole island, but Zale? She needed him. She would use him to . . .

Wait. Why *did* she need him? In fact, why wasn't he Redeemed to keep him out of trouble? He'd been wandering freely around the palace for weeks—she should have Redeemed him as soon as she'd seen him in the . . . wherever it was that she'd run into him after he and Calandra had destroyed the Heartstone, so she could gain the power from his *sklavia* bond as her mother had. Holding his bond had been different than holding a human's—Adonia had actually used fire. Of course, Narcissa had used fire without Redeeming Zale, but still. But there was no need to banish him—his powers could become useful someday. Especially if she bonded Zale as consort—the *syzagos* gave so much more power than the *sklavia* did.

But whoever was in charge of her mouth didn't plan to bond Zale— they wanted to send him away. And who was this Tamiel they kept discussing?

Something the dark-eyed man said set off alarm bells—something about enemies watching, or being about to move against her, and an armada of human ships on their way here at the behest of someone the black-eyed man refused to call by name.

An armada of ships? Panic surged through her. How had the humans found out about their island? They had to get the barrier up. As soon as she woke up from this terrifying dream, she'd make the arrangements for the stone healers to come. Tomorrow. There was no time to waste.

Her dream-self said she wasn't ready, like she already knew about the ships. But she'd prepared for this—earlier today she'd called . . .

No! Not Calandra! Why was she saying she'd asked her entitled cousin to do what she could do herself—must do, if she wanted the archons to support her? A dim memory stirred—Cleo's and Shinara's surprise when she'd broadcast a message to the rebels and Calandra had responded. But that hadn't happened—had it?

This wasn't a dream. It was a nightmare.

Oh, good, the man was leaving. But instead of walking out the door he'd come through, he disappeared into nothingness.

Definitely a dream. She relaxed.

"I know you're watching, Narcissa."

The voice—a deep, resonant voice, but somehow her own—reverberated through her.

Narcissa would have screamed, but she couldn't control her own mouth. Nor could she look wildly around to see who was speaking.

Instead, she watched through her own eyes as her dream-self went over to the gilt-edged mirror on the wall. But it wasn't her own reflection who looked back at her.

It was a man. A man with long black hair, bronze skin, a neatly trimmed beard and moustache, and irises that swirled gold. His lips curved in an arrogant smile.

Who are you? she demanded.

"Hmm. I had your cousin call me Damon, but I find I miss being addressed by my proper name—especially now that everyone is using yours. You, at least, can call me by my true name. Call me Semyaza."

Narcissa struggled again. *Wake up,* she told herself. *Wake up. Wake. UP!*

"Oh, I assure you, I'm wide awake." Semyaza chuckled, but there was no mirth in the sound. "How you managed to wake yourself, I'm not certain. You undines—so difficult to manage. Not like possessing humans, who are so delightfully pliable and their spirits so desperate for something to hold on to. Ah, well. I have found inhabiting you to come with enough advantages to make up for the inconvenience of your heat-blasted difficulty to subdue."

Her dream-self turned from the mirror to look at Matthew, who was visible through the archway leading to her bedchamber, asleep on the bed. Blurry images of intimate moments with the *doulos* swam through her mind, and she realized with horror that this was no dream.

This was absolutely real.

This Semyaza was the reason why she'd been so tired lately, and why her room was always in disarray. He was the one who had been wandering the halls at night, making the servants gossip and fear her. The terrified eyes of a girl screaming and running away flashed in her memory, followed by the image of herself dragging the girl's lifeless body down a dark palace corridor, and she recoiled. She hadn't done that.

Had she?

Semyaza laughed. "You begin to understand. Good. The sooner you accept your lot, the better."

Give me my body back, you cretin!

"Testy, testy. But no, I don't think so. You see, I'd once wanted to use Calandra to rule this island, but now I'm glad she turned me down. Who would have guessed she would have ruined her chances to rule over the most powerful race on Earth? No, my dear, I think you and I see much more eye-to-eye. You *want* to rule. You hunger for it as much as I do. I promise you, we will get our wish."

He frowned, and she sensed dark foreboding in his thoughts. She couldn't read his mind, but for the first time in her life, she could clearly sense the emotions of another being. And Semyaza was afraid of something.

Which meant he had a weakness.

Narcissa stopped struggling. She had to take time to learn about this creature, find out how she could gain the advantage over him. What was he afraid of?

He smiled. "That's better. Yes, you just relax. It will be much better for the baby."

What baby? she asked in spite of herself.

"Oh, did I forget to tell you? You're pregnant."

Narcissa's mind went still in numb shock.

30

THE GRAND TOUR

Robert clutched the reins of his rented horse like they were the only thing keeping him from losing control of his temper. It wasn't far from the truth. Ever since he'd met with Eduardo Romero at the stable that morning, the other man had been a constant source of irritation to him. Romero wasn't vulgar or disrespectful, exactly, unless you counted making Robert wait two hours for him to arrive—just somewhat uncouth, with a tendency to overlook the social niceties that men of good breeding observed as a matter of course.

Romero had kept his dappled grey stud next to Robert's bay mare for the last hour as they climbed toward the inner plateau of the island. Attached by a lead rope to Romero's saddle was a spare horse, a saddled grey roan, which they'd brought for the African to ride back. Robert had thought it had been an unnecessary expense, that the man was more than likely capable of walking, but Romero had paid, so he'd kept his objections to himself.

Ever since they began their journey, Romero had been peppering him with questions about Cornwall, Bristol, his family, and his business. The conversation had hit a short lull, but he could see Romero winding up for a whole new topic and cringed.

"Mr. Cox, have you ever been to Rome? But you must have. All you British lads are big on the Grand Tour these days, no? What did you think of the Sistine Chapel?"

Robert ground his teeth. But just because the other man was acting like an unbreeched whelp didn't mean he needed to stoop to the same level. He kept his tone neutral as he replied.

245

"No, unfortunately, I have not had the opportunity to take the Grand Tour. Both my older brothers have. James was quite taken with the building you—"

"No matter," broke in Romero. "You're on a grand tour now, no?"

He gave Robert a charming grin that probably worked wonders on the ladies but left Robert less than impressed.

How much longer will this unbearable journey last?

"Good sir," he said in a tight voice, "I would appreciate a few moments of silence to compose myself before we arrive at Lord Middleton's estate. Would you be so kind?"

Romero eyed him. "Aye, of course. Good thinking. I'll leave you be, then, and take a few moments myself over there."

He clucked to his steed and guided it to the other side of the road. Guilt flashed through Robert, but the silence was so refreshing, it soon faded.

Robert couldn't make sense of Romero. From all appearances, the man was from a well-to-do Spanish family, probably on his own Grand Tour of sorts—though no one Robert knew of went to the colonies on their tour. But the man's manners were deplorable and his conversation barely civil. He was most likely from a planter family on one of the Spanish islands—propelled into unfamiliar social circles with new money, but still with the vulgar manners of the commoners. Honestly, he had no idea what Miss Bethel saw in him.

Of course! Romero must be from Sirenia. No wonder he'd been such a valuable source of information for Miss Bethel. Why hadn't he seen it before? She wasn't interested in the Spaniard romantically, he'd only been helping her find Zale. Knowing Romero was familiar with the island to which Miss Bethel had gone this morning, Robert's guilt returned—it probably would have been safer for Miss Bethel if Romero had been the one to accompany her. But even though he tried to tell himself she wasn't interested in Romero romantically, he couldn't shake his jealousy. Better that the man was here, where Robert could keep an eye on him. If Miss Bethel had had concerns about her and Berian's ability to find Zale without the Spaniard, she would have said so.

Of course, Miss Bethel was never deterred by much. He'd always admired her boldness, but now, he couldn't help but wonder if there were a reason she seemed so fearless.

The seed of doubt planted by Gryffyn's assertions and watered by Miss Bethel's confidence that she'd accomplish her mission to retrieve Zale from

Sirenia in a single day sprouted another leaf. *It's impossible. And no captain I spoke to had any idea where Sirenia was.*

But that doesn't make them spirits.

Robert glanced over his shoulder to be sure Romero's attention was elsewhere and then, twisting his body to hide what he was doing, he slipped Gryffyn's letter from his breast pocket. Unfolding it, he read the words again. He could have recited the letter by heart by now, but he still felt the need to remind himself that those words had indeed been written by his brother—a man who, while overbearing and often thoughtless, was completely sane as far as Robert knew.

"Excuse me," Romero said.

Startled, Robert tucked the letter back inside his coat and then glanced up, but his companion's words had not been directed at him. Romero was asking for directions from a young black woman with bare feet who was carrying a basket of washing on her head. She pointed along the road and said a few words in the butchered form of English the blacks here often spoke, and Romero thanked her with a graciousness Robert had never seen the man display toward himself.

He frowned. It rankled that Romero would show better manners to a slave woman than to a man above his station. What was this man about?

"What did she say?" Robert asked.

"She says we're nearly there," Romero said to him. "Just around that bend, we should see the entrance to the plantation."

"Excellent. I am ready to be off this horse. And I think she's ready to be rid of me."

Romero laughed heartily at the joke. "Aye, it has been some time since I have ridden, also. Our gaits shall be a match, shan't they, with us wincing every wide-legged step from our sore rumps?"

Robert smiled despite himself at the image of the two of them walking as though they still had horses beneath them. "I suppose we shall."

They rode for a moment in a more comfortable silence, but Gryffyn's accusations and claims made Robert's chest tight. At last, he hit on a way to start weaselling the truth from Romero without being too blunt.

"Mr. Romero, I am aware that you have been seeing Miss Bethel since we arrived here in Barbados. It may be that my companions and I will soon be leaving to find our young friend Zale Teague's mother. Miss Bethel appears quite taken with you, so, as her friend, I must know—what are your intentions with her?"

Romero arched a bemused brow at him. "I can assure you, Mr. Cox,

I have nothing but the most admirable of intentions toward Miss Bethel. I consider her to be like my own family and would never do anything to harm her. But I must commend you for your sense of responsibility toward her. It is not easy to stick one's neck out when it might invite ridicule. Especially from those close to you, or when you feel you have a great deal to lose."

Robert frowned. "Why do you think my defense of Miss Bethel might invite ridicule? She is a lady of good breeding and gentle character. It is my duty as a gentleman to—"

Romero gave a snorting laugh. "Gentle character, uh? Do you know Abela at all? She is the fiercest being I have ever met . . . and that is saying a great deal."

How dare he? The insolence of this man! Robert pulled his horse up short. When Romero noticed, he did the same and wheeled his stud to face Robert's. The bay mare nearly collided with the grey roan following on the lead rope, and it quick-stepped uneasily until Romero clucked a few soothing words to it in a language Robert didn't understand and it settled.

"Mr. Romero, I will thank you to show Miss Bethel the respect she deserves. You say she is as family to you, and yet you call her by her Christian name in my presence and deride her character in this way? How dare you?"

"Her *Christian* name. I see." Romero regarded Robert with a steady gaze. "Mr. Cox, my comments were a compliment, not a criticism. It is not my fault that the men of your country only place value on the parts of a woman's character that make her seem the safest and most congenial to you. But that is how you value all others, isn't it? By their ability to fit into your expectation of them? For instance, you do not like me—do not deny it, it is obvious—not because of what I am, but because of what I am not. Because I have not fit the mould into which you want me to conform to be worthy of your regard. But when someone does jam themselves into that mould, you see what you wish to see and ignore the rest."

"What do you mean by that?"

Romero cocked his head. "Because Miss Bethel speaks like an English lady and dresses like an English lady, you have forgotten to notice how strong she is and that she has absolutely no need of your protection, haven't you? What if, instead, she dressed and spoke like that kind young woman who just gave us directions? Would you be as taken with her then? Or what if she barely spoke your language, or her customs were different than yours, or she was unkempt, or she was poor? What then? Would you still defend her honour? Would you still see her as a woman worthy of protection and respect?" He paused and pinned Robert with a narrowed gaze. "Would you still give her your heart?"

Heat flared through Robert's gut, and he tried desperately to think of a response to Romero's accusations. But he couldn't. He sat there with his mouth opening and closing like a fish.

"I thought not." With a final stare, Romero wheeled his horse around and continued down the road with the roan gelding being tugged along behind him.

Robert had little choice but to follow him.

31

THE PLANTATION

R OBERT HAD INTENDED TO ADVISE Romero to let him do the talking when they got to Huntley Hall. But with his thoughts still reeling in indignant outrage, he said not a word to the man until the sails of a large windmill came into view beyond a row of trees. He turned toward the Spaniard to see him guiding his horse and the spare off the road toward a large bearded fig tree.

"What are you doing?" Robert called.

"Taking a siesta," the Spaniard said over his shoulder. "You think you can handle this much better without me, no? Let us see if you are right. Do not worry—I will be with you in spirit."

After dismounting, Romero dropped his reins and they pooled on the ground beneath the horse's head. After loosing the roan's lead rope from his saddle and dropping it too, he approached each horse in turn and stroked their faces, saying a few words before settling himself in the shade beneath a tree. The horses began grazing on the scrubby tufts of grass.

Robert frowned at him. Romero was going to abandon him, just like that? Not that he needed the man's help—Romero was right about that. But why come all the way out here with him if he was just going to send Robert in to negotiate alone?

He scowled at the napping Spaniard and the horses, who were following their noses to the next clump of grass.

"Those are rented horses. They won't simply stay there."

Romero opened one eye at him.

"So you know better than me about horses too, uh?"

Robert opened his mouth to respond, then closed it. If the man's horses ran off, it would be Romero who would be chasing after them or walking back to Bridgetown, and he who must reimburse the stable owner, not Robert.

Robert clucked to his mare to prod her on, giving Romero a scathing glare before he turned away.

The Spaniard's chuckle followed him on the breeze.

Robert's mount plodded up the palm tree-lined lane past a large pond, a windmill, and a long barn-like structure that must be the sugar house. He pulled the horse up in front of the ornate plantation house and handed the reins to a black groom. Beyond the pond, a few rows of thatched hut roofs were just visible above a hedge-lined fence—the slave village. From the sounds of it, someone was being flogged. The victim was not crying out, but Robert knew the sound of a lash on flesh all too well.

The last time he'd heard it was only weeks ago, when he'd allowed an enslaved African sailor on the *Atlanta* to be flogged for attacking the white first mate, Mr. Crow. The man—Smith, Robert thought his name was— had been defending a young slave woman and Miss Bethel from ravishment. At the time, it had seemed unacceptable that Smith had attacked a white man. He should have known his place. But every time Robert had replayed the event in his mind since, his own actions left a bitter taste in his mouth. Romero's words of moments ago only amplified the shame.

If Robert had witnessed Crow's attack, would he not have done the same as Smith? So what was the difference?

Robert shook his head and repeated the mantra he'd held onto as his lifeline for weeks. *There's a natural order to this world. It's not about expectations—it's about the stations God ordained us to fill.* As a gentleman, he'd been taught to be civil and kind to all—but that didn't mean he must acknowledge all who came calling as an equal. Even he had his betters, and some lines should not be crossed.

But I did cross a line. Several of them.

Since coming to Barbados, Robert had been haunted by nightmares of Smith's ragged back and the human suffering he'd encountered in the slave hold of the *Atlanta*, a slave cargo he'd barely objected to when Gryffyn had proposed it. Once again, he'd caved to the pressure of Gryffyn's will. But he'd failed to count the cost—and he could no longer deceive himself that the good he'd planned to do with the profit would ever be justified by the means. Especially since, of the hundreds of souls aboard when the ship had gone down, only he and his two companions at the Port House Inn had been accounted for.

The pit yawned, clouding his vision with darkness, and he blinked it away.

How many times must I repent before I find mercy?

Romero was wrong. If Robert didn't care about those lowlier than himself, he'd never have tried to take his own life when his sins had become so apparent. His biggest fear was that Miss Bethel, and even God himself, might think the way Romero did. But how could he prove himself? He couldn't free every African in the colonies. He would be lucky if he could successfully free the one he'd come to Huntley Hall to recover.

And as for Miss Bethel, it was her fierceness that made him admire her so, but also her nobility, sweetness, and compassion. Hadn't he already considered the risk he'd be taking by wooing her? Many of his peers would never dream of marrying for love, vying instead for the hands of women of means to ensure financial stability, and yet Robert had been pining over a woman of colour whose background was as muddy as the Thames in spring. If his father knew, he'd roll over in his grave. And Romero dared accuse him of pursuing only safety! If that were Robert's intent, there were several girls he'd met in London last Season who would be happy to consider his prospects—bland girls. Safe girls.

No. It wasn't safety Robert was after. It was redemption.

Robert was still fuming as he followed a woman as dark as Urbi in a white apron and cap through a grand entry hall into a long, well-appointed room with many windows and tasteful decor. A U-shaped sitting area was arranged on a Persian rug near the large hearth centred between two doors on the inner wall, an archway led to a dining room at one end, and a painted pianoforte graced the other end of the room.

He examined the large painting above the hearth of a young man in a powdered white wig and the ostentatious lace-trimmed satin clothing so popular a decade ago—before Marie Antoinette of France had lost her head for such decadence. Robert wondered who he was.

Two men entered the room through the door nearest the piano—the corpulent Middleton with his own out-of-date wig and stockings, now wearing a pale grey jacket over a waistcoat that barely contained his rotund belly, and a man in the red uniform of His Majesty's Royal Navy, sporting the lean figure that always did the uniform the most justice. The man's mouth was a chiselled line beneath a trim sandy-blond moustache.

"Ah, Mr. Cox," said Middleton in his gravelly brogue. "I was hoping to see you soon, but I confess, this early visit does come as a surprise. Have you met Colonel Hayward?"

He gestured toward the soldier, who greeted him with a bow.

"Colonel Fitzwilliam Hayward, at your service, Mr. Cox," was all the man said. The man's use of words seemed as spare as everything else about him.

"A pleasure, Colonel." Robert inclined his head to the man.

Middleton indicated that they should sit. Robert perched on the edge of an overstuffed brocade chair next to a low ornately carved wooden table, the colonel sat in an identical one opposite, and Middleton sat in the matching sofa between them.

"You have a lovely home, Lord Middleton." Robert looked around the room. "It must have taken some time to collect the treasures here. Who is that young man above the hearth?"

A cloud passed over Middleton's face and he glanced at the painting. "That was my son, George. The islands were not kind to him."

He said no more, and Robert heard the dismissal in the man's voice. It was obviously a pain he did not wish to speak of, or had grown accustomed to—more men died in the first few years of coming to the colonies than lived. His manner reminded Robert of the pain in his mother's voice whenever she spoke of his father, who had died a little over two years ago. Robert studied the painting for a few moments more. There had not been much love lost between him and his father. That had obviously not been the case between the baron and his son.

The serving girl brought tea and poured it as they continued speaking.

Middleton cleared his throat. "So, lad, is it possible you have already found what we seek? Did you bring the stone?"

His voice contained an eagerness that surprised Robert.

"No, I am sorry, I have not."

Middleton's brow furrowed. "I see."

Robert accepted a cup of tea from the young woman. With the sting of Romero's words still fresh in his mind, he smiled at her when she gave it to him. "Thank you."

His words seemed to disconcert her. She curtsied clumsily and cast a nervous glance at Middleton, then served the other two men their tea and hurried out of the room.

Middleton glanced after her with a dark look. "It does you credit as a gentleman to show them manners, Mr. Cox, but I fear your efforts are wasted. They don't feel like you and I do. They are like dogs—the only language they understand is the lash. Mary is all right though. She knows her place."

He laughed, and Colonel Hayward offered a quiet snicker in support.

Robert's chest tightened. All the bravado he'd felt when defending Miss Bethel to Romero on the road shrivelled like the sugar cane leaves left in the sun he'd seen on the way here. He wanted to prove Romero wrong about him—but he also wanted to remain in this man's favour and accomplish what he came here to do. He took a breath and gripped his teacup in a sweating hand.

"Lord Middleton, I hope to persuade you to let me purchase that young slave you took from the market yesterday. It is of some urgency that we reunite him to his mother. You see, he was a free black who was unjustly captured in the street, and—"

"And you're here to see justice done, are you?" Lord Middleton stood and went to a liquor cabinet next to the wall. "I think I need something stronger than tea. May I interest you in some rum, Mr. Cox?"

Robert declined with a gesture, but Hayward accepted a tumbler.

After pouring out the liquor and serving Hayward, Middleton stood and swirled the dark liquid around his glass, his eyes narrowed in thought.

"You did read your brother's letter, did you not?"

Robert nodded. "Yes, sir, but—"

"Then you understand what is at stake here."

"No, I'm not completely certain I do."

Middleton looked up. He slowly walked over to the chair and sat down, leaning back and measuring Robert with his watery blue gaze.

"There are those," he said at last, "who would deny the existence of spirits in our world. Though they attend church every Sunday, they go about their daily lives as though the only forces that matter are those they see with their own eyes. From what your brother has told me, you are not one of these. Are you, Mr. Cox?"

Robert frowned at the irony. *I certainly always thought* he *was.*

"No, I suppose not," he said cautiously.

Middleton gave a brief nod. "Millennia ago, men and the gods walked this plane together. It was a symbiotic relationship—man provided the labour necessary to maintain the fertile earth, and the gods provided the knowledge. They taught us many things—woodworking, iron working, medical care, even how to write. It was a golden age, not just of heroes, but when men and gods worked together for the betterment of all. Much of that knowledge has been lost, more's the pity."

Robert realized he was staring and blinked. He took a sip of his tea. It puckered his tongue—he'd forgotten to add sugar—but he took another sip. "You don't say," he managed at last.

He glanced at Hayward to judge the man's reaction to Middleton's claims.

"'And there was war in heaven,'" the colonel said with a small smile, then took a sip of his liquor.

"Pardon?" Was Hayward quoting the Bible?

Middleton smiled. "Not all the gods were happy with the knowledge being shared with humankind. They preferred to keep us oppressed and ignorant, unable to speak up for or defend ourselves."

Robert scooped sugar into his cup and stirred. He flicked his gaze toward Mary, who stood near the door of the room in case something should be required of her. The irony of Middleton's words was not lost on him—but the baron seemed oblivious to the double standard he was embracing.

"Unfortunately," the baron continued, "the oppressors won, and the more benevolent among our benefactors were chained into endless torment. Now all we have left are stories of the heroes of old. Surely you've heard of Prometheus, the Greek name of our most important advocate?"

Robert ignored the question. Of course he'd heard of Prometheus. It was a Greek myth taught to children, the story of the god who brought fire to man, and whom Zeus punished by chaining him to a rock where he'd be doomed to have his liver eaten by an eagle every day. Since he was immortal, it would always grow back. That didn't make it less painful.

"I'm sorry, what does this rather, um, unusual mythology lesson have to do with this stone you've been asking about?"

"Patience, Mr. Cox," Middleton said. "I am coming to it."

He got up and refilled his glass with another two fingers of rum. This time, Hayward declined his offer, but Robert raised his finger to show he'd like a glass of the strong liquid. He tossed it back in a single gulp, and it burned all the way down.

Middleton chuckled. "It is a lot to take in, I know. Your brother must not have shared as much with you as I expected."

I can see why. Gryffyn can't possibly ascribe to this insanity.

Aloud, Robert only said, "He spoke of the heartstone, but not at all about this. Please, continue."

Not that he wanted to hear more, but he surmised it was best to know the full scope of your opponent's madness before deciding on a course of action.

"Not long after the death of the impostor commonly known as Jesus, a priest in the city of Edessa—now in Turkey, though it was part of Rome at the time—discovered an ancient scroll in a temple of the goddess Atargatis that revealed the existence of a key—a key that would unlock the chains around his mistress, and the many other gods whose memories are preserved in religions the world over, but whose powers have been hindered by their captivity. He reinstated a secret order described by the scroll that was dedicated to finding this key and releasing those who would benefit mankind from their prison. Since then, the Order of the Ascension of the Grigori has discovered and kept safe many other secrets—knowledge that helps us toward our goal."

"Pray, tell, sir," said Robert, keeping his voice as steady as he could, "what goal is that?"

Middleton chuckled and moved his arm in an expansive gesture that nearly spilled rum on the carpet. "Why, isn't it obvious? To reinstate the rule of our previous benevolent guardians on Earth."

Robert nodded, not trusting himself to say much. "Ah. Please, continue. Secrets?"

Hayward narrowed his eyes at him. Robert took another sip of tea and forced himself to keep his eyes on the baron.

"Yes," Middleton said, his brow furrowing. "One of which is the stones our benefactors will need in order to materialize in our plane of existence. And that is where you come in."

Robert shook his head. "I still don't understand. You think Miss Bethel is in possession of one of these stones?"

Hayward's lips curved upward, and Middleton leaned forward.

"Yes, a very special one. You see, spirits do not exist on the same plane as we do—when they want to interact with our plane, they must either take on flesh or manipulate the natural world from the spirit one—no easy task. Needless to say, flesh is the preferred option. One way to do this is to inhabit an existing fleshly form, which they must share with the body's host—but only the unprincipled or lowly among them do this, and only on a short-term basis. For those who want to keep possession of their inherent abilities while in the flesh, they must use special heartstones to create a body of their own from the material world."

Robert digested this bit of fantasy. Certainly demon possession was real, but spirits making bodies from stones? He kept a careful expression of neutrality on his face—if there were any useful information to be had from the baron, Robert wouldn't get it by scoffing.

"What is it that makes this *heartstone* of Miss Bethel's so special?"

Middleton gave a knowing smile. "Ah, there are some things you are not yet ready to know, Mr. Cox. First, you must earn your place among us by helping us get what we need. Then you may be ready to learn the deep secrets of the Order."

Robert shook his head. "If Miss Bethel has one of these, I have never seen it. She travels very light, and I doubt such a stone would avoid notice if she wore it. If it is as precious as you say, where else would she keep such a stone but on her person?"

Middleton and Hayward exchanged glances. Robert looked between them in confusion.

Middleton cleared his throat. "It is not *on* her person, but *in* it. You see, the so-called Miss Bethel is much more than she seems. She is a spirit, an agent of the enemy of mankind. The stone we seek is none other than the one she used to create the body she inhabits on this plane."

Robert stared, swallowing hard as he tried to think of a response.

Hayward handed his empty glass to Mary, who had silently appeared at his elbow to take it from him and disappeared with it just as silently. He turned to Robert. "I urge extreme caution, sir. Your golden-eyed companions, Mr. Berian and Miss Bethel, are both agents of the tyrant who banished our lords into eternal torment. They will not give up their treasures easily."

Middleton leaned back, placing his arm along the ornamented wooden back of the sofa. "I'm afraid you will need to take drastic measures to retrieve the stone. Never fear if your conscience bothers you—Miss Bethel is an immortal creature. She will not die, merely be forced to retreat to her own plane until she can find another heartstone. But the opportunity to get our hands on one such as this is too good to pass up. We must acquire it by any means necessary."

Robert's heart froze. What the baron was implying was tantamount to murder! He wanted Robert to *kill* Miss Bethel?

No wonder Gryffyn didn't tell me all this. The stone must be worth a fortune, or he would never have been tempted to throw in his lot with the likes of these.

Robert's brother was a lot of things, and one of them was a very shrewd businessman—a trait he'd inherited from their father. If the reward were tempting enough, even they would have suffered the company of fools in order to gain it. Robert only wished his brother would have warned him what he was getting into before sending him on this wild goose chase.

The seance in Bristol and the beautiful, dreadful golden dragon in the black mirror came to mind, and cold sweat dripped down Robert's back. That creature, who must be one of these Grigori, was the spirit, not Miss

Bethel. Perhaps his brother was doing more than suffer fools—but how could Gryffyn be working with such dark forces?

Another thought chilled Robert. What if the heartstone Gryffyn sought was for the dragon in the mirror? Robert would most certainly not be the instrument of such a creature's physical manifestation. And he wouldn't kill or steal, no matter how valuable the stone may be. But he was getting nervous about the lengths to which these men might go to find their magic stone—their voices held the conviction of zealots, and men like that could be very dangerous indeed. Robert would have to tread carefully.

He leaned forward, resting his elbows on his knees and clasping his hands. "So, if I understand you correctly, you believe the reverend and Miss Bethel are spirits who have made bodies for themselves using these stones?"

Middleton smiled, an unpleasant sight at best. "That's right."

Robert tried to keep his tone measured, but his voice trembled with fear and repressed anger. "What if you're wrong? Say I do as you ask, and I am successful only in becoming a murderer? Gryffyn said he thought my companions were spirits, but he was wrong. And to ask me to murder my friend—the woman who saved my life, no less—is beyond the pale. Why should I ever do such a thing? How do you expect me to believe any of this?"

Middleton stood and walked to a curio cabinet on the wall. He opened it and withdrew a small wooden box with painted embellishments in patterns that looked mystical and old to Robert's eye. Middleton flipped the lid open, then came back and handed the box to Robert.

"Do you recognize this?"

On a bed of black satin lay a small pendant of silver nested rings.

He jumped to his feet. "How did you get this? If you have hurt Miss Bethel—"

"At ease, sir," said Hayward, a hand raised to placate him. "If we could access Miss Bethel, we would not need you, would we?"

Middleton smiled. "I suspected as much at the market. That creature's hidden pendant is one of these." He paused, receiving the confirmation he sought from Robert's tense silence. Middleton gazed at the trinket. "I got this one many years ago at an antiques shop in Italy. It is a chariot of the gods. They are standard issue for lumasi operating on our plane. Do you know it has never tarnished?"

Robert sat down stiffly, still on his guard. "Lumasi?"

Middleton lowered his bulk back to the sofa. "Cherubim. So-called guardian angels. What your friends Berian and Miss Bethel are—a race of winged beasts that come in various forms. Not all of them work for the enemy, but many of them do."

Robert frowned, pushing the baron's explanation aside. He stared at the stone at the centre of the rings. It looked like a simple topaz, though one of astonishing clarity. "Miss Bethel called it a gyroscope."

"Interesting name for it. Most of the time, they're called *chariots*. They function as transportation devices, which is why, I suppose. But trust me, this is like no chariot you have ever seen. In the blink of an eye, it can take you from this spot back to your drawing room in Bristol, or so I understand." He took a sip of his rum and frowned at the device. "Unfortunately, humans are unable to use them. To you and I, it is only an interesting bauble. But in the right hands, and with a chariot of sufficient size, you could move armies across continents in seconds. Can you imagine how that would shift the balance of power? Britain would be unrivalled for the rest of time."

Robert *could* imagine it. His mouth went dry and his thoughts raced. That amount of power—it was unheard of. But it was also completely unrealistic, like something out of a child's storybook or an ancient epic. Spirits he could accept, but this?

"All I see," he said, handing the box back to Middleton, "is a pretty trinket. This proves nothing. And I tire of talking of fairy tales. How much would it take for you to sell me the Negro you brought home from the market? I am prepared to offer you a handsome price."

He tossed the purse Romero had given him for the purpose onto the table between them—it contained much more than Middleton had paid for the man by a fair stretch. Hopefully, it was enough to convince Middleton to give up a slave he valued so highly. One thing that could be said of Romero—he was certainly a generous man.

Middleton watched him for a moment through narrowed eyes and then returned the box to the cabinet. He heaved a sigh.

"Your brother was as difficult to convince, I am told. And I understand. To a rational person, these seem like the ravings of madmen, do they not?"

Robert said nothing, sitting perfectly still, but he tried to work some moisture into his parched mouth. He glanced at his teacup, but it was as empty as the rum tumbler.

Middleton chuckled. "I know it does. No matter. Give this message to your *Miss Bethel*—'We have the key. The woman is lost. The gate will soon be ours.'"

Robert kept his face stony. "And the African?"

Middleton settled his bulk back onto the sofa and smiled. "Is not for sale at this time. I have not finished with him yet, and by the time I do, I suspect he will be of little use to you. His stubbornness will be the death of him."

He gave a hearty laugh, and even the stoic Hayward chuckled a little.

Robert scooped up the purse from the table and stood. "Thank you for your time, Lord Middleton. Colonel Hayward. I will see myself out."

They were still laughing as he stomped out the front door.

32

ALLIANCES

Eric entered the manor through the kitchen door and dipped his head toward Helen, the matronly African cook, who was pounding spices in a stone mortar and pestle on the counter. She acknowledged him with a flick of her gaze. She didn't like him much, and the feeling was mutual. As long as she kept herself to herself, he could care less.

He pushed open the swinging door that led to the dining room, where the table was already laid for dinner. Before he left the room, the voices in the long sitting room beyond stopped him—Middleton, Hayward, and Mr. Robert Cox, if he wasn't mistaken. He paused behind the wall out of sight to listen. He rubbed his shoulder, which had begun to ache from throwing the lash at Winslow's back.

After Cox got up and stalked out the front door in a huff—without the uncouth, laughing Middleton even inviting him to stay for dinner—Eric stepped into the sitting room as though he'd just come in from outside.

"Chapman. Just in time," said Middleton, curtailing his guffaws. "Any news from our stalwart Negro today?"

Eric shook his head. "It is like trying to get blood from a stone, sir. Perhaps we should try the gentler methods my daughter—"

"Your daughter. Pah!" Middleton downed the dregs of his rum and slammed the glass on the table. "If you or your daughter had two wits to rub together, we'd have had that blasted stone or the boy or both already, and we wouldn't be chasing our own tails now. You had him in your grasp for *five years*, and the moment it finally mattered, you let him slip away from you." Middleton narrowed his eyes. "It is almost as though you had done so on purpose. You haven't let your feelings get in the way of your commitment to our cause, have you, Chapman?"

Eric's jaw worked as he swallowed all the things he wanted to say to the baron. Hayward watched with cold disinterest.

"Trust me, sir, my commitment to the cause is, and ever has been, unflagging. There is far too much at stake to let simple affection get in the way of what must come to pass."

And there were too many wheels in motion to stop them now. If only he and Josefine could have found a way other than torturing Winslow to get the information they needed. The Master was getting impatient, and the armada was getting closer. Eric shuddered to think what would happen if he hadn't discovered the exact location of the boy and his sister, and at least one weakness the undines may have, before the ships bearing some of the most influential and military-minded men in the Order arrived. The downed barrier felt too much like a ploy—it would never do for the ships to cross it, only for the undines to raise it and the armada to be trapped on the other side at the mercy of those witches.

Middleton smiled, a wicked, unsettling sort of grin. "Excellent. I believe you. But one can never be too careful, you know."

Eric heard a noise out in the hallway, the sound of quiet feet on stairs. Probably one of the servants.

"Even still," Eric tried again, his voice tight, "I can tell you from long experience that when someone tries to force you to give them what they want, you dig in your heels and vow not to budge a single inch. I see that mettle in Winslow. If you want information from him, you won't get it with the lash."

"You know nothing of these people, and I have been around them my whole life. However, if your enthusiasm is lagging, perhaps David would be a more effective interviewer."

Eric swallowed. The last thing he needed was for these men to start to see him as less than useful. He knew their opinion of him—not of *him*, but of the Roma in general—and what they were capable of. Men like Middleton were why the Roma lived at the fringes of society, which was a curse and a blessing, much like the invisibility it often offered. They accepted the disdain of men like these in order to live their lives free, interacting with the *gorgios* when it served their purpose—trading services for sustenance, creating a niche of usefulness for themselves as tinkers and basket weavers, barrel menders and field labourers. Their usefulness was their shield. Now that Eric had allowed himself to be seen, these men must always see him as eminently useful.

"No, sir," Eric said slowly, "I'll keep doing it your way. I trust you know what you're about."

Middleton gave a peremptory nod. "Good. Right now, I have another task for you and your daughter. We've just had a visit from Mr. Robert Cox."

"Oh?" Eric blinked, feigning surprise.

"It seems he needs some convincing about our cause and the types of creatures we are up against. You and your daughter must go convince him."

Eric nodded, his throat dry. He knew what that meant—another face-to-face meeting with the Master. Assuming he could get Mr. Cox to agree to the meeting. "What about the sphinx guardian?"

Middleton's face darkened and he took a sip of rum.

"He was alone," said Hayward, glancing at the baron.

Eric rubbed his chin. "Was he, now? That makes it easier, it does."

"You must not yet resort to violence," Middleton said. "Cox is not our target. We only want him working with us, not complicating matters."

Eric heard the warning in the baron's voice. *Don't do something that would draw the attention of the authorities, human or otherwise.*

As if he were a child who knew nothing about being clever. He kept his annoyance out of his tone. "Yes, sir. We'll catch up to him. By your leave . . ." He jerked his head toward the door, and Middleton nodded his dismissal.

Eric took the stairs two at a time and half-jogged along the corridor until he reached the small garret room Josefine shared with Mary, the maid. When there was no response to his knock, he went in to collect her obsidian mirror from its hiding place in her pack—they would need it to show Cox what he needed to see.

But Josefine's belongings, and the mirror, were gone.

*

Osaze hung by his tied wrists from the post in the centre of the village, his toes barely touching the ground. Flies had already started to buzz around the sticky fresh blood on his back.

He fought to remain alert. If he lost consciousness, he could die here. He felt it in his bones. But the siren call of blissful escape from the pain was almost as powerful as actual sirensong, and his mind began to drift.

David barked orders to Bussa, and Osaze jerked awake. Bussa unhooked his hands and helped him into their hut, laying him face-down on his mat. The Igbo man leaned close to his ear.

"I will make them, pay, brother," he said in his language. At least, that's what Osaze thought he said. He only understood a few more words in Igbo than when he'd arrived here.

From the door of the hut, David barked something at Bussa, and the other man cast a determined, regretful glance at Osaze before leaving.

David looked down at Osaze with a superior stare and shook his head, clucking under his tongue. "I don't know what the master sees in you. I've never seen such a waste of flesh in my life."

He laughed and left the hut.

Osaze didn't know how much time had passed before soft footsteps padded into the hut. Moments later, something cool touched his flaming flesh. He opened his eyes to find Ifeoluwa squatting beside him, applying poultices to his back. Bunmi was with her, holding the gourd containing the paste and watching him with her big black eyes.

"Rest now. Let your body heal."

"We don't have time for that," came another woman's voice, speaking English. Josefine. "He must come with me at once."

Osaze struggled to lift his head and look at her. She stood at the entrance of the now-cramped hut with her healing bundle in one hand and a large bulky bundle wrapped in a shawl in the other.

Ifeoluwa and Bunmi leapt to their feet.

"He got no strength, miss. He no do no more today."

Josefine's voice was full of determination. "He must, for I fear this may be our last chance to save him."

At this, Osaze roused himself. Grunting, he pushed himself off the mat and sat up. "What save me from?" he said in English.

Josefine came and squatted next to him, unwrapping her bundle. Ifeoluwa peered at its contents in interest. Josefine did the same with what had been applied to Osaze's back, sniffing it and wrinkling her nose.

"What is this?" She pointed at the dried gourd full of dark green paste Bunmi still held.

"Balsam and soldier's bush, for wounds. Barbados Nut, for pain," Ifeoluwa replied.

Josefine nodded. She quickly patted on some mixture of her own. "This will speed healing. Now, you two, help me get him up. We must leave immediately."

Osaze shook his head, trying to clear the fog of pain. Whatever Ifeoluwa had applied seemed to be doing little. "Leave? What you mean?"

Josefine looked at him. "If you stay here, it is only a matter of time before they kill you, whether you tell them what you know or not. There is a man who just left here who wanted to buy you, and The Baron refused. If we hurry, we can catch him on the road. I think he will help us escape."

"'Us'?" Osaze frowned.

Josefine shook her head. "I can no longer stay and be part of this. I am finally choosing a side."

She gave Ifeoluwa and Bunmi a meaningful glance and jerked her chin toward him. They took hold of the upper part of one of Osaze's arms while Josefine held his other one. With their help, he staggered to his feet, though the pain nearly blinded him. He swayed there until Josefine hooked his arm over her shoulders and supported him with her own slender frame, but he could tell his weight nearly toppled her.

Ifeoluwa gave him an earnest stare. "Bunmi go with you. She carry your things. You no send her back. She go where you go now."

Bunmi turned to her mother, her eyes wide. "No, Mama! I will not leave you," she said in Yoruba.

Ifeoluwa took her daughter's hands in hers. "Listen to me, daughter. This is no life for a person to live. If you do not leave me now, with these two, of your own choosing, you will always be the property of others. They will do to you as they see fit. Our master could sell you tomorrow, and we would be separated anyway. We have no say. This way, we have a say. You must try."

Bunmi nodded, her eyes filling with tears, and she threw her arms around her mother. Then she handed Ifeoluwa the gourd and picked up Josefine's bundles. Turning to Josefine and Osaze, she set her jaw.

"I am ready," she said in English.

Josefine nodded. "Fine then. Most of the others are out in the fields, but we must be careful not to be seen by them on our way out to the road. There is a path behind the village that goes around the pond." She looked at Ifeoluwa. "David is in front of your hut."

"I take care of my son." Ifeoluwa set her jaw. "Goodbye, Bunmi. My heart is with you."

With that, she slipped out of the hut.

Osaze swayed and strained to keep from putting all his weight on Josefine, who bowed under his arm. She looked up at him and shook her head.

"I must be crazy," she muttered to herself. "There's no way this is going to work."

At that moment, a man Osaze had never seen before stepped into the hut—a tall man with suntanned skin, black hair, fine clothes, and a rakish swagger. Osaze stiffened. Josefine's body went rigid.

"Perhaps I can be of assistance," the man said, sweeping his hat off his head and bowing with a flourish.

"Who are you?" Josefine demanded.

"I am Eduardo Romero. And I'm going to help you escape."

Osaze stared, riveted by the man's golden eyes.

*

WHEN Robert returned to the place where he'd left Romero, the two horses were still contentedly grazing next to the tree, letting the dangling aerial roots brush over them as they walked. However, Romero himself was nowhere to be seen.

Robert harrumphed, annoyed. "Figures."

Even the rogue's horses seemed determined to show Robert up.

Robert guided his mount around the tree and then a little further afield, but there was no sign of the irritating Spaniard. Perhaps he'd gone to relieve himself. While Robert waited, he swung off the horse and tied it to a sapling, then dug the food out of his pack. He stood there chewing on bread—now a little dried out from several hours in the journey bag—eating dried fruit, and sipping tepid water. Not that he'd wanted to spend the evening with Middleton, but his opinion of the man's hospitality was particularly low at the moment. The baron could have at least invited Robert to stay for tea.

Fifteen minutes later, a scraping, shuffling sound among the trees behind him alerted him to approaching company. He brushed crumbs off his fingers and stood, swallowing his last bite.

Romero came into view, supporting the weight of a tall black man whose arm was slung around his shoulder—the slave from the marketplace. The man had obviously suffered a recent harsh beating, and the criss-cross of stripes and angry exposed flesh on his back made Robert's stomach heave. On Osaze's other side was the gypsy girl, also lending her support. Behind them came a young black girl carrying two tied bundles—one large and one small.

Robert stared at the group, aghast.

"Did you—did you just *steal* Lord Middleton's slave?" he sputtered at Romero.

Romero helped Osaze to the ground in the shade of the tree to rest, and then straightened to look at Robert.

"Is it stealing when the man was stolen into slavery in the first place, or simply freeing a wronged man?"

Romero winked at Robert as though he'd just told a joke. He retrieved his water flask from his horse's saddle and handed it to Osaze. Robert stared at the four of them, eyeing up the gypsy girl, who steadied the flask to help Osaze drink, and the young girl with the bundles, who shifted on her feet under his gaze.

"And what are these two doing here?"

The gypsy girl straightened, looking him in the eye. "We're coming with you."

Robert frowned. "For whom do you work? My brother? Or Middleton?"

The girl shook her head vehemently. "Mr. Gryffyn Cox sent us here, but I *never* worked for him, nor for that despicable baron. I was here because of my father, but now . . ." She drew in a breath. "This is the only way. But they will be coming after us, so we must hurry."

"And her?" Robert indicated the other girl, who must also be a slave.

Romero crossed his arms. "Ah, yes. Well, her mother insisted we bring her. It would seem we were sent to redeem not just one but three people today, uh? The ways of Elyon often surprise me."

Robert glared. "So you did steal one of Middleton's slaves."

Romero shook his head. "I did not steal her. She chose to leave. I simply honoured her choice, uh?"

He grinned and turned to Osaze, speaking to him in his bubbling native tongue, the same language Berian and Miss Bethel had used with Mrs. Urbi. So Romero also knew multiple languages.

It doesn't mean anything. But a lump formed in Robert's throat, Middleton's warnings fresh in his mind.

The man nodded, and Romero helped him to his feet and over to the grey roan, who whickered nervously. After a few words from Romero, the beast stood as steady as a rock.

"Help me get him up," Romero called to Robert.

Robert's shoulders tensed with indecision. While part of him felt obligated to go right back to Middleton and return the escaped slaves, from what he'd seen of the baron, he was inclined to agree with the gypsy girl—the man was despicable, completely without honour. Osaze's horrifying condition after only two days was proof. But could he, in good conscience, take the man's property from him?

Romero narrowed his eyes at him. "Cox, are you coming?"

Blast it.

Robert sighed and stepped toward the two men and the horse. He squatted and cupped his hands for the tall African to step into, and Romero steadied the man's bulk as Osaze swung into the saddle.

Romero turned to the gypsy girl. "Do you know how to ride?"

She smiled. "Of course. What self-respecting Rom does not know how to ride?"

"Good. You ride with Osaze. And you, young lady," he said, turning to the slave girl, "can ride behind me, uh? We'll load your bundles onto the back of Mr. Cox's saddle."

The girl looked fearfully at Robert, but nodded, a determined set to her jaw.

Robert glanced at her with begrudging respect. She looked to be between the ages of thirteen and fifteen. Would he have had the strength to do what she was attempting when he was that age?

He swallowed, the image of his brother's gang tormenting Talwyn and Zale in the woods while he stood by and did nothing answering his question. It also strengthened his resolve. *I won't stand by and do nothing this time.*

"What is your name?" he asked the girl.

"Bunmi, sir," she said quietly.

Robert gave a small smile. "I'm Robert Cox. Let me take those."

He took the bundles and started tying them to the back of his saddle. The gypsy girl came over to help.

"This one has a rather fragile, precious item in it," she said, patting the larger bundle. "Please treat it with care."

Robert looked down at her. In a flash, he saw her as he had in Bristol, in a hooded cloak, summoning a fiery dragon spirit in an obsidian mirror. Was that what the large, flat, disk-like object he could feel in the bundle was?

His heart sped up, but he nodded.

She smiled back. "I'm Josefine Chapman. Pleased to meet you properly at last, Mr. Cox."

"Charmed, I'm sure."

Her brow furrowed at his dry tone, and his face warmed. He turned back to the knots he was tying.

She sidled over to the roan, expertly swinging herself up onto the saddle in front of Osaze, with one leg on each side as a man would sit. Her skirts draped and bunched over the saddle behind her, riding up her legs a little. Robert couldn't help but notice her calves were rather shapely, and his face flamed even more. He kept his gaze firmly on his work until the bundles had been secured, hoping she hadn't noticed his indiscretion.

A few moments later, they were guiding their horses back the way they had come. In the distance, the horizon was obscured by haze coming off the ocean and set aflame by the lowering sun.

Robert directed his horse to walk next to Romero's. Bunmi sat behind the Spaniard, doing her best not to touch him at all, which was nearly impossible. It would have been amusing if the whole scenario weren't so imperilling. Surely Middleton must only be minutes behind them, and when he caught up, Robert had absolutely no idea how he was going to handle the situation.

"One question, Romero," he said.

"Yes?" Romero cocked a brow.

"How did you get these people out of the village undetected? I saw that property. You could see nearly every corner of it from the main house, including into the heart of the slave village."

Romero's smile became secretive.

"I'm afraid you are not ready to know that yet, Mr. Cox. But in time, you will."

Robert blinked. It was so like what Middleton had told him that all the rest of his words dried up. He gave a weak nod and moved his horse to the other side of the road, letting Miss Chapman and Osaze block his view of the Spaniard and his passenger—and hiding their view of himself.

Whatever was happening here, he was determined to get to the bottom of it.

But why was he so afraid of what answers he might find?

33

SIRENIAPOLIS

CALANDRA PEERED THROUGH THE FILMY curtains of the rickshaw at the muscular back of a barrel-chested *doulos* who was hauling her and Judith along the second tier of the Street of Pearls toward the Opal Palace. Sweat tracked through the dust on the *doulos*'s deeply tanned skin. It was early in the day, but the air was already heavy with heat and humidity, and Calandra was thankful Judith had volunteered to dress her hair up to keep it off her neck. The braided crown over an etched silver circlet was a bit fussy for Calandra's tastes—she usually preferred a simple ponytail or braid—but she supposed it was worth reminding those they saw that she, too, was royalty, with a firm claim on the throne, no matter what Narcissa said. She'd drawn the line at wearing a fancy peplos and shawl—it would just be more to take off later before getting into the water of the Mother's Heart Chamber. Instead, she wore a simple short white swimming skirt attached to a tightly woven mint-green hemp belt, and a fitted midriff-baring aquamarine hemp bodice—colours that would complement her tail when she transformed.

Judith wore a belted deep red peplos trimmed in gold embroidery that fell to her knees, her thick black curls bound with a gold circlet and net at the back of her head. Despite her gaunt frame, she was the one who looked like a princess—which didn't bother Calandra at all. She was simply glad her friend had been eager to return to the palace so soon after escaping. "I've been resting for three weeks. I want to *do* something," Judith had said.

Calandra could hardly argue with that.

Despite the heat, their runner marched on with machine-like tenacity and determination. Calandra sighed. One would expect no less of the mind-taken.

Judith eyed the man disapprovingly. "We should Free him."

Calandra shook her head. "Not yet. If we go about Freeing every *doulos* we see, it would only cause chaos and disprove the good faith Narcissa has extended to us. If we can't convince her of our ideas today, when we leave, we can give him the choice to come with us. Besides, between the *douloi* and the sirens, our escort outnumbers us, and we would not be able to Free our runners safely."

On either side of their rickshaw runner, siren singers in vibrant dress-blue tunics and wide tooled dark leather girdles jogged with *deiktes* in hand, their back scabbards empty. The communication stones laced onto their left shoulders below their pins of rank could be used to call for help in an instant.

Narcissa had sent a whole siren pod and a *tapeinos* cluster to greet Calandra and her companions at the harbour when they'd arrived. She'd told Calandra on the commstone yesterday that the escort would ensure their safe travels to the palace, but Calandra was under no illusions. The guard was to make sure she and the others behaved themselves. It rankled to be forced to utilize the runner's services against his will, or rather, *without* his will, but if Calandra had a hope of succeeding in her goals today, she couldn't risk destroying her only chance now. And, despite her misgivings as to who was truly behind her cousin's eyes, she was willing to negotiate with Narcissa *or* Damon if it would serve to provide greater security for their island.

Judith knew this too. Calandra's companion crossed her arms, leaned back against the cushions, and said nothing else.

Calandra pushed aside the curtains to get a good look at their sur-roundings. She'd only been out of the city for three weeks, but seeing it again like this—as an unwelcome guest instead of a rightful resident—made a wave of homesickness wash over her. Judith, who had grown up on the slopes of Mount Melissa near Fire Lake surrounded by farmland and forest, didn't understand her love of the city, with its whitewashed walls, cascading fountains, and bustling activity. They had reached the first tier of the heights, at the top of which perched the Opal Palace on the edge of a sheer drop to the ocean. *Douloi* and servants from the homes on this level and higher moved up and down the street on their way to or from market. Street vendors selling everything from paper lanterns to fresh mangoes to chopped wood moved between homes, and rag pickers from the lower city collected waste the house stewards had put on the street in small wooden carts.

Their rickshaw was first in a procession that also included Rhea and Nelly in a rickshaw behind theirs, and Meg and Airlea in a third at the rear. Airlea had objected to being put at the back with Meg, but Calandra had insisted. The reprieve from the clingy siren and the time spent with her loyal friend was a welcome relief, and the reason she'd insisted Judith be included on this mission in the first place—though, ostensibly, it was because of the girl's knowledge of the palace should something go wrong. But if all went well today, Meg would get her chance to inspect the Heartstone to assess the extent of the damage. Despite her youth, Meg was the most brilliant stone healer besides Calandra among the rebels, and she could hold her own against the island's most prestigious stone healers. Rhea and Nelly had both insisted on coming, and Calandra hadn't argued, much as she resented their supervision. She knew they didn't trust her, but she also knew there was little to be done about it. She hoped their presence would allow her to convince them of what she'd seen in Narcissa, if nothing else.

The procession inched along, and Calandra tapped her fingernails against her thigh while her heart skipped in her chest. Narcissa had agreed to let her and Zale try to heal the Heartstone, but she had given no reason for her sudden change of heart. Calandra couldn't use emotional sensate abilities through a commstone, but her cousin had sounded rattled. Calandra hadn't been the only one among the council who had noticed, but after the arguing died down, the only sensible reason offered was that Narcissa had come to her senses about the barrier. Another large ship had been brought in by the barrier patrol, according to their reports, and already-thin resources were being stretched even further to handle the influx of a couple hundred more Redeemed men. Despite her sudden aspirations to world domination, Narcissa was probably trying to avoid further overburdening of their infrastructure.

At least, that's what Rhea and Nelly and the others thought. Calandra wasn't so sure. Despite the lack of support from her comrades, she couldn't let go of the idea that Narcissa was no longer the one speaking with her own voice. And today, she hoped to have a chance to prove it. However, as far as why Damon would suddenly decide to heal the Heartstone, the only reason she could come up with was that it was a trap.

The council had concurred the whole thing was likely a trap, and had nearly decided against the team going because of it.

"I don't care if it's a trap," Calandra had said. "If there's a chance that I can reach Zale, and that Narcissa will let us access the Heartstone, we have to try. The odds of success are certainly no worse than they were before Summer Solstice, and are a fair sight better if Zale has achieved some measure of control of his powers by now."

They had objected further, but her response had been, "I'm going with a team or I'm going alone. Either way, I'm going."

After that, the only objection had been from the ever-present throbbing between her temples. Which made her think of her mother.

"Judith, you mentioned this morning you found something about the Soulstone. What is it?"

Judith looked away from the scene outside, letting her curtain drop. "Right. With all the preparations for today, I almost forgot." She sat straighter, fiddling with the strap of her small eel-skin dry pouch. "I have not had much time for research, of course, but when I talked to Xeni, she mentioned she had seen the word *Soulstone* in reference to the prison of the Grigori, or the Watchers, as the text called them. It seemed to be separate from wherever Mad undines are kept."

So Calandra had guessed right. "Anything about a connection to the Heartstone?"

"Not that she could think of. But many of the stones are damaged, and she has only been able to review the stones recorded in Atargasian Greek, which are the minority. Most of them are in that other odd script, and Xeni said very little progress has been made on deciphering it. I'll keep searching through other ones, and maybe something will turn up."

"And hopefully someone makes a breakthrough on that script soon." Calandra sighed and leaned back against the chair. "Thank you. Let me know what you find."

Disappointed, she turned toward the curtain, though all she could see through the sheer fabric were indistinct blurry shapes. If she and Zale succeeded in healing the Heartstone today, would she be condemning her mother to an eternity in Tartarus? Or would there still be some way to get her out? There was so much she didn't know about the Heartstone, let alone the Voidstone that took her arm. Damon probably knew, but he'd never once told her anything that wouldn't benefit him in some way. Even if she asked and he answered her questions, she wasn't sure if she could trust his responses.

Shouting filtered through the curtain, and she flicked it aside to see several human women arguing with a priestess in a red chiton standing at the base of the steps of a shrine to Atargatis. Next to the priestess, set up in the shade of a plumeria in full bloom, was a table with several other red-clad women sitting at it, and nearby was a partially full cart loaded with bags of grain with several strapping *douloi* at hand to dispense it. Behind the human women, a long queue of others waited their turn, the line stretching like a string of pearls.

The sirens accompanying their caravan called a halt, then turned to examine the disturbance. One of them went over to talk to the arguing women.

Calandra watched the proceedings, her brow furrowed. Why were these women standing in a bread line? And why were so many of those destitute enough to do so human?

A human woman's hand inserted itself through the window, jamming a rolled piece of rag paper at her. Whomever the hand was attached to stayed behind the window frame so Calandra couldn't see her.

"Here. Take it," said the woman, thrusting the paper at Calandra.

"What—?" Calandra took the paper involuntarily, and the hand disappeared. By the time Calandra stuck her head around the window frame, there was no sign of who had handed her the paper among the milling crowd of onlookers.

Calandra withdrew her head and let the curtain fall.

"What was that about?" Judith asked, peering through the small window slit in the centre of the rickshaw over their shoulders.

"I don't know." Calandra unrolled the paper to see a message written in English.

"Paper?" Judith blinked at the note. "That is uncommon. Why not have a recorder imprint a datastone?"

Calandra scanned the contents, her heart squeezing tighter. "Probably to avoid the possibility of being reported. It's a message from a group that calls themselves the Coalition for Human Freedom. They're demanding that not only the human men of the island be Freed, but the women too."

At Judith's blank stare, she offered Judith the letter.

"What nonsense is this? The women are already Free," Judith said as she took the note.

"Are they, though?"

Calandra pulled back the curtain just as the rickshaw started moving again. Tafrara's words from the other night came back to her. *Not by choice.*

Judith read the note, her face drawing tighter with every word. "At least they are diplomatic about it. Do you think it is safe to go to the meeting they are requesting?"

"No worse than the one we're going to now."

Judith's mouth twisted wryly. "That is the truth." She frowned. "Who do you think this J. W. is in the signature?"

Calandra shrugged. "I don't know. To be honest, I don't know many human women outside the palace. Even most of the ones at Elpida remained behind there, and I've only met them once. What does that say about me?"

Judith gave her a compassionate look. "It says you have had other things to worry about than getting to know every citizen of the city. And, to be fair, you still do. Take this to the council. Someone else can represent you at the meeting."

"They asked for me. And I feel like I owe it to them to show up." Calandra frowned at the note. "Hang onto that for me, will you? Paper and ink don't do well underwater."

Judith carefully rolled up the note and put it in her pouch. "Mother will probably have some suggestions for how to address the concerns of the Coalition. They might even become good allies for us."

"Perhaps." Calandra braced herself against the seat as the rickshaw climbed to the next tier of the city. "But how did we not consider this before? The complaints of the Coalition are requests for personal freedoms every undine takes for granted. How have we allowed the lengths to which we've gone to protect ourselves become such an affront to decency, compassion, and the good of society? Shouldn't a civilization be built from its members willingly bringing their best to the table, not being forced to contribute whatever they have to give?"

Judith chuckled dryly. "It only goes to show how even our empathic kind can miss the truth at the heart of things. If we had been self-aware, our rickshaw would not be being pulled by a man who has been a *doulos* ever since he arrived here."

Calandra gave a snort of acknowledgement. "Indeed."

Besides expressing support for Calandra's declaration of independence for human men, the core of the Coalition's request was that humans brought to the island be permitted to leave. But what could be done about it? Protecting their island was still of the utmost priority—Calandra had taken a risk in sending Osaze and Urbi away, and she wouldn't risk the island further by allowing others to leave who could expose their existence. Even if whomever left didn't know how to direct others back to them, humans were tenacious enough to seek Sirenia out eventually. Unless . . .

She sat straighter and turned to her friend. "Judith, have you ever heard of the song of forgetting?"

Judith frowned. "I do not think so. But it sounds like a bad idea."

"You're not the first to think that. I only know of it because of Tanni. It's the song she was trying to use on Osaze when we were children so he wouldn't report us for being out after curfew, but she accidentally Freed him instead. She found it on one of her Mother's old datastones."

Calandra had wracked her brain for five years to figure out how Tanni had accidentally Freed a boy whose bond she didn't hold, and so had Tanni, who'd been so flustered she didn't even remember what she'd done. Calandra had never discovered the answer—but, fortunately, Thea had, and had revealed it to her not long before she'd died.

"It is the song the Unbinding is based on?" Judith's voice was incredulous.

Calandra nodded. "Kind of, but the opposite—the Unbinding makes you remember yourself instead of forget something else. The song of forgetting is highly regulated though. If someone wants to forget something, they have to apply to the archons and prove beyond doubt the memory is causing more harm than any benefit they gain by retaining it. It's so rarely used, most people don't even know it exists. Unless they're a physic, of course. Or happen to collect old datastones, like Tanni's mother did."

Judith's eyes widened. "If the humans could prove they would be better off without their memories of Sirenia so they could return to their own lands, it might offer a way for them to leave if they wished." She clutched Calandra's arm. "Calandra, you are brilliant. I think it might work."

Calandra harrumphed. "And how many humans do you think will find the cost worthwhile?"

Judith shrugged. "It depends what they have to go back to, I suppose."

"I suppose." Calandra fidgeted with her hem. "I don't feel that brilliant these days. Do you get the feeling the disturbance back there was staged so J. W. could slip us the note? That shouldn't have been necessary. We shouldn't have had to be told about this. We should have known." She paused. "*I* should have known."

Judith shook her head. "You are much too hard on yourself. You are only one person, Calandra. You cannot save the whole world alone. And you don't have to." Judith squeezed her hand. "You've got all of us, remember? There are so many fighting alongside you."

Calandra didn't respond. That was easy for Judith to say—she hadn't been raised with the fate of their people on her shoulders, and she hadn't been the one to fail them so spectacularly. And, as the stab of pain through Calandra's temples reminded her, Judith wouldn't be the one who might have to leave them in the lurch and let the rest of the Free Will Society sort out the mess she would leave behind, just so she wouldn't drag their island to disaster at the bottom of the ocean. The pain today had been almost bearable, but now the throbbing bonds pulsed in the back of her mind like a brazier.

She pushed the curtain aside again, travelling the rest of the journey to the palace bombarded by the silent cacophony of her thoughts.

At last, they climbed the whole length of the Street of Pearls. Two *douloi* in palace livery opened the bronze gates to allow them entry to the palace courtyard. Calandra couldn't see any remaining damage from the earthquake she had caused less than two days before—the stone and plant healers must have been working around the clock. She glanced at the sheltered spot in front of the glass doors leading to the Great Hall. It had only been a little over three weeks ago she'd stood there under the wedding arch, first with Osaze, then her brother. It felt like a lifetime.

The rickshaws stopped in a row in the shade near the walkway leading into the hall. Calandra climbed out of the cart to be greeted by a line of waiting *douloi*, who greeted her with respectful salutes. Letitia, the palace steward, was the sole woman among the waiting servants, and there were no undines at all. Calandra stared at the blank faces of the men. There was Thomas, the man she had sometimes employed as a bodyguard when Osaze was off duty. Narcissa was plainly taunting Calandra. She'd always been particularly good at finding Calandra's weak spots.

The *douloi* helped the women from the rickshaws, or tried. Calandra, knowing the men were only following instructions, grasped the offered hand and allowed herself to be assisted to the pavement. Airlea and Meg had clambered out almost before the vehicle stopped. Rhea refused help, frowning at the assembled men.

Nelly absently accepted the hand out, staring at the white marble and glass face of the palace. "It looks different from the outside. Magnificent."

At the end of the line, Letitia stepped forward. The woman's severe bun of greying black hair made her face look thinner than it would otherwise. She saluted with a deep bow. "Welcome, Princess Calandra. It is a joy to have you home again."

Calandra smiled. "Thank you, steward. It is good to be here." She glanced at the twenty-foot glass windows set in white marble that were as familiar to her as her own hands and as forbidding as a fortress wall. "Though I'm not sure I can call it home."

Letitia's jaw tightened ever so slightly, but she said nothing. Her job had surely been a trial since Adonia's death. The stress of it showed in the bags under her eyes and the tightness of her posture.

"Her . . . her majesty said to bring you to the Observation Chamber." Letitia coughed and cleared her throat.

Calandra nodded, sensing the woman's inner conflict. Whatever Letitia's opinion of Narcissa and her premature claim to the throne, Letitia would be in no position to openly defy her employer, even with something as small as her cousin's preferred styling.

Letitia turned to lead the procession as though Calandra didn't know every step of the way herself, and Calandra and the others fell into place behind her without comment. Even within the palace, the revolution had probably affected the human women, so many of them only trying to survive, like Letitia. No sense making her job more difficult than it already was by standing on the letter of the law. Someone was always watching. Like the army of *douloi* that surrounded them—there were no more effective or honest spies. Their silence made them easy to overlook so you let down your guard, and they would always give a thorough, detailed report to any question they were asked. Which was likely exactly why Narcissa had sent them.

Letitia led the group along the portico on the left side of the vaulted, airy Great Hall, avoiding the dining tables set up in the main area, to the archway near the narrow front of the triangular room. The steps of the raised platform near the archway stood empty but for a few baskets of flowers dotting the back edge and the curved step at the front. Calandra flicked her gaze to the painting of the Heartstone lit up in fiery brilliance that hung high up on the wall, then away. Maybe today was the day they could bring back the Stone's former glory. She hoped so.

They entered the cooler passageway beyond and took a sharp turn toward the core of the building. A short distance down the hall, Letitia stopped in front of the brass-worked wooden door that led to the Observation Room. Two men in *tapeinos* uniforms with blank faces stood at attention on either side of the door. It was open.

Letitia stepped aside and indicated that Calandra and the others should enter. "She is waiting."

Calandra nodded, dipping her head respectfully. "Thank you, Letitia. May the Mother smile on you."

Letitia gave a proper salute, her face stoic, but a ripple of warmth conveyed her gratitude.

Calandra turned toward the chamber, her throat tight. If this were a trap, the small Observation Chamber, with its single, narrow entrance, would be a perfect place to lay it. *Now or never.*

She glanced at her companions. The same trepidation inhabited their faces and leaked through their emotional shields. None of them but her wore a shieldstone this time—they didn't want to reveal that Calandra had found a way to duplicate what her Tear did.

Rhea met her gaze. "Are you ready?"

Calandra clenched her jaw to keep from scowling. "Are you?"

She turned and stepped into the Observation Chamber to meet her fate.

34

THE MEETING

THE OBSERVATION CHAMBER LOOKED EXACTLY as it always had. A long stone table surrounded by comfortable chairs sat in the centre, with a bowl of flowers as a centrepiece—white plumeria blossoms this time instead of water lilies. Mounted along the slightly bowed wall to the right were several storage shelves dotted with tasteful, elegant pottery, some law reference datastones that were kept here for convenience during council meetings, and a couple of stone readers. A few dark lightstones were mounted high on the walls next to sconces holding unlit lamps. The stones hadn't been lit for years, and the lamps weren't needed at this time of day. The room was bathed in the soft glow of light refracting through the floor-to-ceiling glass that made up the curved wall on the left. Through the window, the brilliance of the sunlit Mother's Heart chamber dominated the senses. The upper curve of the Heartstone peeked above the floor level of the Observation Room. From where Calandra stood near the door, the Stone appeared to hover, unconnected to anything.

Narcissa sat at the far end of the table, along with Daskala Amaltheia, the head of the Stone Healing House at the Royal Academy. Despoina Cleo, Zoe, and another siren singer stood at ease behind them, their backs to the wall. Matthew and two *tapeinoi* stood next to the curved wall of shelves, holding *deiktes* erect on the floor in front of them and staring blankly ahead.

When Judith saw Matthew, she tensed.

Calandra glanced at her friend's tight face. "Judith?"

Judith tore her gaze from Matthew and looked at Calandra. "I'm fine."

Calandra nodded.

Narcissa's younger sister, Hebe, with fair, freckled skin and fiery red hair just like their mother's, sat next to Narcissa. Her chin rested on her stacked fists and she stared at the table. When Calandra and the others entered, she sat up and smiled.

"Cali, finally! It's so good to see—"

"Hebe!" Narcissa glared at the younger girl.

Hebe twitched and looked at her sister with a flash of fear, tugging on her long auburn braids. When Narcissa seemed satisfied her sister had been cowed into silence, she turned her glare toward her guests.

Narcissa's becoming more like Adonia all the time.

Behind Narcissa's back, Hebe wrinkled her nose at her sister impudently. Calandra stifled a smile.

And Hebe's as free-spirited as ever.

Narcissa stood, and so did Amaltheia. The healer gave Calandra a deep salute, her mass of black curls poofing out between the ribbons wrapped around the low ponytail that tumbled forward over her shoulder as she bowed. Narcissa gave no gesture of respect of any kind. She templed her fingers on the tabletop.

"Calandra. Right on time."

She seemed neither pleased nor displeased by this fact. Her gaze flicked over Calandra's companions, but she asked for no introductions.

Calandra dipped her chin slightly, an appropriate gesture for the Opal Princess to her own cousin—but maybe more than required to the pretender to the throne, especially one who had just snubbed her.

"Narcissa. Thank you for allowing us to come here today. With your permission, Healer kor'Sybille and I would like to look at the Stone."

Narcissa smiled. "Of course. That's why you're here, after all." She gestured at the glass wall graciously, though even that had an edge of mockery about it.

Calandra studied her cousin's eyes for any hint of a golden flash, but saw nothing. *Was I wrong after all?*

"Thank you." She glanced at Amaltheia. "Healer kor'Herafili, it is good to see you here. Your counsel is appreciated. Would you please join us?"

Amaltheia nodded, smiling nervously, and made her way around the table toward the window behind Meg.

Meg hurried to the glass wall as though she were an excited puppy released from a leash. Calandra remained more sedate as she took the few steps required to reach the window, keeping her gaze and awareness on Narcissa. Airlea moved to stand beside her without waiting for an invitation, evoking a surge of annoyance, which she squelched. The other women in their party moved toward the window to look too.

Her cousin stood and came to stand on Calandra's other side, arms crossed over her chest. Their reflections in the glass showed their family resemblances—and differences. They shared the same fair complexions and fine bone structures, but her own eyes were emerald green to Narcissa's icy green irises. Where Narcissa was taller and athletic, Calandra was short and slender. Narcissa's pale, straight hair was intricately plaited, and she had the red hibiscus of the Opal Princess tucked behind her ear. Calandra's long, thick honey-coloured waves were bound up to keep them out of the way, and she wore no flower. Even still, they both knew which of them had been named the heir to the throne by Adonia, no matter what symbols Narcissa flaunted.

Calandra glanced over her shoulder at the sirens and *tapeinoi*. Despoina Cleo's dark brown face was impassive as she watched every movement being made, her relaxed posture belying the readiness for action Calandra could sense in her like a restrained tiger shark.

Calandra wondered how the *despoina* felt about Narcissa claiming the throne. Perhaps she supported her. Cleo kor'Andromachi had always been a faithful and loyal soldier under Adonia, but that didn't necessarily indicate her current loyalties.

Beside Cleo, Zoe stood at strict attention. As per usual, her emotions betrayed nothing.

Calandra kept her tone casual. "Where is Zale? I thought he would be here."

She extended her awareness to see if there were more people gathering in the hallway outside to trap them in, but sensed only the two guards posted at the door. So far, so good. But there was none of the buzzing resonance she felt whenever her brother was in proximity either.

A burst of annoyance shot from Narcissa.

"He's supposed to be. I expect he'll arrive at any moment." She glanced at the door as though he might appear before her eyes, then frowned. "Perhaps the messenger had a difficult time locating him."

Calandra nodded and turned her attention to the Heartstone. Zale seemed to be as adept at escaping his guards as she had once been. She wondered if he'd found as many places to hide.

"It's been healed," came Meg's wonder-filled voice from her other side. "Not completely. But the core is whole, just like you said. So why isn't it working?"

Meg practically had her nose pressed against the glass. Beyond her, Judith, Rhea, and Nelly peered at the dim sphere with interest and wonder on their faces. The Heartstone was an awe-inspiring sight, even when one had seen it before, as they all had—some of them more recently than others.

"We're not certain," said Amaltheia, her attention on the Stone. "I have inspected it as closely as I dared, and the only thing we can see wrong with it is that single fault which appeared during the, er, Heartstone Healing Ceremony. Everything else has been restored. I've never seen it like this in all my fifty-four years. By all rights, it should be powering not only the barrier, but every other stone on the island."

From this angle, the deep fissure marring the surface of the Heartstone was difficult to see, beginning at the top and disappearing on the far side. But other than that, the spiderweb of cracks and fissures that Calandra remembered was gone. At the centre of the Stone, a strong, red light throbbed like a healthy heartbeat. Calandra closed her eyes. The sense of peace she'd often felt while standing in this room penetrated her. The Spirit was still strong here, stronger than ever.

So why was there no power going to the island?

Meg turned to Narcissa. "May I go take a closer look? See if I can figure out what's going on?"

Narcissa shrugged. "Be my guest. But do take care. Touching the stone can have unintended consequences, so I hear." She gave Calandra a sideways glance.

Calandra clenched her jaw, refusing to acknowledge the subtle jibe. Both times she'd touched it, she'd been overwhelmed with images and emotions and ended up unconscious. How Narcissa had found out, she had no idea.

Amaltheia nodded gravely at her recently raised former pupil. "You are a powerful stone healer, Megara, but even you should not touch the Stone without first being joined in a healer's circle. It is why I didn't inspect it more closely myself. Well, that, and . . ." She glanced at Narcissa, then closed her mouth and turned away as though she'd never intended to say more.

"If you and I were to join, would that be enough for a manual inspection?" Meg asked, turning toward the door.

Amaltheia looked thoughtful. "Perhaps. We can attempt it, anyway." She stopped abruptly and turned toward Narcissa. "With your permission, your majesty?"

There had been an almost imperceptible hesitation before the address, but Calandra had heard it. Apparently, Narcissa's support in the palace was not unwavering.

Narcissa's jaw tightened and she gave a peremptory nod. "We're still waiting for Zale, anyway."

Nelly stepped forward. "Permission to tag along? I have some skill with stone healing. Perhaps I can help."

Calandra raised an eyebrow. This woman never ceased to surprise her.

Narcissa's jaw tightened even more, probably at Nelly's casual lack of address. But she nodded again, and they moved toward the door while Meg made introductions.

Narcissa glanced behind her and flicked her head, and the unknown siren and one of the *taps* followed the two stone healers and antiques merchant as they left the room.

Hebe came and stood beside Calandra—on the opposite side of Narcissa, she noticed, wedging herself between Calandra and Airlea.

"Can you fix it before the ships get here?" Hebe asked, glancing between Calandra and her companions.

Calandra's gaze snapped to her younger cousin, who, at thirteen, was already looking her in the eye. "What ships?" she and Rhea said at the same time Narcissa snapped "Hebe! What did I tell you?"

Hebe glanced at Narcissa, then pressed her lips together, saying no more. Fear oozed from her, and her already-pale complexion went ghostly white beneath her freckles. She returned to her place at the table, sitting erect and anxious.

Calandra exchanged glances with Judith, Airlea, and Rhea.

What has Narcissa done to her? Or what has Damon *done?*

Calandra studied Narcissa. There were still no golden flashes in her eyes, none of the near-Madness she had seen that night in the Archive. She gently tried to delve beyond her cousin's emotional shield, but Narcissa had dramatically improved her ability to create one and she could sense only her surface-level irritation, probably with both Hebe and Zale.

"What is Hebe talking about, Narcissa?" she pressed.

Narcissa glanced at her sister in annoyance, then at Calandra. "There are always ships. We're in the middle of one of the busiest shipping lanes in the Atlantic. Too bad our ancestors couldn't see the future when they chose to settle here. With the barrier out, the sirens have been bringing in a ship every few days."

"Is that what made you change your mind? Is that why you asked me to come back?"

Narcissa drew in a deep breath, and Calandra thought she could sense the sharp tang of fear coming from her cousin.

"Yes. I'm not ready for them. Not yet." Narcissa crossed her arms again and stared morosely at the Heartstone.

Hebe looked sideways at her sister and sucked in her lips as though physically biting back words. What was Narcissa not telling them?

On the far side of the Mother's Heart chamber, directly across from the Observation Chamber window next to the pointed corner of the room, a small rectangular door opened into an access corridor beyond. Healer Amaltheia stood in the opening, highlighted by a wash of light from the luminescent tower chamber. She crouched, and Meg and Nelly became visible behind her. Amaltheia laid her splayed hand on the stone doorsill and closed her eyes. About a handspan below the ledge of the door, a narrow stone walkway slowly extended into the open space of the chamber toward the Heartstone, parallel to the bronze spoke below it. Calandra smiled. It was the perfect security feature, ensuring that only stone healers could access the Stone . . . unless a plant healer were powerful enough to pull water into a column from below, as Calandra had. Few of those living were, and none of those plant healers would want to touch the Heartstone, had they even gained access to the chamber in the first place.

She kept her gaze on the progress with the Stone, but her awareness on Narcissa's every reaction—hers, as well as Hebe's and Cleo's behind her, who had tensed even more at the mention of the ships. Hebe obviously hadn't meant the ships that regularly blundered across their borders now that the barrier was down. *Does Cleo know about them?*

"What do you mean, you're not ready for them?" Calandra asked. "What aren't you ready for? The humans to know about us?"

Despite Narcissa's insane-sounding declaration that she wanted to conquer mankind, perhaps she actually had a methodical plan to do so—it would be foolish to wage a war with the unrest on the island, especially when she hadn't even recaptured all the rogue Freemen causing havoc in the city.

But Narcissa scoffed, then glared at the Heartstone as though it were to blame for all her current problems.

"Like I'd be afraid of humans. No. You know nothing of what I'm dealing with. Why would you?"

Narcissa suddenly seemed very tired. She had black circles beneath her eyes and her rigid posture hid deep exhaustion. Her dismissal wasn't born of the arrogant confidence Calandra would expect from Damon, but an act of desperation from the cousin who would only have asked her for help if she had no other choice. Narcissa had been under as much strain or more than Calandra lately—she, too, had lost people, including her mother and her lover. That was not so different from Calandra's situation. Perhaps the odd behaviour Calandra had heard about was Narcissa handling the pressure and grief in the only way she knew how. Maybe that's what Narcissa was referring to when she said Calandra didn't know what she was dealing with. Typical that she would forget about Calandra's own losses. But that didn't mean Calandra had to do the same.

She bit her lip. "I am sorry about Aunt Adonia and Mari. It's been a difficult time for both of us, I imagine."

Narcissa began to sneer, then stopped, the twist in her lips melting into sadness. From behind her, a spike of emotion came from Hebe at the mention of her mother, but mixed into the sorrow was something else. Calandra closed her eyes and concentrated on it. Definitely fear. Hebe was afraid, and it had something to do with Adonia and Narcissa. But why?

Narcissa turned to Calandra, looking thoughtful, no hint of grief remaining. "When you were talking to your brother, did he mention a woman named Abela who was travelling with him?"

Narcissa's tone was casual, but her sudden shift in mood put Calandra on alert. She frowned.

"Yes," she said cautiously. "Her and a man named Berian. I know little about them, though. Why do you ask?"

"Did he mention anything about her that was unusual?" Narcissa asked.

Unusual? The fact that her brother knew two lumasi, a race the undines had believed to be extinct for centuries, was definitely unusual. But if Narcissa was asking these questions, Zale must not have told her all that, despite whatever befuddlement she'd used on him.

"Why don't you ask Zale? You've spent far more time with him than I have. If you recall, last time we met, he didn't react warmly."

Calandra swallowed her own sudden swell of nervousness. She'd been wondering how he would react today, actually. The fact that he had not yet arrived might be her answer.

Narcissa cleared her throat and smiled, that shark-like smile she'd used in the Archive. "As you can see, Zale is somewhat less than reliable, and has not always been forthcoming. I'd hoped to find out if she poses any kind of threat to him or to this island. Did he mention her carrying a stone device, even something innocuous like, say, a Tear? Or more showy, like a red jewel of some kind? Or even a ring that looks like a wheel?"

Calandra searched her memories, but couldn't come up with anything. She narrowed her eyes and crossed her arms over her chest, glancing at Rhea and Judith. Rhea's jaw was tight, but Judith kept casting furtive glances at Matthew and didn't notice Calandra's questioning look.

"Not that I recall."

Narcissa's eyes narrowed. "Perhaps she had golden eyes, then."

Calandra's breath caught. If Zale hadn't outright told Narcissa about Abela's and Berian's golden eyes, then she was hazarding a guess. But, other than the Free Will Society, Calandra had told no one about golden-eyed Damon, nor Zale's revelation that lumasi, too, have golden eyes—a detail that had never been mentioned in a history stone that Calandra had seen until she'd found her mother's message. So Narcissa could neither be mocking her about her belief in Damon, nor was it likely she would randomly guess that this woman might be of a golden-eyed race.

Unless Zoe had said something. Calandra glanced at the siren, who remained stoic and impassive. No, Zoe was loyal to the FWS.

Calandra swallowed and stared at her cousin's face. There was only one other person she knew that would be aware of a lamassu's golden eyes—Damon.

She opened her mouth to ask what manner of creature had golden eyes to test her theory, but a knock on the door cut her off.

"Come," Narcissa barked.

A dark-skinned siren singer with a powerful build entered, a siren who'd been part of the royal guard for many years—Calliope kor'Renata.

Calliope gave Narcissa, then Calandra, a deep salute. "Greetings, your majesty, your highness."

Narcissa turned and crossed her arms. "Singer kor'Renata, where is your charge? He should have been here fifteen minutes ago."

Calliope swallowed and stood at attention. "We have looked all over the palace and grounds, your majesty. He is nowhere to be found."

"What?" Narcissa lunged a step forward, her rage flaring red and hot and unreasonable.

Hebe jumped, Cleo flexed her hands, and Calliope tensed. Calandra caught her breath. Her cousin's emotions were as unpredictable and volatile as they'd been the other night in the Archive. It wasn't like her.

"He's not allowed to leave the grounds," Narcissa snarled. "He has to be here somewhere. Check again. Check every cupboard and rat hole. Find him."

"Yes, your majesty." Calliope saluted again and turned to leave.

"W—wait," came a small, shaking voice.

Calandra, Narcissa, and the others all turned to face Hebe, whose pale green eyes were round with fear.

"Yes, Hebe?" Narcissa enunciated as though to a much smaller child. Since when had she begun treating her sister with such contempt? Hebe was five years younger than Narcissa, not five years old.

"I—I think I know where he is. I think he went to the city with that siren cadet, Damaris kor'Dione."

Zoe's head snapped toward her. "My sister?" She caught Cleo's glare and shut her mouth, resuming her waiting stance.

"Yes." Hebe drew herself up in her seat, lifting her chin and talking to Calandra. "He's been itching to get out of the city for days, but Narcissa, the big meanie, won't let anyone do anything fun anymore."

Calandra expected Narcissa to react with another outburst of rage at Hebe's cheek. But, instead, she went cold and icy still.

Calandra glanced at her, a shiver running through her. Something about Narcissa had just changed—the set of the lines of her face, the way she held herself. But still, no gold showed in her green irises.

Narcissa glanced at Zoe, her expression and emotions unreadable, then turned to Calliope with her arms crossed over her chest.

"Singer kor'Renata, take these two *taps* and go to Steadfast House to search for Zale and Damaris and bring them here. Do it quickly. I want to get this over with."

Hebe swallowed. "I, um, have something else that might help."

She stuck her fingers behind her woven blue hemp girdle and withdrew a small roll of paper that had become squished and wrinkled in its hiding place. Narcissa jerked her head at Zoe, who took it from Hebe and handed it to the princess. Narcissa broke the mostly-crumbled red wax seal and unrolled the note. As she read, her face darkened by the word.

Calandra took the opportunity to try delving her cousin once more. But this time, when she extended her awareness toward Narcissa, there was no emotional shield. She drew in a sharp gasp. In her mind's eye was a serpentine golden-red dragon with red eyes, roaring in frustration and anger. And Narcissa's eyes were no longer icy green—they burned gold.

Damon!

Calandra glanced at Rhea and Judith to see if they had noticed. They were tense, but no more so than when Narcissa had first exploded with anger. Just like at the Voidstone, Calandra seemed to be the only one who could see him.

"That impatient, foolhardy . . ." Narcissa—or Damon—flung the note aside and marched to the commstone on the wall. Pressing her finger against it to open the channel to the room beyond, she leaned in close, looking through the glass at the three women standing over the Heartstone in the Mother's Heart.

"Come back. You're done. You won't be healing anything today."

The three women looked up from their inspection in confusion and dismay, but whatever they said wasn't audible—Narcissa had cut the connection on the commstone.

Calandra stepped forward. "What is it? What did the note say?"

Rhea scooped up the note and looked it over. "His written Greek is poor, but it says that Zale has gone after your mother. He's gone to Tartarus."

"Chains of Prometheus," Calandra breathed.

35

THE GOLDEN EYES

Calandra snatched Zale's note from Rhea and stared at it in disbelief.

"He's heading to the Voidstone. How? Never mind." She shook her head. That was hardly important right now, and she believed her brother fully capable of doing whatever he set his mind to. She turned to Hebe. "When did Zale give you the note?"

Hebe glanced nervously at Narcissa, whose icy exterior hadn't changed, then at Calandra.

"A few hours ago. He said to give it to 'Cissa this afternoon. I had no idea he wasn't coming back!" She looked truly distraught. "He was so nice—way nicer than I thought a boy would be. I hope he's okay."

Narcissa's jaw worked as she stared at her sister.

Calandra glanced from Narcissa to Hebe. "Only a few hours? Good. We might have time to catch up to him before it's too late. Rhea, radio Nick that we'll be there shortly, but we'll be heading to Atlantis."

Rhea opened her mouth, but Calandra raised an authoritative hand. "Just do it. We don't have time to argue. If he goes into the Underworld, we don't have a way to get him out again. Remember the cost."

She turned her extended hand around to remind those present of the price she had paid to be freed from the Voidstone—and she had only inserted one body part into its sphere.

Rhea nodded and moved to the side of the room, holding the comm-stone on her wristband to her mouth to call Nick, who was waiting inside her submersible in the bay.

Narcissa narrowed her eyes—now their usual cool green—at Hebe.

"You went against my explicit orders. My own sister. You made me look a fool in front of the whole nation."

Hebe scowled and crossed her arms. "You've been doing that pretty well on your own. I thought I was boy-crazy, but I give you the trophy, sis. How many *douloi* have you sent for this week? Three? Or is it thirteen? It's so hard to keep track. You've become worse than Mama was."

Judith glanced at Matthew. "So the rumours are true. You bed him, but you do not care for him."

Narcissa whirled and glared. "Who gave you permission to speak, lady's maid?"

Calandra stepped to the side, inserting her body between Narcissa and Judith.

"She is not my lady's maid any longer, Narcissa, and she is a citizen of Sirenia. Matthew was her friend. It is natural she should feel protective. Recall that our people believe all should have a voice."

Narcissa scoffed. "That might be written in a dusty Tear somewhere, but who actually believes it? If all speak, who decides? Equality is an illusion we feed the masses to keep them sedated."

This declaration caused uncomfortable stirrings among Hebe and the sirens. Airlea stepped forward as though to insert herself between Calandra and Narcissa. Calandra scowled at her and she halted.

Narcissa continued. "You and I both know, *dear cousin*, that without a firm hand and guidelines to follow, the world devolves into chaos. Just look what your little rebellion has already become. Look at the unrest in the streets. Do you know how many citizens of Sirenia have died since your speech last month? Fourteen. Fourteen sirens and citizens have died because of the Wildmen you unleashed upon us. And we have yet to catch them all."

Calandra exchanged glances with her companions and cleared her throat.

"While I'm not sad that those men were Freed, most of those *Wildmen*, as you call them, were Freed when your mother died. She had taken far too many bonds, and it is what drove her insane. Do you not see that?"

Narcissa snorted in contempt, no hint of grief at the mention of her mother's death this time. Her voice was as hard as iron, barely recognizable as her own.

"Adoni—Mother made her own bed, and now she's lying in it. But your so-called peaceful men are still attacking women in their beds and killing for food."

Calandra swallowed, guilt gnawing at her stomach. Attacking women in their beds? That seemed unlikely. But after seeing the desperate look on Cain's face, she'd believe him and his lot capable of killing for food.

She glared at Narcissa. "What do you expect when you hunt them and chain them like wild dogs, only to return them to their original cage once you catch them? How would you react if you knew compliance meant becoming one of the mind-taken?" Her voice softened. "But that's your plan, isn't it, Damon? To sow anger against the humans so no one questions why they must be controlled. You would control the whole world, if you could find a way. Is that why you wanted me to heal the Heartstone for you? Not to protect the island, but so you could somehow use its power to conquer the Earth?"

The room was silent. Rhea had finished her call, and she and Judith looked back and forth between Calandra and Narcissa. Airlea rested her hand on her belt knife and watched Narcissa like a lionfish ready to spring. Zoe shifted her grip on her *deiktis*, and Cleo tensed and took a step toward the two clashing royals.

Narcissa raised a hand at the *despoina* to stop her progress while staring down at Calandra. Her lips curved in a wicked smile, and her irises flared gold once more.

"The time for jealousy and regret is past, little lark. The wheels are set in motion and you can do nothing to stop them, whether or not you heal the Heartstone. You could have ruled with me, but instead, you have set your will against me."

Calandra's breath caught. "It *is* you."

Seeing the spirit who had manipulated and dominated her for five years, she was filled with a mix of rage and terror. She glanced around to see how the others were reacting to this admission, but everyone else in the room was strangely still, as though time had been frozen for everyone but Calandra and the entity inhabiting Narcissa's body.

Damon nodded toward the others. "They can't hear us. This conversation is only for you and me."

"Judith? Rhea?" Calandra looked at the two women, but they didn't react or even blink. Airlea stood beside her, her mouth open as if to speak, but no sound came from her unmoving lips.

Damon smirked. "You never did like taking my word for anything. It's one of the qualities I like about you. Or I would, if you weren't such a thorn in my side all the time."

Calandra scowled, her fear pushed aside by outrage. "What have you done with Narcissa? Is she dead?"

Calandra focused on the presence overlaying Narcissa's mind, trying to find a hint of her cousin beneath. She probed gently, hoping to escape notice.

"Get out of my head, Calandra," Damon snarled.

Her awareness snapped back like a taut rope being severed. She recoiled, stepping back and bumping the skin of whatever bubble Damon had trapped them in.

"It will do you no good, anyway," Damon said. "Narcissa has made me quite at home. Your power has no ability to budge what a willing host has accepted. Her choice overrules yours."

"So she's alive, then?"

That shark smile appeared on Narcissa's lips, and now Calandra knew why it had seemed so familiar. She had seen the same smile on Damon's face many times in her dreams.

"Of course she's alive. Narcissa has simply tasted Redemption."

A chill ran through Calandra. "I don't believe Narcissa would have willingly accepted possession."

Damon's smile grew sly. "Oh, she didn't say the words, but she didn't have to. The darkness in her heart opened the door. Her pride and selfishness welcomed me in."

Calandra could see his point. He and Narcissa were a lot alike. Still, she remembered the feeling of being paralyzed and pushed to the edges of her own mind as he'd poured into her from the Voidstone, and her heart sped up. She wouldn't abandon Narcissa to that fate if she could help it.

Calandra glared at him, trying to look intimidating. "Get out of my cousin, Damon."

"Or you'll do what?"

Calandra held up her hands toward him, preparing to send a bolt of spirit into Narcissa. If she could cause a disruption and loosen his grip on her, maybe she could grasp on to Damon and pull him from Narcissa's body. Adonia had killed with spirit without even a touch. There must be a way to expel a spirit who didn't belong.

But Damon laughed. "By all means, if you wish your cousin dead, go ahead. You will not harm me. I am eternal—I will simply find a new body to inhabit."

Frustrated, Calandra dropped her hands. She was dealing with powers beyond her ken, and he knew it.

"And what darkness did you find in my brother's heart?" She glared. "You're responsible for his reaction to me, are you not?"

Damon crossed Narcissa's arms. "Everyone has something they want. Something they'll pay any price to get. That is often their downfall."

"As your ambition will be yours." She glanced at the Heartstone. "Why did you bring me here?"

Damon scowled. "I told you the truth—I wanted you and your brother to heal the Heartstone and raise the barrier."

Calandra blinked. "Why? And why the change of heart? You told me the other night—"

"I have my reasons." Damon looked at the Heartstone, then the others in the room. "You undines. So unruly. Zale's desires drove him to repel me at last, so it seems, at the least convenient moment."

There were all kinds of reasons why Damon might see an advantage to raising the barrier—not least of which would be getting the archons' support for his host persona, Narcissa, to claim the throne. That didn't matter now. What did matter was that every second she spent talking to him, her brother got closer and closer to doing something irreversibly rash.

Something Damon had driven him to.

"Why do you waste time by holding me here? If you want us to catch him, you need to let me go." Calandra extended her awareness to the edges of the pocket of reality that held them, trying to discern what Damon had done. She watched him carefully to see if he noticed her psychic explorations.

"There is a way out, you know," said Damon.

Calandra drew in a sharp breath. Had he figured out what she was doing already? She played dumb. "For Narcissa?"

He snorted in contempt. "No. For Zale, from the Underworld. Unlike humans, undines can go into Hades and survive, but to come out again, they must unlock the gate. To do that, they need a key. There used to be one here on Sirenia in the care of the undines. If only your brother had been a little more patient, I could have found it before he left."

Calandra narrowed her eyes, still mentally poking at the wall of the bubble that held them. Was this key what Narcissa—Damon—had been searching for?

"Why would you help him?"

Damon flicked his gaze at the Heartstone. "Let us say our interests coincide." He snorted. "It seems you and Zale truly are this island's only hope. Ironic, isn't it?"

Calandra sensed an opportunity and decided to take a risk. "But if we heal the Heartstone and restore the barrier, won't we also be trapping your companions in the Soulstone forever?" she bluffed.

By the sharpening of Damon's gaze, she must have hit a nerve. "And your mother." He stepped toward her, her cousin's face looming above her. "But apparently that's a risk we are both willing to take."

Calandra bit her lip. If he could be believed, there was some kind of connection between the Soulstone and the Heartstone. How could she get him to tell her more?

"Surely there's a way to heal the Heartstone *and* free someone from the Abyss," she said, following her gut.

He smiled. "Oh, there is. But, again, you need the key. Which, despite my best efforts, continues to elude me."

The hair on Calandra's arms stood on end. Was he telling the truth about the key? Not everything Damon said was a lie. He'd been honest about needing a male and female undine to heal the Heartstone—other than that deep crack, it appeared she and Zale had almost succeeded in restoring the Stone to wholeness. Of course, at the time he'd been trying to convince her to take him as her consort and use his ability with fire in conjunction with hers so he could escape his prison, but—

Damon could use fire! That's why Narcissa had begun to wield the element. It wasn't her ability, it was his. Maybe the reason Calandra had seen the fire while tuned in to the Matrix was because he wasn't an undine—it made sense his abilities would be different from hers.

Calandra crossed her arms. "Why can't *you* heal the Heartstone? For what remains, surely your abilities combined with someone like Amaltheia or Meg would be sufficient to—"

"Do you think it is easy for me to admit that I can't do this without you? That I haven't exhausted all other options first?" Damon snapped, and scowled. He took a breath. "If I could have done this another way, be assured, I would have. It must be Zale."

Calandra pressed her lips together.

"Then you best release me from whatever plane you've put us in and let me go after him. Or do you intend to join me at the Voidstone as well?"

An inexplicable spike of fear flashed from the dragon possessing her cousin, but he only waved dismissively, an aloof expression on his face.

"No need. I will send sirens to accompany you. Quite handy that the most powerful woman on this island has welcomed me so enthusiastically, wouldn't you agree? Oh, don't pout, little lark. You had your chance. If you're very good, perhaps we'll let you live here with us when we establish our New Order. A rare bird like you deserves a prettier cage than what I have in mind for most of this plane's inhabitants."

Something about the way Damon talked about a New Order made Calandra shiver again, but she didn't have time to consider it. What he said about the keys gave her hope—that she could go in to the Underworld and free her mother, allowing Delphine to return while Calandra remained behind, out of harm's way. Her plan to save her island and her mother could work. But before she went after Delphine, she needed to raise the barrier. And for that, she needed Zale.

But what if she were too late to intercept Zale? She needed to get out of here, now.

Someone outside was trying to reach through the distortion in reality. She pushed her mind in that direction. If they could touch . . .

"So what do these keys look like?"

Damon frowned. "The key to the Abyss is a crystal, an amethyst with perfectly formed terminals on both ends."

Calandra stared at him. She thought of the crystal-studded cavern below the palace. "A specific amethyst? Or will any fully formed amethyst work?"

Damon cocked his head. "Why? Have you seen one like I speak of?"

Calandra frowned. Surely Damon, who must have taken possession of Narcissa the day of the Heartstone healing ceremony, had been to the cavern? How would the subterranean room have escaped his notice as the only escape route Calandra and her people could have used that day? And if it had, why was the passage to it now so well-guarded?

If neither Narcissa nor Damon knew of the cavern, Calandra didn't want to alert them.

"I'm not sure. How big is it?"

"I am not certain, to be honest." He frowned. "The other key you need is for the Soulstone. It would probably be shaped like an eight-spoked wheel with a stone of some kind in the centre. The queen of the undines is supposed to carry one that opens not only the Soulstone, but the Voidstone as well."

Calandra shook her head. "I've never seen anything like that. Is there another way to open these gates?"

Damon gave a wicked grin. "Destroy the Heartstone. Though that's counter to both our desires at the moment."

Calandra frowned. "I mean a different way."

"I suppose you and your brother could destroy the Soulstone instead," Damon said thoughtfully.

"Wouldn't that also destroy its inhabitants?"

"The Soulstone is a gateway, much like the Voidstone and the Heartstone in some ways. Destroying it would only unlock the prison, not hurt those it encloses."

So the Soulstone was a portal, not the actual prison. But she'd never heard the Heartstone called a gateway before. "But destroying the Soulstone would release a cloud of Grigori on the world. Or the Underworld. And it also wouldn't open the gate back to our plane." She paused, hoping Damon might betray a secret method of getting out of the Underworld he'd been withholding.

"True," he said. "But unless we can find the key, there is no other way."

Calandra boldly met his stare. "Then how did you get out?"

He gave a knowing smile and said nothing, but before she could press him on it, the world sprang back to life. Airlea stood panting, staring at both Calandra and Narcissa as though she'd run a mile. Meg, Amaltheia, and Nelly hurried into the room followed by their escort, demanding an explanation for their cancelled examination of the Heartstone.

Airlea jumped between Calandra and Narcissa, holding up her *deiktis* defensively against the taller girl. "You will not have her, you monster!"

Cleo lunged forward to intercept her, with Zoe only a step behind. Hebe sprang from her seat, wide-eyed.

"Peace, Airlea!" Calandra shouted, grabbing the siren's arm. "We're not here to fight."

Airlea whirled to face her, her relief palpable. "Your highness. You're all right!"

Calandra gave Airlea a tight smile. "I'm fine. Now let's go save my brother."

Damon grabbed her arm. "If he has gone beyond the veil, you must return and help me find the key. Believe me when I say that without it, you will be as trapped as your mother is."

Calandra glanced at Narcissa's hand and stared into the golden irises she alone could see. She held up her regrown hand.

"Trust me. Thanks to you, I'm fully aware of the dangers. Now unhand me."

Damon nodded and let her go.

Zoe stepped forward. "Your majesty, may I have permission to join them? My sister has apparently joined this foolhardy boy."

Damon gave a sharp nod. "Go. Despoina kor'Andromachi, take a full pod and go too. Do not, under any circumstances, touch the Voidstone."

Both sirens saluted crisply and fell into place with Calandra and their party.

As they rode down the mountain to the bay, Calandra fingered the small amethyst she always kept in her belt pouch. It came from the crystal-studded cavern below the palace, a reminder of Osaze and the time they'd spent there when Calandra had taught him to swim. She didn't know if it would be enough to break into the Abyss. But surely, if she could find a way to make a shieldstone, she could duplicate a key made of amethyst.

But what about the other key? The one she'd need to get her mother out? Could she recreate that, too, when she didn't even know how it worked?

She hoped it didn't become necessary to find out. If she could get to Zale before he went through the Voidstone, she could tell him about the keys and the Soulstone and what they'd learned about the Heartstone. She could convince him to come back with her to restore the barrier before they went after their mother. Maybe she could even convince Damon to allow her safe passage around the island to Release the men whose bonds continually branded her mind before her mental health declined any further—or, if she could convince the archons it was Damon, not Narcissa, behind her cousin's eyes, she could remove him from the seat of power and begin ridding herself of the bonds immediately.

But if they were too late . . .

She clutched her Tear and breathed deeply, trying to still her racing heart and convince herself the sense of doom that oppressed her was a product of her own fears and the constant throbbing in her head. Maybe she had been destined for this journey to the Abyss all along. For if she carried the burning bonds much longer, she may no longer be able to live safely among her kind. And then there would only be one safe place for her to be—the Abyss that harboured Mad undines from throughout their history.

No, I'm not ready!

She bit her lip, praying with every breath they would reach Atlantis in time to bring her brother back, terrified she'd have to make a decision she wasn't prepared to make.

"Are you all right, Calandra?" Judith asked with a concerned look.

Calandra gave her a tight-lipped smile, trying to ignore the pounding in her temples. "Just worried about my brother, is all."

"We will find him," Judith said reassuringly. She squeezed Calandra's hand. "And we'll figure out what to do about Damon too."

"So you believe me?" Hope sparked.

Judith nodded. "I do not know what happened in there, but I know something did. That was not Narcissa. I will back you up with the council—if Aunt Rhea and Nelly need any more convincing. They had to have seen something."

Gratitude rushed through Calandra. Someone believed her. "We have to find a way to free Narcissa. No one deserves that."

Judith stared at the floor. "And Matthew."

"And Matthew," Calandra agreed. "I'm so sorry, that must have been hard to see."

Judith nodded, keeping her gaze downcast.

Calandra regarded her friend, red pain clouding the edges of her vision. If Judith believed her about Damon, others might too. Which meant there was a chance something could be done about him—that she didn't have to work out the solution alone. But how could the council help when most of them didn't even believe possession was real, let alone understand it? No, she couldn't count on them. And she couldn't shake the feeling she was responsible for Damon being here in the first place. The look in his eyes when she'd asked him how he'd escaped haunted her. *I brought him here. I have to find a way to be rid of him.*

The answers lay beyond the Voidstone, she could feel it. But what good would it do to find them if she couldn't return to act on them?

Trust me, came the voice. But instead of peace, the idea evoked fear.

Why? she asked the Spirit she could barely feel.

I'll go with you. You won't be alone.

She felt alone. Even with Judith right beside her, she felt alone. But for some reason, she *did* trust that the Spirit would help her and be with her, no matter how unprepared she might be.

That didn't make the thought of facing the Voidstone less terrifying.

A sudden urgency to explain herself came over her. If she ended up going to the Underworld today, never to return, she wanted someone to know her plan, to know why she'd done it—that she hadn't abandoned everyone. That she was fulfilling her duty the only way she knew how. Even if it meant she could never come back home.

"Judith, I need to tell you something." The words choked her, and she paused.

"Yes?" Judith glanced up, her brow furrowed.

"Damon told me about some keys that let undines cross through the

Voidstone. I don't know if he was telling the truth, but he said it's the only way to let someone on the other side return."

"We will get there before Zale," Judith said. "You won't have to worry about any key. And Damon was probably lying anyway, just like he did about your Tear, remember?"

How could Calandra forget?

"Even if we arrive at Atlantis before Zale, there's still my mother to consider," she said.

Judith nodded. "All right. If the keys exist, we will find them." She patted the hand she held with her other one. "Don't worry, Calandra. We will work it out. On the way back to the rickshaws, Meg told me she is sure the Heartstone can be fixed. It is not the Stone, but something to do with one of the spokes that is the issue. You and Zale did it. So relax. We will find a way to get the barrier up. It will just take time."

Calandra blinked with relief. The Heartstone wasn't the issue? Even still, every day the barrier was down increased the danger to her people, and the thought of the ships Hebe had mentioned niggled at her. No matter what Damon said, Hebe knew something—and she was terrified of her sister.

No, she was terrified of Damon.

"We need to follow up on what Hebe said about the ships. And maybe we should get her out of the palace for now."

Judith nodded, frowning. "I agree."

Pain and worry built inside Calandra like a volcano ready to explode. *No. Not now. I need to find my brother!* She closed her eyes and breathed until the pain had receded to a manageable level, but the pressure had only been reduced, not eradicated. What would have happened if she hadn't been able to prevent another attack? Here, on this busy street in Sirenia-polis?

"There's one more thing." Calandra's terror was probably washing over Judith in waves through their touch. She pulled her hand away and put it in her lap. *I will not cry. I will NOT!*

"Calandra, you are scaring me." Judith studied Calandra's face.

Calandra gave a tight smile. She couldn't do it. She couldn't tell Judith that, keys or no, Zale's choices notwithstanding, today could be the day she exiled herself to the Abyss. "I've decided you're right. I'm doing too much on my own. Could you talk to the council about the Coalition's meeting? I have enough on my plate already."

Judith studied her. "Of course." But she didn't look convinced.

"Thank you. You're a good friend."

Judith laughed nervously. "That is hardly a test of friendship. Wrangling your hair into that up-do just so you could ruin it by swimming, now that is a different story."

Calandra forced a laugh, then turned toward the rickshaw curtain, moving it aside so she could watch the city she loved pass her by.

It might be the last time she ever did.

36

DISCOVERIES

The trip to Atlantis passed in tense silence. Despoina Cleo had sent her pod of sirens in a crown submersible but had insisted on accompanying Calandra and the others in the *Luz de Paz*. At Calandra's suggestion, Zoe had come on board their ship too.

Nick had been less than impressed—her cover as a salvage operator for any future missions was completely blown. However, it was this or abandon hope of intercepting Zale before he got to the Voidstone, and that was not an option. Even if Calandra wouldn't be returning today, Zale must.

Calandra sat in the passenger cabin between Meg and Airlea and anxiously fiddled with her Tear pendant. She kept her senses on high alert for either Zale's presence or a hint of betrayal on the part of Cleo or her siren pod, whom she could dimly sense in the other sub. Through the porthole across from her, Calandra could see the blue sky meeting the dark blue ocean beyond—as a state-sanctioned trip, they'd been able to stay on the ocean's surface for faster travel without fear of being stopped by the guard. The view of the horizon helped with the sense of claustrophobia in the tight quarters, but not much.

The people in the passenger cabin with her were all in various states of alertness, or lack thereof. Next to Cleo, Nelly had laid her head back and closed her eyes—how she could sleep at a time like this, Calandra had no idea. But, other than Nelly's, the emotions in the room were tight enough to pluck a tune on.

For her part, Calandra couldn't stop thinking of the Voidstone that awaited her—the Voidstone that had taken her hand. The place where the Mad undines were sent. After the constant pain she'd been enduring for

302

only a few weeks, she wondered if, by the time those undines were exiled, the escape to the oblivion beyond were a blessing instead of a curse.

Finally, she could take the tension no longer.

"I'm going above." Calandra stood.

Airlea leapt to her feet.

"Alone." Calandra gave her a pointed glare.

Airlea hesitated and then nodded, obviously not happy about it. But she didn't sit down again. Instead, she came to stand next to the door of the passenger cabin.

Calandra went to the forward cabin, where Rhea and Judith were standing behind Nick to allow more room in the back for the others.

Calandra leaned into the room, holding the door frame on both sides for support. "We'll be on the surface for a while yet, won't we?"

Nick glanced at her instruments. "A good fifteen minutes yet."

"Good. I'm going above for some air."

Judith studied her. "Do you want some company?"

"No, thanks. I just need to think."

Judith gave her an understanding nod, then returned to looking out the glass.

Calandra scrambled up the ladder. Why couldn't Airlea pick up on Calandra's cues that easily? For a siren, she was surprisingly unaware of others' emotional states. Even though Calandra's emotions were shielded, it's not like she'd made her feelings about the young woman a secret or anything.

Leaning against the brass rail of the deck above the front cabin, she closed her eyes and relished the salt spray of the ocean misting her face, thankful her hair was contained so it couldn't blow around in the wind. The last time she'd stood here like this, Osaze had been with her and she'd drawn comfort from his gentle strength. This time, she had to draw on her own strength. A twinge of loneliness made her heart stutter. She wiped away a tear and stared at the blue horizon.

Someone started climbing the ladder, and Calandra's melancholy turned into annoyance. *She can't leave me alone for two minutes, can she?*

"I would speak to you, your highness."

Calandra whirled. It was not Airlea standing behind her, but Cleo, her face full of determination. Calandra was instantly on guard, grateful for the Tear hiding her emotions. However, she sensed no malice, only caution, from the *despoina*.

"Of course, *despoina*. I have always considered your counsel wise.

Please, join me."

Cleo came to stand at the rail. She said nothing for several moments, and Calandra sensed an inner struggle.

"You may speak freely, *despoina*."

Cleo nodded. "Your abilities must have become quite strong to see beyond my emotional shield, your highness."

Calandra turned to face her, keeping one hand on the rail. "It wouldn't take an empath to surmise your loyalties are being torn during these turbulent times. Know that I don't begrudge you for serving my cousin under the circumstances."

A shot of relief burst from Cleo, and Calandra was hit by a flash of clarity.

"You're doing it to protect the people, aren't you?"

Cleo nodded, her forest green eyes clouding even darker. "Narcissa has become unhinged since her mother's death. I assume you've heard the rumours?"

"Indeed. It's all anyone talks about." Calandra studied the siren. Would Cleo believe the truth if Calandra told her? Best to proceed with caution. "Why do you bring this to me?"

Cleo reached inside her belt pouch and withdrew a delicate silver quaternaria pendant hanging from a fine silver chain. The hammered silver wire was twisted into a four-pointed knot like a compass rose bound together with a circle and polished to a high shine. In the centre of the pendant was mounted a round amethyst. *The queen's tiara!*

"I believe she's looking for this," Cleo said, handing the pendant to Calandra.

Holding the stone felt like holding a tiny bead of spirit. She stared at the amethyst, watching the sunlight play in its depths. Could this be the key? But delving it revealed nothing unusual about it other than the concentration of spirit, which seemed inherent to its structure, not infused to alter its composition such as the Voidstone key would surely be. She pressed her lips together in disappointment.

"How did you come by this?"

"I was the first to find Adonia's body and took it from her. Despite what Narcissa has told the people, I do not believe her story that Thea and Adonia killed each other. There were far too many inconsistencies in how the queen died. I believe she is lying, though it is exceedingly difficult to tell when she is being false these days. There is something different about her, something unexplained by the ravages of grief. At any rate, I have not felt . . . comfortable revealing to Narcissa or the council that I have the quaternaria in my possession. If she had this, what little keeping her from claiming the throne outright, despite the council's fin-dragging, would be gone."

Calandra's heart quickened. "Be wary of her, *despoina*. She's no longer herself. There are other powers at play here."

Cleo studied her. "What do you know?"

"What have you sensed?"

Cleo gazed at the horizon. "There are times . . . There are times when it feels as though the princess is a completely different person."

Calandra drew a breath. *Time to take the plunge.* After all, what was there to lose?

"I know this will be difficult to understand, but Narcissa has been possessed by an ancient dragon spirit who goes by the name of Damon. His sole ambition is power, and Narcissa is helping him get it, however inadvertently. I believe she is alive, but she may not be aware of what he is using her body to do. And I am not aware of a way to rid her of her possessor."

Calandra swallowed. What would Cleo say to that? Would she scoff, as her fellow rebels on the council had done?

But Cleo only nodded. "I believe you. What I have sensed confirms it."

Calandra drew a deep breath. Just like that?

"Despoina Cleo, there is a place for you in the Free Will Society if it should become too dangerous in the palace."

The *despoina* placed her hands on the rail and looked out toward the horizon. "If I leave, who will protect the *tsirakis* at the Academy? Or the staff or other members of the royal household? Who will keep watch on this being you describe and mitigate the damage it is doing in Narcissa's name?"

She was right. The *despoina* turned to face Calandra, her expression full of resolve.

"No, your highness," Cleo said. "This island needs you to come and challenge this Damon and take back the throne. It needs you to step into your place as the queen of Sirenia."

Calandra's throat tightened, and she turned away. "I don't want the throne. And I'm far too dangerous to have it. My power grows ever more unstable, and will continue to do so until I can be rid of these bonds that chain me."

Cleo's eyebrows rose. "The bonds? What have those to do with it?"

The hatch opened, and Judith's head appeared above deck.

"Time to come below," she called.

Calandra called acknowledgement, and then thrust the tiara back toward Cleo. "Hang onto this. I'm not abdicating my responsibility to our people, and I won't allow Narcissa *or* the dragon to topple our island into ruin. But neither do I want the throne. Keep this safe until we find someone who is worthy of it. Keep our people in the city safe." She paused. "And keep Hebe safe. I charge you with this, *despoina*."

Cleo reluctantly took the pendant and tucked it into her pouch.

"As you wish, your highness."

She placed a hand on Calandra's forearm, and Calandra sensed her unwavering loyalty through the connection.

"Thank you, *despoina*."

Cleo cleared her throat. "One more thing—you should be aware there is a mole in your ranks. I don't know her identity, but Narcissa—or rather, this Damon creature, I suppose—regularly receives information from her."

Calandra blinked. She supposed she should not be surprised. But who could it be?

"I will inform Rhea," she said.

"You trust Rhea kor'Eudoxia?" Cleo arched a brow. "I remember her from her days at the Academy. She was quite the wild one then."

Calandra smiled, trying to imagine the staid steward as a younger, less restrained version of herself. "So was I, not so long ago."

Cleo pressed her lips together, but the corner tugged upward. "Yes, I suppose you were. There is more than a bit of wildness in you yet."

Calandra chuckled in acknowledgement. "We may not always see eye to eye, but I trust Rhea with my life. So did my mother. If something happens to me, seek her out. She knows about the bonds too."

"Yes, your highness. But . . . the Mother grant you remain unharmed."

Calandra followed Cleo down the ladder so they could submerge, praying all the while that they had arrived before Zale went through the Voidstone. Just because she must go beyond the veil to fulfill her duty didn't mean he must—she could free their mother without him, and she wouldn't risk that he'd be trapped there along with her. But thinking of the cold black stone that had swallowed her hand, she cringed. What would the journey through the stone be like? And what awaited her on the other side?

"I hope so too," she breathed, though Cleo could no longer hear her.

Her chest tightened, and her regrown hand tingled. She knew what she had to do.

As long as she could find the strength to do it.

*

Cleo returned to the aft cabin, and Calandra went to the fore and told the others what Cleo had told her about the mole. Rhea and Judith exchanged concerned looks. Nick was too busy navigating between the crags and spires of Atlantis on their descent to do more than glance at them over her shoulder.

"Do you think it is one of the girls we just brought back?" Judith whispered.

"Perhaps," Calandra said, thinking of her misgivings about the chatty Polyxo kor'Theano and her difficult-to-check background.

"If it's been going on for some time, it must be someone else." Rhea's face darkened. "I hate to think one of ours would betray us. Who?"

"Or there may be more than one," Calandra added.

Rhea's eyes became even more troubled. "Keep this to ourselves for now. We'll have to give everyone the truth test as soon as possible so we can clear this up."

Calandra nodded, though she wasn't happy. The truth test wasn't a pleasant experience for the administrator or the recipient. But they could ill afford to worry about an invasion of privacy when the lives of so many were on the line.

Nick flicked some switches and shifted her splayed, slightly webbed fingers on the semi-spherical guidestone on the console, and the pod touched down on the sandy floor of the city next to the spire Calandra recognized as the Archive from her last visit. A short distance beyond, the other sub set down in a cloud of billowing sand. This far below the surface, the midday light above had filtered to a murky green-blue.

"We're here," Nick announced, whirling to face them.

Calandra stared at the impressive marble building with the vaulting tower rising from the centre, its sides carved in tiny figures depicting stories she'd never heard, overcome by a sense of destiny.

She swallowed the lump in her throat. "Let's go."

Before descending through the moon pool, she gathered everyone in the aft cabin to outline the plan. They crammed in cheek by jowl, and the small space grew stuffier by the second.

Those who had come to Sireniapolis in more elegant clothing than a swimming skirt had changed while Calandra was abovedeck. Rhea and

Nelly now wore ill-fitting bodices and skirts Nick must have supplied. As sirens in the royal guard, Cleo and Zoe had already been clad in vibrant blue swimming skirts and bodices. Airlea, who dressed for swimming on every away mission, wore a teal green set to match her tail instead of the turquoise blue of her former uniform. Meg had also come dressed to swim in the Mother's Heart chamber. Judith must have been wearing a slim-fitting swimming outfit beneath her elegant red peplos, for she was now tying a diving knife onto a natural hemp belt over a deep red swimming skirt that just reached her thighs. Nick was prepared, of course—she wore a swimming bodice and short skirt under a sarong as everyday wear, dark green today—and was now handing out collection bags of fine netting, commstones, and lightstones to everyone who needed them.

Rhea looked around the circle, holding up her bag. "Thank you, Nick. Our people's history has been too long neglected, so let us not waste the opportunity. Gather as many datastones as you can, but don't let that distract you from our primary mission."

Calandra caught the steward's eye and gave an approving nod. Rhea gave a small smile in return. Yes, Rhea would be able to handle everything just fine until Calandra returned. She didn't let personal pride interfere with practical considerations—the mark of a good leader.

"And if you see anything else that might be valuable, I'd appreciate you bringing it on back for my trouble," Nick added, handing a bag to her sister with a pointed look.

Nelly eyed her sharply. "If I find anything valuable, what makes you think I'd hand it over to you?"

Nick glared at her. "Huh. Well, it wouldn't be the first time you cut me out of a deal."

Nelly gave a sardonic snort. "Are you ever going to let that go?"

"Are you?" Nick locked eyes with Nelly.

"Please, ladies," Rhea said. "Can you save the bickering for another time?"

"I will if she will," Nelly muttered, but when Nick didn't respond, she fell silent.

Rhea clucked her tongue as though at two recalcitrant children, not two grown, middle-aged women.

Yep. Just fine.

Calandra accepted a collection bag and tied it to her belt. Then she checked that the rolled and tied closure of the small waxed canvas dry pouch next to it was secure. Satisfied, she turned to address the group.

"Keep your eyes peeled for Zale and Damaris," Calandra said. "Rhea, Judith, *despoina*, you search the Archive. Nick, Nelly, Airlea, you search the surrounding buildings." She ignored the consternation of the Nyx sisters at this order. Served them right. "Take your diving bags and bring back all you can. Meg and Zoe, you're with me. We'll stand watch on the Void-stone. Despoina Cleo, have your pod fan out outside the building to watch for the approach of Zale and Damaris. None of them are to interfere with my orders or the activities of this group. And no one is to go anywhere alone."

"I will supply each group a pair of feldspar cuffs, just in case," said Cleo.

"Do you really think that's necessary?" Calandra asked.

"Unfortunately, yes. The boy's powers are still unstable, though they are improving. While I've never seen him willfully lash out at anyone, his in-structors have reported several incidents that required healing. He clearly has his mind set on going through the Voidstone, and we don't know how he'll react when we interfere. If he should choose to fight back, we must be prepared."

Rhea's face was twisted in withheld objections, but Calandra spoke before the steward could.

"Fine. But sirensong is to be used only to calm, not to Redeem. And cuffs should only be used as a last resort."

Cleo acknowledged this with a flick of her eyelids and then stepped into the corridor to give orders over her commstone.

"And if Zale has already gone ahead of us?" Zoe said, her eyebrow raised.

Calandra's gut tightened. She shared Zoe's fear. "Do you think Da-maris would follow him?"

Zoe scowled. "She better not. But I didn't expect her to come this far."

"Hmm. Well, we'll either find Damaris, who will tell us where Zale is, or we won't find anything. Report in every hour. We'll wait as long as seems reasonable before deciding what to do next. I'm not sure how they were planning to get here, but if they were foolhardy enough to swim, it could be a full day before they arrive."

Though Calandra hadn't felt a hint of buzzing on the way here, that didn't mean they hadn't passed right over Zale's head and she missed it. And if Zale saw them drive past, changed his mind, and returned to the island, so much the better.

Airlea raised her hand slightly. "I would go with you, your highness."

Calandra was about to object, but Rhea interrupted. "That's an excellent idea, Calandra. You never know what you may encounter at the stone. Airlea, please accompany the princess. Meg, you go with the Nyx sisters."

Calandra glared at Rhea, but swallowed her anger. There was no time.

"One last thing." Calandra met each gaze in turn. "Under no circumstances is anyone to touch the Voidstone, no matter what you may see there. Damon may no longer be trapped there, but we don't know what manner of creatures may still be trying to escape. The Grigori seem to need bodies like ours to move through our plane. But while we may be their escape route from the Underworld, for us, it's a gate that only goes one way."

She held up her regrown hand for emphasis, but she probably didn't need to. Every person in the room gave grim acknowledgement of the command. No matter what they thought of her experiences with Damon, the fact she'd lost a hand to that stone had been irrefutable.

"All right. Let's go."

*

THE Atlantean Archive chamber would have been even grander than the Archive at the Opal Palace in its heyday—larger, with a higher ceiling that looked like it had once held rose skylights at the top of each dome. It was exactly as Calandra remembered it—most of the shelves toppled, the datastones scattered on the floor and partially obscured by sand, with sea plants growing between them and fish darting through the shadows. One wall displayed the confusing mural showing Hadad and Atargatis being thrown into a pit in chains. And beyond, the corridor with the short branch leading to the tower where they would find the light-absorbing black sphere of the Voidstone suspended—a mirror image of the Heartstone in the Mother's Heart chamber.

Calandra, Airlea, and Zoe swam through the Archive, leaving Rhea and her team behind to scour the debris for the precious datastones by the halos of light cast by their handheld lightstones. They swam the short distance to the Voidstone chamber, whose door still hung open from Calandra's last visit. She quickly swam the height of the entire Voidstone tower, careful not to touch the golden spokes that connected the oily-looking obsidian sphere with the crystal-tiled walls, or to even look too closely at the mesmerizing black ball. She peered through the window of an observation chamber slightly higher than the stone to inspect the room beyond, but it was empty. There was no place to hide in the tower itself. Seeing no sign of Zale or Damaris and not sensing the tell-tale resonance, Calandra signalled Airlea and Zoe to stand guard.

Where are you going? Airlea flashed in diving hand signs.

Something about the strange mural on the wall of the Archive was niggling at Calandra's brain, and she wanted to take another look.

I need to go check on something.

Airlea bit her lip. *You shouldn't go alone.*

Calandra sighed, heaving a rush of water through her gills. Airlea was right—those had been her own orders, so she'd better follow them. She beckoned to Zoe and held up her hand to show the frowning Airlea she should stay put.

Be right back.

Airlea nodded unhappily.

Calandra swam back to the main Archive chamber and suspended herself before the mural with the occasional flick of her tail to maintain her position above the floor. Zoe paused nearby, looking around while Calandra studied the details of the painting.

When Damon had appeared in her dreams, it had often been in this very room, but Calandra hadn't known the room's location was Atlantis until the first time she'd visited it in person. Unlike the real thing, the mural in her dreamscape showed him and Atargatis receiving praise and adulation as benevolent deities, not being thrown into some kind of pit in shame.

The chains binding the two shamed deities were held by an undine man and woman in *ichthys* state for Atargatis, and for Hadad, by the mouths of a sphinx and a dragon. Above the disgraced gods' heads, a winged disc-like sun floated like some kind of vengeful star.

Zoe floated next to Calandra, regarding the mural with a tight expression. Calandra wasn't sure if it was the siren's anger she felt, or her own. Who had dared to create such blasphemous art on the walls of the very City of the Goddess? Had it been Nadia, the queen who had finally sunk the city in her Madness?

There was a deeper mystery here, peeking at her from around a corner, but she couldn't glimpse enough for it to take form and substance. She hoped the datastones Rhea and the others were scooping into their diving sacks from the lopsided shelves would reveal more clues.

Two datastones—a faceted blue sapphire Tear slightly grungy with age and an unusual cabochon Tear with black tourmaline shards in criss-crossing lines through transparent quartz—sat at the foot of the mural, partially obscured by sand, and she picked them up. As soon as she touched them, that weighty sense of destiny filled her once more. She rubbed away the film of grime on their surfaces, her heart a rapid drumbeat in her ears.

What was on these stones? She'd never reacted that way to any data-stone she'd ever held, not even her Tear with the life-changing message her mother had left for her. She was tempted to delve them right here and now, even knowing the data she would see that way would be confusing and jumbled.

But no. They had a job to do. She'd left Airlea alone too long, and it was time to get back in case Zale and Damaris showed up.

The commstone on her wrist vibrated with Judith's hummed signal, followed by the melody that meant *Come to me*. Calandra looked around and saw Judith's slim figure in red down the corridor at the back of the room. She hovered near an open doorway, rapidly flashing the lightstone pattern for *Come here*. White light poured through the doorway, illuminating Judith and the corridor around her in a soft glow.

Beckoning to Zoe, Calandra sped toward her friend. When she got there, she saw why Judith looked so shaken up.

The room beyond the door was ablaze with artificial white light. But more than that, it was empty of water. Looking into it was like looking at the sky through the surface of the ocean—her own face reflected back at her, revealing her open shock.

Cautiously, she pushed her hand through the vertical surface. When nothing untoward happened, she changed to *podia* state and stepped into the room. Two echoing splashes behind her told her Zoe and Judith had followed.

She stared around at the wet chamber, which had obviously been full of water until recently. It looked like a meeting hall of some sort. Smooth stone columns lined the edges of the room, their surfaces oddly clean for being submerged for so long. Water beaded and ran down every surface and drained through the cracks between the flagstones on the floor. Tall cylindrical illuminated rods of rock quartz between the columns bathed the entire room in brilliant but comfortable white light. At the centre of the room, several steps led to a dais with a plain stone altar of some kind, but no statues revealed the identity of the one who was worshipped here. At four points around the central dais, aligned between the corners of the altar and the corners of the room, stood chest-height circular stone pillars with nothing on them.

"What is this place?" Zoe breathed.

Calandra stared in awestruck wonder. Her next words were out of her mouth before she consciously composed them.

"An answer."

But all she had were more questions.

37

THE CITY OF THE GODDESS

"How . . . ?"

CALANDRA'S VOICE TRAILED OFF as she looked around the dripping marble room. She had so many questions, she didn't know where to begin.

Judith pointed at an upright ornate silvery rod next to the door that was fixed into a semi-circular casing on the floor. "I came in here searching for stones and all the lights came on. I was so surprised, I backed up and accidentally bumped this lever, and all the water drained from the room. I can't believe the mechanism hasn't crumbled to dust."

Zoe walked up to the altar, staring at it. "What is it for?"

"The bigger question," said Calandra, circling the room and inspecting every detail, "is why a mechanism exists to drain water from a room in a city that was never meant to be underwater."

The wide-eyed stares of her companions told her that thought hadn't occurred to them.

"Look at this," Judith said.

She pointed to one of the empty pillars near the altar. She hadn't raised her voice, but Calandra could hear her perfectly from her position near the door.

"The acoustics in here are amazing." As Calandra moved to join Judith at the pillar, she sang the opening bars of "The Mother's Light Shine on You," marvelling at the way the music resonated around the room.

Judith and Zoe listened, awed.

When Calandra reached the pillar, she saw what had intrigued Judith. In the centre of the platform was a dimpled impression, very similar to the niche on a stone reader that held a datastone.

314

Judith began to fish one of her stones out of her bag, but Calandra put up her hand.

"I want to try this one." She held out the sapphire Tear she had found beneath the mural, placed it in the impression, and stepped back.

Nothing happened. Judith put her thumb on the stone and sang the trill with which stone readers were typically activated, but still nothing happened.

Zoe crossed her arms. "Maybe it's broken."

"Or maybe our ancestors used a different audio signature," Judith mused.

"Let me try," Calandra said.

Judith moved aside. Calandra held both hands above the stone, palms flat, and closed her eyes to heighten her awareness. The golden threads of the Matrix of Creation came into sharp focus, and she extended her intention along them into the stone, into the pillar, and along the lines of power that connected the two, nudging the switch that would enable the stone reader to come to life.

Judith's gasp made her open her eyes.

Projected above the Tear in a cone of light was a moving image with as much depth and colour as the three of them standing there, and nearly as tangible.

"I've never seen the like," Zoe murmured, staring. "Perhaps the ghost stories about this place were true."

Calandra gave a sardonic snort. "I think those ghost stories were meant to keep people away from the Voidstone and nothing more. For good reason."

Judith squinted at the image. "Is that Atlantis?"

No sound accompanied the moving images, but whatever device had captured them appeared to be moving through the streets of Atlantis. The city appeared much as it did on the history stones Calandra had seen at school, with several important differences—while the occupants of the busy city were walking on two feet, the light was odd. Closer inspection showed some kind of glimmering dome over the city, with pale blue light filtering through the water beyond. Most of the light in the images appeared to be artificial.

Another oddity was the people—men and women alike of all races, confirmed by the many-hued varieties of human eyes and the various luminescent greens of undines. There was even the occasional golden-eyed person who glanced into the recorder, reminding Calandra of Damon's swirling irises.

And every man among them was Free.

Calandra swallowed as she watched an undine couple walk along a boulevard, holding hands as they passed the recorder. The person capturing the images rose to follow them, making their way into a magnificent structure with a grand portico and, beyond an enormous entrance with two open doors twice as tall as a person, an open courtyard full of people with an ornately carved marble altar at the centre, similar to the one in this room. Calandra remembered seeing the building as they'd come in, still amazingly intact. Men and women in white robes with purple sashes stood next to the altar—priestesses and priests, Calandra realized with a start. But that wasn't the most incredible part.

Zoe gasped, and Judith covered her mouth with her hands. Calandra swallowed, trying to make sense of what she was seeing.

The priests and priestesses were conducting some kind of worship service. People would bring them their gifts of fruit or vegetables or flowers or the works of their hands, such as fine cloth or metalwork or stonework. Then the giver would join the other worshippers in prostrating themselves before the altar, surrounding it on all sides. Calandra could see their mouths moving in song and wished the recorder had captured it. But the priests and priestesses who were laying gifts on the stone were what had caught Calandra's attention—each beautiful man or woman had golden eyes and exquisite, powerful-looking feathered wings folded against their backs.

The lumasi. They once lived among us? But whom are they all worshipping? Where is the Mother's effigy?

The commstone on her wrist squealed with an urgent hummed pattern from Airlea—the one that meant *Come immediately, something is wrong.*

The resonance she'd been waiting for buzzed through her.

Her gaze snapped to her companions. "Zale's here."

She snatched the sapphire from the column and the light went out. Then the three of them ran as one to the arched chamber entrance and dove through the water's surface into the corridor, transforming in mid-jump.

*

Around half an hour earlier

ZALE swam between the buildings of the wrecked city, which looked surprisingly intact for having been sunk by a Madwoman. White and pink marble spires and pyramids decorated with elegant carvings and friezes made the squat square buildings of Sireniapolis—even the more ornamented ones—look like a child's effort at architectural grandeur in comparison. Through the sand that littered the streets, he could see the occasional patch of a black basalt flagstone cleared off by ocean currents. In its heyday, this city must have been a truly magnificent sight.

Swimming along the abandoned streets, he wished he knew what they were looking for, but all he really knew was that here, in one of these abandoned, watery tombs, was the gateway to the Underworld. He'd found out that much from Abela. He didn't know what it looked like, but he hoped that, being as it was the entrance to hell, he'd know it when he saw it.

Damaris beckoned to him from the door of a tall, official-looking building, and he followed her. He would have preferred to come alone, but the truth was, he wouldn't even be here if it weren't for her. Having the student resistance help him get to Atlantis was the price he'd negotiated for his silence to Narcissa—though he'd still had to fight the urge to tell his cousin the truth every moment until they'd left, even after seeing the strange, creepy man in her hallway and knowing what he knew about her. Damaris and the others were right—there was something wrong with him.

He was so tired of being used as a pawn.

They swam through yet another vast hall filled with seaweed and the occasional snake-like creature—he'd have to ask Damaris what those were called later—whipping between some plants in a building that had probably been undisturbed by undines for millennia.

Or had it? He glanced around. This place was different than the other buildings. It had rows of shelves, most of which were askew or laying on the floor, with dozens, maybe hundreds, of tear-shaped precious gems strewn around. A huge mural on one wall caught his attention, and he stared at the two chained beings and the lumasi and undines who guarded them, wondering what it could mean.

Just then, he felt a shiver course through him—the strange resonance he experienced every time his sister was nearby. But she couldn't be here, could she?

Damaris grabbed his arm. She had been exploring the room, but there was now alarm written all over her face. Damaris had shown him a few signs from the sign language the undines used while diving in the sub on the way here, but he wouldn't have needed a prior interpretation to understand the one she was flashing at him now.

Danger!

She pointed frantically at a corridor. Unable to question her but sensing her alarm flowing through her touch, he followed.

They bolted down a curved corridor with doorways going off to the left and right. In some ways, this building reminded Zale of the Opal Palace. Flicking into one of the arches, they found stairs leading upward and swam up the stairwell, emerging into an unfurnished dimly lit room with a single wall of glass overlooking a vast, empty space beyond.

No, not empty. Zale's jaw dropped and he floated toward the glass, pressing his hands against it as he stared at the enormous obsidian-like globe beyond. It pulsed with a dark energy that pulled light into itself.

I think we found it.

The question was, how could he get to it?

The chamber was much like the Mother's Heart in the Opal Palace. Even though it was sitting beneath a mile of water, it still caught the small amount of light that filtered from above and refracted it a million times from the rock crystals lining the walls until the column glowed softly. The light had no effect on the globe, which absorbed it as though the stone were not even a real substance, but the absence of a substance.

Zale pressed his face to the glass and looked up as far as he could. The Mother's Heart was capped with a glass ceiling, but from what he could tell, the top of this column was open, though it might have once held glass in the spoke-like frame that remained.

He looked downward and froze.

Small figures had entered the column. He saw a flash of golden hair on one, another one with a long, dark braid, and a third woman with her brown hair cut shorter than most boys'. The resonant vibration became stronger.

Calandra! How did she find me?

The figures began swimming the boundaries of the tower, and he and Damaris darted toward the wall beside the glass, pressing themselves against it so they couldn't be seen. He looked at his companion, whose eyes—so tantalizingly close—were wide with alarm.

He was surprised she'd even warned him. Damaris had tried, repeatedly, to convince him not to do this, that they should go to the rebels for help. But Zale had remained firm—going to the rebels meant talking to his sister, and that was the last thing he wanted.

And now, here she was. Had Damaris told Calandra where to find him, despite her promise not to?

He grabbed her arm, and she jerked her gaze to his. He didn't know enough signs to ask her what he wanted to know, so he pointed subtly toward the window, then at her, then at himself, and then held his hands out in question, scowling.

She followed his movements and quickly discerned his meaning. Her eyes widened more, and she began flashing signs at him with jerky, emphatic movements close to her body so they wouldn't be seen through the window. He didn't understand her gestures, but he understood the adamant shaking of her head and the pleading look in her big green eyes. She was denying his accusation. She grabbed his arm, and her anxiety, fear, and sincerity flowed through him.

He stared into her eyes a moment longer, then nodded. He believed her. So far, she'd kept every promise she'd made him—including using her family connections to get them this far, even using money her mother gave her to hire the sub that brought them here—and a little extra for the driver's silence. For the first time, he wondered what would happen to her if others discovered what she'd helped him do. What had she risked?

No more than she risked by being part of the resistance, he supposed. Is that why she was helping him? Because of the beliefs of her resistance?

The beliefs my sister imparted to them.

He swallowed. Would his sister risk her life to tell her people to free and respect men, and then try to kill him? Damaris and the others had been right. That didn't make a lot of sense.

The resonance faded somewhat, and he dared a look through the glass. His sister's blond head and the girl with the long braid had disappeared from the room, but the woman with the short hair and the deep teal-coloured tail was floating some distance below the enormous black sphere with something in her hand—a staff. On her swimming belt hung a pair of feldspar bracelets.

He rubbed his wrists. He hadn't enjoyed wearing the bracelets the girls had put on him while he was unconscious, which surprised him. They'd proved only partially effective, anyway, but the cuffs revealed the purpose of his sister's visit to Atlantis—she'd come for him. How she had found out he was here, he had no idea. Hebe should only just now be handing the note he'd left for Narcissa to her sister, and other than the sub driver who was waiting for Damaris in an abandoned building near the edge of Atlantis, no one else knew they were here.

Maybe it was merely coincidence. Calandra and her rebel friends might have come looking for something else. But if so, why the cuffs? Whatever the reason, he couldn't risk the rebels interfering with his mission. He had to find a way through the Voidstone without them noticing.

He looked around the room. Opposite from where they'd entered, a narrow door hung slightly ajar. He pointed at it, and Damaris nodded.

They skirted around the room along the far wall, watching the glass to see if the remaining siren had decided to go exploring. When they reached the door, Zale gave it a tug, but the ancient hinges were stuck. Another pull, and pieces of the metal flaked away. Damaris grabbed the door with both hands and they pulled together.

The wood and brass disintegrated in a cloudy heap. Zale and Damaris flitted backward in the water, waving the billowing debris away from their faces. Then Damaris grabbed his arm again, alarm flowing through the connection once more. She pointed at the chamber beyond and indicated that the siren was coming toward them. Zale nodded, and they darted through the door.

They swam down a dark, narrow corridor containing a short downward flight of stairs that ended in an equally narrow stone door. Judging from its position, the door led into the vast column housing the stone portal beyond.

This was it! Zale was only a few yards away from the gateway into the realm where his mother was being kept. But how could he get to it?

In the darkness of the corridor, he could barely make out the dim outline of Damaris's face and her sandy hair, which billowed from her ponytail in a cloud. Her seafoam-green eyes shone softly. Even without touching her, he could sense that she was worried. For him.

He took her hands, hoping to reassure her that he knew what he was doing, even though he had no idea. His life hadn't felt this out of control since he'd first discovered his powers and fled from his home in Madron as a child. But he didn't want her to know that.

She gripped his hands, and her concern coursed into him. He wavered. Maybe this wasn't the best way to go about this. After all, he knew nothing about the place he was going to. What dangers would he face? How would he even find his mother when he was there? If she were still alive, as Abela and Berian had believed, the plane beyond must have physical substance, but what if the rules were completely different than the world he knew? He was utterly unequipped for any of this. Maybe he ought to wait . . .

He shook his head, strengthening his resolve. No. He had started with nothing before, and he'd always found a way. This time would be no different. Alone or not, in a strange place or not, he had to do this.

And he had to get away from the strange, unnatural pull he felt toward

Narcissa. Golden ooze stuck to the thought, and a jolt of fear banished it.

He couldn't make himself trust Calandra, even if she hadn't tried to kill him. He couldn't trust Narcissa or the feelings he had toward her that demanded trust for no reason. He trusted Abela, but he had no idea where she was. And, he realized, he had some small amount of trust for the girl before him, the girl whose emotions seemed to be begging him not to do this.

But he *had* to do it. It was the only thing he was truly certain of. According to what Abela and Berian had told him, he was the only one who could save his mother. He only regretted waiting this long to try.

He couldn't sense the siren in the room beyond as clearly as he knew Damaris would be able to, but his sister's presence seemed to be far away. He made a few gestures he hoped would convey his question, pointing toward the room through the door, pointing at himself, and moving one hand in a swimming motion and making it collide with his other balled fist. He pointed at the room again, then at his other hand, which he now had swim up and down like the siren they had seen on guard. Then he held his hands out to the sides questioningly.

Damaris gave a quick nod of understanding. She closed her eyes. When she opened them, she shook her head and pointed toward the bottom of the chamber to show where the guard was.

Good. I guess this is it.

He looked at Damaris long and hard. Now that the moment was here, he wasn't sure he could go through with it. She grasped his hands as though to say, *You don't have to go. Stay here. Stay safe.*

He closed his eyes and the image of his mother's sweet face filled his mind. He'd run away and had never told her where he went. She'd gone looking for him and had fallen into the hands of whomever had taken her beyond the veil. If it weren't for him, she wouldn't even be there, facing whatever tortures Tartarus could produce.

He owed this to her. That was the one thing he was absolutely certain of.

He opened his eyes, released Damaris's hands, and heaved open the door to the chamber.

The siren he'd been hoping to avoid was waiting for him, feldspar cuffs at the ready.

No!

Closing his eyes, he lashed out with his powers.

*

When Calandra, Zoe, and Judith reached the chamber, Zale's tail fin was just disappearing into the inky surface of the Voidstone. The resonance disappeared like a lightstone turning off.

"No!" Calandra screamed aloud. The word was muffled by water.

Damaris hovered near the stone, staring at it with her staff extended. Airlea stood in a giant air bubble floating nearby, pounding frantically against its surface. The feldspar cuffs she'd carried were resting on the floor of the bubble.

Calandra stared. Had Zale done that?

Zoe was already halfway to her sister. Seconds later, the bubble burst, and Airlea transformed, snatched the cuffs, and swam toward Damaris at full speed.

Damaris looked at them in alarm, then back at the stone. Her face set into decisive lines. She turned and plunged into the Voidstone after Zale.

Calandra stopped and stared, and so did the others. They turned to look at each other. Zoe's face was twisted in distress. Her emotions, usually so carefully concealed, pelted Calandra like hailstones.

They mirrored Calandra's own, whose mounting anguish was accentuated by an increasing pounding in her temples. The pain almost blinded her. Screaming, she pressed her hands to her head, her mind filled with red-hot pain. Power surged through her and exploded from her gut, but she could do nothing about it. It was all she could do to maintain her grip on reality as the tsunami of pain raged on.

Airlea's cool hand on her forehead and calm humming pushed the pain back to a manageable level, and she focused on the water moving through her gills until she could control herself once more. When she opened her eyes, Zoe and Judith were both pressed against the walls of the chamber as though held there by an invisible force, and Airlea looked like she'd just been through a war. Hairline cracks had splintered the walls of the chamber.

Calandra looked around in horror. That had been the worst seizure she'd ever had. Zoe and Judith peeled themselves off the wall and swam toward her. She spun to look up at the Voidstone.

Her moment of decision was upon her. She hadn't intercepted Zale in time, and now Zoe's sister had followed him into the void. Should she go back—back to Damon, as she'd promised, and help him find the keys she'd need to safely travel back from the Underworld and free her mother from the Soulstone? Or should she jump in now, when she had the best chance of finding her brother? What would happen to him and Damaris if she waited?

Glancing at the damage her seizure had caused, she didn't think she had time to wait. If her episodes continued to get worse at their current rate, by the time she returned, she might have caused so much worse than a few cracked buildings. She could do irreversible damage, perhaps killing people she cared about and hundreds or even thousands more, just like when Nadia sank the very city they were now swimming in.

No, she didn't have the keys—but she did have a perfect, double-pointed amethyst. And hopefully in the Underworld, whatever power Damon held over Zale would be weakened, if not broken. If that were the case, the two of them working together might be able to find a way to free their mother from the Soulstone, with or without the keys. If the Soulstone was connected to the Heartstone, maybe they could restore the barrier from the other side, even if they couldn't find a way back. After all, who knew what she and Zale would be capable of if they were working in unity?

She'd been uncertain before—uncertain if she could dive into the Voidstone without being sure she could get out again. But she knew what she had to do. She would go and find Zale and her mother. She'd figure out a way to get them out, one way or another. But as for herself?

She didn't know if she could ever come back. The void that had tormented her for so long in her nightmares might be the only place she could prevent what she'd always feared would happen—destroying everything and everyone around her.

She looked at her companions and hummed to get their attention.

I'm going after him, she signed, *to free him and my mother. Tell Rhea. Help the cause. Protect the island. Don't follow me.*

Airlea's big eyes grew even rounder than normal, and she shook her head.

No, signed Judith, desperation streaming from her. *We'll find another way.*

But there was no other way, not one that would protect the island from her own Madness. And if she didn't go now, she might lose her nerve—and never see Zale and Damaris again. She exchanged glances with Zoe and saw the same determination she herself felt.

Their family was inside that stone. And they were going to go get them back.

As one, she and Zoe swam toward the stone, and Calandra surged ahead of the siren. This time when she reached the oily surface, she didn't hesitate. Images of Damon capturing her hand flashed through her mind, but she dove into the stone, feeling as though she'd been enveloped in cold tarry sludge.

I'm coming, Zale.
I'm coming for you and Mother.

38

INTO HADES

CALANDRA BURST THROUGH THE GATE into thin air and darkness, tumbling onto an irregular stone surface strewn with sharp rocks in a practised roll, though it was less easy in *ichthys* state than when she had legs. She changed to *podia* state and got up in a seamless motion, standing ready to let loose a blast of air against whatever might try to attack her.

Nothing did. And there was no sign of Zale or Damaris. But it was so dark, she couldn't see her own hands. She'd never been anywhere that was so completely, utterly without light.

She touched the lightstone laced onto her bodice to activate it, but nothing happened. She frowned, trying several more times, desperate to get a sense of her surroundings. *Breathe,* came a voice in her head.

She stopped and closed her eyes, reaching out with her senses. She was in a large space enclosed by stone. There was water nearby with presences in it. When she opened her eyes, her vision had adjusted somewhat, and she appeared to be standing in a gloomy halo of light. She turned to look back at the Voidstone, but there was nothing behind her but more darkness. She was alone in a void. Her heart thumped.

Where's the gate?

She glanced at her stinging shoulder and swiped at a trickle of blood running down it. A small, jagged cut continued to leak. She pressed her fingers against it, hoping the flow would stop soon.

Zoe tumbled to the ground beside her and, seconds later, so did Airlea, both in *ichthys* state. They appeared out of nothing—no sign of a black sphere anywhere. They transformed and leapt to their feet in a defensive position, blinking until their eyes adjusted enough to see each other. Zoe tried her lightstone, touching it repeatedly when it failed to light and then giving up with a frustrated growl.

Calandra looked at Airlea in dismay. Of all the people to follow her into the bowels of hell, did it have to be her? Why couldn't it have been Judith? Or neither of them, as she had commanded?

She understood why Zoe had come—even knowing she must protect her people from the threatening Madness, the pull of family was what had brought Calandra this far. But why Airlea?

"Calandra?" Airlea asked, blinking blindly.

"I'm here." Calandra sighed. "Your eyes will adjust soon. We're alone, as far as I can tell."

She closed her eyes again. There were now two more living souls she was responsible for getting out of the Underworld—and she still had no idea how. Not only did she not have a key, she couldn't even see the portal.

When she opened her eyes, they had completely adjusted to the gloom of her surroundings. She and the two sirens looked around the chamber in wonder.

"I've never seen anything like it," Airlea murmured.

The floor, walls, and ceiling of the vast chamber were covered in enormous jutting clusters of hexagonal purple crystals, some of them up to a full pace in length and as thick as a tree trunk. The violet shade faded to translucent clear crystal at the base where it attached to the black stone of the cavern wall—what could be seen of it between the close spires and spikes. A short distance away was a murky lake, and whatever lay beyond was lost in darkness, even to undine eyes.

"I have," Zoe said. "It's very similar to the cavern beneath the Opal Palace."

"The resonance is wrong though." Calandra closed her eyes to get a better sense of the space. "The crystals beneath the palace are much smaller, but they practically sing with energy. Even though these ones are larger, they're dull and hollow, as if merely holding on to the appearance of what they are without the substance."

Zoe stared around, her *deiktis* drawn and at the ready. "Everything is dull here. Maybe that's why the lightstones aren't working."

"Like the spirit element has been clouded." Airlea cautiously touched a nearby cluster of stones. "I feel it too, Calandra."

"Do you have stone healing abilities?" Calandra asked.

It was rare for anyone with earth abilities to join the siren corps—they were usually conscripted into the stone healing trades as novices—but it did happen.

Airlea shook her head. "No. But every substance normally has a little bit of spirit running through it. These do too, but it's weak and difficult to sense."

"What happened to the gate?" Zoe stared at the empty space where they'd entered the chamber.

Calandra shook her head. "You two came out of nowhere. Perhaps that's why it is so difficult to leave—you can't open a gate you can't find." And if she could find it, she still wouldn't be able to open it without a key. No sense mentioning that now and panicking her companions further.

Airlea drew her *deiktis* and stabbed toward the general location where they'd entered, but hit only air. She frowned. "I can't sense anything either. On the other side, the gate felt like an unnatural nothingness. But here, everything feels the same—hollow and insubstantial, like the nothingness is all that remains."

Calandra took her hand away from her shoulder and inspected the cut. The bleeding had stopped.

Airlea's brow furrowed. "What happened to you?"

"Nothing. Just a cut when I got here. Nothing serious." She dabbed her thumb on her tongue and wiped off the last of the blood from her skin around the fresh scab.

Airlea frowned. "Not this time. But we'll all have to be more careful."

She didn't say that if something serious did happen to Calandra, there would be no healer to help her and the other two would be stranded in this place, but she didn't need to. *If she was worried, she shouldn't have come. I can only be responsible for so much.*

Guiltily, Calandra remembered how Airlea had halted her seizure in the Voidstone chamber, despite how difficult it must have been to get near her. *I should be more grateful.*

She was about to offer an apology when a sharp pulse of pain throbbed in Calandra's temples, eclipsing the stinging in her shoulder. She ground her teeth, determined not to let her anguish show, but the pain had been rising since they had stumbled in here. She wasn't sure how much longer she could contain it.

Another pulse, stronger. She bent over, holding out her hand.

"Airlea—" she managed in a choked voice.

In moments, the siren was at her side, hand on her forehead, singing her calming song. It helped—but not as much as usual. However, the pain subsided and the red fog behind Calandra's eyes cleared. She stood and composed herself.

"Thank you," she said. "And . . . I'm sorry for last time, in the Voidstone chamber."

Airlea shook her head. "Don't mention it."

Gratitude rushed through Calandra. It may have been better for Airlea if she hadn't come, but Calandra couldn't help but be glad she had a reprieve from the full power of her seizures, thanks to Airlea's touch. Despite her gratitude, the pain left her irritated, as usual.

"Let's go," she said brusquely. "Zale and Damaris can't have gotten far."

Zoe watched her with a neutral expression, and Airlea smoothed the worried frown from her face. Thank the Mother for that. Her episodes were embarrassing enough without others making a big deal of them every time.

She didn't know how the siren was able to soothe the pain at all—Xeni had guessed that because the pain was caused by bonds of spirit, a song that invoked spirit might be able to mitigate the effects, and she'd been right. Airlea had quickly volunteered to try, and ever since, she'd been just as quick to offer respite whenever Calandra needed it—but besides irritability, a heavy lethargy often remained. The exhaustion felt worse than ever this time. With effort, Calandra forced herself to take a step forward.

"Wait." Airlea's voice pulled her up short.

Calandra turned to see Airlea raise her staff and pound the end of it into the base of one of the enormous crystal spikes. The resounding crack bounced off a million other surfaces in the space around them.

"What are you doing?" Zoe demanded.

Airlea barely glanced up.

"Maybe the gate is here, maybe it isn't. But if we ever want to find it again, we need to mark this place." She pounded again, but the only effect was the rebound of her arms and the echoing thuds from her strikes.

"Stop!" Calandra stepped forward. "Do you want everyone in Hades to know where we are?"

Airlea ceased pounding and looked up in consternation. "I'm sorry."

"Here. Let me."

Calandra brushed Airlea aside and squatted. She'd been too harsh, but couldn't find it in herself to apologize. After all, Airlea should have known better. Of all the foolish, dunderheaded . . .

A splash from the lake made her whirl to see something indistinguishable disappear beneath the surface some distance out, and the ripples roll toward them in warning.

"Did either of you see what it was?" she whispered, eyeing the water.

They shook their heads, their expressions sober.

"Guess we won't be going for a swim any time soon," said Zoe. "That water is full of hate."

She wasn't wrong. Airlea looked embarrassed, probably for attracting the attention of whatever lay beneath the water.

Calandra returned to her task, shoving the throbbing red bundle of pain in her temples aside as best she could. She placed her hands around the base of a crystal about the length of her forearm. Closing her eyes, she focused on separating the bonds that kept the stone rooted to the floor, laying it gently on the ground when she'd finished. Then she did the same for two more that were about the same size.

"Help me," she said, gesturing to the others.

They each took one of the crystal shards and propped them in a three-legged tripod on top of a black boulder near the lake shore, with the sharp terminals leaning against each other at the top and the flat bases splayed out against the stone in three directions. Laying her hands on the pointed spire, Calandra created bonds between the ends so they became one joined piece.

She stepped back to admire her work, and the way that what little light there was in this place became concentrated in the depths of the crystals.

"Good idea." Zoe nodded approvingly.

"It's not the most obvious sign," Calandra said, "but that unusual formation should stand out against all the natural ones growing the opposite direction if someone's looking for it."

Airlea nodded and said nothing, still looking a little shame-faced. Guilt pinched Calandra. She hadn't needed to be so harsh. What else could Airlea have done with what she had to hand? But still, a little lack of caution in this place filled with unknowns could mean their deaths, and no one on the outside would ever know.

Of course, almost all the people she cared about most were already here somewhere. She swept hair that had come loose from her braid out of her eyes and turned away from her companions, grateful that her Tear would hide her sudden surge of emotion. Would she see Thea and Tanni here in the Underworld? She shook her head to push the thought away, but it wouldn't leave.

She composed herself and turned to the others, making sure to keep the edge out of her voice this time.

"Are you ready to go?"

Airlea and Zoe nodded, and she started walking along the shore of the lake, knowing they'd follow behind.

She'd hoped that once she got moving, the lethargy that had hit her after her seizure would dissipate as it usually did, but the further around the lake they got, the more exhausted and heavy she felt.

She glanced at her companions. Their faces were furrowed with effort, taking careful steps so as not to place their bare feet on the sharp crystals.

Zoe glanced at the lake. "Maybe we should just swim after all. We don't know that whatever's in there is dangerous."

Calandra stared at the water. Dim light that emanated from nowhere illuminated only a half-dozen lengths of the water's surface before the lake, like the rest of the cavern, was lost in darkness. No light at all pierced the murky depths. The surface was as still as glass—but it was what was beneath the surface that concerned her.

"I don't think that's a good idea," she said.

"Why?" Zoe frowned.

"Can't you feel them?" Airlea stared at the water. "There are thousands of presences in there. Hostile ones. Perhaps they're the spirits of the dead." She took another step away from where the water lapped the black sand.

Zoe pressed her lips together, but she didn't argue. With a last glance at the water, she continued on along the rocky shore.

Calandra pointed at a shadow in the wall of the cavern ahead. "I see something."

A tunnel of bare grey stone several spans wide and tall came into focus, illuminated with the same mysterious gloom as the cavern. Standing at the mouth, she could see no more than a dozen paces along it. There was something unusual about the light here. It seemed to follow them, enveloping them in a dim sphere, for if it were the same intensity everywhere, Calandra expected she should be able to see the entire room at once.

How very curious.

She looked back the way they'd come. Everything more than a dozen paces behind them was obliterated by darkness, and their triangular signpost was nowhere to be seen. It reminded Calandra of what it was like to swim in the ocean—she could usually see, even in very deep water, but only so far. Panic rose in her throat, and she pushed it down. She didn't often go swimming in open water, where the only other creatures were the big hunters or whales—it reminded her too much of the nightmare of empty ocean she'd endured for years.

Shuddering, Calandra turned to face the tunnel. "Well, I suppose we should go this way. If we keep circling the lake, we'll just end up where we started."

"Why don't you leave a mark here too?" Airlea suggested.

Calandra nodded. "That's a good idea."

She gave Airlea a small smile, and the girl gave her a grateful half-smile back.

This time, however, instead creating of a laborious cairn, Calandra simply placed her hand flat on the wall and concentrated. It took time to create channels in the stone with only her powers and no tools, but eventually, she'd imprinted a tiny triquetra on the wall of the tunnel where it joined the chamber.

With that, they began making their way along the curving passageway, always only a few steps away from utter darkness.

39

THE LABYRINTH

Hours or days later—it was impossible to tell time in this place—Calandra was getting tired of the overwhelming sameness of their surroundings. They'd seen nothing but countless tunnels crisscrossing each other since they'd entered, and still hadn't found Zale or Damaris or any evidence of other inhabitants of this place, save the malevolent presences in the lake.

All the tunnels were curved, with smooth walls that had obviously been hewn and polished, not formed naturally, but the lay of them made no sense. At their first crossroads, they had decided to continue straight. But after that tunnel had turned sharply back on itself and they'd come to another crossroads that looked identical to the first, they decided to always take the tunnel to the left. Calandra would have sworn it *was* the same crossroads, except she'd marked their route, and there was no engraved triquetra to be seen. No matter how many left turns they'd taken, or how many marks she'd imprinted on the walls, they hadn't come across the same turning point more than once.

She hadn't yet admitted her fear out loud—that they were hopelessly, utterly lost.

They emerged in the stone chamber of another crossroads, and Calandra wanted to weep.

"Zale and Damaris could be one tunnel over and we'd never know," growled Zoe, running her hands along the wall, which was surprisingly dry. "Have you noticed how all the stone here is warm?"

Calandra placed her hand on the wall to see for herself, confirming Zoe's observation. She hadn't thought about it while she'd been marking walls—she'd been too worried they may not find their way back to the mark she was making again.

"Why wouldn't you know if Damaris were that close?" she asked, turning to face the siren singer. "Couldn't you feel her?"

Zoe shook her head. "Not through solid rock when the tunnels are this far apart from each other. No one can sense someone from that distance." She frowned at Calandra. "Why, can you?"

Calandra sank onto a nearby boulder to rest her feet. "Not just anyone. But I think I could sense Zale's resonance if he were not too far away."

"His . . . resonance?" Zoe cocked an eyebrow.

Calandra glanced up. "Don't you have that with your sisters? I assumed everyone must feel that with their siblings."

At Zoe's and Airlea's blank looks, she expanded.

"Whenever Zale is nearby, I get this strange vibrating feeling, as though our bodies are two tines of a tuning fork reacting to the vibration of the other." She took in their incredulous looks. "You don't have any idea what I'm talking about, do you?"

Airlea shook her head. "I've never heard of that before. We can sense our siblings using spirit, the same as we could with anyone else. Do you think it's because he's not just a sibling, but male?"

Calandra picked up a pebble from the floor and fidgeted with it. "I don't know. Maybe. Judith never mentioned anything about it with Zeke, but I never asked her."

Zoe cleared her throat and said nothing. The siren had never quite gotten over her discomfort with men, even though she fought for their cause. She wasn't the only one. From experience, Calandra knew overcoming a lifetime of misconceptions and prejudices didn't happen in a single day. She had to admit that even she'd been frightened by Cogger's outbursts when he had been Freed. When he was Released at Margaret House, he'd been just as uncooperative as Kofi had predicted until he'd been given the choice of Redemption, incarceration, or work on one of their labour crews, which he'd only accepted once he knew the crew supervisor was as pale-skinned as he was. She hadn't objected at all when Nelly kor'Nyx had suggested someone skilled in sirensong be assigned to that crew as well, just in case. Guilt pricked her. Cogger's prejudices made no sense to her, but how could she champion these men if even she couldn't see past the prejudices she'd been raised with?

Zoe gave an exaggerated yawn. "Well, I'm beat." She squatted next to Calandra. "This place really takes it out of you. And if we don't find some water soon, we're going to have to retrace our steps and take our chances with the lake monsters just to get hydrated. They can't be much worse than a hungry hammerhead."

Airlea shook her head. "I think they could. Hungry sharks don't hate you—they see you as prey, something they need, nothing more. Those things . . . they were angry. They felt vile." She shuddered.

Zoe said nothing.

Calandra's stomach growled. Time had lost meaning here, but their bodies still had needs. Since they hadn't exactly been planning on a trip to the Underworld when they'd left Margaret House, they were remarkably unprepared. However, she did have some trail food in her belt pouch.

She untied and unrolled the top of the waxed canvas pouch, pulled out some dried anchovies, and passed a couple to each of the others. "This is all I have. Until we find food, we'll have to make this last."

Airlea withdrew some dried pineapple and an orange from her pouch. She peeled and segmented the orange and handed a small chunk of wedges and a pineapple ring to each of them.

"I didn't bring much either. This is it."

Zoe looked at the offerings. "Sorry, I don't have anything with me at all. We were supposed to be back at the palace before supper."

Calandra examined the meagre meal in her palm. "It's okay, Singer kor'Dione. I'm sure we'll find something to eat eventually."

"Will we? We're in the Land of the Dead. I've always assumed spirits don't need to eat much."

Calandra had no response. She was afraid the truth behind Zoe's observation could prove their undoing. She took a small bite of salted anchovy and ate an orange wedge to banish the dryness.

"I never expected the greatest danger of the Underworld would be starvation," she mused.

Airlea sat cross-legged on a roughly even patch of floor next to her and took a few small nibbles of her own food. "In general, this has been one of the more unexpected missions I've ever been on."

Zoe looked incredulous. "*One of?*"

Airlea smiled—a rare sight, in Calandra's experience.

"Well, it's not like I've been on a lot," Airlea said self-consciously. "But there was that time during Tanni's and my last year at the Academy when I was part of an expedition to Dolphin Cove—you know, after that big hurricane two years back hit the east side of the island so hard? The siren force was stretched a little thin, so Daskala Lida volunteered our year to assist with the rebuilding efforts."

Zoe nodded. "I remember that. My pod was assigned to Haven. It would have been a nice break from guard duty if Haven hadn't been such a mess at the time."

Airlea continued. "Our student pod was helping supervise a *douloi* reconstruction crew under Rhapsodist Stamatia kor'Zylina's command for a village that had been nearly flattened. This was before she was teaching at the Academy. Anyway, it was dreadfully boring, so Tanni suggested we pitch in alongside the men and start plastering bricks. When Rhapsodist kor'Zylina found us, all our uniforms were a torn, dirty mess. Rhapsodist kor'Zylina was going to write us all up for shoddy appearance, and when she demanded to know who was responsible, Tanni stood up. The rhapsodist dressed her up and down for destruction of Academy property, but Tanni just said, 'We could have done it naked, I suppose, but that would have been against dress code. But isn't it better to replace a couple uniforms than for these children to go another night without a roof over their heads?' And that with six little girls whose apartment we were rebuilding watching the incident with big guppy eyes. The rhapsodist was so embarrassed, she unslung her *deiktis* scabbard and joined in with the rest of us."

Calandra snorted a laugh, despite herself. "That's exactly what Tanni would do. She was always so calm and generous about everything, and she always lent a helping hand wherever one was needed."

Airlea's smile became bittersweet. "I know. I miss her a lot." She shook her head, looking off into the distance. "Anyway, Rhapsodist kor'Zylina never said another peep about our ruined uniforms. She just had them replaced when we got back to the palace. I suspect she might even be part of the reason Tanni got promoted to rhapsodist so quickly—she probably put in a good word with Piper kor'Dimitri, and that's why Tanni was assigned to one of the piper's pods right after she graduated."

"And why were you?" Calandra asked.

Airlea flushed. "I don't know, actually. Luck of the draw, I suppose. It was nice to stay close to home. My mother lives just up the Paradise Valley, and I was able to visit her pretty often." She looked at her crossed legs. "Well, I used to be able to. It's not safe now."

Calandra watched Airlea while chewing a tiny piece of pineapple slowly to gain as much value from it as possible. She'd known Airlea and Tanni had served together on the same pod and had been in the same class at the Academy, but she'd had no idea how close they were. In reality, there was a great deal of Tanni's life she'd never known about, despite the telepathic emotional bond they'd shared since she was twelve and Tanni thirteen. An unexpected pang of jealousy stabbed her that there were things about Tanni which Airlea had seen and Calandra had not.

She frowned and opened her pouch, shoving in her few leftover remnants of food for later. That was ridiculous. Tanni was gone now. Calandra should be glad her friend had been so loved and admired. And on top of that, it was obvious Airlea had made sacrifices to join their cause, just like everyone else had. Why couldn't Calandra be more grateful for that?

As she put her food away, she noticed the double-pointed amethyst in her pouch and thought of the night she'd collected it from the Crystal Cavern after a swimming lesson with Osaze, not long before their ill-fated wedding. That was before guards had been posted in the lower hallways at all times, because no one suspected anyone was using them—even still, that night, they would have been caught if not for a well-placed alcove behind a pillar, in which they had hidden while a siren patrol passed by, protected from detection by Calandra's Tear. The moment the patrol had passed, Osaze kissed her deeply, but she'd been caught by surprise and off-balance, and they had fallen out of the alcove into the hallway. Thanks to the curves of the Opal Palace design, the sirens were already out of sight.

At once, something that had been niggling at her mind came into sharp focus.

"It's a triquetra!" she blurted.

"What?" Zoe frowned.

"These tunnels. They're curved and interconnected, just like the wings of the Opal Palace. The Opal Palace is a triquetra around the Mother's Heart chamber. I think this is a triquetra around the crystal cavern. Or maybe the lake. It might be important somehow."

Zoe looked thoughtfully at Calandra, then shook her head. "No. You might be right about the lake being the centre, but I was counting our turns, and even assuming we'd been travelling along the outer channels of a shape like that, we would have found one of our marks by now."

Airlea stared at the ceiling in thought. "Actually, I think she's on to something. Not a triquetra, maybe, but it might be an eternity knot shape like that. Which means if we go that way"—she pointed at the tunnel directly across from the passage from which they'd entered this chamber—"we should end up back at the lake."

Calandra's heart fell. "So we've been going in a giant loop all this time? Why haven't we seen Zale and Damaris?"

Zoe scowled, obviously as frustrated as Calandra. "They could be in another part of the loop and we'd never know."

"Maybe they saw your marks and are following us," Airlea suggested. "Perhaps we should turn around and retrace our steps."

Calandra's perpetual headache spiked in pain, and she clenched her fists and drew in a breath to control her reaction.

Airlea studied her. "Your pain seems worse here."

Calandra nodded, her eyes still closed. "Sending Mad healers to the Abyss might help protect the mortal world, but I'm guessing it did absolutely nothing for the healers who were banished."

Granted, there had not been many in their history who had required that extreme fate. But Calandra had a new appreciation of what those who had come here before her must have experienced. And they would have been alone—no companion with the skill to subdue the pain, however temporarily.

"Well, I say we rest here for an hour or so before we continue on." Airlea looked between them. "We'll do no good to Zale and Damaris if we're only staying one step ahead of them. This will give them a chance to catch up. And us a chance to sleep." She let loose with a big yawn. "I can't remember the last time I was this tired."

Calandra looked sharply at the young woman. "Would you say you feel more tired than usual?"

"Definitely." Airlea found a place next to the wall and sat down, leaning against it. "Like I could sleep for a thousand years." She closed her eyes and looked as though she might nod off that second.

"Wait!" Calandra said.

Airlea and Zoe started, staring at Calandra with with wide, bloodshot eyes.

"This place makes you tired, don't you see? We're in the Underworld. What would happen if we all fall asleep at once? It must be some kind of trap."

In truth, though, she could barely keep her own eyes open. Sleep sounded like the best idea anyone had ever had.

"We need rest though," she continued, covering her own yawn with the back of her hand. "Let's take turns keeping watch. I'll go first. One hour each, so we can each have two hours rest."

Zoe shook her head and stood. "No. I'll go first. You need it more than I do."

Calandra wanted to object, but the bundle of bonds throbbed and a corresponding red pulse momentarily obliterated her vision. She put her hand in front of her eyes, took a breath to control the pain, and when she was feeling more composed, nodded to Zoe.

"Fine. Wake me next. No more than an hour, or your closest guess."

"Yes, your highness."

Calandra thought she detected the slightest hint of a sardonic tone in Zoe's voice, but surely not. It must be the pain and the lethargy talking.

She found a relatively clean spot on the ground and stretched out on her side, resting her head on her arm.

Mother, protect us in this strange place. And may we get out of it alive.

40

UNCHARTED WATERS

JUDITH RESTED HER HEAD AGAINST the seat back in the passenger cabin of the *Luz* and closed her eyes. Despite the healing she'd received yesterday, it would take time for her body to recover fully from the three weeks of inactivity and neglect in the dungeon. But it wasn't just the physical activity that made her limbs heavy. An ocean of sorrow crushed her into the seat.

What would happen to their island now that both Calandra and Zale had gone to the Underworld? Who was strong enough to challenge the possessed madwoman in the palace—the one holding the love of Judith's life captive?

They'd found the sub that Zale and Damaris had hired waiting in a building near the edge of the Sunken City. After asking the jumpy skipper a few questions, Cleo quickly determined the woman was only a taxi driver who'd been desperate enough for a fare that she'd jumped at the money Damaris had offered her to go to "haunted" Atlantis—paid in advance. With ships crossing into Sirenian waters almost daily and making women nervous about being too far out to sea—or even travelling around the island much—business had been slow for the water taxis. When the driver found out Damaris wouldn't be returning, she was all too happy to return to safer waters as soon as possible.

Feeling someone watching her, Judith opened her eyes to see Rhea taking her measure. She hadn't told her aunt about the mysterious room in the Archive or the images on the datastone yet—she wanted to wait until they had some privacy. But the lines on Rhea's face indicated she had enough to worry her as it was. Her aunt looked as though she wanted to say something, but was hesitating.

"What is it?" Judith asked.

Meg and Cleo, the only two others in the cabin, turned to look at her.

"If you're feeling up to it, I want you to find the mole," Rhea said. "You don't know many of the new people who have arrived, so you won't be as biased by past experiences and connections when you give the truth test."

Judith clenched her teeth. She hated that it was even necessary, but she was glad Rhea had given her the job—it would give her something to take her mind off of Calandra and Matthew. Even if truth testing could be a gruelling process. "Certainly."

She thought of the paper from the Coalition rolled up in her pouch, which she'd left on the sub while they'd been in Atlantis, just in case. She glanced at Cleo. Best to wait to mention it. No telling what the *despoina* would do with that information.

But Cleo was studying Rhea.

"Calandra says I can trust you," the *despoina* said. "She implied there's something more about the bonds I should know."

Rhea pursed her lips. "So you believe what she said at the Court?"

"About the *sklavia* bond preventing the conception of boys? Her mother has proven that. As have the rest of you. Do you have a son?"

Rhea shook her head. "No, but I have a grandson. Jason." She gave a small, proud smile, her eyes looking at something the rest of them couldn't see. Then her gaze sharpened. "But that's not the only problem with the bonds."

Cleo nodded gravely. "The Madness. She said it was caused by creating a *syzagos* bond with a Redeemed man. But if that was true, why did Adonia go Mad so many years after her consort died? Especially because she wasn't that powerful to begin with?"

"The *syzagos* bond isn't the reason a healer or siren is prone to Madness. It's the way the bond pulls at someone with high empathy when a *sklavia* bond is also in place. The cognitive dissonance tears at the mind's stability. I believe the same effect can be created by holding a great number of *sklavia* bonds, whether or not a consort bond is in place."

Cleo nodded thoughtfully. "Adonia was holding at least a thousand bonds, by my calculations."

Meg leaned forward. "And Calandra is holding several thousand." She met Judith's gaze, understanding in her eyes. "She was going Mad already. That's why she did it."

Judith swallowed. She'd seen evidence of Calandra's duress, but she hadn't realized how bad it was until her seizure in the Voidstone tower. It made sense, though, with her abilities. Calandra had had her first seizure in Fire Lake, less than two weeks after she'd started her tour to collect the bonds. The condition must have progressed quickly for her to cause an earthquake only weeks later. No wonder Calandra had chosen to dive into the Voidstone after her brother with no guarantee she'd ever return. She knew she didn't have time to wait.

Cleo looked at Rhea. "Several hundred of the men that were Released when Adonia died are still unaccounted for, but despite the rumours flying through the city and the occasional person going missing, I have seen little recent evidence of marauding. Most of the women coming to the bread lines Priestess Shinara has set up have been human—our undine citizens seem to be fending fine for themselves. Narcissa has had me check to make sure the human women are consuming the food themselves and not abetting escaped Wildmen, and the answers have been inconclusive. How many of the Freemen are with you?"

Rhea narrowed her eyes at the *despoina* calculatingly, before heaving a sigh. "One hundred fifty-two of our members are from Sireniapolis. Do you intend to come retrieve them?"

"Are they going into the city to steal food and kill our citizens?"

"No."

Cleo arched a brow. "Then my answer is also no. Do you happen to know where more might be sheltering?"

The two women eyed each other like circling orcas.

Cleo clasped her hands in her lap, looking as though she chose her next words carefully. "As mistress-at-arms, it is my duty to serve the throne, and it is a duty I have always taken seriously, Healer kor'Eudoxia, despite the challenges that it presents. Queen Helena's daughters were ever divided, and now, it seems, so are her granddaughters. But before my duty to the throne comes my duty to the people the throne serves. And I don't believe Narcissa is the best choice as our next sovereign. I also believe, as disruptive as Calandra's revolution is, it is necessary. Our people are long overdue for this change. But I can't work to protect the Free human men of this island if I don't know where they are."

Judith swallowed her surprise.

After several more unblinking moments, Rhea cupped her hands over her knees. "A human woman who joined us only yesterday tells us she's been helping Freemen escape the city and smuggling them to a safe location in the hills, but she didn't tell us where it is, nor who's helping her. She's a cagey one, she is."

"Tafrara Baya, I presume?"

Rhea nodded. "Indeed. I thought you'd know of whom I spoke."

Judith watched her aunt. What Rhea said about Tafrara was true, but not completely. Tafrara hadn't told them the exact location of the refugee camp to which her mother, Baya Damya, was sending the men they successfully smuggled out of the city, but she'd said it was on the Irene River in the mountains between the Irene Plains and Valerian. Tafrara had promised the FWS could visit when they took her home, if they wished. A thought occurred to Judith—were Baya and Tafrara part of the Coalition? Their family had run the Irene Human Cooperative, a *latifundium* east of Sireniapolis, for centuries. Baya's connections among the human community on Sirenia must run deep. It would explain how her meek, soft-spoken daughter had found the resources to smuggle men out of the city in her produce wagon. For half a second, Judith wondered if Tafrara could be the mole, but decided against it. It would be foolhardy for her to be in that position, and besides, she'd only arrived yesterday. Judith would have to be careful not to let her new duty destroy harmony in the camp.

Cleo gave a wry smile, glancing at Judith and Meg. "That was gutsy, what Calandra did to break you all out of prison, and then to face Narcissa to try to reach her brother. She would have been a great queen."

Judith's heart squeezed, the despair returning. Then she straightened and frowned. "And she still will. I have not given up on her yet."

Rhea's mouth tightened. "I've read a lot of history stones, and I've never seen anything about a Mad undine returning from the Abyss."

"That's because they need a key. Calandra said Damon told her about it today during the meeting."

Rhea's gaze sharpened. "So you believe her claim that Narcissa is possessed? Did you see something?"

"I did," Cleo said quietly. "And I felt something. Narcissa has been off ever since her mother died. I didn't know what it was until Calandra told me about this creature while on the way to Atlantis. Damon, did you say his name is?"

Judith nodded, then looked at her aunt. "You are telling me you still could not sense him?"

Rhea hesitated, then her shoulders slumped. "I didn't know what it was. I suppose it must be Damon, unless we were *all* hallucinating. And it would explain a great deal. But if Narcissa is possessed, what can we do about it?"

"Maybe you could arrest her," Meg suggested to Cleo.

Cleo shook her head. "On what grounds? You can't arrest the acting monarch on a hunch with no evidence." She frowned. "Trust me, if I had enough evidence to arrest her, I would have already, possession or no."

"Why?" Rhea asked.

Cleo hesitated. "I'm fairly certain Narcissa killed her mother. But I have no way to prove it."

This news was so shocking that silence settled over the cabin for several moments.

"What about Hebe?" Judith asked.

"What about her?" Rhea frowned.

Cleo peered at Judith with interest. "Yes, I have considered her, and I take consolation that if Narcissa is removed, there is still one successor for the throne, but—"

"No," Judith said. "I mean, yes, Hebe could take the throne, and, with guidance, she might even turn into a good queen. But I was trying to say maybe she knows something about Narcissa and Adonia. Did you see her today? The poor girl was terrified of her sister. Something is going on. It might be Damon's behaviour, but there could be more to it."

Cleo nodded. "Calandra was concerned about her too. I'll look into it."

"It would seem we each have problems to solve," Rhea said quietly. "Thank you for the tip about the mole. I assume if Narcissa—or Damon, as the case may be—wanted to squelch our activities, he would have given you the order to bring us in by now. You must know where we're located?"

Cleo gave her a shrewd look. "If Narcissa knows, she hasn't told me. And please don't tell me now, or I shall be forced to divulge the information if she asks." She blew out air. "I don't look forward to telling her about today's events in Atlantis. She might have claimed to want Calandra and Zale to restore the Heartstone, but I'm sure neither she nor this Damon creature will mourn their loss. The bigger concern is that without Calandra here, the archons no longer have cause to dither, so what will stop Narcissa from securing her claim?"

"Keep looking for a reason to arrest her," Rhea urged, "and we'll try to find a way to restore the barrier." She glanced at the sodden collection bags against the wall. "Maybe one of those has the answer." She glanced at Meg.

"I can't wait to find it," Meg said with determination.

In the silence that fell, Judith considered mentioning the message from the Coalition again, but, tipped off by her aunt's discretion, she decided to wait. The *despoina* may support their revolution, but she was a woman of honour and had a reputation for forthright honesty. There was no sense putting her in a difficult position with information she might be required to pass on to Damon if asked, or risk herself trying to conceal.

But there was something the *despoina* might be willing to do.

"Despoina Cleo?" Judith's voice quivered. When the siren looked up, she cleared her throat. "Would you please do what you can to safeguard Matthew, Narcissa's bodyguard, as well? I know you may not be able to do much, but I fear she is mistreating him, and . . ."

Tears welled in her eyes, and she blinked them away, angry with herself.

Not that the *despoina* wouldn't be able to sense her emotion anyway.

"I'll do what I can, Kore kor'Ignatia." Cleo's face was impassive, but her tone was kind.

Judith gave a tight smile. "Thank you."

"And see what you can find out about the key Judith mentioned," Meg added. "If we can find that, we can still hope for Calandra and Zale's safe return."

"Maybe even Delphine's," Rhea added.

Cleo gave a tight-lipped acknowledgement. "We must have hope. Without that, we have nothing."

Rhea met her gaze and smiled, and a hopeful flame burned in Judith's chest.

Nick's voice vibrated tinnily from the commstone on the wall. "We're pulling into Manta Ray Bay."

Cleo stood and touched the stone. "You can drop me off here. I could use a good swim to clear my head. I'll make sure you get away cleanly, but please use a circuitous route, regardless."

"Will do," Nick replied.

The submersible slowed to a stop. Through the small window, the buildings of Sireniapolis gleamed white in the moonlight around the glittering bay.

Cleo gave the occupants of the cabin one final look. "I am out of my depth. But times like these require us all to explore uncharted waters."

Rhea gave her a smile of understanding. "Indeed, *despoina*. Should you ever need us, please call. And alert us if there is something we should know."

"Like, say, some wandering Freemen who need a place to go?"

Rhea dipped her chin, amused. "As one example."

Cleo's lips stretched into a rare smile. She gave a crisp, deep salute, then spun and took the two steps to the ladder before clambering to the deck above.

Judith clasped her hands together to steady them. They were all in uncharted waters now. But, for the first time in weeks, she dared hope there might be safe harbour on the other side.

"We'll keep the island safe for you while you're gone, Calandra," she whispered. "But please don't be gone too long."

41

MYSTERIES

CALANDRA WOKE WITH A START. She'd been dreaming of the nightmare void of failure that so often haunted her, where she was alone, hanging in a black, empty ocean. But when she opened her eyes, nothing seemed any different—she was still lost in black nothingness.

She could have sworn she had heard someone calling her name, but as she lay in the pitch dark, trying to remember where she was, there was not a whisper of sound around her. Why was her bed so hard? The small chambers of Margaret House weren't exactly luxurious, but Ignatia and her crew had managed to scrounge up straw-stuffed mattresses for everyone, at least.

Then she remembered everything—Narcissa's eyes, the journey to Atlantis, her dive through the Voidstone, her wanderings in this strange place.

Calandra sat up, and the darkness shifted to the dim gloom that had accompanied them so far. Not far from her, Airlea still snoozed near the wall—now laying curled on the floor instead of propped against it. She couldn't see Zoe anywhere.

Leaping to her feet in alarm, she took a few steps into the dark, her globe of gloom moving with her. She found Zoe a few paces away, also sound asleep.

Her heart still thundered against her ribs. What had awoken her? She couldn't shake the feeling they were not alone.

She put her hand on the hilt of her diving knife, which seemed laughably useless against the incorporeal sense of doom that pervaded this place. She wished she had a *deiktis* staff of her own to protect herself from small threats. Would the lulling tones of sirensong even have an effect

346

on creatures of the Underworld? She supposed she could use her other abilities to defend herself, as Thea had against Adonia at the end—Zoe had told her it had taken the best stone healers in Sireniapolis days to repair the Fountain of Atargatis, which Thea had evidently cracked in two during their fight.

Looking around, she surveyed her options. The tunnel walls and floor were smooth, offering no readily available rocks to hurl at an attacker. The nearest water—the only element she could use without touching it—was the lake, which was too far away to summon. Her best defense would be air, but it was the element she was least adept with. Besides, she'd never used her abilities for anything so destructive before—not intentionally, anyway. Though the stone healers who had repaired the damage her miniature earthquake had caused might disagree, she wasn't sure she could bring herself to do something like that on purpose.

Still, she kept her awareness on the element in case it would prove handy, one hand ready to summon and send. With her other hand, she slid her diving knife out of its sheath on her belt—the one with the ornate carved-bone handle and sheath Tanni had given her as a bonding gift before her failed wedding—and took careful steps around the perimeter of the chamber, her senses straining to find whomever had called to her.

By the time she returned to her sleeping companions, she'd found nothing. She had tried to follow the thread of that ominous presence, but it led in no defined direction. Still, the uneasy sensation of being watched remained.

Uncertain what to do but still on guard, she sat on the floor between her companions where she could see them both and sat erect and cross-legged, eyes and mind straining toward the darkness. To still her nerves, she began unravelling her braids, which had come unpinned while she slept. She didn't have a brush, but her waist-length locks were easily finger-combed. The circlet wouldn't fit in her pouch and she hesitated leaving it behind, so she carefully repositioned it over her head before restyling her hair into a single braid falling down her back, with some of the hair holding the circlet in place.

Calandra . . .

She bolted to her feet, holding her knife at the ready. She hadn't so much *heard* her name being called as sensed it. There was definitely some-one—or something—here.

"Who's there?" Her voice barely even wavered.

No one answered. After a few more moments, the sensation faded. Ten minutes later when it hadn't returned, Calandra cautiously sat back down and laid the knife on the stone in front of her.

The hopelessness of their situation pressed against her mind, and she cursed her own impetuousness. They hadn't found a hint of where Zale and Damaris had gone, they didn't know where to find a gateway out of here, and even if they did, they didn't have the key to leave the Underworld and go back home. She'd hoped she and Zale would be able to find a way to open the gateway using their powers instead of a key, since their powers working in unison had had such an effect on the Heartstone—but that would only work if she found both her brother *and* the gate. What if she'd led Zoe and Airlea here, and instead of rescuing Zale, Damaris, and maybe even her mother, all she did was condemn three more souls to hell?

And what had Zale been thinking, coming here with only Damaris for help? If only he'd listened to Calandra, they could have come up with a plan, found the keys they needed, and had a much better chance of success. Instead, they could all very well be stuck here for eternity.

She wondered if Damon had been telling the truth about the keys. He'd told her the truth about needing male and female powers to heal the Heartstone, so not everything he said was deceitful—just revealed in such a way as to manipulate others to his will. The problem was, he was so skilled at it that she hadn't known his intention with the Heartstone until it was too late. She wondered what he was hoping to accomplish now—he certainly wanted something, or he would never have told her about the key in the first place.

Isn't it obvious? He wants to free the Grigori.

She shook her head at her own argument. He probably did want that, but he also hadn't wanted her to come to Hades without the keys to do so. Why had that been so important to him?

She glanced at her sleeping companions. Should she tell them what Damon had said about the keys? She thought about it, then shook her head. That would only worry them and would solve nothing. Better to try to find a solution on her own first. But how?

Her hand went to her pouch and the amethyst she carried—a miniature version of the enormous crystals in the lake cavern somewhere nearby. She loosened the drawstring and pulled out the small violet stone, along with the two datastones she'd taken from the Atlantis Archive. She frowned at the stones, remembering the confusing images she'd seen on them, and placed them on the floor of the chamber beside her knife. Then she examined the amethyst.

Like everything else here, the energy in the stone seemed sedated—but not in the same way the energy in the giant crystals that had grown here felt hollow and false. More like the vitality of the stone had simply been turned down, as though it were affected by the lethargy too. Even now, despite the blood pumping through her veins at her strange awakening, she could feel the unnatural weight of the gloom pulling at her soul.

She closed her eyes and concentrated on the amethyst. Could she somehow make it into a key like the one Damon had said he was looking for? She touched the stone gently with her mind, exploring the ways its energy interacted with the strange energy of this place, but she found nothing useful.

Frustrated, she opened her eyes and set the crystal on the floor. Next, she picked up the two datastones.

She couldn't stop thinking about the strange images the stone reader in the temple had shown her, Zoe, and Judith. Where had the statue of the Mother been in that room? Who were the lumasi, undines, and humans worshipping?

And then there was the mystery of the chamber itself. Why was there a mechanism that would drain and keep the water from a room that had never been meant to be immersed? And how was such a thing accomplished?

She put down the tourmalinated quartz Tear, with its slivers of black crisscrossing the translucent stone, and cupped the faceted teardrop-shaped blue sapphire stone in her palm. Closing her eyes, she extended her awareness into the Tear, delving it for what images she could find. She saw snippets of a male and female undine on thrones in a palace she didn't recognize—perhaps one in Atlantis, for the light seemed to be artificial, like the images she'd seen on the other stone. There were other creatures there too—lumasi of various types, including winged bulls, winged lions, and griffins. Images of dragons seated blithely on either side of the thrones made her blood run cold. There was even a water-bound race with blue-green skin, angular features, slanted black eyes, green hair, and spines along their backs and the ridges of their forward-curling tails swimming along canals between beautiful buildings that had to be to Atlantis in its heyday. Tritons? No one had seen them for ages. But the more she concentrated, the more the throbbing bundle of bonds in her mind glowed red-hot, the pain ascending to a blinding crescendo of white light—until it all went black.

This time, she awoke to Airlea shaking her arm, hard.

"Calandra, wake up. Calandra!"

She sat up slowly, her head still throbbing, but not as badly as before. The chamber had been altered—cracks ran along the floor and a few boulders had tumbled from the ceiling.

Calandra stared at the debris and gingerly touched a tender bump that had formed on her forehead.

"What happened?" Then she gave her head a small shake. "Never mind. I know what happened. Me."

Airlea's round green eyes were troubled. "Let me try again."

She lifted her hand toward Calandra's forehead, but Calandra put up an arm to stop her.

"It's no use. Something about this place accentuates the pain of the bonds. They're about as good as they're going to be right now."

She glanced up and froze. On the far side of the chamber, floating as though in water, was Damon as he used to appear to her in her dreams—a beautiful undine man in *ichthys* state with a golden-scaled tail, a billowing cloud of long black hair around fine-boned, sensual features, and eyes that swirled with golden light.

She scrambled for her knife and leapt to her feet, holding it aloft.

"Get behind me," she said to her companions.

Damon's lips curved in a cruel smile.

"Calandra, what are you doing?" Airlea cried in alarm.

She put a hand on Calandra's shoulder, but Calandra didn't dare look away from the creature who had already caused her so much pain.

"Don't you see him?"

Zoe raised her staff defensively, but she peered into the darkness without focus. "Who?"

"Damon. He's right there. Don't you see him?"

Damon laughed, but no sound came from him.

Airlea shook her head. "There's nothing there, Calandra. It's just us here. You're staring at a wall."

Calandra looked at Airlea. The siren held her half-*deiktis* aloft in her hand, but without the readiness she would have if there were an apparent threat.

"You can't see him?" When Calandra looked back toward the far wall of the chamber, the apparition was gone.

Had she been hallucinating?

She looked back at her companions, at their alarm and concern, and lowered her knife. Her blood still surged through her ears like the deafening report of a pistol shrimp's attack. Zoe was looking at her as though *she* were the threat.

"I'm fine. I—I thought I saw Damon, but he's gone now. It was nothing, like you said. Perhaps that is one of the dangers of this place—seeing your fears."

Zoe nodded uncertainly. "Perhaps. We'll all be careful."

"Yes. Before you trust your eyes, check with the others to see if the vision is real." *But I was the only one who saw Damon in the Voidstone when I lost my arm, and that didn't make him less real.* She hid her consternation by sheathing her knife.

"If we're safe, I'm going over there to relieve myself." Zoe pointed at the far side of the chamber, near where Damon's apparition had been moments before. "I sense no one here but us."

Calandra swallowed and nodded, her senses confirming they were alone. She hadn't sensed Damon when he was floating in front of her either, but she'd always had a hard time sensing him—until he'd possessed Narcissa. But how could he be in Sireniapolis and here at the same time? *He wasn't real. Accept it. It's one more sign of your fracturing mind.*

She glanced at the floor. Her amethyst and the two datastones were still laying there. She scooped them up and dropped them in her pouch.

"What are those?" Airlea adjusted her swimming belt and back scabbard harness, then slid her half-*deiktis* into it.

Calandra tightened the pouch string, fighting simmering resentment at having to answer Airlea's questions. *That's not fair. She's in the same danger as me. I can't hold it against her forever that she came without being asked.* Still, Calandra practically had to force out her explanation.

"I found the Tears in Atlantis just before you called us to the tower. I've been trying to figure out what's on them."

Airlea checked her diving knife blade and tucked it back in its sheath. "And did you find anything?" She widened her stance and started doing some stretches.

Calandra frowned. "Not really. What I could see didn't make any sense. I'll need a stone reader to get a proper look at it."

A few stretches to work out the kinks of the uncomfortable sleep on a stone floor—and her lingering irritation from the seizure—would be a good idea. Calandra moved away from Airlea so she'd have space to stretch.

Zoe rejoined them. "The light here is so weird. Did you know it's brightest over here? I could barely see a thing on that side. I can't remember ever being someplace so dark."

Calandra pulled her arm sideways across her body with her other hand to loosen her shoulder muscle. "It seems to follow us, which *is* odd. Almost as though we're the source."

Airlea glanced at the edges of the halo of gloom. It illuminated a half-dozen paces on either side of them. "Yet another mystery of this place. But if that's the case, it might be stronger when we're in a group."

Zoe cocked a brow in thought. "That must be it. Because whenever I move away from the two of you, I can barely see a pace in front of my nose."

"I guess that's one more reason to stick together." Calandra managed a smile. "As if we needed one."

Airlea smiled back. "Indeed." She glanced back at the floor, and her eyes widened. "Are you two seeing that?" She pointed at the floor.

Calandra followed her gaze, and her jaw dropped. "What in the name of the Mother?"

42

ZOE'S SECRET

C ALANDRA, A IRLEA, AND Z OE STARED at one of the cracks in the floor of the tunnel, which had begun to seal itself up again. The boulders were eroding into sand that streamed along the floor and walls to fill in the large cracks above and below, resolidifying as smooth stone once more. The cracks had all but disappeared.

Calandra watched in amazement. "I'm seeing it *and* feeling it. But I still hardly believe it."

"That explains why these tunnels are in such great shape." Zoe crossed her arms and snorted. "I bet the stone healers at the Opal Palace wish repairing damage were that easy."

Calandra's face flushed with heat. Zoe glanced at her and stopped smirking, but didn't apologize.

Calandra turned away to hide her embarrassment. "Indeed." She resumed her exercise stance. "Join us, singer."

Zoe took up position near them as they transitioned into the next form of the *Tropos Hydor Zon*. Spring Rain on Palm Leaves flowed into Mountain Stream Bubbling Over Rocks, then several other forms before finishing with the Pool of Stillness, as it always did.

As they finished the forms and stood, Calandra closed her eyes and clenched her teeth, taking controlled breaths to hide the still-persisting pain.

Of course, Airlea noticed.

"Can you tell me why you must keep doing that?" Airlea asked. "What's worse than before?"

Calandra wasn't sure she could, but she may as well try. She forced

353

the words out between gritted teeth with her eyes still closed. "It's like the bonds I hold are stronger while I'm here than they were in the mortal plane. I don't know what it's like for the men, but for me, it's all I can do just to think about anything else for even a second." The distraction of speaking and having to explain it helped. The pain receded slightly, and she opened her eyes. "It's a little better now."

Zoe watched her with a cool expression.

Airlea smoothed her short hair with her fingers and stood, obviously ready to go. "Maybe because this place is less substantial than the mortal plane, matters of spirit become more obvious."

Calandra shook her head. "Then why does it feel as though spirit is what's missing from the structures here? I mean, these stones are solid." She gave a little jump to emphasize her point. Her feet barely made a sound as they landed on the warm grey rock. "It's like they're *more* solid somehow, and that means there is less room for the spirit element. All they are is earth, packed so tightly that spirit has no room to breathe."

"But we brought spirit with us, in us, as part of us. Maybe the lines of spirit that connect you to the men are accentuated because of the lack of it anywhere else."

A chill ran over Calandra, a subtle recognition of truth. "Maybe that's how Damon was able to contact me when he was imprisoned here. And maybe I didn't just hallucinate him—maybe I'm still connected with him somehow."

She placed her hand on the warm stone wall to mark the tunnel they were about to walk down. Zoe stood in the tunnel entrance, waiting.

Airlea shuddered. "I hope not." She walked over to stand next to Zoe.

Calandra concentrated on her work. "Me, too. And honestly, I don't think that's the case. My mind is free of him, and he won't find it so easy to ensnare me again."

The mark complete, they began walking down the corridor, enveloped by the strange gloom.

"How can you be sure?" Airlea asked.

"I . . . have protection I didn't before. It's difficult to explain."

Airlea didn't press her. Zoe gave her a look, but also said nothing.

Calandra was glad. She hadn't been able to put into words to anyone exactly what had happened to her in the Heartstone, how the web of golden threads that Damon had bound her with for so many years had torn—not because of her, but because the Spirit of the Heartstone had empowered her to break free.

That was it! *That* was why Zale had resisted her—Damon must have done the same thing to her brother that he'd done to her for five years. But he'd only had Zale in his power for a few weeks. How was he able to deceive her brother so deeply? But she thought she already knew the answer—Zale was innocent of the ways of the undines. It seemed their mother had taught him almost nothing of his past, which would leave him open to believe almost anything he was told now that he was here, even the lies Damon fed him about her. She knew from experience how Damon could deceive someone so completely they had no idea they were being deceived, and the bonds were strong and tight. How could she help Zale break free?

You are not alone.

The words fell into her heart, washing her in gentle comfort. The Spirit. The Spirit was guiding her, even here—it had kept its word. The Mother still favoured her.

For the first time since they'd arrived in the Underworld, she felt a glimmer of hope.

"Calandra," said Zoe from a few steps ahead of them, "if you can sense those bonds better here, perhaps you would be able to sense Zale better too. I've already tried reaching for Damaris, but I can't even feel the presences in the lake from this distance, so she's at least that far away. You might have better luck, though. With your greater sensitivity, I mean. Along with that resonance you were talking about."

Calandra stopped, and the others turned to look at her.

"That's brilliant, Zoe. Let's try that before we wander another step to who-knows-where. I've been keeping my senses open for Zale, but haven't done an intentional search. Here, let's hold hands. I can use your spirit to amplify my senses further, just like a deep healing."

Airlea immediately took Calandra's hand and offered her other hand to Zoe, but Zoe hesitated ever so slightly before returning the gesture. Calandra glanced at Zoe, curious about her hesitation, but the singer's eyes were closed in preparation for joining the circle, and the emotions coming through their physical connection were anxious and determined.

Perhaps Calandra had imagined Zoe's reluctance. Or maybe Zoe was more worried than she wanted to let on and didn't want Calandra and Airlea to see the full extent of her fear, so she'd taken a moment to compose her shield. Zoe was a warrior—she would want to appear strong, even if she were terrified.

Calandra understood the feeling.

She closed her eyes, channelling the spirit her companions poured into her along with her own into a single cord, then sent it questing into the void around them. The sensation was a little bit like creating the *pisti* bonds she'd shared with Tanni and Osaze. The bond with Tanni had been broken when she'd died—an emptiness that had been largely eclipsed by the pain of the bonds of late—but Calandra had unravelled the bond with Osaze herself when she'd set him free and sent him back to Africa. She still missed them both so much—she missed having the gentle awareness of the two people she loved most in the world sitting at the edge of her mind. All she was left with these days was the flaming red wound created by the *sklavia* bonds she carried—bonds undines were never meant to form. But this sharing of spirit—this was nice. It was soothing, like when Osaze would send her calming emotions through—

"I feel something!"

Calandra wanted to open her eyes, but she kept them closed, concentrating on the presence her mind had touched.

In her mind's eye, a blurry male figure stood with his back to her in a field of grey fog. She wondered if she could communicate the way Damon had when he'd connected with her.

Zale?

The man turned, and his features came into focus.

Calandra?

It was Osaze. He seemed to be in pain, his mind unfocused.

Calandra, is that you?

A surge of emotion—love and desire and rage all mixed together— flowed toward her like a slap. Calandra's eyes flew open and she released her companion's hands. The connection was lost.

"What? What happened?" Zoe demanded. "Did you find them?"

"I . . . I found Osaze. Somehow, I touched him. But how could I find him more easily than Zale? He must be a hundred times further away. Maybe a thousand."

Airlea frowned. "I don't think *here* is particularly close to anywhere on Earth. Or maybe it's close to everywhere. It might be just as easy to contact one person as another."

"You found *Osaze*?" Zoe put her hands on her hips. "You were supposed to be looking for Damaris. And Zale." Zoe turned around and stared at the darkness, her chest heaving. Anger rolled off her, but beneath it, Calandra sensed a deep unease.

"I'm sorry, Zoe. I got distracted and started thinking about him, and there he was."

She wished the moment had lasted longer. That brief touch was like tasting a single drop of water after wandering in a desert. Her chest tightened with restrained tears.

Zoe crossed her arms and spun. "Your lover isn't even here, and you still found him first. I know you've been doing nothing but mope around because of him the last few weeks—Kynthia told me all about it when you came to get Meg and Judith. But you sent him away, so it's time to grow up and get over it. Stop wasting all your time thinking about him and be present, Calandra. You've got responsibilities, but he is no longer one of them. It's almost as though he holds a *sklavia* bond on *you*."

Calandra stared at the siren, stricken. Zoe was right. She *had* been stewing in her losses, letting it cloud her decisions and keep her stuck in a mire of self-pity. Tanni, Thea, Osaze—they were with her every moment, constant spectres to remind her of the poor decisions she'd made.

"Zoe . . ." Airlea began.

"No," Calandra said. "She's right." She swallowed, the words thick in her throat. "I've been selfish and self-centred, and look where that got us. If I had been spending more time thinking about Zale the last few weeks instead of Osaze, perhaps we wouldn't be in this situation. Let me try again."

But this time when their hands connected, she could sense what lay beneath the irate siren's shield. There was more to Zoe's anger than concern for her sister.

Calandra opened her eyes. "Singer kor'Dione. Zoe."

Zoe flinched, then opened her eyes to look at Calandra. Airlea looked between them with a furrowed brow.

"Yes, your highness?" Zoe's shield became impenetrable once more.

Calandra clenched her jaw. "I know you're hiding something. Tell me."

Zoe pulled her hands from Calandra's and Airlea's grips. "My emotions are my business."

"This isn't about your emotions, and you're trying to distract me. There's something you've been keeping from me. What is it?"

She stared into Zoe's eyes, sensing the war raging there. Whatever it was, Zoe didn't want to say anything.

The siren dropped her gaze to the floor.

"Osaze may not exactly be in Africa," she muttered.

"What?" Calandra stepped back in surprise. "Where is he?"

Zoe tensed and glanced at Calandra. "Barbados."

Calandra stood still in shock. "Barbados! That's a slave colony!"

When the undines brought in ships for the summer Redemption Moon harvest to replenish their male population, they usually targeted slaving ships because there were so many people aboard, most of them male. The slaves on board were almost invariably from the African lands across the ocean to the east, and they were frequently suffering from neglect, ill-treatment, and disease. The tales the Redeemed men told—and the women who'd come on the ships with them—confirmed the abuses of power that had always justified the undine practice of Redemption. If Calandra hadn't known Osaze as a child, and hadn't received the eye-opening message from her mother on her Tear, she would probably never have questioned her people's fear of Freemen and their belief that Redeeming them was the right thing to do. And without that, she would never have Freed Osaze in the first place.

But once she had, she came to see men in a completely different light. Osaze was nothing like she'd been told to expect a human man to be. He had been gentle and strong, honest and protective. He had been a better bodyguard as a Freeman than when he'd been enslaved. He'd put her needs before his own, and made her realize that she hadn't really understood what love could be until she'd met him. Love *had* to be free, or it wasn't love at all.

The whole reason Calandra had sent Osaze away was to protect him and his freedom—which was why she'd told Zoe to take him and his mother back to their home in Africa. There, they should have had the autonomy to find their family and live in peace—unlike the colonies on the islands nearby, where class was determined by distinctions in shades of brown Calandra would never understand. On Sirenia, Osaze had been enslaved because of his gender. On Barbados, he would be in constant danger of being enslaved because of his skin colour.

"Why would you take him there?" Calandra demanded.

Zoe's voice was as tight as her posture. "When he woke up, he didn't want to go to Africa. He became enraged and demanded to be let off at the nearest island. Urbi didn't argue. So I took him there."

Osaze had been *enraged*? That seemed unlikely. Then again, he'd been pretty angry when she'd touched him moments ago. Guilt twisted its knife in her gut.

"But . . . Barbados is nowhere near the route you should have been taking, and his people are treated like animals there. You should have taken him somewhere else, somewhere he would have had a fighting chance."

Zoe's eyes stared at the darkness behind Calandra. "I did what I thought was best at the time, your highness. I'm sorry to have disappointed you. He seems to be a resourceful man, skilled at deception. He's probably doing just fine among his own kind."

There was a hard edge to Zoe's voice. Calandra wondered if her grudge against Osaze had less to do with his status as a male and more to do with the fact Zoe had associated with him for weeks as a Freeman before she'd realized the truth. Zoe's emotional shield had definitely become more impenetrable since she'd committed to their cause at Elpida. Given her position in Narcissa's inner circle, that had been a blessing. Now Calandra wished she could pry a chink from it and sense what Zoe was feeling—but she hesitated to touch her again and violate her companion's privacy.

"I understand. Thank you, Zoe. I trust you."

Zoe's shoulders relaxed slightly, and she met Calandra's eyes at last. "Shall we resume our search then, your highness?"

Calandra couldn't help but notice that Zoe had not gone back to the more informal personal address they often used in private. She sighed.

"Yes. I can still sense nothing of Zale, so a manual search is our only— wait."

Her nerves vibrated faintly with the resonance that indicated Zale's proximity. She couldn't tell where it was, but she once more got that impression of someone calling her name and felt drawn toward the corridor ahead.

"I can feel him. I think he's up there. Come!"

She broke into a run and heard her companions jogging beside her. The further they ran, the more presences she could feel—all of them malevolent. Was Zale in trouble?

Calandra . . .

Just before they reached the end of the tunnel that would take them out into the crystal-filled cavern beyond, Calandra stopped short. Near the end of the tunnel stood a beautiful woman in an orb of light, wearing a fine white linen peplos trimmed in delicate gold embroidery along the hem that brushed the tops of her bare feet. The top of the tubular garment was folded down to the woman's thighs and snugly belted with a gold chain, and gold clasps on her shoulders and upper arm revealed her creamy shoulders along the upper edge. Long walnut-coloured hair was pulled away from her face and fell in thick waves down her back, and her eyes glowed faintly emerald in the gloom of the cavern. She looked as regal as a goddess.

When she saw them, she smiled.

"Hello, Calandra."
Calandra stopped short, her mouth as dry as the stones.
"M—Mother?"

43

THE ONCOMING DARK

Osaze swayed on the back of the horse behind the girl with the thick black curls, gripping the seat of her saddle to keep from falling off. Flies buzzed lazily around his bloody back, and the evening heat and humidity made sweat trickle down his palms and temples.

He fought to stay conscious, but between the warm air and the gentle movement of the animal beneath him, he found himself fading.

He jerked his head up and clutched at the saddle. He'd nearly lost his grip and had started sliding off to one side.

Josefine glanced over her shoulder. "Hold on to my waist. I'll help you stay on."

Osaze didn't know what else to do, so he did as she instructed, slipping both arms around her tiny frame. She grabbed his forearms with her free hand, curling her arm around both of his. He doubted her grip would do much besides take her down with him if he were to fall off, but the human connection was nice.

He closed his eyes. Her curly hair was soft against his chin, and she smelled like rosemary and sweat—the fresh, sweet sweat of a woman who kept herself clean, like Calandra's. He hadn't bathed since he'd been unceremoniously dumped on this hunk of rock and could no longer even smell his own foulness. She didn't shy away though, for which he was grateful.

With his eyes closed, he could almost imagine it was Calandra's slim waist his arms encircled. They had never had the time nor freedom to be together openly, and he'd never been able to hold her close while they travelled anywhere, needing to keep up the pretense that he had been

Redeemed. But in private, he and Calandra had had nearly a month of discovering each other after she'd freed him from the *sklavia* bond, both while he'd been guarding her while she toured the island to gather more bonds at Adonia's behest, and after she'd been sent back to the capital to have her hand regrown by Thea and had Freed him from the bond Narcissa had laid on him. In the end, it hadn't been the bonds or Narcissa's scheming or even the laws of the land that had separated them, but Calandra herself.

Now, every time he thought of those tender kisses and loving words, the sweetness of the memory was blurred by anger and betrayal.

How could she have ever thought he'd prefer this to whatever might have come of them being together?

Josefine guided her horse over to the man who'd helped them flee the plantation—without attracting any notice, a fact Osaze found astounding. Romero glanced at her.

"Yes, Miss Chapman?"

"Mr. Romero, we should get off the road. I am certain my father will soon miss me, and what we have done will not go undiscovered for long."

Romero gave her a warm smile. "Do not worry, Miss Chapman. You are safe with me. Do you believe me?"

She regarded him for a long moment. "Yes. I do."

He gave a small nod. "Good."

Osaze said nothing. The gist of their words was clear to him, if not the individual meanings. He had shared Josefine's concerns, but for some reason, the golden-eyed man's manner assured him completely. He didn't know what these lumasi were capable of, but after growing up among the undines, he suspected Romero had abilities he wasn't telling them about.

Indeed, a few minutes later, a work gang of slaves in indigo-and-red striped clothes and with their cane knives over their shoulders walked along the road toward them, followed by an overseer in a straw hat and pale suit astride a horse. Osaze stared at the ground as they passed, waiting for the alarm to be raised, but they barely even acknowledged the odd group. The overseer tipped his hat to Romero on the way by, who returned the gesture without smiling.

Osaze relaxed and looked at Romero. "What you do?"

Romero glanced at him. Though he replied in English—so Osaze thought—his words were perfectly intelligible to him.

"This time? Nothing. Act as though you belong, and others will usually not question it. But do not fear, Osaze. You are under my protection. I will not give you up easily."

Osaze nodded. Bunmi, who was seated behind Romero with her arms wrapped around his waist, glanced at the back of his head and relaxed slightly.

"Indeed, Mr. Romero." Josefine sounded amused.

He arched a brow at her. "You know of that which I speak."

The amusement left her voice. "Indeed, Mr. Romero."

With that, she let the horse fall back a bit so conversation was not quite so easy.

What does she know?

But his fuzzy mind wouldn't let him work it out. The moment he grasped a question, the thought would slide away like a slippery fish. Osaze closed his eyes to rest them, aware only of the swaying of the horse, Josefine's warm presence in front of him, and the ever-present pain in his back.

That's when he felt it. A mental touch he would know anywhere.

He became instantly alert.

Using the skills Calandra had taught him for focusing his thoughts, he turned his awareness toward the touch, trying to block out the pain in his body. A voice he couldn't hear with his ears came to him—something he'd never experienced before.

Zale?

It was her. The woman he loved. The woman he hated. How was she doing this?

Would she be able to hear him too?

Calandra?

Osaze?

The word echoed in his mind along with an outpouring of emotion. It was like having the *pisti* bond back and more. The longing and sorrow in the stream flowed through him.

He went rigid.

"Are you all right, Osaze?" Josefine asked without turning around.

As suddenly as the sensation had come, it faded. He waited to see if Calandra would reach out to him again, wondering if he had only imagined it. He didn't think he had. But when nothing further happened, his shoulders drooped and he swallowed convulsively to get rid of the lump in his throat.

"Yes," he lied. "I am fine."

*

WHEN the group of slaves and the overseer had passed by, Robert's gut had coiled as tight as a watchspring. He had been sure the man would notice something odd and would turn on them any second to raise the cry. But the overseer had offered only a polite gesture—to Romero, not himself, of all people. Robert was still trying to decide if he were more relieved or indignant at the man's behaviour.

Still, when Middleton did come for them, they would not get off quite so easily. No matter what Romero said, every law of this island would condemn them for stealing Middleton's property. And the officials in Bridgetown would not be charmed by Romero's winks and good looks.

"Mr. Cox," came Romero's voice at his elbow.

Robert jumped so high he nearly fell off his horse.

When he twisted to glare at the other man, Romero seemed to be trying to repress a smile, but doing a mighty poor job of it. He'd directed his horse between Robert's and Miss Chapman's, and Robert could hear her give a snort of laughter beyond.

"Yes?" Robert didn't try to hide his irritation in the slightest.

"I wanted to ask how your meeting with Middleton went, now that we have some time."

Robert clenched his reins. "Well, he didn't let me buy his slave. But you must have guessed that would happen or you wouldn't have gone and stolen him while I was trying to negotiate the deal."

"Freed him."

"If you say so."

Miss Chapman watched the exchange with open interest. Behind her, Osaze seemed barely aware of his surroundings. All this trouble for a slave who would likely die before long. Robert hoped it was worth it.

Still, seeing the way Middleton had misused his slave in the few days he'd had him, Robert couldn't help feeling a twinge of gratitude for what Romero had done. Perhaps they could do something for this man. Blacks had few rights on Barbados, but their owners were not supposed to beat them to death. One more day of the treatment he'd been getting and Osaze may have been too far gone to save, judging from appearances.

Romero arched a brow. "And Middleton said nothing else of import?"

Robert swallowed. He'd done nothing but think of all the things of import Middleton had said—his claims about Miss Bethel and Romero being spirits, the secret society he had invited Robert to join, and more. He glanced at Bunmi, who was watching him with dark eyes. She dropped her gaze when he looked at her.

The sun had sunk beneath the waves in front of them, and despite the oncoming dark, traffic on the road was getting heavier the closer they got to Bridgetown. Miss Chapman kept watch on a man guiding a donkey pulling a nearly empty cart along the road, but the man didn't even look up at them.

The curious behaviour of the people they passed had not escaped Robert. It was unnatural how others ignored their motley crew. And why hadn't they been pursued yet? Maybe there was something to Middleton's claims about Romero.

But no. He couldn't believe that Miss Bethel had anything to do with a nefarious conspiracy. He wouldn't.

There was a way to test it, of course. Only Robert wasn't sure he *wanted* to know this truth. There were too many strange circumstances in his life already.

He shook his head at himself. That was a lie. He was tired of being the one with his arms flailing, the only one unable to see the mysteries that had blinded him. He *did* want to know.

He studied Romero, whose posture of patient waiting had never faltered. The man might be uncouth, but he had the patience of Saint Job. Even that was irritating.

"He did—" Robert's voice cracked, something that hadn't happened in years. He cleared his throat, his face aflame, and tried again. "He did, in fact. He had a message he wanted me to give Miss Bethel."

"Oh?" Romero tensed, which was unusual. "May I hear it?"

No going back now.

Robert steeled himself. "He said 'We have the key. The woman is lost. The gate will soon be ours.'"

The effect on Romero was instantaneous. His roguish demeanour slid from him like a masquerade ball mask falling away. He went completely rigid, his golden eyes narrowed, and his nostrils flared. Robert thought he heard a low growl like that of a wild animal and glanced around in alarm, but there wasn't even any underbrush to hide such a creature. Then he realized the sound had come from Romero.

"I assume they said a great deal more than that," Romero said at last, his gaze on the low, lumpy buildings of Bridgetown growing larger before them with every clop of the horses' hooves.

Robert gave a small nod. "Indeed."

When he said nothing more, Romero gave him a hard stare. He seemed to come to a decision.

"You have already seen enough to know the truth, Mr. Cox, yet you still persist in denying it. May Elyon help your unbelief, and the grace of our Lord go with you."

Robert's gut twisted, and he frowned as Romero turned and gave some instructions to the slave girl. She replied with something that sounded doubtful. After a hurried, quiet conversation in that bubbling language Robert didn't understand, she reluctantly nodded.

Romero stood in the stirrup and carefully, so as not to hit Bunmi with his leg, swung out of the saddle and hopped onto the ground, all without the horse breaking pace. He grabbed the reins near the bit, pulled them from around the horse's neck, and held them as though they were a lead rope. Once he was on the ground, he helped Bunmi up into the seat, then called to the young gypsy woman over his shoulder.

"Miss Chapman, would you take my mount's reins? Bunmi has never ridden before and she doesn't know what to do."

"Aye."

Miss Chapman rode up to take the proffered reins from the Spaniard's hand and looped them around her saddle horn. The horses whickered but rearranged themselves accordingly.

"What are you doing?" Robert demanded.

Romero reached inside his breast pocket and pulled out something which he kept concealed in his hand.

"You must hurry to the inn and give the message to Miss Bethel and Mr. Berian. Tell them I've gone to follow up."

"Gone? Where are you going?"

Romero moved to the horse's head and murmured soft words to the beast as though giving it instructions.

Robert watched the process in annoyance. This man's lack of forthrightness was quickly becoming one of his most unlikeable features, which was saying a great deal. That, and his tendency to ignore Robert.

Romero glanced at Miss Chapman. "By your actions, you have chosen the side of the Light. Once you get to the inn, you must tell them all you know."

Josefine paled slightly, but nodded.

Romero walked, holding the stud's bridle and whispering more words to the beast, but Robert wasn't sure if he were talking to the horse or to himself.

Robert ground his teeth in frustration and a tinge of fear. What was all that about *choosing the Light*? When Miss Chapman had joined them, she had claimed she was choosing sides. That implied battle lines had been drawn.

Which implied a war.

As much as he wanted to deny what Middleton had told him, Romero was not making it easy. There were too many things about the Spaniard that didn't add up, much like Miss Bethel. Every interaction Robert had with either of them only produced more questions than answers. They were certainly not spirits, but they may be secret agents of some kind.

Of course. A *Spaniard*. How had he not seen it before? His throat went dry. Had he been aiding and abetting agents of the Spanish crown? Alarm flooded him, and he glanced at Bunmi and Osaze. Perhaps he could still redeem himself and his family's good name if he reported the scoundrel and the stolen slaves, and Robert could escape the repercussions of Romero's actions. But he'd have to find a way to do so while protecting Miss Bethel. She couldn't possibly know what she had gotten herself into.

He shook his head. Miss Bethel was no fool. But she couldn't be a spy—not that divine creature. Maybe there was something else going on. For her sake, he should give Romero the benefit of the doubt.

"Mr. Romero, please. Explain yourself. Why did you help these slaves escape? And what nefarious activities have you involved Miss Bethel in?"

Romero glanced up at him in surprise, as though he'd forgotten Robert was there. He shook his head.

"Cox, you have so much potential, but you worry far too much about what matters little, and not enough about what matters most. Darkness conceals the truth, and light reveals it. Choose the Light. All the rest is moths and rust."

Dark and light? Moths and rust? What is the man blathering on about?

Romero raised his closed fist to his chin and opened it, palm up. Robert tensed when he saw what had been concealed there.

On Romero's palm sat a gyroscope exactly like the one Miss Bethel wore around her neck—what Middleton had called a *chariot of the gods*.

With one final glance at his companions, Romero breathed on it. The stone in its centre glowed red and the fine silver wheels spun and blurred. In the next instant, he disappeared.

Robert stood in his stirrups with a shout, and his horse reared slightly and skittered sideways, neighing and chomping at the bit. Robert sat and pulled the beast's head sharply to one side, turning it in small circles until it once more complied with his guidance.

When he'd calmed his horse, he glanced around at his companions.

Miss Chapman had halted the mini caravan when Romero disappeared. Bunmi's eyes were round as saucers. Osaze looked mildly interested.

But Miss Chapman did not even look surprised. She regarded the place where Romero had been standing and then looked up at Robert.

"Nice handling." She gestured to his horse. "Let us make haste to your inn. Osaze will not last much longer."

"Are you going to tell me what's going on?" he demanded. He knew his tone was barely civil, but he could no longer contain his annoyance at being left in the dark once more.

"Yes."

She glanced at the buildings on either side of them. They'd reached the outskirts of the town, which had been plunged into the fading grey of dusk. Dim figures moved between the structures—the bawdies and drunken sailors of Bridgetown's dubious night life.

"But not here. Without *him*, we are much more vulnerable. We must hurry."

Robert stared at her. She seemed to think Romero had been protecting them somehow.

Maybe he had, though Robert had no idea how. One thing he could no longer deny—Mr. Eduardo Romero was no ordinary man. And somehow, he'd endangered Miss Bethel.

Robert clucked his tongue at his mare, a rope of fear around his chest squeezing his words to silence.

44

OFF BALANCE

WHEN ROBERT AND HIS UNLIKELY companions reached the Port House Inn, the fat waxing moon was well above the horizon and the lamplighters had finished their initial rounds. The common room was loud with revellers enjoying a pint, so they went around back to avoid notice. Robert had Mr. Varley's son, a boy of about fourteen, take the horses to return them to the stables down the street, pressing a bit into the bony lad's palm for the trouble.

Osaze stood on the dirt courtyard, swaying on his feet, and Robert took the big man's arm from the gypsy girl and draped it around his own shoulders. He gave Josefine the key to his room. He supposed he'd have to see if there were another available now. Part of him thought Osaze could sleep on the floor, but after Romero's reprimands, he thought twice.

Romero. Once again, Robert saw the man disappear before his eyes and his mouth went dry. When he spoke, his voice came out as a croak.

"It's fourth on the right—"

"I know." Miss Chapman picked up her bundles from the ground and started up the stairs.

She knows? He thought of the times he'd spotted either her or the gypsy man since they'd arrived in Barbados and realized she had been watching him. Or maybe Berian and Abela. Or all of them.

Spies?

Of course she was. He already knew that. But spying for whom—Gryffyn or Middleton?

He couldn't wait to hear the answers she had promised to give. He hoped she could begin to make sense of the madness his life had suddenly

369

become.

Romero simply disappeared. How is that even possible?

He followed Miss Chapman up the outdoor back stairs next to the kitchen, helping the tall injured slave—ex-slave—manoeuvre the steps with his dragging feet. At one point, the man nearly lost his balance, and Robert was afraid they would tumble down on top of Bunmi, who followed them, but Osaze grabbed the rail and righted himself.

"I do it," he said gruffly.

Osaze took his arm from Robert and propelled himself the rest of the way up the stairs. Robert was impressed with the man's fortitude.

But when they reached Robert's room, Osaze sank on the narrow bed and lay on his side, staring at the wall with an expression of controlled pain. Miss Chapman placed a hand on his forehead.

"You're burning up. And your back is still oozing. Let's get you cleaned up."

She hastily unwrapped her smaller bundle to reveal a collection of herbs and tools.

Bunmi peered at it in interest. "I can help you."

Miss Chapman gave a perfunctory nod and issued some sharp instructions to find water and a cloth, and Bunmi brought her the pitcher and towel from the washstand at the end of the bed.

Robert cleared his throat. "Miss Chapman, I must know what Mr. Romero was speaking about. What it is you know. How did he—?"

"Soon." She scowled. "Can't you see I'm busy?"

He watched the women work for a moment, nonplussed at her manner, then mumbled excuses and backed into the hallway. He had a message to deliver anyway.

He backed right into someone and whirled. "So sorry, Mrs. Urbi. I—"

"Is he here? You find him?"

She didn't wait for an answer, but pushed past him into the room, running to her son and laying a hand on his cheek. Robert didn't understand what she said to him next, but he understood the tears running down her face very well—tears of joy at Osaze's return, tears of sorrow at his condition.

Robert turned away, uncomfortable with the display of emotion. If Urbi had heard them, why wasn't Miss Bethel here too? Perhaps she hadn't heard their return.

But when he knocked on Miss Bethel's door, there was no answer. The same with Mr. Berian's. No light seeped around the jamb. They must not have come back from their information-gathering foray yet. Or perhaps something had happened to prevent their return.

He stood in the dimly lit hallway, uncertain what to do next. He should probably go back to talk to Miss Chapman, or go ask the innkeeper if he had seen Robert's travelling companions.

But the truth was, he was too relieved at the delay to pursue more answers right now.

Something Gryffyn had told him long ago, after they'd had another argument about the truth of what had happened that day at Chyandour Brook, came to mind. Robert had been pressing Gryffyn to admit something strange had occurred, that the lightning which had just happened to hit the exact tree Robert had been standing beneath, stirring up the wasps and sending them all running for cover—as well as leaving Robert with the scars he still carried—had been no freak accident, but brought about by something supernatural, the blurred figure he'd taken as a demon through his agony.

Gryffyn had denied any such thing were true, telling Robert he'd been too delusional with pain to understand what was happening.

But now, he'd found out his instincts had always been closer to the truth than even he'd realized—the lightning had been called by Zale, who was unlike anyone else Robert had ever seen. Not a demon, but not a human either, at least not in the usual sense. But what about his other childhood friend, Talwyn, whose death he still bore the burden of? The girl with the golden eyes—just like Miss Bethel and Berian.

Someone with golden eyes is a spirit in disguise.

There's no way she had been a spirit. He'd grown up with her. He knew her parents. And when she'd died, he knew he'd been to blame.

But he'd only *assumed* she'd died. She'd disappeared after the incident at Chyandour and, shortly after that, so had her parents. He'd assumed they'd been consumed by grief and had moved elsewhere to start over, especially since that's the gossip that had gone around the village. Times were hard for everyone. Mr. Penrose had probably wanted to find less dangerous work than tin mining, especially after the explosion that had killed Zale's father.

Besides, Talwyn's parents had both had golden eyes, just like she had. It had been a family trait.

Unless . . . could they have all been more than they seemed?

No. She was only a child.

And Miss Bethel was only a young coloured woman. And Mr. Berian was only a fat old Methodist preacher from a backwater village in Cornwall. And Romero was only an irritating, uncouth Spaniard.

No. Romero was obviously much more than that. But . . . was he a spirit?

Could they all be spirits?

Robert's denial was no longer so adamant.

These were the agents Middleton accused of working against the good of humanity. These were the cohorts whom Romero had implied were working for the Light—and they'd just been joined by a young runaway slave girl, a gypsy witch, and another escaped slave who was nearly on death's door.

If these were the agents of the Light, the Light was in trouble.

A noise came from behind Miss Bethel's door, and a flickering light appeared beneath it where moments before had only been darkness and silence.

He frowned at it, thinking of Romero disappearing before his eyes less than twenty minutes ago, and the chariot pendant Miss Bethel wore around her neck. He *knew* that room had been empty. Yet now, plainly it was not.

It was high time he found out who he was dealing with. He would get answers this time, and no one would stop him.

He pounded on Miss Bethel's door. "Miss Bethel? Are you there? I need to talk to you."

The latch rattled and the door swung wide, but Robert's demanding questions stuck in his throat at the barely constrained anger and outrage on Miss Bethel's face.

"What is it? What has happened?" he asked instead.

"It's Berian." She said darkly. "He's gone."

*

It took ten minutes for Miss Bethel to calm down enough for Robert to get a word in edgewise. He sat on her bed in the small room while she paced in the narrow lane between her and Urbi's beds, moving back and forth between the door and the window and expounding in broken thoughts about the old codger and his stubbornness while clenching and unclenching her hands. Robert felt a bit awkward being alone with her in her room, but she had hurried him in and shut the door without allowing him a moment to object.

So far, he'd gathered that she and Berian had succeeded in reaching Sirenia but failed to find Zale. However, they had discovered where he'd gone—chasing after his mother to this Tartarus place Robert kept hearing about. He'd had help getting there, but her sources said he'd gone alone. So Berian had gone after him.

"Can't you simply follow him?" Robert said. "We'll take passage on another ship and . . ." He trailed off, staring at the chain around her neck.

"You don't understand," she snapped. "This place . . . it's worse than Tortuga or Port Royal, and you cannot simply sail there. No ship in the harbour would be able to take us. And I'm afraid the passage would be rather lethal for you, Mr. Cox. Humans go in, but they never come out."

Robert gave his head a shake. *Humans? Lethal only for me?* Foreboding tightened his gut. All his questions about spirits and the day's strange events swirled in his brain. A place named Tartarus you couldn't sail to . . .

He went rigid, his fingers digging into his knees through the cloth of his breeches. "When you say Tartarus—"

"And I was supposed to go. Erel gave the mission to me. Zale is *my* responsibility. That bullheaded codger." She wrung her hands.

Mission? That sounded like spy talk. Robert's chest tightened further, his fears choking him. The foundations of his reality had already taken several blows today, and he began to wonder if they had been quicksand all along.

"Who is Erel?"

She blinked at him as though just remembering he was there.

"He's . . . a friend of mine."

He remembered Miss Bethel and Romero bent together in earnest conversation and shook his head. *No, couldn't be.* "And why is Zale your responsibility?"

She stopped pacing. "Because I'm his guardian."

Robert almost laughed. Miss Bethel? A guardian? Of what? She was too young, and too *female*, to be legally responsible for anyone. But assuming she was, why Zale?

Lumasi. Cherubim. So-called guardian angels, rang Middleton's voice in his mind. His spine tingled with cold shivers, and dread made his stomach knot. "H—how did you say you knew Zale?"

She stared at him, looking as though she were wrestling with herself about how much to say. Her pretty round eyes caught the lamplight, glinting gold.

"You see," Robert continued cautiously, "I've known Zale since he was a child. His family lived in our parish. And until I saw you on the *Atlanta*, I'd never met you before in my life. So why would you be his guardian, especially if his mother is still alive somewhere, as you suppose? And Zale is, what, sixteen now? He hardly even needs a guardian anymore."

"Because . . ."

She wrung her hands again. He looked at them and noticed for the first time a bracelet on one wrist, peeking out from beneath her sleeve. It was made of a metal that looked like gold, but it was supple like leather. He'd never seen anything like it before. The band anchored a circular face on the back of her arm. And inside the gold setting was a multi-faceted round gem the colour of burgundy wine. More so than even her eyes, the jewel pulled in the lamplight and scattered it into the room in a brilliant array, as though the light came from inside the gem itself.

Robert's breath caught.

The heartstone.

It might be a garnet. No, an enormous ruby—the reddest ruby he had ever seen.

Middleton had said it wouldn't be something she wore but that was part of her. Seeing it there, plain on her wrist, brought an enormous sense of relief. If Middleton had been wrong about that, he could be wrong about other things too—like golden-eyed spirits. But Robert could certainly see why Gryffyn, or even Middleton, would want such a gem. It must be priceless.

But what about Romero, disappearing before his eyes? And what about Miss Bethel appearing in her room so suddenly?

I am his guardian.

Miss Bethel's words echoed in his mind. He thought of Zale, the boy he'd thought was a demon and had only been a young merman with powers he couldn't control. If anyone needed an angel's help, it was likely him.

There was so much more going on here than Robert understood. It was time to stop flailing blindly and see the truth.

The thoughts that had been swirling through his mind all afternoon fell into place like pieces of a puzzle. Middleton had been right about the chariot. And Miss Bethel had just called herself a guardian. If Zale could turn into a merman and call lightning from the skies, why couldn't Miss Bethel be a spirit who used a ruby to make a body of flesh?

"They were right," he murmured, staring at the stone. "They were right about the heart. And that means . . . you are a spirit."

Her gaze snapped to his face, then followed his attention to her wrist.

She pulled her sleeve over the band to hide the stone.

"What? That's outrageous. Why would you say such a thing?"

"You. Berian. Romero. You're all spirits, just like Middleton said. He was telling the truth."

Miss Bethel looked like she wanted to deny his words again, but instead, she squared her shoulders and sighed.

"You're right. My name—my real name—is Guriel of the city of Bethiyel. I am a guardian of the Order of Cherubim. And I have been sent here—well, came here more than sent, really—to prevent a war. Zale is the key. Unless we find him, all could be lost."

Robert was glad he was already sitting. He stared at her, trying to absorb her words.

"Zale is the key," he echoed stupidly. Guriel, is that what she'd called herself?

Her words tweaked something in his memory through the haze of shock.

"'We have the key. The woman is lost. The gate will soon be ours.'"

She glanced at him sharply. "What's that?"

"The message Middleton gave me for you. He told me who you were, but I didn't believe—"

"Oh, no. Zale," she whispered, looking stricken. "Let Berian not be too late."

She shook her head and closed her eyes, then opened them. She covered the bracelet with her hand and spoke, as though to herself. "He's in Elyon's hands now."

Then she looked at Robert with earnest eyes.

"There's something else you should know, Robbie. Something I've wanted to tell you for a long time, but my oaths prevented me. I have now been released from those oaths by you discerning the truth on your own. Talwyn—you didn't kill her. She is alive, and she forgives you for your cowardice."

His breath caught, and shame burned in his belly. "How could you know about that? You weren't even there. Did Zale tell you?"

She shook her head. "He didn't have to. You see, Talwyn . . . she's me. I'm Talwyn Penrose."

45

BEYOND THE GATE

ZALE SQUINTED AT THE STRANGE horizon, looking for landmarks or variation in the terrain, but found none. Stretching from where he stood to where the purple fields met the weird orange sky were waves of white blossoms, their sweet scent both tantalizing and cloying. They bobbed in a breeze he could not feel. Sweat trickled down his spine and his damp shirt clung to him, with no relief from the still, hot air.

Beside him, Damaris turned in a full circle, her gaze roaming over the fields.

"What are you looking for?" he snapped. He hadn't forgiven her for following him in here—and he still didn't know why she had. What did she want from him?

"Water." She licked lips that had begun to crack. "We're undines. We need more of it than humans do. Aren't you thirsty?"

He was, but he didn't want to appear weak in front of her. He shrugged. "I'm fine. But you can have some of mine, if you wish."

He hadn't known what he should pack for a trip through the Underworld, but he'd brought a few supplies. He had enough water to last for a couple of days, if he were careful, and food for the same. Since it was impractical to carry much more, he had hoped to find his mother and leave with her before his supplies ran out, or find a source of sustenance. After all, he assumed she was staying alive here somehow.

That was, he'd *had* enough to last two days—for one person. Damaris being here changed all that.

She shook her head. "I brought some, but I've been saving it, same as you. I just wanted to find a source to replenish it from."

376

She untied and unrolled the top of the waxed canvas cross-body dry bag on her hip and withdrew a water skin. Removing the stopper, she took a small sip, just enough to dampen her lips and mouth. "You should have some too. Dehydration will do no good to anyone."

"I'm fine," he snapped again.

She frowned and put her water skin away in her bag. "So's your temper," she muttered.

He didn't respond, just started walking again. The swishing of the grass behind him told him Damaris was keeping up.

An hour later, he stopped again, and this time, he did take a drink of his water. It was all he could do not to guzzle several mouthfuls, but he restrained himself to a single sip, which satisfied him not at all.

Their surroundings were completely unchanged, and they hadn't seen another soul, living or dead. Just miles upon miles of purple grass, white flowers, and orange sky.

The worry that had been gnawing at his belly since they'd popped through the gate into this place—with no sign of the portal they'd taken to get here—grew to outright fear. What if this meadow was all there was? What if he died here in the Underworld, right here in this nightmarish field, without having gotten any closer to freeing his mother?

He sat down cross-legged, and Damaris joined him. She peered at him through eyes squinted against the otherworldly harsh light that came from everywhere and nowhere, but said nothing. He peered at the ground. Even the dirt was strange—instead of loamy or even rocky clay soil, the grass appeared to grow out of solid black rock. And instead of the wholesome, refreshing scent of grass and earth beneath the sickly sweet perfume of the flowers, the air was permeated with a harsh sulfuric tang.

His legs hurt, but more than that, his heart ached. Inexplicably, he longed to go to Narcissa and tell her everything, to run back and apologize for his rebellion and beg her to forgive him. The urge pestered him as he took a few small bites of his trail food—biscuits and an orange. Damaris surprised him by pulling some food from her own pouch.

"Were you planning to come with me all along?" His voice sounded accusing, even to his own ears.

She glanced at him, then away. "I hadn't decided for sure."

"Why?"

"Why what?"

"Why would you come with me?"

"Why not?" she shot back.

"Fine, then, if you won't answer why, then why not?" He popped an orange piece into his mouth.

At first, he thought she might not answer that either. She studied the food in her hands, then said softly, "I was afraid I'd lose my nerve."

He gaped at her. "You? Afraid?" he said with his mouth full.

He'd never seen her so much as balk at any challenge set before her. True, he'd only known her for a few weeks, but still . . .

"We all feel fear, Zale. My mother says you can only be truly courageous if you're afraid, otherwise you're simply ignorant. Or foolish."

He swallowed the last of his ration. "When was the last time you were afraid?" He looked around for something to clean his sticky hands, then settled on licking the juice off his fingers.

"Right now." She indicated the horizon. "I'm afraid this is the last thing I'll ever see. And you're the last person I'll ever see. No one will ever know what happened to me." She glanced away. "To us."

Her thoughts were so close to his own that he was taken aback. He'd been thinking only of himself. How selfish could he be? Damaris had come here, and her fate was tied to his now. He still didn't know why, but he didn't need to be rude to her either.

In a softer tone, he asked, "What about before coming here?"

Damaris studied him. "That day you and I first touched."

He blinked at her. "What? Why?"

"I had no idea what would happen. And did it ever occur to you that it was a risk for me to let you see behind my shield like that?"

It hadn't. Zale felt like an idiot. He tested her shield now, but her door was firmly closed.

He supposed he deserved that.

"You're so confident, and everyone likes you. What would you have to worry about?"

She gave a scoffing laugh. "Looks can be deceiving, Wonder Boy."

When she didn't expand, Zale got to his feet. "I guess we better keep walking."

Damaris got up too. "What if walking's not the answer?"

Zale glanced at her. "What do you mean?"

She spread her arms wide.

"We've been walking for hours already, and nothing's changed. We haven't even seen a tree. This isn't like our world. There's supposed to be a river in the Underworld, but I haven't seen anything but these stupid flowers. Maybe the stories about the Underworld are wrong. What if this ghastly meadow goes on endlessly, and the way out isn't by walking, but by, I don't know, going through another gate of some kind, just like the Voidstone that brought us here?"

Zale swallowed. That made a terrible sort of sense. Terrible because he'd never thought of it and had no idea where they might find a gate, nor if it would even look like the Voidstone. Everything looked exactly the same—if there were something to differentiate one particular spot from the other, he hadn't seen it yet.

"Any ideas what that might be?"

Damaris's face fell. "No."

Zale sighed. He suddenly realized how very unprepared he was for this. He'd known he didn't know much, but figured he'd figure it out as he went along.

What if the mystery were too knotted to unravel?

"Me, either," he said. "So until we get one, I think we should keep walking."

Damaris scanned the horizon once more. "Fine. We were going that way." She pointed.

He squinted in the direction of her pointing finger. "How do you know?"

"Because, Icarus, I marked it."

She stooped and picked up her *deiktis* staff from the black rock, which had been carefully laid to indicate the direction they were travelling.

He chuckled despite his annoyance. Maybe having her around wouldn't be so bad.

If only he could figure out a way to get them out of here again.

"Okay. I'll follow you." He gestured for her to walk ahead of him.

She gave him a wary look, then a half-smile.

"About time," she muttered on the way by.

The warmth that had been blooming toward her crumpled in his chest. "Like a tame mare one moment and an unbroken filly the next," he muttered.

"What's that?" she asked.

"Nothing," he said. He ground his teeth and fell into step behind the siren cadet.

*

"I have a question," Zale said after they'd walked some distance in silence.

He snapped off the head of one of the flowers and stroked the petals. They looked smooth and velvety, like flowers should, but the texture was rough as sand against his thumb.

Damaris still walked ahead of him, forging a fairly straight trail through the blossoms, though Zale couldn't be sure. When he looked behind them, there was no evidence they had even been there. As far as the impact they'd had on the landscape, they may as well have been standing still.

"Well, are you going to ask it?" she said finally.

Zale tore a petal off the flower and tossed it away, frowning. "Maybe not."

"Suit yourself," Damaris said over her shoulder. A moment later, she continued. "But you know, since we have all this time to talk, it would be the perfect opportunity to fill in some of those lamentable gaps in your education. You should probably ask questions, or I might start lecturing anyway."

That sounded exactly like something Abela would say. Zale tugged at his earlobe. If he were going to be lectured, he wanted to choose the topic.

"Fine. What's your deal?"

"What do you mean?" She tossed her ponytail over her shoulder, and the sandy curls swung against her olive-skinned back like a pendulum in time with her strides.

"I mean," he grabbed her arm and whirled her around to face him, "why did you come in here with me?"

She stared up at him. Through their physical connection, he sensed curiosity, anger, and something else—unease. Was she still afraid of him after all this time?

Instead of answering, she shook her head. "We all have our reasons, Wonder Boy. And our secrets."

She shook off his arm and kept walking. But Zale couldn't let it go so easily.

"No, I need to know. I mean, c'mon, you're right. We might die here. Each of us might be the last person the other ever sees. What's the point of keeping secrets now?"

She stopped and looked at him steadily. "You show me yours, and I'll show you mine."

He blinked, taken aback.

"Yeah, that's what I thought." She resumed walking.

"Wait, no," he said, catching up to her in a couple long strides. "Fine, I'll tell you one, and then you tell me one. Deal?"

She glanced sidelong at him, then nodded.

He studied the horizon. He wanted to know why she'd come, so he may as well tell her why he had.

"I'm the reason my mother is here."

He took another two steps before he realized she was no longer beside him. He stopped and turned around to face her. She was looking at him in open-mouthed shock.

"You sent your own mother to Hades?" she choked out at last.

He shook his head vigorously, his palms out to ward off the misunderstanding. "No, never."

He tucked his hands in the pockets of his trousers—or tried. The undine fashions didn't use pockets, and his hands slid fruitlessly over the fabric on his legs. Instead, he awkwardly folded his arms across his chest.

He cleared his throat. "When I was younger, I had a few, er, accidents when my powers first manifested."

If she'd been shocked when she thought he'd sent his mother here, no sense in letting it slip that he'd succeeded in sending his father when he'd blown up the minestack near Madron.

His stomach clenched. Would he see his father while he was here? What would it be like to see Papa as a spirit? Different than when he'd had Josefine channel him when he'd first joined the Roma, to be sure—and he still wasn't certain she hadn't been faking the whole time. At any rate, he'd never had her do it again.

He continued through a dry throat.

"I hadn't ever heard of the undines or Sirenia—my mother had never mentioned them to me—and I had no idea what was going on and no ability to control my powers. So I ran away. I only found out a few months ago that there are some bad people looking for me, and they kidnapped my mother and brought her here as bait."

Damaris's eyes were even rounder. "Let me get this straight. First, you run away from home to protect your mother."

"Yep."

"Then, your mother gets kidnapped because you ran away from home."

"Yeah."

"And now the people who kidnapped her are tracking you down."

"Uh-huh."

"But you did exactly what they wanted you to do and followed your mother to a trap in the worst place ever."

Zale bristled. "Wouldn't you?"

Damaris frowned and ignored his question. "And did they know where you'd gone? Did anyone know you were coming here?" She looked around. "Well, not here. But to Sirenia?"

Zale pursed his lips. The only people on the *Atlanta* who had known where he was actually going were Abela, Mr. Berian, and Robert Cox. All three of them knew where his mother had been taken—though Robert hadn't seemed especially cognizant of the reality of the situation, which had probably been for the best.

"As far as I know, only my three travelling companions, and two of them were lumasi, so they knew all about Sirenia and Tartarus. The other one was . . ."

He thought of Robert's shocked disbelief when he finally realized that Zale was responsible for his scars, how he'd fled from him in horror. Would he have turned against Zale because of that? Zale hadn't had a chance to find out—the *Atlanta* had been taken by the undines immediately after, and he hadn't seen Robert since.

"I don't know what he knew. Or where his alliances are. He went to great lengths to warn me about his brother and tell me about my mother being here, though. Gryffyn Cox—that's his brother—is one of the people who are chasing me."

Damaris stepped toward him, setting her jaw and staring up into his face through narrowed eyes. "So the brother of a man willing to kidnap your mother and imprison her in the Underworld just to get to you knows where you were going—to my home, which is now vulnerable to human attack for the first time in thousands of years, thanks to you? That's just great."

She whirled and stalked on through the endless field.

Something she said clicked in Zale's brain.

"Wait. Is that what's been bothering you?" He strode after her, hurrying to catch up. "That the barrier went down when Calandra and I tried to heal the Heartstone?"

She threw her hands in the air. "Of course that's been bothering me. All our culture has ever known is that humans—and especially male humans—are dangerous, that they would attack us, murder us, and use our abilities to their own ends if they ever knew we existed. These people who took your mother seem to have done just that. And if it weren't for you, who knows how much longer the barrier would have lasted?"

"So now you're mad at me for trying to do what none of you have been able to do for thousands of years? You're right, we failed, but there was a chance we could have succeeded. Bet you wouldn't be so huffy with me if it had worked, would you?"

Damaris gave a half-shrug and scowled.

"And you know," he continued, "I didn't really want to do that, but Calandra convinced me to. As far as I know, she sabotaged the whole thing to make me look bad and cause the revolution in the city."

Damaris rolled her eyes. "Calandra would never do that."

"How do you know?"

Conflicting images flashed in Zale's head about what had happened that day in the Mother's Heart chamber and, later, in the Archive. Had Calandra been trying to kill him or had she helped him? Was she on his side or was she his worst enemy? He shook his head, trying to clear his muddled thoughts.

"I just know." Damaris whacked at the heads of some blossoms with her *deiktis* staff. "You think you've got her all figured out, but you don't even know her. All you really know is what Narcissa told you, because you won't listen to anyone else."

"That's because Narcissa is the only one who even cares whether I live or die. The rest of you could rot in hell, for all I care."

He stopped short, realizing what he'd just said. Rot in hell? He wouldn't wish an eternity in this weird place on his worst enemy, and it wasn't even as bad as he'd expected it to be.

She looked at him with wide, hurt eyes.

"I'm sorry, Damaris. I didn't mean that."

Where had that even come from? His thoughts oozed with golden sweetness, fuzzy and warm at the thought of Narcissa . . . but that wasn't right. There was nothing here to feel good about, and Narcissa couldn't help him now.

He gave his head another shake. He'd felt this way before, when . . . when . . . he couldn't remember when. And when he looked back at Damaris, she was watching him with wide-eyed shock.

"What's wrong with you?" she asked.

Her tone was curious, not surly for once, but even still, rage at her accusation exploded in his stomach.

"What do you mean, what's wrong with me? I'm fine. I'm—" The last of the golden fog cleared with his outburst of anger, and he stopped, realizing he hadn't been making any sense. "I . . . I don't know."

Tears pricked at the backs of his eyes, and he blinked to get rid of them, turning away so Damaris couldn't see his face. Thank goodness she couldn't sense his emotions while he had his bracelet on either.

He could sense hers, though, which meant her shield had slipped. She was upset, understandably. But also concerned, and more than a little afraid—a sharp, immediate fear this time, not a more general unease like he'd noticed before. Probably about the fact she was keeping company with an unstable crazy person. An unstable crazy *male*. Isn't that why she and everyone else on the island were so guarded around him all the time? They were afraid of him simply because he was a *him*?

He couldn't blame her for being frightened. Though the reasons for her fear were foolish, in his opinion, the fears themselves weren't completely unfounded. He didn't know what damage he could do in this weatherless place if he lost control, but he wasn't eager to find out.

"So, these guys who are after you," Damaris continued in a more even tone. "Why do they want you anyway?"

Zale shrugged. "How should I know? This is all new to me, like I said. I didn't know anything about undines or Sirenia or any of that until Abela showed up, and she couldn't do a thing to help me control my powers."

"Abela, your friend from the ship?"

"Yeah, that one. She and Berian were a load of help—always telling me I didn't know anything and then not telling me what I really wanted to know. All they wanted was to use me to get in here or something. They didn't want to help me."

His voice was rising in pitch again and his thoughts were clouded, but he was sure he was remembering that right. Wasn't he?

"It's the same with you not telling me why you followed me here," he said accusingly. "Or finding out my foster family of five years had been using me all along."

Rage bubbled hot and dangerous in his belly. Damaris backed up a step and fear flowed from her, but he couldn't stop.

"My own mother didn't tell me who or what I was. No one in my whole life has truly helped me understand anything. Except for Narcissa. If it weren't for Narcissa, I wouldn't even know how to do this."

He thrust his open palm toward a spot in the field and a ball of flame erupted from it, shooting into the grass and instantly turning it to charred white ash.

Damaris jumped back. "What are you doing?"

The breeze that didn't touch Zale or Damaris picked the ash up and swirled it away, revealing a small crater where the fireball had landed. The inside of the crater looked darker than it should be in the harsh white light.

Zale stepped toward it. What was down there?

Damaris grabbed his arm, glaring at him. "Look, Icarus, I get that you have these abilities that make you special, or whatever. But your powers are about as stable as an active volcano, which means you're dangerous. You're just as likely to hurt one of us as you are to do what you intended to do. So I'd appreciate it if you wouldn't do *that* again."

He scowled. "*That's* why you're afraid of me? I thought it was because I was one of your hated males, but it's not that. It's my powers?"

She swallowed and nodded, staring up at him with round, anxious eyes. By the saints, she was pretty. Zale's throat went dry, and he felt like he had more in common with this Icarus character than he'd thought. All those things he'd been saying about how he got here and what had happened to him—they were true. He was sure of it. But none of them were Damaris's fault.

And, he realized, he hadn't lost control just now. He'd been angry, sure. But the fireball hadn't been random happenstance, the weather reacting to his emotions. He'd *chosen* to do it. He'd lost control of his temper, but not his powers.

He took a breath and spoke more calmly, embarrassed by his outburst.

"I, well, I get it. I've spent years being afraid of my powers. But I'm not afraid of them anymore. I haven't had an accident in weeks. What I just did? I meant to do that."

He pointed at the spot he'd hit, a feeling of triumph swelling in him. He really had come a long way in a short time.

But then he saw the look on Damaris's face as she followed his pointing finger, and he looked down at the ground to see what she'd noticed.

He hadn't only made a crater. He'd made a hole with no bottom. Through the layer of black rock was dark, empty space.

He and Damaris exchanged glances. Her expression was a mixture of anxiety, annoyance, and awe.

He grinned, his spirits lifting.

"I think I found a way out."

46

BENEATH THE SURFACE

"Do you see that?" Damaris pointed at the edges of the hole Zale had made. "It's healing itself."

The edges of the hole were shifting and changing, bubbling out of themselves to cover the empty space beyond like a slowly closing wound. Zale hadn't expected hell to have regenerative properties—but nothing about this place was quite what he'd expected.

"It's pretty slow," he said. "I'm going to see what's down there."

He squatted and peered through the open hole to see if he could make out what was beyond. When that revealed little, he lay on his belly and put his face right up to the opening. The sour stench of rotting plant matter hit him in the nose. He pulled back and took a deep breath of sweeter air before looking again.

It was gloomier below, and though he should have been able to see easily, the contrast between the bright meadow above and the darkness below meant he could only make out vague shapes.

He lifted his head and spoke over his shoulder. "Hold onto me." He pointed at his midriff.

Damaris grabbed his waist and planted her feet to brace him as best she could against the rocky ground. He squirmed forward and stuck his head and shoulders into the gap. There was a fair amount of space around him, and the hole was closing slowly enough that he should have plenty of time to see what was down there.

Once his head was below the level of the harsh white light, he was able to make out a few skeletal shapes stretching downward in the dark space. Grey mist billowed up from beneath them and obscured the ground.

386

"It's some kind of weird upside-down forest, with the trees growing downward." He squinted to let his eyes adjust to the gloom. "Wait. Those aren't trees, they're roots. Tree roots."

"Tree roots?" Damaris sounded as incredulous as he felt. "Where are the trees?"

"I know, right? There are trees growing up from the ground below too, but they all look dead. And it stinks like a monkey's backside in here. Actually, it's worse than that—it smells like a street in Liverpool."

"What's a monkey?"

Zale thought of the friendly little creature he'd once seen perched on the shoulder of a man from another Roma family, a distant cousin of Eric, Merle, and Sal Chapman, at the Appleby Horse Fair, the annual gathering of gypsies and Travellers in Cumbria. The little beggar had been the best pickpocket Zale had ever seen, lifting a few precious trinkets before his owner had scolded him about stealing from family and given them back.

"Trouble, that's what."

The stark forms of the skeletal branches below reached toward him as though beckoning him downward to the swampy depths. A sense of dread and foreboding came over him. His skin puckered in goose pimples. He had the strangest sensation of someone watching him.

"Zale . . . ?" Damaris sounded concerned, and anxiety flowed through her hands on his waist.

Something pushed against his shoulder.

"Hey, what's happening out there?"

"The hole is closing, and it's getting faster."

Zale's heart started thumping and he squirmed backward, but the gap had already closed enough that he could barely move, his arms scraping against the rock.

"Pull me out," he called in alarm, wiggling his torso against the constrictions.

Damaris tugged on his hips until he could use his hands and forearms on the ground above as a lever. The rock was pressing against his chest now too. Finally, panting with exertion and fear, he was able to wriggle out and away from the hole.

He sat up and looked at it. As soon as he was clear, the remaining gap closed in moments, the ground as solid and hard as if it had never been there. He blinked, and the barren spot was covered once more in waving purple grass and white flowers, exactly the same as the rest of the field. It was like the hole had never even existed.

He and Damaris exchanged glances.

"That's a little disturbing," she said.

He nodded, willing his heart to slow down. "I guess this place doesn't like change."

He'd said it tongue and cheek, but as he looked around, he couldn't help but feel as though this place truly did have a mind of its own. He checked his stinging shoulders. There were some shallow scrapes in his skin, but nothing serious. It could have been so much worse.

He couldn't shake the feeling that if they were down in that strange swamp, it would be.

Damaris looked at the grass where the hole had been. "That swamp down there might be a way out of . . . wherever this is. And I felt something while the hole was open—other beings. I think that might be our best bet to find your mother. Do you think you could make another hole to get us there?"

Zale tried to appear nonchalant, despite how victorious he felt that he'd successfully thrown a fireball. Every time he'd tried to do that during training, his attempts had been pitiable and had drawn Narcissa's ire. This time had been so much easier for some reason—he'd barely had to think about it. It had even felt good to control fire like that.

"I know I can." He gave up on nonchalance and grinned.

Damaris rolled her eyes. "Don't get cocky, Wonder Boy."

He sobered. She was right. This was no time to start getting over-confident. But at the idea of returning to the swamp, his gut hardened and everything in him rebelled.

"I *can* do it. But I don't think I should. I don't like that place, Damaris. I think we should keep looking."

She frowned and gestured around them at the unending fields. "Looking for what? I've been looking for hours with more than my eyes, Zale. There's no one else here. Just us. And there were people down there."

"People? You're sure that's what they were?"

She crossed her arms and her jaw worked.

"No," she said finally. "But there were presences. And my gut says that's the only way out of here. Now that I know it's there, I can still sense it. Can't you?"

Zale blinked. He closed his eyes, picturing a hatch that opened to the swamp below. But whenever he opened the portal, the only thing he saw beneath it was the black rock beneath their feet. He opened his eyes.

"No."

His frustration at his lack of ability simmered in his veins. Things he wanted to learn usually came so easily. So why was this so hard?

Damaris's expression shifted to mock sympathy. "So there's one thing you're not good at. Look at that. Even Wonder Boy has his limitations."

He glared at her.

"Don't pout," she said with a curve to her lips. "Being fallible makes you undine."

Undine? The word still sat uneasily on his shoulders. He'd thought he was human for so long—not the same as other humans, to be sure, but human none the less. He still didn't feel comfortable with the identity that truly belonged to him. Perhaps because he found so little about his kind that appealed to him.

He scowled at the field where the hole had been and remembered the skin-crawling sensation he'd experienced while investigating the swamp below.

"I think you're right," he said at last. "There were presences down there. But not welcoming ones. There was something off about that place, like someone was watching me. Or more like some predator was waiting for me to climb into its mouth. I think we should keep looking for another way out. It's only been a few hours. This place can't go on like this forever, can it?"

"Can't it?" She arched a brow. "This is the Underworld. We have no idea how the rules work. And are you sure it's only been a few hours? I'm tired enough to have been walking for days."

Zale remembered a comment Abela had once made about Tartarus, the part of Hades where his mother was being kept, being as big as the Ground, and cleared his throat. If that were true, they could search for his mother for the rest of their lives and never find her. But if they didn't find food and water soon, that end would come sooner rather than later. Still, despite the humidity he'd felt below, he couldn't shake the unease tightening his belly.

He crossed his arms. "It's not safe."

"Safe? You dove into the Underworld, and that's what you're worried about?"

Zale scowled. "No sense being more foolish than necessary."

She scoffed. "Look, Zale, if you want to be safe, then you may as well go back home. There's nothing safe here."

He clenched his fists. "There was nothing safe there either. Not for me. And I thought you didn't want me to use my powers."

Damaris set her jaw and said nothing for several moments. Then she drew in a shaky breath, looking like she'd reached a decision.

"I'll admit, your powers frighten me. I mean, controlling the weather? Throwing fire? That seems like too much power for one person, like you're some kind of weapon of the gods."

Zale swallowed. He hoped that wasn't true.

"But on the other hand," Damaris continued, "Calandra has always had immense power too, and I trust her. So I'm going to make you a deal. I'll try to stop being so jittery about your abilities. And you start trusting my instincts. Deal?"

"Why should I trust your instincts over my own?"

She cocked her head. "Seems like your instincts haven't exactly led you true north, have they?"

He wanted to object, but she was right—hadn't he just admitted his poor judgement was why his mother was here in the first place? And he'd never once suspected that Eric and Josefine and Gio and the rest of his Romani family had intended to betray him.

She was right. His instincts were atrocious.

"Fine. I'll make that deal with you. But before we go down there, I think we should rest."

"My instinct agrees with you." She tilted her head, smirking. "So I guess you get it right sometimes. Deal."

He glared at her, and she snorted a laugh—but as he turned away, he caught a pitying expression on her face, and his shoulders tensed.

Zale flattened some grass with his feet to make a bed for himself, kicking at the dry, crunchy stalks with a vengeance. It felt good to take out his frustrations on something. When he had sufficient space prepared, he pulled his cloak out of his pack and spread it out, then laid down on it.

Not far away, Damaris did the same. He hated to admit it, but Damaris's argument about there being no one else around actually reassured him. *At least we don't have to worry about predators.*

Despite his exhaustion, he couldn't sleep. The harsh, unchanging light penetrated right through his eyelids. He'd been tired since he arrived, but considering how little sleep he'd gotten the night before they left for Atlantis, that didn't surprise him. His stomach gnawed at him and his throat begged for water. He allowed himself another sip from his water skin, but took no food. After the drink, he felt no more satisfied than he had before.

After lying there for what felt like an eternity, he rolled over and looked at his companion.

Her eyes were closed, and her lovely face was partially concealed by stray locks of sandy blond hair. Now that her rosebud lips weren't spouting sarcastic comments at his expense, they were pink and inviting. He resisted the urge to push aside the hair so he could get a better view of her thick lashes on her cheeks.

"Stop staring at me, Icarus."

He started guiltily. "I wasn't staring."

"No?" Her eyes opened, and their seafoam-green irises contracted.

He rolled onto his back, his face hot. "I can't sleep. It's too bright."

"Me, too," she admitted, sighing. "Tired but can't sleep. Hungry but can't eat. Thirsty but can't drink. I'm starting to figure out why this place is called hell." She sighed.

"To be fair, it's not like it's exactly set up for the living. I did think we'd see a few more of the dead, though."

A puffy black cloud scudded across the sky. Zale thought it looked like a bat. Or maybe a dragon.

She watched the cloud pass. When she spoke, she sounded thoughtful. "Do you think if we die here, we'd stay in this field? Or would our spirits travel somewhere else? Like, if you die in Hades, but you're in the wrong place, would your spirit know what to do next?"

Zale smirked, despite his annoyance. "Maybe there's a guide that shows up to take your spirit to wherever it's supposed to be." He blew air through his nose. "It would be nice if one of them would make an appearance right now."

Damaris chuckled. "Maybe. Or maybe it would be Cerberus the three-headed dog, upset that you're blowing holes in the place, and we'd be running for our lives. Most of the stories of the afterlife aren't exactly comfy, cozy tales our mothers tell us on cold nights by the fire . . . unless they're trying to frighten us."

"Why would they do that?"

"It's a tradition on the Festival of Spirits, when the veil is supposed to be especially thin. It's coming up in a few months. Haven't you heard of that either?"

Zale shook his head. "No, but we, er, humans where I'm from, in England, celebrate All Hallow's Eve around that time. Perhaps the same day. And," he said and smiled, despite himself, "one of the traditions is to tell each other scary stories."

Damaris gave him a half-smile. "About the afterlife?"

"Not really. More like how the denizens of the afterlife are coming after folks who are still alive."

Damaris laughed. "Yeah, that sounds about right."

Zale thought of what his mother had mentioned about the afterlife, which was precious little beyond what the Bible or the Greek myths she'd taught him talked about. Maybe she hadn't known much.

Or maybe, like his true identity and his powers, she hadn't wanted to tell him.

He frowned, his jaw tight. "Well, I hope we don't have to find out if Cerberus really stands guard here. Or anything else."

Berian and Abela hadn't mentioned much about this place either, only that Hades was somewhere his mother could be in and not be dead. His lumasi companions hadn't spoken of it so much as an *afterlife* as simply another place, and another plane, in which to exist. Humans couldn't come to the Underworld while alive though, just undines, which was weird. Undines and humans both had flesh bodies. What was the difference?

There was so much he felt he should have been told before now. It was like everyone he knew had been conspiring to keep him in the dark—even Damaris, whom he couldn't help but notice had never told him why she'd come here, despite her promise. And then she'd had the gall to throw his secrets in his face to get him to agree to another deal.

He was so tired of secrets. But more than anything, he was tired of being manipulated and betrayed. If that's how she was going to be, he wouldn't share another word about his past. Thanks to his Tiger's Eye bracelet, she wouldn't be able to read his emotions either. They'd almost be on equal footing.

Damaris propped herself up on an elbow. "What are you thinking about?"

Grim satisfaction made his chest ache.

"Sleep well, Damaris."

He rolled away from her onto his side and stared at the waving purple stalks until he drifted into unconsciousness.

*

ZALE awoke to Damaris shaking him. He'd been dreaming Eric had been drowning him while Gio, Josefine, and Sylvie had sat by and laughed. Of course, Zale couldn't actually drown, but in his dream, it had felt real. And when he remembered where he was, the sense of drowning intensified.

Stiff silence lay between him and Damaris as they ate a little, drank a little, and walked a short distance away from each other to take care of their bodily needs. Not that that took long—Zale hadn't consumed enough to need to excrete anything.

He returned to where they'd slept, then rolled up his cloak and put it in his bag, dreading what they were about to do next. Damaris was sitting cross-legged on her make-shift bed. She withdrew a perfect translucent white crystal from her belt pouch, held it carefully between palms pressed together in front of her chest, and closed her eyes. It looked like she was praying.

Not a bad idea. He drew a breath and turned a little away from her. Then he clasped his hands and closed his eyes as he'd been taught as a child. *Elyon, I could really use your help to find my mum. And to keep us safe in this weird place.*

As soon as he thought the words, new energy stirred inside him, and he felt a little less hopeless. It was like his mind had been bound in layers of blankets, but the prayer had removed a layer, letting some light shine through. He still didn't have the answers, and their situation was no different than it had been seconds earlier. But he felt different.

Damaris tucked her crystal back in her pouch, stuffed her cloak into her bag, and stood.

"Are you ready?" she asked.

"As I'm going to be."

She gave him a brief scowl at his terse tone. His throat closed and he turned away. He'd started to like her, and that was where things always went wrong for him. Better to keep his distance.

"Stand back," he said over his shoulder. He held up his hands palms-down in front of him and pulled energy into them from the hot, moist, unmoving air that belied the waving blossoms around them.

He let fly.

After a brief blaze, the ash and smoke blew away to reveal a circular hole the width of two people laying end-to-end. It immediately began to regrow.

"That should be big enough to let us through before it closes."

Damaris went over and inspected it. She waved her hand in front of her nose. "You weren't joking about the smell." She bent over, bracing her hands on her knees, and stared into the darkness below.

"Well?" Zale came to stand beside her. The skin-crawling sensation was back, and he repressed a shudder. "You still think this is our best bet?"

Her brow furrowed. "I wish I didn't, but yes." She pulled some rope out of her pack—*she brought rope?*—and looped one end around her waist, then handed the other end to Zale. "Lower me down first. I'll guide your descent from below."

Zale opened his mouth to object to her being the one to be down there, alone and defenseless, while he found a way down without rope. But then he closed it.

Damaris may not have fireballs, but she was hardly defenseless. And better him lowering her than the other way around.

Zale braced his feet against the dense grass roots and slowly lowered her down with the rope. She'd let her shield slip, and he could sense anxiety floating up to him along with the foul odours of the place—and that strange sensation of being watched. He shivered.

"It's cooler down here," she called to him quietly.

"Good. I'm ready for a break from this heat," he said.

"Slowly. I need to avoid this tree."

"Okay."

He halted the rope's progress, then started feeding it through his hands more slowly than before. Then it went slack, followed by some rustling, scuffling, and cracking sounds.

Zale bent over the hole to try and see her, but it was too dark below to see anything. "Damaris? Are you okay?"

The silence stretched.

"Damaris?" Zale tensed, looking around for the quickest, safest way to get down after her quickly. He was about to spring into action when her voice floated up to him.

"I'm fine. I'm down," she called.

Zale took a deep, shaky breath to calm his racing heart.

There was nothing to tie the rope to, so he released it. The distance from the lip of the hole to the ground below had looked to be about three storeys, and besides the stark, black tree branches rising from the fog, should be a fairly soft landing. But he was going to see how far down he could get before he let himself drop.

He slid himself backward to the edge of the hole, took a deep breath of the sweeter air of the meadow, and lowered himself into the opening. Fortunately, one of the thick tree-like roots was within reach, and, unlike the flowers, its rough-looking surface matched how it felt. He grabbed the root and slowly, carefully handed himself lower, grunting with the effort. Before long, though, the root ran out, and there were no others near enough to reach.

"How high am I?" he called over his shoulder.

"About five paces. There's a grassy hillock below you, and no trees. You should be able to drop."

Five paces. Fifteen feet. He strained to see around his own body, but couldn't make out the hillock Damaris described through the swirling mist below. He was just going to have to trust her. Her, and Elyon, that he was looking after them even in this hellish place.

He glanced toward Damaris . . . and saw a hulking shadow rise from the deeper shadows beyond.

"Damaris, look out!"

She whirled, but not quickly enough. The creature sent her flying with a single backhand.

He let go of the root.

47

CLASHING BEASTS

Zale crashed to the spongy ground, rolling as he'd been taught in sparring practice and leaping to his feet, hands at the ready to defend himself. He didn't have to try hard to call fire this time—his anger and fear had already awoken his inner flame, and his hands glowed with energy.

Some distance away, Damaris lay crumpled at the foot of a barren black tree, barely visible through the mist. The ground near her was moving, but of bigger concern was the monster that was stalking toward her.

The beast's head had a square frame and a pointed snout like a dog's, but it was covered in copper scales, with some leathery frills beneath the jaw and ebony horns twisting from where the ears should be. The eyes were strange, with vertical black slits in golden irises, like a snake's or a lizard's. A forked tongue flicked from between its lips, and it walked with a bow-legged gait, its claws digging into the soft surface beneath them.

A dragon.

The dragon pushed through the tangled roots, which trailed over a ridged back that nearly scraped the ceiling in places. Despite its squat bulk, it moved with surprising speed.

And it was focused on Damaris's limp form.

"Hey! Over here," Zale called.

The creature's head snapped toward him, then turned back to Damaris and kept advancing.

Zale ran to intercept it. "Hey, you big galoot. Look at me when I'm talking to you!"

Zale threw the fireballs he'd prepared. They hit the creature square in the forehead . . . and slid off like he'd thrown a handful of snow.

396

The dragon roared. This time, Zale had its full attention. It charged toward him.

Zale tried to summon more fire, but fear made his hands clammy. Instead, wind answered his summons, roaring through the trees so the skeletal branches knocked together . . . but it had absolutely no effect on the beast.

Not now! This wasn't the time for his powers to fail him.

"Come on," he muttered. He rubbed his palms together, trying to pull heat into his hands once more. At the same time, he backed into the trees, away from Damaris, as fast as he could. "Burn, darn you!" he yelled at his hands, to no avail.

He glanced up. The dragon was almost upon him.

Zale gave up on calling fire. Instead, he turned and ran, dodging through tree trunks and around squishy clumps of grass, trying not to run into anything in the gloom. The beast crashed through the woods behind him, gaining on him.

There was nowhere to hide. Climbing a tree would be useless—the creature was as tall as the tallest tree here. Zale rubbed his hands together, concentrating, and was gratified when his hands lit with a soft yellow glow.

"Yes!"

He twisted and threw a few more fireballs behind him, but that only made the dragon angrier.

This is it. I'm going to die here, and so will Damaris. If we do stay where we died, I kinda wish we'd been up in that meadow instead of in this reeking pit.

A boulder loomed out of the darkness and he scrambled behind it, turning to see how close his pursuer was.

The creature towered above him, rearing on its powerful hind legs with a roar that shook the trees.

Zale braced himself for the inevitable blow, hunkering down and squeezing his eyes tightly shut . . .

But an answering bellow and a crash made him open them again.

Above Zale, a sinuous black dragon formed of shifting shadow caught the copper dragon's torso with a massive tail that solidified as it swung, tossing the first dragon aside. The heavier reptile landed with a crash, then heaved itself to its feet again, its leathery wings fluttering at its sides in ominous warning.

The shadow dragon roared and charged.

Zale scuttled backward, out of the way of the fighting spirits. The copper dragon swiped at the black one, which dematerialized and then rematerialized on the copper dragon's other side, landing another blow on the surprised beast. It took longer to recover that time.

Zale huddled with his back pressed against the boulder and watched two creatures he wouldn't have believed existed only a few months ago fight in a wretched swamp in the bowels of hell. He wanted to help, but he wasn't entirely sure the shadow dragon was on his side. It must be a seraph, like the friend Abela had mentioned. For that matter, they might both be seraphim. Zale didn't know how the designations worked—were all seraphim dragons? If so, were they all the same kind?

Before long, the shadow dragon had dealt the heavier copper beast so many blows that it seemed addled. It gave a few parting roars and slinked off to lick its wounds.

Then the shadow dragon turned to stare at Zale with burning red eyes. It blew hot air from its nostrils and folded its wings against its back.

"Rise, boy," the creature said in a voice as vast as the night sky. "What are you doing here?"

With shaking knees, Zale pushed himself to his feet, back still pressed against the stone. His throat had never been so dry, but he forced words through it anyway.

"I'm . . . I'm here to find my mother. Her name is Delphine Teague."

As far as it was possible for a dragon to look impatient, this one did. The shadows that formed it swirled and twisted like smoke in a dragon-shaped container, so at no point was its body completely whole.

"I know who your mother is. I meant, why didn't you wait for me?"

Zale stared. "Why . . . why would I wait for you? Who are you?"

The immense dragon shrank in on itself, the shadows contracting and solidifying into the shape of a man—tall, muscular, and bronze-skinned, with wavy black hair and golden eyes. He wore a belted, loose-fitting long black robe that crossed at the front, with long sleeves trimmed in red and splits on the sides of his legs that revealed matching long trousers beneath. Folded on his back were two leathery black wings. His shifting face was never visible all at the same time. Bits of it would come and go, leaving hollowed-out pockmarks or missing features that would be filled in a moment later while something else melted away.

Zale stared, dumbstruck. He'd seen a man like this once before, when Berian had revealed his true forms to him on the *Atlanta*. But the sight was no less impressive for that.

The man smiled through half-formed lips. "Rumiel sent me to find you," he said in a voice as insubstantial as the rest of him. It didn't quaver, it only wheezed as though he were speaking while breathing in as well as out.

Zale tried to work moisture into his dry mouth. "Who's Rumiel?"

"You know him as Berian. He sent me to you while he goes after your mother. My name is Bezaziel. You may call me Bez."

Zale swallowed, trying not to stare at the man's constantly shifting features. "O—okay, uh, Bez."

The spirit helped Zale to his feet. "Now, let's go find your friend."

48

MOTHER

CALANDRA STARED AT THE WOMAN in white in stunned shock. Delphine was a little taller than Calandra—most people were—with a heart-shaped face surrounded by cascades of brunette hair. The hair on top of her head was pulled back into a pearl-studded gold comb before falling to her waist. Calandra didn't know what she was supposed to do. Hug her? Shake her hand? Salute her?

She opted for the last one, pressing her bunched fingers to her forehead and bowing slightly to hide the moisture in her eyes, breathing deeply to still her pounding heart. She'd spent hours daydreaming about what it would be like if she ever got to meet her mother. She'd never imagined it would be like this—in a tunnel on the shores of a black lake in a dark cavern in the bowels of the Underworld.

"It is wonderful to meet you at last, Delphine kor'Helena," she said, kicking herself for sounding so formal.

Delphine was far less awkward. She smiled and rushed toward her. Calandra stood still, wondering if her mother were going to hug her— half-hoping she would. But once Delphine stood before her, she stopped and clasped her hands together. Calandra smiled to hide her disappointment, thankful for her shielding Tear.

"Thank the Mother we get to meet at last," Delphine said. "I didn't think anyone would find me. How did you come to be here?"

"Um, it's a long story." Calandra looked beyond Delphine to the tunnel entrance. "But how did *you*? Have you escaped the Soulstone on your own? Or were you in the cavern the whole time?"

Delphine flickered like a candle caught in a draft. She looked at her

400

slender hands, which flickered again before solidifying once more. "No, I am still imprisoned. This image is merely a projection." She met Calandra's gaze. "Before you tell me how you know of the Soulstone and how you found me, please introduce me to your friends."

Projection? That explained why Calandra could feel no emotions from her at all. But how was her mother being projected?

She had so many questions for her mother—a lifetime of questions. But those would have to wait. She only hoped they would soon have time to find out all she wanted—no, *needed*—to know.

Calandra gestured toward each of her companions in turn. "These are Sing—" At Airlea's glance, she caught herself. "Kore Airlea kor'Phile and Singer Zoe kor'Dione."

The two women saluted Delphine as their names were mentioned, and Delphine returned each salute with a stiff nod. Zoe studiously avoided Calandra's gaze, which suited Calandra fine. Anger at Zoe's betrayal still simmered beneath the surface, but with this newest development, she'd have to address that issue later.

"They're both working for our cause," she finished.

Her mother arched a brow. "Cause?"

"The Free Will Society."

Delphine's brow furrowed. "Free Will Society?"

Calandra frowned. "Yes, you know. The one you started with Rhea and Ignatia kor'Eudoxia at Elpida."

Another moment passed before understanding flooded Delphine's face. "Right. That. Well, how wonderful."

"It's a pleasure to meet you at last, your highness," Airlea said.

Delphine barely acknowledged Airlea's comment before turning back to Calandra. "And why are you here, in the Underworld?"

Calandra exchanged glances with Airlea. Her mother was certainly not behaving as she'd expected. Perhaps Delphine was more nervous than she was letting on.

"We came to rescue you. You and Zale."

Delight registered in her mother's emerald eyes. "Zale? Is he here with you?"

She glanced around as though he might be hiding in the darkness, looking much more excited than when she'd greeted Calandra. But of course she would be—Zale was the child she knew.

"Yes. Well, no. Not *here*, here," Calandra said. "We've been looking for him. He came through the Voidstone a few minutes before us, and we haven't found out where he went yet."

Delphine glanced at Calandra's expression, which must have shown her displeasure at Zale's foolhardy move, and her face fell.

"Oh," she said, frowning. Then the smile crept back. "But that's wonderful. With you and Zale both here, you can help me escape. If you know about the Soulstone, I assume you also brought the keys?"

Zoe frowned. "Keys?"

Airlea looked at Calandra in confusion.

Calandra sucked in her lips, glancing at her companions. "I heard that's what, er, Narcissa has been looking for. But she hasn't found any yet."

Delphine's face grew hard. "You don't have the keys? Not for the Soulstone, nor for the Well of Souls?"

Panic closed Calandra's throat. "Well of Souls?" Was there *another* key she would need to complete her task?

"The Abyss," Delphine said impatiently. "You need a key for each."

"Oh."

Delphine meant the crystal key. Calandra thought of the unaltered amethyst in her pouch. She couldn't count that. She didn't even know what would need to be done to it to turn it into a key, let alone whether she were able to do it. If a perfect amethyst were all it took, this place was full of them—much larger than the one she'd brought. So simply having one was not enough. "No. I . . . I didn't have time to wait for them to be found."

"Calandra, what's she talking about?" Zoe demanded. "What do you know of these keys?"

Calandra turned to her companions, her stomach clenched in trepidation. "In the Observation Chamber back at the palace, my fears were confirmed—Narcissa has been possessed by Damon, the dragon spirit who haunted me for so long."

Delphine covered her mouth and Zoe's face twisted in disbelief. Only Airlea looked unsurprised.

"That's impossible," said Zoe.

"I know it seems so," Calandra said tightly. "Many of the Free Will Society Council members thought the same. But I assure you, I'm not making this up."

Airlea twirled her staff absently. "I still didn't see him," she said quietly. "But I did experience . . . *something*, something very strange. It was like being trapped in sludge and being unable to move, watching the two of you speak. I didn't know if I was going to break through."

Calandra blinked at her, impressed. "*You're* the one who broke the bubble?"

Airlea gave a small shrug. "I guess. I didn't know what was happening, but I knew I had to get through to you. Eventually, it worked."

Calandra regarded the siren defector with begrudging gratitude. Airlea had never told her why she'd joined the FWS, and maybe that's why Calandra was so bothered by her constant clinging presence. She knew she *should* be grateful to the girl. Especially since Airlea constantly used her abilities in service of Calandra's needs . . . even to the point of following her to the Underworld unbidden. Perhaps it was time Calandra started giving her a little more credit. She promised herself she'd at least try.

"When was this?" Zoe asked.

"Just after we found out Zale had gone to Atlantis," Airlea replied.

"I didn't notice anything strange," Zoe muttered. "But what does that have to do with the keys?"

Calandra flicked her braid over her shoulder. "When Damon manifested, he told me we'd need a key to open the Abyss, and another to unlock something called the Soulstone, where Mother is being kept. He'd been looking for them but hadn't found either. That's why he didn't want me to dive in after Zale if we got to the Voidstone too late." She glanced at Delphine, who had her lips pressed together in displeasure, and her gut twisted. The throbbing in her temples reminded her why she'd defied Damon's admonition—but what good would it do to find both Zale and her mother with no way to send them home? Them, and the three other souls who had followed her and Zale to the Underworld.

Airlea glanced at Delphine unhappily. "So we've come all this way and we won't even be able to rescue your mother? Do you think Damon was telling the truth?"

Delphine clasped her hands in front of her. "He was," she said. "I'm surprised he didn't also mention the key you'll need to return home."

"What?" Zoe spun to look at her. "We'll need a *third* key?"

"No soul, living or dead, leaves Hades without a key," Delphine replied calmly. "Can you imagine the chaos that could be unleashed otherwise?"

"Actually," said Calandra, her face burning, "he did mention that key." She glanced shamefacedly at her companions. "Except he said the one that would open the Soulstone would also work to open the gateway home."

Zoe's eyes bulged in outrage, and she clenched her fists. "So you knew you didn't have a way to return home, and yet you jumped through the Voidstone anyway. Why?"

"Why did you?" Calandra shot back, straightening. She was in no mood to accept accusations from Zoe.

Zoe glared. "Because I didn't know we'd be trapped here forever."

"You had to know it was a risk," Calandra said. "And if I'd told you this earlier, would it have stopped you, even though your sister might have been lost?"

"Maybe. I could have gone back for the keys before I joined you." Zoe crossed her arms, glaring sullenly at Calandra through narrowed eyes.

"I did tell you to stay behind, if you'll recall," Calandra snapped. "Not the first time you've disobeyed my orders recently, is it?"

"Calandra. Zoe," Airlea said, looking back and forth between them. "This won't solve anything."

Calandra glared at Airlea, irritated at the reprimand, but even more that the girl was right. Pain spiked inside her skull. She closed her eyes and drew a deep breath. She couldn't afford another seizure—not right now. When she opened them, Zoe was watching her warily, and Airlea looked ready to spring into action.

She turned to Zoe. In a more measured tone, she said, "After all the damage you've seen me do this past week, you wonder why I was willing to fling myself into the Abyss? Should I have gone back to Sirenia and risked collapsing the safe house or the Opal Palace with my next seizure?"

Zoe stared at her, then shook her head and dropped her gaze. "No, your highness. That you would go to extremes to fulfill what you see as your duty doesn't surprise me at all." She glanced up hesitantly.

Softening, Calandra gave a brief nod in acknowledgement of Zoe's statement, which the unsmiling siren returned.

"I have some good news," said Delphine gently. "You may not actually need the Soulstone key in order to open it and free me."

Calandra and the others turned to face her.

"Because Zale and I can free you without it, right?" she asked hopefully.

Delphine blinked. "You see astonishingly clearly, daughter. So you and Zale must have healed the Heartstone, as I hoped would be possible." Delphine's voice had an undercurrent of tension Calandra didn't understand. Was she being sarcastic?

Calandra swallowed, her chest tightening. "We tried, and I thought we'd failed. Now, I'm not so sure."

Delphine tilted her head. "What do you mean?"

"The barrier around Sirenia has gone down," said Zoe flatly.

Delphine's eyes widened slightly, her nostrils flaring. "Indeed?"

"But the Heartstone doesn't seem to be the problem," Airlea added with a glance at the siren singer. "The stone healers are working on a solution."

Delphine nodded, her face unreadable. "Well, as disappointing as that news is, it might work in our favour. You see, like the Heartstone, the Soulstone is suffering from many years of neglect, and it is weak," Delphine said. "I haven't yet ascertained how, but it seems to be connected to the Heartstone in some way."

"That's what Damon said," Calandra broke in. "That if we healed the Heartstone, you'd be trapped in the Soulstone forever unless I found the right key. I wasn't sure whether to believe him."

"That part was true. However, since the Heartstone has not yet been returned to full strength, if you were able to find your brother, the two of you might be able to break the Stone and release me, even without a key."

"Break the Soulstone?" Calandra asked incredulously. She shook her head. "Even if we could, we shouldn't. The Soulstone also holds others like Damon, a malevolent group of rebels who were imprisoned for their crimes. If we break the Stone, those spirits will also be freed." *And that's assuming we even find Zale.* She pushed that thought aside. No matter how long it took, she *would* find her brother. She had to. She had to succeed in doing at least one thing she'd set out to do. And maybe together, they could find another way to free themselves from Hades.

Delphine's eyes widened slightly. "You know of the Grigori. Good. And yes, you're probably right about what will happen if you destroy the Stone, but perhaps not. You see, the Soulstone is more of a gateway to the plane where the Grigori are held captive. It's possible to access the Stone itself without flinging open the doors on their cells."

Calandra's breath caught. "That's not what Damon said."

Delphine's gaze grew hard. "Damon wants you to free his companions, no? So why would he tell you of a way to free me without freeing them?"

"That's a fair point," Calandra said, her chest tight.

Delphine continued. "I believe you could free me while sealing them in—like a tunnel cave-in that opens one passage while closing others. I trust the recent incident that drew me to you was not indicative of your true skill."

She arched a brow at Calandra, who flushed. So that's how Delphine had found them—her seizure in the tunnel. Then she thought of the crack marring the Heartstone and the unprotected island she'd left behind as a result of her and Zale's last attempted joint effort and bit her lip. "But what if we get it wrong and release them anyway? Zale is largely untrained, and even with me guiding him, we may not be able to perform such a delicate procedure."

Delphine stepped close to Calandra and dipped her head. "Isn't my freedom worth the risk?" she asked softly.

Calandra swallowed, her heart yearning to agree that it was, but something held her in check. What Delphine said gave her hope, but she couldn't shake the feeling she was missing something. If only she had more time to think . . .

"Your freedom is worth everything to me, Mother, but there has to be another way."

"There is no other way," Delphine snapped.

Calandra jumped in surprise. Delphine's gaze pierced her, reminding her of all the ways she'd failed her mother until now. After so much failure, would she fail Delphine again by risking her eternal imprisonment in a place where only the Mad and wicked were sent?

On the other hand, would the woman who had left all that was precious to her behind to prove a theory that could one day save her nation, no matter the cost to herself, encourage Calandra to risk that same nation for personal gain? Why did Delphine seem so unwilling to even consider another option? The unease in her spirit grew.

She looked at her companions. Zoe's face was unreadable, her emotional shield as tight as ever, but Airlea's brow was furrowed slightly. She returned Calandra's gaze, but said nothing.

Calandra turned back to Delphine. "Rest assured, Mother, I will do everything in my power to free you from your prison. If you believe this is the only way, we will attempt it."

Delphine smiled. "Excellent. I knew you would grow to become all I hoped for and more."

Calandra flushed under the praise. Why, oh why, did the thing she'd agreed to do to earn it seem so wrong?

49

THE QUEST

"Now," Delphine said brusquely, "the first order of business is to locate your brother, as you will definitely need him to release me. Where has he gone?"

Calandra exchanged hopeless glances with Airlea and Zoe. The slight vibration she'd felt in the tunnel had faded, and she sighed. "We wish we knew. He was only minutes ahead of us when he went through the Void-stone, but we've been wandering these tunnels for most of a day and haven't found any trace of him. I thought I sensed him just before you appeared, but the feeling is gone now."

"He can't be far then, can he?" Delphine said, and closed her eyes. After a moment, she opened them and frowned. "I can't sense him at all. Too many other souls interfering." She looked at Calandra and her two companions, concentrating. Then she turned back to her daughter. "I can't sense you either, daughter. I can sense your two companions, but not you. How are you doing this?"

Calandra wrapped her hand around her Tear. Why would Delphine have forgotten about the properties she herself had woven into it? This wasn't the first time Delphine had said something odd. She must be under a great deal of strain, and it was making her mind fuzzy. Calandra could certainly understand what that was like.

"He's wearing some kind of shield," Zoe broke in. "Like the one you have, Calandra. I could never sense him either."

"A shield?" Delphine frowned at Calandra's hand, and she dropped it, self-conscious.

"I suspected that must be what his bracelet did, especially when I

407

couldn't sense him in the Archive the other night." Calandra turned a curious look on her mother. "But if that's a shield like my Tear, didn't you make it?"

Delphine blinked, glancing at the green opal Tear on Calandra's neck with a flash of understanding on her face. "Of course I did. Aren't I clever? I managed to foil the devices and abilities of our pursuers for years, all with a simple piece of rock. I'm so glad he's still wearing it after all this time."

She smiled, but there was a hard edge to her voice. Calandra exchanged glances with Airlea. Something about her mother's behaviour was decidedly unusual.

"How is it that you were able to sense him while he had it on?" Delphine asked sweetly.

"We have a . . . connection." Calandra shifted her weight. "I've never experienced it with anyone else. If he's close by, I can tell."

Delphine frowned. "Interesting. How far does your ability to sense him reach?"

Calandra's face grew hot. "I . . . I'm not sure. We haven't exactly been able to test it. Zale and I, we've only met a couple of times, and neither were very peaceful."

"Oh?" Delphine arched a brow, inviting explanation.

Calandra sighed. "The first time, we tried to heal the Heartstone. As you know, that didn't turn out well. Zale's powers were too strong for me to guide him. And there were, um, complications. With Damon."

"This Damon seems to be quite the grit in your gills," Delphine said.

You have no idea.

"And the second time?"

Calandra resisted the urge to clench the fabric of her skirt. Instead, she stood erect and kept her hands at her sides. "Damon seems to have brainwashed him somehow, and now he doesn't trust me. We had a fight."

"I see." Delphine drummed her fingers across her leg absently. "That's rather inconvenient."

Inconvenient? That's what she calls this?

"Is that why he came here without you?" Delphine asked.

Calandra nodded morosely. She wished a hole would open in the stone floor of the cavern and swallow her.

Her whole life, all she'd wanted was to fulfill her duty to her family and her people by finishing what her mother could not. When she'd finally heard the message on her mother's Tear and discovered Zale existed and could help her heal the Heartstone, she had thought she'd found the answer she needed. But when it came down to it, not only had she failed to heal the Stone, but she'd also failed to protect her brother from both Damon and the dangers of the palace . . . and she'd lost her best friend and foster mother in the process. She'd once hoped that, if she ever met her mother, she'd get to proudly show her that she'd fulfilled the mission Delphine had given her. Instead, all Calandra had to show for her efforts were a fractured Heartstone, a fractured family, and a fractured nation. And Delphine's disappointment in her was plain.

She drew in a breath, her face aflame, and clenched her teeth against the pounding in her temples. "We need to find him as quickly as possible. Before someone or something else does."

"Well," Delphine said, clasping her hands once more and pacing in the small space offered by the tunnel, "if Zale is wandering through the hells alone, we must find him immediately. He could be in great danger."

"He's not alone," said Zoe.

Delphine's smile tightened. "He's not?"

Zoe shook her head. "My sister is with him. But she's nearly as inexperienced as he is."

"I see."

Was that relief in Delphine's voice? Without the ability to sense her emotions, Calandra felt almost blind. But the signals she was getting from her mother were so confusing. Delphine seemed remarkably composed and assertive one moment, proud the next, and scornful and disappointed the next. She reminded Calandra more of her sister, Adonia, every second. Disappointment squeezed Calandra's heart. She'd spent hours imagining what her mother might be like, but this woman before her was nothing like her fantasies.

How could she have been so foolish?

"How do we find Zale? And then how do we get to him?" Calandra gestured around. "There doesn't seem to be any way out of these tunnels. I'm pretty sure we've been going around in circles."

Delphine gave a small smile. "You're right. The tunnels are in the shape of a four-pointed eternity knot, and you could wander them forever without finding an end. And since there are no gates on this level, you must go through there, along the river." She pointed out the tunnel entrance into the darkness in the general direction of the lake.

"That looks like a lake," said Zoe dryly.

"Oh, it is. And it's also an entrance to the river that connects the planes of the Underworld. It will take you where you need to go."

Calandra took a few steps out of the tunnel into the darkness, and Airlea and Zoe crept cautiously along beside her. Once she was in the main cavern, the pain of the bonds intensified again, and the light that moved with them extended far enough to see the lake beyond. She turned to talk to her mother and found Delphine was still standing at the entrance to the tunnel behind them, her hands clasped before her.

"Aren't you coming?"

Delphine heaved a sigh. "I wish I could, dear, but the nature of my prison will not permit me. You must go on alone." She glanced at the lake, her expression tight.

Calandra swallowed rising panic. "But how will we know where to find Zale? Can't you find him the way you found us?"

"Is he in the habit of causing earthquakes too?" Delphine said, an edge to her voice.

Calandra's face grew warm once more. She shook her head. "His powers are much different than a woman's. If he has a mishap, it will likely be with fire or air."

Delphine cocked her head as though listening to something they couldn't hear. "Wait here a moment."

She disappeared, and Calandra exchanged frustrated glances with her companions.

Just then, something broke the glassy water behind them with a splash. Calandra and the others whirled to see it, but all that remained were concentric ripples emanating toward the shore. Her gut tightened. The malevolence she'd sensed before was even stronger now. This was the way to find her brother?

Delphine reappeared. "Great news! I think I know where Zale is. There's been a disturbance in the Sleepless Swamp. Not an earthquake, but definitely something that has upset the balance. It might not be him, but it seems unlikely to be anything else, especially given the timing. But if I can sense it, others will too. You must hurry to reach him before anyone else does. Follow the river until you reach the flaming dragon."

"The flaming dragon?" Calandra frowned. She moved closer to her mother once more, who still didn't budge beyond the edge of the tunnel into the cavern.

Delphine smiled. "That's right. You can't miss it."

"And once we find Zale, how do we find you?"

"Return here and I'll find you. My prison is very near this place, and trust me, I'm not going anywhere. However, unless you find the key laying around the halls of Hades somewhere, finding Zale is your only hope of freeing me."

"Your highness," said Zoe with a small salute, "we know almost nothing about this realm. What if we get lost?"

"I have made a few allies here," Delphine said coolly. "I will contact one of them and send them to keep an eye on you."

Calandra's throat tightened. Her mother had left Calandra to be raised by her aunt before Calandra was old enough to remember her, and she was terrified of losing Delphine again. But at the same time, Delphine's assurances sounded somehow hollow and vaguely threatening. What was wrong with her to think that of her own mother?

Airlea frowned at the lake. "What's down there?"

"Oh, don't worry." Delphine flipped her hand dismissively. "They're mostly harmless . . . when you're going upstream. Their job is to guard what's below, not what's above. It's when you come back for me that you'll have to worry about them, but I've got a plan for that too."

Zoe stepped toward the water, her staff at the ready. "But what *are* they?"

"Why, they're the Mad undines, dear." Delphine smiled. "The ones condemned to the Void. This is it—otherwise known as the Pool of Tears."

Calandra blinked at her mother, then at the water as dark as the ocean of her nightmares. *That's* where she would go if she lost her grip completely?

Delphine's image flickered again. "I grow weary from keeping this connection with you. I will await your return." She met Calandra's gaze. "I'm counting on you to succeed. You can do that, can't you?"

Calandra nodded, hoping with all her heart she didn't let her mother down again.

With one final smile, Delphine flickered out of existence.

Calandra and the others looked at each other in stunned silence.

Zoe peered at the lake, which was barely visible in the gloom. "Do you think she was telling the truth? This lake is full of Mad panaceas?"

Calandra frowned. "Why would she lie?" Few undines ever lied. It was too easy to tell, so there was little point. Why would Zoe even consider it? Then again, her mother had been away from undines for a long time—and they couldn't sense her emotions either.

Airlea studied the water. "About the lake, I think she was telling the truth."

Calandra cast her a questioning look, but Airlea was checking her waterproof bag to make sure it was secure. It would seem she wasn't the only one who'd felt something off in the exchange with her mother. She still didn't think Delphine had outright lied—but there were times her mother certainly seemed to be keeping things from them.

Guilt pricked her. There she went, doubting her mother for no reason again. She had to stop. It was only this creepy darkness and the pain of the bonds messing with her mind, just as her mother's imprisonment was likely affecting her.

She focused on the lake, testing the state of the creatures—*undines*—who lived there. Their minds seemed fractured, disjointed, and full of malice. If they were the Mad panaceas and sirens, that meant the lake was full of all the most powerful undines in their history, every one of them out of control of their faculties.

She swallowed and clenched the muscles of her legs to stop her knees shaking.

"Let's dive in."

50

SPIRITS OF THE DEEP

As soon as Calandra touched the water, the pounding in her head intensified. She stopped, standing in the shallows in *podia* state while she composed herself . . . or tried.

Airlea paused a few steps beyond her and looked over her shoulder. "What is it?"

Calandra shook her head, her fingers pressed to her temples.

"The . . . bonds," she managed through gritted teeth. She panted, but it did nothing to control her headache. "They're . . . worse."

She scrambled out of the water, and the pain lessened to a more manageable level.

She stared at the lake. Why had the water done that to her? More importantly, how was she supposed to swim through it to her brother if her brain was on fire the entire time?

But she had to. There was no other way.

Zoe and Airlea stood in the shallows and watched her. Zoe's face was unreadable, but Airlea's was etched with concern.

Steeling herself, Calandra took a step into the water again. Agony shot through her temples, blurring her vision with involuntary tears.

Wondering if the pain would be less noticeable in *ichthys* state, she stumbled several more steps into deeper waters and transformed, sinking up to her shoulders in the shallow water. But there was no difference.

Once again, she scrambled out of the water. She bent over and propped her hands on her wet knees, staring at her two companions in the lake.

"I can't . . . the bonds . . . it hurts too much."

Airlea, who had been treading water, changed back to *podia* state and

413

clambered out. She came over and took Calandra's hand.

"I'll go with you this time. Maybe I can help."

Calandra shook her head. "I don't know if you can."

A ripple broke the surface beyond, and Zoe looked over her shoulder, edging closer to the shore.

"The inhabitants are getting restless." She turned toward the open water, her diving knife in one hand. "Whatever we're going to do, we need to do it soon. Calandra, maybe you should stay here. Airlea and I will go on alone. We'll be coming back this direction anyway."

Calandra considered it. With how Zale had been acting the last time she'd seen him, maybe it would be a better idea for Zoe and Airlea to bring him back. Then she shook her head. "No. We must stick together. I don't know why the water triggers the bond pain, but there has to be a way for me to get through. When I get in the water, though, I'm in so much pain I can barely think, let alone swim. I . . . I'll need your help to get to the other side, wherever that is."

Airlea squeezed Calandra's hand. "I'll be right with you the whole time. I'm not going anywhere."

Airlea's concern and compassion flowed through her touch. Calandra swallowed, struck by sincere gratitude. Why was this girl so devoted to her? What had Calandra ever done to earn such esteem?

Calandra swallowed. Nothing. She'd let Tanni die, and it had all been for nothing in the end. Now Airlea was trying to take Tanni's place, but there was no place to take—Calandra didn't *want* anyone to be that close to her again. She always disappointed the people she loved, which was why it was safer to keep Airlea at a distance. If she could, she'd tell Airlea to go back to Sirenia right now, that Calandra couldn't keep her safe—especially not in her current condition.

But there was no going back, not yet. They had no keys, and they didn't even know where the gate that would take them home was. The only way out of here was by going farther in.

And that meant she was going to have to accept Airlea's help.

She nodded at the siren. Still holding hands, they walked back into the lake together.

The pain was instant and blinding, as before. Calandra kept sloshing through the water until she was deep enough to transform, then sank to her shoulders, panting with shallow breaths, her eyes streaming with tears.

Airlea's cool hand touched her forehead, and the song she sang brought mild relief. It wasn't enough—not by a long shot—but it allowed

Calandra's mind to regain control instead of simply reacting to the pain.

She nodded to signal her readiness, and Zoe dove beneath the surface.

Calandra hesitated, her heart racing. It hurt so much! Would she fail her mother and Zale again before she'd even begun?

"I'm not letting go," Airlea whispered.

Despite her fear, Calandra squeezed Airlea's hand and followed her beneath the dark water.

*

The water was warm, which surprised Calandra. The deeper they got, the warmer the water grew.

The halos of light they'd noticed around themselves in the cavern stayed with them beneath the surface. Through the pain, Calandra strained to detect any movement among the presences surrounding them. But the beings only circled at a distance—warily, Calandra thought. Once in a while, she caught the flash of a luminescent green eye, but nothing more than that.

Is this where Nadia is? And Lydia? Are these really the Mad undines I've read about in the stones? If so, are they dead or alive?

She swallowed and looked away, focusing on where they were going. She wasn't sure she wanted to think too hard about that question—and, in the end, it probably didn't matter much.

Nor did she have the extra mental space. It was all she could do to keep the pain from obliterating her senses completely. *I must . . .* keep going. I must hold on.

They swam downward for what felt like an eternity. After some time, spires and pillars of black rock appeared, their bases lost in the murk. They reminded Calandra of tree trunks. *Strange trees.* Soon, they were swimming among them.

The pressure mounted, and as they got deeper, even their auras dimmed. Zoe swam nearer to Calandra and Airlea, but the light continued to fade.

Soon, there was no light at all. Calandra's only connection to anything was Airlea's grip in hers, and the bonds that threatened to turn her mind into a wasteland. But something had changed—the pain diminished somewhat, as though it had overwhelmed her capacity to feel it.

She was becoming numb. She couldn't feel anything. Even Airlea's hand in hers was a mere impression.

Calandra swam alone through a black void. She had no idea where the boundaries of the water were. She'd lost all sense of up or down. Not a speck of light reached her. She could no longer feel Airlea's hand or the water moving past her. Her own heartbeat pounded distantly in her ears.

It was the ocean of her nightmare. She fought the urge to scream. Then she collided with a stone spire and stopped, stunned.

Sensation came rushing back. Airlea's hand tore from hers. Calandra sensed her companions moving away from her and called out, the sound muffled through the water.

"Airlea! Zoe! I'm here." The words were lost in bubbles, but the sound would travel.

Her companions sent locater audio signals in response, but the cries were impossible to trace.

Frantically, Calandra ran her hands along the stone pillar, straining to detect the shape of it, but pain had numbed her senses once more. Her throat closed in mounting panic. She extended her senses toward her companions. They moved about aimlessly but seemed no nearer, and soon she could no longer sense them either. A spike of distress from one of them signalled their own fear and possibly pain—maybe they had met a similar obstacle. She thought about removing her Tear so they could sense her, but the only way to be rid of its shielding influence was to leave it behind, and she didn't want to lose it—for years, it was the only connection to her mother she'd had.

She bit her lip. She'd found her mother, or very nearly. Did she still need a memento?

She wrapped her hand around the stone pendant, about to take it off, but doubt niggled at her—the same doubt that had been bothering her since she'd seen Delphine standing in the tunnel entrance.

She shook her head, trying to clear it, but the pain washed over her in waves that threatened to drown her. She thrashed, no longer caring if she beat herself to a pulp on the stone pillar, desperate for a boundary to prove all her worst nightmares hadn't come true.

Spirit, help me!

The peace was instantaneous.

The pain was gone like a flame being doused. Calandra pulled water through her gills, her eyes closed, relishing the sensation. She hadn't had respite this complete since the seizures had begun. Could it be permanent? She dared hope.

Thank you. The gratitude was more than words—it infused every layer of her being.

She could sense her companions swimming near each other some distance away. She began swimming toward them, her hands outstretched to prevent collision with a rock spire, and was immediately glad for the precaution. The stone pillars were everywhere, always another one within arm's reach. Navigating them in the dark would take more time than she had, and her companions were getting farther away, not closer.

I need to see. But how?

The lightstones, came the response, like a voice in her mind—the gentle prompting of the Spirit she'd barely heard for weeks.

The lightstones? What could she do with those? Sure, she'd learned how to make lightstones at the Academy, but these ones were already processed. If they weren't working because of the properties of this plane, what could she do about it?

Still, the compulsion to try stayed with her.

Closing her eyes, she concentrated on the lightstone laced to her bodice, willing it to work.

Handheld lightstones usually made their own power, a property of the quartz that undines had long ago learned to take advantage of. What was preventing them from lighting?

She explored the stone's matrix with her mind. The stone, normally alive with vibrations, seemed sleepy and subdued, like so many other things here.

Wait, that was it. If the stone was asleep, maybe Calandra could wake it up. But how?

She opened her eyes, though the darkness remained unchanged. Concentrating, she extended a thin line of spirit to her lightstone. As soon as it touched the stone, the quartz vibrated in response and a dim spark glowed in its heart. But when she withdrew her spirit, it went back to sleep.

She extended the spirit again, but this time, she didn't withdraw it. She threaded the line of spirit into the stone and filled the matrix with it, saturating the stone with her own spirit—and, somehow, the Spirit within her.

The stone flared to brilliant life, piercing the murky water with white light.

She smiled. *Thank you, Mother.*

Using a mental trick Thea had taught her, she anchored the spirit to the stone while freeing up most of her awareness, then glanced around.

A thick forest of black rock spires surrounded her. Closing her eyes in concentration, she located her companions and the altered stones that must be their own lightstones. Using the same method she'd applied to her own, she supplied each stone with a line of spirit.

Two more bubbles of light flared to life some distance away, their sources hidden behind black pillars. Calandra swam toward them, and they drew nearer to her, until she, Airlea, and Zoe converged near the edge of a large clearing between the crags. The water rushed downward past them in a gentle current—they'd found the river.

Airlea reached out to grasp Calandra's hand again, her face twisted in guilt, but Calandra waved her off, her hands flashing in diving signs.

It's okay. I'm okay now.

Airlea nodded, her brows bunched.

Did you do this? she signed and pointed to the glowing stone on her left shoulder.

Calandra nodded. Zoe nodded briefly, but Airlea gave a proud, impressed smile. The lines of spirit that connected her to their stones tugged at her awareness, but they didn't irritate her like the *sklavia* bonds did.

The spires of rock around their clearing were so close together, they would barely admit one person at a time between them. Only a little deeper, the bases of the thick trunks merged. The three of them must be near the foundations. No wonder Calandra had collided with one in the dark—it was almost impossible not to.

The current comes from that direction. Zoe pointed back the way she and Airlea had come.

Calandra nodded absently, her attention on a speck of light some distance below them. She could still feel the Mad undines in the water, hovering at a distance—but that dimly glowing dot seemed to hold scores more living presences.

Calandra . . .

The voice was almost audible in her head, though she knew that was impossible. She looked around, trying to locate the source.

Calandra, be careful.

She stared at the dot of light below. Had it come from there? Was one of those presences calling to her? Maybe even her mother, trying to show her something.

She did a flip in the water to start making her way downward, but Airlea's hand on her shoulder stopped her.

I don't think that's a good idea.

Calandra shook her head. *Just a quick look.*

Airlea pressed her lips together and nodded, drawing her *deiktis* staff and swimming alongside Calandra on high alert while Zoe hung back.

As they descended, the dot solidified into blue-white light streaming through a circular iron-like grate at least four arm spans across. The heavy bars formed a familiar four-pointed eternity knot—just like the pendant on the tiara of the Queen of Sirenia and the secret tattoo worn by adherents of the Free Will Society. And, apparently, the tunnels above.

A quaternaria.

Calandra peered through the grate and drew a sharp rush of water through her gills. Next to her, Airlea's jaw dropped.

Below them was a circular chamber with walls covered in translucent rock quartz tiles that refracted the light, transforming the chamber into a column of dimly glowing blue fire. But it was the light source itself that dominated her view—an enormous translucent blue sphere with light playing from its multi-layered depths glowed softly in the centre of the chamber. Cracks and craters pitted the surface, and long silvery spokes connected it to the walls.

It looked like another Heartstone, this one made of nearly transparent blue moonstone—at least, that's what Calandra thought it was. She'd never seen such an enormous specimen. But as lovely as it was, it had obviously seen better days. But it was definitely the source of the thousands of presences she'd felt, all of them in abject misery. *Chains of Prometheus. The Well of Souls. Which means that must be the Soulstone.*

Why hadn't her mother told her how close they were? She looked at the grate. If the Abyss was supposed to open with a crystal key, this must be the gate it unlocked—the only barrier between the pool above and the chamber below. But where—?

There! In a silvery panel next to the grate was a small hexagonal hole. Excitement surged in Calandra's belly. Might it be the right size for her little crystal? She fumbled with her pouch, loosening the wet cord and unrolling the flap, knowing her remaining food would get wet and soggy but not caring.

The crystal fit perfectly, almost as though the hole had been made for it. What should she do now?

She tried twisting it, but it wouldn't budge. It must need some kind of elemental power to make it work, but what? She explored the grate with her mind while Airlea kept anxious watch above them. Empty channels of power were laced through the unusual metal, but she couldn't find a way to activate them, not even when she flooded her crystal with spirit until it glowed, as she had the lightstones.

A huge beast with a triangular snout slid through the water beyond the grate like a lunar eclipse, leaving hate in its wake. Calandra withdrew involuntarily, backing away from the grate and the malevolent beast between her and the moon-like orb . . . and accidentally dropped the crystal.

She flew to the grate, wrapping her fingers through it. By the time the monstrous beast had passed, her crystal had disappeared in the waters of the vast chamber below, too small to see. *No!*

Calandra, look out! The words in her mind hit her in an impression of danger and alarm.

Airlea's hand on her arm yanked her backward, and she narrowly missed being bowled over by a shadowy fluke-tailed figure who had been hurtling toward her. The ghoulish undine whirled and glared at them with wild green eyes, claw-like fingers raised as though to project power toward them. She let out a shrill, wordless shriek of warning, then charged—right into the butt end of Airlea's staff. A second blow to the creature's temple stunned her, and she floated backward, shaking her head.

Calandra gave the *let's go* signal and sped upward against the current. Above them, Zoe hovered in the water with her half-*deiktis* drawn, watching impatiently as they drew nearer. Her eyes widened and she sang a short, wordless tune that indicated danger behind them.

Calandra whirled. Another undine wraith charged into the light toward them. The creature's hair streamed behind her in knotted black ropes. Her skin was probably once a warm brown but was now grey and death-like, her green eyes so pale they were almost white. The scales on her tail were loose and patchy, almost as though she were moulting—or rotting. Hanging from a tarnished slim silver circlet on her forehead was a silver crescent moon with a star between the tips.

Just in time, Calandra raised her hands and solidified the water in front of them like a shield. The creature collided with it and paused, looking stunned and confused, before a creepy smile twisted her lips. She raised her own gnarled hands toward the barrier, channelling power to break Calandra's wall. With effort, Calandra maintained the water's rigidity.

The creature looked dismayed that her efforts had proved futile, and let out a screeching cry. Other figures moved out of the gloom behind her and placed their hands on her.

They're forming a circle. A circle of panaceas. I won't be able to hold them!

Calandra had often been told that she was the most powerful healer in three millennia, or had the potential to be. She'd so often been compared to Nadia, the Mad queen responsible for the sinking of Atlantis, that she almost felt she knew her ancestor. But all the Madwomen who had been banished to the Void ever since Nadia's exile working in tandem would be enough to overpower even her.

We have to get out of here!

The undine sorceress—for Calandra could not think of her as a healer—grinned wickedly, her green eyes flashing. She was making progress against Calandra's shield, and she knew it.

A hand on Calandra's shoulder made her turn her head. They were high enough in the water that the spires had thinned, with several lengths between each one. Airlea pointed at a black vaulted passageway beyond. Zoe hovered near it, watching them.

Upstream this way, Zoe signed.

Calandra nodded, slowly swimming backward and keeping the solid water shield between her and their attackers, but they advanced faster than she could retreat.

Spirit flowed into her from Airlea's hand on her shoulder—the siren was giving her a boost. Calandra hoped it was enough.

Slowly, they inched their way backward to the tunnel, keeping the wraiths at bay. One of them saw Zoe and charged toward her. The singer raised her *deiktis* and her diving knife, prepared to meet the onslaught, but Calandra knew her weapons would be useless against the powers of a panacea. She took one hand and directed it toward Zoe, creating a protective bubble around her, too.

The lightstones flickered, but stayed alight.

They had nearly reached the tunnel. When the sorceress leading the charge saw that her victims were about to escape, she screeched in frustration and redoubled her efforts. Suddenly, she broke off her attack on Calandra's shield and surveyed the rocks around them. She extended her hands toward the rock spires on either side. The stone began to quiver.

Calandra glanced at the spires in horror. *She's going to pull them in on us.*

She whirled to face Airlea, dropping the shield.

"Go!" she yelled.

The word was lost in bubbles, but Airlea understood, none the less.

They sped through the water, away from their pursuers. Zoe saw them coming and turned toward the channel too. In moments, Calandra collided with a streaming current, caught by surprise with its force. She fought against it, working her way to the edge where it was slower but still at a safe distance from the sharp edges of the stone channel, then turned to face their pursuers.

But the undines hovered around the edge of the tunnel opening behind them, allowing the current to pass between them and not giving chase. Calandra beckoned for Zoe and Airlea to keep swimming upstream, keeping her attention on the wraiths behind them. Soon, their ghastly faces were beyond the reach of the lightstones and she turned to face what was ahead.

The channel broadened and the force of the current diminished, making it easier to swim. Immediately upstream from the widening bottleneck, Zoe hummed caution to them, then pointed at a strange figure sitting on the river bottom. They stayed in place and waited, watching, but the figure didn't move. It had no presence either.

Calandra swam nearer and saw the frozen gaping jaws of a stone sea serpent. The statue was enormous—Calandra had never seen an actual sea serpent, but she thought this representation might be life-sized, its long ridge-backed body coiling and looping along the sandy river bottom, its alarmingly life-like eyes staring toward the hole through which they'd just come.

They circled around it, then Calandra indicated they should continue on. It was obviously not the flaming dragon her mother had told them to watch for—but it now made sense how such a creature could indicate when they should leave the river highway.

It was only when Calandra turned to keep pace with her companions that she realized what the undine sorceress had been wearing around her neck—a pendant of a perfect, double-ended amethyst, the stone that had been described to her by Damon.

That sorceress had the crystal key.

And then she remembered where she'd seen the moon-and-star symbol the sorceress had been wearing before—in a history stone about the seals of the monarchy.

That wasn't just any undine sorceress.

That wraith-like creature who had nearly overpowered Calandra was Nadia herself.

Calandra swallowed. She wasn't sure if she were more amazed that she'd been able to hold her ancestor off, however narrowly, or more terrified that the woman she'd just fought was the harbinger of her own fate.

Either way, Calandra knew one thing—she'd have to face her again.

51

REVELATIONS

Judith sat in the meeting chamber next to her mother, listening to several of the archons bicker. By the time she'd arrived at the after-supper council meeting—in which she'd only been included so she could give an eye-witness report of what she'd seen in Sirenia and Atlantis—exhaustion had seeped into every bone. She'd lost track of what the others were saying three counter-arguments ago. All she could think about was how much time they were wasting—time they didn't have. Precious time she could be using to find the mole or sift through the new Atlantis datastones to find solutions to their other two problems—raising the barrier and finding the keys to help Calandra and the others escape the Underworld.

Time she could be using to Free Matthew.

Her mother gave her an understanding look and an encouraging smile. On Ignatia's other side, her father, Jacob, frowned at the arguing women. The seat on Judith's other side was empty, since Meg stood tall in the centre of the room between all the dissenting voices. Like Judith, she'd cleaned up since they'd returned to Margaret House, and she now wore a belted plain knee-length lavender peplos, her long, thick black hair held back by two pearl-encrusted gold combs. Her resemblance to her late great-aunt, Thea, was striking. She'd been invited to the meeting to give her opinion about what could be done about the Heartstone, and she looked like she was enjoying it about as much as Judith was. Less, maybe. Judith glanced across the table at Ewelike, who had been instated as a council member at the beginning of the meeting. His furrowed brow made her wonder if he regretted his request to join.

"So, what you're saying," Stella kor'Panorea repeated, as though saying it again would draw a different answer, "is that you think the Heartstone is completely fine, but there's something interfering with the connection? If that were the case, then why is the barrier down? And what connection has the Heartstone ever needed before? Most of the things it powers have no physical connection to it whatsoever. I'm no stone healer, but there must be more going on." She narrowed her eyes. "What aren't you telling us?"

Judith frowned, biting back the urge to retort that since Meg actually *was* a stone healer and had actually looked at the Heartstone, she might actually know what she was talking about. Judith had known Stella in Fire Lake, having seen her on her occasional trips to town from Elpida, and the girl had been as insufferable then. Why she was on council and Judith herself had not been allowed because she was *too young* could only be attributed to Stella's connection with Councillor Iris kor'Lucilla, the Fire Lake archon. At least the girl's opinion seemed to be treated with as much weight as Judith's would have been by the others around the table—about as much as Stella was giving Meg's now.

"Like I said," Meg said evenly, twisting her blue opal stone healer's ring around her middle finger with her other hand, "the Stone itself is almost completely intact. I'm certain of it. Other than that one big crack, I've never seen it look so whole." She turned to Rhea. "You saw it. What do you think?"

Rhea nodded slowly. "What you say may be true, but I am no stone healer either. What did Daskala Amaltheia say?"

"She came to the same conclusion as I have. We did not have much time to discuss it, but—"

"Amaltheia?" broke in Nelly kor'Nyx with a dismissive wave. "Why, that old scavenger fish couldn't tell a geode from a toad. She's been teaching too long and has lost touch with how most stones are even used on the island these days. Adonia should have replaced her years ago. You're going to trust her opinion?"

Meg opened her mouth to object to Nelly's harsh statement, but she was cut off by Rhea.

"Kyria kor'Nyx, your experience with antiques does not make you an expert on the Heartstone, no matter how skilled you are at refreshing old datastones. Healer Amaltheia kor'Herafili has been working with the Heartstone for three decades, and is one of the most skilled and respected stone healers on this island. If we are to trust *anyone's* opinion, it will be hers." Rhea flicked her gaze at Meg. "That, and her star pupil's astute observations."

Meg's mouth remained in a firm line, but her tense posture relaxed slightly.

Rhea nodded at the young woman. "Thank you, Healer kor'Sibylle. You may be seated."

With an unreadable expression, Meg resumed her place next to Judith.

"Well, that was a bust," Judith muttered for Meg's ears alone. Though she was gratified that her aunt had stood up to Nelly on Meg's behalf, many of the other councillors looked as unconvinced as Stella.

The other girl glanced at her and said nothing.

Nelly laughed. "I was there, too, remember? That crack wrapped around that sphere like sea kelp, strangling the light right out of it. Unless we fix it, we'll never get the barrier up."

Stella crossed her arms on the table in front of her, tapping her immaculate nails on the stone surface. She looked as though she had just come from the spa, not living rough in a cavern in the hills. Her lady's maid must be kept very busy.

"And how are we to fix it now that both Calandra and Zale have disappeared through the Voidstone?" Stella said. "Despite what we've been told Calandra's whole life about her vital role in healing it, my understanding is that *he* is the key component." She frowned, looking around the room. "We have no other young men who have displayed even a jot of his ability. Alexander bet'Kynthia has some ability with air, but he has displayed no talent for fire as of yet. And the boy is only eight."

Judith met Rhea's gaze. After dropping Despoina Cleo off, she, Rhea, and Meg had agreed not to mention the keys to the general population at Margaret House. Morale was bad enough when they told everyone why Calandra hadn't returned with them—no sense adding she may not ever be able to come back. Talking about the keys would also require the council members to believe Damon had told Calandra about them in the first place—and until they'd crossed that hurdle, discussing the veracity of his claims seemed pointless.

At the memory of the sub ride, Judith's thoughts wandered back to the contents of the note from the mysterious J. W. When she'd finally told the others in the sub about the Coalition's note, Rhea had taken it off her hands, thankfully, promising to handle the situation. One less thing for Judith to worry about. But Nelly had been about as gracious toward helping a human rebel organization as she was being about healing the Heartstone now. Judith frowned. If the woman hadn't passed the truth test less than an hour ago, Nelly would be a prime suspect as the mole.

But then, being difficult to get along with didn't make one a traitor.

"I think we can assume healing the crack in the Heartstone will have to wait until Calandra and Zale return from the Underworld," said Rhea to the others, "which makes it likely that we won't be able to restore the barrier until then, though Healer kor'Astera has her team combing the Atlantis datastones for anything about the Heartstone's workings that might help."

Healer Erigone kor'Astera was a stone healer from Haven who had joined them the week before. She had passed her truth test just fine, just like everyone else Judith had tested so far.

Rhea continued, "Healer kor'Sibylle, I hope you'll join her. Perhaps the two of you together can come up with a solution to test your theory about connection." She dipped her head to Meg, and the young healer gave a brief salute. Meg would also be looking for information about the keys, but Rhea didn't add that. "In the meantime, we have to explore other options. Judith, I believe your report may give us some. Why don't you go next?"

Judith startled, blinking away her fatigue. She stood and moved to the space in the centre of the horseshoe-shaped table, then turned to face the archons, bolstering herself with the thought that after relaying her report, she could finally, blissfully retreat to bed. She glanced at her mother, who sat next to Rhea. Ignatia gave her another encouraging smile.

She straightened and told the council about the strange room she'd discovered in the Archive in Atlantis and Calandra's observation that it had been designed to be drained. She told them how, in the images made of light, it looked like the whole city was underwater, protected by a dome. She also mentioned the streets full of humans, undines, and a winged race she'd never seen before. She didn't mention the strange ceremony they were partaking in, which didn't seem relevant.

Her revelations were met with increasing reactions of shock and wonder.

Ignatia spoke first. "What a wondrous technology, to enable an entire city to thrive at the bottom of the sea. I have seen many beautiful things under the waves, but never anything like that. Judith, were you able to find any means for activating the dome over the city?"

"No. There was not time to seek one out." Judith met her mother's gaze. Since returning to the safe house a few hours ago, she'd barely had time to eat, change, and truth-test the council members in time for the meeting, let alone tell her mother what had happened. "But one must exist somewhere. I am certain Nick would be happy to return to look for it."

"I'm sure," her mother agreed.

"I'll go, even if my sister doesn't," Nelly broke in. "I want to see this for myself. Now that the *despoina* is on our side, even you have to admit the risk has been greatly reduced." She gave Rhea a pointed look.

"Indeed," Rhea said, her lips pursed. "In fact, I was going to suggest that a team go find out more. If we can find a way to drain Atlantis, the city could become a viable option as a refuge from—"

"The ships," Stella said.

Rhea frowned at the interruption, but nodded. "Yes, or other potential attackers."

At the mention of the ships Hebe had hinted at, the faces around the table grew tight. As soon as the group that had gone to Atlantis had returned that afternoon, Rhea had sent a small pod to investigate whether the threat had merit, but no word had come yet. Judith had been praying ever since they would find nothing out of the ordinary . . . but she doubted they'd be so lucky.

Meg spoke up. "The winged creatures are called lumasi. We learned of them in history class at the Academy. They went extinct a long time ago."

Judith nodded, feeling foolish. Her education at Elpida had been thorough, but she had not had access to the breadth of knowledge an Academy-raised girl would have.

Rhea clasped her hands on the table in front of her. "You're partially correct. They are, indeed, lumasi. When Kyria Eudora sent word this afternoon about the birth of her and Kyrios Ewelike's child, she mentioned she'd been visited by a lumasi woman named Abela Bethel who was looking for Zale."

Judith stared at her aunt, and a chorus of sharp gasps filled the room.

Alarm filled Ewelike's face. "She said nothing of this to me. I must speak to her at once." He began to rise, and Rhea extended her hand to stop him.

"Peace, brother," Rhea said. "Your family is perfectly safe. Abela is one of Zale's allies. She contacted your wife yesterday because she'd sensed Calandra there using some special device her kind have and thought Calandra was Zale—something about an inverted signal the siblings both have. You must have narrowly missed meeting her yourself, in that case."

Judith shook her head in disbelief, her heart thumping in her chest. The lumasi were real? "Why did you not mention anything about this before?"

Rhea looked around at the shocked faces. "And have rumours fly out of control? I wanted to bring it up with everyone at once during the meeting, and fortunately, the young lady on commstone duty kept the secret as I requested. Although Abela herself is not a danger, she revealed a hidden danger I never would have imagined—spirits not apparent to our senses who have been able to access our island now that the barrier is down. This next part is significant—she believes at least some of the spirits may be working with an escaped Grigori who is located in Sireniapolis, probably the palace. As if we needed more proof after this morning's event's, Calandra appears to have been right about Damon."

"What?" Nelly's head whipped toward Rhea. "You believe Calandra about that dragon spirit? Even if this lamassu is right about the Grigori, that doesn't mean Narcissa is possessed."

Rhea nodded, her brow furrowed. "You were not in the Observation Chamber when he manifested. Narcissa changed personality before our eyes, and she and Calandra froze up for several seconds. I can't explain it, but I've never seen anything like it."

A shiver ran through Judith. It had been terrifying watching Calandra's face go slack and unresponsive, just like when her hand had been caught in the Voidstone. Judith had wondered for a moment if *Calandra* had been possessed. Luckily, Airlea's quick thinking must have distracted Damon, and the enchantment had broken.

"What else did Eudora say about Abela?" Hammad asked his wife calmly.

"Not much," Rhea said. "Abela and a lumasi man visited again today, once more looking for news on Calandra and Zale, right after Despoina Cleo had paid Steadfast House a visit to tell them about Zoe and Damaris going through the Voidstone. When the two lumasi heard what had happened, they became quite agitated and left in a hurry. In fact, they said something about going after Zale and the others to bring them back."

"Bring them back?" Judith blurted. Her exhaustion lifted a little. Maybe they wouldn't need keys after all. Not if these lumasi could bring their friends back.

"Indeed." Rhea gave Judith a smile tinged with hope. She turned back to Meg. "At any rate, healer, the lumasi are not so extinct as we once believed."

Meg blinked. "I see."

An urgent knock at the door drew their attention. Xeni got up and opened it. After murmuring with whomever was on the other side for a moment, she stepped back and Bryce, Polyxo's lady's maid, hurried into the room. Judith frowned. Bryce had been on commstone duty since supper—a work duty she'd quickly volunteered for after she'd arrived—and her shift wasn't over yet.

"I bring news," Bryce said, "from Kynthia kor'Amphitrite. I thought it best to bring it myself instead of sending a messenger."

Judith tensed. Kynthia had led the pod who'd gone in search of the ships Hebe had mentioned.

"Well, hurry up, girl, spit it out," Rhea snapped.

Bryce stiffened. "She said a large armada of vessels has been located sailing west across the Atlantic. The vessels are running flags from a variety of human nations, yet they are on a common trajectory—not to the human colonies, but to here."

Gasps and murmurs rippled around the room.

Rhea's jaw tightened. "Anything else?"

"Yes," Bryce said, her face pale. "Kynthia thinks that at their current speed, the vessels will be here by Panselinos."

Judith's blood ran cold.

"Chains of Prometheus," breathed Nelly into the dead silence.

For once, Judith agreed with Nelly on something.

Panselinos was only three days away. Whatever they decided to do next, they would have to do it soon.

52

DECLARATIONS

JUDITH SAT STIFFLY, LOOKING AT the faces around the council table as they absorbed Bryce's news. Most of them looked shocked or even afraid, and a hubbub of murmurs filled the room as the women exchanged comments with their neighbours. Gerrick drew his wild, steely eyebrows together and looked intently at his hands. Tafrara, who'd joined the meeting at Rhea's request, stared at Bryce with an unreadable expression in her big dark eyes. Ewelike, ignored by the women on either side of him, looked straight ahead of him with a stern expression.

Rhea leaned toward Hammad. Jacob and Ignatia leaned in, away from Judith, and the four of them shared a whispered exchange. Judith wished she could hear what they were saying, but the noise in the room meant even her parents' words were lost.

Finally, Rhea stood. "Silence, please."

She waited while the furor died down and the gazes of the assembled turned toward her.

"Thank you, Bryce," she said. "You may go. Alert us if there is anything else."

"Yes, *kyria*." Bryce gave a respectful salute and left the room, glancing over her shoulder before slipping through the door.

Judith shivered, exhaustion forgotten as every limb screamed to spring into action. Narcissa possessed, visiting lumasi, invisible spirits on the island—maybe here in this room—Calandra trapped in the Underworld. And now, their worst fear had come upon them—they would soon be under attack by the humans they'd spent millennia hiding from. Judith had spent her whole life as a rebel, hiding on a small *latifundium* on a small

430

island only miles from the seat of power, and she'd never felt so vulnerable and exposed. She looked at her aunt, hoping Rhea had a reasonable solution to offer, but even Rhea's face looked tight and drawn.

"This is a dire situation indeed," she said evenly, "and the necessity to find a place to hide is all the more urgent. I propose we focus on two things—finding a way to drain Atlantis so we can evacuate the island beneath the sea and restoring the Heartstone's connection, based on Meg's observations, so evacuation may not be necessary."

The suggestions were met with murmurs of dismay. The humans—Ewelike, Hammad, Jacob, and Tafrara, who had joined the meeting as a representative of the Irene Cooperative—looked uncomfortable, probably at the idea of living underwater. The ocean would be as much of a wall for them as it would be for any attackers trying to reach them—they would probably feel even more trapped than they already might.

Gerrick watched, still saying nothing.

Judith's gut tightened—as much as she wanted to do something constructive, both of those solutions seemed like fool's errands in light of the threat bearing down on them.

Amaryllis kor'Yianna, the woman who had once been a friend of Adonia's, shook her head firmly. "The time for trying to restore the Heartstone is past. I've been trying to tell Adonia we needed a backup plan for when it failed for years, but she would never listen. I'd rather spend our efforts on a plan that relies less on luck and more on things we can control. We should start evacuating the island tonight to somewhere the humans can't find us. One of the uninhabited lands, maybe."

"And where would that be?" Nelly snapped back. "Humans grow bolder by the day, and there are few lands they haven't touched. No matter where we go, it is only a matter of time before they follow." Her normal brazenness had a sheen of desperation to it as she turned to Rhea. "I will prepare the team for Atlantis tonight, and we shall leave before sunrise."

Amaryllis frowned. "A temporary solution to buy us time would be better than doing nothing. And I don't see Atlantis as a viable option. If it used to be habitable underwater, why do the history stones say Nadia sank it and drowned every human on the isle? Why have our people not used it for so long? If it was once an underwater fortress, the mechanism must have failed and the city been abandoned."

Meg stood, looking apologetic. "If I may?" she asked Rhea, who nodded. "Unfortunately, it may not be the mechanism that failed. The dome around Atlantis may have simply been another casualty of the Heartstone's long deterioration. If I'm right, it's a wonder a single room could be drained with the limited flow coming from the Stone. Which means that unless we find a solution to restore the flow of energy from the Heartstone, we'll have neither an island nor an underwater refuge when the ships come."

She sat down again.

Tafrara stood, and all eyes turned to her. She cleared her throat. "Have you considered that these humans may not be coming in war, but in peace? Perhaps they only want to explore and establish trade with us. There is no indication their intentions are bad. If we were to make contact with them, it might be possible to establish diplomatic relations. Perhaps this could be the beginning of a new era of peace between humans and undines."

Judith stared in stunned surprise at the girl as she sat down. Tafrara was right—they were so used to fearing humans, their first thought had gone to what the humans wanted to take from them, not what they might want to give.

The lines of Rhea's face deepened. "Unfortunately, with a power-hungry spirit possessing our acting monarch, even if the humans are approaching with the best of intentions, such a utopian outcome seems unlikely," she said heavily. "However, it also seems unlikely that an entire armada of ships from so many nations would be coming to offer the olive branch of peace, especially so soon after we became vulnerable. Archon kor'Yianna has a point—while I believe we should keep exploring our other options, we should start evacuating. I believe Cleo will see the reason and support the evacuation, and without siren support, Narcissa or Damon will have little power to prevent the effort."

"But how could we possibly evacuate the entire island in only three days?" Ignatia asked, brow furrowed. "We only have a few submersibles, all of them small. Even if we could somehow convince Despoina Cleo to aide the effort—"

"We can't, that's how," snapped Nelly. "We'd move a few hundred at most. Our people would be able to flee the ships underwater, yes, but what about the humans we leave behind? There's no guarantee the attackers would show them mercy. And what of all of our possessions?" She crossed her arms. "We've fled from humans long enough. If it's a choice of running or fighting, I say we fight. And keep trying to raise the barrier."

At that, the room erupted into a cacophony of women shouting. Rhea tried to restore order with little success, despite the escalating pitch of her voice. Hammad crossed his arms disapprovingly. Ignatia placed a hand on Jacob's arm and murmured something in his ear. Ewelike blinked in frustrated shock.

Judith and Meg exchanged askance glances and watched the madness in silence, for what else could they do? They weren't even on the council. If the archons weren't giving each other the respect they were due, what respect would they give to two young women brought in only to report? Judith watched the women carefully for signs of treason—despite the truth test, the idea of possessions and moles and invisible spirits had her on edge—but with everyone dissenting about everything, it was difficult to know what was inspired by lack of loyalty and which comments were simply from fear.

Gerrick stood, his grey mourning robe falling gracefully to the ground and lending his quiet presence an air of dignified gravity. Slowly, silence fell, and all eyes in the room turned toward him.

Judith blinked. She'd never heard Gerrick string more than two sentences together. When she'd once asked her mother why Gerrick was on the council, Ignatia had replied that it was out of respect for Thea and the sacrifice they had both made. Was the old man actually going to speak?

He steadied himself with his fingers on the tabletop and looked at each person in the room, staring especially long at the squabbling Nelly and Stella. Nelly glanced away uncomfortably, but Stella lifted her chin in defiance, her dark green eyes glittering.

"You should be ashamed of yourselves, acting like children. You call yourselves the leaders of these people?" He gestured with his arm to encompass not only the room, but everyone in the safe house beyond.

Judith's mouth fell open. Remembering herself, she closed it. It seemed Gerrick thought of himself as more than a token memorial.

The man's pale blue eyes were hard as steel as he continued in his lilting accent. "You pride yourselves on being a peaceful people, but tales of mermaids dragging sailors to sea have persisted among my people for centuries. Your kind are not so peaceful as you might think. Did you think your attacks would go unnoticed?"

Judith flushed with heat. She'd fought for male emancipation her whole life, but she couldn't help feel responsible for the sins of her people's past anyway.

Gerrick met Tafrara's eye. "Your people have been sheltered here for a long time, and I think you may have forgotten the ways of our kind. Unfortunately, I don't believe these ships are coming in peace—not a peace that benefits the island, anyway. And, as difficult as life has been for me here, I have become fond of many of you and would not see you come to harm." Gerrick's sharp gaze roved around the room. "But it's time to wake up. You have been at war with humans for as long as your history and ours remembers. The humans beyond your barrier simply haven't known how to find you until now."

"But how could they have found us so soon?" Stella demanded. "The barrier only went down a few weeks ago, and human travel is slow. Has someone told them?"

"The spirits," Judith said, putting the pieces together. "Damon must have used them to send messages."

Gerrick eyed her. "Possibly. But what matters is that now humans are sending ships to meet the enemy they have finally located, and you cower in your stone halls. Yet you have abilities and technology far beyond human capabilities, even without your Heartstone. No more talk of how best to hide. Perhaps it is time for you to learn from humans and fight to defend yourselves. Fight to protect the island Thea served, and that Calandra . . ." His voice broke, and he looked down at his hands. "And find a way to get Calandra out of that place. That is all."

He sat down and stared at the table, his face set in heavy, sad lines.

"Fight? I'd expect no other suggestion from a man," sneered Amaryllis. "It's like that's all you know how to do."

Rhea's voice took on a warning note. "Councillor kor'Yianna, that hardly seems—"

"Doesn't it? We've had three fights among the Freemen here just in the past week. This morning, there was one about a sleeping mat, for the love of the Mother! One can see why our ancestors chose sirensong instead of the incessant violence. Perhaps that's how we should deal with the oncoming threat. It's always worked for our people in the past."

"And defeat the whole purpose of our rebellion?" snapped Ignatia. "I think not."

"I, for one, think defending ourselves is a brilliant idea," Nelly said. "And a familiar one." She raised her brows at the archons, but she cast Gerrick a grateful look.

"What would we do with that many ships?" Stella asked. "We can't bring them here. We can barely handle the new humans we've got."

Judith had to agree. Cogger, the belligerent sailor Calandra had brought back from Steadfast House, had quickly become a problem on the work crew he'd been assigned to and was now back in a temporary holding cell—captive in body, though not in mind. The more captives they brought to the island, the more men like Cogger they'd have to police. She thought of the song of forgetting Calandra had mentioned that morning. Could that be a solution? She opened her mouth to suggest it, but was cut off by her father leaping to his feet.

"They only lack purpose," said Jacob—to the surprise of everyone, including his wife. "The Freemen, I mean. They still know so little about Sirenia or their place in our society. Their minds are free, yes, but they have very few options open to them. How else do you expect them to take out their frustration?"

"With something besides their fists, for a start!" shot back Amaryllis.

The room erupted again. Some were in favour of Gerrick's suggestions, some against, and the additional element of the constant tensions among the men in their camp only confused the issue.

Judith tried to catch someone's attention to bring up the song, but no one paid her any mind. She sat back in her chair, frustrated.

She wasn't the only one who'd had enough. With an angry glance around the room, Gerrick got up and left.

Moments later, Judith, Meg, and Tafrara trailed after him, escaping to the relative peace of the Great Hall beyond the door. No one even noticed them go.

The council may not want to fight the oncoming human ships. But they certainly had no problem fighting each other.

Polyxo sat leaning against the wall in the portico, reading on a stone reader. As soon as she saw Meg, she stood, her face wreathed in smiles, and bustled over to them. Tafrara was frowning, deep in thought. Judith thought about telling her about the note from the Coalition to see if she knew who the mysterious J. W. was, but before she could, Polyxo broke in.

"Finally. I thought you'd never be done! I have something important to tell you."

Gerrick paused to listen. Polyxo cast him an uncomfortable look, then turned back to Meg.

"You're going to be *so* surprised." She wore a knowing smile.

Tafrara excused herself with a perfunctory salute and walked away down the hallway toward the sleeping quarters. Judith frowned after her, feeling bad that the council had never even gotten to the Coalition's note, the order of business for which the human girl had been invited. She promised herself to go talk to Tafrara soon.

"Couldn't Erigone have handled this?" Meg asked, sounding as tired as Judith felt.

Polyxo rolled her eyes. "She's been in bed for hours. Remind me never to get old."

Judith frowned. "Erigone is only thirty-two."

Polyxo raised a brow at Judith as though she'd just proved her point.

"Just tell us already," snapped Meg.

A flash of hurt crossed Polyxo's face, but it was soon overcome by the excitement of whatever news she was brimming with. She actually bounced on her toes a little.

"I found it," she said. "I found the reason the Heartstone isn't working."

Meg straightened. "What is it?"

Polyxo's face flushed with embarrassment. "Well, er, it's probably best if you read the stone yourself. It's a lot of technical talk I barely understood, which is why I wanted you to take a look at it."

Meg gave a sharp nod. "Let's go take a look then. Lead on, Kore kor'Theano."

Judith said nothing, but caught a slight shift in Polyxo's shield that made her look twice at the young noblewoman. Was that deceit she had just sensed, or was Polyxo simply worried about something behind her excitement?

Just then, sounds of a brawl in the Great Hall beyond reached their ears. The three young women ran along the portico until they could see the source—two Freemen had been having a fistfight and had been pulled apart by several others.

Polyxo scowled at the cluster of milling men. "Do you ever wonder if maybe Calandra didn't know the whole story before she made her big announcement?"

Judith eyed the scuffle. A statement like that might be due reason to question someone's loyalty. But perhaps Amaryllis had a point about how men solved conflicts.

Gerrick arrived, having followed them at a more stately pace. He stood at her elbow and looked over the disgruntled men in consternation.

"If you have truly found the answer we need, Polyxo, it isn't a moment too soon," said Judith. "At this rate, Damon won't need to defeat us. We'll do the job for him. We need something to focus on to give us hope."

"So do they," Gerrick said, staring at the men milling in the hall. "Jacob was right. They need someone to teach them how to belong here."

Meg gave him a sidelong glance. "I can't think of anyone more suited to the job than you, Uncle Gerrick. Perhaps you should be the one to teach them, yes? Find out what they're good at and how they can be useful here. Teach them how to survive among the undines." She swallowed. "You could even teach them how to . . . to fight. With the *Tropos Hydor Zon*, I mean, with discipline and purpose—not to just brawl out of boredom."

Surprise registered in Gerrick's eyes, and he nodded. A small smile touched his lips—the first Judith had seen him wear for weeks.

"Thank you, er, Meg."

He gently squeezed Meg's arm. She looked slightly taken aback by the gesture before she gave him a wide smile. Then he shuffled down the walkway toward where the scuffle had occurred.

Polyxo bounced on her toes with barely restrained urgency. Judith's irritation, already elevated, rose even more at the young woman's eagerness, but when Meg spoke, she only sounded amused.

"Yes, Kore kor'Theano," she said. "Show us your great discovery."

Polyxo's face broke into a wide grin. "Finally," she said, sounding relieved.

She nearly ran as she led the way toward the compound's temporary archive.

Judith cast a glance toward Gerrick, who had already captured the attention of the milling men. They stopped to listen to whatever he was saying. Despite their hostility toward each other, they obviously respected him—Judith knew not how he'd earned it. But she sensed Meg's suggestion would serve to give more than only the newly Freed men purpose, and smiled.

She followed Meg and Polyxo down the corridor, with the latter chattering the whole way about how she'd discovered the stone that held her big revelation. Judith allowed a spark of optimism to light in her chest. Perhaps they could resolve more than one problem today, all without the interference of the bickering archons.

And then she could finally find a way to Free the man she loved.

53

REELING

Robert sat in a corner of the common room of the Port House Inn, quietly sipping his brandy—which Barnum had delivered post-haste in response to Robert's haggard bark when they'd entered the common room—while the voices of his companions rose and fell around him like waves against the Bajan shore. He couldn't stop staring at Miss Bethel, but he didn't try either. Outwardly, she appeared calm, but her face was set in tight lines as she listened to Miss Chapman recount their flight from Huntley Hall. Nowhere in that face could he see a trace of the girl he'd known as Talwyn Penrose.

When Miss Bethel had seen Robert's face after her revelation about her past—no doubt he'd looked truly dreadful—she'd insisted they go get something to eat to regain their equilibrium. And, he was sure, to give them something else to focus on. Since neither of the escaped slaves could show their faces for fear of being discovered, Miss Bethel had instructed Bunmi to watch over the sleeping Osaze while the rest of them went for supper. Once they settled in the moderately busy common room, Miss Bethel had a tray of soup and tea sent up to the room while she, Miss Chapman, Mrs. Urbi, and Robert occupied a corner table to regroup. When Anne-Marie came to take their order, he deferred to Miss Bethel, claiming not to be hungry. In truth, he didn't trust his own voice.

Robert looked around at the three women, brooding. What was a gentleman like himself doing in this position—sitting at a table in an inn of questionable reputation with a gypsy woman and two black women?

And how could one of them be a spirit—and the same village girl he'd given up for dead—when she was sitting right across from him, ordinary

438

as can be, ordering tea, bread, and cold cuts?

And *how* could Gryffyn and Middleton have known the truth about her long before he'd even suspected?

As he thought about it, he realized he *should* have suspected. After all, there was the fact she spoke every language he'd seen her encounter. And how she and Berian were so comfortable talking about demons and other spirits. And the way the light caught in her eyes, glinting at him as though it were a secret she couldn't wait to tell him. Indeed, as the lamplight glinted off her dark brown curls in golden flecks brighter than seemed warranted by the smoky flame, he couldn't believe he hadn't seen it before. Light was drawn to her like bees to sunflowers.

With consternation, he realized he'd been given ample evidence of her true nature, but, as usual, he had wilfully turned a blind eye. And who could blame him, when his past claims about spirits had earned him nothing but derision from everyone he knew? He could still see the mocking scorn in his sister-in-law's expression as Amelia, with her perfect porcelain-doll face and pouting lips, jibed him about claiming to have seen spirits—a story Gryffyn had told her, not him. Gryffyn, who had known the truth all along, and had made Robert feel a fool for his whole life. Why would he do such a thing?

He'd once thought that encounter a one-time event, a defining moment in his life. But now, it seemed Robert encountered spirits at every turn.

First Zale. Then Romero. Now Miss Bethel, who was apparently one and the same as Talwyn Penrose. And then there were Mr. and Mrs. Penrose and Mr. Berian.

Was there anyone he knew who wasn't a bloody spirit?

He took another sip of the burning liquor and peered at the woman he apparently didn't know at all. Miss Bethel finished placing her order for the table and fastened Robert with a glower as the server hurried toward the kitchen.

"Really, Mr. Cox. Can you stop staring, at least?"

He glanced away, studying the brown and green bottles lined up on shelves behind the proprietor's counter, but he couldn't help peeking back at Miss Bethel every few seconds.

She folded her hands in front of her chin, her elbows resting on the table. She almost looked as though she were praying.

"Are you all right, Mr. Cox?" she said eventually.

He made a noncommittal sound and stared into his drink.

"I don't know what to think of you Miss . . . Guri—"

She cut him off with a hand on his arm. "Miss Bethel will do fine, thank you. Or Abela, if we are now familiar enough to use proper names."

He met her intense look, reading her wish to keep her true name concealed.

"All right . . . Miss Bethel," he said stiffly.

She gave him an exasperated look.

"Mr. Cox. Robbie. I'm still just me. I'm no different than I always was." She smiled, the same smile that had been making him weak-kneed for months, and he could almost believe nothing had changed.

Except everything had.

"If you say so, Miss Bethel." He studied the bottom of his glass, which was bare already.

She frowned, then sighed. Apparently giving up on Robert, she turned to Miss Chapman and gave her a long look. The young woman lifted her chin and stared defiantly back.

"Miss Chapman, I confess to being surprised to see you here. Given your key role with the enemy, I thought you'd made your choice long ago. What has prompted the change of heart?"

The handsome gypsy girl glanced at the three of them hesitantly, tucking an errant black curl beneath her mustard yellow headscarf and straightening her spine. Robert frowned, thinking of Miss Chapman in a hooded robe in that nefarious ceremony, and said nothing. She, at least, wasn't a spirit, though she seemed to be neck-deep with them.

"I am not a bad person," she said. "I've always tried to honour my father and our family, even when I haven't understood or cared for his methods. I always thought he was working for the good of the family and our people. But lately . . ."

She fidgeted with the ends of the long black curls that hung over her shoulder.

"I never expected Zale to become family too. Nor did I expect Father to turn against him, not after sharing our *tan* with him for so long. Father has become someone different. Someone . . . cruel." She frowned at the table. "The man I once knew would never have laid a hand against another man, let alone flog him so mercilessly."

Urbi's brow furrowed. "Your father, he the man who beat my son?"

Miss Chapman bit her lip and nodded, her eyes bright. "Your son is the bravest man I've ever seen. What he endured . . ."

She blinked and looked toward the window, though all was dark beyond it save the stars.

"These men my father is in league with," she continued. "They are not good men. And my father is becoming like them, but he won't see it."

Miss Bethel folded her hands in front of her on the table. "And what can you tell us of their plans?"

Miss Chapman glanced around the room, then leaned in and lowered her voice. "You know of Sirenia, where Zale's people are from?"

Urbi and Miss Bethel both nodded. Robert couldn't hold in his frustration any longer.

"How do you all know of this place when I have never heard of it before this ill-fated journey to the tropics? What the devil is going on?"

Miss Bethel looked at him kindly.

"There is a reason you've been kept in the dark, Mr. Cox. The undines—that's what Zale's kind are called—have been protected from discovery by humans for thousands of years."

"Protected? Protected how? And why?"

"They have a special barrier that surrounds their lands which deflects attention from those beyond it. Such protection became necessary once humans began distrusting and fearing undines and their abilities. The undines were once hunted nearly to extinction."

Robert wished he could deny humans would do such a thing, but he knew it was not true. Why, wasn't even he capable of such inhumanity, for lack of a better word? The memory of the stench of the slave-filled cargo hold of the *Atlanta* wafted through his nostrils, and he nearly gagged.

"How do you all know of it then?"

Urbi pressed her lips together. At Miss Bethel's nod, she sighed and turned to him. She switched to Greek instead of using stilted English.

"When Osaze was a small boy, still a babe in arms, he and I were taken as slaves and put on a ship to a place like this." She indicated the island beyond the walls with an encompassing gesture, and Robert's throat closed. "The undines took our ship before we arrived and we have lived on their island ever since . . . until a few weeks ago."

"How did you escape?" Miss Chapman asked with interest.

Urbi gave her a dark look and shook her head. "I do not wish to say."

The gypsy girl and the older woman gave each other a hard stare. Miss Chapman looked away first.

"You have good reason not to trust me," the gypsy girl said in her clipped West Country lilt, "but I want to change that, so I will tell you what I know. My father is part of a secret order whose goal is to release some ancient spirits known as the Grigori from their prison in the Abyss." She met Robert's gaze with her dark eyes. "He has been working with your elder brother, Mr. Gryffyn Cox, ever since Lord Alverton died."

"Your father is part of the Order of the Ascension?" Robert said involuntarily, then clamped his mouth shut. His father had made no bones of his opinions of the gypsies. That he would suffer one to gain admittance to an order of which he was a part surprised Robert greatly. He'd thought the gypsies had been employed by his father, nothing more.

"Aye," she said. "Your father and mine have known each other for many years. I know not how they met." She cast Robert a sideways glance. "I'm sorry for your loss."

Robert acknowledged her condolences with a stiff nod.

"And you were their medium, I presume?" Miss Bethel asked.

Miss Chapman nodded, and the bangles on her wrists clinked softly beneath the table as she spoke.

"For years, they have used my abilities and training as a *shuvani* to contact a dragon spirit to whom they have sworn fealty." Her burnt umber complexion went a little sallow. "Once he discovers what I have done, he will certainly order my death. So know that I did not make the decision to join you lightly." She flicked her gaze at Urbi. "I couldn't keep watching my father become a monster like them. And . . . I couldn't let them keep hurting your son."

She glanced at her hands and swallowed. Urbi gave her a shrewd look, studying her.

Barnum brought the tea service and poured it out. As soon as her cup had been filled, Miss Chapman snatched it up, sipping the steaming liquid black and bitter.

Miss Bethel gave Miss Chapman a compassionate, closed-lipped smile. Then she began doctoring her tea with sugar and milk while she spoke to Robert.

"Of course, you know why *I* know about Sirenia—it is Zale's home, though I've never been there until recently. The gyroscope I showed you allows me to—"

"I know," Robert said.

She gave him a dark look—for his tone, no doubt. "Even my kind have been unable to penetrate the barrier, thanks to the machinations of the same foe that threatens us now." She turned a questioning glance on Miss Chapman. "With which spirit do you communicate?"

She shook her head. "He goes only by 'the Master.'"

Robert shuddered involuntarily.

Miss Bethel tilted her head. "That could be any number of the leaders of the Rebellion. Or perhaps one of their sympathizers. Ah, well." She patted Miss Chapman's hand. "You did a brave thing. And you made the right decision. There are worse things than death."

Miss Chapman nodded, some colour returning to her cheeks. "If it's all the same to you, I'd much prefer to remain alive."

Miss Bethel smiled. "Right. Don't worry, we shall keep you alive and fighting on this plane for as long as we are able." Her expression darkened. "Of course, that would have been easier if both Mr. Romero and Mr. Berian hadn't left on the very same day."

She sighed and shook her head.

Robert shifted in his seat and fixed his gaze on Miss Bethel. "And where did they go, exactly? What is it your kind do when you're not getting falsely drowned in streams or rescuing merfolk lads from gypsies?" His voice dripped with sarcasm, but he didn't care.

Miss Bethel's mouth twisted sardonically, and her hand tightened around her teacup. "You forgot 'rescuing English gentlemen from mermaids' in there."

Robert's mouth went as dry as though he'd eaten sand. His knuckles went white around his brandy tumbler.

"The *Atlanta* didn't sink, did it? Tell me the truth. It got . . . taken by these undign—"

"Un-*dine*," Josefine corrected him. "Like *unseen*."

He cast her a baleful glance and turned back to the golden-eyed girl.

"Un-*dine* creatures somehow. That's why I could never find anyone from the ship here."

Another thought hit him like a blow.

"And you and Berian and I didn't get picked up by a passing ship. You brought me here with that"—he pointed at the chain on her neck, the pendant concealed beneath her neckline—"the same way Romero used one to disappear before my eyes today. Wait." He blinked at her. "That's how you were able to get to Sirenia and back so quickly, isn't it? With one of those . . . those chariots."

Miss Bethel, Miss Chapman, and Urbi sat through his diatribe with increasing astonishment on their faces. At his final words, Miss Bethel gave a surprised blink, then her face broke into an amused, cautious smile.

"It takes you a while to spot the truth, Robert Cox, but once you see it, you see it all at once. How did you know this is called a chariot?" She placed her hand over her dress where her pendant was concealed.

"Middleton. He has one just like it, said he couldn't use it. Only *spirits* could." He glanced away. Then he frowned, struck by sudden curiosity. "Why is it called a chariot? It's just little rings."

Miss Bethel's mouth tugged upward in amusement. "You've read of them, I'm sure, in the Book of Ezekiel? The wheels within wheels that bore the throne of the Almighty, directed by the cherubim?"

It was Robert's turn to be cautious. "I remember the passage. I can't believe I'm about to ask this, but are you saying the throne of God sits on little gyroscopes such as the one you wear around your neck?"

At this, the tension fell from Miss Bethel's face in a peal of laughter that ended with a snort. Robert, whose insides were stretched to the point of snapping, watched her, nonplussed. The bracelet with the red stone peeked out from beneath her sleeve, and his gut tightened further. He thought he might be sick.

"No," Miss Bethel said, stifling her giggles, "those ones are much bigger than this. This one is only for personal use, to move someone a short distance at a time."

Robert blinked at her as more of her words sank in. She'd already admitted to being a spirit, even an angel, but now she'd confirmed what Middleton had told him. A cold weight settled in his gut.

"So you are a . . . cherub?"

She nodded, still smiling. "So you believe me. Good. We have much to discuss."

Robert frowned. "All this time while I tormented myself over Talwyn's death, she was never really dead. Because she's you."

"Yes, that's right," Miss Bethel said expectantly, as though waiting for him to grasp one final important piece. "And that's why I told you I forgive you. Please, Robert, forgive yourself. It was only a test. You've had others, and you'll have a few more, I'd warrant. Don't let that choice define your entire life. Elyon has his eye on you, Mr. Cox. So keep your eye on him, and all will be well."

Rage curdled in Robert's belly, melting the icy shock. He stood up suddenly, startling the women so they sat back in their chairs. Miss Chapman gasped, as did a few of the surrounding patrons.

"But it *has* defined me, Miss . . . whoever you are. It was the reason I've tried so hard to earn redemption. But it was only a test? Who ordered such a test? What kind of sick, twisted god would be capable of such a thing? No god I want to serve. And you . . . you let me believe every soul on the *Atlanta* but us had been lost, knowing the torment I've been suffering because of it. Were any of them lost? Or did they all end up on this Sirenia?"

Wide-eyed, Miss Bethel nodded. "From what I understand, all or nearly all are safe, but—"

"Was that a test too?" he said coldly, then narrowed his eyes at her. "I gave you my heart, but, all along, you only saw an awkward schoolboy in need of a lesson . . . no matter how your lessons might make him bleed."

With that, he snatched up his coat and strode from the common room into the moonlit darkness beyond, ignoring the curious gazes that followed him.

Elyon has his eye on you. The weight of that gaze fell on him like a vest of lead. What had often been a comfort, knowing that he was never beyond God's view, had now become a burden, an ominous threat that he could never hide from the stern, judgemental God who never missed anything he did, nor would let any sin go unpunished.

Well, privacy might be an illusion. But it was an illusion he'd sink his teeth into if he could find it.

54

THE HEART

Osaze lay on his side on the hard bed with his eyes closed, the flames in his back coming into focus as he awoke. He felt somewhat better after the sleep. Whatever poultices Josefine and Ifeoluwa had slathered him with were finally having an effect, for the pain had lessened considerably. The tangy, woody scent of the poultices wafted around him, and the savoury smell of something cooking nearby made his stomach rumble.

His mind wandered between reality and the dream he'd left behind. He'd held Calandra in his arms as they stared at a black bowl of sky streaked with a ribbon of stars. That had been at Fire Lake, the night before everything changed—before Adonia named her the Opal Princess and the seizures had started.

Thinking of Calandra filled him with a different kind of pain. Were the bonds she carried the reason she had sent him away? Had she even been in her right mind?

Despite the comfort it would have given him to blame the bonds and encroaching Madness for her rejection, he knew she hadn't been that affected by them when she sent him away. And his mother had certainly been of sound mind when she'd agreed to the plan. Both of them had treated him like a piece in their game of stones, and it rankled. *I will not be a* doulos *again.*

Osaze . . .

Osaze pushed himself bolt upright, causing Bunmi, who'd been sleeping on the room's other bed, to startle awake and sit up.

"What is it, elder brother?" she asked.

The mental touch had been faint, desperate, and unmistakable. He

446

closed his eyes and tried to sense Calandra again, but her presence was gone.

His heart ached with the void of it.

A cool hand on his arm made him open his eyes to see Bunmi's dark, worried irises staring back at him. He shook his head.

"It was nothing. Only a nightmare."

She nodded and went to sit on a nearby chair, watching him. He lay back down, facing away from her.

He didn't want anyone to see his tears.

*

WHEN the door swung open and admitted Josefine, Osaze sat up again. Behind the slim girl in bright clothing came the golden-eyed Abela, followed by his mother.

Urbi rushed toward him in open relief.

"Osaze, you're awake." She put a hand on his cheek. "When you first arrived, I feared we were too late."

He turned his face away, and she let her hand drop, obviously stung. His conscience pricked a bit, but he just looked at the lamassu.

"Abela, it is good to see you again," he said in Greek. "You kept your word about my mother, and I am grateful."

Even though he was angry with his mother, he still wouldn't have had her suffer the indignity of becoming a slave. But though his mother looked safe and well, the true surprise was that Abela had found a way to free him as she'd promised. If she hadn't, he wasn't sure how much longer he would have held out. He'd thought he was strong, stronger than all their pain. Lord John had nearly proved him wrong.

Abela smiled, but cast a concerned glance at Urbi. He didn't look at his mother again. He didn't want to see the pain he knew he'd caused, though he was glad she'd felt it.

Her fault. She had no right.

Abela turned toward him. "And I'm grateful we were able to rescue you, too, before the worst happened. I am only sorry we did not reach you sooner."

She turned to Josefine, who sat on the bed beside him, checking the dressings on his back.

"How soon do you think we can leave?" Abela asked.

The Romani girl looked up at her. "It would be best if he could rest here for several days. But I know we don't have that luxury."

Abela shook her head. "Correct. Romero's safeguards will only protect us for another few hours, I'm sure, and then Middleton and his people will be able to get to us. We must go somewhere they won't be able to find us. And I must report what you told me about the Order's plans." She tapped her lips with a forefinger. "My source didn't know the exact location of the rebel base on Sirenia, but I think I could work it out if we could only get to the island. Unfortunately, it's too far away for me to blink all of us there together. It was a strain to go that distance alone with the size of my chariot, and it still has not fully recovered. Still, waiting for recharge cycles would be faster than a ship, and safer, even if I only take one at a time. Let's see, if I . . ." She muttered under her breath as she thought through her next steps, ticking items off on her fingers.

Urbi cleared her throat.

"Pardon, miss, but Osaze and I will not be returning to that place. Especially if what you say is true, and Calandra is no longer even there—"

"Where's Calandra?" Osaze broke in, the suddenness of this news jolting him past his determination not to speak to his mother.

The women turned to him. Bunmi sat silently on the other bed, observing everyone with her legs crossed and her ankles tucked under her, though she must understand next to nothing of what was being said of the conversation in Greek.

Abela was the one to speak.

"We have received word that Calandra and Zale have both gone after their mother in Tartarus," she said with a tight voice. "My companion, Berian, has gone after them to assist them."

"Tartarus?" Osaze straightened, trying to push himself to his feet. "Isn't that through the Voidstone? Calandra lost her hand to that thing. How will they get out again?"

Abela and Josefine both put restraining hands on his shoulders. Urbi looked on with anxious eyes, but did not try to touch him again.

"You must sit, Osaze," Josefine said. "You'll make your back bleed."

Osaze wanted to retort that he didn't care, that his back was the least of his worries, but a cracking, pulling sensation made him change his mind. He sat on the bed again, but didn't lay down. He rested his forearms on his knees and sat as still as possible.

Abela gave him a compassionate look. "You would do Calandra no good by going after her. Undines were created to travel in and out of Sheol. For humans, it's a one-way trip. Once you leave your flesh behind, there's no way to come back to it—but for a few special cases throughout history. Whatever good you can do for her will be done here."

Osaze's jaw clenched and his throat tightened. He didn't like this. Not at all. Once again, he felt trapped by circumstances beyond his control. But on the other hand, Calandra had made it clear she didn't want him to do anything else for her.

Does that mean you abandon your vow?

Josefine cocked her head. "Abela has told me Calandra is Zale's sister. But who is she to you, Osaze?"

He stared at Josefine, not even sure how to respond. Urbi spoke up instead.

"Osaze was her consort-elect. They were to be married."

Mercifully, she did not expand on the explanation, and after a nod of understanding, Josefine said nothing more about it. But she watched him carefully for several seconds before glancing away.

Osaze looked at Abela, frustration tightening his gut—along with the conflicting emotions of wanting to both abandon Calandra to her fate and fulfill his promise to protect her. But what could he do from here, especially since she wasn't even on this plane of existence?

But Tartarus was where that ever-chained dragon was, the one who was responsible for her losing her arm in the first place. Damon. What would he do if he got his hands on her?

"Tell me what you know," he said through gritted teeth. "Tell me what has happened."

Abela cocked her head, then pulled the only chair over to sit in front of him. She told him what she and Berian had learned while on Sirenia and what Romero had told them since arriving on Barbados—which, in the end, was quite a lot.

She told him that instead of healing the Heartstone, whatever Zale and Calandra had done had instead weakened it so the barrier around the island had disappeared. The queen and one of the councillors were dead.

"Which councillor?" Osaze asked.

"A woman named Thea kor'Aglaia."

Osaze felt as though he'd been punched. Thea had been like a foster mother to Calandra, but it was her long-standing marriage to a man who was secretly Free that had earned Osaze's respect. Abela didn't know what had happened to Gerrick, Thea's consort, which implied he had escaped. Her informant had told her of Narcissa's erratic behaviour, and between that and Romero's talk of movement in the spiritual planes, Abela was convinced Narcissa had been taken over by some kind of malicious spirit—

"Damon," Osaze interrupted, relieved. If that were true, at least the beast wasn't in Tartarus with Calandra.

"What?" Abela blinked. "Who is that?"

Osaze explained about the spirit who had haunted Calandra's dreams and how he'd tried to draw her into the Voidstone, resulting in her losing her arm. He'd been bent on gaining power.

"He is a trickster, very good at illusion and manipulation. He made Calandra think he'd taken her Tear, but instead, she'd only dropped it at the bottom of a lake while under his influence."

Abela nodded. "That fits what's been happening with the princess. Damon wouldn't be his real name, of course. Did he ever give another one?"

Osaze frowned, thinking. "He claimed to be Alessandro, the Mad Queen's consort."

"The Mad Queen—you mean Nadia? But Alessandro was an undine. He—" Abela stopped, looking like she was thinking hard, remembering something. "He was possessed too. By Semyaza. The description you gave fits him perfectly." Her face hardened. "If Semyaza has broken his chains and escaped the Abyss, then the danger is greater than we realized. That explains some of the reports of Narcissa's strange behaviour. My source says she's been looking for something."

Urbi's nostrils flared. "Do you know what she's looking for?"

Abela hesitated, looking like she was trying to decide how much to share.

"I do," said Josefine.

All eyes turned toward her. Her gaze fastened on the large red stone on Abela's wrist.

"If she's been possessed by one of the Grigori, she's probably looking for that." She pointed at it.

Abela lifted her wrist to look at the stone, then pushed it up her arm and pulled her sleeve over it. "What makes you say that?"

"Because that's what the Master wants. That's why Lord Middleton had my father and me watch you. He knew you had one, and we were supposed to find a way to get it from you."

Involuntarily, Abela drew her arm in close to her chest.

Hurt flickered on Josefine's face. "I'm not here to take it from you. I told you, I'm not working for them anymore."

Abela nodded. She stuck her arm out of her sleeve so the stone was plainly visible and peered at it with a furrowed brow.

Osaze marvelled at the gem. He'd seen many wonderful and beautiful stones among the undines, but this would rival all of them—a red crystal of incredible clarity the size of a large pebble, but cut in such a way that light scattered from its depths as though it emanated from within.

"What is it?" he asked.

Abela glanced up at him. "It is a heartstone."

"Like the one on Sirenia?" How could this small gem be the same as the massive sphere that powered the island?

"Not quite." She peered at the stone on her wrist, absently tugging on one of her curls. "A heartstone can take many forms, but its purpose always remains the same—to organize ether into matter. Basically, it's a way of channelling the building blocks of chaos into a purpose, usually a physical form or energy. This one is for creating a fleshly body. It belonged to Berian, and I am keeping it safe until he returns." She made a face. "He'll have his work cut out for him when he gets it back. He'd been in that form for nearly twenty years. He didn't even have to think about it anymore, I'd wager. Now he'll be starting all over again."

Osaze stared at the stone in fascination. He'd always wondered how the Heartstone worked. Not that he understood much more now than before, but the principle fascinated him.

"Why didn't Berian take his heartstone with him?" Josefine asked.

Abela sighed. "Two reasons—like humans, the erelim cannot take their flesh into Sheol, what you know as Hades or the Underworld—or Tzion, for that matter. It is bound to this plane. Only undines can cross the veil with their bodies relatively unaffected. And though Berian *could* have taken his heartstone so he'd have it when he returned, given the forces he was likely to encounter there, he did not think it wise. He didn't dare risk letting it fall into enemy hands while in the Underworld."

Josefine tilted her head. "Why would that be worse there than here?"

Abela shuddered. "It wouldn't go well, either way. But there, the consequences could shake the foundations of all the planes, not just that one. Here, the worst someone could do is destroy a city or two at a time."

Osaze drew in a sharp breath. "That sounds pretty bad to me. We must be sure this Semyaza doesn't get it. Nor Lord John." He stared at the stone and scowled. Middleton already abused what power he had. What would he do with more?

"Yes, you're right, of course. I've been so upset about Berian that I've been careless with this." Abela clucked her tongue at herself. "How he would scold me if he knew."

She covered the stone with her hand, and when she withdrew it, the bracelet was no longer visible—gone, not merely pushed out of sight. There was no longer even a lump beneath her sleeve. Osaze met her eyes, and her glance gave him confirmation that she had, indeed, used some ability of hers to mask it.

She cleared her throat. "As for Middleton, he wouldn't be able to use it himself. But if it were available, whoever has been directing the Order's movements would likely use it to manifest here. If Semyaza has broken free, it might even be him, but there are likely other Grigori whose chains have loosened and who are looking for a way out of their prison. In fact," Abela paused thoughtfully, "they likely want more than one heartstone."

Josefine nodded confirmation. "They want as many as they can find. I don't know much about their plans, but I do know they are planning more than a jailbreak. They want an all-out war."

Abela paled. "So it's true then," she whispered.

Urbi tore her gaze from the gem's hiding place to look at its wearer. "Where would the Grigori find another heartstone?"

Abela swallowed, and Osaze replied for her.

"In Abela," he said, watching the cherub. "You're using one of these heartstones too, aren't you? And so is Romero."

She nodded. "And the only way someone could retrieve it is for me to discorporate as Berian did."

Urbi gave her a questioning stare.

"This body would have to die," Abela explained.

Osaze shook his head. "I don't understand. If Semyaza is already using Narcissa's body on this plane, why does he need a heartstone? And what has happened to Narcissa? Is she dead?"

His throat closed at the thought. What Narcissa had done to him or had him do while he was her *doulos* still woke him up in a cold sweat on occasion. He wasn't sure how he'd feel if her existence had been snuffed out by the spirit that had threatened Calandra—relieved? Glad? Gratified? Maybe. But he wondered if possession were similar to being under the *sklavia* bond—your will subjected to that of another. A small twinge of compassion pricked him at the thought, but he squelched it.

Narcissa deserved as much compassion as she'd given, which was none.

Abela shook her head. "Narcissa wouldn't be dead. Depending on how cooperative she is being with Semyaza, she may even have some agency. However, a spirit in possession of a flesh form bound to the Ground will have very few of their true abilities available to them. My source said that

Narcissa has acquired ability with fire, a very unlikely gift for an undine female, and yet she hasn't actually burned anything. I suspect the fire is an illusion—something Semyaza has always been skilled in. If he were to acquire his own form by use of a heartstone, though, he'd be able to channel fire in earnest. He'd be somewhat limited by the restrictions placed on the stones, but much less so than now."

Osaze cocked his head. "Restrictions?"

Abela nodded and smoothed the skirt of her dress. "You see, all power in the universe comes from a single source, the creator and foundation of all that is. Elyon made the universe from his own essence, and all that reside here depend on it for existence. When he first gave my kind the heartstones to aid us in fulfilling our duties to serve humanity, we were able to shape and control matter using our own spirit and will, drawing from the chaos beyond the spheres and using it as we saw fit. But after the Rebellion, Elyon limited the stones—the user must still shape the ether with their own will, but the spirit is drawn through the Pneuma, his spirit, like thread through the eye of a needle or water through a pipe. It can only be shaped into a form or energy that conforms to the rules Elyon has set in place for the universe. This dependency means that, no matter how prideful the user may be, they must always remember where the true source of their power comes from. It also means they cannot simply rewrite the rules governing the universe to their own ends, preserving the balance."

Osaze nodded. "So even if Damon . . . I mean, Semyaza were to get a hold of one, he would be limited in the destruction he could create?"

Abela smiled. "Yes. Though not by much. As both humans and the Grigori have proved over and over again, you don't need to wield fire to hurt others or cause great destruction."

Josefine shook her head. "I think there's something more to consider. The Master was very particular about which stone he wanted, which he called *the sphinx's heart*. Lord Middleton and Colonel Hayward—the British officer who is staying with him—were convinced that meant yours. Do you have any idea why?"

Abela looked like a startled doe. "I . . . ." She shook her head. "I am a sphinx in my warrior form. But there's nothing special about the stone I'm using."

As she said it, a shadow flitted across her face—while she wasn't lying, she wasn't telling them the whole truth either.

"At any rate, we're wasting time. We need to get off of Barbados while we still can. The question is, where should we go?" She tapped her pursed lips with her index finger and looked at Urbi. "Where were the two of you trying to get to?"

"Home," Urbi said quickly. "Home to Yorubaland."

Osaze's jaw clenched. "Mother wants to go to her home. I want to return to mine, but . . ."

But where was that? Without Calandra on Sirenia, was it still home to him? And even if she were there, would he truly want to return after what she'd done?

Still, he'd promised to protect her. But how could he do that when she was in the Underworld and he couldn't follow?

"How do we get them back?" Osaze demanded. At their blank looks, he explained. "How do we get Calandra and Berian back?"

"And Zale," Josefine added.

Abela gave them a compassionate look. "We can't. Not from here. We have to trust that Berian will find them both and return them to this plane—after Zale and Calandra have fulfilled their destiny."

"Destiny?" Josefine asked.

Abela nodded. "You see, the children of Delphine are not just exceptionally gifted healers. They are special in a way no undine before them has been. I once thought Zale and any gifted female healer could repair the Soulstone—the Grigori prison—even his mother. But I was wrong. It must be Calandra and Zale. Their path into Tartarus was foreordained."

"Why?" Osaze blurted.

Abela gave him a helpless look, reflecting the way he felt. "Because Elyon wills it. I don't even understand it myself. But know this, Osaze— Elyon will not leave them unprotected. We must trust in that." Her brows furrowed in worry.

Osaze frowned and said nothing. He'd much rather do something than trust some deity he'd never heard of to bring Calandra back. He'd never truly rest until he knew she was safe.

"If it helps," Abela added, "neither Calandra nor Zale are alone. From what my source tells me, three other undines have accompanied them." She looked at Urbi and Osaze. "Maybe you two will know their names. Sisters Zoe and Damaris kor'Dione as well as a rebel, Airlea kor'Phile."

Osaze sat bolt upright. "Zoe went with them?"

Urbi's face slackened. She shook her head, staring at her son with horrified eyes.

Abela and Josefine looked back and forth between them. Bunmi, who had been sitting quietly on her bed, glanced at Osaze anxiously, obviously sensing the shift in the room.

"Why does that matter?" Abela asked.

Osaze clenched his jaw. "Zoe is the reason my mother and I are here on Barbados instead of in Africa, as Calandra ordered. She betrayed us and betrayed Calandra. She wants to return Sirenia to how it used to be. If she has gone to the Underworld with Calandra, all of them could be in even worse danger than before."

Abela's eyes widened. She studied the floor, biting her lip, then looked up at them.

"We can do nothing about it now. We have to trust that Berian will be able to handle it, by the grace of Elyon. He cares for Delphine and Zale a great deal, and he is one of the most honoured guardians of my order. He'll be able to take care of it." She sounded as though she might be trying to reassure herself as much as them.

Osaze stood and placed his hands against the wall, letting his head drop between his arms.

"What can we do?" he said, mostly rhetorically. He turned and asked again in earnest. "What can we do?"

Abela's chin quivered. She looked as though she wanted someone to tell her the answer to that question as badly as he did. Then her face set in determination. She stood.

"We can fulfill our duties here. We must continue the fight."

Urbi shook her head. "No. This is not our fight. I would return home to Africa. We have already done more than our part in a war that does not belong to us."

Osaze clenched his jaw, still staring at the wall. "You can go to Africa. I would return to Sirenia to help the rebels who have taken up Calandra's cause."

"No, my son," Urbi said. "It is too dangerous. What if they enslave you again?"

Osaze turned a gaze like iron on her. "You mean, in contrast to what my own kind has done to me?"

She winced and glanced at his ragged back, but did not turn away.

He scowled. "Danger is not what frightens me, Mother. It is leaving my duty unfulfilled. I have a duty to you as a son, and I promise, I will help you find your way home to Africa. But first, I must fulfill my duty to Calandra."

"Which is what?" she demanded, standing and staring at him defiantly. "What do you owe her now?"

He faltered, glancing at the floor. "I promised . . . I promised I would always be there to fight the battles I can." He looked out the window. Moonlight glinted from the ocean waves beyond. "I don't know how to help her right now. But I will find a way."

Urbi said nothing for several moments. When she spoke, her tone was soft. "As you say, my son. We all have our promises to keep."

He glanced at her in surprise. Her compassionate gaze rebuked his angry heart.

"I'll go with you." Josefine said. They all looked at her. "You never know. I have a magic mirror. Maybe I can contact them."

"No." Abela's voice was firm and sharp. "You are not to use that again. For all we know, it is your communication through the mirror that freed Semyaza and this so-called Master in the first place, loosening the bonds that held them. It could also alert the enemy to our movements and actions and give away any advantage we have while speeding their advantage over us."

Josefine looked shocked, but held up her hands defensively. "Fine. I won't use it again, if that's what you think is best."

"I *know* it's best. It is forbidden." Abela's golden eyes flashed with hidden fire.

Josefine nodded and said no more.

Osaze's gut tightened as his mind raced toward their next steps. "But how are we going to get to Sirenia?"

Abela bit her lip. "I can take you there with my chariot, but only one at a time, and it will need to rest in between to recharge. There is also the matter of Mr. Cox to deal with." She glanced at Bunmi, who still watched the proceedings in wary silence. "We can't very well leave anyone behind either. Even if we don't all go to Sirenia, none of you are safe here."

Josefine arched a brow at her. "Neither are you."

Abela pressed her lips together. "True." Abela pursed her lips. "Perhaps we can resolve several situations at once. Mrs. Urbi, perhaps I can persuade Mr. Cox to see you home to Yorubaland—it is too far for me to take you. He ought to return to England where he'll be out of harm's way, and he cannot come to Sirenia. While I seek him out, you should prepare and rest. It could be a difficult journey."

Osaze caught his mother's forlorn glance at him and turned away.

"Yes, Miss Abela," Urbi said behind him, her voice heavy with reluctance. "That is a good plan."

Just then, a noise outside the window alerted Osaze. He went over and peered through it to see the red-haired young man who'd accompanied them home from the plantation coming up the back stairs with staggering steps.

"Ah, it's Mr. Cox," said Abela at his elbow. "Good. Hopefully he's had time to recover himself. I'll speak to him about our decision, and we'll soon be on our way."

Cox swayed and put his hand against the wall to steady himself, frowning at the stairs.

"Stop moving," he admonished them with slurred syllables. He continued his climb, glaring at each step as though he expected it to object.

Abela sighed. "If he's sober enough to comprehend what I'm saying, that is. Excuse me."

She bustled from the room, and Osaze could soon hear her greeting the intoxicated Mr. Cox from the door at the top of the stairs, though he couldn't see her from here. Her tone was like that of a mother coddling a mischievous child, which Mr. Cox took none too kindly.

"Come away from there, Osaze. You will be seen," said his own mother.

When he turned away from the window, Urbi was gazing at him with an unreadable expression. She glanced at Josefine.

"Would you give me a moment with my son?"

Josefine glanced between them and nodded. Urbi repeated the request to Bunmi in Yoruba, who immediately got up and followed Josefine from the room.

When they were gone, Urbi met Osaze's gaze once more. He pressed his lips together and crossed his arms, waiting.

"Osaze, please. Consider before you agree to return to Sirenia. We were lucky to leave there once—most never do. Do you truly think you'll have the opportunity to do so again?" She took a step forward, her eyes bright with restrained tears. "Please, son. Come with me. Come home."

He looked at her for a long moment before replying.

"I am going home," he said. His knees gave out, and he sank onto the bed once more, keeping himself upright with his arms on the mattress. "I need to rest."

He stared up at her, waiting to see if she would keep talking. But she only nodded and, with one last look, slipped out of the room.

He lay down on his side once more, staring at the wall. A short time later, he heard the door open and someone come into the room. He assumed it was Bunmi, and closed his eyes to feign sleep.

"Osaze?"

It wasn't Bunmi, it was Josefine.

He opened his eyes and peered at her. "Yes?"

She sat in the chair Abela had occupied and pulled it over beside him.

"What do you want?" he asked when she didn't say anything.

She gave him a kind smile. "I didn't want you to be alone."

He let his head fall to the pillow and stared at the wall. Swallowing, he opened his mouth, but the words stuck. Finally, he choked out, "Thank you."

"Think nothing of it," she said, and pulled out a small notebook, which she began perusing by the light of the lamp.

Listening to her steady breathing and the occasional rustling of her skirts or a turning page, he eventually faded off to sleep.

551

INTO THE DARK

Robert allowed Miss Bethel to guide him along the hallway, down the stairs, and into the common room of the Port House Inn, wanting to both lean into and shrink away from her light touch on his arm. The words of the strange man he'd been drinking with at the Rum Runners Tavern still clung to him like oil—*If God really loves us, why does he make us work so hard to earn it?*

Robert couldn't remember how he'd gotten on the topic with the man. He'd been sitting at the bar, minding his own business, when the trim-looking gentleman had come and sat down beside him. William Downing, he'd called himself. He said he owned a plantation on the other side of the island and had come to Bridgetown to conduct some business for a day or two. Robert had been taken by his genteel manners, which stood out in this rustic place that made him think of tales he'd read of the American frontier, despite the lush greenery and tropical birds that populated it.

Downing was, without doubt, one of the most perceptive people Robert had ever met. With barely a word from Robert about his troubles, Downing began rambling about the justice, or lack thereof, of a god who saw all mere mortals as his playthings. He'd held a nearly one-sided conversation about the toils of man, enslaved to a deity who forced all to follow his will while claiming to love them. In fact, his arguments sounded a lot like something Middleton and his lot would say.

"That's not how it is," Robert had objected at last, already several tots of rum deep by that point. Even though he'd been thinking something similar all night, he felt it his Christian duty to defend the deity he'd always tried to please. "If God could make us do whatever he wanted, why would

459

he bother with sending the Christ?"

"It's all a big game to him, isn't it?" replied the well-coiffed man with a wide grin. "Change a rule here, move a piece there, and watch the mortals dance. The only problem is, there's nought we can do about it. How can you fight back against a being who decides your every move and never lets you off the playing board? And do you think there's really a heaven beyond all this?" He gestured around them expansively. "No more than there's a hell, I'd wager. At the end of the game of life, we all end up in the same place, no matter if we played by the rules or not."

"You don't think there's an afterlife?"

Downing grinned. "Maybe there is, maybe there isn't. But who's to say the preachers got it right? Maybe it's more like the pagan idea of the Underworld—you go there no matter what you did in life."

Robert's throat closed—Miss Bethel had claimed Zale was in Tartarus, the Greek pit of eternal torment or hell at the bottom of the cosmic tiers. The Greeks, from whom the word Tartarus had been passed down, hadn't believed in an equivalent concept to heaven, not the way Mr. Berian had taught it. He remembered Miss Bethel talking about a place called Tzion where spirits like her resided—but she hadn't mentioned what happened to folks who'd lived a holy life, only that humans couldn't go there. Could Downing be correct?

And now that he'd found out Gryffyn's letter had been right—that Miss Bethel and the reverend were, indeed, both spirits and spies, he couldn't help but question everything Mr. Berian had taught him. Maybe the minister had been intentionally deceitful in his teachings in order to keep his parishioners passive and easy to subdue. It was far easier to control someone trying to play by the rules than someone who had thrown off all constraints, after all.

He'd been trying to play by the rules for most of his life. He thought the rules would save him, that they'd redeem him from his past mistakes. But what if redemption were an illusion, a construct meant only to confine him?

"You may have a point, Downing," Robert said, his tongue thick with liquor.

The plantation owner clapped him on the shoulder. "Nothing for it but to enjoy life while it lasts, I say. Good drink, beautiful women, a comfortable life—these are the secrets of happiness. Ah, well." Downing tossed back the dregs of his rum and slammed the glass on the bar. "I best be off to bed. Enough philosophizing for one night."

Robert nodded, shaking the man's hand before he left for the night. When Downing had disappeared through the tavern door, Robert had turned to pay his tab and found a small satchel sitting on the bar with a note attached bearing his name.

For retrieving a sphinx's heart, was all it said in shaky script.

Sphinx? He'd opened the bag and found a small bottle of clear liquid and a dagger in a plain leather sheath. *Could they mean Miss Bethel?* He looked around to see if he could ascertain who had left him the package, but no one was watching him, no one was waiting to see his reaction. The bartender came over and picked up his empty glass.

"You want another?"

Robert shook his head. "No, thanks."

He paid for his drinks and thought about leaving the satchel where he'd found it. On second thought, he tucked the bottle in his breast pocket and the dagger in the back of his breeches. It didn't seem safe to leave those lying around. What if someone connected them to him? He'd find a way to dispose of them later.

It was time for him to go back to the Port House Inn to face Miss Bethel.

And now, here she was beside him, urging him toward that same table in the corner of the common room from which he'd so unceremoniously stomped a few hours before. Shame burned in his belly . . . and when he thought of the bottle and the dagger, he squirmed. He'd disposed of the note in a rubbish heap on the way back to the inn, but it hadn't seemed wise to leave the bottle and dagger there. Now the knife was an uncomfortable rod in the small of his back, and the bottle still made a small lump beneath his jacket. Could cherubim read minds? He desperately hoped not.

He cleared his throat and shook his head, trying to organize his liquor-addled thoughts. "Er, Miss Bethel, I must apologize for my previous behaviour. I was upset, but there was no call for—"

"Never mind that," she said, waving dismissively as she allowed him to help her be seated. "We have more important matters to discuss. We must leave at once, and I need you to find passage."

"All right," he said tightly. He wanted to say more, but the drink was making it hard to focus.

She gave him a piercing gaze, then looked at the barkeeper across the room. "Two coffees, please," she called, holding up two fingers. Glancing at Robert, she added, "Make them strong."

The squat man nodded and scuttled between two swinging doors to the kitchen.

Robert sat across from her, his gut tightening further. Even though he'd been upset earlier, he had bared his soul to her, and now she waved it off as though he'd told her he had a corn on his toe. Did he truly mean so little to her? Was he just a piece on the playing board, which she intended to use at will for her own purposes . . . or the purposes of her superiors?

He realized Miss Bethel was waiting for him to respond to something. He hadn't heard a word.

"Pardon?" he said stupidly. Curse the weakness that had made him drink! He could use his wits about him now. His future was riding on this conversation.

The cold glass of the bottle burned against his chest.

"I said," she repeated, "it might be best if you return to England now. The world of the undines has perils for human men I am not equipped to protect you from."

He sat up straight. "Protect me?" He stared at her. "Protect *me*? Is that what you've been doing?"

She pulled back, a guarded expression on her face. "Indeed, Mr. Cox. You are not my primary concern, but I must serve all humanity as the need and occasion arises, as long as it does not detract from my primary mission."

"And what is that mission, exactly?"

She narrowed her eyes at him, folding her hands in front of her. "That, I'm afraid, is not something I can tell you. But suffice it to say I must go somewhere you cannot follow. If you wish to be of service, you can gather information to help thwart the likes of Middleton and the Order to which he belongs."

His shoulders tensed more. Now she was trying to conscript him? "This is about Zale, isn't it? Everything is about Zale." He hated the petulance in his voice.

She studied him, and her gaze softened.

"Mr. Cox, I want you to know . . ." She swallowed and glanced at her hands as though searching for words. "I greatly appreciate your regard for me. But when I told you before that some things could not be, it was because of who and what I am. My kind is different from yours. We do not marry. We do not fall in love. We don't even have physical bodies of our own—what you see is a manufactured construct, a vessel I use to traverse this plane. I am not bound to it—it is bound to me. The sanctions against inter-species coupling are there because such unions simply cannot work." She looked at him earnestly, light glinting from her curls in a soft halo. "It has nothing to do with you. It's not that I *don't* love you in that way, it's that I *can't*."

Robert thought he heard a hitch in her voice as she said this and frowned. "Your voice betrays you. Are you still hiding something from me?"

She tilted her head. "I always tell the truth, Mr. Cox."

"If that's true, then why did you hesitate?"

Her expression hardened. "We must speak of your journey. It's not safe for our group to remain here, possibly not even you. I will be taking Osaze and Bunmi to safety on Sirenia, and Miss Chapman has elected to accompany us. Mrs. Urbi is your responsibility, and she wishes to return to Africa. Can I trust you to return her to her home? Preferably on the first ship on which you can find passage?"

"Just a minute." Robert took a breath, still stuck on her previous revelation. "So you're saying that, no matter your own feelings on the subject, you and I could never be together because you're a . . ." He leaned toward her and lowered his voice. "A *cherub*, and I'm a human?"

"A little quieter, please, Mr. Cox," she hissed, glancing around the room. Then she nodded curtly. "Yes, that's right."

He sat back and regarded her. "And what *are* your own feelings on the subject, Miss Bethel?"

"What?" She blinked in surprise.

"If you were free to do so, would you accept my suit?"

She drew in a deep breath, clasped her hands tightly together, and met his steady gaze.

"I . . ." She looked away. "It doesn't matter how I'd feel about it. I can't feel about it. That's the point."

Barnum brought their coffee service, pouring two steaming cups from a flower-covered porcelain pot with a slender spout. Robert seethed while he waited for the man to leave, and as soon as he was out of earshot, leaned forward.

"You don't have feelings?"

She frowned. "Of course I have feelings! They're just . . . different feelings." As she spoke, she spooned two generous spoonfuls of sugar into first her cup, then three into his. She stirred the coffee and handed it to him. "Please, Mr. Cox."

He took the cup and drank. The scalding liquid burned in a different way than the rum had, bringing him halfway to sober in seconds.

She nodded. "That's better. Now, as I said, I'm one of the lumasi. Our ways are completely different from yours and *falling in love* is something we're not even capable of."

He stared at her, the way the light caught in her eyes, the softness of her expression, and he knew she might not be lying, but she wasn't telling him the whole truth. That's when he understood—Miss Bethel was only a chess piece, too, playing her part. She didn't make these rules. Like him, she was only following them, thinking the rules would save her. But what if they wouldn't? What if they'd been wrong about the rules all along?

His gut clenched. Setting down his cup, he leaned toward her and snatched her hand, pulling her nearer. "Miss Bethel. Abela, please. Look me in the eyes and tell me you do not have feelings for me, and I will believe you. But if you do—if you love me, as I love you—don't we owe it to ourselves to see what we could become together? Without worrying about what others might think, without worrying about the rules others try to confine us with? If we love each other, none of that should matter. So tell me—do you love me?"

He looked in her eyes, wiling her to give the answer he saw there. He was close enough to smell her breath—sweet, despite the coffee. He longed to brush the curve of her cheek. The longer she delayed response, the more his stomach tightened like a jib line under full sail.

Slowly, she shook her head. "No, Mr. Cox. I told you. You and I cannot ever be together." She paused, either in hesitation or to ensure the next sentence would hit home. When she spoke, every word was emphasized. "I do not love you."

Robert's hopes came crashing down around him, and the melted lead in his veins dragged him to the earth. He nodded stiffly and withdrew his hand from hers, swallowing to dissipate the sting of sudden tears. "I see."

She gave him a small smile and folded her hands on the table in front of her once again—but she clenched her fingers so tightly, her knuckles went white. She shifted uncomfortably, then took a sip of her coffee, glancing around the room once more—avoiding his gaze, he was sure of it. He took several more sips of his own sweet brew.

He'd told her he believed her. But watching her now, he didn't. She was only playing her part.

Once more, what he wanted most was on the other side of a nonsensical restriction handed down from above. Perhaps Gryffyn and the others were right—humanity had all been duped into thinking that the Almighty had their best interests in mind . . . but did he? Who was God to say whom he could fall in love with, or whom Miss Bethel could? Perhaps he really had been keeping humanity—and every other race—deliberately in the dark to make them easier to control. Robert began to see the stories he'd been taught in Sunday School in a different light. What would the stories sound like if told from the other side? Would the losers—the imprisoned Grigori his brother and the Order sought to free—be the wronged ones if only their story were heard?

Still, he couldn't see any way to sway her to his side—not as long as the world continued under the current order. But what if there were another Order that could rewrite the rules? What if he, himself, could help bring that change? Not by bringing them her heartstone—that, he would never do. But he didn't need to—the red gemstone concealed somewhere on Miss Bethel's wrist would do just as well. And how would they ever be the wiser?

He was done with following the rules and trying to earn God's approval. It was time to take his future into his own hands. Miss Bethel wouldn't understand at first. But eventually, she would. He was sure of it.

A plan formulated in his mind. He didn't have time to think it through, but he knew it would work. He also knew that implementing it would mean choosing sides, much as Miss Chapman had done earlier.

He swallowed. *It's for the right reasons.*

"Well, I suppose there's nothing to be done," he said, striking as nonchalant a tone as he could muster. "I must simply make the best of it. Please, let me walk you to your room, and then I will head down to the dock to see what passage can be obtained."

"Oh, surely that can wait until morning—"

"There is a ship in harbour that may have sailed by morning. It must be tonight." He put payment for the coffee on the table, then rose and offered her his hand to help her stand. "Allow me?"

She looked up at him uncertainly, then smiled and gave a slight nod, placing her hand in his. When she was on her feet, she slipped her arm through the crook of his elbow and walked silently next to him all the way to the door of her room. He reached into his breast pocket and retrieved his handkerchief, concealing the small bottle inside it, then let it hang out of sight next to him.

It was dark in the hallway, only a single lamp burning at the far end. But when she looked up at him to bid him goodnight, he could still see the light pooling in her golden eyes. It was now or never.

"Forgive me, Miss Bethel," he said.

"I told you, Mr. Cox, there is nothing to forgive, I—"

He bent and placed his mouth on hers, kissing her firmly. Even as her surprised resistance melted into acquiescence, he used his thumb to pull the cork stopper from the bottle, wrapped his handkerchief around the mouth, and upended it to let the liquid seep into the cloth. His other hand came up behind her head to bury itself in her soft curls, and he nearly forgot his true intent. Oh, that there was another way!

She pushed against his chest and broke away. "Mr. Cox! I told you—"

Before she could say another word, he released the bottle and clamped the sickly sweet foul-smelling handkerchief over her face. Her eyes widened in accusation and horror, but she succumbed to the ether-like substance almost immediately, her form slumping against him. He threw the cloth as far as he could into the darkness of the corridor and kicked the bottle into the shadows.

The bracelet reappeared on her arm as if by magic—he had no idea how she'd been keeping it concealed, but he breathed a sigh of relief. After working it over her slim hand, he tucked it into his breast pocket. Finally, he knocked on the door in an anxious rat-tat-tat.

"Mrs. Urbi, are you there? There is something wrong with Miss Bethel."

The door opened to reveal Urbi's flashing black eyes. "What is it? What has happened?"

Robert inserted a desperate tone into his voice. "I don't know. We were about to say goodnight, and she simply fainted. Here, let me lay her down."

Urbi stepped away from the door, and he picked Miss Bethel up and carried her to her bed, laying her gently on the quilt. The older woman came and lay a hand on her forehead, then used her fingers to pry one eye open and looked at the dilated iris before sucking her teeth and releasing it.

Robert looked down at Miss Bethel's unmoving form in concern. She looked so still, he wondered if he'd overdone it on the ether. But then she moaned, and he knew he must be gone before she awoke.

"I don't know what is wrong," Urbi said. "I must go find Miss Josefine to help."

"And I must take my leave and find a ship. I entrust her to your capable hands, Mrs. Urbi." He hesitated, then pulled a sealed envelope from his other breast pocket and handed it to her. "These are your papers of manumission, madam. I had them drawn up yesterday. Safeguard them with your life."

Urbi blinked at the envelope, then at Robert. "Thank you, sir. You are a good man. No wonder Miss Abela speaks so highly of you."

Ignoring his itching neck, Robert bowed and made a hasty exit, careful to snatch up the bottle and handkerchief as he retreated. Once outside, he disposed of them in a rubbish bin near another inn's garden several buildings down—hesitating before he threw out the handkerchief to make sure it was plain, without his monogram. He almost threw the knife in after it, but since he was about to make a long journey in the dark, he thought better of it and tucked the leather sheath into his waistband—near his hip this time, where it would be more accessible.

He made his way back to the stables at the corner, exhaustion pulling at his bones. He had another long ride ahead of him, this time in the dark. He wasn't looking forward to returning to Middleton's plantation so soon, but there was little to be done about it.

But first, he must find a ship and send word to the inn. By the time he gave Middleton the heartstone, he wanted Miss Bethel and the others to be far beyond the man's reach. Robert may be allying with him, but that didn't mean he trusted him.

He patted his jacket, reassuring himself that the bracelet was still there, and stepped through the stable door into the dark.

56

AWAKENING

Narcissa didn't know exactly how long it had been since Semyaza had taken over her body. At first, she had spent most of her time unaware, and the few times she'd fought her way to consciousness, he'd quickly subdued her again.

But she'd been learning. She had figured out how to awaken without disturbing him so she could watch, and wait, and listen.

Every enemy had a weakness. She just had to figure out Semyaza's.

She watched while he manipulated the archons. She watched while he threw wine and food at the servants. She watched while he took his pleasure with *douloi*, sirens, and servant girls alike—frequently with Matthew. Pleasure she couldn't feel, no more than she could feel the baby he'd said was growing in her belly. Maybe it would have been too soon to feel the child, anyway. But she hated him all the more for depriving her of that, then wondered at herself—she'd never particularly wanted to be a mother. But despite not being responsible for the baby being planted in her, now that she was there, Narcissa had an inexplicable urge to protect the child against the monster who had also imprisoned her. If she were to save them both, she had to be smarter than their tormentor.

So far, he'd given her no opportunity to outwit him. And whenever she started fuming, she drew his attention and he subdued her again. So she had to conceal her emotions, to act as though she were one of the *douloi*—brainless and emotionless. She'd never been good at making an emotional shield, but her skills were quickly improving.

At least actual *douloi* had it easier—they had the Redemption bond to protect them. She had to rely on her own self-control.

468

The thought tweaked an emotion she'd never felt before. It took a while to figure out what it was—something about the *douloi* and what it must be like for them to be under Redemption. She didn't know what to call it, but she felt bad for them, and guilty for thinking their lot was easier than hers.

For the first time, when she saw a *douloi*, she didn't see a man getting what he deserved, even needed. She saw a fellow prisoner.

That couldn't be true, though. The *douloi* didn't have to share their bodies with another creature who would torture them whenever they could. She pushed away the reminder of some of the things she'd had her *douloi* do. *Douloi* couldn't feel, nor desire anything, so what torture were they enduring? No, their situation was entirely different.

While Semyaza was creating chaos in her name, turning her island into a boiling cesspool of turbulent dissension, he was also looking for something. He'd searched every room in the Opal Palace, every lav and storage room. Or maybe he was looking for *someone*—whenever a new Freeman was found, he'd have them brought to him and, after having the new palace bondmistress take the man's *sklavia* bond from the arresting siren, interrogate them relentlessly about a man and a woman with golden eyes, people Zale had told him had been present on the *Atlanta*. Narcissa couldn't figure out if he thought they were here on Sirenia, or somewhere else. He was completely paranoid about their activities, though.

He also received frequent visits from the unsettling man with eyes as black as night who appeared out of the air and left the same way. Dagiel. Some kind of spirit.

Dagiel often reported on two people he'd been assigned to watch named Guriel and Rumiel. Another person, Erel, was mentioned often, too. They were also spirits, from what Narcissa could gather.

If what this creature wanted was to contact these spirits, why did he need her body to do so?

Narcissa tried to pay attention, but it was hard to stay focused when she had no ability to influence anything, not even her own body's actions. Sometimes, she'd let her mind wander and imagine the terrible things she'd do to Semyaza if she ever got him out of her body and were able to inflict her revenge.

She perked up one day when she heard a name she recognized. Osaze.

Dagiel was reporting to Semyaza in Narcissa's antechamber. His black eyes glittered, stark against pale skin stretched tightly over thin bones. He looked as though he hadn't seen the sun in centuries.

"And you're certain this man who escaped the plantation is Osaze, the same one Calandra became infatuated with?" Semyaza asked. He lounged in Narcissa's chair—her mother's chair—with Narcissa's clasped hands resting on an abdomen barely covered by her sheer white robe.

Dagiel frowned. "His name is definitely Osaze—he was quite adamant about his real name with that prat of a baron. As for the rest, he wouldn't admit to anything under Chapman's ministrations. Fortunately, the conveyance stone Chapman's daughter has worked fine, and he was much more forthcoming at the inn. How many humans even know of Sirenia, let alone have escaped from it? It has to be the same one. He wants to return to join the rebel cause."

Semyaza scoffed. "Much good that will do him now. But, to be safe, be sure he doesn't find a way back."

"I've already set the wheels in motion," Dagiel said with a cruel smile. "None of that group will find their way anywhere with both Rumiel and Guriel out of the picture." He chuckled. "Humans. So delightfully easy to manipulate. A little nudge here, a touch there . . ." He smirked. "The undines aren't so different though, are they? By the way, nice work getting both the undine brats into Tartarus."

"I'm glad it pleased you," Semyaza said dryly, and Dagiel winced.

Semyaza frowned and sat up, glancing toward the desk not far away that held a stone reader and a few dozen datastones—the aftermath of his most recent search.

"It didn't all go according to plan, though. They went too soon, before I could find the keys. Were you able to retrieve the Key of Og?"

Keys? Is that what he's been searching for? Narcissa stopped herself questioning further, lest she draw Semyaza's attention.

Dagiel's face darkened. "No. The Priest only sent The Baron a sketch to prove he'd found it. He didn't send the key itself. I suspect Valac has already handed it over to that slithering *shedu*. That's why you were supposed to find the undine quaternar—"

"I *know* why I was looking for the undine key!" Semyaza snarled.

Dagiel took a step back and cleared his throat. "Sorry. Of course. But, if you don't mind me asking, without a key to the well, how will Tamiel and the others escape? I know the undine brats can handle the Soulstone— it's so frail, one wrong move on their part should send it crumbling to dust. But it's not much good having a key to the cell if the prison remains locked."

Semyaza stood and walked toward the window, running fingers down Narcissa's long unbound pale hair. "Tamiel's clever. I've sent her everything she needs to escape. She'll have to figure out how to use it. Besides, once I get the sphinx's heart, the key to the well will no longer be necessary." He spun to glare at the pasty spirit. "You delivered the message to Tamiel, did you not?"

Dagiel feigned hurt. "Of course! Does m'lord not trust me anymore?"

Semyaza grinned. "You swore your oath to me six millennia ago and you've never wavered from it. Why would I start trusting you now?"

Dagiel laughed nervously, but Narcissa would have smirked if she could. There were limits to trust, and Semyaza obviously understood them well. Good that he reminded his subordinates once in a while.

"And what of the heart?" Semyaza continued. "Any word on how soon we can extract that from Guriel's hands? Or, rather, her being?"

Guriel had a heart? Wasn't she a spirit? Narcissa pondered this. Did that mean Semyaza had a heart that could be removed, too? How would someone go about removing the lifeforce from an immortal being . . . especially if said being was using your own body at the time?

Dagiel stroked his pointy chin. "Well, you know how you were saying things didn't go according to plan a minute ago?"

"Yes?" Semyaza's voice was dark.

Dagiel shifted his weight, glancing up at the ceiling before continuing. "Guriel wasn't the one who followed the undine boy. It was the other one. Rumiel. He left his heartstone behind with Guriel, I think. And Erel has disappeared. Abandoned the others on the road, he did. I couldn't hear why."

"What?" Semyaza exclaimed in outrage. "You lost track of Erel? By the chains, Dagiel, you had *one* job."

"Actually, m'lord, by my count, it was more like four, maybe five—"

"And Rumiel. I should have guessed he would take Guriel's place. Stubborn old bull. But it's not his heartstone I need. This complicates things." He began pacing around the room.

Dagiel cocked his head. "What's so special about Guriel's? Why does it have to be hers?"

Semyaza sighed. "Oh, Dagiel. For someone so old, you are still so ignorant. When you and your brothers and sisters were bound to the Ground for eternity, the Old Man inflicted a similar punishment on me and mine. Do you not remember?"

Dagiel frowned in confusion, and then comprehension dawned.

"Riiiight. All the heartstones only draw on his essence now, not the unfiltered ether."

"All but one. The Heart of Chaos is the only heartstone that was exempt from that transformation. It is the only heartstone that can draw on the raw material of the cosmos unhindered. That is why we need it. For my plan to work, we must be completely free of dependence on the Old Man."

Dagiel's mouth quirked. "And what makes you think that's the heart the sphinx is using?"

"Because I made sure that's the one she'd find." Semyaza smiled wickedly. "I still have resources, even in Tzion."

Dagiel scratched his scalp through his slick black hair. White flakes floated down like ash and settled on the shoulders of his black coat.

"But I thought Azazel wanted—"

"*Don't* say that name in my presence." Semyaza's intensity startled Narcissa. "I've told you before. Never mention that traitor to me!"

"But isn't he the one who got the heart and the undine boy this far?"

"I *said . . .*"

Dagiel backed up a step, hands raised defensively. "I didn't say his name again."

Semyaza turned to the window and muttered to himself about a betrayer, the rage that bubbled in his mind nearly burning Narcissa. He was angrier than he'd been even when talking of the *Old Man*.

Dagiel cleared his throat. "So I suppose I shouldn't tell you that Tamiel has him, er, helping her out with the situation down in Hades?"

"What?" Semyaza whirled. "Why didn't you mention this earlier?"

Dagiel backed up a step.

"I was working up to it. Not him directly, of course, seeing as he's locked up in Dudael. Tamiel's got Bezaziel touring the boy around. And we all know Bez serves Uriel by necessity, but when it comes to the Grigori, he only answers to, er, you-know-who."

Semyaza began pacing, muttering louder. "It will be fine. She's only using him so she can escape, like we planned. Things were over between them long ago, and she doesn't have the key, so of course she'd use the resources she has on hand, and—"

"M'lord?" Dagiel said hesitantly. "Will there be anything else?"

Semyaza whirled. "Yes. As incompetent as you are, even you should be able to manage this. You mentioned you've been working on the human man, the brother of the one working for the Betrayer."

Dagiel's face clouded. "The Betrayer? Do you mean Aza—"

He cut off at the expression on Semyaza's face.

"Aye. Rather delicate work, that, but I managed it." Dagiel's voice held a touch of pride, but at Semyaza's glare, he straightened. "I've got Robert Cox so turned around he doesn't know his head from his backside. If I did this right, I should be bringing you the heart by tomorrow."

Semyaza raked fingers through Narcissa's hair again and stared at the horizon where the perfect sky met the cerulean sea. "Good. Time is running out. The ships are almost here, and if I haven't taken control of the situation by then . . ."

He leaned on the windowsill. Outside, sirens sparred in the practice court. Narcissa longed to be among them—but Semyaza never sparred. Her muscles would be weak with disuse by the time she got rid of him at this rate.

Dagiel continued, his voice brighter. "I forgot to tell you. Scrunt is workin' for us now."

Semyaza turned again. "Scrunt? Who is he?"

"Y'know, the demon of destruction that Aza—the Betrayer likes to use for inhabiting lackeys. Turns out, Scrunt didn't like always being sent on suicide missions. He doesn't mind making people die, he just hates being in them when it happens. I told him if he'd work for me, I'd give him a better job and let him have fun with his little hobbies too. So he's in that man who's working for the Betrayer's tool, Middleton. What's his name again? Hogsworth? Hardy?" His face scrunched in concentration, then lit up as he hit on the word he was searching for. "Hayward!"

Semyaza had endured this diatribe with increasing annoyance. "I assume you have a reason for that?"

Dagiel beamed, revealing pointed alabaster teeth.

"Of course. I think I finally convinced Cox to bring Middleton the heart, and when he does, Scrunt can pass it on to me instead of their lot. Bam, bang, boom, you've got your heart *and* a double agent in, er, the Betrayer's camp." He grinned. "Scrunt even lets me step in now and again. It's a handy way to eavesdrop."

Semyaza nodded.

"Perhaps I underestimated you, Dagiel. That was well done. It's good to see you've been making use of the time I've spent imprisoned to improve your strategy skills."

"Thank you, m'lord." Dagiel preened, and his pasty face glowed at the compliment.

"What I don't understand," Semyaza continued, "is why you don't just inhabit Robert Cox and be done with it." Semyaza glared at the demon.

"Does he have a Shield of Elyon in place?"

Dagiel gulped, his Adam's apple bobbing. "Ah, no, m'lord. But he's with Guriel and the others so much, there's no way I'd escape notice. I've been going for something more subtle—using the conveyance stone on the Romani girl and hiding in the walls and such. It's been a trick getting information, what with the erelim that follow the Grounded cherubim around all the time. But, like you taught me, it's best to pick a lock with a quill than bash the thing to pieces with a hammer."

Semyaza nodded. "It's no surprise this particular group are being supervised by the erelim, but even Elyon's intelligence agents can miss a determined lone spy like you. You've surprised me twice today, Dagiel. Well done. Now go figure out what happened to Erel. And get me that heartstone."

Dagiel bowed low, his hands touching the tiles in front of him. Then he stood and winked out of sight.

Semyaza looked out the window again, and Narcissa caught glimpses of her friends in the courtyard below.

What were these other heartstones Semyaza and Dagiel spoke of? Narcissa had never heard of any heartstone other than the one that powered their island. If there were more available, perhaps they could use one of those to repair the damage to their own and restore the barrier to keep the island safe.

But first, she needed to know why Semyaza wanted one.

What is the heartstone for? she ventured, steeling herself against the possibility that he might subdue her immediately.

But he didn't. He went to stand in front of the mirror, and a beautiful bare-chested, golden-skinned man with a trim goatee and long black hair stared back at her.

"Heartstones are power conduits, my beauty. They funnel power and substance from a source. The user determines the shape the power takes, but the source determines what it can be used for. Unfortunately, most of them draw power from a single limited source."

The "Old Man"?

The man's eyes darkened.

"Yes."

Who is he?

Semyaza said nothing for several moments, then simply muttered, "A tyrant."

Narcissa pondered this. Her mother had been a tyrant, always overlooking Narcissa and her suggestions in favour of Calandra and ruling the island with an iron fist. Adonia had become erratic and unpredictable at the end, and Narcissa had realized her mother would never see Narcissa with the respect she craved. When the queen had gone Mad at last and started lashing out at everyone—even Calandra and her darling Hebe, the daughter who looked just like the human consort who had rejected her—Narcissa had known she must be stopped.

In that case, Narcissa had killed her mother. But she couldn't very well do that to Semyaza, a spirit who inhabited her own body. She needed to find out what he wanted and use it against him so she could get him out.

Then she might be able to kill him.

Why do you need this sphinx's heart?

"It's not the sphinx's. She's only using it, and she likely has no idea what she has. No." He scowled. "That heart is mine."

The hard edge to his voice went beyond claiming something he wanted—it was like he felt something rightfully his had been taken from him. Much like Narcissa's claim to the throne had been taken from her by Adonia and given to Calandra.

"And," he said, "I need the heart in order to set up a new rule on Earth. The Old Man has had his way long enough. It's time for a New Order to establish itself." He smiled. "What sweeter or more poetic a revenge than to have the cosmos the Old Man created be transformed into my image instead of his?"

In a flash, Narcissa knew what Semyaza wanted. They were alike, the two of them. He craved what she did—power and respect. Barring respect, fear would suffice.

Posing as her, he was already in the most powerful position on the island. But, like her, he seemed to lack true powers of any kind. The fire he was fond of conjuring to scare others was no more than an illusion. It never left a permanent scar on anything—just as she still lacked the ability to use the elements, despite the thousands of bonds she carried in her mind.

More than that, he hadn't Redeemed a single *douloi* the entire time he'd possessed her that she'd seen. She suspected he couldn't even do that much.

The archons aren't listening to you, and you've turned the island against you because of the chaos created by the rogue Freemen you've let wander the island and endanger the people. How are you going to rule the world if you can't even establish power in Sirenia?

"Ah, but all things can serve a purpose, my dear. Even chaos. Especially chaos."

He had a point. She'd often used chaos and disorder as a subtle rebellion against her mother's strict rule. But what purpose could allowing fear and chaos to run rampant on the island serve?

"Fear is a powerful method of control. I shouldn't have to tell you that."

That was true. But it was not the only method, or all she'd have to do to be rid of him was to stop being afraid. She dared to keep pressing for more answers. *How? What is your plan?*

He looked at her for a long moment in the mirror, then smirked. "I suppose there's no harm in telling you. Who are you going to tell, right?"

He gave a cruel grin, but instead of a man's teeth, his teeth were the jagged incisors of a beast—of a dragon. Briefly, Narcissa feared her own teeth had become like his, but if she concentrated, she could pierce the illusion and see her own face. It looked tired and a little haggard, but, other than that, it was as it had always been.

"First, I will align the undines behind me," he said. "Then, I will use them to free my people. Then, I will use the Heart of Chaos and the Heartstone to take over the cosmos with the undines as my personal army."

None of that sounded good. *How do you intend to do that?*

"This world is made from the Old Man's essence. As such, everything in it is dependent on him—even this weak flesh I now inhabit."

What Semyaza was saying sounded blasphemous, but any outrage was obliterated by the anger his description of her invoked. She was anything but weak. Spending hours a day in the training court had seen to that, and it hadn't been that long since he'd taken over her body, had it?

"Even rocks and animals and people who don't know or even deny he exists would collapse if he withdrew his essence for a second," Semyaza continued, either oblivious to her anger or ignoring it. "That's how he can get away with everything he does—because he controls all of it. And no one is allowed to disagree with him without harsh consequences. Not even his favourite son."

And that's . . . you?

He didn't respond, but he started pacing the room so she could no longer see his face.

"This island's Heartstone is a tremendous power source. It's what keeps my brothers and sisters chained unjustly in the Abyss for expressing our dissent against his ways. But if I could change the essence it channels and bend it to my will, it could be so much more."

He stopped in front of the mirror again, and his golden eyes seemed to glow.

"It could rewrite the essence of the cosmos. I could remake the planes in *my* design."

And then the entire world would depend on your essence.

Narcissa couldn't feel cold, but dread and foreboding filled her. Semyaza sounded worse than Adonia had ever been. He was all the things she'd been told to expect of men taken to the extreme.

And he was using her body to do it.

She didn't understand his talk of an Old Man or what this person had to do with the island's Heartstone, though.

The Heartstone was a gift from Atargatis to the undines to protect us from humans. It's not part of any Old Man's essence. It's a gift of the Mother.

He smirked. "Yes, Tamiel did an excellent job with that one. We'd hoped to rewrite the world last time, but instead, all we managed was to rewrite your history. We couldn't foresee that the Heartstone we were trying to kill would be so essential to our future plans." He scowled. "Nor did we anticipate the cunning of Nadia."

Narcissa was completely lost. Did he mean Nadia, the Madwoman who'd sunk Atlantis? And who was this Tamiel he kept mentioning? She wanted to ask, to find out what he knew, but the simmering rage she sensed in him made her wary of asking questions that wouldn't help her solve her immediate problem—getting him out of her.

Why do you need to use me to do this? Couldn't you use anyone? Wouldn't a stone healer like Amaltheia be more useful when rewriting the world?

He smiled. "Indeed. But as you, I can make use of her powers and others', too. Powerful position is frequently more useful than powerful abilities."

Narcissa had no argument for that. She would have gladly taken both, however.

"Of most use would be to have my own body so my true powers would be restored to me," he said. "And that is why I need the heartstone—I need it not only to rewrite the world, but also to give me a form of my own, one not dependent on the Old Man's mercies. Then nothing would stand in my way. *Our* way. I do not forget my faithful servants. Your contributions would not go unrewarded."

If Narcissa could have shuddered, she would have. But she understood one thing clearly—once Semyaza found this heartstone, she and her baby could be rid of him. Right now, nothing else mattered. And if she played along instead of resisting him, perhaps he'd stop subduing her and she could learn what his weakness was. Perhaps even learn how to use this heartstone for her own purposes. It was only a matter of time . . . as long as she could stay conscious.

She tamped down her revulsion and fear and put on a shield of conciliatory obedience.

How can I help?

He smiled wickedly, showing all his scary teeth.

"I knew you'd come around eventually."

A hesitant knock came at the door, and Semyaza turned toward it. "Come!"

A girl Narcissa didn't recognize walked in with her eyes lowered. A scullery maid, by the livery. "Cook said you wanted to see me, your majesty?"

"Indeed. You'll do nicely."

Semyaza smiled and stalked toward her, circling her and admiring her profile. She glanced up, brown eyes limpid beneath pretty lashes.

"You need not be afraid, my dear," Semyaza said, taking the girl's hand with Narcissa's and leading her to the bedchamber beyond.

You do have good taste, Narcissa grudgingly admitted, hoping to put her tormentor at ease.

If you're a good girl, I'll let you watch and learn, Semyaza said internally, smugness oozing from him.

Narcissa said not a word, frozen by the thought he might subdue her again. But as she watched what happened next, she went from mild enjoyment to outright horror. Even she had never taken her entertainments this far. By the end, all that was left of the girl was a lifeless, bloody mess, which Semyaza dragged into a secret passage in the wall Narcissa hadn't even known was there.

Cringing into the far corners of her own mind, she quivered in her resolve.

This monster must be stopped. But Narcissa had no idea how to stop him.

57

SOMETHING SMELLS OFF

By the time Zale and Bez found Damaris in the gloomy swamp, she was on her feet, kicking and punching at any of the wispy souls who came close and shouting curses Zale had never even heard before. But more surprising was Bez's reaction to her. When he saw her, he stopped short, then continued cautiously toward her.

By the time they reached Damaris, she stood in a mistless clearing, breathing hard. When she saw Zale, she smiled a warmer smile than he'd ever seen her have for him before, one that had a strange effect on his stomach. But when she looked at Bez, her expression froze, the smile becoming false.

"What are you doing here?" Bez and Damaris both asked at the same time.

Zale looked back and forth between them. They looked as though they were drawing battle lines, but how could they even know who the other one was?

Bez was the first to break the awkward silence. He smirked. "Looks like your friend has saved herself, Zale. Come, let's go find your mother. This way."

He spun on his heel and stalked off through the trees. Damaris watched him go with a cold expression.

"Damaris? Do you know him?"

Damaris started as though just realizing Zale was there.

"No, of course not. How would I know him?"

"Then why did you ask him why he was here?"

"I only wanted to know who he was and whether we could trust him.

Who is he?" She smiled again, sweetly, and his insides warmed.

Man, this girl is either hot or cold—there's no in-between.

"He said his name is Bez. Bezaziel. He rescued me from the dragon that attacked you, and we were coming to rescue you. He said Berian sent him—you know, the lamassu who was helping me find my mother."

She frowned. "I don't trust him. Perhaps we should try to find our own way. What if he's lying?"

Zale blinked. "Why would he lie? And do you know anything about the Underworld? Because I don't. We've already tried finding our own way, and look where that got us." He swept his arm toward the path of destruction left by the copper dragon when it had charged after Zale.

Damaris flicked her gaze toward it and sighed. "Well, I suppose we could go with him. For a while, at least, just to learn more about him and what he knows of your mother."

Zale eyed her. She was behaving so strangely—pouty and petulant instead of her usual snarky self-assurance—though she seemed as hyper-vigilant to their surroundings as ever, constantly glancing around at the trees and even above them to the cavernous, rooty ceiling.

She turned to follow Bez. It took Zale a moment to recover from the suddenness of it, and when he followed, he nearly tripped over a tree root. Looking down, he realized it wasn't a root at all, but Damaris's staff. He bent and picked it up.

"Damaris? You dropped this."

She halted and stared at the proffered weapon. After a slight hesitation, she smiled again.

"Well, that's embarrassing. Thanks." She took it from him and, after a few awkward attempts, managed to slide it into its sheath on her back.

Odd. Damaris was usually so graceful that her *deiktis* was like an extension of her own body. And she was still graceful—Zale couldn't help but stare at the alluring sway of her hips and her strong legs beneath her swimming skirt as she walked away. In fact, she seemed more captivating than ever, as though everything attractive about her had been magnified. He thought about running his hands through her hair, just to see what it felt like . . .

He shook his head, hard. What was wrong with him? He could only imagine what Damaris's reaction would be to a gesture like that—a sucker-punch to the ribs. And he'd deserve it too. Getting a hold of himself, he started walking after his companions.

"So," he said, catching up to Bez, "what's your, er, designation? Are you a seraph?"

Bez didn't even look at him.

"A cherub?"

Bez flicked a derisive glance at Zale, still saying nothing. Not a cherub, then.

Zale tried another tack. "How do you know Berian? Er, Rumiel?"

"We're both really old, and the cosmos isn't that big," Bez growled, then lapsed back into silence.

Zale frowned. He wished he could sense Bez's emotions, but he wasn't nearly proficient enough with the open-door technique to get a read on him. For that matter, Damaris had her shield locked up like a fortress, so he couldn't sense her either.

Perhaps he was getting worse at this.

On the other hand, with Bez giving him the cold shoulder, did he really need to sense his emotions? It's not like that would tell him anything he didn't already know.

Damaris, on the other hand . . .

He glanced at the pretty girl walking next to him. She saw him looking and shot him a flirty smile. His face flushed with heat. What was with her? Not that he minded, but she just seemed so different all of a sudden.

She leaned close to him and whispered, "Hey. Sounds like Bez isn't going to be much help after all. What say you and I fade into the trees and go looking on our own? He kind of creeps me out."

Her warm breath tickling Zale's ear was more than distracting, and a putrid stench wafted toward him and made his stomach heave. With effort, he focused on her words.

"No," he hissed. "I haven't even got a chance to ask him about Mother yet. Why are you in such a hurry to leave?"

"Why are you so determined we stay?" she shot back.

"Because if some other giant creature attacks us, I'd like to know we have something equally fierce on our side, okay? I don't know how to fight a dragon. Do you?"

"As a matter of fact, I . . ." She seemed to change her mind mid-sentence. "No," she said stiffly. "I suppose you're right." Like a mask being slipped on, her face melted into that inviting smile again. "But I have every confidence that you could figure it out, what with your abilities."

Zale squirmed. She had every confidence in him? He thought about how his fireballs had melted off the copper dragon, but under her adoring gaze, he didn't want to admit the truth. It felt nice to have her be complimentary of his abilities for once instead of calling him names.

He cleared his throat. "Maybe I could."

"So . . . can we leave now?" She took a step nearer to him, standing close enough for him to smell her—

Dear God, what is that? The smell was worse than the swamp around them. He looked around, trying to find the source of the acrid stench, but other than the trees and the mist, the landscape had remained unchanged. He finally realized it was Damaris herself who smelled. Glancing at her eyes, he noticed something odd about them—their typical seafoam-green kept shifting colour to a darker shade. He'd never seen that happen before.

His heart raced. *What's wrong with Damaris?*

Zale took a step back and drew in a breath of air that now seemed sweet in comparison. Keeping his voice even, he said, "For now, let's find out more about this Bez before we lose him, okay?"

She gave a flirty pout. "Why don't you trust me, Zale?"

"I *do* trust you, it's just that—wait. Did you just use my real name?" He stared at her. Something was definitely wrong. But what was it? Had Damaris been knocked on the head harder than he'd thought? He didn't see any blood or swelling. Maybe the strange lethargy of this place was dampening her normal edge.

"Everything all right over there?" Bez broke in, the command in his voice hindered by it cutting out almost completely at the end.

Damaris gave him a sweet smile. "Perfectly fine. We're just talking."

Bez scowled. "Well, don't. It attracts the guardians, and, as you probably noticed, they're not keen on us being here." His tone was pointed and he gave Damaris such a piercing stare, Zale wondered what else he was saying beneath his words.

Damaris gave Bez a nonplussed look. "Fine."

She walked beside Zale for a short while in silence, then leaned close. "Say, did you happen to bring anything with you to help rescue your mum? Like a ring or a pendant shaped like a wagon wheel?"

He scowled at her. Was she mocking him? "You know exactly what I brought . . . My wits. I don't have anything else."

Her brows furrowed. "Narcissa didn't give you anything to help you out?"

He shook his head. "What are you talking about? If Narcissa were helping me, we wouldn't have had to go through that whole rigmarole sneaking around Calandra and the rest of them in Atlantis." He cocked his head. "Are you feeling okay?"

She gave him a bright smile. "Me? Of course. I was just asking."

He gave her a sidelong look, but she fell a few steps behind, making conversation difficult. Zale, wanting to keep an eye on her and Bez both, cast a glance over his shoulder and then decided to ask Bez some of his questions. He'd told Damaris he would, after all. He glanced up at the shifting form of the spirit, totally intimidated. But he'd handled many a lawman and disgruntled *gorgio* in his days on the street. Was this really so different?

He adopted a confident swagger.

"So, Bez," he said, thinking that was just how Gio would say it, "how long until we reach Mother, anyway?"

Bez grunted, and Zale thought that might be his only response. Eventually, he said, "At the edge of the swamp is a ravine through which the river flows. We should get there in about one of your days' time."

"The river?" Zale blinked. Damaris had mentioned a river, but other than the swamp that surrounded them, he hadn't seen any water since they got here. Then he remembered that in the Greek myths his mother had taught him, people would put coins on the eyes of the dead to "pay the ferryman" to take the souls of the dead across the river to reach the Underworld. "Do you mean the Styx?"

Bez snorted. "Sure. That's one name for it."

"But that doesn't answer my question. Once we reach the river, what do we do?"

"You're awfully annoying, boy. Do you want me to draw you a map?"

Zale perked up. "Could you? That would be plummy, actually . . ." He trailed off at the look of scorn on Bezaziel's face. "Oh, you were being sarcastic. Well, could you just tell me how to reach her?"

Bez put on a wicked grin. "Sure. When you get to the river, you hop in and let it take you to the very edge of the planes. But don't go too far, or you'll fall into Tartarus and never be heard from again. Oh, and you'll know you're close when your skin starts blistering off," he added with a sidelong look.

"That sounds, erm, precarious."

"It is. Of course, I know a safer way, but you can't use that one unless I help you find it. So what say you just trust me and we'll get there when we get there, yes?"

Zale frowned. Berian sure had chosen a strange companion to accompany him. Bezaziel was as eccentric as, well, as Berian himself.

"Okay. Of course."

"Now stop talking before another copper shows up," Bez wheezed, jerking his head behind him to indicate that Zale should beat it.

Disgruntled, Zale fell into step beside Damaris, but she would no longer engage with him either. He walked beside her for a few minutes, trying to figure out what he'd done wrong. But after catching another whiff or two of the overpowering cloud of wretchedness that surrounded her, he let himself fall a few paces behind her and brought up the rear, keeping a wary eye on her for other signs of illness. Or maybe dragon dung.

Soon, the murky gloom of the never-ending swamp began to wear on Zale. He felt as though they'd been trudging through it for days. What was with the realms of the Underworld, that once they'd chosen a way to be, they never wavered from it?

There was no way to judge time in the unending twilight, but the exhaustion in Zale's body told him they were way overdue for a rest. Damaris hadn't uttered a word of complaint, and indeed, didn't even look tired. *Some things haven't changed*, he grumbled to himself. Even if she were ready to drop dead on her feet, she'd probably never let on.

Finally, Zale could take it no more.

"Bez . . ."

The man twisted and gave Zale a piercing glare.

"Er . . ." Zale faltered. He almost decided against saying anything, but then glanced at Damaris's stoic face and soldiered on. "We must stop to rest. Mother has been here for months. I suppose she'll be fine for one more night."

The dark man leading their procession scowled, an expression that bubbled and shifted with his constantly reforming features.

"I sometimes forget the frailty of flesh bodies. Yes, of course. Stop and rest."

"There." Zale pointed at a distant clump of trees growing from a rise of soil that appeared less marshy than other places. The trees had thick branches growing some distance from the ground that would be strong enough to hold him and Damaris while they slept. He started walking that way.

Damaris fell into step beside him and beamed a smile at him. "Good thinking, Zale. One mobbing by restless souls is enough for me, thank you."

Zale blinked at her. She'd used his real name again. That was twice in a row.

Bez listened to them, then studied the trees. Comprehension crossed his face. "Ah, I see. You intend to sleep in the crooks of the branches to keep the Sleepless from disturbing you. That is not necessary. I will ensure you remain undisturbed. You will sleep better on the ground. And I could use a bit of sport." He grinned, revealing odd, pointed teeth.

"Er, okay," Zale said, his scalp tingling with unease. "Thanks. You're right, we probably will."

Zale supposed that if having a dragon-man guard them wasn't enough to keep them safe, nothing would be. Still, it wasn't the thought of sleeping on the ground surrounded by dead spirits that disturbed him as much as something about Bez's manner that put him on edge. Perhaps the spirit was simply unused to interacting with mortals, and Zale was reading his signals all wrong. Not surprising when the man's face couldn't stay put for longer than a few seconds at a time.

Their feet made soft sucking sounds with every step they took through the mud. When they reached the spongy grass-covered hill, Zale sank onto a fallen log—one that looked fairly stable, without too many signs of rot—and let his head drop forward, running his hands through his hair. Something about this place clung to him until it oozed from his pores. Not the smell. He didn't even notice the reek anymore, which was odd—he'd never gotten used to the stench of the *Atlanta* once they'd taken on a cargo of slaves despite weeks of travel. Unlike the ship, the stink of this place was all-pervasive, without a single reprieve. Perhaps his olfactory senses had shut down in self-defense.

No, this was something else. He felt as though he were covered in slick oil, except the cloying stuff was only a sensation, not an actual substance.

Bez leaned against a nearby tree trunk where he could see them and their surroundings, his arms crossed and his wings rustling with every minute movement.

Damaris sat cross-legged on a dry clump of grass and patted the hill next to her in invitation. "Sit with me, okay?"

Zale swallowed to hide his surprise and pleasure. Her earlier chill seemed forgotten. When he settled beside her—taking shallow breaths because even his dulled sense of smell couldn't block out her reek—she gave him another glorious smile that warmed him to his toes. He wondered if he were brave enough to mention the smell to her—girls didn't usually take that kind of thing kindly, in his experience. And after two days on the march, he probably didn't exactly smell like a rose either. He decided to grin and bear it.

"Uh, thanks."

"Don't mention it. Long day, huh?" She leaned toward him, her hair falling over her shoulder and almost touching his outstretched toes.

He swallowed and looked away, inspecting the contents of his food pouch—there was exactly one piece of dried cod left, and his light water skin told him it was nearly empty too. "Yeah, and I'm starving. How much food do you have left?"

"Oh. Uh . . ." She fumbled with the clasp on her bag, finally loosening the cord and unrolling the top, then poked around until she found her food pouch. She pulled out a few remnants of food. "Not much, I think."

Zale chuckled. "You *think*? That wouldn't be enough to keep a seahorse alive."

"You know what a seahorse is?" Damaris laughed. "Here I thought you were so sheltered from the sea."

Zale scowled. "It came up in marine life class a few days ago. Or maybe a week ago. How long do you think we've been here, anyway?"

Damaris shrugged. "I don't know. A while, I guess." She tore a bite from a ring of dried pineapple and smiled. "Mmm, that's pretty good."

Zale shook his head. "Haven't you already eaten three of those since we got here?"

"Yeah, but I still like it," Damaris said breezily. She turned away and finished her food in silence.

Zale said a short prayer of thanks and took a bite of the cod, chewing slowly so he could get the most nutrition and enjoyment from it—and perhaps trick his body into thinking it was more food than it was.

Bez glanced at them and barked a laugh. "What are you doing? You don't need to eat here."

Zale glanced up, scowling. "Why not? I'm starving and parched. Of course I need to eat."

Damaris watched the exchange, a bemused expression on her face, and kept nibbling her pineapple.

"Well, of course *you're* hungry and thirsty," Bez wheezed, directing the comment at Zale and ignoring Damaris completely. "It's the Underworld. But it doesn't matter how much you eat or drink, you'll always feel that way. This place isn't meant to sustain flesh, and while here, flesh doesn't need to be sustained. You could live here for years without a drop to drink or a crumb to eat, and when you left this place, your body would be much the same as when you came in."

Zale shook his head. "Then why do we feel the need to eat and drink?"

"Ah, that. It's not a physical need. It's an emotional one. Anyone who once had a body of flesh feels it while in the Underworld."

Zale glanced at Damaris, who shrugged as though to say, *Don't look at me, I didn't know.* Zale thought about his hunger and thirst. He'd noticed that the state of the need never changed, but he'd thought that was only because they'd brought so little with them and had been rationing it so carefully.

"Have you ever taken on flesh?" Zale asked the spirit, using the words he'd heard Abela use to describe her body in the physical realm.

Bez pursed his lips. "Yes, but that was a long time ago now. Millennia, by your reckoning. I lived several human lifetimes on the Ground once—and humans lived longer then."

"So, do you feel it then?" Zale asked. "The need?"

Bez laughed. "Well, it's different for me. My flesh was assumed, not innate."

"But you had it for, what, over a hundred, maybe two hundred years? Surely that counts for something."

Bez frowned. "More like one or two thousand. But that was so long ago now." He nodded slowly. "Still, I suppose it does count for something. Yes, now that you mention it, I do feel a little hungry and thirsty. But you get used to it over time and learn to ignore it."

He shrugged and turned his gaze back to their surroundings. A swirling of the mist near them betrayed movement inside it. Bezaziel grabbed a club of darkness out of nothing and swung at the marauding presence, and the slick grey of a damned soul flew through the air—but slowly, like a leaf that has been thrown and resists the air it's soaring through. It soon floated down to be reabsorbed by the fog. Bez released his club and it dissolved into shadows. His lips, however, were stretched into a satisfied, delighted grin.

"Ah, it's been too long," he said, rubbing his hands together. He turned an imperious eye on them. "What did I tell you? Sleep soundly, little undine. I'll be keeping a close eye . . . on you both." He gave Damaris a pointed look.

Zale and Damaris exchanged glances once more.

Damaris arched a brow and mouthed, "Are you ready to go yet?"

Zale glanced surreptitiously at Bez, who was keeping a watchful eye on an approaching sleepless soul. Yes, there was definitely something off about this spirit, and from the look on her face, Damaris sensed it too. But Bez seemed to be keeping his word about guarding them, so Zale shook his head.

Sighing, she found a place to stretch out on the grass and lay down, and he did the same not far from her—though far enough to avoid the worst of her smell. He thought once again about asking her about it—maybe she'd picked something up somewhere along the way and was keeping it in her pack, failing to notice the smell because of inundation, the way the reek of the swamp had faded into the background of his mind. But just as he was about to ask, Bez smacked another soul to kingdom come and chortled with glee.

Damaris raised her head. "Do you mind keeping it down?"

Bez cast an arrogant glance toward her. "Yes, princess."

She glared at him, then settled down facing Zale, her expression shifting to one that puddled his insides.

Uncomfortable, he rolled onto his other side so he couldn't see her anymore and stared at the surrounding gloom. Now that they weren't moving noisily through the swamp, the murmuring of the dead became clear, flowing over them in susurrations of breathy sound. Zale listened, every hair on his body standing on end. It would be difficult to sleep with that racket.

"What are they saying?" he wondered aloud.

"They're accusing their murderers," Damaris whispered.

Surprised, he turned to face her.

She rolled her eyes, smirking. "Fat lot of good that'll do."

Zale listened intently and discovered she was right. The voices whispered about all manner of unjust, untimely deaths at the hands of others, and the names of those they accused. The voices came and went with the swirling of the mist.

Zale clenched his jaw. No wonder they were sleepless. He wondered if Mr. Crow was somewhere out in the crowd of souls, complaining about his death by electrocution at Zale's hands. Or—and this thought chilled him to his bones—his father, doomed to forever slink through this murky plane, murmuring about how his own son had blown him up.

Zale's heart raced. Sleep seemed impossible now.

"Will they remain like this forever?" he asked Bez.

"Who, them?" Bez swung his club at the mist casually, his tone cold. He batted away another creeping marauder with his shadow club, and Zale flinched. "No, only until their murderers have received justice for their actions." Bez shrugged. "Or one of the guardians eats them." His gaze rested on Damaris, then he turned his attention back to the creeping mist.

Zale sat up, his heart thumping. "The guardians eat the dead?"

Bez looked soberly at Zale and Damaris, but then his face broke into a grin and he cackled. "No, I'm just playing. But even when these souls move on from here, the next place isn't guaranteed to be better. They still have to answer for their own actions while they were alive."

Zale relaxed slightly, but then he thought of his father again. What were the chances Kenver would be here? And if he was, would he even know Zale? "Do—do they remember anything from their lives besides how they died?"

Bez shrugged. "Don't know, don't care." He swung his club again with a gleeful crow. "Whoo, did you see that? I nearly got it to the top of that tree that looks like a fork. That's my best one yet."

Damaris cast him a disapproving glare, and he smirked, but returned to scanning their surroundings with more decorum.

Zale eyed the swirling mist around their little hillock, thinking of the short straw these people had pulled—doomed to purgatory in this miserable swamp until their murderers met justice, and then possibly something worse to follow. He shuddered and wondered how conscious the sleepless spirits were of their own state. Were they even aware of the three of them?

Reaching toward the fog on impulse, his hand passed through a figure in the swirling mist, and his arm went cold and clammy clear up to the shoulder. The figure whipped around to face him and grabbed his arm with moist fingers, staring at him through wide, unseeing eyes. Through the connection, Zale could sense a maelstrom of emotions, but all of them were dark and turbulent. So the soul still felt *something*. But it seemed as though the victim was trapped in hell, not the murderer. His curiosity satisfied, Zale tried to withdraw his hand from the spirit's incorporeal grip, but the ghost didn't let him go.

"Get off!" he cried in frustration, pulling with all his might.

"What are you doing?" demanded Damaris.

Bez whirled to see what was going on. In two strides, he had reached Zale and batted the spirit away with his shadow club. Flailing the club, he made a wide swath in the mist around the hill, pushing the marauders farther at bay from his charges.

Bez spun to face Zale, his face hard.

"Leave the sleepless undisturbed, unless you want them to start disturbing *you*," he growled.

Zale nodded, shaken. He rubbed his arm where the spirit's cold fingers had held him, not eager to repeat the experience. Damaris cast him an unreadable expression, and he could almost hear her thinking the word *Icarus*.

Sighing, he lay down on a somewhat level patch of ground to get some rest.

At least things with Damaris were back to normal.

Why didn't that make him feel better?

58

SLEEPLESS

Z ALE AWOKE TO THE SOUND of whispered arguing. He let himself become alert before he cracked his eyelids. The gloom around them remained unchanged, but Damaris no longer lay beside him. Instead, she and Bezaziel were standing next to Bez's tree. The arguing was coming from them.

"Yeah?" Bez sneered in a low, wheezy whisper. "Well, as far I'm concerned, you can just go on back to your den. I don't need a crèche mother keeping an eye on my every move. If he didn't trust me to do this, why did he even send me?"

"You know as well as I do he doesn't trust anyone," Damaris snapped in a quiet voice. "I was as surprised to see you as you were me. I guess this keeps us both honest, doesn't it?"

He? Zale kept his eyes closed and his breathing slow and measured, despite the sudden increase in his heart rate. *Who's* he*? Berian?*

He'd often been suspicious of Berian's intentions, but that was before he'd gotten to know him and the lamassu's loyalty to the Light. And besides, Berian wasn't the distrustful sort—he trusted people more than he should, probably. He trusted Zale, though Zale had no idea why. Zale had certainly done nothing to deserve it. No, they must be talking about someone else. But who?

Who could Damaris and Bez both know? And how did they know each other?

A sinking feeling settled in the pit of Zale's stomach. He tried to push it away, tried to deny it. *No, Damaris hasn't betrayed me too. Not her.*

Why not? asked another voice. *If Eric and Josefine and Gio could betray you—if your own sister could try to kill you—why not Damaris? What does she owe you? Nothing.*

"What does your brother think of you working for Papa?" Bez asked.

"*Don't* call him that. And Asmodeus doesn't control me, I make my own decisions. If the High Lord sends me on a mission, I certainly don't need the prince's approval to go."

Papa? A brother? Damaris doesn't have either of those. A thunderstorm brewed in Zale's heart, trying to burst free. He focused on containing it—in this lifeless swamp in a cavern, his companions would know he was awake immediately if some strange weather conditions appeared. He swallowed, keeping his breathing slow and long like Narcissa had taught him.

Long breaths slow your heart, she'd said. *They keep you calm.*

He desperately needed that calmness now. He wished Narcissa were there with him to tell him what else to do. She would know what was really going on. Narcissa knew everything.

His mind started to float in a golden haze filled with echoes of his cousin's voice, but he was snapped back to reality when Damaris, in a voice not hers at all, hissed at Bez that if he wasn't careful, *he'd* end up in the Abyss with his brethren, she'd see to it.

Just who was this girl? He tried the open-door method to see her emotions again, but there was nothing there—literally nothing, like the space where she should be was a vacuum instead of a living being. The sinking feeling twisted to terror as all the pieces fell into place—her strange behaviour, the horrible smell, and the nothingness in her soul. This wasn't Damaris. But who—or what—was it? And what had happened to his friend?

Soft footsteps came toward him. He lay perfectly still, focusing on his breathing, while the Damaris impostor lay down beside him. He hoped whatever this creature was couldn't read minds. Or that his mother's river stone bracelet would protect him from that too.

He drew in a sharp breath and opened his eyes as though he had just awoken. The false Damaris was laying with her head resting on one bent arm, watching him from those beautiful green eyes that were so like the girl's she'd stolen them from. Zale gulped. Had she actually stolen them, or merely copied Damaris somehow? What kind of creature was this?

When she saw him stir, the girl gave him a languorous smile. "Good morning, sleepyhead. Or whatever time of day it is."

He propped himself on one elbow and forced a smile. "Good morning. Did you sleep well?"

"With you beside me, how could I do anything else?" She propped herself up, too, so their faces were only inches apart.

When Zale was very young, before his powers had manifested and before he knew he was an undine, he had once seen a man fall through thin ice on a pond in the winter and drown. The man hadn't realized the danger he was in until it was too late. Zale glanced at Bez, who stood with his back to them and his shadow club over his shoulder, scanning the perimeter for the sleepless. Zale felt a lot like that man—one wrong step now could mean the end of him.

How could he get himself out of this mess? He needed to act as if nothing was wrong until he could safely get away.

"Tell me," the false Damaris said, interrupting his thoughts, "When did you first know you liked me?"

Zale started. Damaris—the real Damaris—had sensed his attraction to her that first day they'd touched in the sparring courtyard. But this wasn't her, and she didn't know that. Perhaps, if he were clever, he could use this opportunity to find out something about her, or at least where to find his mother.

"Uh, I'd say it was that day when I first told you about my mother being here in hell."

False Damaris snorted. "Your mother's not in hell."

Zale stiffened. "What? She's not even here? How do you know?"

False Damaris shook her head in alarm. "No, I mean she's *here*, in the Underworld, obviously. I only mean that there are many levels to the Underworld, and the fiery pit of hell isn't where your mother is being kept."

Zale arched a brow. "How do you know?"

False Damaris's face went slack, but she quickly recovered and gave him a coquettish smile. "Why, I managed to get Bezaziel to tell me. He's not as impervious to my charms as he'd like to believe."

Zale realized he was staring at her blatant display, and forced himself to blink. How had he ever suspected this girl was his friend Damaris?

Her lips curved upward even more. "By the chains, you're yummy. It was all I could do not to eat you up while you slept."

Zale swallowed. The words sounded both inviting and threatening at the same time.

"Er," he stammered, taken aback. What does one say to that?

"Come on, Zale. I know you think I'm pretty. It's just us here. Ol' Bez is busy. Why don't you satisfy your curiosity? See how I taste." She leaned toward him and inclined her head, the invitation abundantly clear.

Her sour breath washed over him, and Zale fought his gag reflex. He'd thought about kissing Damaris since the first time he'd met her, but this creature was not her. However, he remembered how Berian had first revealed his true forms to Zale—through a simple touch which he said was due to Zale's abilities, not his own. If he really wanted to know who he was dealing with, he was going to have to touch her. And how much harm could a simple kiss do?

Swallowing bile, he leaned forward and pressed his lips to hers. She responded hungrily, wrapping one arm around the back of his neck and pulling him closer to her. Despite what he knew, Zale allowed himself to be pulled closer, his body responding without his mind's agreement.

Focus. Who is she?

No sooner had he thought it than the form of a beautiful dark-haired woman with blood-red lips, copper skin, and black eyes flashed in his mind. The most startling part of all was that from the waist down, instead of legs, a thick, coppery tail like a serpent's lay in a coil in the soft moss.

He gasped and pushed her away, scrambling backward and leaping to his feet.

Or, at least, that's what he *tried* to do.

In reality, he was stuck in her grasp, unable to break free from her kiss. He was paralyzed.

He opened his eyes, panic welling in his chest. The girl's eyes had gone black, and her olive skin was now copper. Her facade had been stripped away.

He tried to cry out, though the sounds were muted. Still, it must have been enough, for, moments later, Bez was pulling the Damaris impostor off him by her curly hair—which was no longer sandy blond, but luscious black.

"Stay back, you viper!" Bez snarled. "I knew I couldn't trust you."

The woman wiped her mouth, which was curled into a seductive smile. Zale stared at the coiled serpent's tail that supported her—copper, with black and white diamonds along its length, just like his vision.

"Aw, Bezzy," she said, pouting, "you ruined my fun. I wasn't really going to eat him. I was just softening him up a little."

Zale had started to get feeling back in his face, though his arms and legs still wouldn't move. He tried to call air or fire, but even the elements seemed far away and sluggish, like his mind.

"Who're you?" he slurred, his tongue thick. "What've you done with Damaris? If you've hurt her . . ." He let the threat hang. They both knew there was little he could to the serpent woman at the moment.

She tsked. "Now, now, Zale. Is that any way to address a princess?"

"It's a fine way to address anyone who's just tried to kill me," he tried to snap. What came out was as intelligible as a sailor on shore leave at dawn.

The woman stood. Or, rather, she raised her body to approximately standing height, her snakey coils in a pile beneath her, and dipped in an approximation of a curtsy. "Lamia, princess of the shedim, at your service."

Zale wiggled a toe, which he took as an encouraging sign. He needed to keep her talking, her and Bezaziel both, until he figured out what was really going on. He also needed to distract this snake-woman from any further notions of eating him until he could do something to defend himself.

Fortunately, Lamia didn't seem averse to talking. She gave a mock pout. "Oh, Zale, nothing to say? You were more fun when you thought I was your sweetheart."

"Damaris isn't my sweetheart. What's a shedim?"

"Oh!" Lamia lifted her hand to her heart as though she were aghast. "You don't even know of my kind? What has education come to among the the undines and their ilk?"

Bez rolled his eyes and crossed his arms, standing within arm's reach of the serpentine woman—Zale suspected it was to intervene if she tried to reclaim her prey and felt a small modicum of gratitude, dangerous as Bez likely was.

"The shedim are the offspring of the bene elohim and humankind," Bezaziel said. "Normally, they don't hang out around these parts, being bound to the Ground and all." He turned to Lamia. "Why *are* you here? Did Azazel really send you? Or did you just happen upon this spry young chap and decide to have a little snack on your way by?"

Zale's fingers twitched. "Snack?" His voice squeaked a little, and he hated himself for it. "Snack?" he asked again, deeper. She'd meant that literally?

Lamia laughed and slithered around him. "Aren't you the cutest thing? Why, yes, darling. I believe you're just my type. Unfortunately, I'll have to delay satiating my appetites for a while. You're far too valuable alive."

"Bez?" Zale asked. "She's just joking, right?"

"No, she's a real man-eater," he wheezed, smirking. "Though she's a sucker for young men's souls. I knew she was up to something." He narrowed his eyes at the woman. "Can you move yet, boy? The river is only a short distance away, and then we'll be on our way to your mummy." He eyed Lamia, tracking her movements. For a creature formed of shifting shadows, he was certainly tense.

Lamia sighed and turned to Bez, laying a possessive hand on Zale's shoulder which he could feel, but not shrug off. "Now, Bezzy, we both know you're not planning to take young Zale to his mother any more than I am. The question is, what *are* you planning to do with him? What does the High Lord have in store for our young captive?"

A shadow club appeared in Bezaziel's hand, but he let it hang limply at his side—a warning, not an attack. Not yet. "It's not my business what Lord Azazel and the Lady Tamiel want to do with him. I was ordered to retrieve him, and that's what I'm doing."

"Wait," Zale said, playing dumb. His legs and arms were afire with returning sensation. It wouldn't be long now. "You weren't sent by Berian, er, Rumiel? What do you want with me? And *where* is Damaris?"

Lamia patted his shoulder. "Isn't he adorable? Oh, I might just eat him anyway, consequences be bound." She slithered around in front of him and stooped to his eye level. "Bezaziel here is one of the Grigori, one of a few who escaped an eternity being chained in the Abyss. But I'm not sure he sees his freedom as a blessing—not when he's spent the last few thousand years sweeping the corners of Elyon's Keep. Poor, malformed Bezzy, couldn't be chained. Poor, shifty Bezzy will always be blamed. How has ol' Abaddon been treating you, anyway?"

Bez growled somewhere deep in his throat—the resonant warning rumble of an asthmatic dragon.

Zale reached out to the elements again and was thrilled when a trickle of heat responded. He let it pool in his hands while he kept talking, remaining on the ground as though he were still paralyzed.

"And you are, what, a demon? Is that what a shedim is?"

Lamia moved behind him and wrapped her arms around his shoulders.

"A shedu, dear," she said into his ear. "Grammar, please. But we'll also answer to jinn. *Demon* is such a negative word. We don't use that here."

Her reeking breath triggered his gag reflex again, and he swallowed, focusing on the fire in his palms. *Almost there . . .*

"As for your little friend, the undine girl," Lamia continued, and smiled. "Don't worry. You'll see her soon."

She gave a short whistle, and without warning, the hillock was surrounded by other creatures like Lamia who had emerged from the trees, half-serpent men and women laughing and hissing and slithering around in a dizzying circle.

"Lamia, what are you planning?" Bez demanded in a wheezing bellow even as he swung his club high, circling to keep an eye on as many of the shedim as he could at once. He inserted himself between the black-haired serpent woman and Zale.

"What am I planning?" hissed Lamia. "I'm planning to finally gain the shedim the respect we deserve!" Her voice had risen to a shriek, and with the last syllable, she rose higher, swaying back and forth in a mesmerizing pattern while her lackeys drew in closer around Zale and Bezaziel.

Bez brandished the club, swirling and occasionally swinging it to keep the encircling shedim at arm's length.

"Can you move yet, boy?" he asked again quietly over his shoulder.

Whoever this spirit was, Zale decided that Lamia posed a greater threat than Bezaziel at the moment—he'd take his chances by siding with the dragon.

"Yeah." Zale scrambled to his feet, crouching with his hands poised to throw fire if any of the shedim attacked.

Lamia was still talking. She hadn't noticed their little exchange. "Everyone always overlooks us—the vassals of the spirit world. But wait until we have the key to the Soulstone in our hands. Who'll be looking down on whom then?" She grinned hungrily at Zale.

Key? Does she mean me? And what's a soulstone?

Bez rolled his eyes. "By the High Lord, will she ever shut up?" He hissed wheezily at Zale from the corner of his mouth, "Okay, on my signal, I want you to run that direction." He pointed his club off to one side. "When you get to the ravine, wait for me. I'll come get you as soon as I take care of this lot."

"And then what?" Zale demanded. "You'll take me to my *mummy*?"

Bez gave him an inscrutable look. "Eventually." He said it on an intake of breath, so it sounded like a question.

Zale scowled, seeing few other options. "Fine," he muttered.

Bez grinned, showing pointed teeth, and his shifting face grew and transformed into the shadowy dragon once more. When Lamia saw the transformation, she shrieked and produced a sword out of nowhere, then ordered her demons to attack and turned her attention back to Zale, her arms outstretched as she swooped toward him.

The shadow dragon turned one baleful eye toward Zale even as he reared to meet his attackers. "Now, boy! Run!"

Bezaziel swung his great head around in time to blow fire at the ring of attacking shedim.

But Zale was done with running. He'd done plenty, and nothing good had ever come of it. Instead, he hurled his fireballs straight into the gaping maw of the descending serpent-woman. She screeched and recoiled, hissing and sweeping the flickering flames away with her hands. Zale tried to recharge, but his connection to the elements was still sluggish.

Her face had contorted into a hideous caricature of her earlier lovely appearance. The scorch marks on her skin surprised him—his fire had done damage to a spirit?

"I knew I should have made off with you while I had the chance," she seethed. "Get him!" She pointed at Zale.

Three lackeys turned aside from their fight with Bezaziel to close in on Zale. He swallowed, realizing he'd made a horrible mistake.

"Bez," he called, keeping his gaze on the flashing black eyes of the surrounding jinn, his hands raised in ineffectual defense.

"Zale, I'm coming!" was the response—but it wasn't in Bezaziel's wheezing rumble.

Zale glanced over his shoulder to see a man with chiselled ivory features, black hair, and golden eyes flying toward him. The man dodged hanging roots and dead trees with powerful thrusts of his feathered black wings, and his gold-trimmed black tunic flapped in the wind he created himself.

"Berian?" Zale gaped. He'd only seen the cherub in this form once, for a few seconds during that encounter on the *Atlanta*, but there could be no doubt that this was one and the same spirit. He'd never been so glad to see the implacable minister in his life.

Lamia saw him, too, but not soon enough to interfere. Berian, or rather, Rumiel, scooped Zale up under his arms from behind and carried him out of the centre of the melee.

"Zale!" screeched Lamia, launching herself into the air after him—right before being bowled over by the copper dragon that had attacked her earlier.

Zale soared through the air, held firmly in Berian's grip. He squirmed around to look behind him in time to see Lamia sitting up and shaking her head to regather her senses. As they flew away, she yelled after him.

"If you ever want to see the undine girl again, you'll meet me at the Western Wastelands by this time tomorrow. Come to me, Zale, or the girl dies."

She whirled once more to meet another attack from the copper dragon, except instead of fighting, she disappeared in a puff of smoke. Seconds later, so did her lackeys, leaving only Bezaziel and the copper dragon locked in battle behind them.

"Zale!" wheezed Bez in between fending off the copper dragon's blows. Then he laughed. "It doesn't matter what you do. The High Lord has located the Heart of Chaos. It's only a matter of time before the tables turn and he sets up his kingdom on earth."

Rumiel's steady flapping stopped, and Zale thought they might fly right into an approaching tree.

"Berian, look out!"

The flapping resumed and Rumiel dodged the tree at the last second, breaking into the clear above a deep ravine. The sounds of water flowed far below, and above, the cavernous ceiling was sliced with a gash that revealed a bowl of golden sky far above them. Rumiel, no longer restrained by the need to dodge obstacles, shot straight up between the walls so fast that Zale's eyes streamed with tears.

I'll come for you, Damaris, I promise. You'll get out of here alive if it's the last thing I do.

But if it was, who would save Mother?

59

THE FLAMING DRAGON

CALANDRA SWAM AGAINST THE CURRENT of the subterranean river for what felt like an eternity. The glow of the lightstones cast stark shadows on Zoe's and Airlea's determined faces. After some time, a patch of light streaming through an opening above illuminated a statue of a copper-coloured dragon on the cavern floor. Squat and bulky, it sat on its haunches and glared fiercely up at them, looking as though it was daring them to choose its gate. Definitely not the flaming dragon.

Still, Calandra paused and peered at the stone beast in interest. She'd always imagined that the guardians one had to pass to move between the different realms of the dead were living spirits, not road signs. However, as she neared the statue, its gaze darted toward her, following her movements.

Alarmed, she swam backward in the water, holding out her arms to prevent her companions from approaching too closely. But when the statue made no further movements except to observe their passing, she beckoned to the others, and they cautiously swam by. It watched them go, but made no move to interfere.

The next statue was not so easy to classify. Long and sleek, the black stone beast was curled up as though asleep. But instead of plates along its back ridge, it appeared to be on fire, with flames formed of a translucent reddish-orange stone—carnelian, she thought—expertly carved to lick along the dragon's back. It cracked an eyelid and regarded them with a baleful yellow glare as they approached, but made no other movements.

You think this is the right one? Airlea asked with flicking fingers.

Zoe gestured. *Yes, this is the flaming dragon.*

Calandra closed her eyes, and the vibration she'd been searching

500

for pulled at her. *Zale.* She almost surged to the light above in glee, but stopped, certain that was the wrong way to go.

She opened her eyes. *No, we have to continue on.*

She made to continue swimming upstream, but Zoe caught her arm.

This is the one. The siren pointed at the greyish circle of light above with an emphatic jerk.

Calandra looked at the statue, which cracked an eyelid to watch them with a baleful yellow glare. She had only done a little reading about the Underworld, but she had a vague recollection that to travel to different parts, you had to pass through a gate, and each gate was guarded by a different dragon. However, in the datastone she'd read, some of the dragons had seemed remarkably similar—the sitting dragon and the squatting dragon, for instance. She didn't want to hazard a guess as to the identity of the one they had already passed. She'd thought a flaming dragon would be blowing fire, but now that she saw this statue, she wasn't so sure. Maybe Zoe was right—she looked so certain. Calandra wished her mother had been more specific.

How do you know? Calandra signed.

I'll explain later. Trust me.

Calandra looked at the dragon statue once more, wavering. She couldn't really tell which direction the buzzing resonance came from. If this was the flaming dragon, that meant Zale was here, didn't it? Maybe they should check really quick, just in case.

She almost began the ascent to the gloomy light above, but, again, something stopped her.

No. I feel Zale that way, she signed and pointed upstream. *Let's go.*

She flipped her tail upstream, her stomach a tight bundle of nerves. She was relieved when she noticed the glow from both Airlea's and Zoe's lightstones next to her a few moments later.

The next statue left little doubt as to its identity. The graceful red jasper dragon reared back with clawed wings outstretched, letting loose a long stone stream of fire. Calandra thrust herself out of the current to the calmer water alongside the beast, and her two companions followed. The dragon's eyes watched them, but it stayed in its awkward rearing posture, not even closing its mouth.

Zoe looked askance at the dragon and shook her head. *This is not the right one. We should go back.*

Zoe's doubt needled at Calandra, and she took another look at the statue. *Flaming* could be interpreted in several ways, she supposed. However, the dragon certainly had flames coming from its mouth. If that weren't a flaming dragon, she wasn't sure what would be. Besides, the resonance was stronger than ever—she was certain this was the gate they should use.

But what if she was wrong again? What if she made another mistake and made things worse?

At the thought of going back, something in her rebelled. Flaming or not, she knew this was the right way to go.

Zale and Damaris are this way. She pointed toward the light.

Zoe's jaw clenched. Airlea promptly whirled in the water to swim toward the light. Calandra swam after her, easily following the globe of light created by the siren's lightstone and the tug of spirit that connected her to it. Zoe trailed behind, though Calandra felt like she was swimming through a quagmire of Zoe's reticence.

Moments later, they broke through the surface into what appeared to be a peaceful pool surrounded by lush, green jungle. There was no sun, but a clear golden light from some invisible source above them softly illuminated their surroundings.

Calandra blinked against the brightness, getting her bearings. She couldn't see a living soul, but she felt suddenly stifled by the presence of other beings. The emotions were dull and heavy, like when people slept, but there were so many of them, they threatened to overwhelm her. She took a moment to strengthen her emotional shield so she could concentrate, then glanced around. There was no one there. Odd.

"Where are we?" asked Airlea, turning around in the water and staring at the long, trailing branches that surrounded the pool. She shivered. "And where is everyone?"

"You feel it too?" Calandra said. "Like a forest of sleeping people?"

"Yes. It's like that well with the blue stone—full of people, but none to be seen."

Zoe slid her staff from its holster on her back, still treading water. She looked warily around. "I don't see anyone. Chains of Prometheus, that's creepy."

On one edge of the pool, a small stream flowed into the water, partially hidden by lush ferns and mossy rocks. There was no outbound stream that Calandra could see, but since all the water here seemed connected by the same underground river, perhaps none was necessary.

"And it stinks." Calandra wrinkled her nose. Though her eyes and skin said otherwise, it smelled like they were floating in a stagnant marsh, not a stream-fed pool. She was glad for the mucosal layer on her skin while in *ichthys* state that would protect her from whatever made the water smell so bad.

"It does," Zoe said dryly, "but does this look like a swamp to you?"

"It smells like one," Calandra replied. "Maybe that's why it's called the Sleepless Swamp. The swamp smell means no one can sleep here."

"Well, if we're in the right place, where's Delphine's guide?" Zoe asked, scanning the empty bank. But all they could see were the water and the trees. There weren't even any birds singing.

The utter silence made the hairs on Calandra's arms stand on end.

"I don't know. We just got here, though. They'll probably be here soon." Calandra spotted a slight variance in the wall of foliage—an indentation that might be a pathway. "That way," she said, pointing, then surged toward the mark with a strong thrust of her tail.

Moments later, the three of them were on the grassy bank in *podia* state, wringing out their hair, with water dripping from their short linen swimming skirts. The stench of rotting plants in the still, heavy air made Calandra's stomach heave, and she swallowed several times to subdue it.

"Was that big moonstone the Soulstone?" Airlea asked, getting to her feet.

"What moonstone?" Zoe asked.

"The one Airlea and I saw inside the well at the bottom of the pool of Mad panaceas," Calandra explained. "It must be the Soulstone."

"What's this Soulstone you keep talking about?" Zoe asked.

"It's a prison. Or the gateway to a prison, if my mother is correct." Calandra stood, surveying the pool. The water looked almost clear, no sign of algal overgrowth that would cause the stench. "I don't actually know much about it, but from what I've been able to piece together, there was some kind of rebellion among the aerial spirits a long time ago. I think Damon might have been one of the leaders, based on some of the things he told me." She snorted. "He once told me humans used to worship him as a weather god, if you can imagine. Who knows? It might even be true. Maybe that's even what landed him in the Abyss. Anyway, Mother has been imprisoned in it somehow too."

"Why do you think it was so damaged?" Airlea asked.

Calandra shrugged. "It's connected to the Heartstone, so maybe that's why. Didn't Mother say it has been neglected too?" She thought of the wild eyes of the undines they'd passed in the pool. If they were meant to guard the well, they hardly seemed stable enough to maintain the Soulstone. The Heartstone had been carefully restored as much as possible every summer for millennia, and it was still on the brink of failure. Something that had been niggling her came into sharp focus. "The guardians of the deep," she whispered, stunned.

"Pardon?" Airlea asked, glancing at her.

Calandra looked up excitedly at her companions. "From the lullaby. You know:

In the light, the em'rald-eyed protectors of the deep
Will, ever vigilant, defend the gates of Elyon's keep.

The Mad panaceas and sirens get sent to the Abyss, right? And Mother said that was the same as the Well of Souls, where the Soulstone is, right?"

"Yesss," Airlea said, and Zoe nodded cautiously.

"That must mean that crystal cavern is Elyon's keep. Or, the gates to it, I guess. Maybe the well is the keep?"

Zoe shrugged. "Everyone knows that lullaby. But who's Elyon? I never could figure that out."

"I don't know. But, think about it—what if that pool wasn't meant to be a place of exile for our ancestors, but some kind of holy assignment?"

"Assigned by who?" Airlea wondered.

"The Mother, obviously. That is, if Calandra's right." Zoe frowned as though weighing how likely she thought that was. She shook her head. "I don't believe Narcissa is possessed, by the way. Undines can't be possessed."

Calandra sighed. Why did everyone believe that? It wasn't worth arguing about, though, so she let it pass.

Zoe checked her belt knife and adjusted her bag and the sheath for her *deiktis*, though she kept the staff in her hands. "Whatever the reason they're there, I'm just glad those panaceas didn't think it worth chasing us beyond their territory. They certainly weren't keen on the two of you taking a closer look."

"No, they were not," agreed Calandra. "I hope Mother has a good plan for getting past them later. That, and the creature beyond the grate."

At the memory of the huge beast who had blocked the light from below, she shuddered. Apparently, the women in the pool weren't the only defenders of the deep.

Airlea met her gaze, agreement in her serious round eyes.

Calandra saw the path she'd spotted from the water disappearing between two closely set tree trunks.

"There," she said. "We must need to go that way."

Zoe frowned at Calandra. "You're not sure? I thought you said Zale and Damaris were here."

Calandra nodded. "I can feel Zale, which means he must be nearby."

Airlea tilted her head in interest. "Can you tell where?"

Calandra shook her head. "Not exactly, but I feel we should go in that general direction," she said, indicating the path.

Zoe frowned. "Maybe we should wait for your mother's guide rather than chase after your hunch. What if it's wrong?"

Calandra surveyed the still water and the full leaves that hung limp in the unmoving air and smelled like rotting compost. Should they wait for Delphine's guide? Her doubts about the gate marker returned, but she wouldn't let these two know about them. They needed her to be decisive and strong, not show weakness.

"She said her guide would meet us at the flaming dragon," Calandra said. "Perhaps she had a hard time finding someone, or they haven't realized we've arrived yet."

"That wasn't the flaming dragon." Zoe crossed her arms over her damp blue bodice. In the bright light, her singer's triquetra with its single pearl glinted silver on her left shoulder.

Calandra's chest tightened. "What makes you say that?"

Zoe drew a deep breath, and when she spoke, she sounded a bit sheepish. "One of my favourite stories as a child was Inanna's Descent, when the Queen of Heaven went through all seven gates of the Underworld to attend her brother-in-law's funeral. We had it recorded on a child's datastone, and I used to listen to it over and over. The Mother's sister, the Queen of the Dead, barred all seven gates against her, and they each had a gatekeeper. The gate we used was guarded by the spitfire dragon, not the flaming dragon. I'm sure of it. Are *you* sure this is where Zale is?"

Calandra's chest tightened. Zoe was much more familiar with the mythology of the Underworld than Calandra was, and she was so confident she was right that Calandra almost changed her mind and ordered them to go back to the sleeping dragon gate. But then the vibration grew stronger, and a tugging sensation led her on.

"This is where I felt the vibration pulling me." Calandra gestured around them. "It might not be the gate Mother said to use, but it's the way we need to go to find Zale. And, assuming your sister is still with him, Damaris."

Zoe eyed Calandra skeptically, then gave a cursory nodded. "If you're certain."

"I am. Let's go. Mother's guide will have to find us." She pointed at the path. "Zale is that way, and there is no other way to go, regardless. Let's not waste time while we wait."

"All right." Zoe gave her a level stare, then brandished her *deiktis* before her and moved toward the path.

Calandra's gut tightened. Since when had her orders become something that needed to be agreed to? Shouldn't Zoe follow them simply because of her position, out of loyalty to her? She still hadn't decided what to do about Zoe having disobeyed her by depositing Osaze and Urbi on Barbados. Not for the first time, she wondered whom Zoe was truly loyal to. One thing was becoming glaringly obvious—Zoe didn't trust her.

But as she thought about all the ways her decisions had gone wrong, she almost couldn't blame her, and her anger turned inward.

Airlea pointed in front of her. "You should walk between us, your highness."

Calandra gave the girl a half-smile and followed Zoe. At least one of her companions respected her. Calandra only wished she felt deserving of that respect—and that it came from anyone but the clingy Airlea.

Three hours later—she thought it was three hours, but it could have been six, for all she knew—they were still walking along a path that had remained virtually unchanged. They had seen no living things that didn't have roots, and the stench of decay had remained ever-present. Most of that time had been spent in tense silence which had eventually decayed to exhausted silence. Calandra had eaten her last mushy anchovy, though it had done nothing for her hunger. Neither of her companions had more food either. Still, despite her hunger, her energy always seemed about the same. She brought the fact up with her companions and was surprised to discover Airlea hadn't been eating her rations.

"I've been saving them for you," she said sheepishly.

"Airlea," Calandra said in dismay. "You shouldn't have. You need to eat too."

"But it's more important that you do."

Calandra was so shocked by this, she didn't respond right away.

"Besides, I don't feel any hungrier now than when we got here. Maybe we don't really need to eat. It might be one of the strange rules of this place."

As Calandra thought about it, she realized Airlea was probably right. Her own energy hadn't lagged or been bolstered based on how much she'd eaten ever since arriving, and neither had her hunger—it was an ever-present discomfort that was frequently eclipsed by the pain between her temples. Even still, she insisted she wouldn't touch Airlea's rations and the girl should eat them herself, and Airlea reluctantly agreed.

When she turned to face forward again, she stopped just short of running right into Zoe, who had stopped in the middle of the trail.

"What is it?" Calandra asked.

Zoe stepped aside, pressing herself into the dense growth on one side of the trail and revealing a fork in the path.

"Which way should we go?" Zoe asked.

Calandra stared at the paths, which curved out of sight almost immediately. She focused on the vibration, but she couldn't tell which one might lead them to Zale, no matter how hard she concentrated.

"Well?" Zoe demanded.

Calandra looked at her in dismay, her tongue thick. "I don't know."

60

THE FORK IN THE ROAD

"Can't you tell where they are?" Zoe demanded.

Calandra's shoulders tensed, and she eyed the two paths before her. They looked nearly identical. In the distance on either side, tall round hills like giant anthills poked up between the foliage. She wished she had a decisive answer to give. What kind of leader was she?

"Give me a few moments to rest and think about it.," she said curtly.

Airlea squatted on her haunches and remained alert. Zoe gave Calandra an unreadable look, then put a hand on her hip, scanning the forest as though she expected a creature to jump out of it at any moment. Calandra wasn't sure whether to laugh or be impressed by the singer's diligence in the face of all the evidence of vacancy. However, the hairs on her neck hadn't stopped standing up since they went through the Voidstone, so she couldn't blame Zoe for being on edge—especially with that pervasive sense of being surrounded. It was like the trees themselves were alive and slumbering around them.

Calandra took a sip of her water, but her thirst remained unchanged. She gulped her fill, but still, she felt as thirsty as before, even though her stomach could hold no more. She capped her water flask and replaced it on her belt. Maybe Airlea's theory about hunger extended to thirst too. She wasn't sure if that comforted or alarmed her. Surely it was unnatural not to ever need food or drink? Or to not be sated when you had them?

But what about this place was natural?

"I think we should go that way," Calandra said, pointing down the left path.

"How do you know?" Zoe peered down the path in question. "Do you

508

feel any closer to Zale?"

Calandra shook her head. "I can feel him, but nothing has changed. It's like he's moving too, at the exact pace and in the exact direction we are. But no, I can't tell which direction he's in. I simply feel that's the way to go."

Zoe frowned. "If you can't tell a difference, why should we trust your feelings? I mean, it's not like they've been the most reliable source of decision-making in the past."

Airlea glared at Zoe, and Calandra's throat closed.

"What do you mean by that?" Calandra asked.

Zoe arched an eyebrow. "I know you're a powerful empath, Calandra, but your empathy doesn't always make for good choices. If you hadn't followed your feelings, would Sirenia be in a civil war? Would so many people have died? Would we even be here in this hellish place of endless hunger and thirst?"

The siren had taken a few steps closer as she spoke, and Calandra backed up until she bumped into the foliage at the edge of the path.

Airlea rose. "Singer kor'Dione, you forget yourself."

Zoe stiffened, then turned away.

Calandra's heart pounded in her chest, and she forced her knees to lock so they wouldn't buckle. She stared at the siren singer. So this was what had been bothering Zoe. She thought about snapping back, but what was the point? The words coming from Zoe's mouth were merely an echo of the doubts in her own soul.

"You—you're right." Her shoulders slumped. "Of course you're right, Zoe. Every time I close my eyes, I see the faces of those we've lost."

Especially Thea and Tanni. Her heart ached at the thought of them.

"I didn't want anyone to die. I didn't want a revolution and a war. I did everything I could to prevent it. But it happened anyway."

She turned away and stared into the lush greenery that reeked of rot and teemed with non-existent life forms.

Airlea touched her arm. "Their deaths weren't your fault, Calandra. They made their own choices. We all do."

Calandra shook her head. It *felt* like her fault. But accepting the blame on its own was not enough. Her chest tight, she turned to her companions.

"I may not be able to go back and change the past. But I can change what happens to those who remain alive. Let's go. We must find Zale and Damaris so we can free my mother and get you all back to the land of the living where you belong."

"And you, too, right?" Airlea gave her a significant look.

"I still feel we should go that way." She pointed at the path on the left, ignoring Airlea's question.

Zoe clenched her jaw, and frustration leaked from behind her shield. "But if you can't tell which direction Zale is in, you could be leading us to our doom."

Something in Calandra snapped.

"Look, no one asked you to come, did they? Either of you. But if you don't trust me, Zoe kor'Dione, fine. Go your own way. But that's the direction I'm going," she said, pointing down the path on the left. "You can come with me, or not. The choice is yours."

Zoe glared at Calandra, then whirled to stare at the two diverging routes. She shook her head. "I just wish we understood this place better," she growled. "Maybe you're not sensing Zale at all, and we're following a wild hunch. Nothing is as it seems here. Like how my senses say we should be in the middle of a crowd of people, but there's no one here." She gestured around at the forest. "How *can* you be certain you're sensing Zale? I've got four sisters, and I've never had any kind of resonance with any of them like you think you have with your brother."

Calandra drew in a calming breath. *Be water*. Maybe she needed to be more fluid. Her feelings *could* be wrong—but she also knew it was more than her feelings guiding her. How could she explain that she was certain the Spirit of Atargatis was leading her down the correct path without offering proof? She'd seen the scepticism in Zoe's eyes when she'd mentioned the Spirit earlier. Best to offer a compromise.

"Fine," Calandra said. "Why don't we go a short distance down the path on the left, and if I sense a difference in Zale's proximity for the worse, we'll come back and try the one on the right? We'll have more information to work with, if nothing else."

"And what if nothing changes no matter what we do?" Zoe demanded.

Calandra squared her shoulders. "You're just going to have to trust my word, Zoe kor'Dione. This is Zale I'm sensing. Why his distance never changes, I can't tell you, but it is definitely my brother. And it's not like we have much else to go on."

Zoe gave her a measured stare, and Calandra met her gaze, not flinching.

Airlea squatted next to the path and pounded the end of her staff against a moss-covered clod of dirt, looking thoughtful. "Maybe it has nothing to do with distance."

"What makes you say that?" Calandra was willing to take any and all guesses as to the strange properties of this place. Any guesses she'd made had seemed completely ludicrous, but Airlea had already put forth some rather astute observations.

Airlea squinted up at Calandra. "What if this place isn't affected so much by physical distances as metaphysical ones?"

Having fractured the dirt clod, the siren rested her staff on her thighs, picked up the clod, and tore the moss that still connected the two pieces. Wispy green strands stuck haphazardly out of the soil.

"If I hold these pieces at a distance from one another"—Airlea stretched her arms wide—"we would say they are further apart, and all physical connection between them has been lost. Of course, they remain loosely connected through the Matrix of Creation, but what happens to one will not directly affect the other. And, back home, that would be true. But this place operates on different principals. This moss all grew together and was deeply interconnected. What if, no matter if it's touching or not, it remains connected?"

Calandra, thinking she understood Airlea's point, stepped forward and placed her hand over the moss of one clump. She poured energy into the plants in Airlea's left hand—and watched in wonder as the moss in the siren's right hand plumped and grew in tandem with the one she was manipulating, along with several patches near them on the forest floor.

"Hmph," Zoe snorted. She glanced at Airlea. "But what does that mean as far as finding Damaris and Zale?"

Airlea shrugged. "I don't know. I only think the reason Calandra's awareness of Zale hasn't changed has nothing to do with how near or far away from him we are. It probably has more to do with—"

"How connected we are," Calandra broke in.

That might be the problem. She and Zale had a connection of blood, that was true—but that was almost where the bond ended. They barely knew each other, and since Zale had fallen under Narcissa's influence, he'd been actively pushing Calandra away.

But then why had the awareness of his presence been coming and going since she'd arrived in Hades?

She tugged on the thick golden braid falling over her shoulder, which had finally dried. Airlea's theory would also explain why Damon had been able to contact her so easily from here all those years. She still didn't know how he'd found her in the first place, but the longer they'd interacted, and the more of those horrible golden threads he'd connected to her, the more easily he'd appeared in her dreams. But why had he appeared in the tunnel the other day? The chains that had bound her to him had been broken. Were they still connected in some way she couldn't see? Or had that just been a hallucination brought on by the seizures?

Another thought occurred to her—maybe this connection principal was why she'd been able to contact Osaze. Yes, he was on a different plane, but if the rules of this plane made distance obsolete, then it wouldn't matter where he was. He could be anywhere on Earth—so long as they still had an emotional connection, she might be able to find him.

Heat flushed through her. Did that mean he still cared for her, even after what she had done to him? Could she communicate with him even now, apologize for how she'd treated him? Without a second thought, she reached out to him.

Osaze . . .

She thought she felt his mind for a moment, then the sensation was gone. But that single touch had revealed a bleak emotional landscape, one wracked with pain. It confirmed all her worst fears—Osaze wasn't safe. For all she knew, he could be dying.

Oh, my love, what are they doing to you?

With difficulty, she regathered her focus. It wasn't Osaze she was trying to save right now. Wherever he was, whatever he was doing, he was well beyond her reach. She was here to save Zale and her mother. She should be trying to contact them, not her consort-elect.

Ex consort-elect.

Whom she'd sentenced to almost certain slavery and misery, apparently.

The anguish built in her chest, and the pounding in her temples— which had been absent since she'd called on the Spirit in the river—re-appeared and quickly increased in intensity. She clutched the sides of her head and doubled over, red pain taking over her mind. *Holy Mother, help me . . .*

"Calandra?" came Airlea's voice.

Distantly, Calandra felt the siren's touch on her forehead, but it seemed to have little effect. She crumpled to sit in the dirt, clutching her head. The ground beneath her began to vibrate and shake, and the leaves on the trees rattled and whispered in response.

"Calandra!" Airlea cried, sounding far away.

"*There* you are," came a different voice altogether. "It took forever to find you. Why did you choose the spitfire dragon when your mother said to choose the flaming one?"

"Who are you?" Zoe demanded.

Calandra squinted through the ruby haze. A small boy with a curly mop of light brown curls, golden-brown eyes above cheeks like apples, bare feet, and two wings of soft grey feathers nestled against his back stood before them. He wore loose brown cloth breeches that came to mid-calf, and a small bag was slung across his bare chest and rested against his hip. He reached into the bag and held out a small oval stone the colour of milk.

"Here, place this on her forehead and sing the Song of Submission," the boy instructed Airlea.

"O—okay," said Airlea, taking the stone.

She placed the cool stone surface on Calandra's forehead and sang the song that would normally be used to stupefy a man. Cool relief spread through Calandra's body. The ground grew still. The seizure was gone. The throb of the bonds had receded to a barely noticeable pulse.

In fact, she felt *good*. A floating, bubbly feeling that began in the centre of her forehead soon spread through all her limbs. Gone were the exhaustion and the constant hunger. Gone was the pain of the bonds. She looked at the boy in wonder, then giggled. She actually *giggled*. And then she did it again, just because it felt good.

Airlea and Zoe stared at her, their mouths hanging open. Calandra took the stone from Airlea and examined it. She thought it looked like a flattened small white egg, about the size of a drachma. But how could an egg make her feel like this? That was ridiculous! She laughed again at the absurdity of it.

"What did it do to her?" Airlea demanded of the boy.

"Made the pain stop." He looked at Calandra and laughed. "It's like magic, isn't it?" he said to Calandra, and she nodded happily, cradling it in her hands.

"It's very lovely," she said, stroking it. "What kind of device is it?"

He waved his hand dismissively. "Oh, just something I found a long time ago. Your mother said you might need something to calm you down."

Calandra held the stone up to her eyes so she could get a better look at it. She hadn't seen this type of crystal before. Its matrix was convoluted and chaotic, with empty channels that wound through it in meandering, interconnected lines where spirit would normally be. It seemed to be waiting for something to fill it up.

But it wasn't hers. She sighed and forced herself to hold the stone out to the boy. "Here."

"Keep it." He grinned. "It might come in handy."

"Who are you?" Zoe demanded again.

"I'm Valac," the boy said, thumbing his chest. "And that earthquake would have attracted some attention, so we should leg it."

Zoe glanced around, holding her staff aloft. "Attention? From whom?"

A swooshing sound like a rising wind reached them, but the air didn't stir. On a nearby hill, the tops of the trees swayed and bowed, disturbed by something passing beneath. It was big, and it was coming right for them.

"What's that?" Airlea asked, staring at the treetops.

"I don't want to stay to find out," said Zoe. "Run!"

61

THE PUTTI

AT ZOE'S WARNING, CALANDRA JUMPED. She couldn't understand why everyone was so anxious all of a sudden. Maybe it was a game. She took a few steps toward the path on the left.

Valac shook his head impatiently. "Not that way," he said and moved toward the path on the right. "Follow me."

"Why is he going that way?" Calandra asked Airlea.

Airlea tugged at her arm. "Come on, we better follow him."

"Okay." Calandra smiled at her. "You're so nice."

Airlea stiffened, looking at Calandra with wide eyes, and then pushed Calandra ahead of her. "Hurry up, okay?"

"Okay, okay," Calandra said irritably, breaking into a jog. She looked at the path. Weren't they supposed to go down the other one? She was sure she'd meant to go down the left path.

She glanced behind her to look that way, but it was already lost to the jungle. Instead, she caught a gloating smirk on Zoe's face. What was that for?

She stumbled and Airlea grabbed her arm.

"Careful," the other girl chided.

"I'm always careful." Calandra faced forward and realized the running boy was far ahead. "Hey, he's winning." She increased her pace—she wasn't the strongest athlete, but she could definitely keep up to a little boy.

Airlea seemed relieved at that, and Calandra smiled. Airlea was so uptight. Why couldn't she relax and just enjoy things?

The creature that chased them was surprisingly quiet for its size. As they ran, Calandra glanced over her shoulder, trying to see what it was. She caught glimpses of a sleek lionine body with a hawk-like head and huge golden feathered wings—a griffin. It would stop every so often and sniff the air, surveying the landscape with one glaring red eye. In a few more paces, it gave a mighty thrust of its wings and took its search to the air.

"Stay beneath the trees." Airlea nudged Calandra further beneath the canopy.

Valac turned and pointed to one of the hills jutting out of the trees some distance ahead.

"There's a cave in that hill. We're nearly there. Hurry! I'm going to go check it before you arrive." He extended his stubby wings and flitted off, keeping low beneath the spreading fronds above.

Calandra giggled and pointed. "Can you believe . . . those little wings hold him?" she said between panting breaths. "He looks like a . . . chubby bumblebee."

"Ssh," hissed Airlea. "What's gotten into you?"

Calandra sobered, concentrating on running. What was Airlea's problem? For the first time in weeks, she felt happy. Her head didn't hurt. Not only that, her heart didn't hurt. She remembered feeling sad about Osaze and Tanni and Thea, like she'd been trudging through black sludge every moment of every day, but now she felt lighter than air. Couldn't Airlea just be glad she felt good for once?

They reached the cave and, when Valac appeared and gave the all-good signal, piled inside. A large cave mouth opened into a sizable chamber with a sandy floor. Calandra put her hands on her knees, panting and trying to catch her breath. Next to her, Airlea leaned on the wall with one hand, breathing hard and peering out through the entrance from a safe distance away. Zoe leaned against the wall nearer the entrance, doing much the same.

Valac stood in the middle of the chamber, his arms crossed, giggling and pointing.

"You should see yourselves. You're blowing like b'luga whales."

Calandra frowned. "I am not. Beluga whales make a big spray, like this."

Grabbing her water skin from her bag, she took a swig, tilted her head back, then blew it out of her mouth, using air and water to vapourize it into fine mist that sprayed all over herself and Airlea.

"Hey," Airlea said, frowning. She wiped the side of her face with her forearm.

Calandra and Valac took one look at each other and collapsed into fits of laughter.

"Quiet!" Zoe glared at them. "Do you want that thing to find us?"

Valac's eyes still danced with merriment, but he stifled any further mirth. Calandra drew a deep breath, holding in her next bout of giggles with difficulty.

"Okay," she squeaked. "I'll be quiet."

Zoe rolled her eyes and returned to surveying the landscape and sky outside the cave.

"You can relax," Valac said to Zoe. He plunked himself into a cross-legged position on the floor and placed his pudgy hands on his knees. "Ophiuchus is a strong fighter, but he likes to stay above the trees instead of walk around down here. Plus, he gets bored easy. He'll soon go back to his aerie, and then I'll take you back to the river so you can get to the Sleepless Swamp."

Calandra shook her head. "We don't need to go back to the river. We need to go that way." She pointed the way they'd come, then shook her head again. That wasn't right. "No, that way." She pointed in the other direction, then snorted back another giggle. Covering her mouth, she glanced at Zoe, who glared at her and returned to her vigil.

"Ophiuchus?" Airlea squatted next to Calandra. "Like the constellation?"

"Exactly." At a keening cry from the sky above, Valac cast a wary glance at the entrance. Once the cry faded, he relaxed and continued. "The const'llation was named for the guardian, you know. He's a fierce dragon slayer."

Zoe frowned. "I see. And what about an undine slayer?"

Valac laughed, shaking his head like she'd made the best joke ever, and Calandra fought the urge to join in. "He prob'bly won't *kill* you, as long as he doesn't swoop down before he stops to think about it. But when his charges are threatened, he's f'rocious in protecting them. It was the earthquake that woke him up, I bet."

At the mention of the earthquake, Calandra tugged on her braid, then tossed it behind her shoulder, concern breaking through her giddy haze. She'd made that earthquake. Her seizures were getting worse all the time. Then she brightened. Now that she felt so amazing, she wouldn't have to worry about that anymore. Without pain, there would be no seizures, and without seizures, no earthquakes. She opened her hand to look at the little stone she'd clasped there since she'd received it. What a miracle it was.

"What charges?" Zoe asked, peering at the forest. "The trees?"

"They're not just trees." Valac jumped to his feet and went to stand beside Zoe. "Those are the Souls of the Undecided. Well, the trees aren't the souls. The souls are in the trees."

Airlea blinked. "You mean there are *people* in the trees?"

"Just their spirits. They're waiting."

Calandra frowned, trying to make sense of the conversation. "Waiting for what?"

Valac shrugged. "Their judgement."

Calandra looked out the cave mouth, and the awareness of the scores of spirits filling the forest beyond pushed against her. So that's what she and the others had been sensing. A plane devoid of creatures that felt full to bursting with them—they'd been surrounded by spirits all along.

"Judgement?" Airlea straightened. "To decide what?"

"Where they'll go after this, of course," said Valac with an expansive gesture. "This realm is a holding place. They won't stay stuck in the trees forever. Purg'tory is always temp'rary."

Zoe leaned back against the wall and crossed her arms. "Why are the souls called the Undecided?"

Valac tilted his head upward in thought. "'Cause they didn't earn their place in par'dise while they were alive, I guess. They prob'bly meant well, but made some mistakes. They don't let just anyone in there, you know." He rummaged in his bag. "The Forest of Forgetfulness is where those people go until their judgement, when the good things they did are weighed against the bad."

He triumphantly pulled a small coin from his bag, which he began flipping across the back of his fingers. Calandra watched in fascination.

"And then they can go to the Isles of the Blessed?" Airlea asked.

"Yes. That, or Tartarus." Valac giggled again, his focus on the coin. "No one wants to end up there, of course, but lots do."

"You know an awful lot for someone your age," Zoe observed.

The boy gave her a sideways look, the coin not breaking rhythm. "And what age do you think I am?"

She looked at him askance. "Five? Maybe six?"

He broke out in giggles again, clutching the coin in his hand and slapping his leg. "Nope! Try five thousand!"

He kept laughing, and this time, Calandra joined in, howling at Zoe's ridiculous mistake. Then what he'd said sank in, and she stared at him in amazement.

"Wait, you're five thousand years old?"

"Yep!" He dimpled again, then he pulled his lips to the side in thought. "Actu'lly, not quite. I'll be five thousand in . . ." he looked up at the ceiling, doing some mental calculations and counting on his fingers, "a little over four hundred years. So I'm more like four thousand and a half."

"You're forty-six hundred years old," Zoe stated, the disbelief plain in her voice. She gave her head a little shake. "In that case, are you pretty familiar with the Underworld?"

He nodded eagerly. "You bet. I've found all kinds of things down here. Finding things is kind of what I do. Tell me what you need, and I'll find it. That's why Ta—I mean, your mother sent me to find you."

Calandra sat up. The giddy buzz had faded, and Valac's words brought questions with them.

"Can you find Zale, then?"

He pulled a face that showed how ridiculous he thought that question was. "Of *course* I can. That's the next thing we're going to do, if Ophi up there ever goes for his nap."

The keening cry could still be heard in the distance, and Valac glared toward the cave mouth as though he were personally offended by the guardian's tenacity.

"What about the gate back to Atlantis?" Zoe asked. "Can you find that? And the key to open it?"

She cast a cool glance at Calandra, and Calandra's cheeks warmed. A little more of the euphoria faded away.

Valac shook his curls and giggled again. "Any portstone will do for that, silly. But if you don't have the key, you're in trouble." He sobered. "There're not too many keys around these days, you know. I just found one, but that was for someone else, and I don't have it anymore." He looked truly unhappy he couldn't help them, his little eyebrows furrowed in concern. "I guess I could look for one after I get you back to the Pool of Tears . . ."

Zoe cleared her throat impatiently. "Okay, forget the key for a moment. What's a portstone?"

"You don't know what that is either? How did you all even get here?" Valac exclaimed, throwing his hands up in the air.

"We came through the Voidstone in Atlantis," said Airlea.

"You see?" Valac gestured triumphantly. "You do know what a portstone is."

Calandra shook her head. The dull throb of the bonds was tapping a faint rhythm in her temples again. "Are there other portstones? Is that how people travel around here?"

He cocked his head, then leapt to his feet. He traced a small teardrop in the air with his finger, leaving behind a line of white light that hovered there. He drew another line around the original shape, then drew more outlines, all roughly equal in distance from each other.

Calandra watched in wonder. She'd never seen anything like that before.

"It's . . . an onion?" Zoe asked.

"Close enough." Valac finished his drawing with a mess of tangled lines around the outside of the shape, then turned to them, pointing at his drawing. "The onion is the cosmos. All the planes are kind of like the layers of an onion. The centre of the onion and the skin of the onion are both part of the same onion, right?"

Zoe nodded hesitantly, so Calandra jumped in. "The layers are all connected."

She glanced at Airlea, remembering the girl's theory on the path. Airlea's gaze lingered on Calandra, and she realized the other girl was judging her frame of mind. Shame for how she'd been behaving welled in her, and her heart sped up. The pain in her head increased in intensity.

"You guessed it," Valac crowed. "Except the layers of the cosmos aren't actu'lly wrapped around each other. They kind of move through each other"—he demonstrated by jamming his hands together, interlocking his fingers—"but since they're different planes, nobody on one plane sees people on another plane. They're just all in the same space at the same time without messing each other up. Well, most of the time . . ."

Calandra shook her head, completely confused.

"You mean," said Airlea hesitantly, studying the drawing, "the distance between Elysium and the Abyss is more metaphysical than physical?"

He bounced on his toes, and his wings fluttered a little. "Yes! That's it! Metterphys'cal!"

"So this cave could be in the same space as some place back home, like the Opal Palace?" Calandra asked. She frowned. It seemed to make it easier to concentrate.

Valac tilted his head back and forth noncommittally. "Yeah, except it might share space with the Opal Palace one second and the Vatican the next. The layers are always moving around. Have you seen a gyroscope?"

The three young women shook their heads.

Valac began drawing short lines between his onion layers, connecting them to each other. But while each layer's lines were opposite each other, the lines of the next layer were always lined up in a completely different place.

"A gyroscope is a whole bunch of rings that are connected together, but each ring can turn ind'pendently of the other rings."

He took his finger and ran it across the shape as though pulling it, and the lines began to spin and whirl, all in different directions around the axes he'd created for them.

"Whoa," said Airlea.

Calandra stared, stunned at his light show. Even Zoe looked impressed.

"What's the messy cloud you drew around the outside?" Airlea asked, pointing.

"That's the ether. Basic'lly chaos. The further you get from the Essence at the centre, the closer you get to chaos." He shuddered. "That's why Tartarus is on the outside edge. Hardly any Essence gets out that far, and it's just plain miser'ble without it."

"Where's my mother?" Calandra asked.

The spinning white light rings had started to slow, and Valac jabbed his finger into a spot between the outer two layers near the bottom of the onion, leaving a red dot behind. "Right about here."

"And where's Zale?"

He frowned, studying the onion, obviously concentrating. "I don't know exactly. Ta— . . . Delphine said he's wearing a shield, and I can't sense him."

"Can you sense my sister?" Zoe asked. "Damaris?"

After a moment, Valac smiled. "Yep. She's here, in the Sleepless Swamp." He jabbed another ring further in, leaving another little dot. "And we're here."

He poked the next ring closer to the centre, setting it spinning again. Calandra watched the red dots move around, rarely coming within any proximity to each other.

"The river connects the planes, right?" She pointed at his spinning drawing. "Along those connection points." A sharp throb stabbed her temple, and she winced.

Valac gave her a sidelong glance, then looked at the spinning rings. "Yep, but that's the long way 'round. Portstones let you jump from one plane to just about any place on another."

The whirling rings were slowing down, just as though they were made of metal subject to natural laws and not light drawn in air.

Zoe glared at them. "Then why did Delphine have us take the river out of the cavern? Why didn't she just have us use a portstone to go straight to Zale?"

Valac sighed. He flicked the edge of the drawing with his middle finger and it dissolved into a shower of sparkling white dust. Then he sat down.

"That's because there isn't a portstone in Elyon's Keep anymore. Hasn't been for a long time. Not since the guardians in the Pool of Tears stopped healing the Soulstone like they were s'posed to and Uriel had it deactivated, just in case. Now the only way out of the cavern is through the river."

"What about the way in? We were able to port straight there."

He nodded. "Yeah, you can port in—but only into the cavern. No one can port into the Well of Souls, nor the Pool of Tears, neither—you have to port into the Chamber of Tears, then swim down to the well. Of course, to get into the well, you have to get past Leviathan. If you ask me, I think that's why the guardians stopped going into the well in the first place—they forgot how to tame him."

Airlea came and sat next to Calandra, pulling her ankles inward. With the three of them on the floor, they formed a nearly perfect circle. Zoe ignored the space they'd left for her and returned her attention to the forest outside.

"Do you know why the Soulstone is in the Well of Souls in the first place?" Calandra asked.

"Oh, sure!" Valac grinned. "It's because winged spirits like me hate water. And all the Grigori are erelim." At their blank looks, he explained, "Aerial spirits, made of light or fire."

Calandra blinked. "So the Soulstone is in the well, what, just in case any of the Grigori get out? Then the water will trap them?"

He shrugged and fidgeted with his toes. "I guess so. And the Leviathan will too."

Not for the first time, Calandra wondered how Damon had gotten access to her and escaped his prison, especially with all these security measures in place.

"The Leviathan must be the big creature we saw when we looked through the grate," Airlea said.

Calandra nodded. Her head was completely clear now, but the pain of the bonds increased by the second, and she was feeling inexplicably morose. "That thing looked impossible to get past. No wonder the undines stopped going into the well."

"Then how did your mother get in?" Airlea wondered.

Calandra blinked at her. How *did* Delphine get through the grate, then past the Leviathan, and become trapped in the Soulstone? Had she had keys, or had she somehow convinced Nadia to open the grate for her? And had she been extraordinarily lucky in getting past the Leviathan at the right moment, or had she found the secret to tame it, like Valac had said? Maybe she'd waited until it was sleeping. If anyone could find a way to do it, Calandra was sure her mother could. But why hadn't she mentioned all this earlier? A chill tightened her chest—maybe Delphine didn't remember. She'd seemed a little unclear on a few other things Calandra had brought up.

"Do you know how she did it?" she asked Valac.

He shook his head. "I never asked. She always visits me when she wants to talk, if'n I'm close enough, and I never wondered how she got in there in the first place."

"I don't suppose there's another way into the Well of Souls," Calandra said. "Perhaps from the bottom. The river has to go somewhere from there."

He nodded. "Oh, it does. It comes out through a hole in a cliff in Hell's Gate. That's a chamber at the entrance to hell. But no one can get up into the well that way. It would be impossible."

"I thought we were already in hell," Zoe said.

He giggled. "Nope. Let's see, by the terms you undines use, this plane would be . . . the Asphodel Meadows."

Zoe glared outside. "It's not a meadow. And there are no asphodel flowers."

Valac shrugged. "I never said you named it right. We call it the Forgetful Forest. Tartarus proper begins with the Abyss at the Pool of Tears, where the other undines are, and below the Abyss, which includes the Well of Souls, there's hell." He drew his finger through the sand on the floor in a meandering pattern, punctuating his instructions with jabs at descending locations. "It's not any fun there."

The pain had become quite intense, and Calandra found her patience for chatter waning. She gritted her teeth. Maybe she should get Airlea to use the stone on her again. "So we need to find a way into the well somehow if we're going to free my mother. What do you suggest?"

He looked up, his gold-flecked eyes glittering. "You and your brother should blast that Leviathan to little pieces, and then do the same for the Soulstone." He made a sound like an explosion with his mouth, moving his hands apart to demonstrate. Little sparks of light appeared between them in a miniature starburst.

Calandra sat back, startled at this sudden image of violence. Besides her objections to breaking open the prison holding others like Damon, she shuddered at the idea of killing another creature for anything but food, even the monster standing between her and her mother. If she had to, could she do it?

But that wasn't even the first obstacle.

"What about the portal?" she asked. "I saw the key on Nadia—"

"On who?" Airlea's gaze snapped to hers.

"The leader of those undines," Calandra said. "She wore Nadia's crest on her forehead, didn't you see? And she had the crystal key for the grate around her neck."

"Chains of Prometheus," Airlea breathed. "I never imagined. It makes sense, I guess, but, I mean, wow."

Valac tilted his head, looking thoughtful. "Well, I guess you could ask her nicely."

Zoe snorted, leaning against the wall with her arms crossed. "She didn't seem to be the listening type."

The boy leaned forward, his impish smile suddenly becoming sinister. "Then I guess you'll have to kill her too. Same with the others if they get in your way."

Calandra swallowed, staring at the murderous un-child with the face of an angel before her. Where had that come from?

A stab of pain sliced through her brain, and she doubled over, screeching.

"Quiet!" hissed Zoe. "Airlea, shut her up, or that creature will find us, for sure!"

Airlea rushed over and placed her hand on Calandra's forehead, already singing her song, but it barely even touched the pain. Writhing in agony, Calandra held out the stone to her.

"No," Airlea said. "That thing seems dangerous."

Calandra let out another cry and collapsed on the floor, writhing in agony.

"Take it, please. Use it," she gasped.

Airlea hesitated a moment longer, then, when Calandra screamed again, snatched it from her hand, held it to Calandra's forehead, and hummed.

The relief was instantaneous, though not quite so thorough as before. The floaty feeling was back—but this time, instead of flying high above anything that might distress her, she could still sense her pain and sorrow below the cloud of bliss, waiting to envelop her as soon as she sank back into reach. She sat up, staring at Airlea gratefully.

"Thank you, Airlea." She held out her hand for the stone.

Airlea studied her, hesitating. Calandra frowned.

"Give it back, please."

Airlea looked at Valac, who was watching the exchange with intense interest, a small smile on his face.

"Airlea!" Calandra said sternly.

Making a sound of disapproval, Airlea smacked the stone into Calandra's palm and leapt to her feet. "I'm going to go see what's happening outside." With a final glare at Valac, she whirled and padded beyond view through the cave entrance.

Calandra clasped the stone to her breast, caressing it. Zoe cast her a look of disgust, then followed Airlea.

"It doesn't work as well after the first time," Valac said. "You can tell, can't you?"

Calandra stroked the stone, then glanced at the boy and nodded, wishing it weren't true.

Valac leaned forward. "There's a way to take away the pain permanently, you know."

Her gaze snapped up. "There is? How?"

He smiled. "You have to put the stone in your mouth and sing the Song of Redemption. Then you have to swallow it."

She stared at him. That seemed so simple, and she was tempted to try it right then, to remove the vestiges of the headache that still plagued her—and the heart-crushing sorrow that was knocking on the edges of the euphoria, trying to get in. But his earlier alarming comments made her think twice about taking his word at face value. Why the Song of Redemption, the song used to enslave the minds of men and create the *sklavia* bond? That normally didn't work on women, but you normally couldn't use any song on yourself either. What was it this stone did, really?

And what did she actually know about this child-like spirit? Nothing, other than that her mother had sent him. That didn't mean everything he said was trustworthy. As she thought about it, she realized that, despite his constant mirth, she could sense a deep vacancy in his soul—not that she couldn't sense him at all, because she could. It was just as though parts of him were missing. Misgiving filled her.

"Thanks. I'll . . . I'll remember that."

With effort, she placed the stone into her pouch beside the two Atlantean datastones. The fact that her crystal was no longer there brought

Osaze's face to mind, and the sadness seeped through.

Disappointment flashed across Valac's face before fading to his typical dimpled grin.

Airlea and Zoe returned.

"That griffin is still making circles up there," Airlea said.

She crouched next to Calandra, looking her over.

"I'm all right," Calandra assured her, though she wasn't certain it was true. She felt better than she had a few minutes ago, but nowhere near as giddy as she had earlier that day. At least she wouldn't be stumbling around and making a fool of herself this time.

Zoe stood near the entrance, her arms crossed. "He doesn't look like he's going anywhere anytime soon. I think we should get some rest."

Calandra nodded, already looking around for a comfortable place to lie down. Rest sounded amazing.

Before she nodded off, though, she slipped the stone out of her pouch and clasped it in her hand. Just in case.

*

CALANDRA woke up in a sweat. In her dream, she'd watched Tanni fall at Adonia's hand over and over again, with Calandra helpless to do anything to stop it. Her head felt like it was going to explode. She panted, trying to get the pain under control, but nothing she did helped.

Near her, Zoe lay sleeping. Valac was nowhere to be seen, and she could sense Airlea's steady presence outside near the cave mouth, probably keeping guard.

She wheezed, her hands trembling from the strain of moving when she hurt so much. Something clattered on the stone floor and she moved her head to look—the healing stone Valac had given her.

She stared at it, drawn to it as if by a magnetic force. The smooth white pebble offered her relief, and that was what she needed. She thought about calling Airlea to use it on her again as she had before, but she remembered the hesitation in the girl's eyes. No, Airlea wouldn't want to do it again. She hadn't wanted to do it last time. Maybe Zoe?

She nudged the sleeping figure, but Zoe didn't stir. After a harder push with the same result, Calandra gave up. She could sense Zoe—the siren was still alive, but in the deep slumber of the utterly exhausted.

Another spasm of pain rocked through her. She arched her back, us-ing all her concentration to keep from lashing out with the elements. The stone floor beneath her vibrated, and above her, hairline cracks appeared in the ceiling.

No! I mustn't!

The force built inside, threatening to burst out of her like a volcano. If she couldn't control it, this wouldn't result in just a few tumbled boulders and some cracks—she could collapse the whole cave. Somehow, she doubted it would heal itself in time to save her and Zoe's lives.

With a trembling hand, she slowly brought the small white stone to her mouth. Laying on her back spread-eagle with her clawed fingers clutching the floor, she pressed the stone to the roof of her mouth with her tongue and hummed the song she'd sung thousands of times while creating the very bonds that now tormented her. Then she swallowed.

The pain stopped like it had never existed. Bliss spread from her brain through every vein in her body and she sighed, releasing all the tension she'd carried moments before. Blinking, she sat up and looked around.

The cave was different. It was full of light, but she couldn't tell where the light came from. Where was she? She couldn't quite remember.

There was someone sleeping next to her, a woman. Calandra didn't recognize her. She bent close to the woman's face, trying to puzzle out her identity.

"Calandra," called a wistful female voice somewhere in the distance.

Where had that come from? She looked around, trying to locate who'd called her. When she heard her name again, she leapt to her feet.

"Tanni?" she whispered.

How was it possible? She drifted to the door of the cave and out into the light-flooded jungle beyond, searching for her dead friend.

62

THE GRIFFIN

CALANDRA DRIFTED THROUGH A BLISSFUL haze, looking for the source of the voice. No matter how far she walked, it was always just out of reach.

"Tanni, I'm coming!"

The trees stood out in sharp lines, their fronds greener than seemed possible, smelling of the sweetest perfume. The light pervaded everything, shining through leaves and making each vine come alive.

A figure came toward her out of the glaring white, blurry at first, but then coming into focus.

Calandra stopped, her heart full to bursting. There before her, smiling the smile Calandra missed so much, was Tanni, the girl who had been closer than a sister for most of her life, despite their enforced separation for the past five years. She looked as she always had—her thick black hair pulled back into a poofy queue, her siren's uniform crisp and tidy, her dark green eyes alive with joy.

"Tanni, it's you!" Tears streamed down Calandra's face, and she let them. "How is this possible? Am I dead?"

Tanni grinned. "No, silly, you're not dead. But you are in the Underworld, remember?"

Calandra nodded happily. That's right. She'd forgotten. "So this is where you're living now? What's it like?"

Tanni wrapped her arms around herself. "I'm happy. This place isn't so bad, you know? But I came to tell you something. Something important. Are you listening?"

Calandra nodded. There was nothing Tanni asked of her that she wouldn't do.

528

"Good. You need to destroy the Soulstone. Nothing else matters. Do you understand? You must destroy it."

The weight of Tanni's conviction pressed against her. Calandra swallowed and nodded. "Of course. Whatever you say."

"And if an emissary of Elyon tells you otherwise, you must ignore them. They are your enemy."

"Yes, Tanni. I trust you."

Tanni smiled. "I knew I could count on you."

Tanni disappeared, and the path before Calandra stood out clearly among the light-flooded surroundings, demanding her attention. *I have to destroy the Soulstone.* She began walking purposefully toward the river, intent on returning to the glowing blue orb as soon as possible.

A hand grabbed Calandra by the arm, spinning her around. A girl with big green eyes and close-cropped brown hair framing a heart-shaped face looked at her with concern. It took a moment for Calandra to understand the words she was saying, but the girl's distress was obvious.

"Calandra, wake up! Please, wake up!"

Calandra pushed the girl's hand away and turned back to face the trail.

The girl spun her around again, grabbed her by both arms, and shook her.

Calandra blinked, and the forest returned to its ordinary limp, life-less green touched with golden light, saturated with the stench of rotting plants. Airlea looked at her with wide, concerned eyes.

"Airlea. Where am I? What . . . ?" Calandra looked around at the forest. How had she gotten here? She'd just been talking to Tanni, hadn't she? Tanni had wanted her to do something . . .

"Calandra, are you all right?" Airlea looked her over. "You walked out of the cave and started down the trail, but you weren't listening to me. It was like you couldn't even hear me. Were you sleep-walking?"

Calandra swallowed. She'd often had a hard time sleeping, but she'd never actually sleep-walked that she knew of. "I . . . I don't know. Maybe."

She stared around at the forest of soul-filled trees. Was Tanni caught inside one of these trees? Surely not. She'd sacrificed her life for Calandra, for the cause they fought for. If anyone deserved Elysium, it was her courageous friend. She must have been dreaming. What had Tanni wanted her to do?

"I have to destroy the Soulstone," she murmured.

"What's that?" Airlea asked.

She repeated herself, louder, and Airlea frowned. "What about the

Grigori? I thought you were going to find another way."

"There is no other way," Calandra said sharply.

Airlea blinked at her in hurt surprise. "That's what your mother said, and you argued with her."

Calandra pressed her lips together. Airlea was right. Why did it seem so important now?

A huge shadow fell over them, and Airlea looked up in alarm.

"Ophiuchus found us," Airlea shouted. "Run!"

The enormous griffin swooped toward them, claws extended. Airlea grabbed Calandra's arm to tug her back to the cave, but it was already too late. The enormous beast set down in front of them, blocking their retreat to safety. Airlea froze, then whirled and pointed behind Calandra.

"That way! Quick!"

But Calandra didn't run. She stood and stared into the red eye peering down at them from the cocked hawk-like head, mesmerized by its depths. Though the beast looked monstrous, she sensed no malice at all. Instead, the griffin emanated only wary caution and sharp curiosity.

She stepped forward, hand extended with the palm out. As she did, she projected calm as she had done many times for animals and people, though she'd always been touching them before. She hoped this worked.

"I am Calandra of the undines," she said in a low, soothing voice. "I mean you no harm."

The griffin blinked and twisted its head in jerky movements.

Airlea watched her, frozen, and glanced at the beast, which lowered its enormous head to get a closer look at its prey.

"Your highness . . ." she said in warning.

Calandra took another step forward and stopped, waiting.

The griffin's form began to shift, the great head shrinking, its talons transforming into a man's feet and hands, and its posture becoming upright. Calandra stepped back. Before their eyes, the griffin changed into a tall man with a slim, athletic build, golden eyes, a long, sharp nose, and golden-brown skin beneath a shock of black hair. He wore a belted garment fashioned completely of golden feathers that hung from one shoulder and fell to just above the knee, revealing muscular thighs. Above his sandalled feet were two burnished bronze greaves covered in intricate knot-work designs, and matching bracers covered his forearms. Two reddish-gold feathered wings curled against his back.

Calandra and Airlea stared at him in astonishment. This was the first time Calandra had ever seen one of the lumasi, the flying race of spirits she'd thought were extinct until Zale had told her about his friends Abela and Berian. Other than Valac, she supposed—*was* Valac a lumasi? She had no idea. Now that Ophiuchus had transformed, he was both more impressive and less terrifying than she'd expected. Nothing like the chubby boy-spirit.

"Greetings, Calandra of the undines," he said. "I am Kassiel Ophiuchus. I have been looking for you."

"You have?" Calandra blinked. "You don't mean to attack us?"

He gave a small smile. "Indeed not. I have a message for you. Be strong and courageous, for the Spirit of Elyon is with you."

The hair on Calandra's arms stood on end, and something in her gut twisted. "I'm afraid you're mistaken, sir. The Spirit of the Mother guides me."

The man's face darkened. "This *Mother* you speak of is no more than an impostor who has taken the glory that rightfully belongs to Elyon for herself. She has long deceived your race, and the time has come to undeceive you. The Shield of Elyon you bear gives testimony to the presence of the Pneuma in you. Why do you persist in your false beliefs?"

As he spoke, anger grew in Calandra's belly and she glared at the man. "How dare you? The Mother has always guided and protected her daughters, even when we have chosen wrong ways and created much travail for ourselves. It is by the Mother's grace we will find the right ways once more. That is why *she* has chosen me."

Ophiuchus stepped toward her, his face softening. Calandra tensed, despite the unadulterated compassion coming from him. She didn't know why, but she didn't trust him.

"Atargatis, the spirit you worship, is also known as Tamiel. She is one of the imprisoned Grigori your kind was set to guard in the Abyss. Like Semyaza and Azazel and her other co-conspirators in the rebellion of old, they sought to lord themselves above those they had been created to serve and to usurp the throne of Heaven itself, and are now reaping the consequences. However, they ever seek to escape their bonds."

Calandra clenched her fists. This man had some nerve—now he claimed that the Holy Mother was of the same ilk as Damon? She half-expected Atargatis to strike him down for his blasphemies right there.

"Who were the Grigori created to serve?" Airlea asked, glancing back and forth between Calandra and the winged man.

"Humans, of course," Ophiuchus replied. "And it was not only the Grigori who were tasked with this purpose, but all of the races—including the undines."

"What?" Calandra stepped back, outraged. Now she knew why she didn't trust him—only an enemy would claim the race they had feared so long, who had hunted them nearly to extinction and wreaked so much havoc on the Earth, was meant to be their masters. "You lie."

He shook his head. "I never lie. Though much has gone awry, the races of light, fire, and water were meant to guide and protect the youngest race, the race of clay."

"Where is your proof?" Calandra demanded, her hand on the hilt of her belt knife.

"Your highness," Airlea said, laying a hand on Calandra's arm. Calm flowed through it, warring with another force in her belly. She snatched her arm away and glared at her companion.

"Leave me alone!" Calandra snapped, and Airlea jerked her hand back, hurt flashing from her.

Ophiucus glanced at Calandra's hand, then inclined his head. "You do not need to fear me, daughter of Aikaterini. I will not harm you. You *should* fear the deceiving worm in your midst, the demon Valac. He has long been an associate of Tamiel, and has probably been sent to deceive you. I'm only sorry I didn't find you sooner so I could give you fair warning. I pray you haven't—"

"You *lie!*" Anger raged through Calandra's veins, and she raised her hands, ready to call air and earth and blast this deceiver and blasphemer away from them. "Valac is my friend. He helped me more than anyone else ever has. How *dare* you?"

She let loose, picking up stones and moss with earth and air and anger and hurling them at the man. Ophiuchus expertly ducked and wove, deflecting oncoming matter with his bracers, protecting his head with upraised arms while he drew nearer to her, leaning into the wind. No matter what she threw at him, he continued his steady progress forward.

"Airlea, help me!" Calandra called.

Airlea hesitated, her brows drawn in concern. "Calandra, stop. I believe him. He means us no harm."

"How can you say that after what he just said about Atargatis and Valac?" She braced herself, connecting to the earth around them through her bare feet, and worked on loosening a huge clod of dirt from the path to hurl at her attacker.

"Valac has a sweet face and a viper's cunning," Airlea said. "I believe Ophiuchus's words about him. The boy is not here to help us."

Calandra cast an irate glance at the girl, which was her undoing. With a mighty effort, Ophiuchus pushed forward the last few steps and placed the flat of his hand against her belly.

Abruptly, Calandra's stomach heaved, and she ceased her assault to clutch it. Turning aside, she doubled over and retched. When she'd finished, a small white stone lay in the mess she'd deposited alongside the trail, and her head had once more begun to throb.

Ophiuchus bent and picked up the stone, wiping it on the grass. "It is as I feared. Valac intended to control you with this bliss stone."

Airlea stared at it, then looked at Calandra, her expression a mix of shock and disappointment. Calandra wiped her wet mouth with the back of her hand and glared back.

"Don't look at me that way. You have no idea what it's like to go through every moment of every day besieged by pain and heartache. That stone is the only thing I've found that's offered any respite at all. Whatever you were doing was barely helping."

Airlea put her hands on her hips. "What about in the Pool of Tears? What happened then?" she asked. "You went from torment to peace in a matter of moments."

Calandra frowned. She had, indeed—after calling on the Spirit that guided her. And that peace had come without the cost of losing her wits. She glanced warily at the man, unwilling to admit as much.

"Who is this Elyon you all seem to know so well here?" This time, the mention of Elyon's name caused no surge of rage or anger—but a severe exhaustion pulled at her.

Ophiuchus closed his fist over the stone and grasped his wrist in his other hand, standing erect and at ease. "Elyon is the Creator of all. It is his essence that runs throughout the universe. By him we live and breathe and have our being. Where Elyon is not, there is no life, just everlasting death. And he has chosen you and your brother to awaken the undine race to their true purpose once more."

Calandra sighed. "And what purpose is that?"

Ophiuchus inclined his head, studying her. "I believe you already know."

She did. The words came unbidden to her lips. "We're the guardians of Elyon's Keep. It is our duty to tend the Soulstone and guard those it imprisons."

He nodded gravely. "Yes. And to serve as guides and protectors of the seas and the ways of the deep."

The weight of her task fell heavy on her, and she took a faltering step back. Airlea looked as confounded as she felt.

"How can we have forgotten something so important?" she whispered.

"Great deceptions often don't begin that way," Ophiuchus said solemnly. "They start small, with a lie based on partial truth so it sounds plausible. Once a few people believe the small lie, more error can be added on top of it, until what remains is so far from the truth, it is barely recognizable. Over time, these lies become ensconced in tradition, and no one even questions them anymore."

"Like Redeeming the men," Calandra said, her voice tight.

She could see the thought progression of her ancestors as though it had been laid out before her—*humans are cruel. Men are violent. They persecute us. Therefore we must protect ourselves. The easiest way to do that is to enslave them. Maybe the only way to do it.* She didn't know how the lie had begun that men were any more dangerous than women. But someone had started it. In the right circumstances, propelled by the right person, that lie could easily be spread throughout a nation and beyond. It would take some time to see the consequences of the lie, but by the time her ancestors realized they were no longer producing boys, that effect could have been laid at the feet of any number of things. Without men to work with the women in unity, the Heartstone had begun to fail, and, apparently, so had the Soulstone, weakening the very barriers and bonds their kind had been charged with maintaining.

Who would benefit from a lie like that?

She knew exactly who. Those who were imprisoned.

And she also knew who had spread that lie—Damon. He'd told her he'd once been Alessandro, king-consort of Nadia, the first woman in their history to go Mad. Damon must have taken over Alessandro, Calandra's flesh-and-blood ancestor, much as he'd possessed Narcissa. Except by the time Nadia had enslaved her consort, Damon's damage must have been done. He'd been re-imprisoned somehow afterward, and there were still other missing pieces to that puzzle, but Calandra could see more of the picture clearly.

And now that Damon had once more escaped his chains, the fruit of his previous deception was paying off . . . the Heartstone and the Soulstone were both failing and weak, ready to collapse and release the Grigori on an unsuspecting world.

"I have to destroy the Soulstone," she said absently.

"Pardon?" said Airlea.

Calandra looked at her, tears pricking at the back of her eyes. "I thought I saw Tanni while I was sleepwalking, and she told me I had to destroy the Soulstone. But that's what Valac wants. Valac, and . . ."

"Delphine," Airlea finished for her. "Calandra, I'm sorry, but that wasn't Tanni."

Calandra saw the same realization in Airlea's eyes that she'd just had.

"I know. And that wasn't my mother we saw in the crystal cavern either, was it?" She wiped away a tear and turned to face Ophiuchus. "Besides Damon, have any of the other Grigori already escaped?"

Ophiuchus cocked his head. "Damon?"

"A red dragon. I don't know another name for him. I think he possessed my ancestor Alessandro, king-consort of Nadia, queen of the undines, around three millennia ago. He has recently escaped once more, and is now possessing my cousin, Narcissa."

Understanding lit the man's face, and he raised his thick black brows. "Ah. Semyaza. I wonder how he got out this time."

Calandra's face felt hot, and she hoped Ophiuchus wouldn't notice her blush. She still didn't know quite how Damon had done it, but she knew he had used her to escape his prison and felt responsible, even if she'd never intended for that to happen.

"As far as I know," Ophiuchus continued, "none of the other Grigori have escaped, but with the failing of the bonds in the Abyss, Tamiel has found a way to project an image into our realm, and has won many sympathizers to her and her companions' plight. Uriel is aware of her activities, but unless the Soulstone is repaired, there is little that can be done about it. Perhaps it was her you saw."

Calandra's mouth went dry. "Why did she look like my mother?"

Ophiuchus sighed. "Normally, bending light is a power reserved for the cherubim, but some of the seraphim, like Semyaza, have also learned the ability. It would seem Tamiel has also discovered the method."

"Tamiel. The woman you say has been posing as Atargatis all this time?" Airlea asked.

Ophiuchus frowned. "She is not simply posing as Atargatis—that is one of her names. It is thanks to Tamiel that the undines stopped serving Elyon and hardened the barrier to my kind, which is why we've been unable to correct this error for so long."

Calandra's heart beat faster. She wished she could sense deception from him so she could discredit his words, but there was none. He believed everything he said. Worse than that, *she* was starting to believe it.

Then she thought of another puzzle piece—the empty room in Atlantis and the images of the worship service on the sapphire Tear where the Mother's likeness was so glaringly absent. Could it be? Could her ancestors, alongside all those other races, have been worshipping this invisible Creator, Elyon, the Essence whom Kassiel Ophiuchus claimed permeated everything?

Thunderstruck, she had one more alarming thought. As a panacea, she knew exactly what connected all of creation—the spirit element was the most ubiquitous and easily accessible of any of the five, and rare was the undine who couldn't detect it. Could that be what Ophiuchus meant by the Essence of Creation?

No. If he was right about that, that meant he was also right about Atargatis, and the Spirit whose voice she had so often heeded. But he *couldn't* be right about that. She wouldn't let him be.

She shook her head, her throat tight. The bonds flared red and hot in her mind, and she clenched her teeth in pain, her breath coming quick and shallow as she tried to subdue it.

The man looked at her compassionately. "You bear such a heavy burden, Calandra of the undines, but you need not. Elyon is gracious and merciful to his children. You have only to ask, and he will free you of your bonds."

She shook her head. It sounded so easy, and she knew she should believe him—the Spirit had already answered such a call once to provide temporary relief. But she was afraid. If it worked—if the Spirit answered such a request—what would that mean for her, her island, and everything she'd ever believed? "Why should I believe anything you say?"

Ophiuchus regarded her steadily. "It is not my task to convince you to believe me. The Pneuma has already provided you plenty of evidence. You either trust in Elyon or you don't. But consider this—I have done nothing to try to manipulate you into doing as I say. I have only told you truth. As far as what you do with it, the choice is yours. Even if you choose wilful oblivion and to let someone else do the choosing."

He opened his fist, revealing the white stone and offering it to her. Hesitantly, she reached out and took it from him, staring at it for a moment before wrapping her fist around it. The compulsion to consume it once more and be free of her torment pulsed through her veins, and her hand shook.

"Calandra . . ." Airlea said in warning, shaking her head, eyes wide with alarm. "Don't."

The stone was hard in Calandra's hand, offering relief from the pain that clouded her vision. She looked away from Airlea and drew in a trembling breath, raising her hand to her mouth.

But what if what Ophiuchus said was true, and Valac intended to control her with the stone? What damage could be done with her abilities if she were not in control of her own mind? She didn't dare risk it. Closing her eyes, she lowered her hand and concentrated on the stone. When she opened her hand again, the bliss stone was nothing more than a pile of dust on her palm. Relief rolled from Airlea.

Ophiuchus nodded in somber approval. "You have done well, daughter of Aikaterini. To be free of the worm himself, you must use your gift of song to repel him. Praise the Creator and he will flee from you."

"What about my mother?" Calandra said. "She is trapped in the Soulstone, and I have no key."

"What leads you to believe that?"

Calandra opened her mouth to reply, then froze. She'd first heard of Delphine's location from Damon. That had been confirmed by her mother—who, she now realized, must be Tamiel, not Delphine. Regardless of whether Ophiuchus's claims about Tamiel's identity as Atargatis were true, the evidence pointed to the spirit impersonating Delphine to deceive Calandra and get what she and Damon wanted—the freedom of their kind by destroying the Soulstone. And the final confirmation of Delphine's location had been Valac, who was also in league with Tamiel. What if everything had been a lie? Was her mother even in Hades?

No. Zale had been the one to tell Calandra their mother was here, and he'd heard it from his lumasi friends, who were most definitely not working with Damon. Besides, when Calandra had been in the Pool of Tears, she could have sworn she heard her mother calling her. Maybe Tamiel was using her mother's image as bait, but that didn't mean she was lying about Delphine's location.

"I . . . I heard her." She glanced at Airlea. "In the Pool of Tears. While we were looking at the Soulstone, I heard someone call my name, and before that, too, in the tunnels. I'm sure it was my mother—my actual mother, not the impostor."

Airlea hesitated, then nodded. "Okay."

Ophiuchus inclined his head in acknowledgement. "The intuition of the undines is still widely known among my kind, so if you believe this to be true, I trust your word. You may be interested to know that my associate Rumiel has uncovered the method Delphine used to mask the frequencies of you, your brother, and herself from our finders. But even though he has found a way to work around it, the result is much less accurate than we'd like. From that, we have confirmed Delphine kor'Helena is, indeed, in the Abyss somewhere. We couldn't locate her with more accuracy than that."

"Can't you just go in there and find out?" Calandra asked.

He shook his head. "Thanks to the decline of the undine guardians, Uriel long ago sealed the lower gates of Elyon's Keep, which was directly accessible from the ceiling of the cavern where the Pool of Tears is located. We can port in and out of the cavern with a chariot—that is a small hand-held portstone usually reserved for use on the Ground—but my kind still cannot access what is sealed by the waters below. Your ancestors designed the prison well."

Calandra stared at him. "My . . . my ancestors *designed* the Abyss?"

"Yes." Ophiuchus smiled. "They were brilliant designers and architects. That's why Elyon entrusted the task to them."

No wonder the Mother's Heart chamber, the Well of Souls, and the Voidstone chamber in Atlantis were all so similar. She felt a strange pride that her ancestors had been given such a task, but it was quickly overcome with the distress of knowing they'd failed at it terribly for millennia—and knowing the origin of the Soulstone didn't resolve her problem.

"I still don't know how Mother accessed the Soulstone in the first place," Calandra said, "but I'm certain she's there. If Tamiel is as manipulative as Da—Semyaza is, then she could have tricked my mother into believing she must enter it. And one thing I do know about my mother—if she believes something must be done, she'll go to the ends of the world to do it."

Ophiuchus frowned. "It would appear that now, Tamiel is trying to use her to lure you and your brother to her own ends, as well—to convince you that in order to free her, you must destroy the Soulstone. Judging from what Valac and Tamiel said, they want to use you to break their remaining bonds and free the rest of their kind from prison."

"It does seem that way," Calandra agreed. It was a smart plan, and she cursed how well Semyaza knew her—if it came down to destroying the Soulstone or saving their mother, Calandra wasn't sure which one she'd choose. Which duty was stronger? "This would be easily resolved if we had the appropriate keys. I don't suppose you know where we might find those?"

Ophiuchus gave her a kind look over his hawkish nose. "No, and neither can I tell you how to free your mother—that is beyond my knowledge and purview. You must work it out with the help of the Pneuma. That brings me to the message I was sent to bring you: you and your brother have been brought here for a single purpose—to restore the Soulstone and renew the bonds that have been failing for so long. Ask for wisdom, and the Pneuma will provide it. Trust the path down which your heart guides you."

He clasped his hands in front of his chest with a firm motion in an odd gesture of respect that reminded Calandra of one of the blocks in the *Tropos Hydor Zon*. Calandra frowned. What did he mean, they were *brought* here? By whom? He obviously didn't mean the machinations of Tamiel and Semyaza. But if it weren't for them, she and Zale wouldn't be here at all.

But, aside from who brought them, now she was being given *another* task? She shook her head, everything in her rebelling at the responsibility.

"I'm sorry, but I can't heal the Soulstone. I was already supposed to heal the Heartstone, and I couldn't even succeed at that, not even with Zale's help. I'll be lucky if I get Zale to work with me to free Mother, let alone work together on restoring the Soulstone. You've chosen the wrong person. All I want to do is find my brother, find my mother, and find a way to get us all out of the Underworld."

Ophiuchus gave a small smile. "Elyon is with you, daughter of Aikaterini. The time is coming when you will be called upon to lead many to redemption. But first, you must learn to heed his voice." He stepped toward her and placed his right hand on her right shoulder in a strange gesture of camaraderie. "The prayers of the holy erelim will be with you. May Elyon uphold you in his mighty right hand."

Sensing the interview was over, Calandra pressed her bunched fingers to her forehead and bowed at the shoulders. But without her normal invocations of the Mother, she was at a loss as to how to bless him. She settled for an awkward, "Thank you."

But she wasn't grateful. She was reeling from all he'd just told her, staggering under the weight of the responsibility he'd laid on her.

How was she supposed to free her mother from behind two locked doors with no keys and without destroying the lock, but rather *fixing* it?

Beside her, Airlea gave a deep salute to the griffin-lamassu before he turned and walked away. His feathered tunic clung to his growing, changing form more with every step, melding and covering his warm brown skin, until he was once more the golden lion-like griffin. Ophiuchus padded a few paces along the path before turning his great hawk head to regard her with one red eye. Then he leapt away and broke into flight, his powerful wings creating a down draft that blew dust and debris into Calandra's and Airlea's faces.

Calandra lifted her arms to shield herself from the swirling leaves and dirt, and when she dropped them, Kassiel Ophiuchus was no more than a small figure in the white, sunless sky.

Calandra fought the urge to crumple to the ground right then and there.

"How do you think he does that with his clothes?" Airlea asked. "Is it a special fabric do you think, or does he make them with his mind when he transforms?"

Calandra stared blankly at her. "What?"

Airlea tore her gaze from the sky. "His clothes. They just appear out of nowhere when he changes to *podia* state, or whatever erelim call it. How does he do that?"

Calandra glared at her. "*That's* what you're thinking about? At a time like this? When I'm apparently supposed to save the world *again*? Why does everyone keep expecting me to do that?"

She spun and crossed her arms, scanning the path back toward the river and taking slow breaths to try and still her racing heart and aching head.

Airlea stood in silence for several moments before touching Calandra's shoulder.

"You asked me earlier why I came to Hades with you." Airlea tilted her head and arched a brow. "You want to know why?"

At the moment, Calandra wasn't entirely certain she did. But she heaved a sigh and turned to face her companion.

"Why?"

Airlea hesitated before answering, looking as though she were searching for words. "Did you know my mother is discordant? Not that it matters much in our family—we're farmers, you know. My family grows cotton and flax near Serenity. My aunts are skilled plant healers, but when my grandmother died, she passed the title on to my mother. They still work the land together, and my mother is one of the most respected suppliers in the district."

Calandra frowned uncertainly. "Why are you telling me this?"

Airlea twisted her staff in her hands. "My mother is the best person I know. She would often tell my sisters and me that you don't need spirit to sense someone's character—all you need to do is watch their actions. When I was tested and selected to go to the Academy, she told me never to forget that kindness and integrity are more important than achievement and recognition, and that true courage is doing something you know is right when you have everything to lose. And I haven't."

Airlea met Calandra's gaze. "I know you and I were never very close, even though I was only a year ahead of you. But I've had ample opportunity to observe your character, Calandra kor'Delphine. Narcissa's motivation was always to get power and recognition for herself, but I watched you put others first over and over again. When you stood up in the Court of the Redeemed and risked your life to defy Adonia so our people could know the truth, I knew right then and there that I would do everything in my power to help you succeed."

Calandra regarded the girl steadily. She had no idea Airlea had been present at the Court of the Redeemed on the Harvest Moon, but it didn't surprise her—Tanni and Airlea's pod had brought in the Harvest. Still, sticking her neck out for her beliefs didn't make her a good leader. "But many of my decisions *have* been poor ones. You can say as much as you want that the revolution on Sirenia wasn't my fault, but I know it is. It never would have happened without me. If it weren't for me and my cuttle-brained ideas, no one would have died. Tanni—" Her voice broke, and she swallowed. "Tanni and Thea would still be alive."

A shadow passed over Airlea's face at the mention of Tanni's name, and then disappeared. "You can't know that. There were already revolutionary forces smoldering—you were simply the spark that lit the fire. Our nation was sick, Calandra. And when a sickness is being purged, it's messy." She shook her head, her expression soft. "I know you often doubt yourself. I suppose all great leaders do. And I know you've made mistakes. But you've also done many admirable things, Calandra kor'Delphine. I've seen what you can do when you're following your heart, and I believe in that person. That's the person I followed to the Underworld . . . and I intend to follow her out."

Calandra bit her lip. "I . . . I thought . . ." She shook her head, dropping her gaze. "This is stupid, but I thought you were here, that you'd joined the FWS, out of loyalty to Tanni. Like you were trying to take her place."

Airlea's brow furrowed. "I loved Tanni like a sister, and she always spoke highly of you. But do you honestly think I would follow you into Hades to honour a dead friend?" Moisture filled her eyes. "Tanni's gone, and I miss her every instant. But it would not honour her sacrifice to throw my own life away. No, I didn't come here for the dead, but for the living."

Calandra's throat thickened and her eyes stung with unshed tears. She repented of every unkind thing she'd ever thought about Airlea. The girl's loyalty and kindness were more than Calandra deserved.

Airlea's words about how throwing her life away would do nothing to honour Tanni burned. Calandra had briefly hoped, while under the influence of the bliss stone, that she wouldn't need to stay behind in Tartarus in order to save her people from Atlantis's fate. But now, she didn't see any way she could avoid it. She didn't know if Tanni would understand, but she wanted to think so.

There is a way, you need only ask.

She ignored the unbidden thought and forced herself to concentrate past the pain to what she must do next.

"Come, let's go get Zoe. It's time to find my brother." She turned back toward the cave. "And we'll be taking the left path."

63

TRUTH BE TOLD

As soon as Zale and Rumiel cleared the lush green jungle that blanketed the ground above the swamp, a familiar vibration buzzed through Zale.

"Calandra!" he said involuntarily, and shuddered.

"Your sister? What about her?" Rumiel asked, his deep, melodic voice rumbling into Zale's back through his chest.

"She's here. I can feel her."

"Interesting." Rumiel paused, as though absorbing this tidbit of information. "Where is she?"

Zale scanned the unending carpet of green fronds below them and shook his head. "I don't know exactly, but if I did, I'd send you somewhere else. I don't want to see her."

"I beg your pardon?"

Zale sullenly gave a small shrug, which was not an easy feat while being carried around by the armpits. The cherub took a sharp dip, and in seconds, they descended into a small clearing in the jungle that was surrounded by dense trees. Rumiel dropped Zale on the spongy moss and he sat, gulping air that smelled like a wildflower meadow compared to the swamp they'd just come from. There was still something off about the scent—like rotting plants. But that was so much better than the sulfuric stench of what he was sure were rotting souls in the swamp, he didn't care.

Rumiel stood above him with his arms crossed. Other than the golden eyes, he looked almost nothing like the man Zale knew as Berian, and it was disconcerting. Instead of fleshy jowls, there was a chiselled jaw. Instead of a pear-shaped middle, there was a trim form that had felt as hard as stone through the soft fabric of his tunic while he'd carried Zale.

No wonder Berian had always moved with such surprising grace.

"Come, boy, out with it," Rumiel said. "Why don't you want to see your sister? What's happened since I saw you last?"

At least his voice was the same. And his attitude.

Zale pulled his knees up to his chin and wrapped his arms around them. He told Rumiel about being taken by the undines and Freed by Calandra. He talked about trying to heal the Heartstone and failing, probably because Calandra planned it, and how she'd killed Thea and Tanni—her own mentor and best friend. How he thought he'd killed Calandra, but she'd been faking, and then how she'd tried to kill him in the Archive. He told Rumiel about Narcissa training him, about the other undines shunning him, about the rebellion, and about Damaris and the student rebels. And then he told Berian how he'd decided to come here to save Delphine himself, but Damaris had come, too, and now she was in danger because of him.

Through all this, Rumiel's expression didn't change. He just nodded and made encouraging sounds for Zale to continue, or asked the occasional clarifying question.

"So," the cherub said at last, "you don't want to see your sister because you think she tried to kill you."

"She *did* try to kill me." Zale pounded the moss next to him. "Why does everyone keep saying it's all in my head?"

Rumiel squatted next to Zale. "Because, boy, I'm afraid it is. I can see the web on you plain as day—thanks to your Shield, it's not rooted to your soul, but whomever made this has done a fine job weaving it so tightly around you that you can't even tell it's there."

Zale blinked. "What are you talking about? What web?" Were the effects of his kiss with Lamia still lingering?

"Let me show you," Rumiel said.

He laid his hands on Zale's shoulders, one of which glinted with an unusual golden ring. Rumiel closed his eyes and prayed, "Elyon, in the name of the Logos, reveal the web of deceit that has ensnared your child."

Zale examined his arms and hands, expecting to see some kind of spidery threads appear, but nothing happened. He looked up at Rumiel and shrugged. "I don't see anything."

Rumiel wore a knowing expression. "Close your eyes and look again."

Zale stared at him in confusion. Obediently, he closed his eyes.

Then he saw them—memory after memory paraded before him, imbued with sticky golden sweetness. His training sessions with Narcissa that helped him hone his powers. Watching Tanni die at a gesture from Calandra. Calandra in the Archive when she tried to kill him. He could still see her coming at him with the knife.

Look, came an impression in his heart. *Look again.*

Zale concentrated on the memory of that night in the Archive when Calandra had attacked him. As he looked at it, he realized there was some kind of golden weave glossing the memory, like a translucent tapestry screen that showed a different picture than what was behind. The memory was a lie—but even as he accepted that, he still felt a strong compulsion to turn away, to let the memory be. What if the truth was even worse?

He pondered for a moment, then shook his head. No. Without the truth, he would be caught in a whirlpool of illusion, and that was no way to live. But how could he see behind the screen?

As soon as he'd made his decision, however, the golden weave unravelled in thousands of tiny threads, falling away from the memories until he saw them as they were, raw and unvarnished. He opened his eyes and stared at Rumiel, who was watching him with a compassionate expression.

"Calandra never tried to kill me. And she never killed her friend either. How did this happen? How could I have been so deceived?"

Rumiel sighed and pulled his hands away from Zale's shoulders, sitting cross-legged before him so the loose black pants the cherub wore beneath his split ankle-length tunic showed.

"Humans—and their half-undine kin—have an amazing capacity for self-deception, unfortunately. Though you bear a Shield of Elyon that prevents your soul from becoming possessed by one of the enemy, you can still be oppressed if you choose to believe lies instead of the truth. Fortunately, when you accept the truth, it shall set you free. How do you feel?"

Zale straightened. Despite being stuck in an unknown level of the Underworld, with Damaris under threat of death and his mother imprisoned somewhere, he felt better than he had since he'd arrived on the island of Sirenia.

"I feel great!" He scowled. "I'm not sure I want to be an undine anymore, though. They are seriously messed up, you know?"

Rumiel smiled. "The undines of Sirenia have much to learn, but this wasn't done by an undine. Your kind's abilities do not work this way. No, this was the work of a seraph, one of the fallen Grigori. The question is, which one?" He frowned. "Abela and I suspected the bonds holding them were weakening when we heard Robert's story about the dragon in the mirror. Perhaps they are weaker than we thought and one or more of them has already escaped, perhaps even inhabiting one of your kind."

"Inhabiting?" Zale asked.

"Possessing."

"Ah." Zale shuddered. He'd often wondered if he were possessed by a demon, or perhaps even *was* one, before he'd met Abela and found out the truth of his own past. Confronted with a whole nation of people like him, it had never occurred to him that one of them might have succumbed to that very fate.

Rumiel tapped his strong chin. "Was anyone there acting oddly or inconsistently?"

Zale snorted. "Yeah. Like, all of them. As I said, they're crazy there!"

Rumiel arched a brow and shook his head, and Zale sobered, thinking it over. Then the answer occurred to him.

"Narcissa. Everyone said how she had started acting like a Madwoman after her mother died. I only met her briefly before that, and she seemed a little off-balance even then. But I guess she was acting *really* weird after. And . . . and she was the one training me." He sat bolt upright. "I spent two hours with her every day, but now that I think about it, most of that wasn't even training. She was always asking me questions about you and Abela, and she was obsessed with my abilities with fire. The weird thing was, she was training me to use the elements, but most of the steps forward I made were things I discovered myself or I figured out accidentally because of one of her rants. I thought she could use fire too, but nothing her fire touched ever seemed damaged, so maybe it was all an illusion. Can seraphs, er, seraphim use fire?"

Rumiel nodded, looking thoughtful. "They don't use the element in the way undines do. Undines use the underlying matrix of the cosmos to draw fire energy to themselves and manipulate it. Seraphim are made of fire energy, so they can manifest the different aspects of fire in many more ways than an undine can—when they're in their own forms. But their abilities are limited while inhabiting another, even an undine. Especially an undine, actually—your kind have flesh, but it is tied so strongly to your spirits that it does not easily accept another's. Your description does narrow down who the culprit might be, and I suspect your intuition as to Narcissa being the host is right."

Zale dropped his gaze. "I wouldn't trust my intuition, if I were you."

"Why not?"

"It's been wrong more than it's right. I keep getting betrayed by the people I trust most."

Rumiel crossed his arms again. "Oh?"

Zale sat up. "Yeah. Eric, Josefine, Gio. Calandra . . ."

He stopped. That had been a false memory. Calandra had never betrayed him. And it turned out Damaris hadn't either—that had been Lamia plotting against him. His heart pinched with guilt when he remembered he had assumed the worst of Damaris when he'd overheard Lamia and Bez talking.

"What about Abela?" he said defensively. "She's my guardian, but she abandoned me on that island where I was basically living under house arrest and being, I don't know, bewitched by a possessed crazy person. Where is she, anyway?"

At the mention of Abela, Rumiel's expression became unreadable. "She and I weren't able to follow you at first because of . . . other considerations. And when we did, we weren't able to get near you—I suspect whichever seraph is inhabiting Narcissa is responsible. We knew you were in the palace, but the place was surrounded by principalities of the air. I suppose that should have been a clue that one of the Grigori was in residence, but it could just as easily have been Lamia or one of the other shedim, or a demon of a different race."

The realization that Berian and Abela had been on Sirenia should have been the most shocking part of that revelation, but—

"Wait, the Opal Palace is surrounded by demons?" Zale shook his head. "I never saw any."

Rumiel pressed his lips together. "You wouldn't. Though they are bound to the Ground, they rarely ever materialize there—taking on a visible form requires a lot of energy. It's different here, but on the Ground, even the Middle Ground where Sirenia is usually located, it requires manipulating the natural realm. Not to mention the advantages of being able to operate completely incognito, even if they can't do much but whisper to the impressionable and keep an eye on things. Since Sirenia is open to the outside for the first time in three millennia, everyone has been trying to find out as much about it as they can. We thought they were there doing surveillance. Our own operatives have been doing the same."

"So if I couldn't see the demons, why could you?"

"In my flesh form, I couldn't see them either," Rumiel said patiently. "Though I can sense one who is nearby. You remember my finder?"

Zale nodded, picturing the odd pocket watch with a face like a red stone cat eye that Berian had shown him. The minister had been in raptures because he'd discovered how Zale's mother had used his river stone bracelet to keep him hidden from exactly that kind of device.

"Do you remember how I told you it amplifies the abilities of my kind to find spirits by their frequency?"

Zale nodded.

Rumiel continued. "Not just flesh-bound spirits. Any spirits. We knew the enemy spirits were there before we ever got to Sirenia. We had found you, too, thanks to my little discovery"—he looked a little smug—"and my superiors posted some incorporeal operatives to keep an eye on you. But had we tried to come get you earlier, we would have been spotted by the enemy immediately and their leader warned long before we reached you. You were surrounded by those demons at all times, and we feared the worst would have happened to you if we made a move. So we decided to employ another method."

Zale shivered, his skin crawling at the idea of being surrounded by demons. "What was that?"

"Abela found someone she trusted who swore to protect you with her life, which she has done. It took a while for her to understand the importance of it, but once she did, she willingly agreed. And she has kept her end of the bargain."

Zale's mouth fell open. "Who was that?" He thought of his siren guards at the palace. Perhaps Singer kor'Renata?

Rumiel gave him a piercing stare. "I think you know."

A hole opened in Zale's chest, and his mouth went dry.

"Damaris," he croaked, and Rumiel gravely nodded confirmation.

It all made sense now—why she had taken the risk to befriend him, why she had helped him get to the Underworld, and most of all, why she'd followed him in here.

"So she wasn't befriending me just because she liked me." His heart caved in a little.

Rumiel put a hand on Zale's arm. "That's not true. By the time we contacted her, she had already become friends with you. That's why she agreed to help, and why we believed she would. She also left word with our contact—her sister, Eudora—about where you'd gone. That's why I'm here." He sobered a little, as though there was more he didn't want to say.

Zale felt ridiculous that this tidbit of news made him so happy. Then his heart fell again. "And now she might die here because of me."

"Aye. And because of me, because I let my fleshly emotions cloud my judgement, Abela might suffer and the Grigori might win the coming war," Rumiel said quietly. "Even the very aged like myself can still sometimes make mistakes."

Zale blinked at the cherub's admission. Rumiel had made a mistake because of his feelings? That seemed so unlike him. What feelings could possibly have swayed him so?

"This is no game we're playing here, boy," Rumiel continued. "The fate of the cosmos is at stake, and you're right in the centre of it. But one thing none of us can do is change the past. So let's not mope. We must do what we can to change what we can while we can, yes?"

Zale stared at him, the full weight of the cherub's words sinking into his soul. Not so long ago, a statement like that would have overwhelmed him and sent him fleeing in whatever direction he could. He still felt the pull to run, to let someone else deal with the difficult things to come. But he knew there was no one else. Rumiel was right—for reasons Zale didn't know, he'd been born with abilities he never asked for. And he knew enough to believe that his abilities would be the key to either maintaining or changing the balance of power in the universe, which was why he was in this mess in the first place.

The key. I am *the key.*

"All right," he said, standing, "what do we do first?"

Rumiel smiled proudly. "There's a good lad."

A sound in the trees behind them made them turn in time to see three young undine women stop short at the edge of the clearing—a tall siren with her long brown hair pulled back in a braided ponytail whom Zale recognized as Damaris's sister Zoe, the slim girl with the pixie cut and big green eyes in the blue bodice that had been present when the Archive burned and whom he'd fought off in the Voidstone chamber . . . and Calandra.

"Zale!" his sister said in surprise.

64

FAMILY REUNION

Zale leapt to his feet and stared at his sister, who looked as though she were sizing up an unbroken stallion. He'd seen Eric's brother, Sal Chapman, wear the same look many times. His gut twisted as he remembered the true unfolding of events that night in the Archive—how she'd tried to get him away from Narcissa, but he'd struggled like a fresh-caught carp. No wonder she had that look of caution in her eyes.

"Er, hallo, Calandra. Nice to see you."

He shifted his weight, that strange vibration he felt whenever she was near zinging through him. He supposed he had some apologies to make, but he didn't know where to start. He glanced at Rumiel, who crossed his arms and jerked his chin toward Calandra encouragingly. Zale looked at her again, clenching sweaty fists.

"I need to tell you . . . er, that is, what I mean to say is, um . . ." Why was it so hard to say this?

Perhaps because he knew what it was like to be treated like nothing, distrusted, and disbelieved, for no fault of his own. He'd believed the worst of Calandra the way the girls at the Academy had believed the worst of him—and Damaris was right. He knew almost nothing about her. Shame burned in his chest.

"What I mean to say is, I've been a paper-skull. And I'm sorry."

"Zale," Calandra said again with relief in her voice, rushing toward him. She glanced up at Rumiel warily, but when he made no move to stop her, she came to stand right in front of Zale, looking him over. "Are you okay? Are you hurt?"

Calandra reached toward Zale's head with an open palm, probably to test him for injuries, but he shook his head and pushed her arm aside.

"I'm fine. Physically, anyway."

"Where's Damaris?" Zoe demanded, only a step behind Calandra

The third girl hung back a little, but inserted herself between Rumiel and Calandra, glancing up at the cherub on occasion. Rumiel clasped his hands together in a solid knot with the palms perpendicular and his fingers wrapped around the other hand, and touched them to his chest with a slight inclination of his head toward her in what must be some kind of lumasi greeting.

Zale clenched his clammy fists and turned to Zoe. "Damaris was taken by a demon, a . . . a shedu named Lamia. She said I need to meet her at the Western Wastelands by tomorrow if I want to get Damaris back, wherever that is."

Zoe looked stricken, standing stock still.

Rumiel snorted. "It's a trap, obviously. But one we'll have to enter if we want to retrieve her."

Zoe looked at Rumiel through narrowed eyes. "We? Who are you? And why do you care?"

Zale stepped forward. "This is, er, Rumiel. I grew up calling him Mr. Berian. Calandra, he's our mother's guardian."

Calandra looked at the cherub in frank curiosity. "Mother's guardian? If you were guarding her, how did she end up here?"

Rumiel's mouth grew firm. "It's a long story."

Zoe tilted her head, examining the cherub from head to toe, her gaze lingering on the feathered wings folded against his back. "So you're Berian. Not at all what I expected from Zale's descriptions of you."

Rumiel inclined his head slightly. "I can't say the same, Zoe kor'Dione."

She blinked. "You know me?"

"Only by reputation. I had the good fortune to meet a former governess from the palace on Barbados before I came after young Zale here. She happened to mention you. As did your sister, Eudora, when I spoke with her."

At the mention of the governess, Zoe paled, but Calandra stood bolt erect, her body quivering with sudden tension.

"You met Urbi?" Calandra demanded of the cherub. "Was Osaze with her?"

The hitch in her voice as she said this made Zale look twice. He'd met Osaze, the man his sister was supposed to marry before Adonia had gone crazy, but they'd been in the middle of fleeing for their lives. Rumour around the palace was that Osaze and his mother had died during the coup, but Zale knew better—he'd seen Calandra send the two away to escape an island no human was ever supposed to leave. Narcissa hadn't known he knew otherwise, so she'd never tried to gloss the memory. But he'd known, that night in the Crystal Cave, that what Calandra and her consort-elect shared was something many people didn't. He'd seen that kind of love and affection between his mother and father, but rarely anyone else.

Rumiel's face filled with compassion. "I'm sorry, Calandra. When I met Urbi, Osaze had been sold as a slave to an agent of the enemy. But my cohorts, Guriel and Erel, were going to retrieve him"—he turned to Zale—"with the help of young Mr. Cox, you may want to know."

"Guriel and Erel? Who are they?" Zale asked.

"Ah, yes. Guriel is Abela's true name. You met Erel when he was on assignment in Madron as Mr. Penrose—you know, Guriel's father as Talwyn. Though now he has taken on a different form better suited to our current purpose."

"Yes, very nice," said Zoe patiently. "Can we get back to the part where we're rescuing my sister from a demon?" She glared at Rumiel, then Zale, as though she weren't sure who to blame more for the fact that her sister wasn't with them. "Do any of you even care what happens to her?"

Zale crossed his arms and glared at her. "I know you're her sister, but I'm her friend, and I most likely owe her my life." He thought of what Rumiel had told him about Damaris's promise to watch over him. He had no idea if she'd actually intervened for his life, but he certainly wouldn't have made it this far without her. "I swear to you, I'll do whatever is necessary to get her back."

Zoe gave him a sullen look and turned to Rumiel. "Where are the Western Wastelands?"

Rumiel heaved a sigh. "Far away from here. As far as Underworld districts go, its where the least desirables reside. Fortunately, we should be able to jump very close to the shedim's lair using a portstone, so that's the easy part. Unfortunately, the lair of the shedim is nigh impregnable and Lamia one of the most cunning and devious of her kind. Negotiating Damaris's release or finding another way to free her will be the difficult part."

"A portstone?" Zale asked.

"Like the Voidstone," Calandra explained. "It lets you instantaneously go from one place to another, no matter how far away, so I understand."

"Oh!" Zale said. "A chariot!"

Rumiel nodded, smiling. "Like a chariot, but much larger, and anyone can use it, not just lumasi. There are a few portstones on every plane to facilitate travel for those without the innate ability to teleport. There's one not too far from here."

Zale blinked. If only he'd known about that, he wouldn't have blasted a hole in the ground and landed him and Damaris in the swamp in the first place. But how could he have known? They'd already been travelling for hours or maybe days with no change in the landscape. Even if he'd been told there was a portstone there, he wouldn't have known how to find it.

"Great," he said. "So we can get there in time, but how do we get her back?"

"What did she want in exchange?" Zoe asked sharply.

"Only me." Zale frowned. "Wait. In the swamp, when I still thought she was Damaris—"

"What?" Zoe asked.

"She's a shapeshifter. Anyway, she asked me about a key, some kind of jewellery like a pendant or a ring or . . ." Zale's gaze fell on Rumiel's hand and his unusual gold ring. "Something like that." He pointed.

Rumiel held out his hand and frowned at the ring. It had a round blue stone flecked with gold set in the centre of a symbol that looked like an eight-spoked wheel.

"What is it?" asked Zoe.

"It's an *ichthys* chainbreaker," Rumiel said. "There aren't many working chainbreakers left. This one was once in the care of King Solomon himself. Erel brought it to use to free Delphine and return her to the Ground."

He glanced away as though he were holding something back. Surely not. Zale had often suspected Reverend Berian had been hiding something, and it turned out, he'd been hiding nothing at all—his intentions had always been what he'd said they were. Zale must be reading him wrong again—the man could be surprisingly opaque.

Calandra's eyes grew wide. "That's . . . that's the key!" She turned to Rumiel excitedly. "The key we'll need to unlock the Soulstone and free Mother!"

Zoe squinted at it. "*That's* the key? Are you sure?"

"What's a Soulstone?" Zale asked.

Rumiel raised his brows. "I'm surprised you know that, your highness. Your kind have not maintained the Soulstone for so long, I thought the knowledge of it had been forgotten."

"What's a Soulstone?" Zale tried again.

Zoe whirled to face him. "It's a giant moonstone at the bottom of an enormous well guarded by a sea monster and a bunch of Madwomen where your mother is being imprisoned," she snapped.

Zale glared at her, crossing his arms. "Didn't have to be so snippy about it."

Calandra frowned at Zoe, then turned back to Rumiel. "Unfortunately, the knowledge *has* been lost. I only know of it because one of the Grigori, Semyaza, has escaped and possessed my cousin, and he told me about it."

Rumiel's eyebrows climbed higher on his forehead. "So you know of the fallen also. I suspected Semyaza might be the one who escaped."

Calandra blushed, and she cleared her throat before continuing. "My friend Judith found a reference to the Soulstone in a datastone we recovered from Atlantis. Semyaza said I'd need a key to free my mother, or Zale and I would have to destroy the Soulstone to release her."

"Oh, you mustn't do that," Rumiel warned. "That would fling open the door on every soul keeper in the Abyss, and then—"

"It would release all the Grigori. Yes, I know." A shadow crossed her face. Then she looked at Rumiel's ring and brightened. "But now that we have a key, that's one less universe-altering decision I'll have to make. Thank the Moth—I mean, er, thank goodness."

Rumiel smiled warmly. "Yes, Elyon has a way of bringing plans together at the last minute."

Her smile grew strained, and she winced a little as though in pain. The girl with the short brown hair looked at her sharply, but Calandra gave a small shake of her head.

"Semyaza," said Zale, watching the exchange between his sister and the other girl with concern. "That's who's possessing Narcissa?"

Calandra glanced at him compassionately. "Yes. He's quite the deceptive trickster, isn't he?"

Zale's face flushed warm, and he nodded. Rumiel looked at Calandra with obvious curiosity, but she spoke before he could.

"Why do you have the key if you can't even access the Soulstone?" she asked. "I was told the winged races can't go in water."

Zale blinked at Rumiel. That was news to him.

Rumiel made a wry face. "It's not that we *can't* so much as we really, really hate it." He shuddered. "The more water there is, the less likely we'll risk it. The dragons hate it even more than we lumasi, especially seraphim."

Zale thought of Abela coming to find him in the ocean when he'd fled the *Atlanta* in shame after accidentally killing Mr. Crow, and his chest tightened. He had no idea how much of a sacrifice that had been—and she hadn't even said anything.

He sighed. He missed Abela. He wondered what she was doing now.

"Anyway," Rumiel said, "the plan all along was to enlist you and your brother to help free your mother, which is why Guriel and I were bringing Zale to Sirenia in the first place. But circumstances on your island being what they are, arranging both of your cooperation proved difficult. By the grace of Elyon, he arranged it for me, even if not in the way I would have chosen."

He glanced at Zale. Heat bloomed in Zale's stomach, but Rumiel gave him a kind smile. "I'm not blaming you, boy."

Zale swallowed and nodded.

Rumiel held out the ring and examined it before continuing. "Once we'd found and freed Delphine, I was to use the ring to unlock a port-stone and return the three of you to the Ground—and the rest of you, too, now." He looked at Calandra. "But no one has pinpointed her location closer than somewhere in the Abyss, and I haven't yet been able to go to the Chamber of Tears to try to get a more accurate reading. Why do you believe she's trapped in the Soulstone itself?"

Calandra bit her lip. "I, er, heard her. While I was at the bottom of the Pool of Tears looking down into the well."

Zale perked up. "You talked to Mother?"

His sister shook her head. "Not exactly. It's more like she talked to me in my mind. I've done the same thing a couple times since I got to Hades, but with someone else."

Rumiel arched a brow. "Telepathy? Interesting. That is a rare gift, your highness."

"Telepathy?" Calandra's brow furrowed. "I suppose that's what it was, but it wasn't really my doing. Something about the Underworld must make it possible for people to connect with their minds, like so many other things that are different here." She brightened as though something had just occurred to her. "Maybe that's how Damon contacted me all these years. I mean Semyaza."

Rumiel shook his head. "Semyaza has many gifts, but he's no telepath. Trust me, child, when I say the gift must be yours."

Calandra looked at him, dumbfounded. "Well, uh . . . I'm not very good at it, then." She turned to Zale. "I was trying to contact you, but it didn't work."

Zale didn't know whether to be awed or alarmed at the idea that someone could talk to him right inside his head. After his recent experience with Narcissa, and his brief bout of Redemption at Adonia's hand before that, he wanted his mind left well enough alone, thank you.

"So, how are we going to get Damaris back?" Zale asked.

"Finally!" growled Zoe, who had been tapping her toe with her arms crossed. "The sooner we rescue my sister and get out of this chained place, the better."

Calandra scowled at her, and Zoe frowned.

"And Delphine," she said begrudgingly. "I meant her too."

The pixie-like undine girl cleared her throat and gave Calandra a significant glance. "You need to tell them what Ophiuchus said."

Rumiel perked up. "You saw Kassiel?"

Calandra gave the girl a look of reluctance, then sighed, nodded at Rumiel, and turned to Zale. "We've been given another task, by . . . by Elyon." The word sounded like it choked her a bit.

Zale's heart sped up. Elyon had given them a task?

"What is it?"

Calandra swallowed, shifting her weight. "We're supposed to heal the Soulstone."

Zale's stomach twisted, and he pulled back. "Wait, we couldn't even heal the Heartstone, and now we're supposed to repair this prison stone? What if we fail and break it like we did the Heartstone, and then all the Grigori are free? No, we can't."

His panic had escalated as he spoke, and Calandra's lips pressed together. She looked as impressed by the added responsibility as he was.

"You didn't fail," the third girl said flatly, glowering at Calandra.

Rumiel made a rumbling sound in his throat. "Indeed. I have it on good authority the Heartstone has been almost completely restored."

"Then why is the barrier down?" Zale demanded.

"That is not our problem to solve," Zoe said shortly. "What *is* our problem is how to free Damaris and Delphine and get out of here in one piece."

"Count me in," said a new voice from the other side of the clearing.

Zale whirled to see a squat man with a barrel chest and copper-coloured leathery wings alight and stride toward them, still morphing into cherub form.

The pixie-like undine girl leapt between him and Calandra, her *deiktis* raised. "Who are you?" she demanded.

An amused smile quirked his mouth. He stopped, placing meaty fists on his hips, which were clad in some high-waisted loose brown pants with tight ankles. At the waistband, a long piece of shimmering cloth had been wrapped around his thick, muscular midriff several times before being tied in a neat knot in front. His chest was bare but for a yolk collar made of overlapping round copper plates that looked like scales and a baldric made out of a supple metallic material. The baldric held a magnificent tooled sheath with a leather-wrapped sword hilt protruding from it. Reddish-brown hair fell to the man's shoulders in gentle waves.

"Chazdiel, Gatekeeper of the Fifth Legion of the Chthonic Guard under her excellence, General Uriel," he said. "Who are you?"

The young woman narrowed her eyes, studying him.

He glanced at Rumiel and gave a sharp nod. "Hey, Rumiel." He made the same gesture Rumiel had given Calandra's friend earlier, his clasped hands thudding against the decorative yolk he wore—though it seemed fairly casual in execution. "Long time, no see. How are things in the heavenlies?"

Rumiel looked bemused. "I haven't been there for some time, but given recent developments, I'd say they're busier than Saint Peter on Judgement Day."

Chazdiel chortled.

Zale didn't get the joke.

"You're a gatekeeper?" Zoe broke in, her tone making it clear how credible she thought that was.

Chaz smirked. "Show me a gate, and I'll keep it for you just to prove it."

She glared at him and said nothing more.

Rumiel shook his head with a long-suffering expression. "Thank you for your help back there, Chaz. I'd hoped you might come back with the young undine girl, solving one of our problems."

"Sorry to disappoint you, old friend," Chaz said.

Zale frowned. "You know him?" he asked Rumiel, gesturing to the newcomer.

Rumiel nodded. "For millennia. You've met him too, in a way. He was the one trying to rid you of Lamia and Bezaziel before I found you."

Zale's gaze snapped back to the copper-skinned man. "You're the copper dragon?"

The man folded arms the size of tree trunks across his chest. "In the flesh. Well, okay, not really. Been a long time since I took on flesh, actually. You know what I mean. That's quite the arm you have there, young man."

Zale remembered the fireballs he'd thrown at the dragon, and his face flamed. "Er, sorry about that. I didn't know you were trying to help."

Chaz waved a dismissive hand. "It's all ashes and dust now, boy. Not like I had a chance to introduce myself."

The slim siren relaxed her stance and lowered her staff. "Airlea kor'Phile."

Everyone turned to her, Zale and the two lumasi looking at her in confusion.

"My name is Airlea," she said to Chaz. "Thank you for asking."

Calandra's face grew red. "Right, sorry. Speaking of introductions . . . this is Zoe kor'Dione," she said to Chazdiel, gesturing at the other siren. "I assume you know my brother Zale, at least by name."

The seraph nodded and grinned at Zale. "And by reputation."

Zale's gut clenched, and he squirmed. How had a spirit of the Underworld heard of him? From some of the souls he'd sent before him, however unintentionally?

Did Chazdiel know Zale's father? His heart pounded, but he dared not ask that here. He glanced at his sister—he hadn't told her what had happened to Kenver, and wondered how she'd react when she found out.

"And I'm Calandra kor'Delphine," she finished.

"Opal Princess of Sirenia," added Airlea with a glance at the petite panacea.

Now Zale stared at Calandra, who looked embarrassed, as though the title felt uncomfortable on her shoulders, though she didn't correct her bodyguard. There had been a great deal he and his sister hadn't been able to cover in their brief initial meetings, one of which was any of their personal history. What little he knew had been gleaned from snippets of overheard conversation and what Narcissa told him, or what he'd managed to wheedle out of his younger cousin, Hebe, before Narcissa had cowed her into silence.

Narcissa had been demanding the styling of *her majesty* since the death of her mother, as though she were already crowned, and insisted she bore the title of Opal Princess until she could garner the united approval of the council to name her queen. Zale had assumed that's because she *was* the Opal Princess, but perhaps there was some debate on the subject. It had been shocking to find his mother was sister to the queen of a nation—but was his own sister his aunt's true heir? Or was *Opal Princess* a title given to all the royal family, making him an Opal Prince? He squirmed more at the thought—he barely felt at home in his undine identity, but the idea of being a royal made his flesh crawl.

However, Airlea's statement implied only one Opal Princess, and if the respectful "At your service, your highness" and clasped-hand salutes Chaz and Rumiel were giving his sister were any indication, the title meant much more than simply *related to royalty*.

For her part, Calandra held her head high and smiled graciously at the two lumasi, though her resonance changed slightly. She was definitely uncomfortable. Maybe she didn't like being royalty either.

"So, when do we leave?" Chaz said, rubbing his hands together. "That viper Lamia knows better than to encroach on my turf. I'm looking forward to teaching her a lesson. Or five." He flexed his fingers and curled them into a fist with a grin, then sobered and glanced at Zale. "Sorry about your friend. By the time I was finished with the decoys, Lamia had gone."

Zale shook his head. "Damaris was gone already. She had been since"—he thought about the scuffle he'd heard when Damaris dropped through the hole from the meadow—"well, I guess since we arrived in the swamp, just before you showed up. I don't know why Lamia didn't just take me while I was sleeping, if that's what she wanted all along."

He should have known something was off when Damaris started flirting with him. He'd been used to that kind of behaviour from the Romani girls he'd met at large gatherings like the Appleby Horse Fair—girls outside the Chapman family—but none of the undine girls he'd met had so much as said a peep to him, let alone been so flattering. Even Damaris, with her sharp tongue, had been bristly as often as she was nice.

Chaz waved a hand. "Oh, that's easy. She needs you to come willingly, because she can't keep you any other way. You're too powerful, and she couldn't force you to do what she wanted. If you give your word you'll stay in your friend's place, you must."

Zale blinked. "I can't just lie?"

Chaz snorted. "You could try. But I wouldn't advise it."

"Lie?" Calandra gave him an incredulous stare.

Zale bristled. "Only if it became necessary."

Calandra's mouth gaped, and then she closed it with a small shake of her head. Why did that bother her so much? But the shock he felt from Airlea answered him—he supposed in a society where everyone could sense duplicitousness, lying must be almost unheard of. There didn't need to be a taboo—being outright deceptive would be completely ineffectual most of the time. Could a shedu sense a lie as easily as an undine would?

He rubbed his river stone. With that on, it shouldn't matter if they could.

Rumiel turned to Zale. "Words form powerful bonds, Zale. Chazdiel is right—if Lamia wants to use you to gain power for the shedim, she needs you to agree to the idea, as she likely wouldn't be able to hold you against your will. Only your own words could do that. Even a promise given under false pretenses would create a bond that would keep you beholden to her."

Zale's heart fell.

"What?" Zoe interjected. "What form of magic is this?"

"The oldest magic in the universe, sweetheart," Chaz said cheekily. "In fact, it's the magic that made the universe. Words are the most powerful and most binding magic of all."

Zoe paled a little and closed her mouth, not even glaring at the impertinent seraph.

Zale looked between the three of them in confusion. "So even if I were just pretending to go along with Lamia in order to rescue Damaris, I'd still have to stay?"

Rumiel nodded. "That's why you must always be careful what words you speak, or you may incur a debt you cannot repay."

Zale had never been much of a liar—he'd always avoided it when he could. But when it seemed harmless—such as telling Gio's mother, Britannia, her new homespun dress was pretty in order to soften her into giving him an extra helping of rabbit stew, even if the dress was as plain as a summer hare, he'd indulged. Still, he was glad he'd never promised something he couldn't deliver.

That could be a problem when they were trying to free Damaris. Unless . . .

"If Lamia is as cunning as you say, then we'll just have to be more cunning," Zale said. "As my friend Gio would say, it's all about directing their attention where you want it to go."

Calandra looked at him with interest. "What do you have in mind?"

"We'll give Lamia exactly what she wants—me."

65

THE MESSAGE

JUDITH HUFFED, CLIMBING THE LAST few steps to the commstone room in the observation tower overlooking the falls. Voices filtered through the closed wooden door, and she froze. The smooth wood was new and pleasant-smelling—Uncle Hammad and several of the other men had replaced this and the other missing doors that had long since mildewed and rotted beyond repair not long after the FWS had moved in to Margaret House. It was a shame they might soon be abandoning the safe house—and not just the safe house, the entire island. Judith pushed the thought away. The Sunken City wouldn't have been her first choice, but it was better than some distant island—or declaring outright war on their attackers. Saving a few hundred lives by evacuating to another place had been outvoted after Judith had left yesterday's meeting. Gerrick's words rumbled in her chest. If Nelly's team didn't come back from Atlantis with good news, they'd have no choice but to heed his warning and prepare for war. She prayed it wouldn't come to that.

Judith had ascended the tower not to make a call, but to truth-test Bryce, who was once again on duty. It seemed a bit unnecessary, since Bryce hadn't even arrived at Margaret House until the day before Cleo had warned them of the mole, but Judith had already tested everyone who'd been at the safe house for longer—even the people she'd grown up with at Elpida—and had come up dry. Now she was on to the less likely options. It gave her something to take her mind off the armada of doom bearing down on them, among their other problems. Bryce wouldn't be the mole, of course—of the remaining options, Polyxo seemed a more likely informant than her quiet lady's maid, who'd been only too eager to volunteer for the duty roster. Anything to keep her away from her flighty mistress, Judith guessed.

But as she listened to the rise and fall of words through the door, her gut tightened harder and harder. Maybe she'd been foolish to leave Bryce so long.

"No, I told you, I looked for . . . plenty of food now. The plant healers have been busy, so . . . almost two hundred Freedmen, and I couldn't find . . ."

Judith stared at the door in horror. Whoever was speaking was reporting to someone about Margaret House. She'd caught the mole red-handed! But what could she do about it? All she had was her diving knife. She suddenly regretted not taking her father's suggestion to wait until he could accompany her to do the truth-testing. What would the mole do if she burst in and surprised her?

She decided to play it casual, and quickly invented an alternate reason for her presence here so she could go in and confirm that the mole was, in fact, Bryce.

But when she stepped inside the octagonal room, the person speaking into the faceted yellow commstone in the centre of the octagonal table wasn't Bryce, but Tafrara.

Tafrara looked up at Judith in alarm, her face tense. She looked back at the commstone. "Mama, I . . . I have to go. I'll send word as soon as they let me know when we'll be coming for you all."

"All right, Tafri. God's peace be with you," came the tinny response.

"And with you, Mama. Give my love to everyone. Bye."

"Bye."

Tafrara looked up at Judith, then pointed awkwardly at the stone. "Would you mind severing the connection for me?"

"Pardon? Oh, of course."

Judith hurried forward and touched the commstone, singing the trill that would end the call while keeping her burning face lowered. It seemed unlikely Tafrara would be the mole, at least not one reporting to Narcissa. But why would she be passing that information to her mother? If that's who she'd actually been speaking to. But no, Judith sensed anxiety from the girl, but no fear or deception. Sadness too. This girl was often sad. Maybe she simply missed her family.

But why the report?

"I—I came looking for Bryce," Judith said.

Tafrara pointed through one of the six windows. Following her finger,

Judith saw Bryce sitting on a large rock at the edge of the river with her tail draped in the water, staring toward the sea.

"She's giving me some privacy," Tafrara said.

Judith's face grew even warmer—Tafrara had simply been calling home. But she had to ask. There was too much at stake not to.

"Why were you telling your mother about our rations and numbers?" She thought of the cryptic note that had been shoved into Calandra's hand in Sireniapolis the day before. Could Tafrara and her family be part of the Coalition? But why would they care about the safe house food stores? Was the Coalition planning a raid?

Tafrara leaned back in her chair and sighed, her hands resting in her lap. "Because she worries. She wanted to know if she should send food here from the Cooperative, but I assured her we have plenty. It's amazing what a few plant healers can do with a few acres of vegetables." She sounded wistful. "If only I could convince her to hire some to work at the farm year-round instead of only seasonally. She says food grown without magic might not be as big or fruit as early, but it tastes better and has healing powers of its own."

The tension in Judith's shoulders eased somewhat. "But why was she interested in how many Freemen we have? Does she want to know if we have room for more?"

Tafrara frowned, distorting the geometric lines of her forehead tattoo. "No. Well, yes, but that wasn't why I brought it up." She looked out the window, then turned to Judith. In a cautious tone, she asked, "When you worked in the palace, did you know a man named Thomas? A *tapeinos*, I've been told."

Judith straightened. "Yes. He was sometimes assigned to bodyguard duty for Calandra. Why?"

A little of the dejection lifted from her countenance. "Did he have golden skin and dark eyes like mine, and dark brown hair, and a scar on his arm, here?" She pointed to her own arm at the spot.

Judith frowned, thinking. "Yes to how he looked, but I don't know about the scar. When the *taps* get injured in training, the healers make sure they don't have any scars, and I assume they heal old ones when the boys are brought in. In any case, I do not remember a scar. Why do you ask?"

The cautious hope didn't leave Tafrara's face. "Because I think he might be my brother."

Judith blinked at her in surprise.

Bryce came in the door and looked at the two of them but sat in another chair, saying nothing.

Tafrara frowned. "Why did you think I was telling my mother those things?"

Judith cleared her throat. "I, um, I came here to truth-test, just to follow up on some, er, discrepancies. Would you mind if I do you next?"

Tafrara shook her head. Judith took the girl's hand, making sure their physical and emotional connection was solid by asking some simple questions to gauge how well she could sense Tafrara's response. The girl had no emotional shield, but most humans didn't. Even those who were very guarded in demeanour did not usually know the undine technique for hiding emotions from another empath. Of course, Judith also had to let down her shield for the procedure, but with a human, that mattered less— they wouldn't sense anything more than they usually did. Bryce looked on steadily, her shield almost impenetrable—or maybe Judith was concentrating too hard on Tafrara to pick up on Bryce's mood.

After repeating her questions about Tafrara's conversation with her mother and about other people she'd been communicating with since coming to Margaret House without any concerns, Judith asked about her brother.

"I have two, in fact," Tafrara answered. "They were both taken and Redeemed when they were twelve, of course. I barely remember Gwafa."

Bryce stirred, but said nothing.

Tafrara continued. "But I was already eight when Thomas was taken. My mother and sisters and I have never given up hope we might see them again. Now that things are, well, different, we'd hoped that maybe, you know, if we found them, we could find a way to Free them. Or that they would be Free already." Moisture welled at the corner of her eyes. "I'd hoped they might be here, but none of the men I've talked to have heard of Gwafa. A couple who came from the palace recognized Thomas's name. But they didn't know about the scar either." She bit her lip. "I'm so worried that if we leave them behind, I'll never see them again."

Judith stared compassionately at the other girl, her heart pounding with a similar fear. She'd asked her aunt about going on tonight's mission to meet up with Despoina Cleo so she could retrieve Matthew to take to Atlantis, and all she'd received in return was a harried, *I don't know, Judith.*

"I have someone in the palace too." Judith's vision blurred, and she blinked the moisture away, releasing Tafrara's hand. "You're clean. Thank you." She turned to Bryce. "I need to test you next."

Bryce blew a dark curl out of her eyes. "Why?"

Judith shrugged, her thoughts with Matthew. "Precautions. I will come around—"

The commstone whistled, and Bryce whirled toward it. She touched the stone and sang the trill to open the line, giving Judith an apologetic shrug. "Margaret House."

Judith frowned, trying to puzzle out Bryce's odd reaction.

Kyria Dione's shaky voice came on the line and asked to speak to Rhea at once.

"Yes, Kyria kor'Eirene," Bryce said. "I'll go fetch her." She glanced up at Judith and Tafrara. "Can you two stay here and keep watch?"

Tafrara stood. "I can take the message. I was just leaving—"

"No need." Bryce stood, smiling. "I need to stretch my legs. Be right back."

She hurried out of the room.

"Who else is there?" came Kyria Dione's voice.

Judith leaned closer to the stone. "It is Judith kor'Ignatia. Tafrara Baya of the Irene Cooperative is also here. She can be trusted."

She met Tafrara's gaze, and the girl smiled. Judith felt an unexpected companionship with this girl. She smiled back.

"Oh, thank the Mother." Relief flooded Dione's voice. "I don't know how long I have—Narcissa's *douloi* tend to pop in at the most awkward times. Would you carry my message for me instead, Judith?"

"Of course, *kyria*. I am ready."

"Another girl has gone missing." Dione's voice quivered. "A scullery maid. And I think I know who's responsible."

Judith's chest tightened, afraid whatever Dione said next might make it even harder for their cause to justify Freemen to their countrywomen.

"Who?" Judith met Tafrara's gaze, and noticed she wasn't the only one holding her breath.

"I think it's the princess," Dione said. "I think it's Narcissa."

Fear gripped Judith. That was both worse than expected and horribly unsurprising. "Matthew," she whispered involuntarily. She looked up at Tafrara. "I have to get him out. Tonight."

Tafrara gave her a determined look. "And Thomas too."

Judith ended the call just as Bryce re-entered the room with her aunt.

"What is it?" Rhea asked when she saw the look on Judith's face.

Judith steeled herself. She and Tafrara were going on that mission, and there was no way she'd take no for an answer.

66

THE RING

CALANDRA LISTENED IN INCREASING CONSTERNATION as Zale outlined his plan to trick Lamia into giving up Damaris while not telling a single lie—have Zoe pretend to bring him to Lamia as her prisoner, drawing Lamia outside her lair to negotiate an exchange for Damaris, all while Zale himself committed to nothing. As Damaris's sister, it would be believable Zoe would betray Zale to free her. While Lamia and her kin were distracted by the negotiation, the rest of them could find positions around the dry gorge Chaz said lay in front of the shedim stronghold and get into position. Once Damaris had been freed, the undines, the seraph, and the cherub could swoop out of hiding and incapacitate the shedim while they made their escape.

The plan had some good elements, but there were about a million things that could go wrong.

Zale finished his speech, then looked around with a hopeful expression, his gaze landing on her.

Calandra frowned. "Won't they just teleport Damaris back into their stronghold at the first sign of trouble?"

Zale's smile faltered. Guilt pinched Calandra, but she wasn't about to lose Zale to an ill-conceived plot when she'd only just found him again.

"Fortunately for us," Chaz said, "no one can jump directly into Lamia's stronghold. She doesn't like surprises, not even from her own people. The bigger challenge will be keeping them busy long enough to make our escape."

"I could call lightning," Zale offered, shifting his weight. "That would distract them."

Calandra's heart thumped. She was convinced his out-of-control lightning was the reason for the crack in the Heartstone that brought down the barrier. How much better could he have gotten in only three weeks? His guilty glance at her implied he might be wondering the same thing.

She cleared her throat. "I don't know if—"

"Great idea, Zale," Rumiel said. "I'm proud of you, boy."

Calandra closed her mouth, watching her brother beam under Rumiel's praise. She forced cheer into her voice. "And I could probably do something with earth—cause an earthquake, maybe?"

The thought of causing an earthquake on purpose gave her shivers, but better that in service of their plan than the random seizures that seemed to be increasing in intensity. At the thought, a sharp stab of pain sliced through her brain, and she winced.

"Would this work?" Zoe pulled an odd-looking bronze device from her bag. It looked like a human gun, but with sleeker lines. Instead of a barrel, the business end bore a small red crystal.

Chaz's eyes widened, and he whistled. "I haven't seen one of those since before the Sinking of Atlantis. Where did you get a stunner?"

Zoe met Calandra's gaze, then looked at Chaz. "Atlantis."

Chaz wobbled his head back and forth. "All right, then."

Calandra stepped forward to peer at the device. "You got this from Atlantis? What does it do?"

"Just what the man said. Knocks people out." She pointed the gun at a tree trunk a short distance away and pressed the trigger. A beam of red light shot across the clearing and left a scorch mark on the bark. "And makes sure they remember it too."

Rumiel eyed the tree with a disapproving sound, a muscle in his thick neck twitching.

"Cool!" Zale eyed the device. "Will it work on demons?"

"Used to, back in the day." Chaz rubbed the back of his neck. "I think that's why the undines invented it, actually."

Calandra's ancestors had invented this? She glared at it, then shook her head. "No. That's way too violent. We can't use that."

"Oh, so you're okay with earthquakes and lightning bolts if they're wielded by you and the other special ones," said Zoe, "but not a tool that gives the rest of us an even playing field?"

"You have ways to defend yourself," Calandra said, trying not to sound plaintive. "You have the *Tropos Hydor Zon* and sirensong."

Zoe snorted. "Lot of good those will do against a murderous shape-shifting teleporting demon."

"Actually . . ." Chaz said.

Calandra and Zoe turned to see him rubbing his chin.

"What?" they demanded in unison, then glared at the other.

Calandra's head throbbed, and she took a deep breath, trying to ignore it.

"Sirensong might do a little something," Chaz said. "Enough to cause a distraction. Should slow down the men, anyway. Unless Zale knows how to . . . ?"

"Sirensong?" Zale glanced between them. "I . . . I don't know what you're talking about. Is sirensong what you all use to do that mind thingy?"

Calandra shook her head. "No. Well, kind of. Unlike bonding, sirensong is used to stun, not enslave. The effect is temporary. As soon as the song stops, the sedative effect disappears."

"I don't know how to do that."

"No," Calandra said, "you wouldn't. The technique takes months, sometimes years to learn, and I don't even know if males can do it. Hmm." She crossed her arms, a shiver running through her. *Could* male undines stun women the way women could men? "I think we need to have other options in place. Stunning would be easiest, but we should plan for the worst case scenario."

Chaz shrugged. "Well, even just stunning the males will help a little anyway."

"But not as much as a device that doesn't care what gender you are, I guarantee it," Zoe said.

"True." Chaz looked deflated.

Zoe gave Calandra a pointed look. "And it will only knock someone out, not violate any ethical principles about bonds. You can hardly be upset by that, healer."

Zoe's meaning wasn't lost on Calandra, who had used the physicking technique of knocking someone out more than once in time of need. But it wasn't so much the gun that bothered her, but the fact that Zoe had hidden it from her this long. Calandra stalked over to the tree, where a small tendril of smoke curled from the charred starburst on the trunk. She hoped whomever was sleeping inside hadn't felt that. Laying her hand on the tree, she restored the bark to wholeness in seconds.

"I don't see why she couldn't use the stunner. Set a little lower than *that*, of course," Chaz said. "It would keep those popping slither-tails busy while Rumiel and I blink the rest of you out of harm's way."

Airlea, who had been listening to the discussion with pursed lips and a furrowed brow, spoke up at last. "And what if Lamia doesn't fall for it?"

"I agree," Calandra said. "This is obviously a trap, and it feels like we're walking right into it. I'm not going to send Zale into Lamia's hands without any form of protection."

"You don't think I can handle myself?" Zale glared at her.

Calandra thought of the burns she'd left the Archive with, and how he'd trapped Airlea in a bubble in the Voidstone tower. "No, I do. But it seems foolhardy to go into a situation like this without some sort of backup plan."

"A backup plan like that?" Chaz pointed to Rumiel's ring.

Rumiel glared at the coppery seraph and crossed his arms, concealing the ring. "No, Chaz. You know that's not an option."

"What? Why not? What haven't you told us?" demanded Zoe. "Every asset matters. This is my sister's life we're talking about here."

"And my brother's," Calandra said at the same time Zale said, "And mine."

Zale gave Calandra a glare before glancing away. She pressed her lips together. She needed to tread more carefully with him.

"That blue stone is lapis lazuli, which interferes with demon powers," Chaz said, "just like green feldspar hampers you undines and selenite hampers us dragons. Cherubim like ol' Rumiel here can't stand jet." He frowned. "I don't much care for jet myself, though. Such a hungry stone."

Chaz shuddered. Rumiel looked uncomfortable just thinking about it.

Zoe put her hands on her hips. "So if we've got a ring like that, why wouldn't we use it?"

"This isn't a simple dampening cuff, young lady," the lamassu said testily.

She scowled, and he sighed, pulling his hand from its hiding spot so they could see it.

"Chainbreakers like this ring don't literally break chains. They create doors and pathways in spiritual strongholds, permitting someone so bound to escape their bondage. But, like so many things in this world, they can also have the opposite effect—closing and destroying those doors, creating bonds and walls where they never existed. It depends only on the will of the one who wields it. This very ring was once used by the famed King Solomon of Israel to force Ground-bound spirits to assist in building the temple. When Archon Michael found out, he was furious. Removing someone's will to choose is one of the most offensive things possible to Elyon. That's why we mustn't even consider it."

Zoe crossed her arms. "Sounds like a silly reason not to use it to me."

Calandra hated to admit it, but she had to agree with Zoe. Shame tightened her gut. Would she really enslave a demon to get Damaris back?

Yes. Yes she would, when that demon had kidnapped Damaris in the first place. Lamia had made her nest.

"Why is it called an *ichthys* ring?" asked Zale. "It doesn't look anything like a fish."

Rumiel's lips curved upward. "Ah, no, but look carefully at what it spells." He held it up so the wheel was vertical, its eight sections perfectly aligned with the points of a compass if upward were north.

It took Calandra a moment, but she finally saw what he meant. "*Ichthys*," she said, working out the letters in her mind.

Zale cocked his head, straining. "I speak Greek, obviously, but I was never much good at writing it."

Airlea nodded, an appreciative smile on her face. "Iota, chi, theta, upsilon, sigma." She traced each letter on the ring as she said it, and then turned to Zale. "Do you see it now?"

His face brightened. "Oh! That's neat."

Ichthys. Fish. A bond-breaker or -maker.

"It was made to replicate our abilities, wasn't it?" Calandra stated more than asked.

Rumiel nodded and sighed. "Indeed. The undine makers created several devices that would enable other races to access and monitor the Soulstone and its inhabitants so they could assist the undine guardians in their duties. The problem is, the stones themselves become discharged with use and must be recharged by an undine pair wielding all five elements. That, and the Soulstone remains completely inaccessible to most other races. No one counted on the mental deterioration and isolation of the guardians themselves . . . or the lack of male undines that would ensue."

"Another thing that's been affected by the *sklavia* bonds." Calandra's chest tightened. Would there be no end to the consequences of her kind's mistakes?

Rumiel eyed Zale and Calandra.

"That is, of course, probably why the Grigori wanted you here in the first place—a key alone couldn't free them. Once one, maybe two, had been unbound, it would become useless. But you two can keep replenishing the key's energy until every last one of them has been freed—all ten thousand rebels."

No wonder Rumiel didn't want to let the ring out of his sight. "I don't think they have a key. If they had, why would Tamiel and Valac have gone to such trouble to convince me destroying the Soulstone was necessary?"

Chaz's mouth quirked. "How'd you run into those two?"

"Tamiel appeared to us in the crystal cavern," Zoe said flatly. "She was pretending to be Delphine."

The siren's anger at being taken in by the ruse leaked through her shield, but Calandra could empathize. On the walk here—after Zoe had finally agreed to follow Calandra's choice of path, which Calandra had been both gratified and relieved to find had led them to Zale in short order—Calandra and Airlea had told Zoe what Ophiuchus had said about Valac, Tamiel's projection ability, and how Valac had tried to control Calandra with the bliss stone. Calandra hadn't mentioned his blasphemous claims about Tamiel being Atargatis. She still wasn't sure what to make of it herself.

"I guess we'll have to think of something else." Zale frowned, whacking at a nearby fern. "If Gio were here, he'd come up with an amazing plan."

"I like your plan," Airlea said gently.

Zale looked up, an embarrassed look on his face. "Thanks."

"Me, too." Chaz glanced around the group. "I think it's our best option. It's almost our *only* option. Is it settled? Zoe and Zale will distract them until Damaris is out of their den, then the sibling act hits them with fireworks and a rock show and Miss kor'Dione stuns the tarnation out of them until Rumiel and I can blink everyone away? Maybe Miss kor'Phile can throw a little sirensong in there to slow them down even more?"

"Won't sirensong affect the two of you?" Airlea asked.

Rumiel chuckled, his face transforming with his smile. "We'll be fine, my dear."

"I won't, though." Zale frowned.

Calandra wished she had some songstoppers with her. She wondered why the erelim wouldn't be affected by sirensong.

"We'll make sure you get out first," said Chaz.

"Let's go then." Zoe tucked the stunner into her belt. "The longer we talk, the less time Damaris has left."

"Your highness?" Rumiel looked to Calandra for approval.

Calandra chewed her lip, staring at her brother. Zale shifted his weight under her gaze.

"There are too many ways this plan could go wrong," she said. "What's stopping Lamia from just taking you from Zoe instead of negotiating for

Damaris?"

Zale shrugged. "Lightning?"

"If you use lightning before Damaris is safe, you could ruin everything." Calandra's head throbbed, and she blinked to clear the burning pain. "I think we should use the ring."

Rumiel drew himself up. "Didn't you hear what I said? We—"

"Not to control anyone, but as part of the deception."

Deception? Did I just say that? But desperation left few options. Besides, Osaze had pretended to be Redeemed for a month, and Wilhelmina had deceived the sirens to save her and Airlea. Chains, she and Tanni had shared a secret bond for five years and hadn't told a soul—they hadn't lied, but they hadn't been forthcoming. Sometimes deception was necessary. Pain pulsed, and she took a deep breath before speaking again.

"Let Zale wear it to distract Lamia while Zoe negotiates for Damaris's freedom. Lamia might be terrified he'll use it on her, which would give Zale and Zoe an advantage, and might prevent her noticing us sneaking in from elsewhere."

Zoe nodded. "Yes, let's do that. Except if I'm pretending to hold Zale hostage, I should wear the ring. It wouldn't make sense for him to be Redeemed and to be wearing a ring of that power."

"What?" Zale's head jerked around, his voice cracking.

"You're not going to enslave him," Calandra snapped. She wasn't certain how comfortable she was with Zoe having that much power on her hand either. She wished she still trusted Zoe implicitly, but the truth was, she didn't. Still, other than taking Osaze to Barbados against Calandra's wishes—but apparently in alignment with Osaze's—and neglecting to mention the weapon from Atlantis, what had Zoe done? She'd continually risked exposure serving as an agent for the rebellion in the Opal Palace. Wasn't that worth some trust?

But Calandra couldn't squelch her misgivings. She thought about delving Zoe's shield, then decided against it. She clenched her jaw. Until Zoe proved otherwise, Calandra would choose to see her as trustworthy. Still, sometimes she wished the siren weren't so adept at concealing her emotions. Deception definitely had a dark side.

"Then how are we going to make it convincing that I've managed to subdue him?" Zoe asked. "If he looks like he came willingly, I'll lose all my bargaining power."

"I'll tell you how." Zale turned to Airlea. "Do you still have those feldspar cuffs I saw in the Voidstone Tower?"

Airlea blinked in surprise. "Well, yes, but . . ."

Zale held out his wrists.

Airlea looked at him doubtfully. "Are you sure?"

He nodded. "It's for Damaris. Trust me, I've worn these for less noble reasons."

"No way." Calandra crossed her arms. "The point was to make your chances better, not worse."

He planted his feet, glaring at her. "Don't you trust me, big sister?"

She narrowed her eyes at him. She wanted to trust him, but other than his apology, he'd given her little reason to do so lately. And she'd be chained if she'd send him into that nest of vipers with his powers dampened, not when the only one close enough to help him was Zoe.

His defiance broke, and he nodded. "Okay, I know I haven't been a beacon of trustworthiness. But I promise, I'm different now. And I'll be okay, even with the cuffs on. Do you believe me?"

Calandra glanced at his shielding river stone bracelet. "May I touch you?"

He nodded. She laid a hand on his arm, and his sincerity surged through her. For whatever reason, he certainly believed what he said. She stepped back.

"Okay."

She nodded at Airlea, and the ex-siren pulled the two green bracelets out of her pack and placed them on Zale's wrists, their gold clasps clicking closed. Zale kept his eyes on her, and their hurt expression needled her. *Trust is earned. I learned that the hard way. So will you.* But his gaze still pricked her heart.

"And the ring?" Zoe held her hand toward the black-clad cherub expectantly.

"No, absolutely not." Rumiel glared around at all of them. "You're all a bunch of guppies in shallow water here, and you don't know what you're playing with. This ring is no trinket, and not just anyone can use it."

"Why would I use it?" Zoe asked. "I can stun them when the time comes. If that doesn't work, you'll all be there to help. This is only to give us an advantage until then."

Rumiel hesitated, studying Zoe.

Zale cocked his head, pointing at the dark-haired man. "I thought you said Erel brought it to Abela. So if *she* was meant to use it, why do you have it instead?"

Rumiel's mouth opened, but no sound came out. He closed it and worked the ring off his finger. Zale gave a satisfied grin.

Calandra leaned toward her brother. "What's that about?"

She gestured subtly toward Rumiel, who scowled fiercely. Maybe cherubim weren't permitted to curse, because he certainly looked like he wanted to.

"I'll tell you later," Zale whispered.

She glanced at his wrists as she pulled away, biting her tongue.

He caught her look and scrunched his lips to the side. Then he sighed and leaned closer. "Don't worry, I'm not completely helpless with them on."

Calandra stared at him. *Does that mean he can still use his powers with the cuffs on? That should be impossible!*

But before she could ask, Rumiel handed the *ichthys* ring to Zoe. She slipped it on her middle finger, and it resized itself to fit. Calandra stared at it in astonishment.

Zoe turned to Chazdiel. "Where's this portstone you said was so close?"

Chaz pointed into the jungle, and a path appeared out of nowhere.

Zoe gave a decisive nod, slipping her *deiktis* from its scabbard on her back as she went to stand by the path. "What are you all waiting for?"

Without waiting, she strode off down the path. Airlea and Zale fell into line behind her.

Calandra took a deep breath, looking after them.

"What's the matter, your highness?" rumbled Rumiel's kind voice beside her.

She glanced up at him and shook her head. "I'll just be glad when this is over."

His golden irises swirled beneath partially closed eyelids. "Who's to say what comes next won't be worse?"

She swallowed the fear that choked her, then turned and trotted down the path after Airlea, pursued by Rumiel's words and a pounding headache.

THE GARGOYLES

CALANDRA COUNTED HER STEPS, PANTING as she jogged after Airlea down the trail Chaz had mysteriously created.

Directly behind Calandra, Rumiel spoke. "Did you hear Semyaza has escaped?"

Calandra stiffened and stopped counting.

"What? How?" Chaz's voice was full of dismay.

"I wish I knew. Probably a consequence of the failing bonds."

"They're not that weak yet, or Uriel would have implemented precautions," Chaz replied staunchly.

Calandra focused on her footing, ducking her head to hide her burning face from the guardians who followed her.

"I believe she has, albeit a little late. Semyaza, at least, must have had a key," Rumiel said, "but he most likely drained it when he escaped, making it useless. Which one do you think it is?"

"The Key of Og?" Chaz mused. "No one's seen that for hundreds of years. It's been lost on the Ground somewhere."

Rumiel made a noise of dismissal. "If Semyaza has inhabited a princess of the undines as Zale and Calandra believe, the one he used is more than likely the quaternaria."

Calandra's heart skipped. She stopped and turned around. "What did you say?"

The two guardians looked at her.

"The amethyst quaternaria worn by your queen," Rumiel explained. "It is another *ichthys* circle, a powerful key to the Soulstone entrusted to the undines after the Rebellion."

"The quaternaria *is* a key?" Calandra's mouth went dry. Here she'd been offered exactly what she needed by Cleo, and she'd turned it down. How much grief could she have saved herself had she known? But she hadn't—and they had Rumiel's ring now, anyway, so it didn't matter. But even though Semyaza didn't have the quaternaria, he might have found a different key to help him escape. *That would mean it wasn't my fault. Right?*

Airlea came up behind him. "Everything all right?" she asked Calandra in a low voice.

"I'm not sure," Calandra whispered back, watching the two tall warriors.

She glanced behind her. Zale had noticed their halt in progress and was whacking at a frond near the path in a bored way, but Zoe had already disappeared around a bend and was obscured by greenery. She sighed. She could understand the siren's urgency, but running into the fray without all the information could cost them in the end—she hoped Zoe would at least wait before jumping through the portstone.

Chaz nodded at Rumiel. "Yeah, you're probably right about the key. That changes things. And of all the chainbreakers to get their claws on." He gave a low whistle.

Calandra shook her head. "Narcissa was definitely looking for the quaternaria, but she—er, *he*—hasn't found it."

"How can you be sure?" Rumiel asked.

She hoped Cleo had been keeping a close eye on the quaternaria. But if there was anyone Calandra could trust inside the palace to not give in to Narcissa's tyranny, it was Cleo.

"Trust me, he hasn't," Calandra said. "By the fins of Venus, he won't."

Chaz and Rumiel exchanged glances.

"You're right, though," Chaz said to Rumiel. "They must have one, or Semyaza would still be bound. That means all they really need to bust out of there is Zale. Between him and his mother, they could keep recharging their key until every last one of them was free, even if the Soulstone never loses another speck." The seraph shuddered.

"On the other hand," Rumiel said, "if they had a key, why would Tamiel try to get Calandra to destroy the Soulstone on her own instead of collecting Zale to help recharge the key first?"

"Who needs a key when you have a battering ram?" came a familiar childish voice from behind the two spirits.

Chaz and Rumiel whirled and tensed, hands at the ready—to do what, Calandra wasn't sure.

Airlea leapt forward between Calandra and the smug-looking boy on the path, her staff in defensive position. "Valac," she spat. "You've got some nerve."

The little boy grinned, but all the innocence Calandra had seen there before was gone. He put his hands on his hips and gave Calandra a chastising glare, which looked quite comical on his childish features.

"So this is what's taking so long. I thought you'd be back at the river hours ago. I see you found your brother without my help, though." He frowned at Chazdiel and Rumiel. "And you picked up some strays."

Rumiel drew a flashing sword that looked forged of light.

Where did he pull that from?

"What have you and Tamiel done with Delphine?" Rumiel demanded.

Zale jogged up behind Calandra and Airlea. "What's going on? Who's that?"

"The devil in disguise," Calandra growled, her hands at the ready to channel power. But even as she said it, part of her longed to ask the little spirit if he had another bliss stone to relieve her pounding head.

Some demons were hard to exorcise.

Zoe came sprinting up behind Zale and Airlea, her stunner at the ready. "That little leech is back?" She growled and pointed the weapon.

"Don't," Calandra said, and Zoe glared at her, but relaxed her raised arms—only a little.

"Where were you?" Airlea asked over her shoulder.

"You didn't tell me we were taking a break," Zoe said.

Zale hissed at them to be quiet.

Valac pouted and crossed his chubby arms. "I hain't done nothing with the undine woman," he declared to Rumiel, eyeing the elegant glowing sword pointed in his direction. "She got herself stuck in the Soulstone. Too bad—if she'd just destroyed it like we asked, we never woulda needed these two at all." He pointed at Zale and Calandra. "She's not doing so great, though. You two better come get her out soon, or there may not be much of your mother left to free." He giggled, but it had a maniacal edge to it.

Calandra's stomach churned, and she raised her hands threateningly. "What have you done with Mother?" she said in a low, controlled voice she'd perfected on misbehaving novices at the Academy.

"Why do you all keep blaming me? I haven't done a thing." Valac shook his head, obviously unconcerned by her gesture. "But the Soulstone ain't exactly a fun place to hang out. It's a door, not a lobby."

Calandra tried to imagine being trapped in the cold emptiness of the

Voidstone indefinitely—like being trapped in her nightmare ocean. She shivered. Is that what the Soulstone was like too?

"We'll be there soon enough, Valac," she said. "But tell Tamiel to wear her own face this time."

His eyebrows disappeared beneath the curls on his forehead. "Oh, so you figured out who she is, did ya? What a clever girl you are. Just like your mama. No wonder Delphine keeps calling for you. The question is, can you actually save her?"

Calandra blinked. She really had heard her mother's voice in the Pool of Tears? Her heart skipped.

Chazdiel, who was closest to the boy, leapt forward with a resonant snarl, but Valac reacted just as quickly and darted backward into the air, his stubby wings flapping like a bumblebee's. He crowed with laughter.

"Uh-uh. Too slow, old man," he taunted, but when Chazdiel spread his wings, Valac flew a little higher, then called down to Calandra and Zale. "In case your mother's imm'nent demise ain't enough motivation, I'm sending some friends of mine to help you along." He spotted Rumiel's ring on Zoe's hand and did a double take. "Is that what I think it is?"

"I thought you wanted a battering ram, not a key." Rumiel feinted, and Valac fluttered back a little further to avoid the fiery sword.

Valac's grin spread wider. "That ain't just a key, and you know it." He looked at Zale and Calandra. "New deal: bring Solomon's Ring when you come too, or you'll never get your mother back."

"You're never getting your hands on the ring, Valac," Rumiel said.

The boy shrugged. "You'll share your toys with her but not me?" He faked a pout. "Fine, then Delphine will die. Up to you. But hurry, either way." He giggled and winked at Calandra. "Don't make me come back again."

Zoe took aim at him and pressed the trigger, but Valac blinked out of sight before the red bolt of energy made contact, and it dissipated in the golden sky.

"I guess that answers the question about the key," Chaz said, his big hands on his hips. "Partly. How *did* Semyaza escape?"

Calandra's gut tightened. She couldn't *know* Semyaza had used her to escape. It didn't make sense. But if he hadn't had a key, how else could he have done it? She was relieved when Zale whirled to face her.

"What if Valac is telling the truth and Mother is on death's doorstep? We have to go there first."

"You'd risk Damaris's life because of that little twerp's lies?" Zoe gestured after Valac with the gun.

"No, of course not. But if he's not lying, then we'd be risking Mother's life instead." Zale pressed his palms into his eyes. "I told Damaris not to come with me. Why didn't she listen?"

"Good question," Zoe muttered under her breath. She tucked the stunner back into her belt.

Calandra's chest twinged in sympathy for her brother, and she suppressed the urge to glance at Airlea. It wasn't Damaris's fault she'd been captured by shedim. But it certainly presented a difficult decision.

"Perhaps we should split up," suggested Chaz. "Manage both angles at once."

Calandra shook her head. "There's no way to split up that would accomplish both goals. Besides, the plan to free Damaris won't work if we're not all there."

"We could revise the plan," Zoe said. "I think Zale and I would be better off with a smaller team. Less likely Lamia will discover Zale brought backup and break her word. We've got the stunner and the ring, so—"

"You're not to use the ring," said Rumiel.

"I know, already." Zoe crossed her arms and glanced down at the ring. "I only meant it would deter them from attacking until we got away. Isn't there a portstone in the Wastelands?"

Chaz nodded. "Yeah, near Dudael, a hunk of rock not too far from Lamia's lair—but it's far enough. Five hundred paces. You think the shedim would be wary enough of that ring to let you get that far?"

"You tell me."

Zoe raised her hand, pointing the ring at Chaz, and he backed up a step with his hands raised.

"Whoa, no need to get nasty."

"We're not splitting up," said Calandra. "We need the ring to free Mother from the Soulstone too. We'll have to do one, then the other."

Rumiel clasped his hands before him and regarded her with his unusual golden eyes. "What do you think we should do first, your highness?"

All eyes turned toward her, and Calandra's stomach tightened. What *should* they do? It seemed like a no-win situation. She was getting so tired of being given impossible choices.

"Well, I guess I think we should—"

The sound of flapping wings and piercing screeches filled the air, and the ever-present golden light dimmed. Calandra looked up in time to see hundreds of misshapen humanoid figures with bat-like wings and grotesque faces coming at them out of the turmeric sky and charging from behind the dense undergrowth.

"Valac has sent galla demons," Rumiel called while shifting into an enormous winged bull. He spread his wings wide, curling them around the undines like a shield.

"Oh, Kassiel is going to freak out," Chaz said. He grew into a bulky, squat copper dragon, not unlike the one on the river bottom, and turned to meet their attackers. "Go! I'll meet you at the portstone," he roared over his shoulder.

Zoe lifted her weapon and started shooting at the twisted figures.

"Save your charge," rumbled the bull from his massive chest. "Follow the path." He jerked his horns forward, his wings partially extended above them to deflect oncoming gallas.

Zoe put the gun in her belt and drew her staff, then took off down the path. Calandra and the others bolted after her—first Zale, then Calandra, then Airlea. The winged bull took up the rear.

A gargoyle's scream grew louder in Calandra's ears. Zale whirled, throwing a fireball at the creature just before it made contact with Rumiel's head. It yelped and flapped backward, avoiding the missile. Calandra swallowed her surprise at this new skill her brother had acquired and threw her own weapon at the next attacker—a blast of air that blew the monstrous creature aside. Airlea and Zoe brandished their staves, but there was little they could do unless the beasts got within range, and the galla seemed hesitant to do that. Suddenly, a beam of red light shot into one of the flying beasts and it fell to the ground. Calandra whirled to see Zoe taking aim with the stunner at another demon. She had to admit, the weapon certainly had advantages.

"Rumiel said to save your charge."

"I am," Zoe snapped. "I'm saving it for sure shots."

Up ahead, a circular white stone tower with a crenellated top rose above the trees.

"That must be it!" Zale called.

"Run," Rumiel called to them. "I'll take care of these and meet you there."

They did as he said, dodging fronds and leaping over moss and roots in a mad scramble to get away from the flying gargoyles. Calandra wondered whether she ought to stay behind and help. A glance over her shoulder revealed Rumiel rearing while tossing his head back and forth to ward off the harrying galla. However, he and Chaz seemed to be winning, for there were fewer beasts than before. An enormous hawk-headed griffin came swooping into the fray, sending gargoyles flying left and right—Ophiuchus.

Calandra turned and kept pace with the others. As they approached the tower, an enormous polished black sphere came into view. It balanced on a short, wide silver pedestal inside the arched tower base. The tiled platform upon which it sat was easily reached by a short flight of steps. The tower didn't appear to be protecting the portstone so much as signalling its location.

They had nearly reached the tower when the shadow of a large gallu fell on them.

"Duck!" Calandra shouted, diving to the ground just as long, evil-looking claws clacked where she'd been standing a moment before. She looked up to see the creature circling around, with two others following behind in close succession. Some distance away, the bull, griffin, and dragon were busy fending off a hoard of other galla.

Zale threw some fireballs, which the creatures easily dodged, screeching in annoyance. Calandra blasted them with air, and when that barely fazed them, drew some large clods of dirt from the ground and used earth to hurl them at their attackers. The only effect was for the beasts to screech in rage, circling once more with increased determination. Zoe took one of the diving creatures down with the stunner, but when she tried to shoot a second one, nothing happened.

"Chains of Prometheus," she muttered, stuffing the gun back in her belt and drawing her staff once more.

As the two red-eyed creatures bore down on them once more, the eerie sound of sirensong reached Calandra's ears. She glanced at Zoe, who stood singing the wordless tune, then she and Airlea joined in. But their song had no effect—the flying demons kept coming, and they all ducked once more, blasted by wind from the creature's wings.

Zoe huddled on the ground, scowling. "That answers that question."

Then Calandra remembered what Ophiuchus had told her about how to rid herself of Valac. *Praise the Creator and he will flee from you.* But which creator? Atargatis, whom she had been taught her whole life had created and cared for the world, the Mother of all the undines? Or Elyon, the impersonal Essence whom Ophiuchus and Rumiel claimed allegiance to?

She stood and sang one of her favourite hymns.

Great Lady of Heaven, roar,

Speak the words that devour
Place your enemies beneath your feet
Let all heaven and earth know your power.

The creatures swooped down on her once more, and she dropped to all fours. Zale flattened himself on the ground next to her, and Airlea and Zoe swung at the creatures with their staves without making contact. Calandra opened her mouth to sing the next verse.

Zale looked at her incredulously from his position hugging the ground. "What are you doing?"

"Sirensong didn't work. I thought I'd try something the griffin told me to do."

"What's that?"

"Praise the creator."

Zale frowned. "The *Great Lady of Heaven?*"

Calandra closed her lips, too irritated and afraid to answer.

The shadows turned for one more pass. This time, Zale stood and planted himself. He opened his mouth and sang in English:

A mighty fortress is our God,
A bulwark never failing:
Our helper He, amid the flood
Of mortal ills prevailing.
For still our ancient foe
Doth seek to work his woe;
His craft and power are great,
And armed with cruel hate,
On earth is not his equal.

His voice rang out pure and strong, projecting over the trees. As soon as he started singing, the creatures flapped to a stop, screeching and tossing their heads.

"It's working," Airlea hissed. "Keep singing."

Zale glared at the creatures as he launched into the next verse.

And though this world, with devils filled,
Should threaten to undo us,
We will not fear, for God hath willed
His truth to triumph through us.

The Prince of Darkness grim,—
We tremble not for him;
His rage we can endure,
For lo! His doom is sure,—
One little word shall fell him.

Calandra stared at her brother. As he sang, a golden aura appeared around him, glowing like a skin-tight shield. She'd never heard the song he sang before, but it invigorated her. And it was having the desired effect on their attackers, too—as Zale continued singing, their screeches of hatred and fury turned to terror and pain. Every word he sang seemed to intensify the assault on the demons, and by the time he sang the last note, they had flapped away, whimpering, not even joining their companions in the thinning fray beyond.

Zale stopped singing, panting and staring after the disappearing galla demons. Calandra, Zoe, and Airlea all stared at him. Calandra rose from the ground and approached her brother in wonder. The light around him had faded, but when he met her gaze, the intensity of it still burned in his eyes.

"You might not know sirensong," she said, impressed once more, "but, brother, you can sure sing. You need to teach me that song."

"And me," said Airlea.

Zoe glared, giving Zale a sidelong look. "Not now. But, Zale, keep that in your pocket for when we face Lamia and her hoard."

Zale nodded. "I'd be happy to teach you. But I don't know if it was the song so much as the intention."

"It is much the same with sirensong," Airlea said. "The notes themselves don't matter, only the will you put into it. You're a quick study, with great intuition. Maybe it wouldn't take you so long to learn, after all."

Calandra drew in a breath. Zale's song had never mentioned Elyon, but it was obviously not directed to the Mother. Why hadn't her own song worked? She'd certainly intended it to repel the demons, just as Zale had.

You know why.

She shook her head, pushing away the thought. Why couldn't the winged races worship their deity and she worship hers? What made them right and her beliefs wrong? Elyon might have created the erelim, but that didn't mean Atargatis couldn't have created the undines and protected them all these years.

But how could there be more than one Essence flooding the universe?

"Go, Calandra," Airlea said with a nudge. "Zoe and Zale are almost to the portstone."

Calandra shoved her disturbing thoughts aside and sprinted after her brother and the siren.

They gathered at the foot of the steps, looking behind them to where the battle waged on, though there were few of the gargoyles left.

"Should we wait?" Zale watched the fighting beasts, looking as awed as Calandra felt.

"We don't even know where we're going yet," said Airlea. She looked at Calandra. "What did you decide?"

Calandra swallowed, her heart racing from more than the run. "I . . . I think we should go after Mother first. After we free her, we can go save Damaris. They gave Zale a day, and it's only been a few hours. We have plenty of time to do both."

Zoe shook her head. "No, we have no idea how long it's going to take to free your mother, and time is so strange here. What if we misjudge, or what if Lamia doesn't keep her word? The sooner we free my sister, the better. Wouldn't you agree, Zale?"

Zale gulped. "Er . . ." He looked back and forth between Calandra and Zoe, facing Calandra at last. "I promised I would do whatever it took to get Damaris out of here alive."

Zoe gave him a grim smile. "Thank you."

"But," he continued, turning to Zoe, "I trust my sister. I'll go with what she decides."

Calandra gave a nod of acknowledgement to her brother, her mouth dry. Whatever Semyaza had done to him must have well and truly worn off. But what should she choose? No matter which decision she made, someone would be at risk. How could she possibly decide?

Save the girl, came the quiet voice in her heart. *It will be all right.*

She frowned. If that voice truly was the Pneuma, the spirit of Elyon, she no longer trusted it. Zale's song notwithstanding, how did she even know it was trying to help her?

"We'll go after Mother first," she said, ignoring the disappointment in Zoe's and Zale's eyes. "Once we have freed her, we'll return for Damaris. With Mother free and the Soulstone healed, Lamia will find her leverage much diminished."

"And she might kill my sister on the spot," Zoe said, scowling. "No, we must go for Damaris first."

"You're questioning me *again*, Zoe? Do you wish to try and free your sister by yourself?" Calandra stared the taller woman down.

Zoe ground her teeth, then relented, stepping back. She turned toward the portstone. "We should hold hands as we go through so we don't get separated again."

"Good idea."

Calandra stepped on the bottom stair, glad Zoe hadn't fought harder than that. She held her hand out to Zale. Zoe clasped Zale's other hand.

Airlea stepped forward. "I'll go first in case there's danger on the other side."

Calandra was about to object, but, feeling Zoe's eyes on her, she smiled. "Thank you, Airlea." She took Airlea's hand and spoke over her shoulder. "We're always stronger united, wouldn't you agree, Zoe?"

Zoe inclined her head in the barest of nods, her lips pressed tightly together. As per usual, Calandra could sense nothing behind the woman's emotional shield, but it wouldn't take an empath to know how Zoe felt. Calandra would probably feel the same way if their roles were reverse. Had she made the right decision?

Rumiel and Chaz jogged up, once more in the forms of winged men.

"Are the galla demons gone?" Airlea peered back the way they had come.

"Yeah," Chaz said. "Kassiel came to help and chased the last few off. I think they were only what Valac said—motivation. Tamiel must be getting impatient."

"So have you made your decision, your highness?" Rumiel asked.

Calandra gave a curt nod. "We'll free my mother first. We're holding hands to make sure we don't get separated in transit like when we all came through the Voidstone." She was dimly aware of Zoe and Zale whispering behind her, and hoped they'd come to terms with the decision soon.

Rumiel smiled, visibly relieved. "Bless you, girl. I knew you'd make the wise choice."

Calandra studied him as he took Airlea's hand. Why was he so happy she'd chosen her mother? She supposed his position as her mother's guardian may have biased him. At least not everyone was upset with her decision.

Chazdiel declined to join the line. "I'll meet you in Elyon's Keep," he said. "I'll go tell Apollyon you're coming." He disappeared into the black sphere.

Calandra glanced over her shoulder to see Zale and Zoe exchanging meaningful looks.

"Are you ready?" she asked curtly.

Zale whipped his head around. "Huh? Yeah. Of course."

Calandra turned toward the front of the line, where Airlea stood on the steps. "Lead on, Singer kor'Phile."

Airlea flushed. "Yes, your highness."

"Think of Delphine as you go through," Rumiel said, "and we shall arrive as near as the portstone permits, which should be the lowest level of Elyon's Keep. I'll stand here until you're through and come right after."

Airlea gave a cursory nod, her lips pressed together, then stepped into the portstone.

As Calandra stepped in after her, Zale gave her hand a squeeze. "I'm sorry."

"For what? Ouch!" Calandra released her grip on Zale's palm, which had suddenly become too hot to touch. She turned to snatch at it, but she was already being sucked into the cold void of the portstone jump. "Zale!" she shouted, or tried—the sound was sucked away by the vacuum.

She tried to corral her anxious thoughts, concentrating on her mother's image. The cold void pressed against her, barely cooling the pain in her palm. In seconds, she stumbled out the other side still clutching Airlea's hand. They surprised some winged warriors who were seated cross-legged on the floor of a vast stone torch-lit chamber filled with hundreds more. The guardians leapt to their feet as Rumiel stepped into the room out of nothing behind her, their split robes swinging with their movements.

"What's this?" asked one of them, a man with a topknot bound by a golden ring.

Calandra looked around, holding the wrist of her scalded hand, though the pain was subsiding—Zale had only meant to make her let go, not injure her. The room was filled with similarly dressed winged erelim, sitting or standing roughly in groupings, obviously with not much to do. But there was no sign of her brother or Zoe anywhere.

One of the men—tall, dark-skinned, with broad shoulders, fierce goldenrod eyes and black feathered wings, in a predominantly red uniform—approached and gave Rumiel that lumasi chest-touching gesture that must be their equivalent of a salute.

"Captain Rumiel, it has been a long time," the man said in an unusual language Calandra had never heard before—so why did she understand it perfectly?

He surveyed the two young women. "And you have brought undines. What a welcome surprise." He repeated the gesture for Calandra and Airlea, bowing his head slightly at the same time.

"Greetings, Commander Apollyon," Rumiel replied in the same tongue. "Why do you have so much company?"

"Abyss watch. Things have been getting a tad testy down below." He stamped his foot to emphasize his point. "General Uriel thought it best to station extra legions here, just in case."

They stood in the centre of a huge circular stone trapdoor, though it had been sealed with some kind of metal. The shiny golden metal that filled the grooves of the door and surrounding stone casing was completely untarnished but had worn away with use in places.

Panic rose in Calandra's throat. She still couldn't see Zale and Zoe. "Excuse me, did you happen to see an undine boy and a siren singer appear a few moments ago? Maybe somewhere else in the hall?"

The man blinked. "I'm sorry, m'lady, but you're the first undines I've seen in thousands of years, since the general ordered the lower gates sealed." He pointed at the sealed stone door beneath their feet.

"May I see your finder?" Rumiel held out his hand expectantly.

The man handed him a flat, round gold case. Rumiel flipped it open and rubbed his thumb across the stone face, studying it. The pattern on the smooth stone looked like a green cat eye.

"He's not here," the cherub said at last.

Calandra's heart sped up. "Where is he, then?"

Rumiel looked up, scowling. "The Western Wastelands. And the nearest working portstone is hours away. I'll have to take us to him with my chariot, but that means we'll have to use the portstone there to leave—my chariot won't be recharged enough yet."

Calandra's heart fell. Why had Zale done such a thing after saying he'd abide by her choice? She replayed the moments before they walked through the stone—his murmured apology and her scalding hand . . . and Zoe's look.

In the few seconds Calandra had been turned away to talk to Rumiel and Chaz, Zoe must have said something that changed Zale's mind. She clenched her fists, ignoring Airlea's understanding look.

Airlea kor'Phile might believe in her decisions. But apparently few others did—not even her own brother. Maybe not even herself.

"What about that?" Airlea pointed at the end of the chamber behind them. "Isn't that a portstone?"

Calandra turned to see stone arches leading into another room that had a dais and a large round object covered in white cloth.

The winged commander shook his head. "That one's been

decommissioned for centuries."

Chaz flew up and alighted in front of them. "Sorry I'm late. I've been talking to Captain Shriniel, and she said her troops are at our service, should it become necessary." He took in their shell-shocked expressions and stopped. "Whoa, who put the nettles in your tea?"

Calandra gave a small growl of frustration. "Zale. He and Zoe went to the Wastelands after all. And we're stuck here unless we take the long way around or use up Berian's chariot." She turned to the tall cherub in red who'd spoken earlier. "Unless you have more we could borrow."

Apollyon shook his head. "I'm sorry, m'lady, we have no need of such devices here. The only guardians stationed here must be able to teleport. But I could spare a few to take you, if you wish."

Calandra was about to respond in the affirmative when pain throbbed in the back of her skull, radiated down her neck, and bloomed across the top of her head. The bundle of bonds glowed fiery red in her mind. She began panting, trying to control the mounting agony.

"We have to go after him." She turned to Rumiel. "Now."

Rumiel looked at her with concern on his face. "Your highness, I think you should send someone else. Chaz can lead Captain Shriniel's flight to the right place. You look like you should lie down."

"NO!" Red surged in front of Calandra's vision, and she fought to maintain control. It wasn't supposed to go like this. How did this happen? "I have to do it! I have to help him. It's my duty. I need him to save Mother and heal the Soulstone. I have to go after him!"

The ground beneath her feet began to tremble and sprays of dust tumbled down the shaking walls in little rivulets. Airlea leapt toward her and placed one hand on Calandra's forehead and the other on the back of her head, singing anxiously.

Calandra pushed her away. "It's not helping. I can't control it. Get out of here, Airlea! Save yourself!"

Airlea shook her head vehemently. "No, Calandra. I'm not leaving you."

Rocks began falling from the ceiling. The chamber was in chaos as commanders shouted orders at their troops. Around them, warriors ran or flew this way and that before popping out of sight.

Rumiel dodged a rock fall and hovered in the air. "Get back, Singer kor'Phile. Calandra, call on the Spirit!"

"Mother," she said through gritted teeth, begging the protector she'd always known to respond. "Help me!" Panting, she curled up in a ball on the floor, laying on her side. Tears flowed from her eyes, only some of which were from pain. "Please, Airlea, I'm . . . begging you. . . . Don't die here. Rumiel," she called, "take her . . . away."

Airlea clung to Calandra's shoulders, hunching over her body. "No. I told you I'd follow you out of this place, and I mean to do it, one way or another."

A resounding *crack* filled the air.

"Look out!" came a shout.

Rumiel looked up in time to see the boulder and dodged it in mid-air. Chaz dove toward Airlea, grabbing her around the waist. Airlea's hands were ripped from Calandra's shoulders, and she whimpered. Rumiel looked like he was trying to get close to Calandra, but he kept having to avoid falling rocks. One fell close to Calandra's head and shattered. She flinched, weeping.

"Calandra, call on the Pneuma!" Rumiel called.

If she'd been able to, she probably would have. But pain was all she knew. It consumed her.

Then, with the roar of sundering stone, the bottom fell out of the world and she plunged through darkness.

68

THE SHEDIM

Zale materialized in a desert ravine shadowed in weird grey twilight and bumped into Zoe's back.

She whirled. "Watch it, numbskull."

"Sorry," he muttered.

His conscience pricked him for abandoning Calandra, but Zoe was right—Damaris needed him *now*, and Calandra would be fine without him. They'd catch up to her once their task here was complete. Now that he'd found a way to repel demons, he wasn't as worried about it being just him and Zoe. Between his song and hers, they should be able to handle Lamia and her nest.

He hoped.

He took a few steps away from the siren, craning his neck upward to survey the rugged stone cliffs around them. Against the eerie light, their silhouettes were the black of dried blood.

"They weren't joking about it being a wasteland, were they?"

Zoe turned in a slow circle, her *deiktis* at the ready. "Something is off."

Zale snorted. "You think? I mean, there isn't a single plant. There isn't a single animal. There isn't anything but rocks, and sand, and—wait, are those human skeletons?"

"Ssh!" Zoe hissed with a wave of her hand.

Zale tore his gaze away from the scattered bones. With his senses on high alert, he craned his neck to see what she had detected, but he couldn't see anything. After a few seconds, he whispered, "What is it?"

"Nothing." She cast a derisive look his way. "I just wanted you to be quiet."

Zale scowled and adjusted the strap of his bag, the heavy stone cuffs already starting to chafe. After a few minutes, he asked, "So, which way to Lamia's lair, do you think?"

Zoe pointed partway up the hills to some dark smudges that might be cave openings. "I think we're already there."

Without warning, a dozen shedim slithered out of the sand around them, laughing and jeering. Their putrid stench made Zale's stomach heave. Lamia, in a gold-trimmed off-the-shoulder red bodice that bared a supple midriff above her serpent's tail, materialized in front of them and slithered to loom just inside the circle of her kin. Her smoky black eyes flashed, and when she placed her beringed hands on her hips, dozens of slim gold bangles on each wrist tinkled like a rattlesnake's warning.

"How observant you are," Lamia purred to Zoe through blood-red lips. She turned to Zale. "So nice to see you again, Zale. I knew you'd be back for more."

Zale crouched, drawing fire into his gut in preparation. It was a strain with the cuffs on, but he could do it if he concentrated. He hoped it would be more effective against a snake than it had been against a dragon. "Where's Damaris?"

Lamia clucked her tongue in mock reproach. "What, no warm greeting for your sweetheart? I'm hurt." She bent toward him, and her visage shifted before his eyes so when she drew near, it was Damaris's head and body on the copper serpent tail. "I'm right here, my love. Do you have another kiss for me?"

Her fetid breath washed over him, and a slimy black tongue flicked out of her mouth. He pulled back, warding her off with raised hands. "Once was more than enough."

"Oh, pumpkin, you're breaking my heart." She walked her fingers up his arm, then changed back to her own face, laughing in delight at his shiver of disgust.

"Enough of this," Zoe said, brandishing her staff in front of Lamia's face and raising the outstretched fist bearing the *ichthys* ring into Lamia's field of vision. "What have you done with my sister?"

Lamia retreated, eyeing the ring warily. "Where did you get that?"

"Does it matter?" Zoe held her fist high in challenge.

Lamia shook her head, not taking her eyes from the ring. Calandra's intuition about Lamia's reaction had been right. Zale dared to hope this could work.

"What do you want?" Lamia asked.

"My sister for the boy." Zoe jerked her chin toward Zale.

"You'd give up one of your own kind?"

Zoe cast him a snide glance. "*He* is not my kind."

Ouch. He frowned at her. She was getting a little too into the act.

Lamia smiled lazily. "Any chance you'd part with that ring, as well?"

"No," Zoe said. "I need it to get Damaris and me out of this chained place and get us home."

Zale blinked at her, a whisper of alarm tickling his throat. What Zoe said was true, but something about the way she said it made him think she wasn't planning on going back for Calandra and the others first.

Lamia turned back to Zale. "And what about you, dear boy? Do you agree to take your sweet Damaris's place? Come with me willingly?"

Zale looked at Lamia through narrowed eyes. *Don't commit to anything.* "Let me see her. I want to know she's safe."

Lamia arched a brow, and Zoe jerked her fist. Lamia glanced at it, looking as though she were trying not to look nervous, then gestured to the sandy rise behind her and called something in a language Zale had never heard before. It made him want to wash out his ears.

Moments later, a male and a female shedu appeared from a cave entrance halfway up the cliff where it started sloping downward to the ravine floor, urging a haggard-looking Damaris down the shifting slope. Her sandy curls cascaded in tangled clumps over her shoulders, and her hands were bound in front of her with green stone cuffs.

Feldspar. But she wouldn't be able to force power through them like Zale could. And, unlike his dampening cuffs, hers were connected together with a short gold chain, hindering her mobility.

Zoe never took her eyes off her sister's progress down the hill until Damaris was standing just beyond the ring of shedim. When she saw Zale and Zoe, she stiffened her neck, holding her head high.

"See?" Lamia said to them both. "She's safe, just like I promised."

"Are you hurt?" Zoe called.

Damaris gave a wary glance at her two guards and then shook her head.

"So," said Lamia, slithering around behind Zale, "do you agree to this exchange?"

Damaris's brow furrowed. "Exchange? What's she talking about?"

Zoe gave him a piercing look. "Oh, he agrees. He already agreed. Didn't you, Zale? Whatever it took, you said."

Zale stared at Zoe uncomprehendingly. This was the part of the plan where the others were supposed to attack and distract the shedim while he, Zoe, and Damaris made a run for it—only, there were no others. It was just them. Was Zoe's meaningful glare meant to signal he should call lightning anyway? Keep the demons busy so they could get away?

But she gave him a slight shake of her head. "We're outnumbered and out of our league. This is what it takes, Zale. Wouldn't you agree?"

Realization dawned. Zoe had no intention of freeing Zale. She was sacrificing him to save her sister without even a fight. The two of them might have stood a chance at fighting the shedim together, but him alone? He didn't dare risk it. He wouldn't risk Damaris's freedom on his failure.

Slowly, he nodded his head. "I did say I'd do whatever it takes for Damaris to leave the Underworld alive." Even without whatever binding magic his words may have put on him, he'd meant every word.

Zoe gave a small, victorious smile, then turned to Lamia. "See? He'll stay, no arguments."

Lamia had been looking back and forth between them and now broke into a wide smile. "Then we have an accord. You and your sister may go."

She moved aside, and Zoe walked past her to Damaris. The two shedim who held her arms released her, and one of them used a black iron rod with a glowing red gem on one end to open her cuffs. Two more male shedim with brawny arms and bare chests blocked Zale's way.

"Zale—" Damaris tried to go to him, but Zoe grabbed Damaris's arm to stop her.

Zoe tugged on her sister, trying to turn her around. "Let's go."

Lamia pointed along the ravine. "You'll find the portstone around the curve that way, my dear. Mind the gap on the way out." She laughed.

"Zale?" Damaris said as Zoe tugged her away. "Zoe, what are you doing?"

"What had to be done," Zoe said tightly.

Damaris struggled against Zoe's handhold. "No! We can't leave him here."

Zoe grabbed her sister's arm with her other hand, and Damaris winced. "This is the only way to get you out of here. Zale wants you to leave. Don't you, Zale?"

He drew a breath, trying to look brave. "Yes, I do. Damaris, it has to be this way. Go with Zoe. I'll be fine. They need me alive."

Damaris tore her hand from Zoe's and began to run back to him. The two shedim who had dragged her down the hillside grabbed her arms and stopped her in her tracks.

She looked at him with pleading eyes. "No! Zale, I promised too. I promised I'd look after you, no matter the cost. I won't leave you here alone."

"Please, Damaris," Zale said. "Please. You have to go. Go with Zoe."

She looked at him with moisture in her big eyes, her chin quivering. Even with her hair in disarray and her pink lotus lips trembling and twisted, she was still the prettiest girl he'd ever seen.

"Please," he said quietly, fervently.

At last, she nodded, and the shedim released her. With trudging steps, she turned and allowed her sister to guide her away.

Lamia watched the two of them walk until they were beyond earshot, then turned her wide, grotesque smile back on Zale.

"Now, my love, it's just you and me. Oh, such a shame I have plans for you. You would be absolutely delicious."

She slithered around him and trailed a finger along his arm and across the nape of his neck. He shivered, watching the figures of Zoe and Damaris get smaller in the distance. They would soon disappear around a bend in the ravine. *Just a little farther . . .*

Lamia looked at her minions and snapped her fingers. The two shedim who'd been guarding Damaris snapped to attention.

"Go get me that ring," Lamia hissed.

The two shedim pressed their palms together and bowed in acknowledgement of the order, then disappeared into thin air.

"No!" Zale cried, his gut tensing, fire boiling in his veins and straining against the feldspar. Without the ring, Damaris would still be stuck here, and all this would be for nothing. "You promised!" he shrieked.

A flash of light and heat struck the hillside above them, followed by a roaring thunderclap that made many of the shedim around him cover their ears. Rocks tumbled down the hill from the place the lightning had struck it.

Lamia flinched, then turned to stare at him. "I see those cuffs are just for show. Very clever. We'll have to do a better job than that." She snapped her fingers at her minions. "Manacle."

Before Zale could look to see who was obeying her order, a thick manacle of green feldspar closed around his ankle from behind, and all the fire in his belly guttered. He whirled to see a man with yellow slitted eyes and a tail covered in a black and yellow diamond pattern retreating back to the circle. Zale strained to rekindle the flame, but the extra feldspar had done its job.

"Hey!" He glared up at Lamia.

She shifted to *podia* state and stood before him, her hands on her hips.

"Now, you and I must come to an understanding. You play nice, and I'll let you live. Does that sound fair?"

He glared at her. "You broke the deal. Damaris needs that ring."

She clucked her tongue. "Not as much as I do."

She held up her hand to show him her fingers. A ring very similar to the one Zoe wore glinted from her hand. It looked clunkier and the stone in the centre was white instead of blue, but the gold eight-spoked wheel setting was unmistakable.

"You see," she continued, "once I have all the keys, plus the boy who can help charge them, I'll have all the power. Then dear daddy and Tamiel and Semyaza and all the others will have to give us what we want, because if they don't, they'll rot in their cages forever."

"And why should I help you?"

Lamia grinned maliciously. "Because, if you don't, your dear Damaris will still die. Whether in this world or the other one, I'll see to that."

An unaccustomed chill ran through Zale's veins, and he stared at the serpent woman. These creatures were bound to the Ground—they could come and go from the mortal plane as they pleased, and he wouldn't even know they were there. How could he protect Damaris, or how could she defend herself, from a threat neither of them could even see?

"Ah, I see I have your attention now," Lamia hissed. "So, are you ready to do your part?"

Zale nodded miserably, his shoulders slumping. He should have been more specific when he made his deal.

She slithered around him, drawing in a deep breath with a look of bliss on her face. "Ah, the misery. You're full to bursting with it. Like sweet nectar."

She nodded at two more of her minions. Two shedim, a man and a woman, grabbed Zale by the upper arms. He tried to shake them off, but their grips were like iron.

"Where are we going?" he demanded.

Lamia leaned close and he tried to pull back, but couldn't.

She grinned. "Tamiel may have laid claim to you first, but that doesn't mean I can't have a taste as my bounty."

Her wicked laugh filled his ears as she pulled away, leaving him feeling covered in slime. But when his guards urged him up toward the cave entrance, he didn't resist. The heavy stone manacle made him limp a little as he walked.

He glanced at the woman who held his arm and caught his breath. There across her back was Damaris's *deiktis*.

"Get moving," she hissed, giving him a shove. "The Dark Princess has a surprise for you."

That couldn't be good. He looked at the forbidding hole of the cave entrance above and tensed. What did Lamia intend to do with him?

69

THE DEEP

CALANDRA HUDDLED IN THE DARK, still water, hugging her tail to her chest in the tight space of the crevice she'd found, her back pressed against jagged rock. A typhoon of memories of how she'd gotten here swirled in her head—frantically lashing out from the blinding pain when she'd hit the surface of the Pool of Tears, wrestling the crystal key from Nadia's neck, her crazed drive to reach the Soulstone, how she'd encountered the Leviathan the moment she'd opened the quaternaria grate, how she'd fled the monster until she'd found this crevice in the side of its grotto, how she'd shaken the earth on purpose to close herself in . . . though she didn't know if she'd started a new earthquake or if the ground had even ceased shaking since her seizure had started. The serpentine sea monster had banged against the wall of rocks she'd created for ages before it finally stopped.

She sobbed into her scales, her tears lost to the salty water around her. Her heart pounded a frenzied rhythm in her ears and water rushed through her gills like a sub's turbine. The pain, the ever-present pain that wouldn't release her even in unconsciousness pulsed through her, until she *was* the pain. Beyond the rock slide that hemmed her in, she could sense the enormous sea monster circling. She shuddered, remembering the long snout with sharp, tearing teeth, the beady eyes, the sinuous body the size of a large ship, the enormous flippers, the black, blubbery hide. Most of all, she remembered the hate. The beast didn't just want to eat her. It wanted to erase her from existence.

For a moment, the promise of relief that death offered had even tempted her.

Calandra . . .

She stopped crying and looked around at the darkness.

Mother? Mother, I can hear you. Where are you?

Several moments of silence went by with no response. She stopped straining to hear one, curling in on herself once more.

What have I done? Her shoulders slumped. *I've failed Mother. I've failed Zale. And I've failed my people. Is there anyone I haven't failed?*

The list went on. Tanni. Thea. Gerrick. Damaris. Judith. Rhea and the Free Will Society. Little Melany and Charis. Even Zoe.

Osaze.

At the thought of her former consort-elect, despair clenched her heart. What if she didn't get out of this? He'd never know how sorry she was for what she'd done. She hoped Rumiel's companions had successfully freed him, at least. If only she knew he was safe, she could face her fate.

You can find out, said a voice. The voice she wasn't sure she wanted to hear.

But it was right.

Forcing herself to concentrate through the pain, she bit her lip and closed her eyes, questing with her heart as she had done before. At first, all she sensed was the void, pulsing with agony. She tried again, and this time, she found him.

But this time was different than it had been before.

Instead of quivering in a small rock cavern off the Leviathan enclosure near the Well of Souls, she was swimming in the Crystal Cavern beneath the Opal Palace. Above her, the cavern walls and ceiling were covered in thousands of clusters of amethyst crystals, and light sparkled from light-stones beneath the surface of the water around her. Treading water in front of her swam Osaze.

He stared at their surroundings, looking as surprised as she. Then his gaze landed on her.

"Calandra, you're here." He started swimming toward her, then stopped, looking dazed. "Is this a dream? It feels . . . different. Real."

"It's real, in a manner of speaking," she said softly.

She drank in the sight of him. He looked just as she remembered, but he seemed . . . tired. Discouraged. Even still, he searched her face as hungrily as she searched his.

"Are you safe?" she asked, not knowing if she wanted to hear the answer.

He frowned in thought and winced. "Safe enough."

She caught her breath. Would he even tell her if it were otherwise? But the question stuck in her throat, fear of the truth silencing her. He looked fine, but what did that mean in this fabricated place? What she saw was probably not how he was. Not with the way pain twisted his features every so often. She wondered what injuries the dreamscape concealed.

When she'd encountered Damon in her dreams, it had felt like this. The dreamscape version of the inundated Atlantean Archive had been nearly identical to the real one, but there'd been some key differences— differences that reflected a version of reality Damon had wanted her to see. If their meetings were because of her own gifts, Damon had still managed to influence how she'd perceived him.

Or she'd willingly deceived herself.

"Osaze, are you sleeping?"

He gave her a confused look. "I . . . I think so. I must be, otherwise we wouldn't be here. Together. Abela said you're in the Underworld."

His voice cracked, and the hurt and anger she'd felt from him each time she'd contacted him washed over her again, flowing from him in violent waves. She wanted nothing more than to rush to him, to wrap her arms around him and take all the pain away—but she knew it wasn't that simple. Not when she was the one who'd caused it.

A distant crash reached her awareness—the Leviathan had resumed its repeated blows against her hiding spot. Calandra gasped, looking around, but the dreamscape didn't even waver.

"Listen, I probably don't have much time." She swam nearer to him. "I want to tell you . . . no, *need* to tell you how much I regret sending you away. I knew almost immediately I'd been wrong to do it, but it seemed too late to do anything about it—better to let you be than drag you back only to apologize."

She was near enough to touch him. Oh, how she yearned to reach out and caress his face, to feel his lips on hers once more . . . but she hesitated. The guarded expression on his face matched the hurt in his heart. And then she couldn't sense him anymore—he'd put up his shield.

"You had no right to do that," he said in a low, controlled voice, tight with anger. "You treated me like a *doulos*. You promised to protect me, and I promised to protect you. You broke your promise."

Tears flowed down Calandra's face, but she did nothing to stop them. "I know. I'm so sorry. If I could go back and change the past, I would. I only wanted to ask your forgiveness before . . ."

She couldn't say it. She couldn't tell him she was sure the Madness was about to take her—that she would soon be joining her Mad sisters in a futile attempt to guard condemned spirits trying to escape from the failing Soulstone. That it would only be a matter of time before the bonds holding the power-hungry spirits would dissolve, and all she loved, the very earth itself, would be destroyed, thanks to the dragon she'd allowed to escape.

She couldn't say that she'd failed him. She'd failed everyone.

"Before what?" he demanded. "Calandra, what's happening to you? Are you in danger?"

She almost laughed. Even in his hurt, even though he could do nothing to help her, his first concern was still for her.

How could she have ever thought he'd chosen her only by default?

"Please tell me you forgive me, Osaze."

She looked into his coal-black eyes, begging for the release he could give her with his next words. He searched her face, the only sound the swishing of the water around them and the distant crashing of the sea monster's attacks, like surf pounding on the cliffs outside the palace.

At last, he shook his head.

"No, I cannot forgive you. I won't, not if it means you're going to give up and—"

Searing pain through Calandra's head brought her out of the dreamscape and back to her little cave. The rocks shuddered from the force of the sea monster's blows, and she shivered in fear, trying her best to shore up the wall's connections with her scattered mind.

Osaze wouldn't forgive her. And she didn't blame him. Not when she couldn't even forgive herself.

Consumed by pain, she waited for the absolution that only the Madness would bring.

70

THE RETURN

Osaze jolted awake, a sharp pain of longing slicing his chest. He kept his eyes closed and listened. The sound of steady breathing came from the other bed—two people, both sleeping.

He opened his eyes. The room was barely illuminated by whatever light sifted through the filmy curtain in front of the window. Which made it easier to remember what it felt like swimming in the Crystal Cavern with Calandra.

The longing intensified, tightening around his stomach like a rope. Had he really been talking to Calandra, or had it been a dream like so many times before?

And he'd denied her request for forgiveness—not out of cruelty, but because he heard the resignation in her voice. She was giving up—and if Calandra was giving up, she must be in deep trouble.

She could die in that place, and no one would never know. He would never know.

If she gave up, how would she fight her way back to him?

He curled his legs up to his belly. "I'll forgive you, Calandra, but only if you come back to the land of the living. You have to live, so I can find you."

*

"Osaze! Osaze, wake up!"

Osaze roused to find Bunmi shaking him by the shoulder. Behind her, Josefine was tying up her bundles.

He struggled to sit up, foggy tendrils of his encounter with Calandra

601

still clouding his emotions.

"What is it? What's happened?"

Bunmi looked at him with worried eyes. "It's Miss Bethel. She says we must leave, now. Mr. Cox—"

"Robert Cox has betrayed us," said Josefine in a severe tone as she yanked the last knot in her shawl tight.

Osaze was wide awake now. He swung his legs off the side of the bed, wincing at the pain the action evoked in his wounds. Taking Bunmi's proffered hand, he used it and the wall for support to raise himself to standing. He moved the curtain aside to see a cityscape lit only by the occasional street lamp that had not yet guttered. The stars had already begun to fade—it was nearly morning.

In the alley below, a pudgy man in a brown jacket stood staring up at his window. He thought the man resembled Thatcher, the baron's plantation foreman. Osaze dropped the curtain and withdrew into the shadows, then peeked around the frame through the sheer fabric. Yes, the man was definitely looking at this window.

And it was definitely Thatcher.

"We are being watched," he said in Yoruba and then Greek so both of the women would understand. "Thatcher is here."

Bunmi drew in a sharp breath and shook her head. "How did he find us already?"

Josefine came and took a quick look, barely moving the curtain and taking a quick glimpse before dropping it again. "It was only a matter of time. I doubt he's alone." She picked up her shawl and slung it over her shoulder. "We have to get out of here. Now."

She put her arm around Osaze's waist on the side opposite Bunmi, and he flinched. She looked up at him in concern, but he gritted his teeth.

"It is fine. Thank you." He looped his arm around her shoulder and used her and Bunmi as support to shuffle out to the corridor.

When they got there, his mother and Abela were just leaving their room. Urbi looked only slightly less worried than Bunmi when she saw Osaze's hunched form. She came and took his hand from Bunmi, who moved aside for her. Osaze stiffened.

She looked at him with piercing eyes. "I am your mother. It is my job to support you. Do not rob me of this, my son."

He nodded and relaxed as she took up her post next to him. Guilt pricked his heart. He'd been angry and distant with her ever since coming to this island. What good had it done? After so many years of being separated from her by the *sklavia* bond, he'd wasted the last few weeks in resentment. Even still, she'd never stopped being kind, never stopped looking out for him. They may not always agree, but did that mean he needed to punish her with silence forever?

"Thank you, Mother," he whispered, and squeezed her shoulder. She looked up and gave him a hesitant smile.

"All right?" Abela looked them over.

"Middleton's plantation foreman is in the street watching our window," said Osaze.

Abela tapped her lip. "Hmm. He arrived much sooner than I expected. Of course, I'd planned to be gone by now too."

"You were expecting him?" Urbi asked.

Josefine cleared her throat. "My father knew where you were staying. Even though I didn't tell him where I was going, it wouldn't have taken much for him to surmise I'd left with Mr. Cox. Frankly, I'm surprised someone didn't arrive earlier. Mr. Romero's doing, I suppose."

Abela nodded. "Indeed. Mr. Romero would have set a guard of erelim to prevent you being followed. It would only have worked for a while—unmanifested erelim prefer to use weapons such as confusion and misdirection to distract rather than enter into an open confrontation, and eventually, humans work their way through such tactics. The erelim could block their path, which would alarm their animals and prevent progress, though not indefinitely. But usually such safeguards last much longer. How long was I unconscious, anyway?"

The last question was directed at Urbi, who frowned.

"Not so long."

Abela shook her head as though pushing away an unpleasant thought. "Even still, only one of our own, a person not under the influence of the erelim, should have been able to lead them directly to us—no one else could have gotten through."

Osaze didn't understand all the English words, but he understood the meaning perfectly. "Did Cox show them?"

She glanced at him and shook her head. "Not possible."

"They have a Dragon's Eye," Josefine said.

"Pardon?" Abela said sharply.

Josefine's cheeks flushed rosy. "My father has a finder. Could that have done it?"

Abela pressed her lips in a firm line. "That explains a great deal. Yes, that is likely why. A Dragon's Eye. Indeed." She shook her head as though in disbelief. "There are more Dragon's Eyes on this island than dragons," she muttered.

Reaching into the small yellow silk drawstring bag she carried, she withdrew a thick gold disc attached to a gold chain with a hook on the other end. When she pressed a clasp on the side of the disc, the face flipped open and revealed a smooth circular stone encased inside. The stone's colouring reminded Osaze of a red lizard's eye.

"This is Berian's finder," Abela said. "The ordinary sort we lumasi use, not a Dragon's Eye. He left it to me along with his other tools for safe-keeping. When I woke up, I used it to look for Robert and found he had returned to Huntley Hall, where he remains. After learning he'd drugged me, that doesn't surprise me terribly." She gazed at the face as though it was revealing more to her than the rest of them could see. "Just disappoint-ed," she said quietly.

Osaze peered at the finder in wonder. He'd never heard of such a de-vice. *Could something like that be used to find anyone? Even someone in the Underworld?*

Abela closed the instrument and tucked it back into her pouch. Then she turned a sharp gaze on Josefine.

"You're familiar with the supernatural. Do the men you and your father were working with have what you humans would call a familiar? Or have any of them manifested a demonic presence?"

Josefine shook her head. "I've never seen Lord John or Colonel Hay-ward with any animals at all. As for possession . . . I'm not sure. Possessing spirits often cause their hosts to be quite slovenly and uncouth, and I've never seen such a punctilious man as Hayward. Middleton? Well, you've seen him."

"Indeed. Though an evil spirit who possesses a man for only a short period of time or sporadically wouldn't leave any defining marks of their presence. What about Mr. Thatcher?"

"I barely know him," Josefine said.

"And your father?" Abela arched a brow.

Josefine paled slightly. "I . . . I don't think so."

Abela frowned, tapping her lips once more. "Well, we can chew on that mystery later. Come, now, it's time we're gone." She frowned. "Too many for a single chariot trip, and we don't have time to wait for the re-charge. I suppose we'll have to sneak out through the kitchen into that little alley. Let's—"

Footsteps coming up the stairs at the end of the corridor made them freeze.

"Stand along the edge of the corridor and don't move a muscle," hissed Abela, gesturing them aside.

Urbi and Josefine helped Osaze shuffle backward a step so he was next to the wall, and Bunmi pressed herself against it beside them. Abela spread her fingers as though grabbing hold of something, then moved her hands toward them as though pushing it in their direction. The shadows in the corridor intensified, clinging to Osaze and his companions while leaving Abela standing in a pool of light from the flickering lamp hanging from the wall. She turned to face whomever was coming.

A young teenage girl with a single brown braid appeared, dressed neatly in a clean work frock. Osaze caught his breath—if she saw him, would she sound the alarm?

Seeing Abela, the girl rushed toward her, not even looking at Osaze and the others. In fact, she hurried right past him as though she couldn't even see him there.

What sorcery is this?

"Miss Bethel, this came for you from Mr. Cox," said the girl, handing Abela a folded slip of paper.

Abela smiled graciously. "Thank you, Mildred."

The girl smiled and curtsied, but didn't leave.

Abela opened it and scanned the contents. "Oh, that confounding man. He's arranged passage for Urbi on the Molly Merrow. At least he followed through on that." She gave her head a shake, a perplexed expression on her face. She turned to the girl. "No response is needed. You may run along."

"There's one more thing, miss, from the gentleman as was comin' to see you so much. He said you'd know what to do wit' it."

Mildred pulled a small carved wooden box from one apron pocket, and a familiar-looking lumpy, dirty cloth drawstring bag from the other, which drew a soft gasp from Urbi, and offered them to Abela. Abela took them, feeling the contents of the bag before opening it and peeking inside. Smiling, she pulled the string tight again and tucked it under her arm, then turned her attention to the box. When she opened the hinged lid, her eyes widened. On the silk pillow inside lay a bauble of nested silver rings around a small translucent golden stone bead.

Abela reverently took the trinket from the box. "When did these come?"

"He come and gived 'em to me father hours ago, but said to bring 'em to you at precisely four in the mornin'. An' that's what time it is."

"Thank you," Abela breathed, holding the pendant to the light by the small ring at the top. "You have no idea what this means to me. Here." She tucked the box in her bag, then fished a few coins out and handed them to the girl. "The pieces of eight are for your father, to thank him for his kind and excellent service. And the bits are for you. Run along to the kitchen now. I'm sure Cook is looking for you to help with breakfast."

The girl blushed and curtsied. "Yes, miss. Thank you so much."

She turned to hurry away, then stopped and looked back over her shoulder. "You're all right, miss. I wish more of our customers was like you, no matter what the other guests say." Her mouth twisted. "Especially the ones as said it."

With that, Mildred turned and dashed back down the stairs.

Osaze let out a breath, staring wonderingly after the girl. "She didn't even notice us. What did you do?" he asked in Yoruba.

Abela glanced up at him, then back at the trinket in her hands. "Nothing but a little light bending. Oh, Erel, you wonderful malak, you," she said to no one in particular. She handed the cotton bag to Urbi. "I believe this belongs to you."

When Urbi opened the bag and peered inside, Osaze caught a glimpse of the handful of amethysts they had buried in the sandy dunes along the shore some distance away. He looked at his mother, wanting to ask how they had been retrieved, but before he could say anything, Abela continued in an excited voice.

"Do you know what this means?" She pulled another identical pendant from where it hung behind the neckline of her dress on a long fine silver chain, holding them beside each other in her open palm.

Osaze looked at the identical baubles on her hand. Urbi tucked the bag into her dress pocket and bent close to the devices, fascinated. Bunmi looked at them in a mixture of fear and curiosity.

"No. What do they mean?" Urbi asked for all of them.

Abela smiled. "It means that between my chariot and this extra one from Mr. Romero, I can take us *all* out of here, all the way to Sirenia. We can get help from my contact there to reach Atlantis. We don't even have to sneak past our unwanted visitors." Her gaze darkened and she looked at her wrist where the heartstone bracelet was most likely hiding, then shook her head, frowning. "I'll deal with that later."

"Sirenia?" Urbi glanced at her son.

Abela caught the look. "Only temporarily for you, Mrs. Urbi. I will make sure you get to Yorubaland as soon as possible after that."

Urbi nodded hesitantly.

Bunmi stepped forward, her wondering gaze on the trinkets in Abela's outstretched palm. "These can take us away from here?"

Abela smiled. "Yes. Each one should last a couple blinks before draining completely. Hold on."

She let go of the trinket attached to the chain around her neck and withdrew a thin silver rod about a handspan long from her bag. When she touched the rod to the trinket, a small red stone set in one end of it lit up, and white light shone from the stone at the centre of the rings, then faded. She replaced the rod back in her reticule and closed her hand around the gyroscope.

"I almost forgot to re-key it," she said, rolling her eyes. "Don't want to make that mistake again."

A disturbance came from downstairs, and Josefine tiptoed along the hallway to peek down the stairwell. A man's voice echoed up the stairwell, demanding to be allowed to the rooms above, and her eyes widened in alarm. She hurried back toward them as silently as she could.

"It's my father!" she hissed, waving them back toward Osaze's room. "Hide!"

Abela glanced toward the hubbub, then around at the group. "You hide," she whispered to Josefine and Bunmi. "I'll take these two and be back in a few moments for you."

Before Osaze could object, Abela placed her hand on Osaze's chest, lifted the pendant in her open palm toward her face, and blew on it.

The rings started spinning and the gem glowed once more. Something tugged at Osaze's chest.

In the next instant, he was no longer standing in the dimly lit corridor of the inn.

He was looking at a wizened old woman with long curly grey hair pulled into a low ponytail who sat hunched next to a brazier in a paved courtyard under completely different stars—stars he'd know anywhere. Beyond her, a wooden gate was set into the plastered wall, and the other three sides of the courtyard were surrounded by a house made of whitewashed brick. Sweetly scented air from the trailing flowers along the walls enveloped him, and he breathed deeply, ignoring the pain the movement caused in his unhealed back.

Next to him, Urbi yelped in surprise. The old woman looked up and did the same. Then her face changed to recognition. She hastily rose to her feet and moved to the gate, peering through the gatekeeper's hatch along the street both ways and issuing a whispered command to the guardswoman on duty there. Giving a satisfied nod, she turned and approached them.

"So you're back, are you?" she said to Abela in a gravelly voice. She spoke the familiar Greek of Sirenia.

Of home.

"Greetings, Wilhelmina," Abela replied in the same tongue. "I've got no time to explain what is happening. Please see to my companions. I'll be back soon with more."

Wilhelmina pressed bunched fingers to her bowed forehead. "As the mistress has commanded. It is our pleasure to serve the lumasi."

"Thank you." Abela blew into her open palm again and disappeared.

Wilhelmina ran her gaze over Osaze and his mother in frank appraisal. Osaze half-expected her to raise the cry about the Freeman in the courtyard any second.

No such cry came. She went to the brazier and poked it with a rod, banking the fire and casting glances toward the back of the courtyard. Then she shambled over to the guardswoman once more to exchange urgent whispers. Somewhere in the house, an infant wailed, and Osaze startled. The babe soon quieted.

"She will betray us," Osaze whispered, glancing around the courtyard. The layout of the house reminded him of another along the Street of Pearls which Narcissa had often visited while he was in her service. "We must flee. There should be a servant's entrance over there."

He gestured toward the back of the house with his head and made to turn, but Urbi wouldn't budge.

"Wait," she said quietly. "Wait for Miss Abela."

The guardswoman, who obviously had siren training, hurried toward a room in the back of the house, and Osaze tensed, though no cry of alarm went up.

Wilhelmina gave a satisfied nod and returned to them. "About time we dealt properly with those spies," she muttered, gazing after the guardswoman. She turned to face her guests. "The lamma must have been detained. No matter." She gestured for them to follow her. "We'll get you settled while we wait."

Then she turned and shuffled toward one of the enclosed rooms at the back of the house. Osaze met his mother's glance. He expected to see the same anxiety and distress there that suddenly bunched his own gut— Wilhelmina was human, but her employers wouldn't be, not if they lived on the Street of Pearls. He was one sirensong away from being Redeemed once more. Despite his weeks of yearning to return here, he felt naked and unprepared without the songstoppers Calandra had made him for protection.

But Urbi's face was calm. "Miss Abela wouldn't have brought us here if she didn't think it was safe," she said.

Osaze studied his mother's face, then nodded. If she trusted Abela, so would he.

Wilhelmina stopped and turned. "Are you two coming? Do you even speak Greek?"

"Yes," Osaze replied. "We're coming."

He and Urbi followed the old woman at Osaze's slow, hobbling pace. Wilhelmina stepped into one of the doorways along the back portico and spoke to someone. When she emerged, a servant girl with luminescent dark green eyes and dark hair hanging in braids down her back followed her, the thin nightdress falling to her thighs her only covering. She offered a hurried salute to Osaze and Urbi, then dashed off to one of the rooms at the far corner of the portico.

How odd. In his nineteen years on Sirenia, he'd never been saluted by anyone before, let alone an undine—even a servant. And how refreshing to be back somewhere where his naked torso was not looked down on as barbaric, but considered appropriate dress for the climate. Even Wilhelmina's shawl was probably more for warmth for her old bones than for modesty. His mother, wearing a long-sleeved green gown in the fashion of the Europeans who lived on Barbados, suddenly looked overdressed.

"*Kyria* Eudora will want to meet you," Wilhelmina said over her shoulder as she led them along the walkway. "And she'll want to get your wounds seen to. Come. You may rest in here while you wait."

She picked up a small oil lamp from a nearby table in a sitting area near an elaborate fountain, then led them into a room covered with plush carpets and cushions in rich patterns around the edges and a low square table in the middle. An unlit brazier sat off to the side. A servant wearing a flowing belted white tunic with a red-and-blue striped hem entered through a door on the far side, carrying a wooden platter that she set in the centre of the table. It was covered with a selection of sliced fruit, cheese, and flatbread. She was followed by another girl carrying a tray with a clay teapot and two bronze cups. Both girls saluted before withdrawing.

Wilhelmina surveyed the room, then gave them a glare that immediately softened. "Rest yourself. I'll go back to wait for the lady lamassu. The mistress will be with you shortly. And be assured, *anthropos*," she said, meeting Osaze's gaze, "the House of Dione is a safe haven for Freemen like you."

With that, she withdrew, leaving Osaze with fresh alarm twisting his insides.

"The House of Dione?" his mother asked in a strangled voice, her previous calm gone. "As in Zoe kor'Dione?" She glanced nervously toward the doorway. "What's taking Miss Abela so long?"

Osaze glanced toward the door in time to see two men with the glazed look of the Redeemed step through, followed by the guardswoman.

The men took up posts on either side of the door and the woman turned a stern expression on Osaze, whose heard thundered against his ribs.

He swallowed. *Just when I thought I'd come home.*

71

THE BETRAYAL

THE MOMENT ABELA DISAPPEARED FROM the hallway of the Port House Inn with Osaze and Urbi, Josefine hustled Bunmi into Osaze's room.

"Stay here," she whispered.

The girl nodded, the whites of her eyes flashing in the dim predawn light coming through the window. She looked scared stiff.

"Here," Josefine said, handing Bunmi her smaller bundle of healing herbs. "Keep this for me. I'll be right back."

Bunmi nervously licked her lips and hesitantly accepted the bundle. She didn't look convinced.

"I promise," Josefine added, infusing her voice with all the assurance she could muster.

"You should stay here and wait with me for Miss Abela," Bunmi said. "She said she will return soon."

Josefine shook her head. "Yes, but my father is already coming up the stairs. If he and Hayward find you, you're going back to that plantation. My father is probably angry with me, but my consequences will be much less severe. I'm going to delay him."

Bunmi gave another nod and clutched Josefine's bundle to her chest like a shield.

Satisfied, Josefine stepped into the hallway to greet Eric, her larger bundle slung over her shoulder. He was being followed by Mr. Varley, the good-natured innkeeper, who wore a perturbed expression.

Eric reached the top step and stopped short, causing the innkeeper to bump into him and let out a surprised cry.

"There ye are, m'girl," Eric said gruffly. "Where are the others? Cox?

611

The slaves and the lumasi creatures?"

Josefine drew in a deep breath and stepped toward him—away from the door concealing Bunmi. So Abela was right—Robert hadn't sent them. That fact was not enough to redeem the young gentleman in her eyes. Her father probably felt the same way about her right now.

"They're gone. I'm the only one here."

The innkeeper leaned toward the wall to see Josefine past her father's broad-chested form. "You know this man, miss? He said his daughter was staying here, but I didn't know whether to believe him."

Josefine gave a resigned nod. "Aye, he's my father. Thank you, Mr. Varley. Best leave us alone to work this out. 'Tis a family matter."

Mr. Varley glanced between them and gave an uncertain nod, then retreated back down the narrow stairwell.

She sized up her father. Eric crossed his brawny arms over his rich red waistcoat and leaned against the wall, looking like he was doing much the same to her.

"Well, daughter, I trust ye 'ave a good reason for your actions this day? You left me in a very awkward position with The Baron."

"Middleton is a brute and a cad," Josefine snapped. "Why are you even working with him?"

"Ye know why, m'girl. For the restoration of the Romani people. Sometimes for the greater good, personal sacrifices must be made."

"Sacrifices like Zale?"

He shifted, and she could see she'd hit her mark. She softened.

"I know you care for him, Father. How can it be worth sacrificing one of our own family for a deal with a *daeva*? Can you truly be certain he isn't playing you for a fool as we have often done to the *gorgios*?"

"Of course he is," growled Eric. "But I know what he's up to, so we'll see who gets caught with their hands in the pickle jar."

"Marin always warned you not to play with things you don't understand, Father."

At the mention of the Wise Woman who had been training Josefine as a *shuvani*, Eric shifted uncomfortably and his gaze darkened.

Josefine pressed her advantage. "And look where it's got us—our family fractured, Zale in the Underworld, and you at the beck and call of a malicious spirit. If you won't listen to her, listen to me—no good can come of this path. You're changing. You're becoming like them—and you frighten me." She paused and took another step closer, tilting her head in that way he said always reminded him of her mother. "Do you truly think this is what Mother would want?"

Another arrow landed home. Eric turned aside, staring at a point be-yond her on the floor.

"You know nothing, daughter. Hold yer tongue. Now get yer things and let's go. Is that the mirror?" He pointed at the tied shawl over her shoulder.

The mirror. Of course. It wasn't Josefine her father wanted, but only her abilities and her connection to the Master that he needed. Her heart crushed inside her, and she blinked back the prickling of tears. But she'd made her choice, and she knew he needed her much more than she needed him. If he was ever going to change, she would have to do the hard thing now.

She drew herself to her full height, still barely reaching his chin. But she infused her voice with the full weight of the power she'd been trained to harness.

"You will not silence me, Father. And you will not command me any longer. I will no longer serve the Master. Please, turn aside from him and join me."

She held out her hand, a metaphor for the peace offering she was making.

He studied it, his face sad, then stood up and unfolded his arms. For the briefest of moments, she thought she'd convinced him.

Then without warning, he pulled his belt knife, grabbed her hand with his free one, and spun her back into his chest, pressing the cold blade to her throat. The rigid edges of the mirror dug into her ribs.

"Some choices cannot be unmade," he said.

She grabbed the arm pinning her by the waist and tried to drag it away, but couldn't budge it.

"Father—?" Her voice trembled. She'd never thought he would turn on her. She tried to twist to see his face, but he held her fast. A sting at her throat made her cease her struggling.

"Don't make me do this, daughter," he said against her ear. "The Mas-ter doesn't need to know you ran away, and Middleton can be appeased if we show him you're still loyal." His voice was gruff with restrained emo-tion. "Your mother didn't understand, but you do, don't you? Don't make me beg. I don't want to lose you too."

Something in his voice made Josefine's heart stop. With cold dread, Josefine recast the circumstances of her mother's unusual death in her mind in an instant. "She got in your way too, didn't she?" she choked out.

"She didn't die at the hand of that *gorgio* merchant—you killed her."

A tightening of his muscles betrayed his reaction and confirmed what she'd said. Horror gave her strength, and she elbowed her father in the gut, then twisted away from him as soon as his grip slackened.

"How could you?" she asked, her heart tearing in two.

Eric's face twisted with guilt, and he opened his mouth to speak, but she never heard what he said. Abela appeared next to her and laid a hand on her arm. In the next moment, she was standing in a large stone sugar house in the predawn light.

Josefine placed her face in her hands and shook.

72

THE MISTAKE

It was after midnight when Robert, by now completely sober, once again turned up the long treed lane of the Huntley Hall estate. The stable keeper had tried to send a local boy with Robert as a guide—not because of the fear of large predators, for the island had none, but most likely to make sure Robert found his destination in the dark. Robert had refused the offer—he'd been at the estate only hours before and, with the nearly full moon, was certain he could find it again. He suspected the worst vagrants were inside the city and that he had little to fear once he was beyond its borders.

Still, it hadn't taken him long to regret the decision. With nothing but the sound of his horse's hooves clopping against the hard dirt road, the moonlight turned the half-harvested cane fields into a crowd of broken spectres that tormented him with guilty regrets. But each time he thought about turning back, he remembered the soft pressure of Miss Bethel's kiss as she leaned into him, and his resolve hardened. He *would* find a way for them to be together. She'd understand in the end.

When Middleton's butler answered the door—his nightcap askew and an irritated look on his face, a brass candlestick in one hand—Robert practically fell inside.

"Rouse your master," he said curtly, too exhausted to be gracious. "Tell him I brought what he asked for."

"As you say, sir," said the man stiffly.

The butler led him to the sitting area in the Great Room and lit a lamp on a nearby table before leaving Robert to go fetch Middleton. Robert wandered to stand in front of the portrait of Middleton's son. The painter had done an excellent job—the boy's expression was hauntingly lifelike, especially in the flickering light of the lamp. Judging from the lad's attire, he'd be nearly the same age as Robert's mother, Genevieve, had he lived. Robert gazed at the portrait sadly. If only his own father had held him in as much esteem as George's father did. Had Robert died before James, Lord Alverton I, there would have been no painting of Robert over the mantle at Alverton Manor to remember *him* by.

He turned away from the portrait and his gaze fell on some papers sitting on Middleton's open roll-top desk next to it. He froze. The letter on top bore a familiar hand—Gryffyn's.

He brought the lamp over to the desk, glancing over his shoulder to see if anyone else was in the room. Still alone, he bent close to the desk and flattened the letter to read its contents.

Gryffyn had written to Middleton to update him on the progress of the Order's plans in England, with a list of those who had been won to their side. Nearly everyone on the list was someone prominent, including many of the landed gentry and peers and members of the House of Lords. *The Exchequer is part of the Order of the Ascension?*

These were the people he'd be joining if he joined the Order. These men of position, rank, and power. Perhaps some of them had even become men of influence *because* of their association with the Order. No wonder his father and Gryffyn had thrown their lot in with these men. Something stirred in Robert's chest—a longing to belong on a list such as this, with men who could influence the very direction of the British Empire. No more invisibility because of his scars. No more being overlooked by even his own family. He'd be a great man, rubbing elbows with other great men.

But first, he'd have to prove he belonged there.

A noise in the hall made him turn. He stepped away from the desk and returned the lamp to the table next to the sofa.

Middleton came in fully dressed, though his wig had been removed, revealing a mostly bald pate. Hayward was only a pace behind him, still in full uniform. He nodded to Robert coolly. Had the men still been awake?

"Mr. Cox," said Middleton in a greeting that was not altogether welcoming. "Two surprise visits in one day—and that's not the most momentous thing to have occurred this day. Did you know two of my slaves disappeared right after you visited? One of them was the lad you were so keen on purchasing."

Robert's heart froze. He'd been so distracted with thoughts of Miss Bethel and what he was about to do that it hadn't occurred to him the baron might associate him with Osaze and Bunmi's departure.

"I . . . I did not. Have you sent men out to recover them?"

Middleton arched an eyebrow and studied him, then went and poured them each a drink of rum. "Yes, it took longer than we expected, but we have discovered their whereabouts, and Chapman and Thatcher, my foreman, are out leading a posse now. Seems Chapman's daughter was involved."

Robert tensed to prevent his hand from shaking as he accepted the tumbler. Hayward took the glass and sat on a chair, watching Robert steadily. At the baron's gesture with his own glass, Robert sat, resuming his position on the brocade chair he'd sat in last time. Despite his determination to eschew any more drink this night, he took a swig of rum while Middleton settled himself on the sofa once more.

"How remarkable," Robert said, and wiped his mouth with the back of his hand. "That young woman made off with two slaves? Where does she think she can take them? What does she hope to do?"

"Where and what, indeed?" Middleton kept a steady gaze on Robert. "They're at the Port House Inn. For what purpose, I do not know. Do you know it?"

Robert coughed. "I've seen the sign, yes."

His heart thundered in his chest. *How could Middleton know exactly where they are? And has he discovered the three of them left with me?* But there had been so many witnesses of their odd troupe along the road, it would not have taken much to put the pieces together, no matter what Romero had arranged. Barely breathing, Robert pulled the bracelet from his pocket.

"I brought what you were looking for."

He tossed the bracelet toward Middleton, who caught it with a snap of the wrist.

The baron studied it with beady eyes. "It's magnificent," he murmured, turning it over and watching the light scatter from its depths. "Truly astounding." He looked up at Robert. "I confess, I had my doubts. I didn't think you had it in you." He turned to Hayward. "Did you?"

"I was reserving judgement," Hayward said quietly. Still, by the look the colonel gave Robert, he was obviously impressed.

Robert's insides warmed. Why had he been so worried? These men couldn't tell it was the wrong heartstone, and he'd earned credibility with them by bringing it. Berian wasn't using it anymore, and though Robert knew it would be an inconvenience to Miss Bethel, she would find another one for the reverend to use when he came back. If he even did. And if

Middleton had proof to associate him with the missing slaves, he surely would have said something.

Middleton rubbed his thumb across the stone, his eyes glittering. "What was it like to watch her discorporate? Did she bleed as a human does, or did she sort of just"—he wiggled his pudgy fingers, keeping the bracelet tucked into his palm with his thumb—"melt away?"

Robert shifted uncomfortably. "I do not wish to discuss it."

Middleton gave a sound remarkably like a giggle and tossed the bracelet to Hayward to examine. "Oh, never mind. It doesn't matter how you did it, only that you did. Well, sir, you've shown your worth. Your brother will be extremely gratified to hear of this."

Robert's heart sped up. Gryffyn would approve of something he did? That would be a first.

Middleton clapped his hands and rubbed them together. "It looks like you've earned your place in the Order, Mr. Cox. Fortuitously, we were preparing for a communion with our master when you arrived. Are you ready to be confirmed tonight?"

Robert's heart sped up. That was it? It seemed too easy. But while the affirmation felt good, part of Robert cringed. *They're excited because they think I killed Miss Bethel and took her heartstone. Are these really the kind of men I want to help rule the world?*

He brought that picture of him and Miss Bethel living happily together back into his mind and took a deep breath. "Yes, sir, I would like that very much." His voice cracked, and he cleared his throat. "What must I do?"

Hayward handed the bracelet back to Middleton and stood. "I'll go fetch a robe for him and meet you in the parlour." He left the room.

Middleton heaved his bulky frame to standing, gesturing for Robert to follow. As they left the room and went down a narrow hallway, Middleton said, "I apologize for the crudeness of the method we're about to use. Miss Chapman's mirror is our best method of communication with our spirit partners, but since she isn't here and she's taken it with her, we must resort to other means."

Robert's gut clenched in foreboding, remembering the sight of Miss Chapman, her father, and Gryffyn, along with several other supplicants in an empty warehouse in Bristol, talking to a dragon spirit in a large mirror. Would he be facing that same spirit soon? His knees felt weak, and he stiffened so they wouldn't knock together.

They entered a room at one of the front corners of the house, with windows on two adjoining walls. The room was as large as the study at Alverton Manor. A small fire burning in the hearth cast a flickering light over furnishings that had been pushed against the walls to make space on the floor. But it was what the space had been cleared for that made Robert's blood run cold.

The dark hardwood floor had a large circle of white powder that looked like wheat flour in the centre. Kneeling on her bare feet in the circle was a middle-aged black woman with her hair pulled to the nape of her neck and wrapped in a red scarf. Her hands rested on her skirted knees, and she sat with an air of expectation. In front of her on the floor was a large wooden bowl filled with water, a smaller empty copper bowl, and an unlit white pillar candle, though it had obviously been lit in the past. A dagger similar to the one Robert had concealed in his waistband lay next to a small circle of cloth upon which rested a bundle of dried herbs tied with red string.

The woman's face barely registered surprise to see Robert.

"Lulu, do you know this man?" Middleton asked.

Robert looked at the baron. Why would Middleton ask that?

The woman shook her head. "He no the one who took my daughter."

Robert's breath caught in his throat. That's why. This woman was Bunmi's mother. So the baron had been suspicious after all.

Middleton gave Robert an apologetic smile. "I had to check, you understand. One of the slaves I lost today was this woman's daughter, a fairly strong, handsome female. Her loss is not insignificant."

Robert glanced at the woman's tight expression, thinking more of Lulu's loss than the baron's. Had Bunmi left of her own accord, without even telling her mother? Ashamed, Robert realized he hadn't once wondered why the girl had fled her home until this moment, nor who she might be leaving behind. Perhaps Romero had had a point—he didn't spend nearly enough time thinking about what mattered most.

The memory of the golden-eyed man pricked his conscience, and he pushed the thought aside. Romero would never approve of what he was about to do. Neither would Miss Bethel, if she knew, and that gave him pause. But following the rules hadn't benefited him yet. He'd simply have to find a way to convince her that this had been the best way to break through the obstacles between them.

Middleton picked up a black hooded robe from where it lay across a chair near the door. Another robe still occupied the chair, and the baron's white wig lay on a small table next to it.

Hayward entered with a long black robe over his arm, which he held out to Robert. "I borrowed Chapman's for you," the colonel said. "The fit isn't that important."

Robert took it reluctantly and put it on. By the time he'd finished, Hayward had donned his own robe and both of his hosts had their hoods pulled up over their heads.

"What will I be expected to do, exactly?" Robert asked, pushing the long cuffs of the robe up his arms.

Middleton adjusted his robe over his shoulders. "Oh, it's a fairly standard devil's pact—a little cut on the hand, some blood dripped on herbs, an oath, and we burn the herbs to seal the deal. That doesn't bother you, does it, Mr. Cox?"

It did. Quite a lot. But Robert daren't show his aversion to the idea. He'd come too far now.

He clenched his fists. *It's for me and Miss Bethel.*

Middleton and Hayward settled themselves on the floor facing each other on either side of Lulu—the baron with some difficulty, though he managed it—leaving space opposite her for Robert. Feeling foolish, Robert pulled up his own hood and knelt in the remaining spot, careful not to disturb the flour as he stepped over it.

Once they were all settled, Lulu gracefully went to the fire, took a slender stick from the cup on the mantle and lit it in the flames, then came back and lit the candle wick with it. The flame smoked black for a moment before the flame took hold, and she waved the baton to extinguish it.

She looked at the men in turn. "Whom do you wish to address this night?"

Solemnly, Middleton replied, "Azazel, Giver of Light. Mr. Cox has this offering to present." Middleton placed the bracelet with the red gem on the floor next to the candle.

Lulu nodded. "We must hold hands."

Robert offered his hands to the men on either side of him. Middleton's was clammy, and Hayward's warm and dry. Once the circle was complete, Lulu closed her eyes. She spoke a few sentences in her own language, then switched to broken English.

"Oh, great ancestors, I beseech you. Bring Azazel, the Giver of Light, to us. It me, Ifeoluwa of Akure, daughter of Babalawo Ademola, who make this request."

Silence fell, and Robert held his breath, resisting the urge to shift nervously on the hard floor. After several seconds, Lulu opened her eyes.

"He here." She paused and inclined her head as though listening. "He

want to know why you talk through me instead of to him like before."
She looked at the candle blankly, though it was more like she was looking
through it. "The mirror is no here," she said. Then she focused on their
faces once more. "He want to know why you call him tonight."

Middleton and Hayward exchanged glances. Robert watched Lulu in
fascination. Was she truly in communication with a spirit? Maybe even the
same dragon he'd seen his brother addressing in Bristol?

Middleton looked toward the ceiling, as though the spirit might be
hovering there. "Oh, great lord, we come to you tonight with information,
offering, and a request. We have a new supplicant in our midst, Mr. Robert
Cox, and he has found that which you seek—the heart of the sphinx."

The candle flame sputtered and grew. Robert stared at it in alarm as
it filled the space between them and transformed into the pointed head
of the horned dragon he'd caught a glimpse of in Miss Chapman's mirror
months ago. His heart raced, his chest constricting with dread and fear.

Lulu, Middleton, and Hayward looked as surprised and alarmed as he
felt. As the flame grew, the candle wax hissed and spat, and sweat rolled
down Robert's face. He let go of Hayward's and Middleton's hands and
inched away from the image. The rest of the room closed in on them, becoming darker while the fire grew.

"Wherrre isss it?" the dragon hissed. "Wherrre isss the heart?"

The dragon's head twisted, staring at each of them in turn. When its
gaze locked with Robert's, he pointed at the bracelet with a shaking hand.

"There it is, er, S-Sir Master."

The dragon swooped low to examine the bracelet. It opened gaping
jaws and closed them around the gem, then screeched and spat it out as
though the beast of fire had been burned.

"Thisss is not the heartstone I sseek! Which of you is resssponsible for
this treachery?"

Middleton and Hayward sank low on their faces. Robert scooted even
further backward.

"No, Mr. Cox," cried Lulu, stretching out a warning hand.

But it was too late. Robert felt the fine grit of the flour beneath his
hand and looked down to see he had broken the circle.

The dragon roared, rattling the windowpanes. Flames leapt from
the fireplace, and the dragon pulled them into himself, until he was no
longer just a head, but an enormous dragon of flame that nearly filled the
room. The sinuous creature floated in mid-air, his leathery, bat-like wings
of flame partially extended behind him. Robert and the others scrambled

away, pressing themselves against the divans and tables at the edge of the open space to avoid being burned.

"I will repay this disssloyalty ten-fold," the dragon howled. "Who has done this to me?"

Without looking up, Middleton pointed at Robert with a shaking hand.

Robert met the creature's fiery eyes and almost melted in terror, one thought clear in his mind:

He'd made a terrible mistake.

73

RECKONING

JOSEFINE GATHERED HER SCATTERED EMOTIONS and looked around at the sugar house Abela had taken them to. A huge brick furnace dominated the space, flanked by rows of copper kettles of various sizes—some large enough to fit a person, or several, inside. Large flat trays for drying the sugar lined one wall, most of which were full of either crystallizing liquid or crystals of various shades of golden brown. The harsh lines of the sugar works were softened by the glow of predawn light filtering through the open spaces below the rafters.

Josefine blinked at her surroundings and adjusted the heavy shawl over her shoulder. "I know this place. We're back at Huntley Hall." She whirled to Abela. "Why did you bring us here? And where is Bunmi?"

With a quick glance around, Abela pressed a finger to her lips and then gestured for Josefine to follow her. Josefine closed her mouth, following the lamma into the shadowy crevice between a copper boiling vat and the wall. Abela turned around and leaned close.

"Bunmi is safe on Sirenia. I took her there while you were talking to your father. We're here because I need to retrieve Berian's heartstone," she whispered. "Robert stole it from me. That's why he came here—to take it to them."

"And you thought the two of us alone could come and get it back?" Josefine said, incredulous. "They don't want Berian's heartstone. They want yours, remember? This is the last place you should be. Do you have any idea what kind of protection this place has?"

"Of course I do!" Abela hissed. "That's why I didn't blink us straight into the great house. We need to get the lay of the land first. Besides, it's not like our side doesn't have anyone in the Hidden Realm around here."

Josefine swallowed. She was much more concerned about the corporeal dangers than the incorporeal ones. "I thought your chariots only had limited energy before they'd be useless. How do you intend for us to leave here again?"

"Not useless. They recharge, it just takes time. By the time we need to leave, the one I used to take Urbi and Osaze to Sirenia should be ready to—"

Abela stiffened and her eyes widened. She spread her hands high and wide and stepped forward into the light. Then a strong hand grabbed Josefine's arm from behind and shoved her after Abela into the aisle running the length of the sugar house. A tawny-skinned man stood behind Abela with the stock of his short multi-tailed whip pressing into the small of her back.

"Well, what have we got here, Chidindu?" David, the slave foreman, glanced at Josefine's captor. "Miss Chapman has returned, and she's brought a friend." He glared at Josefine. "You missed quite an eventful day around here yesterday. What have you done with my sister and Winslow?"

"I don't know what you're talking about," Josefine said, deciding to play dumb. There was no evidence besides the timing that would connect Bunmi's and Osaze's disappearance to her—in her note to her father, she'd only said she could no longer be part of such a wicked cause and would find her own way home. Eric would never have shared the contents of that note with Middleton or the staff—he would have been too embarrassed for anyone outside the family to see their dissension. She was sure he would have consulted his finder immediately, but whatever Romero had done to prevent being immediately pursued may have even foiled such a device—it wouldn't be the first time the finder had failed. She wouldn't be surprised if her father had made up some excuse about sending her to town after Robert to spy on him. "What has happened to your sister and the new slave?"

David narrowed his eyes at her. "You truly do not know?"

Josefine shook her head. "Miss Bethel and I just arrived here after a long walk from Bridgetown. I have an urgent message for my father. Please let me take it to him."

David stepped away from Abela, but didn't lower the whip. "Mr. Chapman went to town with Thatcher to track down that Cox fellow. The Baron thinks he stole the slaves. Your father thought you'd gone with him."

"He thought no such thing," she said, her voice dripping with derision, though her heart sped up several notches. Maybe she'd been wrong about what Eric would have told them. She didn't let her doubt show in her voice, though. "Everyone here knows my loyalty to my father and my value to The Baron. Since my father is out, I'll take Miss Bethel to the kitchens to get some breakfast while we wait. We've been on the road for some time, and we're quite tired."

"Yeah?" David arched an eyebrow. "Then why aren't your boots dusty?"

Josefine's heart raced. "Because we washed them. That's why we're in here. I didn't want to track filth into the main house."

She exchanged glances with Abela, who raised her eyebrows as though to say *I'm sorry, I can't help you.*

David snorted. "It's too early in the day to start shovelling dung, don't you think?" He pressed the whip against Abela's back again. "I don't know what's really going on here. But I do know Lord John has given orders to bring any suspicious intruders straight to him. So that's where we're going."

Behind Josefine, the other man chuckled. She considered swinging her heavy bundle into him and making a run for it, but she didn't think much of her chances against the muscular man. And what would happen to Abela if she did? She glanced at Abela, who gave a soft sigh and dropped her hands.

"Lead on, sir." Abela gestured toward the entrance of the sugar house. "The whip won't be necessary, I assure you."

David studied her with an askance expression, then shook his head. "No, I don't trust you. Something about your eyes. Let us go."

Josefine didn't resist when Chidindu urged her along behind Abela and the far-too-observant David. There seemed to be little point.

But when they emerged from the sugar house, an orange glow of flames licking through the windows of one of the corner rooms of the main house—and the overwhelming sensation of evil emanating along with the smoke—pushed all other considerations aside.

David's eyes widened, and he shouted at Chidindu in a language Josefine didn't understand. The man ran toward the slave village a short distance beyond, just visible through some frond-type trees, hollering as he ran for people to wake up and help him.

"Don't go anywhere," David ordered them. "I'm going to get buckets." He ran back into the sugar house.

As soon as he'd left, Abela said, "Hurry! There are people in there. Robert is one of them." She broke into a run, hiking up her skirts and racing straight toward the burning building.

Seeing little other choice, Josefine dropped her bundle to the ground next to the wall of the sugar house and did the same.

*

THE dragon raged around the room, setting furniture and drapes on fire. Lulu had been cornered near the hearth. She stood waving her hands in ritual gestures and calling on names Robert didn't recognize to contain the beast, but it didn't help. Middleton and Hayward scrambled to the door and let themselves out, cowering and watching from the other side of the glass.

Robert pressed himself into the feet of a divan, crouching low to avoid the fiery monster darting around the room above him. Smoke had started to fill the upper half of the room. Robert lost sight of the woman, though he could hear her coughing. He had to get Lulu out of here, as well as himself.

Peering beneath the smoke, he saw the circle and its objects in the centre of the room. The candle was disappearing at an alarming rate, the flame of its wick still connected to the monster by a thin stream. Flames from the hearth still licked outward, fueling the monstrous image. The line of flour had been scuffed and broken in multiple places.

Maybe if the circle were repaired, the beast would be contained once more.

He peered cautiously above him, but the dragon seemed bent on touching every object it could and setting it alight, ignoring the people in the room. Creeping forward on elbows and knees, Robert made it to where he'd broken through the circle. Glancing above him occasionally to check that the dragon was still preoccupied elsewhere, he swept the white dust back into an unbroken ridge.

When he looked up the next time, Lulu was creeping beneath the smoke on the other side of the room toward another break in the circle. He nodded at her and started moving toward the hole left behind by Middleton.

He had just reached the spot when the room's other door slammed open. Miss Bethel stood there like a vengeful fury in green, her eyes reflecting the dragon's fire so they looked made of flame, not molten gold.

"In the name of Elyon, be still," she shouted at the flying beast above the roar and crackle of the flames.

No! Hide! Robert wanted to yell, but his throat was hoarse and dry from smoke and fear. What was she doing here? She was supposed to be long gone. Behind her, Miss Chapman stared at the fiery spectre, her mouth agape.

The dragon whirled, roaring, but when it saw Miss Bethel, it stopped, hovering.

"Ah! I sssee sssomeone has brought the Heart of Chaos after all. I only need to unwrap it firssst."

The dragon grew even larger. The remaining logs on the fire roared as they were consumed, and the candle was nearly half gone. If the beast could be distracted until its fuel had been consumed, would it disappear?

But, looking around at the burning curtains, the fire licking up the mantle, and the smouldering beams above them, they may not be able to wait that long. If the room collapsed, they would have worse problems. He coughed, feeling faint. A glance at the door his hosts had fled through showed Middleton had disappeared—hopefully to get help. Hayward was watching the scene with intense interest, and his eyes looked like black pools through the glass of the door. Robert shuddered and kept sweeping the flour back into the circle.

Miss Bethel faced the monster, undaunted. Suddenly, she began to change. Robert froze, watching as the woman he loved transformed before his eyes into a winged lioness whose shoulders rose nearly as high as the mantle.

"Have at thee, foul beast," she shouted. Roaring, she reared and charged the monster, meeting him in the air above the casting circle.

Robert stared at the snarling, roaring spirits above his head in shock. Miss Bethel had told him she was a cherub, that her kind were different, but it wasn't until that moment he truly understood how different. *This* was the creature he'd been wooing? No wonder his suit had appeared so paltry to her. For the first time, he saw her not as a frail lily in need of protection, but as the fierce warrior she'd been all along. She was a soldier of light, and he'd thought he could convince her the ways of darkness were the better choice. How could he have been so foolish?

He swept the flour before him into an unbroken line and glanced across the circle to measure Lulu's progress. She had just reached Hayward's break and was feverishly working to repair the damage. The glint of the heartstone bracelet caught Robert's eye, glowing like fire in the brilliant light streaming from the candle.

A glance upward showed the dragon and the sphinx engaged in even combat, circling each other in the air. Occasionally, one would dash forward and strike, then the other, and then they would engage in close confrontation, wings flailing and teeth glinting as they tried to deal each other a harsh blow. But how could Miss Bethel win against a spirit made of flame?

He stripped off his robe and tossed it aside. Then, careful not to disturb the flour he'd so painstakingly put back in place, he crawled into the circle and grabbed the heartstone, tucking it into his breast pocket. The hair on his hands singed from the heat of the flames. Wax flowed down the sides of the candle and pooled on the floor around the knife and the bowl of water.

"Mr. Cox, you must get out," Lulu called to him.

Glancing at her, he could see she had one more small section of the circle to repair and it would be complete. She was waiting only for him to leave the magical space. Perhaps he'd guessed correctly that closing the circle would once more contain the flaming spirit. But if that were true, perhaps also cutting off his fuel source would send him back whence he came. They did not have enough water in the room to put out all his sources of flame—besides the logs on the hearth, the creature was now pulling flame from the various things he'd set on fire.

"Close it," he said. "I have an idea."

He placed both hands on the sides of the bowl of water. She saw what he was doing and nodded, sweeping the last of the flour to remake the circle.

I hope I know what I'm doing.

As soon as the circle was closed, flame from all sources but the candle stopped feeding the monster. Fire still raged from the surfaces around them, but the dragon could no longer access it. The beast howled above Robert in rage, but before he could turn his wrath on him, Robert flipped the water from the bowl onto the stream from the candle, drowning it.

He looked up in time to see the fiery monster blink out of existence, just as the sphinx was about to deal another blow to its shoulder. Instead, her paw passed right through the space and she spun in the air. Robert sat up, crowing in victory.

"Miss Bethel, we have to get out of here!" he called to her. "The place will come down around us."

The sphinx shifted back into a woman and stood looking down at him. The sadness and disappointment in her eyes left him feeling naked, and he glanced away.

"Miss Bethel!" called Miss Chapman's voice somewhere through the haze. She coughed. "Ifeoluwa! Mr. Cox!"

"Here," said Lulu, and crawled toward the sound.

Robert crouched. "Come down here, Miss Bethel. It will be easier to breathe."

"Breathing is the least of my worries," she said shortly. "Quickly, whom did you call upon?"

Robert coughed. "The Baron called him Aza . . . Azazel."

She frowned and turned to Miss Chapman. "So Azazel and Semyaza have both loosened their bonds. The undines must repair the Heartstone before—" She stopped short as though she'd hit an invisible wall, her foot hovering over the line of white dust on the floor. She set it down within the circle and turned to Robert. "Please break the circle so I can leave."

Robert frowned. The circle had entrapped her too?

"Of course," he said and turned to comply.

But before he could scuff the circle open once more, flames flared from the flour like a lit cannon fuse, spreading from the place Hayward had just lit with a baton. The colonel shuffled back a step, giving Miss Bethel an unpleasant grin. His eyes were still as black as night—it had not been merely an illusion created by light reflecting from glass.

"How nice of you to join us here at Huntley Hall," Hayward said, but his voice was different—resonant and harsh, like boots on gravel. Chills ran up and down Robert's spine.

"Colonel Hayward, what are you doing?" Robert demanded.

"You can call me Erebus," the black-eyed creature said. "And I'm retrieving the Heart of Chaos for my master."

"Whom do you serve?" Miss Bethel demanded. "The dragon?"

Erebus shook his head. "Not this one," he said, indicating the casting circle and the fire with a derisive flip of his wrist. "Azazel can rot in his desert prison, as far as my master is concerned."

"Semyaza," she said matter-of-factly.

Erebus laughed. "How very astute of you."

The sound of cracking wood came from above their heads, and Robert glanced nervously at the beams, then caught the glint of the knife in Hayward's hand—the one Lulu had been using earlier to cut herbs. Behind Hayward, men began rushing into the room with buckets of water, dousing drapes and furniture and splashing water on the mantle and even into the hearth. The room grew darker with each doused section of flame, though the progress against the fire seemed slow. Erebus advanced on Miss Bethel.

"Mr. Cox, the circle, if you please," she said tightly, her eyes fixed on the approaching demon-possessed man.

The intense heat from the burning circle of wheat flour was already starting to flare out. Wincing, Robert scuffed through the remaining ash. In the hardwood floor beneath smouldered a black line of charcoal.

He couldn't break the circle. Miss Bethel was trapped.

He glanced up at her in horror. "Miss Bethel, I'm so sorry. I was trying to find a way for us to be together. I never intended for all this to happen."

Erebus laughed and casually stepped over the circle, holding the knife aloft and keeping his wary gaze on Abela. "Save your breath, Cox. The kedoshim may suffer a spineless sack of meat like you, but I have no stomach for it."

Miss Bethel walked around the inside edge of the circle, keeping Erebus opposite from her. Between them, Robert crouched over the destroyed candle and the pool of wax, which had hardened after the water had spilled on it. The air in the room was clearing slightly, but he still coughed every few minutes.

"Mr. Cox, you should get out into the fresh air before your lungs take damage," Miss Bethel said.

He shook his head. "No. I will not leave you. Not again."

"Aw, he fancies you," sneered Erebus. "Is that why you came—to save your love? Be careful, lamassu, or you'll end up in God's Cauldron with the rest of them."

Abela drew herself to her full height. "I am a guardian, third class, of the Cherubic Order of Raphael. I made my choice long ago."

Erebus scoffed. "It can't be that long. I've never heard of you before. When were you made?"

She hesitated before answering. "Three hundred ninety-three years ago. But though I'm young, I am resolute. That is why I was given this task."

"Oh? Is that why you were entrusted with that heartstone you carry in your chest?"

Abela faltered, then kept pacing, staying out of reach of Erebus and his knife.

"Ah, I see. It wasn't bequeathed to you. Which means you must have taken it. That's it, isn't it? You stole the Heart of Chaos, which is how it's come to be on the Ground."

Miss Bethel flushed rosy, her face twisting. "I do *not* steal! I . . . borrowed it. And I'll return it when my mission is complete."

Erebus chuckled. "The master said he'd made sure you found it. It appears he was right. He's very good."

Miss Bethel's hands clenched, and she stopped moving to face Erebus. "What is your real name, demon?"

Erebus's face darkened. "That is no concern of yours. All you need to know is that I am the darkness that will consume you, lamassu."

He lunged toward Miss Bethel, and Robert launched himself upward, planting his shoulder in the man's stomach and forcing him out of the circle. A man with a bucket scrambled to get out of the way. By now, nearly all the flames were out except those above the magic circle, which the water carriers hadn't touched, staying a safe distance back from the confrontation. Robert glanced over his shoulder at Miss Bethel, who stood watching him with wide eyes.

Middleton appeared in the door and took a quick look around. "What the devil are you doing, Hayward? The sphinx woman is right there. Get her!" Middleton pointed.

Erebus glared at the baron as he picked himself up. Robert took advantage of the momentary distraction and drew his knife, lunging at him.

The man sidestepped Robert with ease, elbowing him in the kidney as he whirled away from Robert's attempted strike. Searing pain lacerated his side, and he whirled to see a glossy red stain on the edge of Hayward's blade. He touched his ribs and his fingers came away bloody.

"Robert, no!" shouted Miss Bethel.

She pounded on the invisible barrier, then stepped back and examined the charcoal on the floor. Robert parried another attack from Hayward, and when he glanced at her again, she was picking at the pool of hard melted wax. He turned his attention back to Hayward just in time to block another blow.

"So I see you received the gifts I left you at the Rum Runners Tavern, after all," said Erebus. "Here I thought my knife would go to waste. I have to give it to you, you actually had me fooled. I was about to break up your little seance when Azazel revealed the true nature of your tainted heart-stone. Glad I didn't bring my master that one."

He lunged again, and Robert stepped back, narrowly avoiding the wicked-looking blade. Already exhausted from a long, sleepless night and all the prior events, his energy had begun to flag. He needed to find a way to contain or exorcise the spirit in Hayward before he made another costly wrong move. The man was obviously much more proficient in hand-to-hand combat than Robert was.

He charged at Erebus with his own blade, hoping to earn himself some space, but the man knocked his hand aside and his knife went flying. With another step, Erebus clenched Robert's throat in his fist and lifted him against the wall. Robert gasped for air, grabbing at the man's arm to no avail.

"Erebus, leave him alone," called Miss Bethel.

She stood outside the circle, having created a break in the ring of charcoal on the floor with bits of melted wax. Erebus glanced over his shoulder and snarled, swinging the knife toward her while keeping Robert suspended with his other hand. She stepped toward him.

"If you take another step, I'll kill him." Erebus clenched tighter, and dark stars exploded across Robert's vision.

Miss Bethel stopped. "What must I do to save him?"

Robert wanted to tell her to flee, that he wasn't worth saving, and she should protect herself and the heartstone these men were willing to go so far to obtain. But he couldn't say anything, and his futile clawing at Hayward's hands weakened.

"Give me the Heart of Chaos," Erebus said. "Give it to me, and I'll let him live."

"You must swear by the secret name, just as you swore to serve Semyaza all those years ago . . . Dagiel."

Erebus blinked, his black eyes shining. "Aren't you the clever one? Fine. But you must also swear to give up the heart."

Miss Bethel nodded. "I need not swear. I never lie. If you let this man live, I, Guriel of Bathiyel, will give you the Heart of Chaos."

Erebus smiled. "All right, I agree. But mortal ears must not hear the name. Come here, so I can whisper my oath to you."

No! It's a trap! But Robert was far beyond speech. The dark stars had nearly clouded out his vision, but he still saw Miss Bethel come cautiously nearer, saw Erebus lower the knife and lean toward her ear, saw him whisper something in a language he couldn't understand, and saw Miss Bethel step backward, her eyes bulging, with Erebus's knife in her chest.

The iron grip on his throat disappeared, and Robert coughed, his vision rushing back. He glanced up to where Miss Bethel had crumpled to her knees and stumbled toward her.

Erebus laughed. "That's for all the trouble you've caused, Guriel of Bathiyel."

"Miss Bethel, no! This can't happen. Surely you can heal somehow. Here!" Robert scrabbled to retrieve the other heartstone from his breast pocket and thrust it into her palm. "Use this one instead. You can, can't you? Please, Miss Bethel. You can't die!"

He was sobbing now, but he didn't care. She stared at him, dropping the stone from a slack hand.

Dagiel walked over and stood above them, addressing the fallen woman. "Soon, my master will have freed all the rest of his kind, and you and your soldiers of the Light will get a taste of what they have suffered for millennia. All because you fell in love with a human. Oh, how the mighty have fallen."

Robert glared at the man. "She didn't fall in love with me, you despicable creature. She did it because she is pure and good and was protecting me, even if I didn't deserve it." His voice broke, and he clutched her hand in his. "I didn't deserve this. Why did you do it?"

She looked at him with tears brimming in her golden eyes, the ones he'd wanted to stare into forever. "Because," she said, smiling sadly, "when I told you I didn't love you . . . that was the only time in my whole life I lied."

Robert's stomach lurched. Before he could say anything more, brilliant golden light spilled from fine jagged fissures in her face. The fissures soon covered her body, the light shining right through her dress, piercing through the smoke that still remained in the room.

"No!" screamed Robert, catching her as she fell. But all he caught was her gown—the woman herself stood before him like a translucent golden ghost, down to the very dress Robert now held in his hands. Just visible in the centre of her chest was a pulsing red light from a gemstone the size of a chicken egg—the Heart of Chaos.

"Miss Bethel . . . Abela, no! I never deserved your love, no matter how much I wanted it. Don't do this, please. It is not worth the cost."

She looked down at him with a serene expression. "Doing something wrong for the right reasons never justifies your actions. But choosing love is always worth the cost. Know this, Mr. Robert Cox—I have always forgiven you, and I always will. Now you must learn to forgive yourself."

She reached into her chest and clasped the heart in her fist. Piercing him with one last look, she said, "Elyon is with you. Choose the light, Robert Cox."

With that, she withdrew the stone and held out her hand, then blinked out of existence.

Dagiel caught the stone before it even hit the floor.

Middleton, who had stood staring at the proceedings in astonishment, stepped forward. "Well done, Hayward, or, er, whomever you are. The Master will be very pleased with us indeed. Now, finish Cox—he's not worth the trouble to keep alive—and we'll have Miss Chapman call the Master back to present this great treasure." He glanced around at the dripping, charred room. "With the mirror this time. It's safer."

Dagiel swung his knife toward Middleton's nose, and the baron stopped short.

"I don't serve your master," Dagiel sneered. "This stone is going to my master, Semyaza. Cox, get out of here," he said without taking his gaze from Middleton's shocked visage. "I don't ever want to see your face again."

Robert stared at Dagiel, at Middleton holding his hands aloft, at Miss Chapman and Ifeoluwa, who stood frozen near the door, and at the various other men and women at the edges of the room who had stayed to watch what had transpired after the flames had been extinguished. Miss Chapman stared at him with wide eyes, and he could feel their accusation from where he crouched.

Quietly, he rose to his feet, slunk past Miss Chapman and Ifeoluwa, and walked out of the house in time to see the sun peeking over the horizon, red and blinding.

He went and retrieved his horse from the stables and left, not once looking back.

74

TRAPPED

Narcissa opened her eyes and blinked at the messy blankets around her, the pale linens silvery in the moonlight flooding through the open window. It took her a moment to realize what was wrong, and then it hit her—it wasn't what was wrong, but what was *right*. She held up her hands in front of her face and wiggled her fingers in astonishment, her hands silhouetted by the light.

I'm in control. Semyaza is gone.

Could it be true? Could she be free of him? How?

No. She could feel his presence lurking in the back of her mind like a malevolent shadow. He wasn't gone, but he did seem to be dormant, as though his attention were elsewhere. Did even he sleep once in a while? Perhaps he was playing with her, allowing her to control her body as a new way of torturing her. Or seeing what she would do if given a little freedom—a test of her loyalty, perhaps. As though she were a bridled, well-broke horse.

She blinked away the moisture in her eyes, not even appalled at the tears. That metaphor was closer to the truth than she wanted to admit.

She turned her head and saw Matthew sleeping next to her, as well as several empty flagons of wine scattered on the nightstand and the floor of the room. Her hand went to her belly—it was as flat as ever, but that didn't mean the small life inside couldn't be harmed. *How dare he drink while I'm with child?* She glanced at Matthew. While Semyaza hadn't exactly been particular about bedmates, the likeliest sire for the child was her consort-elect—the one she'd stolen from Fire Lake to spite Calandra. She smiled at the memory of getting the better of her condescending cousin, but the smile quickly faded. Calandra had nothing to do with the fix she was in now, much as Narcissa would love to blame her for it.

She sat up and the room spun around her. She waited for it to stop, her hand pressing against her temples in an attempt to alleviate her raging headache. Whether she'd chosen to drink or not, her body was still feeling the effects. Standing, she swept the long tails of the sleeveless white linen robe that was her only covering behind her and stumbled over to the desk in the shadows near one wall of the massive chamber. She leaned on it for support, hanging her head between her shoulders.

On the surface of the desk next to an empty polished brass goblet—which still had a few red drops in the bottom—was a large hexagonal pink quartz stone reader and some datastones. After Despoina Cleo had returned from Atlantis yesterday and told Semyaza what she'd seen in the Archive there, he'd sent a team of sirens to bring him as many datastones as they could carry. He'd pored over them late into the night, stopping only when he fell into bed in a drunken slumber. What was it he'd been muttering about as he searched? A soul keeper? Whatever that was. And a key—he'd been obsessed with finding the key for weeks, even before she was aware of him. Apparently, he'd given up on combing the palace store-rooms for clues, choosing to read ancient stones instead.

She sat in the elegantly carved wooden chair, placed her thumb on the Tear sitting in the stone reader, and sang the trill that would wake it up. The surface of the reader bubbled and formed a shape she recognized—the quaternaria pendant she herself had been seeking since her mother's death. The symbol of the monarch of Sirenia. It had been on her mother's head when she'd fallen in the Grotto, attached to the hair chain Adonia usually wore, but no one had seen it since. Narcissa regretted not snatching the emblem from her mother's body when she'd had the chance.

Narcissa stared at the image. The silver curves of the four-pointed knot with the purple amethyst centre had all been rendered monotone in the soft pink of the quartz, but the four interconnected *ichthyses* and round centre stone were unmistakable as the pendant of the queen. Of course he'd want that. He wanted her to be queen as much as she did.

She touched the right side of the reader and the image shifted, reforming as a ring with an eight-spoked wheel setting with a small round stone in the centre. The next image was strikingly similar—a leather wristband bearing a circular floret with another small round stone in the centre. Then another circular object with spokes and a centre stone, though less finely made. Then an ouroboros bracelet made to look like a snake swallowing its own tail. Were any of these the key he'd been looking for? Or maybe the soul keeper?

She kept flicking through images in what appeared to be some kind of catalogue. The surface of the reader shifted again and again into different pieces of jewelry and symbolic objects—some quite ordinary, others unusual pieces she'd never seen before. They were labelled, but only with serial identifications that meant nothing to her.

Frustrated, she batted the reader aside and it clattered to the floor, the datastone sliding to a stop near the bed.

She glanced at Matthew's sleeping form once more, noticing the fresh bruises and new scabs on his cheek and ribs. Semyaza had been using him harshly. Her friend Zenobia, a physic adept serving under Healer Evadne who had covered up Narcissa's own experiments for years, had barely questioned why she'd been summoned to heal Matthew every morning. After all, Narcissa had brought many other *douloi* to her after her entertainments had gone too far. The one time Zenobia had commented to Semyaza on the increased frequency of the events, she'd been cowed into silence by Semyaza's threats, just like the rest of the palace staff and any former friends Narcissa may have had.

And then there were the ships. War was bearing down upon Sirenia, and the spirit using her body had invited it. But as far as anyone else knew, the fault was hers. Semyaza was systematically destroying her life. And there seemed to be nothing she could do about it.

At least Matthew had survived to be healed, not like . . . Narcissa closed her eyes and turned away from the memory of the broken body of the scullery maid. While part of her had been fascinated by what Semyaza had done, a far greater part had been repulsed. Her thoughts had been seesawing from one to the other ever since.

Last night, after he'd disposed of the maid, she'd managed to arrest control of her body from him. Within seconds, he had regained it and punished her severely for the act of defiance, punching her midriff repeatedly with her own hand while he laughed. She couldn't feel it, of course, but the terror that the baby might be harmed accomplished his goal. She'd begged him to stop, promising to do whatever he wanted. He'd told her she should never rebel against him again.

Semyaza was worse than Narcissa's mother had been. Far worse. And she had to stop him.

But how could she protect her island when she couldn't even protect herself? At any moment, Semyaza could wake up and her temporary freedom would be at an end. The sphinx's heart he'd expressed so much interest in was still not in his grasp, and she had devised no other method of ridding herself of him.

She wanted to be disgusted with the small life inside her that had compelled her to beg, grovelling like a slave. But as she lay her hands on her abdomen, she *felt* it—not physically, but she could sense its tiny spirit flutter beneath her hand, as fragile as a butterfly, and caught her breath. She'd never sensed anyone that strongly before.

It wasn't rational, she knew that. But she would do anything she could to protect that little flutter.

I'll find a way to free us, little one. Somehow, I must.

Perhaps she could find someone, warn them what was happening. Maybe Zenobia—but would her friend believe her after how unstable Semyaza had made her seem?

She needed help. It pained her to admit, but she needed someone who would do her bidding but could not be influenced by Semyaza's bullying and illusions.

Her gaze fell on Matthew, and she chewed her lip. No, that wouldn't work. Sure, she could give Matthew an order, but as soon as Semyaza resurfaced, he could supersede it, and the *doulos* would be forced to obey. If only she held Matthew's *sklavia* bond, she'd consider freeing him, just to see if he were sympathetic to her cause.

She shook her head, standing and pacing in the shadows—away from the bed and its offending occupant. When had she started thinking that way? That was Calandra's mistake. And her mother's.

But still—she'd seen how Osaze had behaved toward his consort-elect after he'd been Freed. He'd risked his own life for Calandra's and stood by her side instead of fleeing, though he'd had opportunities. Zoe had told her how irrational Osaze had become when he realized he'd been sent away, and how he'd insisted on coming back.

Would Matthew be capable of that kind of loyalty? She bit her cheek. She could tell him her baby was certainly his—how would he know otherwise? That might be enough to win some loyalty, assuming he possessed even a modicum of tenderness. Even sharks tended their young. But without holding his bond, the point was moot. She'd held it once, but no longer. She dimly remembered Calandra taking Matthew's bond in the Archive—and Semyaza having Calandra transfer all Matthew's permissions to himself instead of taking the bond back, which was odd. In fact, in all the time Semyaza had been possessing her, he hadn't created a single Redemption bond.

The truth hit her and she drew in a sharp breath, pausing in her stride. *He can't do it, can he?*

Thousands of *sklavia* bonds had done little for her abilities with the elements, but she'd still been able to create them. But that manic insistence that Calandra keep Matthew's bond—even if Semyaza had any true talent with fire, he obviously had no access to Narcissa's abilities and, judging by his frequent use of illusion instead of real fire, little access to his own while inhabiting her. No wonder he was after this Heart of Chaos.

She leaned against the wall near the door to her lady's maid's room, sighing, and watched the steady rise and fall of Matthew's chest. How similar was being under the *sklavia* bond to what Semyaza had been doing to her? Could Matthew understand what was happening to him? Had Osaze all those years? Too bad she didn't know Calandra's trick for Releasing someone whose bond she didn't hold.

Stop it, Narcissa. Desperation doesn't make wishes come true.

It was foolishness to think Matthew would want to help her. Narcissa's father, Frederik, had rejected her mother when Adonia had Released him. Despite Osaze's actions to the contrary, most men had no loyalty. Perhaps she should go look for Hebe. Her sister might believe her if she told her what was happening. But despite Hebe's talent with spirit and water, she was so silly and immature. Even if she wanted to help, what could Hebe do?

Narcissa leaned forward and let her head droop, watching in chagrin as droplets of salty water left dark streaks on her robe.

Semyaza is breaking me. I have to end this now.

But she had no more ideas than she'd had ten minutes ago. *Maybe I should tell Cleo what's happened. Even if she doesn't believe me and locks me up, at least Semyaza won't be able to hurt anyone else. Except me. And my baby.*

Tears flowed in earnest, and she swiped at her face to clear her vision. Absently, she picked up one of the datastones still on the desk. It wasn't likely to give her any more answers than Semyaza, but the cool opal felt reassuring in her palm.

A silent figure slipped through the chamber's main door in the receiving room, barely visible in the shadows beyond the pools of silvery moonlight streaming through the windows. Narcissa clenched her fist around the Tear and suppressed her sniffles, keeping her head lowered as the figure closed the door behind her and stood blinking at the room, which was darker than the torch-lit corridor. It was a slight young woman in palace livery with a long, thick black braid and light refracting from her luminescent dark green eyes—an undine. As the girl's eyes adjusted, she glanced around the room, obviously listening. Narcissa held her breath. Was the girl simply a servant checking on her? But the way the girl scanned the room suggested otherwise.

Had the girl been sent to kill her? Murder was nearly unheard of on Sirenia—or had been until the Redemption Moon. Perhaps someone had surmised the truth of Adonia's and Thea's demise and had decided to mete out their own justice. Or someone had figured out who was behind the missing servants. Narcissa glanced toward the hidden passageway without moving her head. How had Semyaza opened the door again?

The girl crept through the antechamber and slipped through the bedroom archway. She glanced in Narcissa's direction and, when Narcissa didn't move, focused on the man on the bed. She crept around the room on bare feet, keeping to the shadows near the walls, her attention never wavering. When she saw Matthew's face, she gasped and took a step forward to the edge of the patch of light. Then she stopped, staring around the room at the darkness.

Narcissa held her breath and remained frozen. She wore no knife and her staff was leaning against the far wall, covered in dust. Until she knew whom she was up against, it was best to lay low. She hoped the girl would mistake the presence she must feel as her servant who slept beyond the door.

Evidently deciding it was safe, the young woman padded silently forward and placed her finger on Matthew's forehead. Narcissa's throat tightened. Now that the intruder was in the light, Narcissa recognized her—Judith, Calandra's one-time lady's maid. What was she doing?

Judith sang a short trill Narcissa didn't recognize, and then shook the man.

"Matthew," she whispered. "Wake up. Quickly, before she comes back!"

Matthew stirred and moaned.

The impudent sea witch had Released him! How dare Judith think she could steal Narcissa's consort-elect from her? Had Calandra sent her, even from beyond the veil? Narcissa had no doubt her entitled, irritatingly accomplished cousin, who took everything good from Narcissa and turned it to poison, even her claim to the throne, could find a way to orchestrate such an event even from the Abyss.

She leapt to her feet. "Stop!"

Judith withdrew her belt knife and brandished it over Matthew's body, staring into the darkness toward Narcissa, her face a satisfying mask of startled fear. "Do not come any closer!"

Narcissa crossed her arms, still clutching the Tear, and stepped forward into the light. "Or what? You'll kill me with a diving knife? I think not." She laughed. "I could take you with my bare hands."

Judith looked at Narcissa, then the man beneath her, and flipped the knife handle, raising it as though to plunge it into him.

"Not you. I will kill him."

Narcissa gave another mocking laugh. "I don't think so—not after all the trouble you went to in order to come get him."

A look of desperation crossed Judith's face. "Death would be better than what he has been living through."

Narcissa scoffed, but there was a bitter taste in her mouth. Despite all Semyaza had done to her, *she* still had no desire to die. "How can you be so sure he'd agree?"

"Since when do you care what he would want?"

Judith glared at her, then glanced at the unconscious man, and Narcissa wondered if she might be considering whether she could actually kill him.

Narcissa's retort stuck in her throat.

Matthew moaned and put his hand to his head, then opened his eyes and blinked blearily. "Judith?"

The girl's face transformed, a desperate smile touching her lips. She placed a hand on his cheek. "Oh, my sweet Matthew. What have they done to you?"

He wrapped his hand around hers and smiled. "It doesn't matter, now that you're here."

"Oh, to hear your voice! I can hardly believe it." Tears rolled down Judith's cheeks, and the hand holding the knife aloft faltered.

Narcissa's throat tightened as she watched what was obviously the re-union of two people who cared for each other a great deal. If they knew each other, the last time they spoke must have been before Calandra healed Matthew's deafness at Fire Lake, for he'd been Redeemed ever since. A lot had changed since then, including Matthew's clarity of speech.

The scene made her think of Mari, the girl she'd been in love with for two years. But though Mari had often been tender and sympathetic toward her, Narcissa couldn't remember ever being this moved with emotion for her lover—not until Calandra's revolution had taken Mari away from her.

Narcissa sniffled and Judith looked up, surprise written on her face. She pointed the knife at Narcissa once more, hovering protectively over

Matthew.

"Don't come any closer. I mean it, Damon, or whoever you are."

Narcissa blinked. How could Judith know of the monster who oppressed her?

More importantly, could she help?

"He's not here right now. I . . . I mean you no harm." Narcissa closed her eyes and swallowed until the urge to break down in sobs passed. Clenching her fists, she opened her eyes. "I need your help."

Judith stared at her with an incredulous expression. "And why should we help you?"

"Because," Narcissa said, swallowing the lump in her throat, "I'm . . . I'm pregnant."

75

THE DOULOS

JUDITH STARED AT NARCISSA IN astonishment, her hand numb around the knife hilt and her heart cold at the words Narcissa had just spoken. Matthew pushed himself up on his elbow, wincing, and stared at the blonde girl in the long white robe that barely covered her naked form. The sheet fell away from his bare chest, revealing black and purple bruises on his tanned skin.

"Come, Matthew," Judith said, tugging on his arm. "We're leaving. Here." With her free hand, she drew the songstoppers she'd taken from the storeroom at Margaret House from her belt pouch and inserted them into his ears one at a time. "I am taking you somewhere safe."

Matthew sat upright, gingerly touching the amber stones Judith had just put in his ear canals. Then he looked at Narcissa, easing himself off the bed and bending to pick up some black breeches that lay in a heap on the floor. As the sheet fell away completely, it became obvious he'd been wearing even less than Narcissa. Judith tried not to think about why.

"I think the baby is Matthew's," Narcissa added with a touch of desperation in her voice.

Judith felt as though she'd been stabbed with a thousand knives. "That is not his fault, is it?" she said, her voice breaking. "Not when you removed his choice. Now that I have given it back to him, what do you want us to do about it?"

"Don't you see?" Narcissa said, her voice pleading. "That's why he's the only one who can help me. Semyaza is planning something—something big. He says there are ships coming. Lots of them."

Judith's heart raced. "Semyaza? Who is that?"

"He's the monster who . . . who's been . . . using me, the one you called Damon. He's trapped me in my own body, and he's done . . . terrible things." Narcissa's voice cracked. "He'll probably be back any moment. Hurry, please. I don't have much time."

Narcissa clenched her fists at her sides, tears streaming down her face. Judith didn't know what to make of it—she'd never known the princess to cry or feel remorse. Narcissa would have to have a heart for that. And after hearing Kyria Dione's message that morning, some part of Judith had believed Narcissa had been complicit in even this latest crime. Now, that resolve began to waver. But why could she still not sense Narcissa—had the princess somehow gotten her hands on a shieldstone? What Judith wouldn't do to flush out the mole in their ranks . . .

"And . . . and the ships are almost here," Narcissa added, regaining some control of her emotions. "If we don't raise the barrier soon, our island will come under attack. And he's doing nothing to stop it."

Judith chewed her lip. "And the murders?"

Narcissa paled, staring at Judith with guilt in every line of her face. Maybe Judith's instinct had been right about Narcissa's complicity.

"You have been killing the servants, haven't you, Narcissa?"

Narcissa started, a flash of something crossing her face—maybe relief?—then shook her head vehemently. "No, that's him too. I couldn't stop it. I would never, er . . . he's doing it for sport! No other reason than to entertain himself."

Narcissa's voice trembled as she protested, but Judith didn't know whether to believe her. The princess was in full control of her faculties now, was she not? How much control could this Semyaza really have over her?

Matthew had fastened the breeches and now allowed Judith to pull him toward the door, his emotions still the quagmire of the newly Released. She kept her knife raised, though she knew it would likely do little if Narcissa decided to attack—the princess was a skilled martial artist, and Judith would be no match for her.

But Narcissa didn't attack. She stood at the edge of the rectangle of moonlight, watching them go with a dejected slant to her shoulders. If Judith didn't know who she was, she'd never have taken Narcissa for the cruel princess who had demanded the death of Elizabeth, Matthew's mother, only six weeks ago, for the crime of doing what Judith had just done—allowing him to have his free will.

The final wisps of confusion created by the *sklavia* bond cleared from Matthew's expression, and he stopped her just as they reached the door to the corridor.

"Come, Matthew," she urged. "No matter what Narcissa says, it is we who don't have much time."

He hesitated and looked back at Narcissa, who came and leaned on the bedchamber archway, his blue eyes soft. "She's not lying. It was not she who abused me, it was the creature who stole her body."

"Like she stole yours?" Judith shot back. "She does not deserve your compassion. We need to leave. *Please*," she begged. "She will only enslave you again."

"No, I won't," Narcissa said, taking a step toward them. "I need him to be free. And Semyaza can't enslave him, not without me. Matthew's the only one who can help me find a way to get rid of the monster, but he'll have to play the part of a *doulos*. Semyaza has to have a weakness. I just haven't found it yet."

Matthew's face was full of indecision. Judith shook her head, willing him to agree with her. Tafrara and Meg should be finished their missions and would be waiting for them near the servant's entrance by now so they could meet up with the others who'd rendezvoused with the *despoina* in the city. It had taken Judith longer to work her way here than she'd expected.

Matthew gently put his arms around her and she tucked her head under his chin just as she used to do, his love wrapping around her like a blanket. She breathed in his sweat and the jasmine scent Narcissa often wore. Judith closed her eyes against the sting of tears.

"Do not do this," she whispered. "Do not leave me again."

"I'm sorry, Jude," he said into her hair. "You're right, she doesn't deserve our compassion—but the child she carries needs someone to protect it. I've seen that monster torture her by threatening the child. The baby doesn't deserve that."

Judith pulled away. "How do you even know the child is yours?" she said in a choked voice.

He shook his head, lifting her chin with his fingers. "I don't. But does that matter?"

Judith stared into eyes so blue she could drown in them. She wished, just for a moment, that they could have stayed at Elpida as they had as children, oblivious to the horrors of the real world and the threats that endangered them outside the walls of the *latifundium*. But wishful thinking was childish. She had long known that if she ever wanted her and Matthew to be free to love each other openly, she would have to do something to change the world—something risky. So she had volunteered to be the one to surveil Calandra and help guide her toward their cause. The consequences had been both better and more terrible than she could have imagined.

"Think about it," he whispered, clasping her hands between his. He bent to kiss her fingers. "If I'm here, I can find out what is happening and send messages to you and the others. There is too much to explain quickly, but I have already seen a great deal. Narcissa is correct about the ships—Semyaza is planning a war that will encompass the world."

Judith shuddered. A worldwide war? She was both appalled at the creature's hubris and terrified he might actually succeed. On her way here, she had gone to warn the Student FWS of their plans and found Charis and Geronimi. They had told her many of the novices at the Academy and even some of the raised healers and sirens were being swayed to Narcissa's—or, rather, Semyaza's—arguments that the undines should no longer hide, but instead use their abilities to rule the weaker races of the Earth. Judith hid her alarm and gave them their mission—to find Hebe and get her and as many students from the Academy to safety as they could. She had been about to suggest a method, but had been shut down. *We know our way out,* Geronimi had said, her face grim. Judith doubted not a word.

"The ships are why we need to leave. We—" She glanced at Narcissa and lowered her voice even more. "We are planning to tell the island, starting tomorrow, so our people can prepare for war." She spat the bitter word. "There is no telling how Semyaza will react." Unless Meg had succeeded with the Heartstone tonight, but she didn't want to get into that. "I do not want to leave without you."

Matthew's brow furrowed at this. "All the more reason for me to stay then. To help those who remain behind."

"But what can you do?" she whispered in desperation. "You are only one man. And you would be in danger here all the time."

He brushed her cheek with the back of his hand. "We're all in danger. Just look at what you did to come Free me. That was terribly dangerous. And I'm so grateful." He gave her a small smile. "We can't win the rebellion if we won't take any risks."

We can't win the rebellion without risks. She had said that same thing to him the night before she'd left Elpida for her assignment at the Opal Palace. Brushing away her tears, she nodded.

He bent and pressed his lips to hers. "I'm doing it for us."

"I know," she said into his ear, then stepped back and pulled her hands from his. She turned to Narcissa. "You better not hurt him."

But Narcissa was no longer the broken woman she'd been only moments before. Her face had hardened into the mocking, arrogant sneer she usually wore, but with a wicked curve that turned the expression into a stranger's.

"Oh, I wouldn't worry about my *doulos* if I were you, my dear. I'd worry about you." The creature turned to Matthew. "Arrest her!"

Judith met Matthew's gaze with unspoken longing. Narcissa was gone again, and the man Judith loved was staying to try and save her and the child she carried. The princess and Matthew would both be at the mercy of a creature capable of unimaginable evil. How could she leave him behind knowing all that?

"Matthew! Arrest the intruder!" the dragon in the princess's body barked.

Matthew hesitated. "Go!" he mouthed to Judith, keeping his face away from Narcissa so the creature couldn't see.

As Judith fled through the door, he dove after her—too slowly—and made a show of tripping on the inert figure of the siren laying on the floor of the corridor. He landed with a smack on the marble tile. When she turned to see if he was hurt, he waved her onward.

Kynthia, who had been waiting in the hallway crouched behind a plant, joined Judith in racing down the corridor. "He's not coming?"

Judith shook her head, her chest tight. "Not this time."

They reached the stairs that would take them down to the main level. Narcissa's screeching voice hurling insults at Judith's beloved echoed down the stairwell after them, and Judith winced.

It is for the greater cause, she repeated to herself. *It will be worth it in the end.*

If she said it often enough, she might start believing it.

76

UNEXPECTED GUESTS

The mistress of Steadfast House was younger than Osaze expected. He vaguely remembered Eudora kor'Dione from her days at the Academy, and he thought she was around his own age. The only times he'd seen her before had been in the sparring ring while he'd been under the *sklavia* bond. The memory filled him with hot shame. How would she react to a Freeman in her home?

When she saw Osaze, she did a double take.

"W—welcome." Eudora gave him, his mother, and Bunmi—whom Abela had appeared just long enough to deposit before disappearing again—deep salutes that hid her shocked face. As she bowed, she used her other hand to support the head of the infant girl strapped to her chest with a cloth sling. Then she turned to the guardswoman who'd led them to this back room. "Fedra, if you please?"

Osaze tensed. Was this the moment his mother had warned him about, when he'd be returned to his state of blank-mindedness beneath the *sklavia* bond like the two *douloi* standing at attention on either side of the door? He glanced at Urbi and saw his fear reflected in her eyes.

But Fedra stepped not toward him, but each of the other men in turn, binding their hands firmly behind their backs with rope. Once she was done, she stood in the middle of the door with her staff drawn while Eudora placed her forefinger on each man's head and Released him with a look of grim satisfaction.

The men's expressions changed from blank to confused and then afraid.

"Fear not, Purcell and Arthur," Eudora said warmly. "You're among friends."

648

Osaze's chest loosened and he exchanged relieved glances with his mother and Bunmi. Abela had been right to bring them here. He only worried that she hadn't yet returned herself.

As Eudora explained to the men that she had waited to Free them to deflect suspicion from Narcissa until she could send them to safety among the rebels, the two relaxed slightly. No sooner had she finished than Wilhelmina brought in a young physic to tend to Osaze's back, a familiar-looking girl whom the housekeeper assured him was very discreet.

"Niobe's got some sense in her," Wilhelmina said, patting his arm. "Now, if you'll excuse me, I have to make sure the girls have roused themselves to bring food."

After Healer Niobe left, Eudora had a servant girl bring clothes to replace the tattered, worn clothes her guests wore. Urbi and Bunmi were taken to another room to change. Eudora led Osaze to a bedroom upstairs and withdrew a pair of form-fitting dark brown breeches and a sleeveless blue tunic from a basket.

"These belong to my husband, Ewelike," Eudora said, handing them to Osaze. "He's about your size."

He glanced at her questioningly as he accepted the stack of clothes. "Husband?"

She smiled, bouncing the baby, which had started to whimper and turn its head as though waking up. "We've been bonded for about a year, but Ewelike has only been Free for a couple weeks. I'm still getting used to the word, but it seems more accurate than *consort*. We owe you and Calandra a great debt for helping us undines see the error of our ways."

"You recognize me?"

She nodded. "I was there at the Court of the Redeemed after the Harvest Moon and at the wedding. You are much like my husband, you know—kind and courageous."

"Where is he?" Osaze looked around as though the man might be hiding in a corner. Had things on Sirenia already changed so much that this woman's husband could live openly Free?

"He's safe at Margaret House." Eudora sighed. "He hasn't even met this little one yet." She glanced at the baby with an affectionate smile.

Osaze drew a disappointed breath. It had been too good to be true.

Eudora brushed the infant's chubby brown cheek, a sad expression on her face. "This is how it must be for now. I look forward to a day when my husband can live freely by my side. And perhaps our next child might even be a son." She kissed the dark fuzz on her daughter's head. "You'd like a little brother, wouldn't you, Thea?"

"She's called Thea?" Osaze's chest tightened as he remembered the healer who had gone to her death to defend the freedom of her husband and all men on the island.

Eudora smiled. "We had to honour Healer kor'Aglaia somehow."

Osaze swallowed the lump in his throat. "She's perfect."

After he'd changed and been ushered back to the receiving room, Osaze sat on a cushioned stool before a warm brazier eating fruit, cheese, nuts, and pastries he'd piled on a small bronze plate from the spread before them. He tried to eat slowly, but after the healing and his weeks of deprivation, he was on his second helping before he could restrain himself. On one side sat his mother and Bunmi, and on his other the two newly Released men, who'd been untied. They studied their hostesses with uncertain, wary expressions. Eudora, who now suckled Thea, and Eudora's mother, the formidable Dione, a matronly woman with long, wavy, grey-streaked dark brown hair hurriedly pulled back with a cloth band, sat across from them.

Osaze eyed the men. Being Freed was often disorienting, and the process of awakening could be painful and confusing. He'd insisted on sitting next to them in case they decided to do something stupid while they recovered. Not that Fedra looked like she'd need much help if they did. But when he'd offered, Eudora had given him a grateful smile and dismissed the guardswoman to her post by the front gate—one more reason Osaze was inclined to trust the young woman. For their part, the men appeared grateful to have someone nearby who couldn't subdue them with a single hummed note—even if they did keep casting him wary glances. Once he found out they'd been sailors on the slaving ship that had been brought in during the most recent harvest, Osaze had no doubt as to why. He ground his teeth and ignored their furtive looks.

While they ate, Kyria Dione peppered the newcomers with questions. Urbi answered most of them, telling Dione about Barbados and what little she knew of Abela. Apparently, the lamma had been here before, but had told Eudora and Dione little about herself or her activities on Barbados. Her primary concern had been reaching Zale and Calandra.

Bunmi kept staring at the undines with wide eyes, saying very little, even though one of the servant girls had been told to sit next to her and translate. When the girl asked Bunmi a question, she'd respond, but then lapse into silence, staring around her in wide-eyed wonder—and possibly no small amount of fear.

Eudora's long sandy-blond curls fell into her olive-toned face as she stared with pride at the infant girl at her breast. When she caught him watching her nurse the child across the room, she smiled warmly. He took another sip of mulled wine, his face hot, and wondered if she'd surmised what he was thinking—whether he and Calandra might ever have a child such as this little girl, with black curls and plump cheeks and eyes of the deepest green.

At the thought of Calandra, his heart raced. Calandra's apology—that had been real. Even though they no longer shared the *pisti* bond, her love and sorrow when he'd seen her in his dream had been more tangible than the water he'd floated in. He'd spent so long being angry with her, but as soon as she'd asked his forgiveness, he knew there was no way he could hold bitterness in his heart any longer. She'd made a mistake. He'd made some too. But, unlike Eudora and Ewelike, there was much more than a few miles and a revolution between them. Unless Calandra could find a way out of the Underworld, there would be no future children. Or a future of any kind.

The conversation was interrupted when Wilhelmina came in and saluted.

"Yes, Wilhelmina?" said Kyria Dione.

"Tonight must be a night for visitors, m'lady. Judith kor'Ignatia and several other FWS members have just arrived. They have a Free *tapeinos* with them. Shall I send them in?"

Eudora's eyebrows rose. "Of course, Wilhelmina. And have Kelaino bring more mulled wine."

As Wilhelmina went outside to call in their guests, Osaze sat straighter and glanced at the door of the room expectantly. When Judith entered and saw him, she stopped short, causing the person behind her to bump into her.

"Osaze? How can it be?" she asked in wonder.

Judith stepped hesitantly over the threshold, glancing around at the odd assembly. She wore the navy blue linen livery of the Opal Palace. Three similarly clad undines and a human girl with tattoos on her chin and forehead followed behind, as well as a bewildered-looking Freeman in the uniform of a *tapeinos*. Osaze looked curiously at the man and recognized Thomas, who had been quartered with him at the palace and had often served as Calandra's bodyguard when he was off duty. The man looked around the room with a nervous edge glinting in his dark eyes, similar to the men already present.

Osaze leapt to his feet. "Judith. Meg. Thomas," he said, bowing and saluting them each in turn with his fingers to his forehead and his shoulders slightly hunched. "Well met. My mother and I and our companion, Olubunmi, have just returned, with the help of a lumasi woman named Miss Abela Bethel."

Judith closed her gaping mouth. "Abela brought you here? That woman certainly gets around, doesn't she?"

With a slight shake of her head, she turned and offered salutes and polite greetings to the hostesses and the others present, then introduced her companions. The woman with the cowrie shells woven into her long, dark braids was Kynthia, one of the rebels from Elpida. The human girl with the geometric blue lines on her forehead and chin, Tafrara, had Freed her brother Thomas this very night with Kynthia's help.

Thomas's salute was crisp with years of practice. He turned his gaze on the two men on the floor. "Arthur and P-P-Purcell. It is g-g-good to s-s-see you here."

Osaze had never noticed the man's stutter before—not that they'd exchanged many words in their former lives. The two sailors returned Thomas's greeting with hard glances and mumbled hellos.

Thomas frowned. His gaze slid back to Osaze. "Y-You are Calandra's c-consort-elect."

"Was." The word tasted bitter on Osaze's tongue.

"And this is Erigone kor'Astera," Judith said, indicating a slender woman with dark freckles on her light brown cheeks and her dark brown curls held in a loose bun. A white stone Tear gleamed from a silver chain around her neck, and as she saluted, a small satchel covered with whimsical paintings of starfish swung at her side. "She's a stone healer from Haven who has been quite valuable at Margaret House."

The healer darted a quick smile at Judith, dipping her chin.

"Please, sit down," said Eudora, indicating the cushions her serving girls were placing on the floor between the stools. "Take refreshment. Tell us what brings you to us at this hour."

Judith's countenance fell. Osaze sat beside his mother once more, and Judith and Kynthia seated themselves in the empty space next to Urbi. Thomas, Meg, and Erigone all found a cushion and sat.

"I . . . I wish I had better news," Judith began, her expression tight. "This morning, one of Healer Erigone's team found a schematic of the Heartstone on an Atlantean datastone. Erigone and Meg infiltrated the Mother's Heart chamber to see if they could restore the broken connection."

"And did you?" Eudora asked the two stone healers eagerly.

Meg's shoulders slumped, and she glanced at Erigone.

"Sadly, no," Erigone said, pursing her lips and fidgeting with the closure on her starfish satchel. "While we were able to reposition the spoke, it was not enough. To complete the work, we'll need a circle of more than two stone healers. Hopefully three or four will do it." She frowned.

"Hopefully?" Dione raised an eyebrow.

Meg cast a glance at the senior healer before responding. "Healer kor'Astera believes the Heartstone may be too damaged to repair, even with a circle."

"And Zale and Calandra are not here to use all the elements to repair it," Judith added.

"Precisely." Meg gave a sharp nod of emphasis.

Eudora looked back and forth between them. "But Calandra said it was almost completely healed. That doesn't make sense."

"I agree," Erigone said. "But although the connection has been restored, the light inside has dimmed, and I'm not sure why. There were a few things on the schematic I was uncertain of. I will need to study further to see what I missed."

A thought occurred to Osaze, something Calandra had said to him once. "Could the Spirit inside be dormant?"

All eyes turned to him, and he cleared his suddenly tight throat.

"Calandra once told me she could sense a living Spirit in the Heartstone. If it has been, I don't know, injured or some such, that might be why the Heartstone still isn't working."

Erigone nodded. "There were several mentions of *Pneuma*, spirit, being incorporated into the Stone in ways unfamiliar to me. You might be on to something."

"Calandra mentioned the Spirit to me after she rescued us," Meg said. "She said it felt as strong as ever."

Osaze folded his hands and studied them, considering this. "Abela said the heartstones are a tool for organizing matter from ether," he said slowly. He glanced at Meg and Erigone. "She and the other erelim use smaller versions to create the bodies they inhabit while on the material plane."

"Fascinating," Dione murmured, leaning forward.

"The point is, without someone to direct them, the heartstones are just rocks." Osaze scowled, wishing he knew more.

Meg gazed at him sharply. "What else did Abela say about the Heartstone?"

Osaze straightened, trying to remember. He'd been in so much pain . . .

Urbi turned to Meg, answering for him. "She said since the heartstones are a gift of Elyon—the name she gives the Supreme One—ether must be drawn through Elyon's Spirit, the Pneuma, like water through a pipe."

"Pneuma?" Erigone said. "As in the spirit woven into our island's Heartstone?"

"This I do not know," Urbi said.

Osaze broke in. "But if the island's Heartstone is similar to the small lumasi ones, perhaps the remaining damage to the Heartstone isn't the problem. Perhaps the ether is no longer flowing through the pipe. It needs someone to start the flow again."

The two stone healers looked at him in amazement.

"Kyrios Osaze, that is brilliant," said Erigone. "And I believe I know just the song we'll need to use to do it. We need only to gather a circle and return to complete the process." She beamed and looked around the room. "This could work. And once we rekindle the Heartstone's fire, we won't have to worry about fighting or hiding from the ships anymore, because the barrier will keep them out."

Osaze warmed at the praise, then chilled at a new thought. "There was something else."

Meg saw his expression and frowned. "What is it?"

Melina, the servant translating for Bunmi, Purcell, and Arthur, murmured softly in English. A gleam came into Arthur's eye at the mention of the ships—Osaze could practically see the wheels turning in the man's head—but he had a more pressing concern.

"Semyaza is an enemy of Elyon's, and he has gone to great lengths to try to get Abela's heart from her. So far, he's been unsuccessful." Osaze glanced toward the empty doorway. Where *were* Abela and Josefine anyway? "But she said if he ever got hold of one, he could wreak untold havoc. So what damage could he do if he were to use the Heartstone for his purposes?"

"If he could, don't you think he would have by now?" Judith asked.

Meg went pale. "Until now, the connection was incomplete." She swallowed and looked around the room, exchanging alarmed glances with Erigone. "What have we done?"

A sharp cry from the courtyard interrupted them.

Osaze jumped to his feet, as did several of the others, but before they could move, Wilhelmina and Fedra came into the room with their hands held high, prodded along by several tough-looking men holding spears. Several other men flowed into the room behind them, pointing more of the dangerous-looking weapons at the women. Osaze recognized the tattooed man who followed them immediately—Cain, the young man Adonia had been favouring in the months before her death. He strode with an arrogant swagger, his lean figure clad in a farmhand's rough tunic instead of the elegant silks the queen had dressed him in, a long siren's diving knife at his hip. He glared around the room, his eyes bright with intelligence and malice.

Near the door, Wilhelmina gave Dione and Eudora a hapless look, her arms held high. "Sorry, mistresses. There were too many of them."

Eudora clutched little Thea tighter, eyeing the sharp metal pointed at her. She hummed a few notes and Osaze's mind started to fuzz, but Fedra shook her head and cut her mistress off.

"I already tried," she said. "They've got songstoppers or something."

"Quiet, witch!" The man holding a spear to her back poked her, and she flinched.

Cain's gaze landed on Osaze, then Thomas, Arthur, and Purcell. "You four," he barked in Greek with a heavy Spanish accent. "You're coming with me. And any of you human women who want to join." He looked straight at Tafrara. "Nice work, Tafri."

Tafrara stood, ignoring the shocked expressions around her. "Hello, Cain."

77

DIVIDED LOYALTIES

JUDITH CLENCHED HER SWEATY PALMS to hide their shaking. The last time she had seen Cain, he'd been using a stolen ceremonial diving dagger to run through several sirens and Mari kor'Ana, a seventh-year siren cadet, at Calandra's bonding ceremony. What was he doing here? Did he intend to kill them all too? And how did he know Tafrara? She knew there'd been more to Tafrara's story than the girl had explained.

"What is the meaning of this?" Kyria Dione demanded, glancing between Tafrara and Cain and the menacing-looking spear pointed at her own chest.

"Sorry," said Cain with a grin, holding his hand cupped to his ear, "you'll have to speak up. I can't hear you."

Judith noticed small wads of cloth stuffed in the men's ears. It was a less elegant method of blocking sirensong than Calandra's songstoppers, but it seemed to do the trick.

Tafrara crossed her arms and scowled at the burly leader. "Cain, what *is* the meaning of this?" she said loudly. "Explain yourself. You can take out those earplugs. No one here will mind-bond you. And put down those ridiculous spears."

Judith stared at Tafrara. Where had the reserved human girl been hiding that authoritative tone in her voice? More importantly, how did she know Cain?

Cain snorted. "Is that how you thank me for saving you and these men?"

Tafrara gave him an incredulous look. "From whom?" She spread her arms, indicating the others in the room. "From our allies that Freed them?

656

That freed me?"

Cain set his jaw and glared around at those assembled. Then he jerked his chin at his men and they cautiously lowered their weapons—not all the way, but at least they were pointed toward the floor. Slowly, he pulled the cloth out of his ears, though his men left theirs in. They still gripped their spears, watching the undine women in the room like tiger sharks ready to spring into action at any moment.

Tafrara did not look pleased. "You're not needed here, Cain. Take your men and go. This household is a friend to Freemen, as you can see."

Cain glanced at Osaze and the newly Freed men, who were watching him warily. No spears had been pointed at their chests. Osaze shifted his body between Judith and the nearest brigand, and she took a deep, grateful breath. The man flicked a glance up at Osaze, then angled his spear toward the floor, but he watched Judith and Meg with narrowed eyes. He looked like he'd prefer to use it on Judith, even if he had to take Osaze out as he did so. She'd never felt such hate. It made her nauseous.

"Let us take the men and we'll leave peacefully." Cain glanced at the Freemen among the undines and jerked his thumb toward the door as though he expected the men to obey without question.

Thomas straightened. He'd drawn his *deiktis* and held it cross-ways in front of him—lowered, like the spears, but ready for use. "W-why should we g-g-go with you? Y-you are a murderer and a d-d-d-dangerous outlaw."

Tafrara crossed her arms, her mouth hard. "That he is, but he has also been working with Mother and me to help Freemen escape the city. He was the one who told Jane Watson you were in the palace in the first place."

"W-who's J-J-Jane W-Watson?" Thomas asked.

"She's . . . a friend."

Judith had never heard of Jane Watson either. She'd have to ask Tafrara about her later.

"Aren't these ruffians responsible for the girls who have been disappearing from the city?" Fedra demanded, her hands still held wide, her attention on the man before her, who scowled back.

"No," Dione said. She drew her shawl tighter around her shoulders. "That was, er, Narcissa."

Eudora stared at her mother. "How do you know?"

"Why do you think Sabina came home so upset this morning? Her and Hebe—the little scalawags—were sneaking around the palace last night after curfew and saw the princess with . . . well, never mind. Poor child could barely talk about it. That's why I kept her here." Dione shuddered.

"I'd go get Hebe, too, if I could. The young princess isn't safe."

Judith's mouth went dry. So that's how Dione had found out about the murdered girls—her fourth daughter and Hebe were friends. Judith wondered if the girls were both part of the student FWS. Had they been doing what Calandra had asked and following suspicious activity? She hoped Geronimi and the others didn't waste time helping Hebe escape.

"Like mother, like daughter," Cain snarled. "The whole family ought to rot in hell."

Judith noticed Osaze's shoulders tense and his fists clench at his sides.

"Be careful whom you curse. Are you now God?" His voice had a cold, sharp edge.

The pain beneath Osaze's words echoed Judith's own. Why was the one person who deserved Cain's sentiment the least the only one fulfilling it?

Well, not the only one. Kyria Dione's eyes had taken on a haunted look. With two of her five daughters in Hades, she'd probably felt the barb as deeply as Osaze had.

But Cain only sneered. "The mermaids have cursed themselves. And I won't rest until every one of them has paid for what they've done to us and I've found a way off this wretched island."

"There are ships coming," said a man's voice in a lilting English. "Human ships, coming here to attack. Could be our way out of here."

Judith whirled to see Melina staring at Arthur in startled astonishment. At the nasty gleam in Arthur's eye, Judith tensed. It had never occurred to her that the men among them might side with the coming attackers. But why not? What loyalty did these men owe the undines, who had captured and enslaved them, some of them for decades?

On the other hand, the ships might provide the perfect opportunity to do what Calandra had wanted—allow the humans among them to leave if they wished, to truly give them a choice. As long as the undines could protect themselves and implement such a plan.

"Ships, you say?" Cain scowled thoughtfully. "Those could come in handy."

Arthur grinned. "Indeed." He slipped out from between the others and moved to stand before Cain. "If you're leaving this hellhole, I'm with you."

"Wait," Judith said. She stepped around Osaze so she could be seen.

Arthur clapped his hands over his ears and whirled, his eyes narrowed.

Judith sighed, but she could hardly blame him for his reaction. "What if we could get you to the ships?"

Cain's eyes narrowed. "You'd help us escape?"

"Not just me, but the rebels, yes."

"Why?"

She had everyone's attention now. Judith drew a deep breath. "Because the Free Will Society's highest value is that everyone should be able to choose their destiny. The reason no one has been allowed to leave Sirenia was so others would not find out about us. But before Calandra left, she thought of a way to allow humans to leave without endangering our island."

Cain snorted. "Seems the secret's out, don't you think?"

Judith tensed. "For now. But Calandra's idea would allow us to conceal the truth and knowledge of our whereabouts once more, even from the attackers. And once the barrier is up, our island will be as safe as it ever was."

Cain crossed his arms. "So what is this wonderful idea the princess had? Put all the malcontents like us on the ships and then sink them to the bottom of the ocean?"

Eudora looked horrified. "What kind of monsters do you take us for?"

Cain narrowed his eyes at her, his voice filled with venom. "The worst kind."

She closed her mouth, her complexion pale.

Judith continued, her voice barely even shaking. "No one needs to die. But—"

"There's always a *but*," Cain broke in.

"But there *is* a price," Judith added. She swallowed, glancing around the room, noting the held breaths and wide eyes and sensing the fear and anticipation and horror of the others. "The cost is not death. It is life. You'd have to have every memory of your time here wiped from your mind, whether you've been here for three weeks, three months, three years, or your whole life. After that, you'd be free to go out into the world to pursue your own ends. The choice would be up to you."

She glanced sideways at Osaze, who looked grim.

"Rhea has approved this?" Dione said, sounding stunned.

"Aunt Rhea doesn't know. But she and the council will agree. It is the right thing to do." Judith hoped she was right. Judging from the bickering she'd recently witnessed, she didn't know if they *could* agree. "We would also erase the memory of us from the attackers' minds. It is the only way we can once more protect ourselves from the outside world now that the secret is so widely known."

Cain sneered. "I will tell my men of your generous *offer*. But I think they may prefer to take their chances with fate and keep their wits." He glared at the remaining Freemen standing among the women. "You coming?"

Purcell hastened to stand behind him. After a moment's hesitation, Thomas moved to follow.

Tafrara looked at Thomas, her eyes clouded. "You will not come to the safe house with me?"

"If w-what you say is true, he can t-take us to M-M-Mother," said Thomas, his stutter less pronounced than before.

Cain smirked. "He's not wrong, Tafri. Or have you enjoyed your stay with the witches too much to leave?"

Tafrara looked regretfully at Judith and Meg, the sorrow she emanated allaying the concerns Judith had been having about her loyalty, then nodded. "Mother needs to know what is happening so she can prepare. You know, in case the worst happens."

Judith nodded, and Tafrara turned to follow her brother.

"And you." Cain gestured impatiently for Osaze to follow.

"No," said Urbi.

She and Bunmi had been so quiet, Judith had almost forgotten they were there.

Urbi stepped forward and laid a hand on Osaze's arm. "This is not the way, son," she whispered to him.

"Don't worry, Mother," Osaze whispered back. He crossed his arms across his broad chest and turned to Cain. "My place is here."

Cain met his gaze with narrowed eyes—two trained warriors staring each other down. Cain was almost as tall as Osaze, but it was difficult to tell whose force of will was greater. Finally, Cain shrugged.

"Suit yourself. If you change your mind, find Jane Watson at the Mermaid's Curse. She'll get word to me." He arched a brow. "We could use someone like you."

With a gesture, he spun on his heel, and he and his posse retreated to the courtyard and let themselves out into a city bathed in predawn light. Fedra followed and closed the gate behind them.

Judith released a breath she hadn't realized she'd been holding. So she had made a promise she had no real authority to keep. No big deal. The archons would see reason, would they not? Besides, none of the men looked too eager to take her up on it. She hoped they would consider it—she hated to think what could happen if they preferred to fight their way off the island instead.

The commstone on her wrist vibrated, and she placed a finger on it and hummed a trill to open the line. "This is Judith."

"Where are you?" came Rhea's tinny voice. "We've been waiting at the sub for twenty minutes. I've been worried stiff. Is everything all right?"

Judith glanced at the others' shaken expressions. "Everything is fine. We will meet you at Sibyl's Cove. We will have a surprise when we get there too."

"Hurry," came her aunt's reply.

"I'll send Kelaino to guide you," Kyria Dione said, looking around. "Where is that girl anyway?"

"I'll go fetch her," Wilhelmina muttered. "Chained girl can never be found when you need her." She turned to the door, but Meg laid a hand on her arm.

"No need. We'll be fine without her," Meg said. "Calandra told me about the path."

Wilhelmina scowled, still seeming a little discombobulated from the recent home invasion. "I'm still going to find her. Why would she disappear while we have guests in the house?" She hastened through the door, still muttering.

They were on their way in minutes. As Judith led the others down the path behind the mountain, the rising sun turned the tops of the trees bright pink. She gazed out to sea, dreading what she might find there—but no sails littered the horizon yet. They still had time, though it was quickly running out. The sooner they could heal the Heartstone and raise the barrier, the sooner they could work on getting rid of Semyaza so Matthew could be out of harm's way.

With a determined step, she picked up the pace.

78

WINDS OF CHANGE

Oɴ ᴛʜᴇ ʜɪᴋᴇ ᴛᴏ ᴛʜᴇ safe house, Bunmi walked beside Osaze. In fact, she'd barely separated from him and his mother since they'd arrived on Sirenia. She glanced up at him, and he gave her a tight smile.

"Maybe Miss Abela's chariot was not strong enough, like she said," Bunmi said without preamble in Yoruba. "Since she had to make an extra trip for Miss Josefine, I mean. They will come in a little while."

Osaze nodded, glancing at the lush jungle around them. He hoped that was all that was wrong. He'd been torn about whether to go with Judith and the others or to wait for Abela and Josefine. But when he'd tried to insist on staying, Dione had shaken her head.

"That would be unwise. The royal guard is prone to making surprise inspections at unknown times. In fact, it would be safest if you were well on your way back to Margaret House. We will send Cherub Abela and her companion after you when they arrive."

"Perhaps Abela will have word about Zoe and Damaris," Eudora had said, her voice wistful.

At the memory, Osaze's stomach lurched, just as it had at the time. The fact that Calandra was completely out of his reach, but well within Zoe the Betrayer's, made blood surge through his veins once more. If only he had a way to contact them. He thought longlingly of Josefine's mirror and her offer to try to communicate with Calandra and the others. Why had Abela said it was forbidden? Not that it mattered now—the mirror was as inaccessible as Josefine. And Calandra.

He clenched his fists to restrain the sudden rush of energy with no outlet.

Judith, who walked in front of him, turned around. "What is the matter, Osaze?"

He shook his head, glancing at his mother. He hadn't wanted to speak poorly of their host's sister at Steadfast House. No matter what Zoe had done, if she never returned to her family, he didn't want them to remember her as a traitor on his account. But now . . .

"Did you know Zoe kor'Dione betrayed us? She took us to Barbados. She even knocked me unconscious with some weapon she found in Atlantis."

Judith's eyes widened, then her face hardened. "Of course. She must have been the mole all along. No wonder I could not find one at Margaret House." She frowned. "But the Mother has brought you back to us. Let us hope she does the same for Calandra."

"I suppose," he said, his shoulders tight. He took a deep breath, trying to release the frustration tensing every muscle in his body. He felt so powerless to do anything that mattered. For weeks, he'd been at the mercy of the fates, never certain where he'd be laying his head that night nor if he'd survive the day, consumed by hurt and raging against the woman he loved. Now that he'd been restored to health and was out of immediate danger, he was just as powerless to do anything to set right what was wrong between him and Calandra. His words to her in the dream taunted him—had it been real? He didn't know if he hoped it were or not. Had she heard what he'd said to her before the vision ended?

Judith tilted her head. "You know, Osaze, Gerrick has started training the Freemen at Margaret House. But, as spry as he is, he could use the help of a trained young warrior like you."

Walking on Bunmi's other side, Urbi frowned, shaking her head. "We cannot stay long. This is not our fight, and as soon as we are able, we will be resuming our journey back to my home."

Osaze watched his footing, choosing his words, then looked right at her. "Yes, Mother, as promised, I will help you return to *your* home." Her slight wince told him she understood his meaning, though he hadn't meant to hurt her, only to make his position clear. "But this is mine. I helped Calandra begin this fight, so that is mine too. And I have a promise to keep to her." He turned his gaze on Judith. "Lead on, Judith. I look forward to seeing Gerrick again."

Judith smiled. But when she turned away, sadness flitted across her face. They all had many burdens to bear.

Osaze's suddenly seemed lighter, though. He'd promised Calandra to fight what battles he could. He couldn't bring her back from the Underworld, but this was the battle he could fight. As he walked, he considered the change in his fortune. In the course of a few days, he'd gone from being on death's door as a slave on Barbados to being a valued soldier for the resistance supporting the woman he loved.

A breeze played across his face, and he raised his head to breath in the familiar scent of home.

"Thank you," he whispered beneath his breath.

The warm breeze held Oya's response.

When he and his companions filed into the Great Hall of Margaret House, the midday meal was being served. Light streamed in thick beams from skylights above, bathing the hall in a mystical glow. Urbi, Bunmi, and Osaze stared at the vaulted ceiling and magnificent, cavernous room formed of the mountain itself. The centre of the hall was dominated by a raised pool with a statue of a sitting undine in *ichthys* state, her hands raised to receive a blessing from above. Around the pool, rows of wooden tables packed with people eating and talking filled the room with the melodic rise and fall of voices. Rhea, Judith, Kynthia, and Nick, who'd driven the sub, were given friendly greetings by several people as they placed their packs on the floor near an empty table.

First one person saw him and fell silent, then another, then another, until all conversation ceased and the entire hall was full of wide eyes—all staring at him.

Then, a man near him cheered. "Osaze has returned!"

Before he knew it, the entire hall was cheering and clapping. He glanced at Judith, at a loss.

"Oh, yes," she said. "I should have told you—you are a bit of a folk hero around here, thanks to how you helped Calandra stand up to the queen."

Freemen began to crowd around him, clapping him on the back and the shoulders. He met their warm welcome with a dazed smile, clasping forearms and greeting those he recognized by name. Gerrick came and stood a short distance away, a proud smile on his face.

"Good to see you, young man," the old man said once he was able to get close to Osaze.

"And you, sir." Osaze gave Gerrick a firm hug, then stepped away as another Freeman, a tall black man about his own age, approached.

"Do you know Ewelike?" Gerrick asked.

Osaze smiled. "Only by name."

Ewelike saluted. "It is my honour. Calandra has spoken highly of you."

Osaze's gut warmed. Even though he hadn't been here, Calandra had made sure he had a place. Gratitude bloomed in his chest.

"And your wife has spoken highly of you. Here, I have something for you." Osaze worked the leather cord of the aquamarine Tear he wore around his neck over his head. "Kyria Eudora asked me to give this to you."

Ewelike took the stone as if it were a precious piece of fragile pottery. "You saw Eudora? How is she? How is the baby?"

Osaze grinned and clapped him on the arm. "She is well. And congratulations on your beautiful daughter. The message will fill you in on the details, I'm sure."

Ewelike's smile could have lit up the entire hall. "Thank you, Prince Osaze." He clutched the Tear to his chest but didn't leave, as though afraid of being rude.

Prince? Osaze wasn't sure how comfortable he was with that title. "Go," he said, waving his hand. "Go watch your wife's message."

Ewelike nodded and gave a deep undine salute, then rushed away, still grinning.

"You've become quite the celebrity, lad," Gerrick said, surveying the hall of chattering people. Glances frequently directed his way indicated he and the others were still a hot topic of conversation.

Bunmi looked up at him with wide eyes. "Are you a prince, elder brother?"

Osaze shook his head. "No, nothing like that. I'm—"

"Yes," Urbi said, coming and placing her hand on his arm. "Yes, he is. He is consort-elect of the Opal Princess, heir to the throne of Sirenia. That makes him a prince. That, and so much more."

He studied her expression. Sadness. Pride. Hope. Or perhaps the hope was his. Had she finally accepted this was where he needed to be?

Bunmi shifted awkwardly, looking completely overwhelmed. Osaze felt much the same.

"Don't worry, younger sister" he whispered to her in Yoruba. "This is all new to me too. We'll find our place here soon. We'll help each other, all right? Just like we have all along."

She nodded, looking only slightly relieved. Judith, noticing her distress, urged her away toward the food tables, pointing out important places on the way and introducing her to some young women Osaze didn't recognize.

Overcome with gratitude, Osaze slipped his arm around his mother's waist, which was thinner than the last time he'd embraced her before they'd been sent away—before his world had been turned upside down. Not since he had been a young boy playing with Calandra near the Light Spring had his world felt so right.

If the orisha's favour held, perhaps the next change of the winds would bring Calandra home.

79

LAMIA'S LAIR

Zale moved along the reeking corridor, urged on by the occasional jab with Damaris's staff, which was wielded by the shedu woman. Of all the terrible stenches he'd encountered in the Underworld, the shedim lair smelled by far the worst, like the breath of a thousand demons combined . . . which it might very well be.

He cast about for options—his powers were useless with the thick manacle around his leg. While he had gained considerable fighting skill over the last few weeks, he doubted he was any match for a lair full of teleporting snake demons. On top of that, he was alone. If he was going to get out of here, he'd have to do it by himself. He just hoped Damaris was all right.

"Get going, slug," snarled the snake-woman with another jab.

"Look who's talking," he muttered under his breath, but he picked up his pace, keeping up with the slithering man ahead of him.

The tunnel opened into a torchlit cavern, though the flames from the torches were an odd green colour, casting everything in a sickly light. The arched cavern looked like something out of a story his mother had read him as a boy about a man named Ali Baba who found his way into a cavern full of treasure that was the lair of forty thieves. Except there was no treasure, and there were far worse than forty thieves in this cavern. If Zale had to guess, there were at least four or five hundred demons occupying the space—sprawled on rocks, coiled in dusty corners, or huddled together, hissing and laughing. One man reclined on a bench-like rock, cleaning his teeth with what looked like splintered bone. A group Zale passed were playing a game of knuckles with spine bones much larger than a chicken's.

He shuddered, trying not to think what—or who—the bones might have come from.

Zale followed the man ahead of him, ignoring the jeers and laughter and poking that came from the assembled demons as he passed. Some of them even tossed soft lumps at him—putrid, squishy, and warm, it could only be one thing. Where did demons even get excrement? He warded off as much as he could, but it was impossible to deflect it all. He bowed his head and covered it with his arms. In desperation, he reached out for fire or air, looking for some way to retaliate against the taunting horde, but he couldn't feel the elements at all.

That is, he couldn't feel any of them except spirit.

He didn't know what he could do with spirit here, but he grasped on to the gentle life-giving warmth that filled his core and seeped into the cracks of creation even here, deep in the Underworld. The awareness assured him he wasn't alone. Before he'd known Mr. Berian as Rumiel, the reverend had told him how Elyon's essence flowed through the universe, and how his power was made perfect in weakness. Zale certainly felt weak now.

Elyon, if you're here, even in this nest of demons, please show your strength.

Zale didn't notice that the man in front of him had stopped until he nearly stepped on his tail. They'd come to some kind of arena in the centre of the cave, with high, uneven natural tiers of rocks arranged around a large sandy pit. Slithering demons were gathering in the rocky stands to watch whatever entertainment was expected to happen below. But it was the sight at the far end of the arena that made Zale's blood run cold.

There, laying on a black stone altar and tied down with thick ropes made from twisted, thorny vines, was Damaris. She was looking at the crowd with fear in her eyes. Her clothes were torn, blood streaked her skin where the thorns had pierced her, and her sandy hair was matted and clumped. A red cloth was tied over her mouth. When she saw him, her eyes widened and moisture gleamed at their corners.

"No!" he shouted, lurching forward.

The shedu man barred his way with a thick arm, and a whack across the back of his knees with Damaris's staff made him crumple. His knee-caps hit the hard ground at the edge of the sandy bowl with a *crack*. The watching crowd jeered and laughed.

How could she be here? He'd just bargained his own freedom for hers. He'd watched her walk away with Zoe. Unless . . .

The shedim were shapeshifters. Nausea struck him, and he fought the urge to vomit.

"Do you like my surprise?" rang out Lamia's voice. She slithered into the centre of the arena from somewhere on the far side, a wide smile on her wet red lips.

A dread chill came over him. His arms fell to his sides, heedless of the occasional rotten piece of fruit or excrement still being lobbed in his direction. A hint of heat touched his gut, but it wasn't enough. For the most part, his blood ran cold—not a feeling he was used to.

A shedu woman with fine gold chains twisted through her upswept black hair and a black midriff-baring bodice above her black serpent's tail slithered into the arena, bowing and offering Lamia something. Lamia plucked the small item from the woman's hand and slipped it on her finger—it was Rumiel's ring. She admired it, then turned to Zale.

"Nepsi is quite the actress, is she not?" Lamia gestured at the shedu, who transformed before Zale's eyes into the image of Damaris as he'd seen her outside only minutes ago—haggard and vulnerable.

"Oh, Zale," the woman said in a mocking voice—Damaris's voice— "save me!" She clasped her hands in a pleading gesture.

The crowd roared with laughter and Zale's stomach roiled, another tiny flicker of heat sparking and dying in his belly. He glanced at the other Damaris on the pyre, who looked at him with imploring eyes. Could he even be sure *she* was the true Damaris?

Lamia slithered nearer to him, chuckling at the expression on Zale's face. "Yes, you fell for the decoy *again*, all while your sweetheart lay here in torment. How could you be so easily fooled?"

Her words echoed his thoughts. Quivering with quelled rage, he pushed himself to his feet. The shedu guards dragged him into the arena and shoved him toward Lamia. He stumbled to a stop only a few paces in front of her. The stone altar was more than two dozen paces away at the other end of the sand.

Lamia slithered around him, leaning near and breathing deeply once again. She smiled dreamily. "Ah, that's what I needed."

Zale tried to follow her progress as she moved behind him. "How can I know this isn't another trick?" He pointed at Damaris, and the eyes of the girl on the altar filled with hurt.

"That is the question, isn't it, dear cousin?"

Zale's throat closed. The woman walking around in front of him was no longer the sultry Lamia, but Narcissa—arrogant, cold, condescending, but with a wide smile on her face that invited him to believe her.

He knew it wasn't her, it was another one of Lamia's tricks—her fetid stench confirmed it. But even still, seeing the face of the girl who'd deceived him so completely brought a surge of anger to the surface. He roared and lashed out, throwing a punch that Narcissa easily deflected, and another that she dodged, grabbing his wrist and twisting his arm around behind him.

"*Dear* Zale, how could you have been so blind?" the Narcissa figure said, leaning close to purr in his ear and drawing another deep breath. "How could you not have known you were being deceived all along?"

He twisted his body, dipping away from her hold so she lost her balance. He whirled around to face the demon, ready to strike another blow, and froze. She was no longer wearing Narcissa's face, but his mother's.

He faltered, staring at the face that had tormented his days in the tank, the reason he'd come here to Hades in the first place. The false Delphine took advantage of his hesitation and grabbed his extended hand, twisting his arm and flinging him across the arena. He landed in the dirt, staring up at the stone ceiling, panting. The crowd laughed and cheered.

The demon wearing his mother's face came and stood over him with a gloating smile.

"How could you betray me, Zale? If it weren't for you, I would never have ended up in hell in torment and on the verge of insanity."

Her face shifted again, and Zale stared, horrified, at the blond hair and chiselled features of his father, looking as he had just before Zale had blown up the mine stack that took his life.

"If it weren't for you," Kenver said, "I'd still be alive."

Zale's chest constricted, tighter and tighter, and he could feel the sobs building. Kenver closed his eyes and drew another deep breath, bliss registering on his face with the hit of fear the demon inhaled.

No. It's all a trick. Don't let her get to you.

But he couldn't convince himself. Even though he knew the faces weren't real, the words they spoke echoed fears that had tormented him day and night. He'd been betrayed over and over again—but first, he'd betrayed those he loved most.

With another roar, he used his legs and back to push himself to standing. Kenver took a step back, transforming again into the form of Gio, Zale's best friend among the Romani. The teenage boy's thick black hair, black brows, and dark, glittering eyes made him pause.

"You wouldn't hurt me, would you, ol' pal?" Gio grinned, just as Zale had seen him do a thousand times around the campfire or while plying their tricks against the *gorgios.* "Not the way I hurt you. You thought we were brothers. I sure fooled you, didn't I?" He chortled.

Zale rushed forward, charging at the boy's belly, but by the time he made contact, Gio's waist had thickened into the solid trunk of a man—Eric. The man twisted away from Zale's blow, and Zale was carried past by the force of his charge. He stumbled and whirled, glaring at the man whom he'd seen as a father, the man who had taken him in and cared for him when Zale's whole world had been turned upside down—the man who'd intended to turn him over to the Order that had sent his mother to Tartarus.

"I never loved you," Eric said with a wicked grin, "but you were so desperate for approval, for a place to belong, you couldn't see it. You were so easy to fool. And I grew rich off of your blind naivety. That was the best trick I've ever played."

Zale stopped mid-charge, staring into the black eyes and stern face he'd loved so much. How could he have been so willfully blind? How could he have let himself be repeatedly deceived? The weight of all his failures and all the betrayals threatened to crush him, and his eyes blurred, his shoulders slumping.

Eric breathed deep and long as the demon inhaled his misery. "Yes, boy. You should have known a *gorgio* like you could never be part of my family."

Eric's dusky features shifted into the sun-kissed bronze of Abela's oval face surrounded by dark brown corkscrew curls with gold-tipped ends, but her golden eyes were hard and her normally kind smile had a malicious quirk to it.

"And you thought I actually meant to guard you? That you were special? I was using you all along too. To me, you were no more than a means to an end, so I could earn my place among the guardians—and when you wouldn't even use your powers to help save yourself, I abandoned you too."

Zale's throat closed and his sinuses stung. He clenched his sweaty fists at his sides, staring at the face of the girl who had finally told him who he was as the demon sneered at his failures. But really, what more did he deserve? He'd killed Mr. Crow and his own father and left lasting scars on Robert Cox, who would have been blind for life if not for his mother's kindness and skill. He'd hurt Calandra, Abela, and, before that, Talwyn. It was only just that after betraying so many, he, himself, had been easily duped and led astray. That's who he was—a betrayer. A fool. A dangerous monster no one could love.

See past the lie, whispered a voice in his heart. *See what is true.*

He looked at Damaris on the altar. She watched him with desperate eyes. The shedim seated amongst the rocks above her were breathing in her fear, bliss registering on their faces with every deep inhalation. If it weren't for him, she wouldn't be here either. He'd promised to get her out of the Underworld alive, but here she was, demons feeding on her soul. He'd let her down, just like he'd let his mother and father and sister down. If that was even really Damaris. It might be another trick. How could he know?

A tear trickled down her cheek, and she shook her head. She seemed to be begging him not to give up. Would a fake Damaris do that? Still, the demon who had gone with Zoe had been just as convincing, like she had really cared he was staying behind in her place.

On the *Atlanta*, Berian had told him it was the undine ability to see beneath the surface that had allowed Zale to see him as an angel and then a bull without him changing his form. Thanks to Damaris, he no longer even needed to touch someone to do that.

He looked at his friend on the altar, and she stared back at him in anguish. Closing his eyes, he imagined her on the terrace of the Opal Palace on the other side of a door, then opened the door between them to see her standing in a flowing white peplos, bathed in light as though she were an angel.

Her emotions hit him, raw and terrified. But beneath the terror was her own shame, her own guilt, and something more—a desperate fear, not for herself, but for him. She cared about him. And more than that, she had faith in him. He opened his eyes and met hers, and saw, for the first time, the fervent belief beneath her fear that he could find a way out of this, for both of them.

He looked back at Lamia, who still wore Abela's face.

Show me the way out, he prayed. *Show me the truth.*

Abela's face twisted in a cruel smile, and Zale swallowed.

80

DANCE WITH THE SHE-DEVIL

ZALE FLEXED HIS SWEATY HANDS, hoping, praying, for a whisper of fire, a breath of air, to respond to his desperate plea for help. But nothing happened.

Sing, came the response instead.

He blinked. Of course. Why hadn't he thought of it before? These were demons, just like the gargoyles that had attacked him and the others in the jungle. Surely they would be just as averse to hearing a song worshipping the Creator who had condemned them to their eternal misery.

Lamia, still wearing Abela's face, crossed her arms. "So much for the first undine male in three millennia. You turned out to be just as ordinary and gullible as every other fallen being who's ever walked the planet." She snorted in derision. "And you thought you were worth saving."

Zale drew in a deep breath and sang the first song that came to mind—a song he'd once heard in the little stone church in Madron.

Amazing grace, how sweet the sound
That saved a wretch like me.

The effect of the song was instantaneous. From the first note, a furor spread among the listening demons. They clapped their hands to their ears, crying in pain.

Abela recoiled, her face melting into Lamia's enraged features.

"Shut up! Stop that at once!"

I once was lost, but now am found;

Was blind, but now I see.

Lamia slithered several feet away from him, cringing. "Someone, stop him!"

A few of the shedu around the lower edge of the arena slithered hesitantly into the pit with their hands over their ears, some of them transforming to *podia* state as they circled him warily. Every note hit them like an arrow, and they staggered toward him, making little progress before halting under the assault.

He advanced on Lamia as he sang, and she retreated from him, her eyes wide.

'Twas grace that taught my heart to fear
And grace my fears relieved

He reached Lamia, whose hands were pressed firmly to her ears. She'd retreated to the base of the cavern wall on the far side of the pit, and now pressed her back against it. She looked at him, wild-eyed with rage and pain. The spirit that had been a gentle warmth in his core kindled to a roaring fire exploding through his veins, and the gold clasps on the green feldspar manacle melted. With a clatter, it fell to the sand, and Lamia flinched.

How precious did that grace appear
The hour I first believed.

She took her hands from her ears, and immediately clapped them back on. As he sang, Zale reached for Rumiel's ring, slowly working it off her finger, wary of her thrashing tail. When it came near him, he stepped on it, pinning it to the ground. Lamia huddled further into herself, but he didn't let the thrashing member go. The end flailed helplessly behind him.

Through many dangers, toils, and snares
I have already come;

Zale forced Lamia's hand away from her ear and she cowered, struggling to push it back to her head and block out the abhorrent music. He worked the ring off the last knuckle and released her, and she slammed her hand back over her ear. He smiled, slipping the ring on his own finger.

'Tis grace that kept me safe thus far

"You're not as special as you think you are," she spat, keeping her hands on her ears.

And grace will lead me home.

Zale smiled, and his perspective shifted. He didn't pity Lamia exactly, but he couldn't help wonder what had led her to be this way. According to what Abela had told him of the origin of demons, she'd been born the child of one of the fallen angels now condemned to the Abyss and a human. Had she been a monster from birth? Or had she chosen to become who she was, bringing the ire of Elyon on her for her crimes, so he bound her to the Earth as a spirit for eternity? He blinked, noticing for the first time that the gold bracers on her forearms were imbued with spirit—she was cuffed and bound as surely as he had been. She was also living out the consequences of her choices.

Perhaps she'd never accepted her culpability for the wrongs she'd committed, and that's what made her into this. But he had. And more than that, he knew those wrongs didn't have to define him. Like Abela and Calandra and even Rumiel had done, he could accept the consequences of his guilt and choose to do better next time. To do the right thing. He didn't know if he could forgive himself for his past mistakes, but he knew Elyon's grace would lead him home.

"No," he said calmly, "I'm not as special as *you* think I am. But that doesn't matter. Because it's not about me. I'm just a key."

Lamia's eyes widened and she hissed. Zale reached for the second ring, the one that looked so much like Rumiel's, preparing to launch into the next verse of his song. He didn't know what the ring did, but he was sure he would regret leaving it with her.

When we've been there—

Just then, he felt a jolt of fear from Damaris and turned toward her. The shedim Lamia had tried to sic on him had turned to Damaris instead, bending low as they fed on her turbulent emotions, their slimy black tongues licking her face, arms, and legs. She looked like she wanted to squirm away, but every movement caused more blood to appear where the thorns pricked her. Through her gag, she screamed.

The clasps on Zale's cuffs melted through, and they fell away from his wrists. He threw a bolt of fire at the base of the altar, scattering the shedim. Dashing through the fallen demons, he ran toward his friend, his only thought to save Damaris. He ripped the gag from her mouth and pulled it down over her chin, then turned to loose her bonds.

"Behind you!" she cried.

He spun, but too late. The swinging tail of one of the fallen serpent men coiled around his neck, constricting and crushing his vocal cords as the man's torso rose from the ground. Zale pawed at the soft skin, but the compression only increased, the shedu swaying above him on its tensile tail with a gleeful grin and flashing slitted yellow eyes. Channelling fire through his hands, Zale seared the flesh around his neck and it loosened, falling away. He coughed and drew rasping breaths.

With the warding song ceased, the demons filling the cavern had stopped their fearful cringing and were closing in on him. Lamia was shouting orders. He tried to sing, tried to hold them off, but his voice wouldn't comply—all that came out of his mouth were croaks.

Zale tensed. He backed up to the altar, spreading his stance in preparation for the attack he knew was coming. There were too many of them. He knew that. But he wouldn't go down without a fight.

Just then, a man's clear baritone pierced the air from somewhere beyond the gathered demons, his song filling the chamber.

Holy, holy, holy is El Elyon!
Every knee shall bow before his throne.

The demons froze, staring around them in horror and terror.

Demons tremble at his name
All the earth shall sing his praise.
Holy, holy, holy is El Elyon!

Like the song was a signal to charge, winged men and women in red, black, and gold swooped into the space, facing the assembled demon horde with swords drawn. At their head was a beautiful woman with black hair pulled back into a braided bun, a stern, kind face, and thin, hooded golden eyes.

"Guardians, engage!" she called at the same time Lamia called, "Shedim, attack!"

Demons whooped and hollered and leapt from their seats to meet the enemy. Soon, the air was filled with the clash of metal on metal as shedim drew their own curved blades and fought the erelim who had dared to invade their lair. Lamia's head swung back and forth as she tried to follow the battle above her. She lifted the hand with the remaining ring, looking as though she wanted to aim its power somewhere, but the air was a chaotic swirl of demons and angels, and there would be no way to lash out at the enemy without endangering her own.

Zale turned to the altar. Wrapping his hands around the barbed ropes that bound Damaris, he turned them to ash inside his palms. As soon as he pulled her bonds off of her, she pushed herself up and threw her arms around him.

"Oh, Zale, thank the Mother. Or whoever's in charge down here."

He grinned, releasing her and helping her off the altar. "We'll talk about that later. For now, let's get out of here."

A barrel-chested copper-skinned man with leathery bat-like wings and a broad, kind face alighted in front of them. "Can I help with that?"

"Chaz! Boy, is it good to see you," Zale croaked through his raw vocal cords.

"Whew! You sound rough, lad. But I feel the same way." He turned to Damaris. "You must be Damaris. You're much prettier than Lamia made you out to be. C'mon, tuck in here with me, one on each foot." He held his arms open wide and spread his feet.

Damaris cast Zale a questioning look, and Zale nodded. "Chaz is on our side, and he's a lot stronger than he looks, which is saying something. It's okay."

As Zale wrapped his arms around Chaz's thick waist, he sensed the goodness and light emanating from the man's core—a being worth trusting. Just like Abela. Whatever had kept her from him, he hoped she was all right too.

Damaris followed Zale's example, stepping on Chaz's extended foot and wrapping her arms around his waist from the other side.

"You're a dragon, I take it?" She craned her neck to look at him.

Chaz grinned at her. "Yep. Now hold on, little lady. This could be a bumpy escape."

Zale saw Damaris's staff laying on the sand a few feet away. "Wait!" He released Chaz, dashed around a fighting pair, snapped up the *deiktis*, and returned to the angel's side. "Okay."

Damaris grabbed his forearms on either side of the seraph's waist, glancing at the staff and then at him. "Thank you."

He grinned, his chest warming, as he gripped the staff in one hand and Damaris's arm with the other, Chaz's solid torso between their arms.

"Hold tight!" Chaz flapped into the air, dodging duelling angels and demons.

Lamia's voice screamed after them. "Zale, you'll never be safe from me! Wherever you go, wherever your loved ones go, I will find you! Not even your death will stop me. I will haunt you from here until the end of time!"

The cold dread rushed back. Zale looked behind them to see Lamia reared to her full height, her face screwed up as she hurled her obscenities. With a flash of insight, he realized how the ring worked . . . The way the bonds were meant to work. Not by removing choices, but by laying down consequences, just as Elyon's justice was always designed.

He lifted his fist and pointed the ring behind them at the raging demoness, channelling spirit through the blue stone toward her.

"From now until forevermore, may every lie you speak turn against you, may every life you try to ruin bind you further from peace, and may the fears you consume consume you from the inside out. If ever you try to hurt me or my loved ones, may the justice of Elyon protect them and make disaster fall upon you instead."

They were too far away for her to have heard his quiet, raspy words. But he could see the moment the binding curse seeped into her chains. She stared in horror at the bracers on her wrists as the last wisps of spirit burned into them, then her raging eyes found his.

"You'll never succeed, Zale! You were destined to live a pitiful, meaningless life of—"

She cut off with a strangled noise as her own tail wrapped around her throat, cutting off the flow of words. His last view of her before they flew out of the cave mouth into the strange twilight beyond was her staring at him in open-mouthed horror, trying to fight her own body for the right to speak.

Chaz flew down the ravine a short distance before setting them down. An unconscious siren lay nearby.

"Zoe!" Damaris rushed to her sister and placed a hand on her neck. "She's alive."

Chaz frowned down at the siren. "Yeah, she'll be fine. Until she wakes up, that is," he growled. He strode over and hoisted Zoe up, flinging her over his shoulder like a sack of flour before turning to glare at Zale. "You have no idea how glad I was to find you both alive and well. But what were you thinking, lad?"

Zale swallowed. "I . . ." There really was no good excuse for his foolishness. Sure, he'd saved Damaris, but only by the grace of Elyon. He shouldn't have gone against his word. "I wasn't, I guess."

Chaz glanced at Damaris. "It turned out for the best, anyway. Who knows what Lamia would have done to this young lady if you'd waited? But there's no time to celebrate—Calandra's got herself into a spot of trouble, and she needs you, now more than ever."

Zale nodded, handing Damaris her staff. "Yeah, she needs me to help free Mother. I know."

Chaz shook his head. "No, she needs you to help her free herself. She's at the bottom of the Pool of Tears, a place erelim like Rumiel and me can't go. It's up to you, do you understand? I fear she doesn't have much time left before the Madness of the undines takes her."

The Madness? Zale's mouth went dry. Calandra hadn't looked that unstable when he'd seen her earlier, but she'd definitely been in pain. And this was his chance to make up for how he'd treated her since they met.

"Yes, I'm ready."

Damaris gave him a proud look, adjusting her staff in her hand.

"Great. Brace yourself." Chaz placed his hands on their shoulders and closed his eyes.

Zale felt the oncoming rush of an impending blink. This time, though, he wasn't running away from something, but jumping toward something.

His destiny.

81

THE PNEUMA

CALANDRA'S MIND DRIFTED, CAUGHT BETWEEN sleep and wakefulness. She'd lost track of how long she'd been stuck in the hole. She'd lost track of how many times the Leviathan had renewed his attacks on her barricade. She'd tried to light her lightstone, but she couldn't focus long enough to secure the line of spirit, so she'd eventually given up and surrendered to the consuming dark.

Calandra, the voice in her mind came again.

I'm sorry, Mother. I'm sorry.

She repeated it like a mantra, the only thought she could keep in her head.

Calandra, you are not alone.

Calandra tensed, instantly on guard. That wasn't Mother. It was the Spirit she'd met in the Heartstone. The Pneuma. Would it keep pestering her until she healed the Soulstone? Was that the only way to be rid of it?

Let me help you.

Help her? That didn't sound like a demanding deity manipulating her to its will. But, if she were honest, it had never been demanding. In fact, when she thought of all the Spirit had done for her, and how little she'd done in return, her chest heaved with a sob the water stole away. At every turn, the gentle Spirit who guided her had been a boon, not a burden.

So why couldn't she do it? Why couldn't she call on this Pneuma, as Rumiel had said? She'd done it before, and the Spirit had responded. But that had been when she'd thought it was Atargatis responding to her pleas. Now that she knew it had been this Pneuma who had freed her from her bondage to Damon, she could barely dare to think about it—a male god.

A god that represented everything she'd been raised to fear—heartlessness, domination, violence.

That's not who I am. That's a lie you've been told by my enemies.

The voice was gentle, soothing, and the pain in Calandra's head lessened slightly. Her throat thickened.

I don't know you. If that's not who you are, then who are you?

Instead of a responding voice, the memory of her mother singing to her as a small child came to her mind. She hummed the melody of the lullaby, her voice cracking.

In the night, the Dragon waits to ravage in the dark
But Elyon will shield the ones who bear his watermark
In the light, the em'rald-eyed protectors of the deep
Will, ever vigilant, defend the gates of Elyon's keep.
The dragons and the cherubim and undines all as one
Will love and celebrate the race to whom he sent his son.

The second-last line tickled a memory. Fumbling with the ties on her pouch, she fished out the sapphire datastone and clenched it in her fist, thinking of the ceremony in the images where winged races and cherubim had been gathering to worship a deity the recorder couldn't see. Could the deity have been this Elyon? The creator whose Essence flowed through all creation . . . flowed through her, according to Kassiel?

Her spirit already knew the answer. The people whose images had been captured on the stone knew who Elyon was, she was sure of it. So what had happened? Why had her people forgotten him, his name lost but for a nonsensical lullaby?

She didn't have those answers. But she did know that somewhere, somehow, a long time ago, her people had accepted that lie too, on top of so many others. And it was time to turn back to the truth her heart had been trying to deny for so long.

Her throat thickened. What could she say? An overwhelming sense of her own unworthiness crushed her like a flood. After a lifetime of worshipping a false goddess, if Ophiuchus was right that Atargatis was actually the deceiver Tamiel, then how would Elyon feel if the first time she knowingly came to him, she was begging for something? Why would he grant her any boon at all, let alone the release from the *sklavia* bonds she'd willingly acquired? No, she wasn't worthy of freedom like that. But perhaps, if she asked, the spirit might at least relieve some of the pain.

She pressed the sapphire Tear between her palms as she often had with other holy crystals when bringing her petitions to the Mother, her fingers pointing straight up in front of her face. She closed her eyes, though it made little difference—it was almost as dark in her crevice with her eyes open as closed.

She swallowed the lump in her throat.

Elyon, I . . .

Words failed her. How were you supposed to talk to this god?

I'm here, child. The gentle assurance soothed her heart, and the pain receded a little more, allowing her thoughts to organize.

She tried again. *I've been going the wrong way for a long time. I thought I was doing the right thing, but I wasn't. That's no excuse, I suppose. I've made . . .* so many mistakes. I'm sorry.

Her chest heaved with another sob.

I know I don't deserve to even ask this of you, but could you please help me? There are so many counting on me, but without help, I can't do it. I'm going Mad from the constant pain, and soon, I'll be just like my ancestors in the pool outside. If it's possible for you, could you please take away the pain of the bonds, just long enough so I can free my mother and heal the Soulstone like you asked? If you would, I'll never ask anything of you again.

She waited, hoping against hope that the Pneuma would see fit to grant her request.

A small dot of glowing white light appeared in the water in front of her face. She stared at it, mesmerized, as it floated in seemingly random movements until it landed on top of her upright fingers.

The effect was like a jolt to her soul. The speck grew and gushed up her arms, coating her in warmth and energy and peace. It flowed over her chest and up her neck and down her torso until her entire body was enveloped in the pure white glow. It seeped into her very core, stilling what was in turmoil. And in that moment, the raging red bundle of bonds in her mind disappeared—completely severed.

She closed her eyes, letting the flooding peace transport her soul where it would. When she opened them, she was basking on the surface of the ocean on a sunny day with sea birds calling overhead. She'd been here once before—when she'd first encountered the Spirit in the Heartstone. It had been so long since she'd lived without pain, she felt as though she were floating on air instead of in water. The life-giving peace buoyed her up, healing her ravaged heart and renewing her tattered mind.

It is I who determine your steps.

The voice was no longer a gentle whisper, but the roar of ocean pounding the cliffs or the wind rushing through a ravine, and she was caught in the middle of the storm.

It is I who hold your destiny.

Calandra flipped herself upright and spun in the water, searching for the source of the voice.

It is I who heal your wounds.

Sobs wracked her. Overcome with emotions she couldn't even name, Calandra wept away all the fear and pain and heartache she'd been holding on to for so long. She had never known freedom like this. A deep, irrational joy had been planted in her heart, and it now spilled along the lines of the Matrix of Creation running through her, gushing out of her pores. She felt as though all the broken pieces of her were being bonded back together.

It is I who made you, daughter. And I have the power to sustain you. I love you, and you are mine.

This was what she'd been afraid of? This love, this tenderness, this un-tamed power? She'd never experienced anything like it. This wasn't domin-ation by a capricious god bent on destroying her. This was like being held in Osaze's strong arms and knowing that as long as she was there, nothing could harm her. Though that feeling was a shadow compared to this.

"Thank you," she whispered, the saltwater on her face joining that of the ocean around her. "Thank you, Elyon. May I never forget."

A reverberating crash brought her back to her dark crevice. The rocks that protected her from the sea monster were giving way, tumbling down the outside of the cliff where she hid. She tried to retreat farther from the entrance, but she was already as far into the crevice as she could wedge herself. Her cells still buzzed from her experience with the Pneuma, but fear choked her once more.

Protect me now, Elyon. I'm no match for that monster outside.

A few of the rocks grew warm and began to glow red, then white. The water touching them boiled in columns of tiny bubbles. Calandra cried in alarm, adding to the bubbles, but she could do nothing but watch in horror. Just when she thought she would die from the heat, the stones liquified in two places, running down the boulders below them like melted wax and leaving a hole. Hands reached through and pulled on the stones—*has Airlea found me? How did she melt the stone?* But the hands didn't belong to a woman. One of them had a softly glowing lightstone tied to the wrist, and the other wore a hemp bracelet accented by a smooth brown-striped river stone.

Zale!

She peered through the hole and saw his face and his cloud of blond hair illuminated by the white glow of a lightstone—a face she never thought she'd be so happy to see. When he saw her, he grinned. She gestured for him to back away from the hole, and he withdrew his hands, the white light of the stone retreating with them.

She tucked the sapphire stone she still held into her pouch. Then, concentrating, she put her hands on one of the boulders, using earth to push it outward and create a gap large enough for her to crawl through. As soon as the silt displaced by the rolling boulder plumed through the water, Zale rushed forward and pulled her out of her crevice by the arm. She looked around, wondering what had happened to the Leviathan, and her jaw fell open when she saw Airlea some distance beyond them with her hand on the enormous creature's snout. It nuzzled her as if it were a dolphin looking for a treat. She felt a flash of shame that she herself hadn't done that earlier, but she let the emotion roll away—*you can't project peace and calm when your mind is a war zone.* No wonder the Mad undines had lost the ability to tame the Leviathan.

She glanced around cautiously. What had happened to the undine women guarding the pool anyway? They were nowhere to be seen. Beyond the shadowy sea monster, the water faded into darkness in the vast grotto. Beside the creature in the centre of the chamber, the enormous pillar of the Well of Souls stretched upward, stopping well short of the quaternaria grate above, its marble sides covered in rock and barnacles and pock-marked from years of neglect in the salty water. It looked as though the Soulstone wasn't the only thing suffering from the Madness of the guardians—if left unrepaired, the tower itself would eventually crumble, and then what would happen to the condemned spirits within?

Calandra stared at the tower as she followed Zale's silvery-green tail past the docile sea serpent and ascended through the grotto. When they reached the top of the seaweed-slicked tower walls, they floated above the open ceiling of the softly glowing tower toward the partially open quaternaria grate. Calandra looked below at the throbbing blue Soulstone and realized there was some kind of energy barrier on the top of the tower like the one that protected Sirenia, probably meant to keep out the Leviathan, though the creature wouldn't have been able to fit its entire bulk into the tower, regardless. How would they get through? Calandra tugged at Zale's tail and pointed at it. He shook his head and gestured emphatically upward. She swam toward the barrier, but when she touched it, sharp pain made her withdraw her hand. She looked around, trying to determine the mechanism for opening the barrier, but could see nothing. Zale tugged on her arm and pointed upward once more, and she heaved a watery sigh. She supposed they could regroup above and return for Mother when they had a plan.

She turned to follow her brother again just as Airlea topped the edge of the tower, swimming backward and keeping her focus on the Leviathan with a hand extended toward the beast. When they were all through the partially open grate—at least she'd had the presence of mind not to open it all the way and let the monster escape—Calandra turned the crystal key to close it, and the beast bumped its nose against the bars forlornly.

But the biggest surprise was yet to come. When Calandra turned around to ascend to the surface of the Pool of Tears, she saw a woman in *ichthys* state with her back to them, her splayed hands extended wide in a defensive posture, her brunette waves floating in a cloud behind her. Beyond her, the Mad undines floated in a wary pod, watching the woman like caged sharks. Who was she?

As Calandra, Zale, and Airlea passed, the woman turned to follow them, keeping one hand extended to the undines behind, and Calandra finally caught a glimpse of her face. Her mother's face.

Tamiel!

82

REUNION

CALANDRA CLAMBERED INTO THE SHALLOWS of the Pool of Tears, nominally aware of the uniformed winged men and women standing among the crystals. White light glowed softly from the long, thick silvery rods some of the soldiers held propped against their shoulders. It glinted from the gold accents of their armour and helmets and refracted through the enormous sprays of amethyst and rock crystal. Rumiel was there, and Chaz stood next to a tall, golden-eyed woman with feathered wings, a stern oval face, and with her sleek black hair pulled back in a braided bun. Calandra couldn't see Zoe or Damaris.

As soon as Calandra set foot in the shallows, she raised her hands and whirled to face the beautiful woman with the long dark hair climbing out behind Airlea, ready to draw on whatever element necessary to defend herself and those with her.

"Didn't Valac tell you to wear your own face?" Calandra spat.

The woman stopped short, her dripping, slime-coated hair covering her tattered bodice, her knee-length swimming skirt frayed and thin, and water plants clinging to her skin. A scummy striped brown Tear, the stone much like Zale's river stone bracelet, hung from her neck by a short bronze chain.

"Calandra," Zale said, laying his hand on her arm. "That's not Tamiel. That's Mother."

Calandra met his gaze, still hardly believing her brother was there, let alone Airlea and everyone else.

"But I can't sense her. She must be a projection."

"It's my shieldstone," the woman said, touching the Tear on her chest.

"Like the one I made you." She pointed at Calandra's dark green opal Tear. "Besides, the Pool of Tears accentuates the authentic nature of things. It would be very difficult for Tamiel to project anything but her true form here."

"Mother?" The truth sank into Calandra's spirit. A gulping sob shook her. Just when she thought she had no tears left. "Mother!" she cried, splashing forward to throw her arms around the woman's very solid form, tears streaming down her cheeks.

"Oh, Calandra."

Delphine hugged her back, holding her so tightly that Calandra almost couldn't breathe, but she didn't care. She was hugging Delphine just as tightly. The assembled forces watched with barely a clink of metal. The guardians' love and awe filled the cavern around her, as if they were as joyful and overwhelmed as she was.

Finally, she pulled away, her mother holding her by the shoulders at arm's length as though not wanting to let her go but needing to take in every detail.

"Oh, Calandra, I can hardly believe it's really you." Delphine lay a warm, reassuring palm on Calandra's cheek.

"But . . . but how are you here?" Calandra managed. "Did Zale free you from the Soulstone?" She turned to see her brother watching the reunion quietly, shifting his feet at the water's edge. A damp-eyed Airlea and a soft-eyed Rumiel stood on either side of him.

Delphine shook her head. "My mind was trapped, but never in the Soulstone. I had fallen prey to a foolish ruse by a malicious spirit. I was trapped in a dream world of his making while my body remained here in the Pool of Tears with the others."

Calandra staggered, her knees buckling, and she sat in the dark, shallow water, staring up at her mother.

"You were in the Pool of Tears all along?"

Delphine nodded. "Yes. Your brother . . ." She turned to Zale with a proud, happy smile, and Zale nervously swung the side of his fist into his leg, giving her a sheepish smile back. "Your brother recognized me when he came for you. With a little help from Kore kor'Phile and Cadet kor'Dione, they were able to free me from the enchantment."

"She'd swallowed a bliss stone," Airlea said. She came and crouched next to Calandra, placing a comforting hand on her arm. "I distracted the rest of the Madwomen while Zale managed to get her to vomit it up."

"I'm afraid I didn't make it easy on him." Now Delphine wore the sheepish smile.

Zale shook his head. "It wasn't as bad as all that, Mother." Her name sounded like it caught in his throat. He hadn't stopped staring at Delphine since they surfaced. "And I'm sure I deserved whatever you gave me." Now he dropped his gaze, shuffling his feet.

She walked over to him, shallow water swishing around her feet until she reached the shore. Placing both hands on his jaw, she raised his chin to meet her gaze. "No, you didn't. There is nothing you have done to me deserving of punishment, sweet boy. Do you understand that?"

Zale stared at her, moisture in his wide eyes, and nodded, swallowing hard. However, his turmoil was obvious—as much as he might say he understood, it would take time to heal whatever open wounds afflicted his soul.

"You came for me?" Calandra said to Zale. She stood, water streaming from her skirt. "I thought you'd turned against me again, but you came for me. And you found Mother and healed her." It was a statement, not a question. She turned to Airlea, who'd stood when she did. "And you tamed the Leviathan. By yourself."

Airlea nodded with a small smile.

She was not alone, indeed. All this time, she'd been acting as though she were the only one who could fix everyone's problems. How wrong she'd been. She resolved to have a little more faith in others in the future. She briefly closed her eyes and sent a prayer of thanks to her new-found companion.

Delphine looked back and forth between Calandra and Zale. "Oh, my children, I can't believe we're together again at last. There is so much we have to catch up on."

She extended her arm toward Calandra, and Calandra splashed over to join her mother and brother on the shore. Delphine wrapped her arms around the shoulders of both of them at once, and Calandra leaned into the hug. Zale's long arms surrounded her and Delphine, and happiness flowed through her, transferring from her to her family and back through their touch. Rumiel stood to the side with his thick arms crossed, beaming like a proud father. His gaze had barely left Delphine's face, and Delphine gave him a sidelong glance and a warm smile.

When Calandra pulled out of the embrace, she found Airlea next to her, staring at her in wonder.

"Calandra," Airlea said, searching Calandra's face, "you're healed. Your pain is gone. But how?"

Calandra smiled. "I'll tell you all about it when we get home." Then her shoulders slumped. With all the other revelations of the past few minutes, she'd forgotten they didn't have what they required to leave the Underworld—a key to open a gateway to the Ground. She couldn't see Zoe or Damaris anywhere, and she suspected that once Zoe had freed her sister, the siren had taken the ring and fled home through the first portstone she could find. Or maybe she'd got herself captured, too, and they would need to go free her and Damaris both. "If we get home."

Zale grinned. "*When* we get home."

He pointed to Rumiel, who held up his hand. On the cherub's middle finger gleamed the lapis lazuli *ichthys* ring.

Calandra's heart leapt. "Zale, you keep surprising me. But if we have that, where are Zoe and Damaris?"

Zale's smile dimmed. "Zoe is lying unconscious in a tunnel over there." He rose and pointed beyond the assembled guardians to a dark tunnel mouth beyond. "Damaris is sitting with her to keep an eye on her." The hitch in his voice suggested there was more to the story.

"You can tell me about that when we get home too," Calandra said quietly.

He nodded, looking troubled. "Deal."

Calandra looked at all the assembled troops, at Chaz's beaming face, and Rumiel's proud one. "I . . . I guess this means we can leave now then. Right?"

Zale shrugged. "I don't see why not. Just as soon as we can get to a portstone."

Delphine shook her head and turned, grasping both her children by the hands. "No, not yet." She turned a pained gaze to the lake. "Judging by your ages, I have only been here for a few years, but it felt like an eternity in a waking nightmare filled with all my worst fears. Can you imagine the torment of our kin who remain? We can't leave them like this. We must free them." She turned an earnest gaze toward Calandra. "We must heal them."

Calandra nodded. "Of course. If they all swallowed bliss stones, too, that should be easy enough." She thought of the power Nadia had used against her while they'd been defending the well and the undines joining her in a circle and her heart sped up. But Calandra wasn't alone either. She glanced at her companions. "If we work together."

"And," came Rumiel's deep rumble as he stepped forward and came to stand near Delphine, "you have another task to fulfill."

Calandra met his grave golden-eyed gaze, her heart falling. "The Soulstone."

She looked at Zale, and his smile faded. He studied her for a long minute, then nodded. "Yeah, we have to heal the Soulstone."

"Are you up for it?" Calandra asked, trying not to sound as worried as she felt.

He frowned, then wobbled his head side to side with a sardonic twist to his lips. "I think so. I don't know. I think my sister could probably help me through it. I've heard she's some kind of prodigy or something." He levelled his gaze at her. "Can you? You're not going to fake die on me again, are you? Once was definitely enough for that."

She gave a snort of laughter. "I'll try to avoid it, if at all possible."

A look of understanding passed between them.

Calandra turned to Rumiel and Chaz. "There's some kind of a barrier that protects the Well of Souls. Do you know anything about that?"

They glanced at each other and shook their heads. "There are things about the well only the guardians knew. It would appear we must ask them."

Delphine cleared her throat. "And I'm afraid healing them will not be as simple as it was to recover me."

Zale snorted. "You call that simple?"

She gave him an amused look. "Perhaps not, but the others aren't bound by a mere bliss stone. They truly are Mad. Returning them to wholeness will take more than a purgative vomit."

Disappointment tightened Calandra's chest. There was no way to heal the Madness, at least not one she knew. If her ancestors had known how to heal it, none of them would have gone Mad in the first place. Whatever bondage had been responsible for the undines in the pool going Mad should have been broken long ago when the men they had bonded had died—death always broke the bonds, whether of the enslaved or the person who'd created them. How were they supposed to heal something that had never been healed when they weren't even certain what was wrong—and the patients were likely to kill them while they tried?

"How were you holding Nadia and the others at bay?" she asked Delphine, remembering her mother warding off the other undines as Calandra and her companions retreated to the surface.

Delphine's porcelain cheeks turned pink. "Honestly, I'm not sure. I thought they were going to attack any second, so I was praying the whole time. I think it had more to do with that than anything."

Calandra's gaze sharpened. "Praying to the Mother?"

Delphine shook her head hesitantly. "No. You may not want to hear this, Calandra, but I'm afraid the Mother is—"

"An impostor." Calandra gave a tight smile. "Yes, I know. I've recently had an encounter with the true Essence myself."

Delphine's smile broadened, and she wrapped her arms around Calandra's shoulders in a firm hug. "But that's wonderful news."

When Delphine released her, Calandra cleared her throat. "It will definitely take some getting used to."

"So, your highness, what should we do?" Airlea asked.

Calandra turned to face her friend, her heart thumping. Why was Airlea asking her? She didn't know what to do.

Movement caught her eye, and she scanned the group crowding the shores of the lake. Chaz and the commander stepped forward, offering Calandra clasped-fist chest-thumping salutes with sharp bows of their heads.

"Chazdiel, Gatekeeper of the Fourth Chthonic Guard, at your service, your highness," Chaz said.

"Shriniel, Captain of the Third Chthonic Guard, at your service," said the woman in a voice as smooth as melted butter.

Behind Shriniel, her troops gave crisp salutes, and in unison, said, "At your service," their voices ringing and echoing through the enormous chamber. Calandra glanced around and noticed the wide gap in the ceiling where she'd fallen through from above. The edges were regrowing, but it would take a while yet. How big must it have been originally for it to be taking this long to heal itself?

Rumiel clasped his hands in front of his chest and tapped his sternum, inclining his head. "Rumiel, Guardian First Class of the Cherubic Order of Raphael, at your service."

Calandra's throat thickened at the kindness and belief in his eyes.

Airlea pressed her bunched fingers to her forehead and bowed low in a deep salute. "Airlea kor'Phile, protector of the true queen of Sirenia, at your service."

Delphine stepped forward and gave a deep, graceful salute. "Delphine kor'Helena, Princess of Sirenia, at your service, your highness."

When she stood, the pride rolling from her hit Calandra like a wave. Calandra drew in a sharp gasp and stared at her mother, her sinuses pricking. Damaris appeared near the back of the group of soldiers in the mouth of the tunnel and gave a bow and a salute, mouthing *At your service*.

Then Zale stepped forward and gave a fair approximation of a practised salute, though it was a bit sloppy. "At your service, your highness. If you'll have me."

She blinked back the threatening tears. All these people were looking at her, trusting her to lead, to come up with a plan to heal the Soulstone and the Mad undines that protected it.

I can't do this. It's too much.

Yes, you can, daughter, came the reassuring answer in her spirit. *You are not alone.*

Peace flowed over her, and she drew a deep breath.

"Okay," she said, stepping forward, "let's figure this out."

83

TAKEOVER

Semyaza straightened, slamming Narcissa's open palms against the tabletop. "At last!"

He picked up the stone reader with the multicoloured opal Tear in the datastone divot and whirled to face her empty bed. Afternoon light filtered through the open windows, and the sound of gulls floating on the warm breeze with it. Matthew stood next to the main door of the suite in full dress, his *deiktis* clasped in both hands and resting on the floor, his face as blank as any other *doulos*.

The shout brought Narcissa to attention. She tried to make sense of what was on the stone reader, but it was in a script she'd never seen before. It looked like a bird had marched across the tablet's surface in straight lines. A bird with very tiny, sharp toes. Her brain tried to make sense of it, but the script gave her nowhere to start.

What is this about?

"The song! I found it at last! Written in ancient Tritonian. I should have known." He chortled. "That discordant spy you planted at Steadfast House has finally proved her worth."

Tritonian? What language is that? There *were* patterns in the erratic bird tracks. Complex ones that looked like no musical notation she'd ever seen. And when had Kelaino been here?

Semyaza moved to stand in front of the tall brass mirror. This time, instead of the golden-eyed man, he appeared in his dragon form—red-gold scales, glowing red eyes, a sinuous neck leading to a lithe, serpentine body with two bat-like wings flaring behind his shoulders. Narcissa wished she could recoil.

693

"Why, the language of your people, of course. Before you were assimilated into the Greek Empire, as so many other ancient cultures were. Though few, I'll admit, with such abandon."

If Narcissa had hackles to raise, she would have. How dare he insinuate the undines had ever been assimilated by anyone? They'd always been a proud, independent race. They bowed before no others, especially not a human culture.

You lie.

"Oh, come now, my beauty. Surely you've wondered why the language you speak is called Greek? As in, from Greece? And why your art and architecture reflects the Athenian aesthetic so strongly?"

Narcissa fumed. She hadn't, but didn't want to reveal that to her tormentor.

What song did you find?

Semyaza grinned, revealing dreadful pointed teeth. "The Song of a Thousand Days. The song I need to activate the Heart of Chaos to my will."

Narcissa dared to hope. She didn't know that song, but it sounded like the monster was one step closer to leaving her alone.

Now you just need the Heart of Chaos.

"You mean, this Heart of Chaos?"

Semyaza reached into the pouch on her belt and withdrew a large blood-coloured faceted oval stone. It nearly filled her palm. Light refracted from its depths, filling it with red fire.

Narcissa stared.

When did you get that?

It had been an involuntary question, and she cursed herself for the weakness it displayed—proof he could still subdue her awareness, that she hadn't seen him acquire it. That he was still the one in control.

Semyaza's lips curved. "Dagiel—you remember Dagiel? Dagiel brought it to me last night after your little escape attempt."

Narcissa froze.

"Oh, yes," he continued. "I know what you were trying to do. You're lucky you sent that undine girl packing instead of attempting to leave with her. I hate to think what would have happened to the baby then."

Keeping her reaction below the level of conscious thought, Narcissa relaxed slightly, but fear still nibbled at her mind like a swarm of minnows. He'd seen some of what had happened, but he must not have seen everything. If he had, Matthew wouldn't be standing in the room.

Or would he? Had Semyaza heard everything and had someone else Redeem the *doulos*? The fear threatened to swallow her, but she forced it back.

Narcissa chose her words carefully. *Does this mean you can now create a body of your own?* She pushed the idea of her body being free of him beneath the surface of her mind lest it anger him.

"Almost. Now that I have this and the song, there's only one more thing I need." He frowned, clenching his hand around the heartstone. "The *ichthys* key."

She quelled her disappointment and projected only curiosity with her next question. *What is that?*

Semyaza paced over to the desk and removed the rainbow opal Tear he'd been looking at from the reader, dropping it in his pouch and tightening the cord. "Handy little find, that. Not too many shieldstones left." He patted the pouch. Placing the catalogue Tear Narcissa had flipped through a few days ago on the reader, he scrolled through the images until he got to the queen's quaternaria pendant.

"This. I know your mother was in the habit of wearing it, but not what happened to it after her death. Since you couldn't find it either, I assume someone took it, but I haven't been able to ascertain who."

Ridges bulged from the smooth surface of the translucent stone reader in the curving lines of the queen's crest, the same shape as the tiny tattoo on the inside of Matthew's wrist. When he was still under the Redemption bond, Narcissa had asked him about it and he'd said it was a symbol of the rebellion, which was odd. Why would the rebels choose the symbol of the queen to rebel against the throne? Nevertheless, if the rebels were foolish enough to brand themselves, they would be easier to spot.

Unlike the pendant itself, which had eluded her every attempt to find it. She hadn't told anyone what she was looking for, even when she razed the plants at the site of her mother's death in the Grotto. The last thing she needed was for the archons to catch whiff of her intentions and claim she was trying to strong-arm her way to the throne without due process, even if she was. Especially since she was. So she hadn't asked anyone about the pendant directly, even when she'd been chastised in front of the whole council after the plant healers in charge of the palace gardens had complained to them about the mess she'd made. But now that Semyaza mentioned it, it did seem most likely someone had taken the quaternaria from her mother's body, not that it had fallen from her mother's hair during her battle with the panacea. But who would have had the audacity to take it, as well as the opportunity?

Cleo.

Semyaza frowned. "The *despoina*?"

Yes. I'm almost certain.

Why hadn't she realized it before? The *despoina* had been the first to respond to Narcissa's cry that her mother and Thea had killed each other in the Garden of the Mother's Delight. And there was something about the woman's veiled insolence that always rubbed Narcissa the wrong way. She had to admit, the mistress-at-arms had done an admirable job of standing up to Semyaza's bullying, but since Cleo had no way to know it wasn't Narcissa herself, she was less pleased.

Semyaza rubbed Narcissa's chin and paced back and forth. "If she hasn't voluntarily told us about it, she's hiding it for a reason. Perhaps her loyalties are in question."

It would be an easy matter to discern the truth. She can only have hidden it so many places. Summon her and have her searched while her quarters are also searched. If she has it, it will be found. If Cleo wasn't loyal to Narcissa, she saw no reason to protect the woman's privacy.

"No. She holds the loyalty of the siren guard, so I still need her. I don't want to raise her suspicions and have her turn against me. Besides, she strikes me as a very cunning woman and may have prepared for something like this. What if she has given the key to someone else for safekeeping?"

Something as important as the quaternaria? Narcissa was about to add another sarcastic comment, and then paused. What if Cleo had given the quaternaria to those rebel women? Or, worse, to Calandra?

"If she's given it to Calandra, then I'll have to trust that Tamiel will make use of it from the other side," Semyaza mused.

Narcissa went quiet and still, fear gripping her thoughts with pointed teeth. He'd heard that?

Semyaza stopped at the mirror and grinned at her wickedly. "Yes, I hear more than you realize. Don't you ever forget it. You have much more to lose than I do." He flicked his gaze to her still-flat abdomen, and Narcissa's thoughts scattered like a panicked school of fish. She hated inaction, hated that there was nothing she could do to defend herself and her baby against this monster. At least she was no longer alone in her fight.

He turned and gazed at Matthew through the archway, and Narcissa shrank in on herself even further. What else did he know? Was he about to reveal he'd been on to her and Matthew's conspiracy the whole time?

Just then, there was a frantic knock at the door. Semyaza straightened and loped to the archway.

"Come," he barked.

The brass-worked door into the receiving room folded inward and in strode Cleo, flanked by two siren rhapsodists. Semyaza moved to stand in front of the queen's chair and crossed Narcissa's arms.

Cleo stopped at a respectful distance with her two subordinates a step behind. All three gave a deep, proper salute.

"Forgive my intrusion, your highness," Cleo said stiffly, "but this news could not wait."

"And what news is that, *despoina*?" Semyaza demanded.

Cleo stood at strict attention. "I have just received an alarming transmission from Archpiper Ariadne kor'Thisbe of Haven, which has been corroborated by several archpipers from other communities between here and there along our western coast, as well as Lyrista Phaia kor'Ismene from Trinity. Every *doulos* in each community was simultaneously Released. I have already dispatched several siren pods to the larger communities to support the recovery efforts, and am mustering all that can be spared to follow. Some of the men have already been recovered through the quick thinking of citizens who were versed in sirensong, but needless to say, several of these communities are in chaos, and women are huddling in their homes for fear of their lives. Many of the men who were on duty in the mines at Fire Lake have escaped into the jungle."

Semyaza started pacing again. "How could this have happened? Some coup of the rebel forces?"

"I suppose it's possible," Cleo said, "but none of the women I spoke to said anything about foul play or rebel forces. In fact, they were bewildered as to the cause, as was I at first. But it soon became clear to me—the bond of every man who was Released had a single bondmistress."

Semyaza stopped pacing and looked at the *despoina*. "Calandra."

Cleo nodded and stared straight ahead, her hands clasped in front of her.

Calandra. But that means . . .

"So the princess is dead," Semyaza stated without emotion. "That's a shame."

Narcissa's frantic thoughts stilled. She dared not think anything too specific and reveal her mounting desperation to her oppressor. If Calandra was dead, then what would happen to the rebel forces? Who would challenge the monster using her body and defend her island against the invading human hordes? She should have been sickened by the direction of her thoughts, but she was too afraid to be disgusted with herself now. Matthew and his connection to the rebels were her only hope.

"You have done well, Cleo," Semyaza said. "But we must get this under control. Disperse every siren not necessary for essential functions to handle this threat."

"As I said, your highness, with Panselinos tomorrow, I'm already mustering as many as is safe to send away from the city."

"Send more." Semyaza paced toward her. "The confusion will likely cause some delay of incoming visitors from around the Shield, which should help. The sirens will be needed more in the villages than here in the city."

Cleo raised her brows in a rare display of emotion. "If I may speak freely?"

Semyaza gave a curt nod.

Cleo cleared her throat. "The Wildman threat within Sireniapolis itself has not been completely eradicated. Spreading our forces too thin might leave innocent civilians at risk."

Narcissa caught the impression of something about Cain and his band of renegades flitting through Semyaza's mind. Narcissa had suspected Cain was one of the Wildmen roaming the city—but why did Semyaza think he was their leader? Anger stirred. What that man had done to Mari . . .

"And what of the Wildmen in other parts of the island?" Semyaza said in a hard tone. "Are not those communities as important as our own?"

"Of course, your highness." Cleo bowed her head briefly.

"Leave the *tapeinoi* to guard the city with only one siren per human squad," Semyaza said. "Everyone else must be sent to restore order elsewhere."

"But the ships—"

"No!" Semyaza hissed, rounding on the siren. "I told you the ships are not your concern."

"Then whose concern are they?" Cleo said coldly. "They draw nearer by the day, and they will soon be too close for us to deflect using sirensong. It may already be too late."

"Enough!" Semyaza snapped, taking a threatening step toward her. "I'll handle the ships."

Cleo narrowed her eyes and saluted again. "As you command, your highness."

Why did she let the matter drop so easily? Narcissa's hope slipped away. Even Cleo was bowing to Semyaza's tyranny now. She should feel smug that the insufferable woman had been cowed, but couldn't manage it.

Semyaza turned to the two other sirens. "Rhapsodists, carry my orders to Archpiper kor'Sophia. Matthew, go with them and report back to me when the pods have been sent. I need to speak with Despoina Cleo alone."

Matthew gave a crisp salute and turned sideways next to the door frame, obediently waiting for the sirens to leave so he could follow. After a brief nod from Cleo, the two rhapsodists saluted Semyaza and Cleo, then filed out the door with Matthew on their heels. Narcissa watched him go with trepidation—not that he could actually do much to protect her against the monster who possessed her, but his presence had offered more comfort than she'd like to admit. She thought she caught a backward glance at her before the door flattened closed, but Semyaza turned away so swiftly, she must have imagined it.

The look on Cleo's face betrayed none of her emotions. She waited in silence with her hands clasped behind her back.

"Despoina," Semyaza began, "on the day of my mother's death, do you recall if she was wearing her quaternaria pendant?"

Cleo blinked. "I believe so, your highness. It was a ceremonial day, so she likely was. You were sitting next to her in the pavilion. Don't you recall?"

"My memory has been clouded by grief," he said flatly. "I only wanted confirmation." Semyaza paced lazily toward the window, gazing out to sea. Waves edged in white frills lapped the shore. He turned. "No one seems to know what became of it. Do you?"

Cleo tensed, her eyes forward. "No, your highness."

Semyaza walked to stand right in front of the *despoina* and stared into her eyes. Narcissa saw the dragon's reflection in their green depths.

"I believe you're lying," he said. "Like most undines, you're not very good at it. You know exactly where the quaternaria is."

A muscle in Cleo's jaw twitched.

"You have it with you now, don't you?" He smiled. "Give it to me."

Narcissa marvelled. She would never have perceived all that from a muscle twitch. But Cleo's subtle shift in posture belied the truth.

The *despoina* stepped back. "I already told you I don't know where it is. Now, if you please, I have urgent matters requiring my attention."

She began to turn away, and was halted by the ball of fire that appeared above Semyaza's open palm in front of her chest.

"I didn't dismiss you, *despoina*. Now, I'm going to tell you one last time." He leaned into her face until their noses almost touched. "Give me the quaternaria."

A click made him pull back and look at the green feldspar cuffs the *despoina* had just clasped onto his wrists. The ball of flame snuffed out.

Cleo's expression was grim. "Narcissa kor'Adonia, you are under arrest for the murder of Adonia kor'Helena, Thea kor'Aglaia, and Maria Gonzalez, though I suspect there are more." She reached for Narcissa's upper arm, presumably to turn her around so she could steer her away.

Instead, Semyaza clasped the *despoina's* forearms, staring deep into her surprised green eyes. Cleo's shock twisted into pain and she cried out.

Semyaza thrust her away and she fell backward over a chair. "Feldspar only works on undines," he hissed.

Two angry burns glowed on Cleo's skin where he'd been holding her, already starting to blister. But how was that possible? He couldn't *really* control fire. Could he?

And how had Cleo found out about Narcissa's mother and Thea? No one had seen her, she was sure of it. Then again, she hadn't thought there had been any witnesses to Maria's death either. None besides her.

Cleo staggered to her feet, holding her burned arms in front of her and watching him warily as she drew her *deiktis* staff from her back holster. "I've been told you go by the name of Damon. Is that what I should call you?"

Cleo knew of the dragon? A tiny spark of hope rekindled. Narcissa was almost afraid to acknowledge it.

"So you know of me," Semyaza said. "Interesting. But I no longer need that name. Call me Semyaza. Or, better yet, *your majesty*. With Calandra out of the way, it's only a matter of time before the council supports my claim." He held his hands up and conjured a fireball the size of a melon between them. Heat radiated from the fire in little shimmers.

Cleo stared at the flames and stepped around the chair. "I doubt they'll support you once I tell them what I know."

Semyaza spun, blocking her path to the door, keeping the fireball between them. "Oh, I think you'd be surprised."

He stepped toward her, and Cleo retreated half a step, her eyes locked on Semyaza's.

"And Narcissa?" Cleo said. "Is she here?"

Cleo! I'm here. Help me!

Shut up, you whining hagfish, came Semyaza's harsh response. She sensed him trying to subdue her and struggled against his will.

"For now," he said aloud.

What does he mean by that? Narcissa's thoughts thrashed in panic again, pushing against the boundary he used to confine her.

"She tells me you've been hiding something from us," Semyaza continued. "The quaternaria pendant. Where is it?"

Cleo started the tuneless melody of sirensong, but instead of stupefying Semyaza, it only enraged him. With a roar, he pulled his hands apart, separating the fireball into two smaller ones, and threw one at the *despoina*. She sidestepped it and it landed on the stone floor, fizzling out. He lunged at her, grabbing the end of her swinging staff and twisting it over his head, forcing her to let go. She recovered quickly, swinging a leg at his head. Ducking, he hit her leg on the receding side, forcing her off-balance, then swung the staff around before her foot even touched the ground and knocked her other ankle out from under her. Her belly hit the marble floor with a smack and he pounced on her, twisting her arm behind her and placing his knee in the small of her back. Despite herself, Narcissa was impressed. She didn't know if even she could best the *despoina*, especially so easily.

"Now," he said, leaning forward, "let's try this again. What have you done with the quaternaria pendant?"

"I don't have it," Cleo said with a grunt. "You won't get away with this. Once the council finds out what you've done, you'll be locked in the dungeon and they'll throw away the key. You killed the queen and one of the councillors and innocent young girls. Do you think our people will be ruled by fear?"

Semyaza laughed. "That is exactly what I think. But not just you. I intend to rule the world."

Cleo tried to look over her shoulder at him, but couldn't. "You're Mad," she said.

"I am quite sane, I assure you. Now that I have the Heart of Chaos, my fellow Grigori won't need bodies of their own to rule the world. Humans make such pliant vessels, and there are so many more here than the last time I visited. Once I use the Heart to eradicate the Pneuma from the cosmos, my companions and I will have full access to our powers. The undines will be no match, and they *will* follow me. They'll have no other choice."

"And why do you need the pendant?" she said into the tile floor.

"Ah, well, when one is orchestrating a prison break, it helps to have the key. Now, for the last time. The pendant."

Cleo heaved her body, but Semyaza retained his position. He drove his knee deeper into her back, then forced heat into the *despoina* through his hands. She bit her lip, her eyes filled with pain. When she eventually cried out, he laughed.

"Best to submit while you still have a choice, Cleo. Perhaps you could join me and my brothers and sisters when the time comes, instead of being inhabited along with everyone else."

Cleo responded by struggling more, this time succeeding in throwing Semyaza away from her and leaping to her feet. She looked a bit unsteady. Sweat poured down her face and drenched her bodice, despite the breeze coming in the window behind her.

Narcissa felt a small splinter in the glass-like barrier that kept her from controlling her body. Focusing her awareness and whatever spirit she could latch onto, she forced it into the spot like a wedge. Semyaza was too preoccupied with Cleo to notice.

He conjured an enormous fireball and rushed forward, throwing it at the siren at close range. Cleo's clothes, staff, and hair ignited. She batted at the flames, trying to extinguish them, but Semyaza kept running forward, grabbing the siren's belt pouch with one hand and pushing her hard on the chest with the other. The burning belt ties snapped as she stumbled back. The last Narcissa saw of Cleo was her horrified expression before she fell through the window.

Semyaza quickly beat out the flames on the garment while he ran and looked out the window, peering down the sheer drop. But all that could be seen was the white froth of the pounding surf against the black cliffs almost a hundred feet below. Narcissa didn't think anyone could survive that drop.

Turning from the window, Semyaza scrabbled to open the belt pouch, then snagged the silver chain inside and lifted it out, admiring the shining quaternaria hanging from one end.

"It looks like you were right, my beauty," Semyaza said. "Cleo did take the key."

Narcissa kept working at the splinter. It had widened, she thought. If she could break through without him noticing . . . She had to keep him distracted.

So what's next?

Semyaza turned to the window, his gaze roving over the ocean and landing on the cadets practising *Tropos Hydor Zon* in the sparring courtyard below.

"Tomorrow is Panselinos. According to your little spy, the rebels intend to rekindle the flame of the Heartstone. Once dear Matthew informs them that the Mother's Heart will be virtually unprotected, the rebels are sure to plan their next invasion to maximize the effect of the full moon. And I'll use their efforts to free my fellow Grigori. Just wait until you meet Tamiel. I think she'll enjoy Matthew as a host."

Narcissa stopped pushing at the splinter, fear and shock consuming her.

He knew.

Semyaza walked over to the mirror. His dragon mouth was quirked in a wicked half-smirk. "I told you I hear more than you think."

He snapped his fingers, and a few seconds later, that horrid man with the too-pale skin and the too-black eyes stepped out of thin air to stand in the centre of the room. The man bowed deeply, cringing a little.

"Yes, master?"

"Dagiel. We've had a new development that has accelerated my plans. I want you to implement the next phase now. Execute just before the festival begins tomorrow night."

Dagiel smiled, and it left Narcissa feeling slimed to her very soul.

"With pleasure, master."

After a dismissive gesture from Semyaza, the man disappeared again.

Narcissa hesitated to even ask, but she had to know. *What's the next phase of your plan?*

"Why, execute the remaining bondmistresses, of course. My companions can't very well make themselves at home in a bunch of mind-slaves, can they? I have to admit, the timing of Calandra's death is not ideal—Tamiel was supposed to wait until Panselinos, when the island comes to Sireniapolis and leaves their *douloi* home with minimal protection. But chaos is chaos, and I can use chaos. This might even be better in the end. When I emerge as the true Saviour of Sirenia, who will question my right to lead? Especially when I hold the keys to unleashing even more chaos if they don't comply?" He held up the quaternaria with a cold smile.

With every sentence, Narcissa's dread and horror increased. She struggled to understand. *But I'm one of the remaining bondmistresses. I hold thousands of bonds of men around the eastern side of the island. You can't very well kill me while you're using my body.*

"Can't I?"

He withdrew the Heart of Chaos from his pouch, and now the fiery heart pulsed slowly, as though in time with an executioner's drum. Narcissa stared at it, horrified by what his words implied.

No! You can't! You said you were going to make your own body once you got the song and the quaternaria.

"Did I?" He held the heart in front of him, and it consumed Narcissa's vision. "You should know me better than that by now, my dear. I lied. Why would I need another body when I can do everything I need to in the one I'm using? And I'm afraid you've become more trouble than you're worth."

The finality of his words ignited a blind panic in Narcissa. She threw herself at the barrier in her mind over and over while he laughed. The heart drew near her forehead, its fiery core deepening in colour as though pulling darkness into itself instead of light. She froze and stared at it in horror.

"It's a shame you won't get to say goodbye to your sister. But she'll join you soon—and then all the princesses of Sirenia will be together again. Say hello to your mother for me."

He pressed the stone to her forehead, and she felt a rending as a dark, cold force pulled her toward it. *This can't be happening!* She tried to scream, but couldn't. Instead, she faded into oblivion in complete silence and absolute powerlessness.

Her last conscious thought was that no one would even grieve her absence. They might not even know she was gone.

84

BROKEN BONDS

Osaze patiently moved through the form again, showing a soft-bellied middle-aged man named James the proper way to block an overhead attack with a *deiktis*.

"Move your leg outward to create a stable base while you bring the staff up, this way," Osaze said in Greek as he demonstrated.

Next to him, young Alexander translated the words into English for James, and the man nodded. The boy would have his turn to spar with his age-mates later. In the meantime, it was his turn to provide translation services for the men who still struggled with the language of the undines.

James got into the ready stance again, waiting for his sparring partner, Burak, to attack. Around them, the Great Hall echoed with the clack of staves from the other sparring men. When Burak brought his staff down toward James this time, the man met the blow with a solid stance and upraised *deiktis*. Then he countered with an attack of his own that, had he not stopped his staff right before he made contact with the side of Burak's back, would have knocked his opponent forward and off-balance.

Osaze clapped, grinning. "Yes. That is how it is done. Carry on."

As Alexander echoed his words, Osaze walked on to oversee another sparring pair. Across the practice space that had been cleared for them near the entrance of the vaulted common room, he spied Gerrick, flanked by Xeni's son, Jason, working with a couple of men who were likewise struggling with the day's instruction. He caught the old man's eye and smiled.

While showing Osaze to his quarters that morning, Gerrick had asked him to help train the men. Osaze had surprised himself with the fervour of his affirmative response and had asked to start immediately—as soon as

705

he'd caught a few hours of sleep, which Gerrick had laughingly agreed to. The six hours of rest he'd gotten on the hard bed of the Margaret House cell he'd been assigned had felt like a full night's sleep on a feather mattress compared to what he'd been sleeping on for the last several weeks. He'd sought Gerrick out as soon as he'd had a little to eat, refreshed and ready to begin.

Though the men had only been practising for a couple days, he was impressed with their determination and enthusiasm. He threw himself into the instruction, anxious to help them improve. Help them . . . and himself. Because although Healer Niobe had restored his flesh, he needed to be much stronger if he were to restore his spirit.

He paused next to Ewelike, watching him and Kofi spar. Eudora's consort moved with fluid grace and astounding speed. Kofi's staff was a blur as he blocked the taller man's rapid attacks. Most of them, anyway.

"You are doing very well, Ewelike," Osaze said.

The man planted the end of his staff on the ground and flashed Osaze a grin. "I already have some training, thanks to Kyria Dione and Eudora. But I look forward to improving my skill. It's this one you should be complimenting," he said, indicating his partner. "He only picked up a *deiktis* for the first time two days ago."

Osaze raised his brows. "Indeed. Kofi, you must have natural talent."

The wiry sailor looked sheepish and waved a dismissive hand. "I train wit' the spear as a boy. This not so different," he said in Greek.

Ewelike laughed and clapped Kofi on the shoulder. "And he learns languages like an undine. He's only been learning Greek since the Harvest, and listen to him. The man speaks a dozen languages already, and he can break up a fight with words alone. He's quite an asset."

Kofi gave a tight-lipped smile, obviously pleased and embarrassed.

Osaze chuckled. "Perhaps your coming here was no accident. There will be difficult times ahead. A man of your skills will be immensely useful."

Kofi gave him an earnest look. "I no believe in accidents." His brow furrowed. "Though I din't believe in the Underworld until Kyrios Hammad tol' me that's where the Lady Calandra and my *obroni* went."

Osaze's chest pinched. "They'll make it back."

Kofi brightened. "You think?"

"They must." *Because I need her to.*

The sound of bare feet running on stone made Osaze turn. A plump, pretty round-faced girl in a long blue silk peplos rushed toward them along the portico from the back of the hall.

Ewelike leaned on his staff, watching her approach. "What's got Polyxo's tail twisted now?"

Osaze hid a smile. "She's the excitable type, is she?"

Kofi gave a small chuckle and turned his face away to hide his grin.

Ewelike raised a brow and smirked. "You could say that. Kind of the opposite of that girl who came with you. Olubunmi. I hear she's already volunteered to work in the gardens. Ignatia and Jacob are thrilled. She's promised to teach them herbcraft."

"She definitely has some skill in that area." Osaze hitched his shoulders with a prayer of thanks to Oya for all that Ifeoluwa and Josefine had done for his wounds, and even greater thanks that his back had been completely restored to wholeness once he'd returned to Sirenia. No matter what his kind could do with herbs, it was still nothing compared to the healing gifts of the undines. At the thought of the young Romani girl, he frowned. What had happened to Josefine and Abela? Why had they never arrived?

"Kyrios Osaze," Polyxo said breathlessly as she rushed toward him. "Kyrios Gerrick," she called. "Rhea sent me with an . . . urgent message. You are to . . . come to the commstone tower . . . at once." She leaned on the edge of a long stone planter filled with ferns with one hand, wheezing.

"What is it?" Osaze asked. "Have they found Calandra? Is it something with the ships?"

She cast him an unreadable glance. "You should come."

Then she trotted off the way she had come, hurrying up the stone steps at the far end of the portico. Nonplussed, Osaze turned to Ewelike.

"Will you take over the class, please?"

Ewelike gave him a respectful salute. "It would be my honour." He and Kofi saluted each other crisply, and then Ewelike began moving among the men. Kofi continued working through the forms alone.

To Alexander, Osaze said, "Stay here and help supervise until Gerrick and I get back."

"Yessir." The boy walked among the sparring men, his chest puffed a little bigger with the responsibility. Noticing a man in need of help, Alexander gently took his staff and demonstrated proper technique before returning the staff and talking the man through the moves. Osaze smiled. The boy would make an excellent soldier and leader someday.

Osaze waited for Gerrick to join him and then moved along the portico toward the tower as fast as Gerrick could walk—which was at a considerable speed. The old man must be as alarmed as Osaze at the cryptic message.

"What do you think it's about?" Osaze asked when they reached the landing outside the polished wooden door.

Gerrick just shook his head and pushed open the door to the light-flooded octagonal room beyond. Large open windows faced five directions, the back three walls buried in the stone cliff from which Margaret House was carved. The smallish eight-sided wooden table in the centre of the room was carved with intricate images of sea life around a triquetra, its age showing in the spots that had been worn smooth where people had often sat. But of the dozen or so people in the room—almost the entire council, plus a few others like Polyxo, Judith, and Meg—only one person was sitting, an undine girl Osaze didn't recognize who must have been on comm duty. The rest stood in anxious postures, listening to the thin sound of a woman's voice coming through the topaz communication stone in the small console in the centre of the table.

"The local siren pod and the bondmistresses have managed to Redeem many of the Freemen already," said the woman, "but not before significant chaos ensued and several lives were lost, both human and undine. About half the men from the mines remain unaccounted for."

Rhea looked pained, fatigue evident in her posture, her chestnut curls in disarray around her shoulders. She may well have been woken up for this call. "Did you give any of the men another choice? Ask them if they would like to join us here?"

"I'm in a very difficult position here, Rhea," came the other woman's voice. "The guard is watching everything I do, and the bondmistresses keep our town under more scrutiny than any other, as you know. Perhaps I should be grateful—the extra forces her highness stationed here are probably why the confusion was handled so quickly, but there are more arriving this evening, I've been told. So no, other than those from my own household who have already joined you, offering them their freedom has not been an option."

Osaze slipped in behind Judith. "Who is it?" he whispered in her ear.

Judith startled and glanced at him, then whispered over her shoulder in a tight voice. "Archon Iris kor'Lucilla of Fire Lake. Apparently, all the unmarried men in the town were Freed at once this morning. Not just there either. We've been receiving similar reports from all over the island, especially Trinity, Pearl Bay, Serenity, and Haven."

Osaze's heart skipped as he realized the connection between those locations. "But Calandra held those bonds."

Judith looked at him with a pained expression and took a deep, shuddering breath. "I know."

The words felt like a punch in the gut. There was only one way that every bond Calandra held could be terminated at once—she'd died. She had died in the Underworld, where he wouldn't even be able to access her body for proper burial rites. He wanted to flee, to let the grief explode out of him, but he couldn't. He stood in shocked, tense silence, forcing his knees to hold him upright, while Rhea and Iris discussed sending out reconnaissance teams to look for the men who'd run into the jungle and to bring them back to the safe house. He glanced at Gerrick and saw water pooling in the old man's blue eyes. Gerrick gave him a subtle nod of understanding. If anyone knew how Osaze was feeling right then, it was the man who'd already lost his wife of forty-five years to this cause and had just found out he'd lost his foster daughter too.

The discussion continued, but Osaze couldn't follow it. He wove through the press of standing bodies and slipped through the door that led outside the tower. Making his way through the masking greenery, he took the path to the left, which led to the flat rocks along the edge of the Weeping River, instead of to the right to where the gardens were concealed in large clearings a short distance upstream.

Flat black rocks jutted over the pool below, forming a natural plateau. He stood on the edge, the mist from the falls billowing around him, dampening his clothes. From here, he could see far down the valley between the treed black ridges of the volcanic plain known as the Shield of Atargatis. The ocean was a blueish-white haze far away on the horizon. The perpetual breeze of this vantage cooled his skin and sucked moisture from his cheeks left there by the spray mingling with his tears. The people in the tower would be able to see him standing here, but he didn't care. They wouldn't be able to hear him over the roar of the falls, and that's what mattered.

He let out a cry of rage and grief, beating his thighs with his fists. Panting, he stood and stared at the ocean. Above him, a playful breeze pushed puffy white clouds across the sky in silent mockery of his pain.

"I forgive you, Calandra," he shouted. "I forgive you. You were supposed to come back so I could tell you. I forgive you, you hear?"

But his words were torn away by the changeable wind as if he'd never spoken.

*

JUDITH watched Osaze leave, biting her lip, then turned her attention back to the vibrating commstone. Anger and sorrow tightened her belly in equal measure. She'd never given up hope that Calandra would find her way back from the Abyss, but now she was gone. Truly gone. The princess had been their best chance of correcting what was wrong on this island—but not their only hope. Judith was determined her friend's death would not be in vain.

Once the call ended, Rhea put her hand on Bryce's shoulder, who'd been watching the commstone when the message came in. Judith hadn't yet found a good moment to truth-test Bryce. But now she knew Zoe had been the mole, did she even need to keep testing?

"Has there been any word yet from Despoina Cleo?" Rhea asked.

With the eyewitness account Hebe had given of not only the scullery maid's death, but also her mother's and Thea's, the *despoina* had said she had enough grounds to arrest Narcissa, or the creature using her body. Last night, Cleo told Rhea she'd send word as soon as it had been done—but this latest development had likely delayed the plan.

Bryce blew a wispy curl out of her eyes. "No, *kyria*. But before you arrived, Kyria kor'Dione called. She said Matthew brought her a message that the princess is emptying the city of the royal guard in order to handle the threat. *Tapeinoi* are nearly all that remain."

So the princess hadn't been arrested yet. Judith's heart skipped—that meant Matthew was still in danger. She hoped he'd had the good sense to stay at Eudora's after delivering the message. Knowing him, though, he hadn't. Her chest tightened.

Ignatia's brow furrowed and she looked at her sister. "Do you think Semyaza knows how many siren pods are already out to sea deflecting the ships?"

"Let's hope not." Rhea sighed. "Though this situation makes it all the more urgent we raise the barrier. At least we now have the means. Thank the Mother that Meg also found that schematic of Atlantis, but even if Nick and Nelly are able to drain it successfully, I believe we should still view evacuation underwater as a last resort." She turned to Bryce. "Thank you, Kore kor'Dreama. Scan for other reports and keep us informed."

"Yes, *kyria*."

Again, Judith sensed that hint of *something* she couldn't explain in the girl's emotions, but Bryce diligently set about fiddling with the commstone to look for more messages on other frequencies.

Rhea scanned the crowd, her gaze alighting on Polyxo. "Kore kor'Theano, please stay with Kore kor'Dreama to serve as messenger if anything else of urgency should come in."

Polyxo's face—still red from the exertion of delivering her last message—tightened, probably at being asked to serve her own lady-in-waiting, but she nodded. She'd quickly learned how much patience the leadership had for those not willing to pull their own weight. At least her truth test had been clear. "Yes, *kyria*."

To everyone else, Rhea said, "Council members, please adjourn to the meeting room. We must discuss our next steps. I'm not sure it's wise to announce the immediate danger to the island from the ships and Damon when we are so close to resolving both problems. It will only add to the confusion, and our people have enough to deal with."

"That's one opinion," muttered Amaryllis, whirling to march out the door.

The commstone whistled, and everyone halted, turning expectantly to listen. Bryce placed a finger on the stone and activated it with a trill. The voice that emanated from the stone sent a shiver up Judith's spine—the creature speaking through Narcissa.

"Citizens of Sirenia, it is with grave sadness that I come before you a second time today to announce a further blow to our fair island. Cleo kor'Andromachi, longtime Mistress of Sirens, has betrayed the throne. Her current whereabouts are unknown. A reward is being offered for any information that could lead to her being brought to justice. If anyone is found harbouring the traitor, she will be treated as a traitor herself, and punished to the full extent of the law."

Judith's stomach flipped, and she exchanged anxious glances with the others in the room.

"During these difficult times," Narcissa's voice continued, "we need to unite once more under the ways that have brought us this far in safety and harmony. We will not let the rebels who have plunged our island into turmoil have the final say. Calandra's death was a warning from the Mother against the blasphemies she espoused. We must repent and return to the ways of the Merciful Queen of Heaven, who, in her wisdom, hath decreed that men should be subdued beneath a woman's guiding hand. Together, loyal, upstanding citizens shall emerge strong and victorious over every adversary. We are a powerful people, and nothing and no one can stand in the way of our victory. Not even the dissenters in our own ranks. As the Opal Princess, I will overcome those who threaten our health and livelihood by any means necessary. Rest assured, your safety is my highest priority. May the Mother smile on you, my people."

With another whistle, the transmission ended. The stunned silence was suddenly broken by everyone talking at once.

Judith looked at her mother and saw her own worry reflected in Ignatia's kind green eyes.

"This changes things. Quickly," said Rhea over the din, her voice tight. "Let us assemble in the meeting room."

The assembled archons began filing out of the tower, low murmurs punctuating the sound of rustling clothes and feet on stone, both bare and slippered.

Judith pinched the bridge of her nose. First Calandra, now Cleo. Looking up, she noticed Gerrick standing next to her. He held his head high as though afraid if he relaxed, he might break.

She placed a gentle hand on Gerrick's arm. "I'm so sorry, Gerrick. This is a difficult blow."

He nodded stiffly. "Thank you, child." He glanced away and quickly followed Stella kor'Panorea out the door.

She watched him go, thinking of all the man had sacrificed already. That made her think of Matthew, and a lump of ice formed in her chest. If Semyaza had discovered Cleo, had he also found out Matthew had been Released? But no—it had been Matthew that brought the message to Eudora about the guard. She prayed all the more he was still safe at Steadfast House and wished there were a safe way to contact him.

Rhea approached, shuffling forward near the end of the line.

Judith stepped into place behind her. "Aunt Rhea, we must not waste this opportunity."

Rhea frowned. "Yes, I was already thinking that. If we move the stone healers' mission up to tonight, the moon won't be full, but it should be close enough. Despite the grievous circumstances, I suppose we should be thankful for the fortuitous timing that forced Semyaza to lower security at the palace, even if the cause is a heavy blow." She sounded exhausted and somewhat detached, as though she'd separated herself from the emotions surrounding the events of the last several days.

Judith's throat closed at hearing Calandra's death discussed so clinically. She swallowed. "Yes, but that's not what I mean. If most of the sirens have been sent out of the city, this is the perfect time to free the *tapeinoi* and bring them back with us."

"I'm not certain this is the time to add to the chaos." Rhea started down the steps. "Your encounter with Cain and the decisions of the Freed men who went with him prove that just because we Free them doesn't mean they'll do the wise thing. We have enough new Freemen to track down and handle as it is."

"But—"

Judith broke off as her mother, walking ahead of Rhea, turned and reached around her sister to lay a hand on Judith's, her face full of compassion.

"We'll get Matthew back. You know we will."

Rhea looked at Judith with soft eyes. "Like Ignatia says, we'll Free them. But I think it needs to wait. Our first priority is raising the barrier. Then we can worry about the *douloi*. I only hope Semyaza hasn't yet figured out the plans Cleo put in place."

Judith blinked away the pricking in her sinuses and gave a resigned nod. Rhea had been less than happy that she'd made a promise to Cain and the other Freemen without the council discussing it, but she'd agreed it was the right thing to do, as Judith had hoped she would. But just because Judith also saw the wisdom in her aunt's and mother's words didn't mean she yearned for Matthew's immediate rescue any less.

"Excuse me," she choked out, "I just remembered . . . I must still truth-test Bryce. I should do it while it is on my mind."

She turned and fled back up the stairs, barely registering Rhea's and Ignatia's pitying, worried expressions.

When she reached the top of the steps, she leaned against the commstone room door, breathing and getting a handle on her emotions. After wiping away the betraying tears, she turned and opened the door.

Bryce glanced up from the comm with an expression of fear and guilt on her face. Polyxo was nowhere to be seen.

"Please repeat?" came a tinny female voice from the stone.

Bryce looked at Judith, her mouth open and soundless. Unhindered guilt seeped from her like cloying perfume.

"What is happening?" Judith asked.

"Agent Stargazer, please repeat," came the voice again. "I heard, 'The *despoina* has dispatched siren pods to deflect,' but nothing after that. Do you mean the attacking ships? Or are they going to drain Atlantis?"

Judith's stomach sank to her knees. "You *are* a mole," she whispered in stunned disbelief. "Who are you talking to?" When Bryce tensed and said nothing, Judith shouted at the stone, "Who are you?"

The line went dead, and Bryce leapt backward, knocking over her chair. She fled out the door, narrowly missing Polyxo, who jumped aside in astonishment.

Polyxo turned to Judith in surprise. "Well, I go to answer nature's call and miss even more excitement. What's got into her gills? Hey!"

By the time Judith pushed past Polyxo and down the path, Bryce's tail fins were disappearing over the Weeping Falls. Judith ran back through the tower and halted at the sight of Polyxo standing over the commstone, which had a new voice emanating from it.

She looked up guiltily. "I only wanted to try it."

"Hush," Judith said.

The transmission wasn't meant for them, obviously—Polyxo must have hidden skills working with the stones to have intercepted that frequency. The voice vibrating through the commstone sounded like a siren rhapsodist reporting to the palace guard about the chaos that had been unleashed in Dolphin Cove half an hour before.

Polyxo looked up at Judith, her brow furrowed. "Does that mean all the *douloi* on the east side have been Freed too?"

"Can you watch the comm, please?" Judith said, then tore after her aunt and mother without waiting for an answer. She caught up to them just as they were about to enter the meeting room. Ewelike and Gerrick were only a few steps behind.

"We have been . . . betrayed," Judith said between gasps. "By Bryce. Semyaza knows everything. And . . . Narcissa is dead too."

85

THE SORCERESS

THE DARK WATERS OF THE Pool of Tears enveloped Calandra to her shoulders, and she revelled in the pain-free experience. Nearby, her mother, brother, Damaris, and Airlea splashed into the water, transformed to *ichthys* state, and submerged. The *ichthys* ring hugged Calandra's finger. They no longer needed it to free Delphine, but Rumiel had given it to her in case it would be useful when healing the Soulstone or to get through the energy barrier at the top of the well.

One of Shriniel's guards was watching Zoe, mindover at the ready in case she should wake up and cause more trouble. The rest of them had taken up position around the Pool of Tears. Now that the seal to the keep above had been broken, Shriniel had received orders from General Uriel to guard the Chamber of Tears until Calandra and Zale's mission was complete. The troops stood in regimented groups along the edge of the pool, which was much bigger than Calandra had even suspected, a lightrod borne by each flight's light carrier marking its location. Besides the bright posts of light, which reminded Calandra of smaller versions of the light posts in the room in Atlantis, each soldier had a lightstone shining from their helm. The effect was like filling the cavern with candlelight. It was truly stunning to behold.

The plan was to first heal Nadia and the other Madwomen. Calandra hoped at least some of them would be strong and coherent enough to join a circle and help heal the Soulstone while Airlea occupied the Leviathan. Even if they weren't, healing them first meant Calandra and the others wouldn't have to constantly guard their backs against attack while working with the Soulstone.

Calandra had learned her lesson with her and Zale's failed attempt at the Heartstone—yes, they might be the two most powerful undine healers alive, but that didn't mean they couldn't use help. Had there been a circle joined with them to heal the Heartstone, controlling and buffering Zale's power wouldn't have fallen on Calandra's shoulders alone. Besides, the Heartstone had benefitted from the annual healing ceremony, even if all that had been accomplished was slowing the decay. The Soulstone hadn't been repaired at all for possibly millennia, and the damage was likely far worse. Calandra wanted all the help they could get. She'd been pleased and humbled when the others had accepted her suggestions without question, honing the plan with a few comments of their own, and then following her lead. She hoped she'd thought of everything. But what if she hadn't? What if this turned out to be one more disaster to add to her ever-growing list?

Remembering what her mother had said earlier, Calandra sent a shy prayer to Elyon for wisdom and success, then submerged her head underwater.

It wasn't quite as dark in the pool this time—the crystals in the cave above refracted light from the lightrods and lightstones borne by the erelim, magnifying its radiance, and the light filtered through the water in a purple haze. The undines' own lightstones, which Calandra had shown the others how to activate, created small globes of light that marked their locations as they descended. The vacuous hollow sensation of this place still pulled at her, but the Spirit within vitalized her, combating the fatigue with a supernatural energy. She swam purposefully downward with the others, keeping an eye out for Nadia and her pod. Her heartbeat raced in her ears, the sound made louder by the water pressing around her.

They had just reached the tops of the black spires of rock that grew from the bottom of the pool when they were met by the unsettling luminescent green eyes of the dozen or more undine women who'd spread out to block their passage. At their head was Nadia, the black ropes of her hair floating around her head like a cloud, light glinting from the silver crescent moon and star on her forehead. She raised her hands defensively and so did the others, their message clear—*you shall not pass.*

But this time, the intruders had no intention of passing.

As they'd discussed, Calandra rushed toward Nadia while Delphine, Airlea, and Damaris engaged with the other undines, distracting them so Zale could create the bubble chamber that would entrap Nadia, allowing Calandra the time to heal the sorceress without having to defend herself from other Mad undines. Airlea had suggested it, remembering how Zale had entrapped her when he and Damaris had fled through the Voidstone. Zale had been embarrassed at first, apologizing for how he'd behaved, but when asked if he could do it again, he'd said yes.

Zale held his hands slightly apart, one above the other, palms facing each other, and a small bubble of air formed between them. He increased the distance between his palms as it grew and grew. Just as Calandra managed to close her hand around the surprised Nadia's wrist, Zale pushed the enormous air bubble toward them, and the bubble enveloped them.

The force of Calandra's collision with Nadia threw them against the skin of water that made up the far wall of the flexible chamber, and they slid to the valley of the floor, writhing and twisting, tails flapping. Nadia looked around in surprise, her face twisted in rage. Then she shrieked and turned back toward Calandra, claw-like fingernails scraping across Calandra's face. Calandra struggled to touch Nadia's forehead with her palm in order to put the ancient queen to sleep so she could complete the healing, but the woman twisted the arm Calandra held and yanked Calandra backward. Calandra gasped—or tried. The air around her head solidified, and she couldn't draw a single breath. Panic rose in her chest. There was no water for her gills and no air for her lungs. It felt like her face and neck were encased in cement.

She changed to *podia* state and scrambled away from the crazed-looking woman, but the air remained clamped onto her face. She clawed at it, trying to grab it with her mind and force it away, but the force that held it there was as strong as her own. With her thoughts starting to fuzz, she shaped some of the air in the bubble into a pointed tip and jabbed it into the woman's tail—not hard enough to break skin, but enough to break Nadia's concentration. The vice around Calandra's face broke and she gasped in ragged breaths.

The woman laughed. "How dare you attack the Guardians of the Abyss, you insolent guppy?" Nadia shrieked in a voice hoarse from long disuse. She tried to dig her claws into the bubble to pull herself nearer to Calandra. Her hair clung to her back and shoulders in a thick mat, and her patchy tail looked even duller in the dimly lit globe of air than it had in the water.

Calandra tried to press herself against the far wall, but slipped downward toward the centre of the concave floor, narrowly missing the wild woman's grasp. This was the woman Calandra had been compared to her whole life—the woman whose powers hers were supposed to match. But she would never have thought to prevent Nadia from breathing. She began to realize how dangerous the woman before her was—great power combined with three thousand years of Madness. If Nadia had no qualms about simply killing her, how was Calandra going to get close enough to knock her out?

Then again, if Nadia had truly wanted to kill her, why wouldn't she simply pull all the water from Calandra's veins and be done with it? For someone with their power, it was far easier to snuff out life than to preserve it, which was why every girl on Sirenia with any talent at all was required to achieve a certain proficiency with her gifts as a novice at the Royal Academy before determining what pathway her life would take. Maybe there was a mote of empathy left in the woman, after all. Perhaps even some sanity. Calandra clung to the wall, using water to anchor her partway up the side, though she still slipped slowly like a raindrop on a glass window and kept having to scramble farther away again. She was surprised Nadia hadn't changed to *podia* state, the better to pursue her—but perhaps the guardian had forgotten how.

"Nadia, my name is Calandra kor'Delphine. I'm here to help you."

At her name, the sorceress froze and glared at Calandra, fingers still stretched like claws, ready to use the elements against her. Calandra tried to project calm, but it was impossible. Her stomach was so tight, she thought she might vomit.

"How do you know who I am?" Nadia hissed.

"You are my ancestor, many, many generations removed. I'm here to heal your Madness."

At least, she hoped she was. She still didn't know exactly how she would go about that, but her mother had said to trust her intuition and to trust in Elyon. If he could heal Calandra, then why would he not heal the others as well?

The woman stared at her incredulously and then laughed, grey, flaky patches falling from her cheeks. "You? Intend to heal *me*? I am not Mad, little one. I serve the Mother, and she knows of your intention to heal the Soulstone. My sisters and I will not let that happen."

She raised her hand toward Calandra's throat, and, though she still sat on the floor, it was as though a vise had clamped around Calandra's esophagus. Calandra's hands went to the invisible force, but there was no lump of air to claw at—it was just like what Adonia had done to Elizabeth at Fire Lake, closing Calandra's windpipe from the inside, the tissues constricting under the force.

At the lack of oxygen entering her lungs, her body reflexively changed to *ichthys* state, but there was no water from which to draw oxygen through her scales or gills either. She slid down the side of the bubble toward the sorceress, trying to breathe, to focus her mind and retaliate as she'd done before, but all she could do was flail.

The bubble broke and the grip on Calandra's throat disappeared. She refilled her body with oxygen from the life-giving water that surrounded her, looking around to see Airlea floating unconscious and Damaris defending Zale against three attacking women. Zale was sending out small bursts of electricity to get the women to back off, which had probably distracted him from maintaining the bubble.

Calandra whirled to locate Nadia in time to see her knock Delphine out with the very palm-to-forehead technique Calandra had intended to use, then start dragging her mother away. Calandra snapped her tail around to pursue and was blocked by four other women charging at her. She sent blunt missiles of solidified water at them to slow them down, but by the time she broke through their line, she could no longer see Nadia or Delphine. Neither could she sense any undines besides their attackers—her mother's shieldstone would also shield Nadia for as long as they touched.

The other undines accelerated their efforts, attacking with such force it was all Calandra and her companions could do to hold them off. When one of the Madwomen's diving knives bit deeply into her lower tail, Calandra hummed to get the others' attention, then signed retreat. Wrapping her arm around Airlea's body from behind, she made for the surface, thankful the Madwomen simply watched them go.

They clambered on the shore one shorter in number instead of a dozen stronger. The despair piercing Calandra's heart was more painful than the knife wound in her shin. Rumiel scanned the group and caught her eye, his face etched with sadness and understanding.

Calandra dropped her gaze in shame. She had failed again. Instead of healing Nadia, they'd lost Delphine, and with her, a significant amount of their advantage over the remaining undines. She wondered if she would ever see her mother alive again. Grief threatened to engulf her, and she closed her eyes, willing it away. She *would* get her mother back. She hadn't come this far to fail her now.

Shriniel brought a mindover and revived Airlea. Rumiel helped Calandra limp to a flat spot and lower herself to the ground, while Chaz looked on, frowning, his arms crossed over his broad chest. Zale squatted next to Calandra and laid an unusually warm hand on her bleeding shin, covering the wound. The warmth was comforting.

"They took Mother," Calandra said. Her cells buzzed with their synergistic vibration, but it was the grief and compassion pouring through his touch that comforted her.

"I know," he said, keeping his concentration on his hand. "We'll go get her."

She could feel the tissues mending beneath his touch. She was impressed—how had he learned to do that? Surely Damon hadn't taught him how to heal too?

"I'm sorry I failed," she said, her voice breaking. "Nadia was too strong for me."

He looked at her then, his green eyes cloudy under drawn-together brows. "Maybe she was, but that doesn't mean we can't win. Damaris told me you're the strongest, most resourceful person she knows. I was too stupid to see it before, listening to the wrong person's version of the truth. I won't let you do the same thing. The truth is, you were born to do this. Maybe I was too. And we're not alone in the fight—we have Elyon on our side, remember?"

She stifled a sudden sob, then nodded.

He gave a lopsided grin. "Besides, it's only failure if you give up. You're not giving up, are you?"

She shook her head. "Absolutely not."

He gave a satisfied nod, then looked back at his hand. When he pulled it away, no gash remained beneath the smeared blood.

Calandra swallowed, her chest as warm from his words of encouragement as her shin was from his healing touch. "Thanks."

Rumiel and Chaz stood over her. "Where did they take Delphine?"

Calandra peered up at them. "I don't know. I lost sight of her."

She tried to get her feet beneath her, but the exhaustion of healing pulled her back down. Zale scrambled to his feet, then offered her a hand to help her stand, which she accepted.

"Nadia said something strange to me," she continued, straightening her skirt. "She said the Mother knows we're trying to heal the Soulstone, and she and her sisters wouldn't let that happen. If Atargatis is actually Tamiel, and Nadia has been here as long as there's been a need for guardians, how can Nadia believe she serves the Mother when Tamiel has been imprisoned the whole time?"

"Because," said an unfamiliar voice nearby, "she has wisely chosen me over the tyrant."

Calandra's head jerked up to see a strange woman appearing to stand on the surface of the water a short distance away. She was exquisitely beautiful, with dark brown skin, fine cheekbones, and slanted golden eyes. Her long, tightly curled hair surrounded her head like a black halo, and a belted long-sleeved striped bright blue-and-silver robe floated around her in some invisible breeze. The lightrods and lightstones of the surrounding guardians limned her in white light. But though Calandra could see her, she could sense nothing there—it was another projection. The woman smiled widely at Calandra.

"Hello, Calandra. How do you like my own face?"

Calandra took a step forward, standing at the water's edge with clenched fists.

"Tamiel," she spat with all the venom her frustrated, frightened soul could muster.

86

THE BARGAIN

Z‌ALE STOOD AND FACED THE apparition floating above the dark water, his hands clenched into sweaty fists. So this was Tamiel, the woman responsible for capturing Mother and bringing her here. And here she was, looking smug as a June bug, with Mother once more in her clutches—after all Zale had done to free her. Thunder rumbled in his belly, and he drew steady breaths. If he unleashed his anger here, he'd only hurt his friends, not the projection before him. He wished he could inflict just a tiny bit of the misery on her that she and Semyaza had put him through, but he didn't see a way to do it. Maybe if he wore Rumiel's ring . . . but no. The figure before him was an illusion. What good could the ring do here?

Damaris put a hand on his arm. Caution flowed into him, as well as a sense of calm that helped to subdue the storm. Her brief smile was the final bit of fortification he needed. He gave her a stiff nod of gratitude. She dropped her hand and stood beside him, facing the newcomer. He'd never wanted Damaris to follow him through the Voidstone, but she kept giving him reasons to be glad she did. Though if he could have spared her the pain she'd gone through by coming, he would have.

Rumiel stepped forward, stopping at the water's edge next to Calandra. "Tamiel, what have you done with Delphine?"

"Nothing. Yet." Tamiel smiled as though she were a benevolent queen mercifully withholding punishment for a crime.

Zale's stomach twisted.

Calandra planted her feet and called to the floating woman. "What do you want?"

"You know what I want, my dear," Tamiel said. "Freedom for me and for my kind, so we can live our lives in peace."

"Peace?" Calandra scoffed. "Don't you and Semyaza want to subdue the entire earth beneath your rule?"

Tamiel shrugged dismissively. "That *would* bring peace, would it not? When all serve a single master, there are no more wars left to fight. I know of the wars that rage on the so-called perfect earth Elyon created. I know of the misery that abounds there. My kind *will* bring peace—when we subdue the races of the earth, no one will prey on his brother . . . or sister. All will serve us in harmony."

"I've experienced your version of service," Calandra said with a glance at Zale. "It's more like slavery, hardly better than a *sklavia* bond."

Zale remembered how helpless and dopey he'd felt every time the golden mist clouded his thoughts. It hadn't been nearly as hampering as a *sklavia* bond, but he'd been almost as subjugated to Semyaza's will. It was a wonder he'd broken free to come to the Underworld at all.

Except . . . according to Rumiel, that's what Semyaza had wanted. For him to come here, not to free his mother, but to free Tamiel and the other Grigori from their prison. Of course! How could he have been so stupid? He'd thought he was defying Narcissa by finding his own way here. Instead, he was falling right into Semyaza's scheme. His breath caught. What else had he done that had simply been one more step along the path the dragon had baited him to follow?

"You're looking at the bonds all wrong," said Tamiel. "Free will is the true burden. What we offer is far better. Just imagine a world without war, without strife, unified by a common will. We nearly accomplished it on Sirenia once—why do you think your society has been so peaceful for so long? We removed at least half of the reasons for strife when we taught you the *sklavia* bonds. This time, we will succeed. And this time, the whole world will benefit, not just the male undines."

This time? It sounded like Tamiel was claiming credit for the wacky undine practice of mind-enslavement of their men. And, if he understood correctly, she and Semyaza and the rest of the Grigori intended to do that to everyone, everywhere. His blood chilled.

"You nearly caused our extinction," Calandra said, clenching her fists.

"You survived, did you not?" Tamiel gave a languid smile.

Zale had to get Mother away from her. He had to get Damaris out of here. He had to get away from this Madwoman trying to call the shots.

He stepped forward, arms stiff at his sides. "Give us our mother back."

Tamiel turned in curiosity, and when she saw him, her smile became cat-like once more. Or dragon-like.

"If you want your mother back," Tamiel said, "you must destroy the Soulstone, as I've been telling you all along. It is weak and fragile—but not fragile enough for my loyal guardians of the deep to destroy. The bonds that created it used all five elements, and all five elements must be used to unmake them. Sadly, my undine guardians have not a spark of fire among them." She met Zale's eyes, her gaze boring into his soul. "That's where you come in, my dear."

Her guardians? She must have ensnared the women in the pool, just like Semyaza ensnared me. But if she thinks I'll destroy the Soulstone like I destroyed the Heartstone . . .

Zale spoke to Calandra out of the side of his mouth in a low voice. "Mother would never want us to trade her life for the freedom of monsters like Tamiel. She'd die first."

Calandra glanced at him over her shoulder. "I know. If I'm anything like her, I know. But I can't lose her. Not so soon after finding her again."

Zale frowned. "I don't want to lose her either. There must be another way."

"What way?" Calandra hissed.

"Tell her what she wants to hear?"

His sister shook her head emphatically. "No. I'll not have you bond yourself with lies."

"Me, either," Damaris added, and he realized he could sense the determination and fear behind her staunch declaration even though they weren't touching. She looked at him steadily, stirring something deep inside him. "Don't do anything foolish, Zale. Please."

Calandra and Damaris were right—lying to the spirit in order to get their mother back would still create soul ties, and he knew his mother wouldn't condone such a sacrifice any more than his sister and friend would. But what kind of distraction could deflect Tamiel's attention so they could free Mother while she was otherwise occupied? She could project as easily into the water as above it, he'd wager, just to keep an eye on them. The winged guardians around the pool would be useless beneath the water. And should Zale and Calandra try to tackle the Soulstone before healing the Mad panaceas, Damaris and Airlea were no match for them on their own. He also had no doubt that the lives of his mother and the undine guardians meant little to the spirit before them—she was only using them, just as Semyaza had used him.

His chest tightened. Tamiel had no weaknesses that he knew of and many advantages. He didn't even think Gio would be able to trick his way out of this one.

"Well?" Tamiel prompted. "Will you do as I ask? Your mother's life is on the line."

Rumiel ruffled his black feathered wings. "There's no way you can win, Tamiel. You cannot defeat the very Essence of the universe. Release Delphine, or—"

"Or what, you great bullfinch? You'll dive in and make me?"

Tamiel arched her brow in challenge. Rumiel's jaw worked. He crossed his arms and lifted his chin defiantly, but said nothing else.

Tamiel smiled victoriously. "I thought not."

"I will, though." Zale stepped forward, squaring his shoulders. Bluffing was all he had left. "Release Mother, and Release the other undine women, too, or you'll regret it."

Tamiel crossed her arms, her gaze travelling over Zale from head to toe. "Bold words, boy. But what can you do to me that hasn't already been done? The only way would be to enter the Soulstone and repair it, closing off the slim access I've found to the outside world. But my guardians have *chosen* to follow me—their bonds are of their own making. If you attack me or do anything that would hinder my access to them, my guardians of the deep will terminate your mother's life—and then she shall never leave the Underworld. Is that what you want?"

Zale's heart beat like galloping hooves against his ribs, and he clenched his jaw. He couldn't see any way out of this that didn't require sacrifice of some kind.

"What if we freed only you?" Calandra's voice trembled slightly, and she cleared her throat. "We brought Solomon's Key, like Valac told us to. We could open your cell. Would you release our mother and the other undines then?"

Zale glanced at her, startled, and Rumiel and Chaz frowned at her, but she stepped forward into the water, ignoring their looks of consternation.

Tamiel looked thoughtful. "Hmm, intriguing. Yes, I could see the merits of that. But if you'll only free me, I'll free only your mother, and only if you do not heal the Soulstone once you've released me. A life for a life."

Calandra nodded. "Okay."

She sounded confident, but Zale could see the trepidation in the set of her shoulders.

Tamiel smiled. "Oh, and one more thing." She leaned forward, looking down at Calandra as though she were a child. "Once your mother has been freed, you must take her place and serve me, and your companions and mother must leave the Underworld and not return until their appointed time to cross the veil. Agreed?"

Zale's throat closed. Surely Calandra wouldn't agree to that?

Calandra's posture remained firm, but she furrowed her brows. "You must bring Mother to the well so we can see she is alive before we begin."

Tamiel nodded nonchalantly. "Done. Anything else?"

Calandra hesitated. Zale opened his mouth to speak to her, but Shriniel, who'd been standing a little behind Calandra on her other side, cleared her throat.

"Your highness, a word?"

Calandra broke her staring match with Tamiel and glanced at the tall guardian. "Yes?"

"Privately?"

Calandra studied Shriniel, then looked up at the floating apparition above the water. "One moment, Tamiel."

The woman smiled lazily, crossing her arms. "Take your time. I've got nothing to do but wait."

Calandra gestured to Zale, and he, Shriniel, Damaris, Airlea, and Rumiel retreated toward the entrance of the tunnel nearest them, pausing a short distance away from it. Chaz stayed near the water, watching the floating spirit with his beefy arms across his chest. When Damaris glanced at Zoe's prostrate form in the tunnel entrance beyond and the winged guardian sitting next to her, a frown of pain crossed her face.

"What is it?" Calandra asked Shriniel.

The woman spoke in a low, urgent tone. "I must advise against accepting this deal with Tamiel, your highness. Unlike you, she will have no qualms breaking her word."

"I agree," Zale said. "What good does it do to free Mother if you are sacrificing yourself instead?"

Calandra shook her head, glancing at him in compassion. "Duty requires sacrifice. Mother knows much more than I do, and she is almost as powerful. She is liked and respected by many on Sirenia, especially the Free Will Society council, and she has not created as many enemies or caused as much destruction. She has a much better chance of restoring order to the island than I do. Trust me, it is better this way."

Zale shifted uncomfortably. How different would his life have been had he always embraced duty so self-sacrificially as his sister did now?

"You're wrong," he said.

"Pardon me?" She blinked at him in surprise.

"The student rebels weren't inspired by Mother, they were inspired by you. You're the one who stood up to Adonia at the Court of the Redeemed. How many others on Sirenia are finally questioning the things they've been raised to believe because of you?"

"Zale's right, Calandra," Airlea said, her eyes round and earnest. "*You* are the rightful queen of Sirenia. We need you."

"Because my Mad aunt named me heir?" Calandra said gently. "Just because I was the best of the options available doesn't mean I'm the best option. My mother is older, wiser, and much more capable than I am. It was because of her belief and sacrifice that Zale even exists. She should be the queen, not me." Her voice broke, and she paused. "I am not the leader everyone wants me to be."

Rumiel met her gaze. "But you are the leader Elyon appointed for such a time as this. And he doesn't make mistakes."

Shriniel continued in an urgent tone. "You should also consider that Tamiel is an expert at finding loopholes in any contract. She has always been exceptionally sly, even before the Rebellion. You could follow through on your promise to free her and find that Tamiel has twisted your words to suit her purpose, imprisoning both you and Delphine and leaving your people with no true leader at all. She's slippery as a fish."

Zale glanced at Shriniel in surprise. This youthful-looking woman had fought in that long-ago Rebellion? But he supposed that many of the troops around them had. He often had difficulty comprehending how very long these spirits lived. Even Abela was much older than she looked—he'd always thought she was only a year or two older than him, but once he found out what she was, he knew she had to be older than that. Was she as old as Shriniel? Had she fought in the Rebellion too? He shrivelled a little inside. To think he'd wondered if she might be interested in him romantically. How stupid could he have been? At least he knew Damaris was his age. He might stand a chance with her.

He glanced at Damaris and flushed. There was no way she thought of him like that. Lamia's behaviour while she'd impersonated Damaris had nothing to do with reality. He should be thankful for her friendship and expect nothing more. But still, seeing Damaris's anxious, breath-taking eyes turned on him, he couldn't help but wonder. And hope.

"Tamiel likely believes she has a way to free her companions once she is free," said Rumiel. "Or that she will find one."

"What way?" Calandra asked. "The Soulstone is only the prison gate, correct? If we unlock the soul keeper cell that holds Tamiel, and even if we leave the Soulstone unlocked somehow, she will still be trapped by the Pool of Tears. We can retrieve Mother and leave Tamiel there, and very little will have changed from the current state of affairs." *Except one of Tamiel's guardians will be sane and keeping an eye on her.* She swallowed. She had thought she'd already accepted her fate, but now that she was no longer plagued by the bonds, remaining behind in the Pool of Tears was no longer inevitable. Unless she agreed to this deal.

"There's something you should know about Tamiel—" Rumiel began at the same time Shriniel said, "Is that what you were sent to do? Free Delphine?"

Calandra met Shriniel's gaze, then Zale's. His sister hadn't been sent here to do anything—she'd been following him. And he'd come here to free his mother, nothing more. But as soon as Calandra had told him about the mission they'd been given by Elyon, he'd known deep in his bones that healing the Soulstone was what they were meant to do. Maybe it wasn't Semyaza who had brought him here at all, but Elyon himself. But if that were the case, couldn't they find a way to save their mother *and* heal the Soulstone? Why did it have to be a choice?

"Maybe we should pray about it," he heard himself say, then slammed his mouth shut.

Calandra blinked at him in surprise, then nodded slowly. "Yes, that's an excellent idea, Zale. Would you, er, do the honours?" Her cheeks grew pink. "I'm not quite sure of the proper procedure."

He nodded. "Sure. Um, let's hold hands."

The group did as he suggested, and they stood in a ring, almost like a healing circle. Zale closed his eyes to focus his thoughts and offered up a short prayer for wisdom and guidance, especially for Calandra, and for safety for their mother and those who fought to free her. When he was done, he opened his eyes to see Calandra raise her head from a similar posture.

"Thanks," she said.

"Any insight?" he asked.

She looked upward, thinking. After a few moments, she glanced around the circle of expectant faces with a surprised expression.

"You'll probably think I'm crazy, but I really feel like agreeing to Tamiel's terms is the right thing to do. I don't understand it, but Elyon must be aware of the power of word bonds and what is at stake if we fail, so I trust what I feel. The question is, do you trust me?" She looked up into each face in turn, inviting challenge.

Zale looked at his petite sister, seeing not a girl in defiance, but in humble submission to a will she didn't yet understand. He didn't see how complying with Tamiel's demands would be a good idea at all, but he also knew Calandra was not the murderer and liar he'd been led to believe for so long. Everything she'd done had been to try and help him, and now she was following Elyon's voice—a voice he was only just learning to hear himself. If he'd only listened to both his sister and Elyon all along, they might not even be in this mess. He wouldn't make the same mistake again.

"I do," he said. "I trust you."

Calandra flicked her gaze at him in surprise.

"For real this time," he said with a half-smile.

Calandra's eyes grew bright with tears. She nodded and wiped at one of them.

"I trust you too," said Damaris.

"And me," said Airlea quietly. "I'll follow you unto death, your highness. You know that."

Rumiel made a rumbling sound in his chest. "I've only known you for a short time, your highness, but I agree with the others. I trust you, and the Spirit that leads you."

Shriniel glanced around the circle, then nodded. "I trust the Creator is guiding you in the correct paths. I will honour your decision, and your agreement."

Calandra drew in a shaking breath and relaxed her shoulders. "Thank you. Now, let's get on with saving my mother, shall we?"

Zale echoed the others' agreement. Rumiel raised a hand to catch Calandra's attention, but she was already walking back to the pool. He frowned and followed her.

As they made their way back to the water's edge, Damaris whispered to Zale, "Who is this Elyon everyone keeps talking about?"

"I'll tell you later," he whispered back. "Once we're all out of this mess."

"Promise?" Her gaze met his, and she flicked a significant glance at Calandra. "We're *all* getting out of this mess?"

"Of course." He gave her his most confident grin, hoping it convinced her. "Elyon has a plan, I know it. And I have no intention of leaving Calandra here. Her, or anyone else."

Suddenly, Damaris leaned over and gave him a quick kiss on the lips. "I'm holding you to it, Wonder Boy."

He blinked at her in surprise, and she smiled, then turned her attention to Calandra's negotiation with Tamiel. His heart beat so loudly, he was sure the guardians across the lake could hear it. With difficulty, he focused on Calandra's and Tamiel's conversation in time to hear the beautiful apparition's final agreement with Calandra's terms. He hoped Calandra had truly heard the voice of Elyon, and that Elyon did have a plan. Otherwise, he'd do whatever it took to free his sister and mother—soul ties be chained.

87

THE PRINCESS

JUDITH HUDDLED NEXT TO KYNTHIA behind a broad stone pillar at the junction of the royal sleeping quarters and the main corridor bounding the Royal Wing of the Opal Palace, watching the *tapeinos* outside Princess Hebe's door. It had taken some effort to convince the council that she was fit for another mission to the palace already, especially since she had no skill with stone healing and would be no help with the Heartstone itself. But, despite the exhaustion that pulled at her bones, she was determined to find a way to get to Matthew, especially once she found out he hadn't stayed at Steadfast House as she'd hoped. For their part, the House of Dione had evacuated to Margaret House as soon as they heard the news of Narcissa's death—not that most people on the island knew the actual cause of the sudden Releasing of all her *douloi*, since it was the princess's voice that had announced the news. Semyaza had put out another bulletin blaming the sudden Release of all of Narcissa's bonds on a conspiracy by the rebels while diplomatically assuring the population not to get ideas about Calandra—she was well and truly dead.

The price for Judith's inclusion in the mission was guiding Kynthia to Hebe's quarters while the stone healers infiltrated the Mother's Heart. The two of them would sneak the princess out of the palace to the safe house—out of Semyaza's clutches. With Hebe the only remaining potential challenger for the throne, she was bound to be his next target—and she was the rebellion's only remaining hope for success. That condition suited Judith fine—Hebe's quarters were only a floor below the queen's, which Narcissa had moved into weeks ago. If she was going to find Matthew, she'd have to start looking there.

What she didn't expect to see was a blank-faced Matthew coming down the corridor from Hebe's room between a short, stocky siren rhapsodist with a long black braided ponytail and a tall, powerfully built siren singer with close-cropped curly black hair and ochre skin. The young princess walked in front of them wearing a knee-length white cotton nightgown, her red hair aflame in the light of the torches, and in front of her marched the *tapeinos* who'd been guarding her door. Hebe kept glancing nervously around at her escort and biting her lip.

Judith exchanged glances with Kynthia. They were too late.

"Now what?" Kynthia whispered.

"We attack?" Judith whispered back, and was met by Kynthia's worried frown. Kynthia was a skilled athlete, but she was no match for one trained siren, let alone two. And that was assuming Judith could Free Matthew and the *tap* before they could injure her. Perhaps if she used sirensong . . .

"Or," said a girl's voice behind them, "you could let us help you."

Her heart in her throat, Judith whirled to see an open door leading to a dark passageway full of girls of various ages. Geronimi stood at their head, a twig-like young woman only slightly taller than Judith with a belt of physic green over her short *tsiraki* tunic. Next to her stood a long-legged girl with muscular thighs in siren cadet blue who looked only a little younger.

"Geronimi," Judith said. "And the student Free Will Society, I presume?"

Geronimi nodded and gestured to the physic apprentice. "This is Talia."

A child with saffron-coloured braids and a face full of freckles leaned around Talia. "You're Calandra's friend Judith, right? There's a reward out for you."

That was news. Judith smiled. "And you must be Melany."

Melany grinned. "Yep!"

"What are you all doing here?" Kynthia whispered.

"Saving Hebe," Melany said. "Like you told us to."

Judith blinked. She'd nearly forgotten about the charge she'd given Geronimi and Charis only yesterday. It felt like a lifetime had passed since then.

Kynthia eyed the passageway. "That would have been good to know about."

"For certain," Judith said. It could definitely come in handy during their retreat—assuming they successfully retrieved their target. She glanced down the hall at the retreating backs of Matthew and the sirens.

"Quickly, did you girls have a plan?"

Geronimi's brow furrowed. "We *did*, but we only expected to encounter the *tap* outside of Hebe's door."

Talia stepped to the edge of the shadows behind the pillar, a frown of concentration on her face. "We can still do it. Especially with their help." She gestured at Judith and Kynthia with her thumb.

Geronimi gave a slow nod. "I think you're right."

Judith's heart raced, watching their window of opportunity slip away as Hebe's entourage approached the far end of the hall. "What do we need to do?"

Talia smiled mischievously. "Be bait."

*

MOMENTS later, Kynthia stepped into the corridor, planting her feet wide and placing her hands on her hips. With her braided hair, damp green swimming skirt, and bare feet, she looked like some kind of displaced water sprite. Judith stood next to her with her hands clasped tightly in front of her, praying with all her might that this would work.

"Halt!" Kynthia called down the hallway.

The group halted. Matthew and the other *tap* kept a firm hand on Hebe's arms, not turning around as the two sirens whirled, their *deiktes* at the ready.

"State your purpose," barked the stocky rhapsodist.

"State yours," retorted Kynthia. "Where are you taking the princess?"

"We don't answer to you," said the rhapsodist. "Stay here," she said over her shoulder. With a glance and a jerk of her chin, she and the singer started advancing down the hallway toward Kynthia and Judith.

"If you answer to the princess, the only one left is the one in your custody," said Judith. "Narcissa's body has been taken over by a creature of darkness."

The sirens appeared not to hear, slowly continuing their advance. But Matthew stiffened, releasing Hebe and slowly turning around.

"Jude?"

The sirens glanced over their shoulder in confusion. "What the—?"

The students chose that moment to burst from their hiding spots behind pillars and enormous planters. They charged toward the sirens, yelling at the top of their lungs, with Talia and Geronimi in the lead.

The *tapeinos* near Hebe sprang into action, but before he took two steps,

Matthew elbowed him in the gut and then the nose, and the unconscious man crashed to the floor.

The astonished sirens didn't know how to react to the swarm of attacking students and cadets. After only a couple half-hearted swings of their staves, which Talia easily deflected with her own, Geronimi had knocked them both out using her physic training.

"Learned that from Calandra," Geronimi said with a grin.

Judith ran to Matthew, grabbing his hands. "Oh, Matthew, I have been so afraid."

"I'm fine," he said, kissing her knuckles.

"You're a Freeman?" Hebe stared at Matthew, her eyes even more frightened than before. She looked from Judith to Kynthia. "Who are you?" Then she noticed the girls who were gathering beside them. "Charis? Talia? Deedee?"

"I am Judith, a friend of Calandra's. We are all friends of Calandra's. You are in grave danger, Hebe. We're here to take you to safety."

Hebe narrowed her eyes and backed away. "You're lying. 'Cissa said something like this might happen. Leave me alone."

"Hebe, your sister is no longer herself," Judith said as gently as she could. "You cannot trust her. That is why we're here to save you."

Hebe looked between them, her chin quivering, then nodded, tears flowing down her cheeks. "I know. She . . . she killed . . . she's *horrible*." She sniffled and wiped her cheeks.

Judith wanted to wrap the girl in a hug, but there wasn't time.

"None of you girls are safe anymore, not now that Semyaza has taken over." Kynthia said to the students.

"Who?" said Talia.

"It is a long story," said Judith. "You should all come with us. We will take you to the safe house until we come up with another plan."

"But what about everyone else?" Geronimi asked. "All the rest of the girls in the Academy?"

"We don't have the capacity to take them all," Kynthia said, obviously distraught at the limitation. "Could we hide them somewhere instead?"

Matthew squeezed Judith's hand. "If we don't get the barrier up, nowhere on the island will be safe by this time tomorrow."

"Hopefully that is being addressed as we speak," Judith said. "The stone healers are in the Mother's Heart working on it."

Matthew's eyes widened. "Oh, no."

"What?" The hairs on Judith's neck stood on end.

"That's what she meant. She—er, he said he had someone important to meet and sent me to go retrieve Hebe with the sirens. I thought there was a council meeting or something. We were supposed to go to the Observation Chamber. Do you think he knew you were coming?"

Judith thought of Bryce and shook her head in disbelief. "But we changed the mission to tonight because she would not be able to report it."

"Who wouldn't?" he asked.

"The mole," Judith said darkly. She turned to Geronimi. "Does that secret passage lead to the lower levels?"

"Yes."

"Right. Kynthia, it might be best to take the girls down through the Crystal Cavern. With manpower so thin, I doubt you'll encounter any guards in the lower hallways. If memory serves, there is an extra submersible there that should fit everyone. We'll just have to come back for the rest of the students later."

"Where are you going?" Kynthia asked.

"Matthew and I must go protect the stone healers. I only hope we're not too late."

Kynthia gathered Hebe and the students and ushered them back along the corridor. Matthew headed the other direction toward the door that would take them on the quickest path to the Observation Chamber.

"Wait," Judith said.

Matthew paused, looking at her questioningly. Judith stooped and placed her forefinger on the forehead of the unconscious man, Releasing him. She hoped he woke up before the sirens did.

"I cannot take them all with me," she said to Matthew. "But I can give this man a fighting chance."

He gave her a proud smile, then helped her to her feet.

"Still my Judith."

She smiled at him, creeping hurriedly along beside him. "Always."

Judith expected there to be guards in the corridor outside the Observation Chamber, but when they arrived, the short hall was as empty as most of the other corridors in the palace had been. It was eerie.

"Do you think he is in there?" Judith asked Matthew, looking at the closed door of the chamber.

"I suspect so. He said he'd meet us here."

She bit her lip. She wished she could see inside the Mother's Heart chamber from here, but the only window into the tower was beyond that door. The slightly curved hallway going off to their left bounded the chamber's outer wall. At the far end where it met the hallway on the chamber's adjoining wall was the maintenance door that Meg, Nelly, Erigone, and Amaltheia would be using to access the Heartstone.

"Let us check down there," Judith said, pointing toward the far end of the hallway.

She tried to spot Samantha, the woman who was supposed to be keeping watch in the hallway while the stone healers worked, but the lookout had concealed herself well. Judith padded down the hall in front of Matthew, her heart thundering like a summer storm in her chest. When she did see Samantha, she stopped in horror.

The woman's bleeding corpse lay sprawled on the floor outside the open access door, her eyes staring blankly upward. *Oh, no.* Judith's stomach tightened into a ball of marble. She glanced toward the brilliant light beaming onto the floor through the open door from the tower beyond, willing herself to look. There were four presences in the room—exactly what she expected. So the stone healers were still alive. Xeni, who was supposed to be keeping watch in the antechamber below, was too far away for her to sense.

She turned to tell Matthew she was going to investigate and to tell him to warn her if someone came.

Except Matthew was gone.

88

THE TAINT

JUDITH GLANCED BACK DOWN THE corridor, but there was no one to be seen. Everything in her ached to go after Matthew, but she should also check on the healers—the mission to raise the barrier had to come first. She scanned the corridor and raised the commstone on her wrist to her mouth, deciding it was worth the risk of drawing attention to the others, most of whom were in the tower beyond anyway. Whomever had killed Samantha and taken Matthew was probably well aware of the stone healers' presence. And there was only one person she could think of willing to kill to stop them.

So why had Semyaza left the healers, and herself, alive?

"Meg, are you okay?" she whispered.

Several excruciating seconds later, her commstone buzzed. "Please repeat?"

"Is everything all right in there?" Judith said, a little louder. She peered through the door at last to see Amaltheia and Meg standing on the crossbeam above the Heartstone, one on either side of it so they could easily see the woman on the beam below them. Below Amaltheia, Nelly was craning her neck so she could line herself up with the woman above. Erigone stood waiting patiently below Meg, who stood closest to the dark Observation Room window.

Meg raised her wriststone to her mouth. "Fine. We hit some rough seas for a bit there, but I think we figured it out. Someone hung an unusual pendant on the Heartstone, and it was blocking the process somehow. Might be the black goop it's covered with, though why it was there in the first place, I don't know." She held up her hand to show Judith the

737

oval gemstone hanging from a delicate gold chain in her hand. The reddish stone appeared to be smeared with a slick black oil, which was likely why Meg hadn't tucked it away. "Whatever it is, it's very powerful. I can't wait to study it."

"Put it back," came Narcissa's voice, booming through the tower.

Judith jerked her head toward the Observation Room window. Narcissa, or rather, Semyaza stood near the comm button, holding Matthew at knife point with his hands bound behind him. Semyaza wore a floor-length plum-coloured peplos with elaborate silver embroidery along the hem—a regal garment that matched the quaternaria pendant hanging from a silver chain on his forehead. Matthew looked at Judith sorrowfully, fear and warning etched into his face.

"No!" Judith's throat tightened, and she stepped to the edge of door jamb.

"Now, this is familiar," said Semyaza. "Only, last time, I was trapped inside the stone, and it was Adonia calling the shots. This time, it's me."

Judith swallowed and took a step into the chamber along the walkway, carefully not looking down. "Let him go, Semyaza!"

"Oh, so you do know who I am. Good." Semyaza grinned, setting Narcissa's mouth in a cruel curve. One hand was wrapped in a bandage, which was odd—why hadn't he had it healed? He looked back at Meg. "I won't stand in the way of your little operation, but if you don't replace the stone in your hand, healer, I will kill this man."

Judith's breath caught. She knew he'd do it. Matthew meant nothing to this creature.

"What does it do?" Meg called.

"That's none of your concern. Just do it."

Meg looked at Semyaza uncertainly, then studied the stone in her hand. Semyaza jabbed Narcissa's long dagger into Matthew's ribs, and he flinched.

"Meg, please," Judith said, not daring to look away from her love. "Please, just do it."

Meg shook her head. "If that monster wants us to do this, it can't be for anything good."

"But is it worth Matthew's life when we don't even know what it's for?"

Meg looked around at the other women, who stood waiting for her decision. "Amaltheia?"

The stone healer glanced at Semyaza, then back to Meg. "Now that I've seen it, I think I could direct the circle to work despite its presence.

But I don't know what it is, and I would hesitate to throw a man's life away for fear of what it might do."

Meg looked back at the woman beyond the window. "Will it destroy the Heartstone?"

They could see Semyaza laugh, then he opened the channel again. "No. I assure you, I want the Heartstone quite intact."

Meg stared at Semyaza. "I know you killed Narcissa. Why should I trust you?"

He jabbed the dagger harder into Matthew's ribs, and the blond man flinched. "Do it, or Matthew dies."

"Meg. Please," Judith managed through a tight throat. "He already killed Samantha."

"Listen to Judith," Semyaza said. "The stone, if you please?" He jabbed Matthew once more, and the young man stiffened. Blood trickled from his ribs and made a wet mark on his black sleeveless tunic.

"Stop. Don't hurt him!" Judith called.

But Semyaza only grinned wider, then turned his attention back to Meg.

She sighed, then lay prostrate once more and, with some difficulty, attached the chain to a hook recessed into the bottom of the beam. The blackened gemstone dangled directly above the Heartstone, swinging within a finger's breadth of the giant heart's surface.

"Excellent," said Semyaza. "Now, resume your work, please. My dear consort-elect and I shall watch from here."

Judith met Matthew's eyes, begging him with a look not to do anything stupid that would get himself killed, but mostly begging the Mother to spare his life. If Semyaza killed him, she truly didn't know how she would go on. Matthew may have picked up some fighting skills over the past few weeks, but she doubted he could best Narcissa, let alone the evil creature using her body. Semyaza was thousands of years old—he probably knew how to fight.

Meg returned to her place and, with a trembling glance at the form of the princess in the window, stretched out her arms and glanced at Amaltheia to show her readiness.

"Let us begin," the *daskala* said with an unsteady voice.

The four healers closed their eyes and began to sing.

Despite the danger Matthew was in, Judith couldn't help but watch in wonder as the crack around the displaced spoke slowly mended, holding it firmly in place. As the last bit of the crystal casing around the enormous fire opal rejoined, the song changed. Judith suspected this new song was the one Polyxo had found on the Atlantean datastone. With a flash of brilliance, the spherical Heartstone flared to life, blinding Judith. She turned away, holding her arm in front of her eyes, then turned back to see the four healers shielding their eyes from the Heartstone as they shuffled along the walkways to the access doors. Judith didn't wait for the healers to retract the walkways and rejoin her.

"I am going to save Matthew," she said into her commstone.

But then one of the healers shouted.

Judith turned back toward the tower door and saw the healers staring at the Heartstone in horror. She followed their gaze and a sinking feeling dragged at her stomach.

A black, inky cloud was pouring into the Heartstone from the small jewel. In seconds, the entire sphere was filled with the billowing liquid-like substance. A web of oily black veins flowed along the spokes like an invading horde of ants, into the brilliant clear tiles of the walls, and along the beams the healers stood on. In the Observation Chamber, Semyaza watched with glee, one hand still keeping the dagger trained on Matthew.

"At last," he said through the still-open channel. "At last the Old Man will know what it feels like to be erased and shoved into the Void. With words this world was made, but with blood it shall be remade."

He laughed and pressed his bandaged hand against the glass. A long dark stain seeped through the cloth from his palm, leaving an oily black smear behind. A pale angular man with black hair, black eyes, and black clothes appeared out of thin air next to him, watching the event beyond the glass with gleeful delight.

The web reached the corridor floor, spreading like diseased, malevolent molasses, and Judith retreated. Looking up, she saw Amaltheia and Meg rooted to the spot, struggling and whimpering as black veins crept up their legs. She couldn't see the women on the beam below, but she assumed they were similarly trapped. Then she saw Matthew twist, swinging his leg backward toward Semyaza's head—but the blow was blocked with Semyaza's forearm.

The bandage fell away from Semyaza's other hand and Judith gasped. The entire hand was covered in the same oily black taint crawling outward from the Heartstone. Twisting his blocking arm around Matthew's leg to entrap it, Semyaza pulled Matthew forward, catching him on the chest with his blackened palm. Matthew screamed and went rigid, his eyes blank and staring, as the substance crawled over his body with astonishing speed, soon encasing him head to toe in a black web. Semyaza cast him to the floor.

"No!" Judith screamed, turning to run to him—but the black web had rooted her legs to the ground.

Narcissa's fine-boned face peered through the window, twisted into Semyaza's evil grin. He clasped the quaternaria pendant on his forehead with his taint-coated fist. Shadows flowed from him, through the glass window of the Observation Room as though it weren't even there, and surrounded the Heartstone, obscuring it in a dark cloud.

"No longer let it be said that love conquers all," he said. "At last, fear wins."

Black mist covered Judith's vision, and she knew no more.

89

THE SOULSTONE

Calandra stared at the pulsing dim blue orb below her, her heart hammering against her ribs. Next to her, Zale hovered in the water, his eyes as big as oyster shells as he also considered the enormous moonstone with the shadowed heart. When they had approached the Heartstone, its surface had been covered in cracks and fissures and the fire within had nearly gone out. The Soulstone's condition made that seem like minor disrepair. The blue sphere had more veins than an old woman's forehead, and large pieces of the surface had flaked away, leaving it jagged and rough. The fissures went deep—Calandra could sense them wending their way to the very heart of the stone. No wonder Semyaza had been able to escape. It was a wonder he was the only one.

Above them, but inside the boundary where the energy barrier had been until Calandra had disengaged it with the *ichthys* ring, hovered Nadia and several of the other women, supervising. Tamiel had made it clear that if they noticed the slightest bit of reparation to the Soulstone, Nadia and the other guardians would put an end to the process—and to Delphine. Calandra drew in a long draught of water. In her heart, she'd agreed to every one of the objections Shriniel had presented about why she shouldn't agree to Tamiel's deal, though she'd seen little other choice. And even though she *knew* she'd heard the Pneuma's whispered guidance, looking at the stone itself, she questioned what she'd felt. At least the deal meant she was no longer responsible for healing this labyrinth of broken bonds.

Ready? she signalled to Zale.

Even though she knew he didn't understand diving signs well, her meaning must have been obvious, because he nodded and took her hand.

742

She squeezed it and then turned back to the Soulstone. Holding her breath, she and Zale extended their hands and touched the stone at the same time.

In a blink, she found herself hovering next to Zale in cloudy water filling a corridor made of crumbling moonstone. Silt billowed around them in a dirty cloud, disturbed by their entrance. Calandra closed her eyes, reaching out with earth. When she opened them, the silt in the water was settling to the floor of the corridor, revealing a passageway that stretched into the distance and faded into darkness before she saw an end. Frequent jagged openings along the walls revealed equally jagged tunnels beyond—though they looked like rends in the stone, not the careful construction the decaying walls of this corridor implied. Some, however, were more graceful arching entrances to criss-crossing passageways, with sculpted details around the openings in various states of disrepair. The pulsing light of the moonstone filled the maze, casting everything in spooky blue tones.

"Where are we?" Zale asked, then blinked. "We can talk here? Tip-top."

Calandra was only a little less surprised. "Just like in the Heartstone, remember?"

He shook his head. "I didn't talk to anyone in there. It was over too fast."

"For you, maybe."

She spun around, getting her bearings. Behind them, the passageway ended in a grey fog—the way out.

"I think this is the front gate. This passage must have been part of the original design. It looks like it was designed as a labyrinth, even before all these extra fissures and passages opened while it declined."

"And it's bigger than it looks on the outside like the Heartstone too," Zale said.

He released her hand and swam to the nearest gap in the wall. Pieces of stone lay in small piles beneath an opening that was bigger at the top than the bottom. Calandra peered over his shoulder to see a dark uneven tunnel that soon joined another dimly lit passageway much like the one they stood in.

"If we want to find the soul keeper cells, we should probably stay in the original passageways," she said.

He turned away from the tunnel. "Agreed. After you, m'lady." He gestured ahead of him with a flourish.

Calandra began swimming along the passage, scanning with her eyes and senses at each opening for any indication of what they sought. "I'm your sister. You don't need to call me that."

He chuckled, keeping pace beside her. "I know. I was just having a bit of fun. Do you ever do that?"

"Do what?"

"Have fun," he said.

She peered down another crumbling, straight passage. The far end terminated in a smooth clear quartz wall with darkness on the other side. Above it, a word was engraved into the stone in two scripts—an unfamiliar one made up of tiny lines and dashes, and below that, Greek. Studying the word, she realized it was a name.

Kokabiel. She studied the quartz—it looked just like the tiles lining the wall of the Well of Souls outside. *The soul keepers. The tiles are the cells.* She kept swimming, studying the name above the next passageway. *Barakiel. Nope.*

"I don't have time to have fun."

He barked a laugh, then grew sober. "You're serious? You really don't ever take time to just enjoy yourself?"

She frowned at him, trying to remember the last time she'd had fun. Images of her and Osaze in each other's arms, dreaming beneath the stars on the beach at Fire Lake or goofing around during swimming lessons came to mind. That made her think of the last words he'd said to her when she'd seen him in her vision. *He doesn't forgive me.* Without warning, her eyes flowed over and she turned away from her brother so he wouldn't see her pain.

"Whoa, whoa." He swam around in front of her, swimming in reverse so he could see her face. "I didn't know it was such a sensitive topic. Sorry. Please don't cry."

She sniffed, glad the water obscured her tears. She drew a deep rush of water through her gills to get control of herself, then looked at him. "Sorry. I . . . I used to have fun. Lately, I haven't had much opportunity."

He looked at her with his eyebrows drawn together, his shoulder-length blond hair floating in his face as he flipped along the passage backward. He gave her an understanding smile with a mischievous quirk on one side.

"I guess I can understand that. It's not like managing a revolution and rescuing your mother and brother from the Underworld are exactly frolics in the park."

She pointed at the word above the door. "Help me find Tamiel's name, okay? It will start with *tau.* You recognize that letter, right?"

He glanced at the engraved words and nodded. "That's one of the easy ones. It looks just like a *t* in English."

He turned around and resumed his place beside her, scanning passageways on his side in silence.

"Look," he said finally, "I know I apologized before, but I really mean it. I'm sorry for all the trouble I caused. I could blame Semyaza's mind games, but really, it was my own stupid choice. I'd thought I was going to find a place where I belonged, but I got here—to Sirenia, I mean—and nothing was as I expected it to be. I guess I was just looking for something to make sense, and I chose to believe the wrong thing."

Calandra swam past yet another wrong name. "No, I'm the one who should apologize. I should never have left you behind in the palace in the first place. You were dropped square in the middle of a political revolution with no support network in a place you were completely unfamiliar with. I should have come to get you right away instead of waiting. I was just . . ."

She thought of the days after fleeing the palace—days spent evading the royal guard, sleeping rough on land or at sea, and surviving. Wherever she and the others went to find food and shelter, someone always recognized her or Ignatia from the Court of the Redeemed and either reported them or volunteered for the cause. Eventually, they'd set up the safe house at a location Jacob and Hammad had found many years before while hiking through the forest near Elpida—Margaret House wasn't an easy hike from her family *latifundium*, but it could be reached in a hard day's journey over the ridges of the Dragontooth Mountains if one knew the way.

The energy required to simply survive had been a welcome diversion from the hollow ache in her chest. She'd lost so much, so quickly. She hadn't been ready to think about any of it yet. But trying to ignore her pain had meant slowly succumbing to it, causing the ever-increasing turmoil and seizures that had wreaked so much havoc for the last several weeks.

"Distracted," she finished weakly.

"Hmm. I bet you were." He gave her a sidelong glance, but didn't press her further. "I forgive you, too, by the way. We've both made mistakes. Why don't we start again? As Eric used to say . . ." He faltered. "Well, that doesn't matter."

Calandra studied him, waiting for him to finish the thought, but the anger and hurt on his face explained his silence.

"Who's Eric?"

Just when she thought he might not answer, he said, "Eric is the man who took me in when I . . . when I ran away from home." He looked at her guiltily.

"You what?" She looked at him in shock. "Why would you do that?"

"I was trying to protect Mother. My powers had just started manifesting, and I'd had a couple pretty bad accidents." His face paled, and he looked away from her, scanning the passageways with intense interest.

Calandra remembered the fearful boy she'd met less than a month ago who'd been so afraid of his own powers that he wore a feldspar cuff by choice. The pieces started to come together.

"It didn't work, though," he continued.

"What didn't work? Did you end up hurting Mother somehow anyway?"

He nodded miserably. "It's because she came looking for me that she ended up here. I didn't know about it until Abela showed up a few months ago and helped me escape. I—I didn't even know I needed to escape, that Eric had been working for the Order all along."

"The Order?"

He studied the sandy floor of the corridor. "The Order of the Ascension of the Grigori. I told you about them, remember?"

She had a vague memory of him mentioning such an order during their rushed first meeting on the Redemption Moon, but she'd been so overwhelmed by meeting the brother she had barely dared believe existed under such fortuitous timing that many of the details of that night were fuzzy.

Her brother's shoulders slumped, guilt hanging from them like a heavy cloak. Whatever had happened and however he was culpable, he'd obviously been paying penance ever since. He didn't need her to add to his load.

"I almost agreed to become Semyaza's consort," she offered sheepishly. "After letting him train me for five years." Her face grew warm at the admission. "If I had, he probably would have possessed me instead of Narcissa. Can you imagine how bad things would be now if he did?"

Zale met her gaze, his lips quirked. "And I thought Narcissa was the only one who understood me. Zoe's right—I am a numbskull."

Calandra glanced away. "I don't know if I'd trust anything Zoe said." The pain of that betrayal was still fresh. She could hardly believe it when Zale had told her what Zoe had done in the Western Wasteland. At least she now knew the identity of the mole.

"Maybe not," Zale said. "But she did try to save Damaris. That's something, anyway."

Calandra met his gaze, her gut hard. "Something. But not enough."

Movement behind Zale caught her eye. Instinctively, she pushed him behind her to face whatever was hiding in the crack beyond.

"Hey!" he exclaimed, then saw what she was doing and turned to face the potential threat. "I'm not helpless, you know," he whispered.

"Right. Sorry."

Calandra held her defensive posture, her hands raised and ready to blast whatever was moving toward them along the passageway. Confusion, defeat, and hatred preceded the shadowy silhouette. Then it laid a slim creamy-pale hand on the wall of the tunnel in the light next to the entrance.

"Calandra? Zale? Is that you?" came a familiar female voice.

Calandra's chest tightened. *It can't be.*

The figure moved hesitantly into the light, revealing an exquisitely beautiful blond undine girl with ice green eyes, the neckline of her red bodice and the belt of her swimming skirt encrusted with pearls. She looked haggard, her eyes puffy as though she'd been crying.

"Narcissa?" Calandra croaked.

90

THE EXILE

ZALE STARED AT THE GIRL who hovered before them, his mouth dry. Narcissa looked defeated and broken. But seeing her, seeing the face of the person who had bound him up in lies, he froze, gawping like a fish.

"Narcissa? What are you doing here?" Calandra demanded. "Or should I say *Semyaza*?"

The girl's eyes widened slightly. "You know who Semyaza is?" When Calandra's suspicious, defensive posture didn't change, Narcissa shook her head, dropping her gaze. "Anyway, it's me. Semyaza sent me here. Wherever *here* is." She looked around at the broken grey-blue walls and passageways.

Calandra hesitated. "You're in the Soulstone," she said cautiously. "A prison in Tartarus."

"Tartarus. Huh. That explains a lot." She wrapped her arms around herself, a haunted look in her eyes as she studied the two of them. "I don't know how he sent me here. He took me out of my body—my *own* body—using that chained heartstone, and the next thing I knew, I was wandering around here."

Calandra looked startled. "Semyaza used the Heartstone to separate your spirit from your body and send you here?"

Narcissa shook her head. "No, he used *a* heartstone, not *the* Heartstone. It's a device he's been looking for ever since he took over my body. The Heart of Chaos, he called it. Stole it from some sphinx."

Zale snapped upright, fear tightening his throat. "Abela?" he squeaked. "He took Abela's heart?"

Narcissa shrugged, scowling. "Maybe. I don't know. He did talk about

748

a spirit named Abela a lot. At least, I think she was a spirit."

Zale sank to the sandy floor of the corridor, too stunned to even keep himself afloat. Semyaza had asked him about Abela a few times, but he'd thought it was Narcissa being curious about his past. He had no idea he'd been helping a dragon steal Abela's heart. If Semyaza had Abela's heart, what had happened to his guardian angel? Could cherubim die?

No, she said the heart was only used to take on flesh. She's fine. She has to be. Still, he knew that however it had come about, Abela wouldn't have given up her heartstone easily. Especially not to one of the Grigori. He swallowed the choking lump in his throat and flicked his fins to resume his previous altitude. He would *not* let Narcissa see him cry.

But Narcissa started crying instead—he could tell by the way her body shuddered with her sobs, though the tears themselves mingled with the water.

"He . . . he lied to me about the heartstone. He was supposed to use it to make a body for himself, and leave me and my baby alone."

"Y—your *baby*?" Calandra sounded as stunned as Zale felt.

Narcissa nodded sadly, sniffling. "Semyaza's been doing a lot of things with my body that I wouldn't have. But that's not the baby's fault. She didn't ask for this any more than I did."

Zale actually felt a twinge of compassion for his cousin. If it had been difficult for him while enthralled to Semyaza's will, what must it have been like for her, who'd been imprisoned in her own mind while the fallen seraph had used her body as his playground? Much like being under the *sklavia* bond. Zale had only had brief experience with the *sklavia* bond, but he hoped never to repeat it. But he knew a person wasn't responsible for anything they did while under its influence—not when their free will had been removed. Narcissa may look like the same person who'd led him astray with her lies, but she wasn't. In fact, he may never have met the real Narcissa before this moment.

"How could he use a heartstone to make his own body?" Calandra said gently. She looked affected by Narcissa's brokenness too.

Narcissa shrugged, her gaze downcast.

"That's what they're for," Zale explained. "Abela—" His voice broke, and he cleared his throat before continuing. "Abela told me that cherubim and other spirits have to use a heartstone like that to take physical form in our plane. They can use different hearts at different times, and how they look is a choice they make. Berian, er, I mean, Rumiel told me that part."

"That's what Semyaza told me," Narcissa said. "Except he lied. He didn't intend to make his own body. He intended to make my body his own." Narcissa's face hardened, and she slammed a fist into her palm. "Now that he has the heart, he has his powers back, so why bother with making a body no one knows when he could use mine and become queen of Sirenia? He means to use the heart in other ways too. Said he could use it to rewrite the world or some such nonsense. Half of what he said never made sense." She shook her head. "He told me he needed a song to make the heartstone work, but then he used it anyway, so that was a lie too. But he searched for a long time for the song. Why would he do that if it wasn't important? Unless he just needed the song to do something specific. But what?"

"Do you know what song it was?" Calandra asked.

Narcissa looked at her. "Something he found on one of those dusty Atlantis datastones. 'Song of a Hundred Years,' or something like that. Does that mean anything to you?"

She looked at Calandra, who started shaking her head, then froze.

"Was it possibly 'Song of a Thousand Days'?"

Narcissa frowned. "Yeah, that sounds right."

Calandra's eyes widened and she went pale. "That's an archaic name for the song used to repair the Heartstone. We use it every year at the annual Healing Ceremony."

"Oh." Narcissa shrugged. "Maybe he needed to repair the Heart of Chaos. Maybe it wasn't working properly. In which case, I guess he'd need a stone healer to do it, not me." She hugged herself tighter.

Zale's chest hitched. "Did he explain what made the heart so special?"

Narcissa frowned at him in thought. "Something about being able to draw on the raw essence of the universe, not having to go through some deity named Elyon." She snorted. "He sure hated that guy. Called him the *Old Man*."

Zale's heart sped up. He exchanged looks with Calandra.

"We have to get back there," he said. "Whatever he's planning, it's going to be *bad*."

Calandra's expression was tight. "I know. But we have a job to do here first." She turned to Narcissa. "Do you know how you got here, to the Underworld?"

Narcissa shook her head. "I already told you all I know. What are you doing in this maze? Wait, this is the Underworld? Are you two dead?"

"No, we're not dead, we're—"

"Did you find your mother?" Narcissa asked Zale.

So she *did* remember some of what had happened.

"We did, but . . . it's complicated." He looked at Calandra. "We ran into a bit of trouble here too."

Calandra glanced at Zale, then cast a concerned frown at her cousin. "We have to go, but we can't leave you here. Come with us. When we're done, we'll figure out a way to get you home and back into your body where you belong."

The defeated look on Narcissa's face changed to suspicion. "Why would you do that?"

"Because no one deserves what has happened to you. And because we can't let Semyaza take over our home." Calandra pressed her lips into a thin line.

"Even though it means I'd be queen?"

"What makes you think you'd be queen?" Calandra crossed her arms. "Did the archons declare their support?"

Narcissa's nostrils flared, and she opened her mouth to say something, then closed it, regarding her cousin through narrowed eyes. She gestured around them. "You know the way out?"

"It's back there," Zale said, pointing the way they'd come. "Looks like a cloud of mist, which is pretty weird underwater, if you think about it. But then, so is talking."

"Oh. That." Narcissa shook her head, looking disappointed, the brief moment of fire draining out of her posture. "I've tried to get through that, but that mist is as hard as a stone wall. I can never break through."

"Oh," Calandra said. She fidgeted with her braid, looking thoughtful. When she spoke, her voice was tinged with reluctance. "I . . . might know a way to get you out. But you're not going to like it." She gave her braid a tug. "I'm not even going to like it," she muttered.

Narcissa straightened, the slight movements of her tail fins quickening. "What is it? I'll do anything."

Calandra sighed. "I'm not sure how it works, exactly, but I think you might be able to hitch a ride with me somehow."

Narcissa blinked, a confused frown on her face. "You mean, you want me to possess you, like Semyaza possessed me?"

"No! Not at all." Calandra looked momentarily disgusted, then inexplicably guilty. "I mean, I want you to piggyback on me to get back to our plane, the same way Semyaza did. Then we'll find a way to get you back in your body, where you belong. I think I could figure out a way to make it work. Semyaza somehow managed it without me even knowing."

Zale's eyes bugged. "You . . . you were the one who let Semyaza out?"

Calandra nodded miserably. "I think so. I don't know how, but I'm pretty sure it was me."

Narcissa's face darkened. "*You're* responsible for what happened to me? I should have known!" She threw her hands up, jolting backward. "All this time, I thought it was the one thing I couldn't blame you for. But if it weren't for you, he never would have even found me. Forget it. I don't need your help. You turn everything to poison. I'll find my own way home."

She spun and began swimming away.

"Narcissa—" Calandra called.

But then the walls began to shake.

Zale held his arms up to protect himself from falling dust and debris. "Is the Soulstone breaking even more? Or are you doing this?"

"It isn't me!" Calandra beckoned him to follow her along the passageway after Narcissa. "Come on."

While the walls shook and shivered, they sped down the corridor, soon catching up to their cousin. The dim blue pulse of the moonstone walls around them darkened with a blooming cloud of black, as though they'd been injected with ink by a giant squid. With the sudden roar of rending earth, a slab of blue stone shot through the floor in front of them and slammed into the ceiling. Zale jerked his tail in front of him, stopping only inches before he collided with the obstruction.

"What's happening?" he asked.

Next to him, Calandra and Narcissa looked as stunned as he felt. Behind them, another stone wall slammed into the ceiling, blocking their retreat and encasing them in a short corridor of crumbling moonstone. They were trapped.

"Now what?" Narcissa asked, staring wildly around.

"The Soulstone must be decaying even more," Calandra shouted above the din. "But why would it make new walls?"

Next to them, a wall disappeared as though it had never existed, revealing a square tunnel. Zale looked down the new passageway.

"I don't know," he replied. "But whatever's happening, it's helping us to find Tamiel. Look." He pointed upward. Above the passage, Tamiel's name was clearly etched in Greek . . . and English. "Maybe Elyon's giving us a hand?"

"Maybe, but it doesn't feel right." Calandra frowned. "That blackness in the stone, it's just . . ."

"*Wrong*," Zale finished for her, eyeing the ink cloud like it might leap out and attack him.

"This must be what he meant," Narcissa said in a hollow voice, staring at the spreading blight. She put her hands on her head, her momentary bravado once again replaced by the haunted look. "He's rewriting the world. All the worlds."

"How could what Semyaza is doing on the Ground affect the Underworld?" Calandra asked.

"He sent Narcissa here, didn't he?" Zale replied.

Another wall rose from the floor along the passage behind them, nearer this time. Calandra pointed toward the new tunnel.

"We'll solve the mystery later. That's where we need to go, anyway. C'mon."

She sped into the tunnel opening, and Zale followed. With a glance at the surrounding chaos, Narcissa swam in behind him. The billowing ink darkening the Soulstone walls raced to keep up.

They had nearly reached the clear quartz wall at the far end of the tunnel when the ink passed them, seeping into the quartz and spreading through it in black fissures and lines.

"It's . . . it's breaking the bonds." Calandra looked at the wall in horror. "Whatever it is, it's dissolving everything."

No sooner had she said that than the quartz wall exploded toward them. Zale threw up his arms to protect his face from the expected shards, but nothing touched him. Surprised, he looked up to see Calandra with her hands extended and the sharp pieces of rock suspended in a spray pattern in the water. Then, just like she had with the silt when they'd entered, she dropped her arms, and the pieces of rock drifted harmlessly to the floor of the tunnel.

A large lizard-like face—striped bright blue on top, silvery-grey underneath—with a pointed snout, a crested head, and tubular, fleshy whiskers accenting its strangely delicate lines poked out of the darkness where the wall had been. Zale backed up in alarm. The beast drew a long draught of water into the leathery gills along its neck with obvious relish, then peered at the three of them from intelligent golden eyes that looked unsurprised to see them. It smiled, revealing terrifying pointed teeth.

"So," it said in Tamiel's smooth voice. "You see my true face at last, Calandra kor'Delphine—the face of a chalkydra. How noble of you to come all the way here to free me as you agreed. How very expected. But you didn't do this." She looked around at the opening. "Semyaza must have finally come through. You won't mind if I don't honour my end of the bargain, do you? Since you didn't actually free me, that is. I quite fancy leaving you all here so you won't be in my way. Don't worry, your mother will be safe as one of my pets again, I'll see to it."

The water dragon pushed past them, slamming Zale into the wall. As the long, sinuous form passed him, he spotted three sets of spiny wing-like fins undulating along its scaly back to propel it along. Calandra, pressed against the wall on the other side of the tunnel, grabbed hold of one of the spines.

"Tamiel, no! I won't let you do this!" she roared as the beast dragged her along the corridor.

"And how do you plan to stop me, little undine? Soon, my companions and I will all be free, and there'll be no putting the cork back in the bottle." Tamiel gave a mocking laugh, scraping her body along the tunnel sides until Calandra was forced to let go.

"I think you've forgotten something," Calandra called. "You might have escaped your prison cell, but you're still trapped here in the Soulstone. The only way in and out is with a key. And though your cells have shattered, the Soulstone itself is still intact." Calandra gestured around her. "It appears there are some things even Semyaza can't destroy."

Tamiel stopped and whirled, her body flattening improbably in the narrow space as she did so. She glared at Calandra, focusing on the ring on Calandra's hand.

"You mean a key like that?"

Calandra glanced at the ring, drawing it to her chest, and Tamiel launched herself at the panacea.

"No!" Zale darted in between them, hands extended. Electricity crackled from his palms and into Tamiel's snout, causing her to snap her head back. Unfortunately, the jolt didn't only go where he wanted—branches of electricity sizzled in every direction. One struck Narcissa and she screamed, her body arched in pain. He stopped the flow of power and she went limp, drifting but conscious.

"Narcissa?" he called, familiar panic accelerating his heartbeat. *Not again!*

She moaned.

Good, she's alive. Relief exploded through him. But he could only spare her a glance before turning back to the dragon.

The dragon transformed, her sinuous shape shrinking and shifting until she floated before them as an undine woman. The metallic blue scales of her tail extended well up her torso, fading into the russet skin of the beautiful woman he'd seen above the lake when they reached her upper chest.

Even her arms and face bore patches of scales and metallic blue stripes, and her eyes glinted with golden light. On her back, three sets of spiny wings with glittering translucent membranes between them connected to a single point between her shoulder blades, draped behind her like a butterfly in repose. She looked different than any other undine he'd seen in *ichthys* state.

She rushed toward Calandra, who hit her with a blast of water. The attack slowed her down, but she spun and dodged, grabbing Calandra's arm.

Calandra went still, floating in the water as though dead, her eyes looking straight ahead of her.

"What have you done?" Zale cried, staring at his sister. His body still vibrated with the hum of her proximity—she was alive, at least, even if she didn't look it. He rushed toward her, but Tamiel held up a warning hand and he stopped, watching it warily.

"It's a temporary paralysis," Tamiel said. "I just need the ring. If you try to stop me, I'll do the same to you."

Calandra's arm where Tamiel had touched it had swollen in an angry red welt. The chalkydra grabbed Calandra's hand and began to work the ring off.

Zale cast around for options—he couldn't use lightning here, it was too unpredictable. He tried to gather flame into his hands to throw a fireball at her, but it was no use—they might be able to talk normally here, but the water around them still quenched any flame he tried to summon. There was no air to throw, and he didn't have enough skill with earth to do anything with it.

He gathered energy in his hands and stared at the woman. Could he channel electricity right into her? That was how he had killed Mr. Crow, the abusive first mate of the *Atlanta*. He didn't want one more death on his conscience—but Tamiel wasn't human like Mr. Crow, she was an immortal spirit. His bolt to her snout had barely slowed her down. No, this was the only way.

Just as Tamiel slipped the ring off Calandra's hand, he charged forward, both hands in front of him like a battering ram. When he made contact with Tamiel's side, he released the power he'd been holding and her body went tense and rigid. He'd thought it would immobilize her, but she slowly turned to face him. He kept one hand on her side, channelling energy through her, while he reached for the ring in her hand.

That was his undoing. Without warning, she brought her arm down on his, batting him aside. Before he could recover, she darted down the tunnel, slipping the ring on her finger.

Spinning around, he gave chase, but she was faster than he was. Tamiel transformed back into a water dragon as she swam. When she reached the far end of the tunnel, she slammed her whip-like tail with its spiny fluke-like appendages against the opening, collapsing the stone. Zale retreated, his arms held up to protect his face and head from the falling rubble.

"No!" came Calandra's voice from behind. She rushed forward, her arms extended to clear the silt. When it dissipated, it revealed a solid wall of rock.

Narcissa swam up beside them, still looking a little dazed. She stared at the pile of debris. "We're trapped?"

"Not for long."

Calandra extended her hands toward the pile of rubble and concentrated. The pile shook and rumbled and began to move, but when she cleared the silt this time, the rubble had only crept closer to them along the tunnel floor, leaving no gaps. She turned her attention to the walls and ceiling, but the result was more debris falling into the tunnel. Everything she did only added to the pile of rock that blocked their escape.

"Stop!" Narcissa shrieked as another large hunk of moonstone crashed to the floor. "You're making it worse. What are you doing?"

"I'm trying . . . to get us out of here. But it's like . . . the elements are doing the opposite of what I want." She dropped her arms, panting. "This is how my powers used to act when I was taking Semyaza's advice." She turned to face them, frustration on her face.

"Because he's done it," Narcissa said slowly. "He's rewritten the world."

"What if we helped you?" Zale asked. "Like, in one of those circle thingies?"

Calandra looked up. "Brilliant idea, Zale." She turned to Narcissa and held out a hand. "I should have thought of that."

Narcissa held up her hands. "Don't look at me. I've got nothing. I don't even have the *sklavia* bonds anymore. And we both know how ineffective I am with the elements on my own." Her voice sounded bitter.

Calandra levelled her gaze at her cousin. "No, but the *sklavia* bonds weren't what made you strong in the first place. You've always been smart and determined. All you needed to do was to care about someone besides yourself and you would have been a truly amazing leader."

Narcissa frowned and crossed her arms, looking away from Calandra.

Calandra pointed at the walls. "If this black poison is Semyaza's doing, it's affecting more than just Tamiel's prison cell. He said he wants to rewrite the entire cosmos, didn't he? That means everything will be changed. He'll control it all. Just like he controls your body. Don't you want to do something about that?"

"Of course I do," spat Narcissa.

"Then help me," Calandra pleaded softly, "so I can help you." She paused. "You want to be queen of Sirenia? Then you'll need to know when you can't do things alone. You need to let others help you. A queen who rules by her own wisdom and desires becomes a tyrant and a monster—just like Semyaza. Is that what you want?"

Narcissa regarded Calandra steadily. Zale couldn't believe she had to think this hard about it—Calandra's speech would have won over that blackguard Gryffyn Cox.

Well, maybe not Gryffyn. But certainly someone a little less hardened. Narcissa must really hate Calandra if she was being this difficult. Maybe some of the things he'd heard that Narcissa had done after her mother died truly had been her responsibility, not the dragon's who shared her body. But which ones?

"C'mon, Narcissa," he said at last. "What do you have to lose?"

"Nothing, I guess," Narcissa said. "Not anymore." She heaved a sigh and dropped her arms. "Fine. What do I have to do?"

Zale let out a watery breath he didn't know he'd been holding, and Calandra smiled at her cousin.

"Just take my hand," she said, extending her arm toward the other girl.

Hesitantly, Narcissa did.

91

WAR ZONE

Damaris sat cross-legged next to her sister's supine form, fidgeting with a small stone she'd picked up from the cavern floor. She stared at Zoe's face, so peaceful in repose. Avriel, the broad-shouldered, golden-skinned, golden-haired winged guardian in a black and red tunic and pants who sat on a boulder nearby, had assured her that Zoe was perfectly fine and the induced sleep would have no harmful effects, but Damaris couldn't help but worry. She wasn't certain if her concern was more for Zoe's current state, or what she might say to her sister when she woke up.

Zale had told her what Zoe had done to him, and to Osaze and Urbi too. He hadn't wanted to, but she'd dragged it out of him. Now she was trying to reconcile her image of her conscientious, dutiful eldest sister who had deferred her position as heiress of Steadfast House to dedicate her life to the Mother's service with the traitor and liar Damaris now knew Zoe to be. Being ten years apart in age, she'd never been particularly close to Zoe. She'd preferred the company of Eudora or Sabina, who, at thirteen, was the closest in age of her two younger sisters, and who shared Damaris's interest in stories and her taste for adventure.

She'd certainly got more than she'd bargained for with this adventure. Zale may have started out as an interesting way to quench her thirst for novelty, but he'd become so much more. Still, she couldn't believe she'd kissed him. It had been an impulse, the answer to a question that had been burning in her mind since that day on the terrace of the Opal Palace when she'd gone over to talk to him for the first time.

She'd already tried kissing a *doulos*—she'd taken Ewelike into the garden behind Steadfast House a time or two before Eudora had taken him as her consort—and it had been nothing but disappointing. Nothing like the contraband human stories she'd collected over the years had made kissing sound—stories she'd found in water-logged books in the wrecks of ships near the barrier or told by women brought in with the Harvest. Wilhelmina had even told her of a particular boy she'd fancied as a young girl, before she'd been brought to Sirenia. Mother would have been horrified if she found out. But those stories always made romance sound so wonderful and exciting and had made her wonder—what would it be like to kiss a boy who could kiss you back?

Not that Zale had kissed her back. He'd been too surprised. But she could tell he wanted to, and that had made it worth it. She'd thought once would be enough to sate her curiosity, but now, for some unexplained reason, she wanted to kiss him again.

She touched her lips where the memory of his mouth lingered. The look in his eyes when she'd sprung it on him had been priceless. That must be why she wanted to try it again. She did love a good surprise.

But she'd never get the chance if he didn't come back. And she definitely wanted him to come back. Not so she could kiss him—well, not *only* so she could kiss him. She liked him, and she didn't want to see him get hurt.

There. She'd said it. Zale had started off as a story for her collection. Then he'd become a friend, albeit an annoying one. But when she'd seen him being led toward her in that pit of slithering demons, knowing he'd come for her, something in her changed—she'd already believed what Calandra had said that night in the Court of the Redeemed, how men were no more violent and hate-filled than women. But it wasn't until that moment in Lamia's lair that Damaris saw just how loyal and self-sacrificial men could be, the epitome of all that was virtuous and good. She doubted even Zoe would have done what Zale did in order to save her life.

She studied her sister. Well, maybe Zoe would. She'd come to the Wastelands, after all, and it wasn't her fault she'd gotten tricked into thinking she'd freed Damaris when she hadn't. But she'd been willing to sacrifice Zale to do it, and that's not a sacrifice he would have made in return, Damaris was sure of it. Otherwise, he never would have come for her.

"You better come back, Wonder Boy, or I'll never forgive you," she muttered.

Avriel glanced up. "What's that?"

"Never mind." Damaris dropped the pebble and it rattled against the stone floor—and didn't stop. She stared at the vibrating rock. What was going on?

The troops around the lake began shouting. She looked up to see winged men and women jumping to their feet and fluttering over the pool, staring and pointing at the surface of the lake. She stood, straining to see what they were looking at—and her jaw fell open when she realized the lake was no longer there. Oh, there was a hole. But the water was gone.

"Damaris, look out!" called Avriel, pointing at the rock beneath her feet.

She looked down to see dark lines seeping along the rocks toward them from the hole, spreading through the stone like muddy water through a clear pool. When it reached a spray of amethyst spires, it oozed through them from the root like water filling a cut flower.

It felt . . . *off*. And it was getting closer to Zoe by the second.

"Zoe!" Damaris rushed to Zoe, kneeling next to her head and shaking her, but Zoe didn't respond. "Help me," she called to Avriel.

She patted her sister's cheeks while Avriel knelt beside her, taking that slim silver rod the guardians called a mindover and pressing the end with the yellow crystal to Zoe's temple. Her sister moaned, blinking. Zoe saw the guardian's golden face and sat up with a jolt, pressing herself into Damaris.

"Get back," Zoe spat.

"Ssh, Zoe, it's all right. He's a friend," soothed Damaris. "Can you stand?"

Zoe looked down at herself as though taking stock, then rolled over and pushed herself to her feet. She glanced at the chaos by the Pool of Tears in confusion.

"What's happening?"

"I'm not sure," Damaris said, standing. "But something's wrong. We need to move."

The black substance had picked up speed. The clang of swords striking stone rang around her as some of the guardians struck at the black rock. Others were blasting it with fire or trying other methods to eradicate it, or simply staring at it in confused wonder. Damaris grabbed Zoe's hand to tug her away from it, but Zoe resisted, staring at it in fascination.

"Zoe, come on. Whatever that is, I don't think we should let it touch us. Let's hide in the tunnel."

She tugged again, and Zoe finally pulled her gaze away from the oily net to look at her. Just then, the black substance seeped from the rocks beneath Zoe's feet into her toes, creeping up her legs in sprawling veins across her skin.

"Damaris?" Zoe said uncertainly, looking down at her legs and then up at her sister. "I can't move."

Damaris pulled on Zoe's arm, but she didn't budge. She whirled to Avriel.

"Do something!"

He stared at the oozing black substance in horror. "I . . . I don't know what to do. I've never seen this before."

Damaris grabbed Zoe's arm and pulled harder, trying to yank her forward, and Avriel did the same with her other arm, but though Zoe's upper body swayed, her legs stood as rigid as a statue. The black veins had reached her waist and were spreading to her lower arms.

"Damaris?" Zoe's voice had risen an octave.

"Let me try something," said Avriel. He wrapped his arms around Zoe from behind and gave a powerful thrust of his wings—but neither of them moved.

Damaris danced, side-stepping the inky lines, trying not to leave her sister behind but being forced backward toward the tunnel by the creeping black. *Mother, help me.* But she was no longer certain the Mother was any help at all. She didn't understand everything she'd missed while she'd been in captivity, but she did know one thing—not a single guardian here served the Mother. And now, neither did Calandra.

Maybe that's what this was—the Mother's punishment for their rebellion. But why was she being punished too?

She pressed her back against a wall with a small triquetra etched into the stone next to her shoulder, watching the darkness creep closer. There was nowhere else to go—the black cancer had already moved into the walls and down the smooth floor of the tunnel. Avriel squatted next to Zoe's feet and covered them with his hands, concentrating, but the black veins reached her neck and started working their way up her face.

This wasn't a punishment. This was an attack of the purest evil. Damaris didn't know much about Calandra's new god, but she knew he'd healed her from the Madness. And if the erelim served him—the bullish Rumiel and good dragons like Chaz—he must be worth calling on.

Elyon? If you're really as powerful as they say, please. Protect me and my sister.

The blackness reached her and she cringed, expecting to see it creep over her toes and to experience the same rigidness Zoe displayed . . . but instead, the darkness recoiled. She stared, then took a step, watching the blackness under her foot recede ever so slightly as though avoiding her touch, even while it filled in the place she'd just left.

She ran over to where Avriel was still working on her sister.

"Let me try."

Avriel moved aside and she squatted, placing her hands on Zoe's feet. Nothing happened. She looked up into her sister's frightened eyes in time to see the veins close over her head. Zoe couldn't even talk anymore.

"Why isn't it working?" she cried.

Just then, the web of black veins encasing her sister faded as though sinking through her skin, and the fear faded from her sister's face to be replaced by a blank, stupefied expression. It was a look Damaris had seen many times—on the face of *douloi*.

"Zoe?" Damaris stood, shaking her sister's shoulders with no response. "Zoe?" she cried again, nearly shrieking. "Elyon, I asked you to protect her!"

As though in response to an order Damaris couldn't hear, Zoe's hard gaze snapped to Damaris's face. She swung her arm toward Damaris's head, and it was only pure fighting reflex that allowed her to block the blow in time, as well as the next one from the other side.

"Zoe, what are you doing? It's me, Damaris!" Her voice broke in a sob.

Zoe swung her leg around to kick her, and she blocked it just in time.

"Zoe, stop! It's me! It's your sister!"

Zoe snatched Damaris's *deiktis* out of the scabbard on her back and swung it around in a smooth motion. She would have taken Damaris out at the knees if Avriel hadn't blocked the staff with the blade of his sword. He twisted the sword around to pin the end of the staff against the ground, with him and Zoe stooped toward each other.

Zoe glared at him, looking like she meant to launch another attack.

"May the peace of Elyon watch over you," he said, touching her wrist.

She cried out and drew back as though burned, dropping the staff. Glaring at first Avriel and then Damaris, she turned without a word and ran straight toward the empty Pool of Tears.

"Zoe, no!"

Damaris ran after her sister through the crowd of panicked guardians and onto the sandy beach that should have been covered with shallow water—trying to catch her, knowing she didn't have a chance. Helplessly, she watched Zoe launch herself over the edge of the steep drop in a perfect swan dive and disappear into the swirling cloud of darkness that filled the pit below.

Avriel ran to her side and dove over the edge, shooting downward—but as soon as he touched the dark cloud, he cried out, flapping his golden wings in retreat. He tried again and again, with the same result. Finally, he landed next to Damaris, a troubled look on his face.

She turned and pushed him hard in the chest. "What did you do? Why did she do that?"

He held up his hands placatingly. "I only gave her a blessing of protection. This darkness—it is something that is changing the nature of this plane. It seems averse to the presence of Elyon. I thought the blessing would repel it, but I think I was too late—the darkness had already infected her, and my words repelled her instead. Just like the dark cloud below repelled me."

Damaris sniffled and wiped away a tear. "Why did she look like that, like she didn't even know who I was? Like a . . . like a *doulos*?"

He looked over the edge once more. "I wish I knew." He met her gaze. "Only Elyon can help her now. Let us go find Captain Shriniel. Perhaps she'll know what to do."

Movement in the depths caught Damaris's eye, and she looked hopefully below. Maybe the water was coming back. Maybe her sister hadn't just hurled herself to her death.

But that wasn't water. A winged black dragon erupted from the cauldron of darkness below, roaring. It hurtled upward and spewed a plume of flame at the guardians still hovering over the empty grotto before they could even react. It was soon followed by another dragon, and then a flying lion, and a winged bull. Some of the hovering guardians also changed form, to beasts just as fearsome as the ones from the pit below. Soon, the entire cavern was a cacophony of clashing swords and flying, roaring erelim.

"The Grigori! They've escaped," exclaimed Avriel. "Come with me, quickly!"

He clutched Damaris's arm, tugging her away from the edge. She cast one last glance at the war zone the cavern had become, then fled after him into the mouth of the tunnel beyond.

"Run in here and hide," he shouted, but he didn't wait to see if she followed his instructions before he turned to join the melee.

Damaris fled along the dark tunnel, surrounded by a slight aura of light that illuminated her next few steps, until she'd run so far she was certain no one would follow her. Then she collapsed against the wall and slid to the floor, sobbing and panting simultaneously while the black taint flowed around her.

If the Grigori had escaped, something had gone wrong.

"You promised we'd all get out of here, Wonder Boy," she said, sniffling. "Don't make me regret believing in you."

The only response was the distant clash of swords.

OIL AND WATER

WATER RUSHED THROUGH CALANDRA'S GILLS and her heart thudded against her chest. She concentrated on the pile of blue stones in front of her, her hands curling and twisting in the air as she tried to coax the elements to obey her. On either side of her hovered Zale and Narcissa, each with one hand clamped on her shoulder. Even though one was pouring significantly more spirit through her than the other, she was grateful for every bit of help.

Using the elements, she scrabbled at a large taint-soaked stone at the top of the pile, but every time she thought she'd got a hold of it, her cord of power slipped off as though the stone were made of oil, not earth.

With a cry of frustration, she threw her hands down. "It's no use! Whatever this black stuff is, it's repelling my every effort."

"Maybe that's the problem," Zale said quietly. "You're doing it on your own effort again."

"No, I'm not." Calandra glared at him. "What do you think you and Narcissa are doing?"

"Not much of anything, apparently," Narcissa muttered, dropping her hand from Calandra's shoulder. She drifted near the wall and the black ink drew nearer to her, pooling behind her in the blue stone as though ready to pounce the moment she—

"Narcissa, look out!" Zale called, pointing to the wall.

Narcissa jerked away from the wall, glaring over her shoulder in suspicion and fear. The blackness seethed as though frustrated and uncertain where to go.

Zale scowled at the wall where she'd been hovering, swimming nearer to take a look at it.

"Careful," Calandra cautioned.

"I know," he said in a *what-kind-of-idiot-do-you-take-me-for* tone.

Calandra sighed and turned to her cousin. "You *are* helping, Narcissa. I could tell the difference when you joined the circle. It's me. I'm doing something wrong. Again." She pressed her palms into her eyes. Her head had begun to throb—not the deep, searing pain she used to feel when she'd held the *sklavia* bonds, but the surface-level stab of a tension headache, and she'd take that any day over the bondage she'd been under before.

Suddenly, she knew what was wrong. She looked at her companions. "It's the Matrix."

"The what?" Zale asked. He was still staring at the wall, moving his hand slowly back and forth in front of it and watching the effect.

"The Matrix of Creation. The Essence that runs through everything. Elyon. The Matrix is tainted, so the elements won't work right."

Narcissa frowned. "What does the Old Man have to do with it?"

"He's not an old man," Calandra said, exasperated. The memory of the warmth of the touch that had freed her mind from the bonds washed over her and she tingled from head to tail. "Elyon is the Creator of the cosmos, so I suppose he *is* old. And the erelim keep using the male pronoun, but I'm not sure he's an actual man. There's something about him that feels different than any person I've ever met. More complete." She frowned. She'd have to explore that later. "Anyway, it is his essence, his Spirit, that makes up the Matrix. And that's what Semyaza is trying to change."

Her heart sped up at the thought of Semyaza displacing the gentle Spirit who had freed her from her bonds. With the Pneuma running through the Matrix, the bonds of creation had been about order and discipline and freedom of choice, a force of love maintaining the balance. With Semyaza's vile intentions filling all things, the balance would tip toward manipulation and slavery of the worst kind. Could creation even survive it?

Zale glanced at her, his eyes as round as pearls. "That's not good. Maybe that's why this stuff acts so weird."

"What do you mean?"

"Check this out." Zale jerked his head at them to come over, his hand still held aloft in front of the wall.

Calandra and Narcissa swam nearer. Zale moved his hand back and forth an inch or so away from the smooth stone. As he moved, the blackness receded in front of his hand and flowed around it like water, closing behind it again.

"Huh," Calandra said, frowning at the effect.

"It's like it's scared to touch me." He touched the wall with his index finger.

"No!" Calandra reached out a hand, then froze.

Where his finger touched the wall, the blackness flowed away and left behind a little circle of pockmarked blue moonstone.

He grinned. "Spectacular."

"What in the name of . . ." She didn't know how to finish that sentence. Instead, she bent close to the wall, cautiously holding her own hand up to it and noticing the same repelling effect as Zale had created. She laid her hand on the stone and felt the tainted essence flow away from her, leaving clean, if still damaged, stone beneath her hand.

Narcissa narrowed her eyes. "Why does it do that to you, but it looks ready to suck me in and pull me down?"

Calandra glanced over, noticing how the darkness had pooled once more next to Narcissa, allowing for a faint reflection of the girl in the dark surface. Narcissa held her hand up to the wall and the taint concentrated beneath it. Calandra could almost feel it begging for her to touch it so it could soak into her, like she was a sponge to be filled. Narcissa curled her fingers so only her index finger was extended.

"Don't." Calandra held up a warning hand.

Narcissa glared at her, her finger extended toward the wall but not touching it. "As if I would. I was just testing. You know, the rest of us aren't as stupid as you think we are."

Calandra drew back, stung. "I never said you were stupid. I told you I think you're smart, remember?"

"No, but you act like it." Narcissa crossed her arms, arching a brow. "You always think you know what's best for everyone. And you're so talented, everyone listens to you as if you do. Even my own mother thought you were better than me," she said, her voice bitter. "Has it ever occurred to you that you're not the only person who has a clue how to run their life? That if you just give people a chance, they might even have some good ideas once in a while? Better ones than you, maybe?"

"I . . ." Calandra stopped, speechless. Narcissa's words pierced her soul like arrows, hurtful because they were true. Hadn't she sent Osaze away because she thought she knew best? And would Airlea have followed her into Hades, where they might now be stuck forever, if Calandra hadn't seemed so confident in her decisions? And Zale—she'd tried to force him to go against his heart and come after Mother before rescuing Damaris from the shedim, but if he had, Damaris might not have even survived.

That's not your story anymore. I've healed it.

The voice was a balm to Calandra's bleeding spirit. She closed her eyes and drew in a deep rush of water, the pain from Narcissa's words receding.

"Look, I just . . ." Calandra floundered for the right words. "I've made a lot of mistakes, okay? Some of them, there's no coming back from, and I'll keep paying that price forever." The thought of Osaze in pain and in chains clenched around her heart, and she cringed. If she ever got out of here, she'd find him. He still might not forgive her, but she couldn't leave him like that, not if she could do something about it. She owed him that much.

"But you're right," she continued. "I don't always think about what I say before I say it. Sometimes I let my fears affect how I treat other people. I don't think you're not smart enough, Narcissa." She met her cousin's eyes. "I fear *I'm* not. That I'm not smart enough, not powerful enough, not brave enough to do what I have to do."

She looked at Zale, who was watching her with compassion shining from his luminescent green eyes. When she glanced back at Narcissa, though, her cousin's eyes were hard and pale as a lump of ice.

"Like, right now, I'm not sure how to fix this," Calandra continued. "Tamiel, the woman who somehow deceived our entire race into a mistake that has affected us for millennia, is loose again, and so is Semyaza, the deceiver who helped her. They don't just want to take over our island, they want to rewrite the cosmos. I've only just discovered that most of what I've believed all my life has been lies, and even though I don't feel so alone anymore, I'm not quite sure where I fit into the reality of things."

She wrapped her arms around herself, averting her gaze to look at the pile of rubble that had defeated her. Lately, she'd faced defeat after defeat. Some saviour she'd turned out to be.

"My whole life, I've been compared to Nadia, as though my amazing talents would be enough to save us all. But she's stuck in a pool of Madwomen with her mind bound by a sea dragon, so her powers haven't done her much good, have they? And we're trapped in a mystical prison Zale and I are somehow supposed to heal, but if we do, our mother dies. If we don't, we unleash hell on the Underworld, and probably all the planes. And, if my intuition is correct, which—empathy be chained—it usually is, we're too late. Semyaza has already won, and the Grigori have already been freed."

With every passing second, more of the presences that had filled the Soulstone when they'd entered faded away—Tamiel's cell hadn't been the only one that was opened.

"But here we sit, doing nothing about it. Once again, the whole chained universe is counting on me, and I can't even figure out how to move a stupid pile of rock."

She slammed her hand against the wall in frustration, and the murk receded. As soon as she pulled her hand away, it jostled its way back through the softly glowing stone, dimming the light. She stared at the darkness, her chest heaving and shoulders slumped. Defeated, she turned back to her cousin and brother, her gaze on the floor.

"Maybe my fears are right. I'm not good enough. Elyon should have chosen someone else."

Zale's tail kept twitching. He looked like he wanted to speak but didn't know what to say.

Narcissa studied her for a long moment, then shook her head. "You're such an entitled idiot."

Calandra bristled. "Excuse me?"

"You were born with all that talent. Everyone likes you. You're the golden child. And you're still all, *Woe is me, I can't do anything right.* Pfft. Get over yourself." Narcissa gestured toward the pile of rock. "This black stuff in the rock is what's interfering with your powers, right? And it doesn't want you to touch it, right? If you could see past your own nose for a minute, you'd realize the answer is about an arm's-length in front of it."

Calandra stared at her cousin. Narcissa was the only one who ever talked to her like that, and her cousin had derided her so many times before, Calandra's first instinct was to write it off. But this time?

This time, Narcissa was right.

She stared at her hand and experimentally laid it against the wall once more. The taint shrank from it. Closing her eyes, she latched onto the wall, seeing the Matrix that imbued it in her mind's eye like a golden web of light coated with the taint like oil on water. She felt her way along the golden threads, pursuing the black essence, and it receded away from her. She pushed further, pouring spirit into the stone much as she'd done with the lightstones in the Pool of Tears—but it wasn't merely her own spirit that flowed outward through her touch. Just as it had in the Heartstone, the Pneuma flowed through her, energizing her and showing her the next turn she needed to take as she manoeuvred the layers of rock. When she found a fractured section of the rock, she attempted to renew the bonds and make it whole, but the repair seemed incomplete—as though she'd created a patch, not a true healing.

"Whoa," Zale said in awe next to her.

Calandra opened her eyes to see a large oval of the wall around her hand, from the floor to the ceiling, pulsing with a faint but clear blue light. The darkness boiled at its edges like a hoard of gnats waiting to invade again. She kept her hand on the wall and stared at the inky cloud, then turned to face her companions.

"I think I know how to get rid of the taint and repair the Soulstone in one go," she said. "But I'm going to need your help again. Just like Tamiel said—these bonds need all five elements in order to hold." She withdrew her hand and the darkness collapsed in on itself, simmering across the stone once more.

Zale brightened, then his brows drew together in a look of dread realization.

"But Mother . . ." he said, glancing at the ceiling as though he could see her through the stone walls.

Calandra's heart broke. She didn't know if Tamiel's orders to the Madwomen would hold firm now that Tamiel herself was out of prison, but she had no reason to suppose they wouldn't. She'd had so many questions for her mother, and so much lost time to make up for. Could she do this, even knowing her mother could die if she did? But what about all the people who might die if she didn't?

Zale drew a shuddering breath and shook his head. "No, you have to do this. She'd understand. If you can fix this, she'd want you to. And, hey, at least we know where her spirit will go, right? Well, a general idea, anyway." He frowned. "I hope she doesn't end up in that nasty swamp." He shivered, then looked at the floor. "But even if she does, mother would still put duty to her people above her own life. Just like you do." He gave Calandra a small smile. "You're a lot like her, you know."

Calandra nodded, her sinuses pricking, and threw her arms around her brother. At that tight squeeze, the vibration that always sang of his proximity reached a fever pitch, a harmonic resonance she felt to her very core. When she pulled away, the energy still sang through her.

"I can't fix this. *We* can."

They exchanged a look of understanding. She glanced at her cousin, who'd been watching the scene with a guarded expression, her disbelief flowing from her.

"You, too, Narcissa. We're all in this."

Narcissa shook her head. "You don't need me. I don't have powers. I don't have anything, not even a body. What can I do?"

Calandra offered her cousin her hand. "You came up with the solution. As you just proved, we're stronger together."

Narcissa looked at her hand, then glanced fearfully at the blackness and shook her head. "I'll watch."

Calandra glanced at the roiling darkness in the floor and walls, how it followed Narcissa's every move, and gave a nod. "As you wish. You already helped a great deal."

She gave Narcissa a grateful smile, which the girl returned with a doubtful frown. Sighing, Calandra turned to her brother.

"Are you ready?"

"Is a pasty the most delicious thing created by man?"

She stared at him blankly. "What's a pasty?"

He gave a wistful sigh, then chuckled and took her hand. "Never mind. The answer is yes."

She looked at their clasped hands, his power crackling through her.

"No rogue lightning bolts this time. I promise," he said.

Behind them, Narcissa gave a derisive snort.

Calandra chuckled. "I expected nothing less."

As one, they put their other hands on the stone wall.

93

THE CLEANSING

Zale's mind raced through the paths of spirit in the stone, what Calandra called the Matrix of Creation, alongside Calandra's line of spirit. When they'd tried to heal the Heartstone, he'd been bound by fear, worried he'd lose control and hurt someone or something, and he'd done both. But this time, he was no longer at the mercy of his volatile emotions. His powers were like a dolphin ready to play, and he was riding them, leaping forward in a boundless surge of joy. Calandra's spirit flowed like golden water around him, urging him on. In their wake, he and Calandra left the fractures in the moonstone restored and whole.

He laughed, every sense tingling with life. So *this* was what it felt like to be one with his powers. This was what Berian had been trying to get him to do on the *Atlanta*. His mind felt a hundred—no, a *thousand* times bigger. He could see beyond the Soulstone into the Well of Souls, which was inexplicably clear of water, and beyond that into the still-watery Leviathan enclosure. And there was his mother, untouched by taint, Releasing the rigid Madwomen from the web of darkness and lies while Airlea kept the Leviathan occupied. Bursts of golden light moved between her palm and their foreheads as she sang. They blinked and shuddered as though shivering off bounding cords. Already, Nadia had recovered enough to help her.

Wait. His mother was free? And she was healing the Mad guardians! But he'd barely had a chance to take note of the fact before his mind had expanded even further.

He shied away from the heat, despair, and torment in Tartarus below, where the golden Matrix faded to nothing. Instead, he soared upward and outward, above the river falling into the Leviathan enclosure like a waterfall around the well, rushing through a forest of black stone spires into an empty pit where the Pool of Tears should be, then pushed even farther upward into the chaos of clashing swords and teeth and wings in the crystal-filled cavern and the keep above it. Shriniel's guardians had been flagging, but when they saw the darkness clearing from the crystals and stone around them, they redoubled their attacks, slowly pushing the Grigori back down into the pit.

He found Damaris huddled in a tunnel, looking around in amazement as the darkness around her recoiled, swept away by Zale and Calandra's sizzling ecstasy. He found Tamiel in her human form standing next to a portstone covered in a dark cloth with Zoe beside her, a blank look on the siren's face. Tamiel pulled the cloth away and pressed Rumiel's ring against the stone, and the stone began to hum. She glanced over her shoulder uneasily, almost as though she could sense his and Calandra's presence. Then she stepped into the stone, and Zoe stepped in mechanically after her.

Still, Zale and Calandra pressed on, pursuing the infiltrating taint and furling it back on itself. Everywhere they explored, the darkness retreated until it had compacted into a small black ball in the core of the Soulstone. The ball pulsed with palpable malevolence, whispering and pulling at him, pushing at the bounds they imposed on it, but not getting any smaller. Something about it made him shiver.

"Zale," came Calandra's voice, both near and far away at the same time.

He opened his eyes and looked at his sister, keeping his hand planted on the wall of the passage inside the Soulstone. The moonstone around them shone clear and bright, no more writhing black taint and no more lingering damage—other than the pile of rubble that still kept them trapped.

Behind them, Narcissa came forward. "Is it done? It looks done. Did you do it?"

Calandra shook her head. "We have the darkness contained at the core of the Soulstone, but there's a problem."

Narcissa scowled. "What is it?"

Problem? The small black mass tugged at Zale, and when he closed his eyes, he could hear it whispering.

"The taint didn't start in the Soulstone," he said. "So if we want to make sure the darkness doesn't come back, we're going to have to go to the source."

Calandra nodded, keeping her hand firmly against the wall as she twisted to look at Narcissa. "The Soulstone is connected to the Heartstone, which is likely how you got here—Semyaza used the Heart of Chaos to pull you from your body, right?"

"I already told you that," Narcissa said.

"Well, he must have found a way to use it to manipulate the Heartstone and change the source of its power, which is where the taint came from. But that's also how you escaped the Heart of Chaos and found your way here. Fortunately, we carry the antidote in us."

"You do?"

Calandra looked at Zale.

"The Shield of Elyon," he said, the pieces coming together. "That's why the darkness recedes from us."

"Yes." She turned back to Narcissa. "To cleanse the Heartstone of the taint, we need to follow it back to the source and undo what Semyaza has done. And I think this is how we can get you home."

Narcissa looked at her in alarm.

"Narcissa, we're going to need to take you with us," Calandra added when the other girl didn't respond. "Our spirits must travel to the Heartstone to disengage the Heart of Chaos. My guess is we'll find Semyaza on the other side, directing the flow of energy throughout the cosmos and probably quite upset that his plan has just been reversed."

Narcissa shook her head, backing away. "No. I can't face him again. I won't." She turned away from them, her hands fisted at her sides. "Look what he's done to me. I hate that he's made me weak."

"You're not weak," Zale said.

The face of his enslaver looked at him, and he swallowed. *It wasn't her. She was just as trapped as I was.*

"In fact, you were so strong, he couldn't control you. I bet he got rid of you rather than having to keep fighting with you. Isn't that true?"

Emotions warred on Narcissa's face and in her heart, flowing from her in ripples of pain and fear. Other than with Calandra, he'd never felt such an open display without touching someone, not even with Damaris.

"Think of your baby," Calandra said gently. "Do you really want to leave it at Semyaza's mercy?"

Narcissa swallowed and shook her head. "No. But what if I go with you and the darkness finds me first? What do I do?"

"Do you love your baby?" Calandra asked.

"I . . . I suppose." Narcissa looked troubled. "Yes, I do."

Calandra smiled. "I thought so. The taint is the opposite of love. It is fear and hatred and power and pride. Love is service and selflessness and surrendering one's ego for another's benefit."

"It's what connects us all," Zale added, remembering a lesson Berian had taught him. "You. Me. The Soulstone. Your baby. It's what the universe was made from. Elyon made it from himself, and that's why the Essence that runs through the Matrix is love."

The vibration between him and Calandra zinged, and he smiled at her. He'd felt it from the start, but now that he and Calandra were working in harmony, it was electrifying, like the closeness between them had amplified its effect. He still didn't know what the resonance was, but he was starting to understand how it worked.

"And that's what Semyaza is changing," Calandra added. "He's trying to imprint the cosmos with his own essence instead of Elyon's. So if the darkness comes for you, remember why you're doing this, Narcissa. Remember your love for your baby. Choose love, not fear, and the darkness will flee from you too. Can you do that?"

Narcissa's nostrils flared. After a long moment, she nodded. "For my baby."

Calandra smiled. "Excellent. Now, since you're only here in spirit, not in body like we are, I'm pretty sure that once we take you into the Matrix, you'll basically hitch a ride until we find your body and leave you there."

"But what about him? I won't share it with him anymore."

Zale smirked. "We outnumber him. If he thought one undine fighting his control was a lot to handle, just wait until he encounters the three of us. We'll get rid of him for you."

A shadow crossed Calandra's face, and doubt pierced Zale. Did Calandra not think the three of them would be enough? His heart sped up. If she didn't believe, why was she trying to convince Narcissa? Or maybe she was trying to convince herself.

A loud rumble and movement made them turn to face the pile of rubble blocking the tunnel. The stones trembled and shook, and then the rock was torn away with a resounding crash, pulled outward by some invisible source. A cloud of silt billowed through the water, obstructing the view of the passage beyond.

Seconds later, the silt dropped to the floor all at once, revealing at least a dozen undine women in *ichthys* state bathed in the gentle blue light of the Soulstone. At their head was Nadia, looking healthy and beautiful, with clear, green eyes in her dark face, and—

"Mother!" Zale cried and almost let go of the wall.

Delphine smiled at them, and it was the most wonderful sight he'd ever seen.

"Can we help?" she said, indicating the women behind her, all of whom looked bright-eyed and whole.

Calandra beamed. "Definitely." She turned to Narcissa, all hesitation gone. "Make that the fifteen of us."

Narcissa took a shaky breath, staring at the newcomers, and then gave a slight nod and a smile. "Okay. It's worth a try."

94

REDEMPTION

WITH THE POWER OF THE circle of undines pouring spirit into them, Calandra and Zale closed their eyes, and Calandra once more found herself facing the small black mass at the centre of the Soulstone. Together, she and Zale pressed it back toward its source, wedging it along the thick line of spirit that connected the Soulstone and the Heartstone. It was like forcing water to roll in reverse along the Light River Aqueduct. But as soon as they got through the narrow channel that took their spirits to the Ground, her awareness exploded along lines of oil-slicked spirit that were still expanding outward.

Tethered by the Heartstone, Calandra's mind raced toward the outer edges of the swelling cloud of darkness, travelling through parts of her island she'd never visited before, with Zale's spirit beside her the whole way. When she'd been attuned to the Matrix of Creation in the past, it had never been like this—this giddy whirl of sensation and sound and colour. She felt like a bird or a leaf on a joyful summer breeze as she and Zale routed the taint from every corner of their island, right out to the barrier.

The barrier! It had been raised! It, too, needed to be cleansed, but the taint had been contained within its bounds. The more they cleansed, the harder the darkness fought. The effort was taking its toll, but every time she flagged, an extra boost of energy flowed into her from the circle of panaceas and sirens who anchored them and buoyed them up. Narcissa's presence hovered, towed along in her and Zale's wake.

Finally, they'd gone beyond the taint. She and Zale began to contract, working in harmony without words. They pressed inward, purifying the Matrix with the Pneuma's power until they had contained the darkness inside the Mother's Heart chamber and the handful of unmoving people inside, then in the Heartstone.

But the Heartstone was not the centre of the web, nor was the small red gem dangling above it from which the darkness poured. Calandra could see the path clearly now—through the gem, along a connecting line of spirit that led to the source of the evil.

Semyaza.

With Narcissa's face, he looked frantically at the women in the Mother's Heart chamber who had suddenly recovered their wits, then turned to the handsome blond man lying near him who was struggling to sit up despite his bound hands. Another man stood nearby, a tall man with ivory skin and black hair and eyes. As soon as he saw what was happening in the tower, he disappeared into thin air just before every lightstone in the Observation Chamber came on at once.

"What is happening? Why isn't it working?" Semyaza shouted. He banged Narcissa's fists on the window, one greasy hand leaving its shape behind in oily black smears.

Calandra and Zale, everywhere and nowhere, looked down on him. Semyaza seemed so small and unimportant, so pitiful in his need to control, to rebel. But at the same time, great sorrow pierced her, for she knew it was his choice, and she couldn't unmake it for him.

Still, his choices were hurting others. And she had to stop it.

You've taken what does not belong to you, Semyaza.

Semyaza spun around, looking for the source of the voice.

"Uriel? Is that you? Michael? Samael? Show yourself!"

At first, Calandra didn't think she could. But with the Matrix glimmering in her awareness, she realized light was as easy to manipulate as anything else. With a little concentration, she focused her awareness into a figure standing in the Observation Chamber near the curved glass wall. She looked at her hands, which were blurred at the edges and too bright—not quite the same as if she were there in the flesh, but still a visible presence.

So this is how Tamiel did it.

"It's me, Damon. Here to mete our justice for your actions."

Semyaza whirled. When he saw her, his eyes narrowed. "Calandra, you're supposed to be dead. How did you get here?"

"You showed me the way. And now it's time for you to return to where you belong."

To Calandra's senses, Narcissa's form writhed with the taint. It boiled out of her skin and roiled through her core until she seemed made of restless shadow. Even the baby was saturated with it. Calandra could sense Zale with her and the flowing spirit of the healer circle in the Soulstone, helping her contain the darkness within Narcissa's body. But to expunge it completely would mean to exorcise the demon who channelled it, and that part was less easy. Even if they succeeded in rousting him from his position, he could just as easily find a new host.

She needed to get him back to the Soulstone. Only there could he be contained and out of harm's way. But how? She glanced at the Heartstone and the red jewel hanging above it. Now cleansed of the shadowy taint, it was a vessel waiting to be filled with spirit. And it gave her an idea.

Narcissa, wait in the Heart of Chaos. She hoped the thought would be heard and that her cousin would have the necessary control to obey.

The door behind Semyaza opened and Judith charged in, a diving knife in her upraised hand and her face twisted in battle fury.

"Judy, no!" Matthew shouted, but not soon enough to stop the knife from sliding between Narcissa's ribs.

Judith saw Calandra and stopped, staring. "Calandra? How?"

Semyaza stared at Judith, open-mouthed, then stumbled. Fire flared around him and guttered, leaving scorch marks on the table and floor. He sank to his knees, and the taint loosened from the flesh that contained it, shadowy tentacles flailing.

Zale, we need to trap him, now.

Rushing forward, she knelt by Narcissa's form as it sank to the ground and placed her finger on her cousin's forehead, sensing Zale adding his power to hers. The taint—and Semyaza's spirit—thrashed against the constraints she and Zale were placing on it, squirming to break free.

"Judith, I need the Heart of Chaos," Calandra said. At Judith's blank look, she added, "The red jewel hanging above the Heartstone. Be careful not to touch it."

Judith nodded, then went to the commstone on the wall and relayed Calandra's instructions to Meg. Instinctively, Calandra began humming sirensong, which didn't stupefy the spirit, but it did reduce his flailing. Maybe that's what it had been meant for all along—not human men, but rebellious spirits.

Semyaza looked up at her with an expression twisted in pain, Narcissa's eyes flashing gold. "You know I won't die, don't you?" he said, grinning. "You've only killed a piece of flesh. I go on. I always go on."

"And I can think of no one less deserving," Calandra said, scorn in her voice. "I wonder how many chances Elyon gave you to redeem yourself before he condemned you to an eternity in the Soulstone."

Semyaza's smile faltered, and blood ran out of the side of Narcissa's mouth.

"It wasn't his right to decide," he sneered, wincing at the effort.

Meg rushed into the room, holding the Heart of Chaos by its chain. "Here it is."

"Lay it on her forehead," Calandra instructed.

Meg knelt next to Narcissa's body and did as she was told. Narcissa's spirit waited anxiously in the stone. Good. Now for the tricky part.

With a prayer for success, Calandra concentrated her awareness on the stone and on Semyaza, which, to those around her, looked like laying hands on Narcissa's forehead, covering the Heart of Chaos.

Zale, now!

She and Zale started at Narcissa's toes and pushed back the taint, forcing it upward. Calandra thrilled at the power of the Pneuma flowing through her—it felt so natural, so right. She'd never known using the elements could feel like this.

Narcissa's body began to seize—her back arched and her limbs thrashed as Semyaza fought his expulsion. Just as they funnelled the last of the taint into the Heart of Chaos, Narcissa slipped from the stone back into her body. When she opened her eyes, they were their normal icy green—no hint of gold remained.

"Now lift the stone," Calandra told Meg. "Carefully. Don't let it touch anything. Semyaza is contained within it, but he's good at escaping prisons. Wait over there, please."

Meg nodded, standing and holding the stone in front of her by its chain as she went to stand near Judith, who had cut Matthew's bonds and helped him to his feet.

Steward Letitia rushed into the room, two sirens on her heels—Tanni's old pod leader Rhapsodist Danai kor'Panora and Calliope kor'Renata. When they saw what was happening, they stopped short.

"Your highness!" Letitia said to Calandra, smoothing her skirts into place. "You're back. I never gave up hope."

Danai smiled. "Welcome home, your highness."

"One of us is more *back* than the other," Calandra said with a dry glance at her cousin. "My stay is only temporary, but you'll find Narcissa should be more like her old self." She hoped the softer, gentler Narcissa she'd seen in the Soulstone wouldn't disappear now that her cousin was in control of her body again.

"Good heavens, she needs a healer," said Letitia, her gaze sweeping over Narcissa. She looked at Calandra but gave a curt nod of dismissal, obviously deciding she wasn't substantial enough to be effective. Without another word, Letitia swept out of the room.

"Where's Hebe?" Danai demanded of Judith, giving Matthew a suspicious glare.

"Hebe?" Narcissa said, wincing. "What's happened to her?"

Judith shook her head. "She is safe." She met the rhapsodist's eye. "Trust me, she is safer *now*."

Danai gave a brief nod, her expression clouded, but she said nothing more.

"Good." Narcissa cringed, straining to look down at her injury. Her hands were clean, but one palm had a pink gash across it. Bright red blood soaked the side of her gown. "It hurts so much."

"Ssh, I know." Calandra placed her hands on Narcissa's side. The wound went deep.

Matthew looked down at Judith, pained confusion on his face.

"Do not look at me like that," Judith said, looking shaken. "I thought Narcissa was dead, that the monster was all that was left . . ."

"Not so far from the truth," Narcissa said with a strained, wheezing voice.

"Is the baby okay?" Matthew asked, attracting an unreadable glance from Judith.

Narcissa gripped Calandra's arm, her eyes wild with worry.

"The baby's fine," Calandra said.

Narcissa relaxed again.

Calandra laid her hand on her cousin's clammy forehead. "I'm going to try healing you, okay?"

Narcissa searched her eyes, then nodded.

Calandra delved the wound, determining the extent of the damage. Then she began to repair the tissues. After her recent joyride through the cosmos, the process seemed interminably slow. *Zale, this would go faster with your help.*

Her brother's squatting figure materialized on Narcissa's other side. Calandra started in surprise—she hadn't expected that, only a little spiritual boost.

He grinned, his face glowing softly, even in the bright room. "Can't let you have all the fun."

"This is what you call fun, is it?" Calandra shook her head, thinking of his question to her earlier. "In that case, I do this kind of thing all the time."

"You do?" He gave her an incredulous look.

Calandra glanced at the others in the room—Judith and Matthew with their arms around each other, Meg holding out the Heart of Chaos as though it might strike at her, the other three stone healers filing into the room and waiting anxiously by the door, the sirens waiting in expectant shock, Narcissa on the floor in a pool of her own blood, and Zale's semi-transparent form that was merely a projection from the Soulstone in Hades like her own.

"Okay, not *this*. But . . . you know what I mean."

"Zale?" choked out Calliope, her dark green eyes bulging.

Zale glanced over his shoulder. "Oh, hey, Singer kor'Renata." He gave her a lopsided grin. "Have you missed me?"

Calliope smirked and crossed her arms. "Depends how you define *miss*. I don't miss babysitting you every minute of the day . . . but I kind of miss pulling your fine backside out of bed." She arched her brow, and Zale's face flushed bright red. "I'm glad to see you're all right."

Zale gave an embarrassed chuckle and looked back at his sister, his face still pink.

"Do you two mind?" Narcissa said, a little of her old fire back in her tone despite the strain.

"Sorry," Zale said.

Calandra and Zale laid their hands on Narcissa's ribcage. As one, they manipulated the elements to repair the damaged tissue in Narcissa's side and lungs, and then Calandra delved the rest of her. Her body was ravaged beyond anything Calandra had ever seen—Semyaza had been using it hard, but the baby's heartbeat was steady and it seemed healthy. They did what else they could to heal Narcissa's drained systems.

"You're going to be fine," she said to Narcissa. "It's time to sleep now."

Calandra put a palm to Narcissa's forehead and put her into a deep sleep, but she almost didn't need to bother—Narcissa's eyes were already drooping closed in exhaustion.

She stood and stepped away from her cousin, who looked more peaceful than Calandra had ever seen her.

"She'll need to rest for some time. Someone should put her to bed."

Judith nodded. "I'll go find some servants to help. Hopefully they do not arrest me on sight."

"No, you stay," Healer Amaltheia said. She turned to Singer kor'Renata.

"Go fetch a litter. Tell no one what you've seen here."

The woman gave a crisp salute and exited the room.

Fatigue from projecting herself dragged on Calandra. "We have to get back to our bodies."

"And where are you?" Judith asked.

"In the Underworld," said Zale casually. "It's great. I think it's the next big tourist hot spot. Everyone's going to come here." He blinked, then broke into laughter. "Actually, most people *do* come here eventually."

Calandra rolled her eyes at him. He shrugged but reined in his mirth.

Nelly, who was standing near the door, stepped forward, her green eyes sharp. "Did you find Delphine?"

"We did." Calandra frowned. A lot of good that did when she, Zale, and all the others were still trapped in Hades without a key to return. "The key!"

Calandra whirled, searching through Narcissa's tangled hair for what she thought she'd seen there. Yes, there it was! The quaternaria pendant lay among Narcissa's flaxen tresses attached to a hair chain. The amethyst bore the same elemental signature as the giant sprays of crystal in the Cavern of Tears—but full of life and energy instead of dull and lifeless.

"Your highness?" Meg's tone was cautiously hopeful. "Do you intend to claim the quaternaria for your own?"

Calandra glanced at her sleeping cousin, the Girl Who Would be Queen, and wished she knew Narcissa had changed to the point she could be a good leader for their people. But the person Narcissa would become now remained to be seen.

And, now that Calandra had managed to trap Semyaza and correct her mistake, she finally felt worthy of the confidence not only Adonia had had in her when the queen had named her heir, but that her mother, brother, and everyone else had displayed in her before she and Zale went into the Soulstone. If they all saw her as someone capable of being a good leader, maybe they were right.

"If the council wills it, I will accept," Calandra said, to palpable relief from the others in the room. "But that is not why I need the quaternaria now. It is the key that unlocks the passage for us to return from beyond the veil. Without it, my companions and I will be trapped in Hades forever."

Meg's eyes widened. "But can you take it with you? You look like a ghost."

Calandra glanced down at herself, then back at the stone healer. "I have to try."

Judith pulled herself from Matthew's arms and stooped to work the quaternaria loose from Narcissa's hair. Then she stood and held it out on her extended palm.

Calandra went over and stared at the key. She hoped this worked. Laying her hand on top of it, she picked it up by the chain, and murmurs and gasps filled the air. Looking at it through her Matrix-enhanced vision, she could see the key was as much spirit as matter, like Rumiel's ring or the Heart of Chaos.

Healer Evadne rushed into the room with Steward Letitia at her heels, and behind her huffed the short, apple-shaped Councillor Larissa kor'Damiani. Letitia must have forewarned the healer about what to expect, for Evadne gave the briefest of salutes and greetings to Calandra as she hurried over to the figure on the floor and laid her hands on Narcissa. Councillor kor'Damiani, however, stopped just inside the door, bewilderment on her round face.

"She's been healed already," Evadne said in surprise, then looked up at Calandra. "Miracle upon miracle."

Letitia glanced through the window at the brilliant Heartstone, then turned to the stone healers. "I'd originally been coming here to investigate why lightstones and ancient devices throughout the palace were powering on, even those long since disconnected from the source. And, praise the Almighty, the Heartstone is afire!" She crossed herself in a symbol Calandra had seen her make a few times before, though she had no idea what it meant. "I wonder if the barrier has also been restored."

"Yep," said Zale. "Just in time, too. There's an armada of ships about half a day away, and they look like they're coming right for you."

His pronouncement was met with a mixture of cheers and cries of alarm.

Nelly drew a deep, relieved breath. "We knew about the ships. Praise the Mother the barrier is up. One less thing to worry about."

Councillor kor'Damiani's gaze snapped to Nelly's face with a cold look of recognition. The antiques merchant shifted uncomfortably, but neither said anything.

"The *despoina* has had the ships under surveillance for some time, but . . ." Danai glanced down at the sleeping princess. "Well, I don't know what happened between her, um, highness and the *despoina*, exactly. All I know is my pod and several others were secretly assigned to deflect the ships, but there are just too many, and we accomplished little more than creating confusion among them. My podmates will be glad to hear the danger has passed. Especially with the current chaos on the island."

"What chaos?" Calandra asked.

"The Freemen," Judith said. "That is why we thought you and Narcissa were both dead. All of your bonds were released. The sirens have their hands full trying to restore order."

Of course. Calandra would have assumed the same thing in their position.

The councillor turned to address the group of stone healers with a wide smile that became only slightly strained when her gaze passed over Nelly. Calandra hoped whatever lay between them would not become a problem. They had bigger issues to deal with.

"Well. It appears Sirenia owes you a debt of gratitude, healers. You have restored my hope for our island, because, even during darkest times, there are those who would risk their lives to do what is right and bring light to us all." She gave a deep salute, which the stone healers returned with pleased smiles—except Nelly, who only seemed glad of a chance to break eye contact with the archon. Then Councillor kor'Damiani looked at Calandra. "Belief inspires belief." Turning to Matthew, she gave him a deep salute, holding her fingers to her bowed forehead for a long moment. "I welcome you to the Opal Palace at last, Kyrios Matthew bet'Elizabeth. I heard about your mother and what you tried to do for her, and I'm sorry for your loss. May her memory and self-sacrificial love live on in you."

Matthew swallowed fiercely, returning the salute. "Thank you, archon."

Danai watched the exchange with a guarded expression. Calandra knew her to be a dutiful woman, and her inner battle seeped through her emotional shield. It would take some time before the siren corps embraced the revolution fully.

"Rhapsodist kor'Panora," she said, "where is Despoina Cleo?"

Danai's face tightened. "No one knows. It is feared she is dead."

Calandra gave a soft gasp. "How?"

"No one knows that either," Danai said, "but Princess Narcissa condemned her as a traitor after she disappeared."

Calandra digested this, then straightened. "I have obviously missed a great deal, but know two things." She looked around the room, meeting each person's eyes in turn. "For the last several weeks, Princess Narcissa has been under the influence of an evil dragon named Semyaza, sometimes known as Damon, and she may not have been responsible for any action she appeared to take."

Judith and Meg looked unsurprised, but many in the room frowned at this, especially Nelly. Danai gave a perfunctory nod.

"Second," Calandra continued, "Despoina Cleo kor'Andromachi is no traitor. She has ever served the throne loyally, and I hereby nullify any claims Semyaza has made about her or her character. She is still Mistress of Sirens and should be treated as such."

The relief was plain on Danai's face. "Yes, your highness. I—"

"I'm not finished."

Chastened, Danai snapped to attention.

Calandra stood directly in front of her. "I ask that from now on, the siren corps treats all men with the same respect we accord to our fellow women. Men are no longer to be Redeemed, nor treated as dangerous criminals to be subdued. While there are certain to be many confused, frightened men on the island, approach them with the mercy and kindness you would want extended to you if you were suddenly trapped in an unfamiliar setting among hostiles, for that is how they will see you. While they may react with violence to protect themselves, that does not make them inherently violent. The responsibility for redeeming the mistakes of the past is on those of us in positions of power, and the time to do that is now."

The rhapsodist stiffened, then saluted. "I will pass your message to the Archpipers."

That was the most Calandra could ask of a mere rhapsodist, she supposed. Sighing, she turned to the archon. "As for dealing with the new Freemen or the Releasing of men currently under the *sklavia* bond, I ask that the council consults with the archons of the Free Will Society to discuss a plan moving forward."

Nelly shifted her weight, but Councillor kor'Damiani's face broke into an excited grin. She rubbed her tiny plump hands together.

"That sounds like a challenge if I've ever heard one, and I like a good challenge. I'll do what I can to get them to agree." She glanced around at the rebels in the room. "Let's hope their gratitude for the restored Heartstone is greater than their discomfort with change. But you should know, your highness, that many of them have begun to favour Narcissa's claim to the throne. She sounded Mad to me, so I was not one of them." She hesitated, dropping her gaze. "Though I will say that your recent behaviour has also been somewhat . . . concerning."

Calandra thought guiltily of the earthquake and destruction of the palace. "I assure you, that will no longer be a problem. I have been healed of my Madness, and it will not return."

The others looked at her in wonder.

"How?" Judith asked, looking between Calandra and Zale.

Zale chuckled. "You people have a *lot* to learn." His face flushed. "So do I, I suppose."

Calandra smiled affectionately at him, shaking her head. "I'll explain when I return," she said to the others.

Larissa kor'Damiani glanced at the Heartstone, then around the room. "Well, now that I know about this Semyaza character, that explains a lot, even if the idea of a dragon controlling the princess seems a bit Mad too." She cleared her throat. "I may not be able to convince the council of what you've said, but I'll do my best."

"There are perilous waters ahead," Judith murmured.

"Indeed." Calandra gave a small smile. "But I have faith my people will navigate them with wisdom and grace."

Nelly snorted, and Erigone, who stood nearby, gave her a dirty look. Councillor kor'Damiani cast an annoyed glance in Nelly's direction.

Calandra exchanged glances with Judith and Zale. Perhaps Calandra was giving her people too much credit. But she had to start somewhere.

"There is more I must tell you." The overwhelming load of information Calandra had absorbed while cleansing the island was already fading from her memory. "Don't let down your guard. Semyaza has many allies here, not all of whom can be seen with the eyes."

She glanced at Narcissa's sleeping form. Her cousin had been along for the ride while she and Zale had cleansed their entire island. There was no telling what she would remember when she woke up.

"Narcissa probably knows the location of the base."

"I am fairly certain she has known it for a while," said Judith. "Or Semyaza has, I suppose. Also, she killed Adonia and Thea. Or maybe Semyaza did." Judith frowned. "How can we know what she is actually responsible for now?"

"She did what?" Calandra's heart squeezed. She wanted to press further, but she'd nearly lost her grip on the material plane. She turned to Councillor kor'Damiani. "Look into the matter. And keep her under guard for now, just in case."

"Yes, your highness." The archon gave a crisp nod.

"Calandra?" Zale said. "I'm tired."

She nodded. "We must go."

First Judith, then Meg, then all the others in the room gave a deep salute to her and Zale.

"May the Mother smile on your journey and grant you a safe return," the archon said.

"Not the Mother," Zale broke in. "Please not her."

Judith frowned. "What does he mean?"

Calandra chuckled. "Another thing I'll have to explain when I get back. For now, see what you can find on the Atlantis datastones about Elyon. That should lead you to some answers."

She could feel herself fading, her energy gone, even with the continued inpouring from the others in the circle. She went over to Meg and took the gold chain from her hand. Just like the quaternaria, the necklace moved into the flow of spirit as though that were its native realm.

The moment she touched the chain, Semyaza's voice rang in her head—not Narcissa's venomous snarl, but the angry voice she'd known as Damon, the spirit who'd haunted her dreams for so long.

"You're going to be sorry you ever defied me, you little witch! I am immortal, and what are you? A little girl too bound up in her own problems to see what's been right under her nose all along. You're pathetic and weak. I know you, Calandra. I know you better than you know yourself. And you won't get away with this."

He continued on in an unbroken litany of insults, which she ignored.

"Wait," Judith said, and Calandra turned. "You should know Osaze and Urbi have returned. They are at the safe house."

A jolt crackled through Calandra, and she nearly dropped the heartstone. "He's . . . he's safe? He's here?" Joy surged through her, tasting of oranges and honeycakes and a night under the Milky Way.

"Should I give him a message from you?" Judith asked.

Calandra hesitated. He'd come back! How? Why? Had he forgiven her after all? Hope coursed through her veins. "Tell him . . . tell him I'm sorry. And tell him I'll see him soon."

Judith smiled. "I will." She looked up at Matthew, hope on her face. "We both will."

When Calandra turned to Zale to signal her readiness, his image had become almost completely transparent, and she could feel her own energy flagging. But as she faded back to the spiritual plane, an angular man with black eyes and hair and pale skin appeared in front of her.

"I'll take that." He snatched the Heart of Chaos from her hand and disappeared.

"No!" she cried, her voice sounding as though it were coming to her from a distance.

The faces of those in the Observation Chamber reflected the same shock and horror she felt, but it was too late. She was being pulled back to the Soulstone at the speed of thought.

She woke up underwater in the blue passageway next to Zale and surrounded by a small crowd of their history's most powerful healers and sirens. Around her, the Soulstone pulsed clean and whole. The angry, restless presences filling the stone to bursting told her its escaped inmates were once more ensconced in their cells. All except Tamiel, whose vacant cell stared at her like a black cave from the end of the passage.

"Is it done? Did you succeed?" Delphine asked hopefully.

Slowly, she and Zale turned to face their mother.

"Well," said Zale, rubbing the back of his neck, "Narcissa's been healed, and the Soulstone and Heartstone have been healed, and the taint has been cleansed, but . . ." He trailed off, looking sideways at his sister in pity.

"And the dragon?" asked Nadia. "Semyaza?"

Calandra's chest was a cavern as hollow as the Chamber of Tears. "I failed. Again."

95

THE CHOICE

ZALE SPLASHED OUT OF THE Pool of Tears next to his sister and mother, searching out the girl with the seafoam-green eyes. He needed to know Damaris was all right. Once Nadia had closed the water gate—controlled by an unobtrusive lever near the bottom of the well, which she'd opened at Tamiel's behest—the reservoir had soon refilled, allowing the undines to resurface. This time, not only Delphine, but the other women who'd guarded the well for so long came with them. Behind Zale, Nadia and the other healed undine women hesitantly broke surface and made their way out of the pool as he scanned the rocky beach, absently noting the haphazard situation of the lightrods and stones. *Where's Damaris?*

"Zale!"

Damaris scrambled to her feet from where she'd been sitting next to one of Shriniel's troops, a man who appeared made of gold, and raced toward the water, meeting Zale as he sloshed out of the shallows. She threw her arms around his neck and squeezed. He froze, uncertain how to react, then hesitantly put his arms around her and held her close, nestling his head against her soft hair.

"Glad you made it, Wonder Boy," she said into his ear.

"I had no choice. Orders."

She giggled, and he pulled back to stare into her eyes.

"You have no idea how glad I am to see you again."

Without warning, Damaris grabbed his head in her hands, pulled him toward her, and planted a kiss on his lips. This time, he didn't stand there like a stump. Wrapping his arms around her slender waist, he leaned into the kiss and her salty scent, feeling her emotions flow through every inch

790

of his body, his mental door wide open. For several long breaths, they were the only two beings in all the cosmos that mattered, standing on a green terrace surrounded by pink bougainvillea and smiled on by a cloudless sapphire blue sky. It was the most perfect moment Zale had experienced in a long time.

But a thread of sadness mixed with the affection and desire flowing through her touch. He pulled away, smoothing a wayward sandy-coloured curl from her cheek. "What's wrong?"

A tear brimmed in the corner of her eye. "It's Zoe. She's gone. I think she might be dead."

A vague memory of seeing the blank-faced siren follow Tamiel through a portstone tickled his brain. "No, she isn't."

Damaris's eyes filled with hope. "How do you know?"

How to explain that? "Um, it's a long story. Shall we sit?"

She nodded, and he took her hand to lead her to a quiet spot at the edge of the cavern—but then he noticed the exhausted and wounded erelim that stood or lay in various poses around the cavern. They needed healing.

He looked at Damaris, his desire to help the fallen warring with his desire to allay Damaris's fears.

"Go," she said, giving him a shove. "You and I can catch up later."

He grinned at her and put on his best Cornish lilt. "You bet we will, me little Oyster."

She glared at him. "Oyster? What under the seven seas does that refer to?"

"You know—hard and prickly on the outside, but a soft inside that hides a treasure of great price. Hey!"

Her second shove was full of righteous indignation. "Don't ever call me that again, Icarus."

"So you can call me Icarus, but I can't call you Oyster?"

She leaned toward him, narrowing her eyes. "Not if you like those fine pearly teeth of yours."

She turned to walk away, but amusement slipped through her shield in her wake.

Zale chuckled. "So I'll keep working on it then," he called after her. "What do you think of Sea Urchin?"

"No!"

"Snapping Turtle?"

"Too bad," she called over her shoulder. "You had such a nice smile."

Chuckling, he turned to see whom he could help first, the exhaustion he'd felt in the Soulstone all but gone. He stooped to assist the winged golden man, who was examining a red-robed guardian with a deep gash across her forearm. As he healed the fallen warrior, he smiled.

Damaris liked him, and he liked her. His mother forgave him. And he and his sister were finally getting along. For the first time, he didn't feel like a freak and a monster. Not only could he control his powers, he could even use them for good. And he didn't have to hide them ever again.

Maybe being an undine wouldn't be so bad after all, once everyone stopped doing that whole mind-melting thing. No, his people weren't perfect, and Sirenia still didn't feel much like home . . . but maybe it would someday. The closest thing he'd felt to peace since he was a small boy pooled in his chest.

The feeling was almost enough to make him forget the pain of being betrayed by Eric, Josefine, and Gio.

Almost.

*

CALANDRA watched Zale and Damaris's happy reunion in envy. For a brief, delirious moment, she'd hoped she would soon have a similar reunion with Osaze—their joy somewhat tempered by the bridges they would need to repair, but a reunion nevertheless. But now?

How could she return to Sirenia and pretend to be worthy of leading her people, knowing she'd allowed their oldest enemy to once more slip through her fingers right at the moment of victory?

Still, the evidence that her people were changing brought her some small comfort. Her fight, her losses, they hadn't been for nothing. The knowledge would make her next decision easier to bear.

Rumiel and Chaz stood waiting on the shoreline. Chaz bore his typical broad grin, but Rumiel only had eyes for Delphine. With several strong thrusts of his wings, he closed the distance between them and alighted in front of her. She beamed up at him, looking for all the world like she wanted to envelop him in her arms, but holding back. Calandra couldn't hear what they said, but she didn't need to be an empath to understand the emotions passing between them. She turned away to give them the privacy the moment seemed to demand—and to avoid one more reminder of what she'd soon be giving up forever.

Chaz was watching them, too, a troubled expression on his face.

"What's the matter?" Calandra asked. "Haven't you seen two people in love before?"

Chaz turned to her, his eyebrows still furrowed. "Yes, and, in this case, that's the problem. My kind have been given many wonderful gifts, but there are some things that have been withheld from us. Falling in love is one of them. It's forbidden."

Calandra laughed, then caught sight of Chazdiel's serious expression. "Oh, you were serious?"

He sighed, rubbing his chin. "While we can love deeply, we lack the ability to create the kind of love bonds with a single other person that Elyon designed only mortals to have. For the most part, the taboo is a technicality. It's been thousands of years since I've seen anyone, but especially a lamassu, cross the line." He shook his head. "Rumiel should know better."

What would the consequences for breaching such a line be? And who had drawn it in the first place? Surely not Elyon, whose Spirit was love personified. But who else would have the authority? Then again, there was a great deal about the erelim culture she didn't know. She fidgeted with her wet braid. She had her own revolution to deal with—she'd have to let the erelim worry about their own.

Calandra looked back at her mother and the tall cherub, who were having a quiet conversation, their hands clasped between them. When they stepped apart from each other, Rumiel bore a grave expression, and Delphine was wiping moisture from the corner of her eyes. Calandra frowned, her heart aching for her mother. She didn't know much about Delphine's life since she'd fled Sirenia, but she could guess that moments of happiness had been few and far between, especially for the last several years. It didn't seem fair.

Rumiel approached Calandra and gave her the chest-thumping salute of the guardians. "Your highness, I must take my leave of you now. Delphine tells me Tamiel has taken the Key of Elyon, but that you have retrieved the quaternaria and will be able to make your own way home. Now that I have seen my task of rescuing your family from the Underworld through, there is something I must do."

"Of course." Calandra bit her lip, her failure pressing her heart into her toes. "Listen, about the Heart of Chaos—"

Rumiel held up a hand to stop her. "You are not responsible for what happened to it, nor for the escape of Tamiel and Semyaza. You did the best you could do, and that is enough. You must believe that."

Must I?

But she only nodded, keeping her doubts to herself. On impulse, Calandra raised herself on tiptoes and threw her arms around Rumiel's broad neck.

"Thank you, Rumiel, for all you have done for my family. May Elyon's grace shine upon you as you face what comes next." *May Elyon's grace shine upon you.* She'd never heard the saying before, but it came naturally to her lips, and she smiled to herself. She liked the idea of a Creator who had shining grace, who didn't constantly need appeasement for what she'd done wrong.

Rumiel bowed his head, his expression grave. "Thank you. And the same to you, your highness."

He glanced at Zale, who appeared to be comforting Damaris in the shallows of the pool. Perhaps he had just told her where he'd seen Zoe go while they were cleansing the taint.

"Give my regards to Master Teague, in case I don't see him again," Rumiel added. "I don't think he'd care to be interrupted right now."

Calandra peered at the cherub in concern. Rumiel was nervous, but what would he have to be anxious about? What was this task he had to do? "Of course."

The cherub stepped back, fishing a chain from beneath the neckline of his robe. Lifting the small silver nested rings suspended from it to his face, he gave a sharp blow and disappeared. She got the distinct impression he was going to face his executioner—or perhaps the consequences for his mistake of loving the wrong person.

Well, she understood what it was like to make a difficult decision.

Teetering with exhaustion and pushing the threatening despair aside, Calandra turned to face the undine women who were standing awkwardly at the edge of the shore. While the women had been restored to full health—their hair shiny and full and their skin rejuvenated and whole—their clothes were torn and ragged, and some had almost none at all. Several of the winged guardians had lent the women their jackets, and Airlea stood behind one of the women, detangling her hair with her own comb. Already, some of the healed undines were moving among the wounded erelim, healing the fallen. Calandra turned to survey the battlefield. She should help too. It was the least she could do after letting the two dragons who most endangered the cosmos slip through her fingers.

But before she'd taken a step, Delphine came to stand next to her, watching the scene. "It's truly a miracle, isn't it?"

Calandra glanced at her mother. "There have been a lot of miracles recently."

Delphine's emerald-green eyes shone softly in the dim light of the cavern. "I couldn't agree more." Gently, she brushed some hair out of Calandra's eyes, smoothing it behind her ear, then cupped Calandra's cheek. "Look at you. Look at all you've become. I couldn't be more proud of you. You can't know how many times I wondered if I had done the right thing, if your father and I should have taken you with us. You must have so many questions."

A lump lodged in Calandra's throat. All her life, all she'd had was questions, hurt, and resentment for her mother, but especially once she knew Delphine hadn't left because she'd gone Mad, but to raise Zale far away from Sirenia. Calandra hadn't known if she could ever forgive her. But, like Zale said, she and her mother were a lot alike. Looking at her mother now, she knew exactly why Delphine had done what she'd done. She might have even done the same in her mother's position.

"It's water under the bridge." Calandra forced a smile. "You're alive, you're sane, and we're together again at last. That's enough for now."

Delphine smiled, questions behind her eyes. Then Damaris gave a loud exclamation behind her. They turned in time to see Damaris shove Zale playfully and walk away, her grin betraying her affection as they bantered back and forth. As Damaris joined the healed undine women, Zale turned to help heal the wounded erelim.

"He's a lot like your father, you know," Delphine said. "That same playful spirit. That same selfless generosity. Kenver always knew how to make me laugh."

"I can see why you fell in love with him then." Calandra thought of Osaze, how his eyes crinkled so much when he laughed that she couldn't even see their beautiful black depths. And his laugh—it reverberated like a drum, right from his belly, and always made her feel safe. Safe and loved.

Her sinuses pricked, and she blinked to hold back tears. She'd have to wait to cry later. Rumiel wasn't the only one with consequences to deal with.

"Can you do me a favour?" She fished the quaternaria out of her pouch and held it out. "Can you tell Osaze I'm sorry I won't be there to talk things through? Ask him to forgive me—not for me, but for him. I'd hate to see his bitterness fester and turn him into a monster like Narcissa became. Or like Semyaza. He deserves better than that."

Delphine glanced at the proffered pendant, and her brow furrowed.

"Can't you tell him yourself?"

Calandra kept her gaze on the rock beneath their feet, afraid she'd lose control and the tears would erupt before she got through this. "No. Not now. I can't go back to Sirenia. I have to find Semyaza and Tamiel, and then I have to stay here and make sure they never escape again."

"Why would you have to stay here?" Delphine said gently. "The Soulstone already has plenty of guardians."

Calandra shook her head adamantly. "Now that Nadia and the others have been healed, they should be free to return and live their lives. And you'd be a much better queen than I would. Someone has to stay. I let Tamiel and Semyaza escape. I'm the logical choice."

"And you think we'd let you choose our fates for us?" came a woman's sharp voice.

Calandra looked up to see Nadia standing beside Delphine, surrounded by the other guardian undines, giving Calandra a look of challenge.

"You're not the only one who knows her duty, Calandra kor'Delphine." Nadia arched a brow. "I didn't give up my city and my daughter to become a guardian just to let you send me back to a world that is no longer mine. My place is here."

Calandra stared at the woman, her mouth dry. "You . . . you *chose* this? Why?"

Nadia walked over to her with an easy, confident stride—the stride of a woman who knew exactly who she was. She placed her hands on Calandra's shoulders and looked into her eyes. "Semyaza, Tamiel, and I go way back. I know them better than you do—and I won't rest until they're back where they belong, as snug as water bugs. Your people need you, Calandra. Go home."

A weight lifted off Calandra's shoulders, and she straightened, strengthened by the steel in Nadia's eyes. "If you're certain."

Nadia's dark green eyes grew soft. "Absolutely. This is *your* time, Calandra. You must do the task that's been allotted to you. And we must finally do ours."

She dropped her hands and stepped back. Calandra glanced at her mother, who had her arms crossed over her chest.

"And don't you dare try to shirk your duty again, young lady," Delphine chided. "I know Thea taught you better than that. What kind of Opal Princess tries to pass her duty off on her mother?"

Calandra gaped. "I . . . I don't . . ." She straightened, her cheeks aflame. Had she learned nothing from Narcissa's tongue-lashing in the Soulstone?

"You're right. That was wrong of me. It won't happen again."

Softening, Delphine smiled. "As I told you before, I'm ever at your service, your highness, in whatever task you need me for. Even if what you need is a good talking to." She stepped closer, lowering her voice for Calandra's ears alone. "My sister and I may not have seen eye to eye on much, but from what I've seen today, I know why she named you heir. You will make a wonderful queen, my daughter."

Calandra chuckled shakily. "Thanks, Mother."

She closed her hand over the quaternaria pendant and drew it close to her chest, and her fingers brushed her smooth opal Tear, as well as the hard edges of the amethyst pendant she'd taken from Nadia. Sheepishly, she yanked the chain holding the key from her neck and handed it to the queen, who accepted it with a knowing smile and fastened it around her own neck.

"I have so many questions for you," Calandra said, "about the past, about Atlantis. I wish I had more time."

"Time?" Nadia grinned and gestured behind her at the other guardian undines. "Girl, we've got nothing but time."

The other women giggled.

Nadia chuckled. "Feel free to drop by for a visit and we'll tell you all about it. You know where to find us." She arched a brow. "But not too soon. You've got work to do on the Ground, from what I hear . . . and we've got some dragons to hunt."

Calandra nodded, her heart full. "Thank you."

Nadia stepped back. "I'm surprised you all have forgotten so much. Don't you study history stones anymore?"

"I do. We do. But much was lost when Atlantis was abandoned."

Nadia's gaze sharpened. "Abandoned? Why was it abandoned?"

"I'd hoped you would tell me."

Nadia shook her head. "I never abandoned it. That must have been after my time. Do any of you know why?" she asked over her shoulder.

One woman with black hair and dusky skin stepped forward timidly. She reminded Calandra so much of Tanni that her heart skipped. The woman gave Nadia a crisp salute, her fingers pressed to her forehead.

"Lydia?" Nadia asked.

Calandra swallowed, recognizing the name of the Mad siren who had drowned half of Sirenia's humans over a millennia ago before being sent to the Abyss. After what Calandra had experienced at the mercy of the bonds, she could hardly judge her. What would she have done had the

Pneuma not come and freed her?

"It was after the Sinking," Lydia said softly. "After your daughter banished Alessandro to the Void."

At the mention of her consort, Nadia's eyebrows drew together. She turned back to Calandra and Delphine. "Another mistake made by history. Alessandro wasn't banished. He came with me willingly. We were the first, the ones who were supposed to maintain the Soulstone together. As you've seen, women alone are not enough."

Zale, Damaris, and Airlea came and stood beside them. Shriniel and Chazdiel hovered behind at the head of the now-restored erelim troops, who were working their way into formation once again. Nadia's troubled gaze encompassed them all, then swept back to Calandra and Delphine.

"You need to find the truth. We did what we did to save our people, not destroy them. If that's been forgotten, no wonder all the women who've come to me since then have been Mad. I left some journals behind. Seek them out." Her voice grew distant. "They still won. After all I gave up, they won." Sorrow flowed from her, sharp and bitter.

"So you never sank Atlantis?" Airlea asked.

Nadia glanced up in surprise. "Oh, no, I did that. Carefully and on purpose." She looked at them, her eyes bright with moisture. "You should go. You've got a job to do, and so do we."

Her companions had started retreating to the pool, and she turned to follow.

Shriniel stepped forward, looking at Calandra and her companions. "We can take you to a working portstone." She indicated Chaz and her troops.

"Thank you." Calandra was about to follow, then spun toward Nadia's retreating back. "Your majesty?"

The woman turned expectantly, her long black curls flowing softly around her shoulders, her posture erect, her eyes bright beneath the star and moon emblem on her brow. Despite her ragged clothing, she looked every bit the great queen Calandra had always imagined her to be.

"What happened to Alessandro?" Calandra said. "If he came here with you, where did he go?"

A tear escaped Nadia's restraint and slipped down her russet brown cheek. "I don't know. But if you find him, come tell me, all right?"

Calandra barely had time to nod before Nadia turned and splashed into the Pool of Tears after her companions, transforming into *ichthys* state as she dove beneath the dark surface.

Calandra's heart clenched, trying to imagine what it would have been like if she'd spent all those millennia without Osaze, at the mercy of Tamiel, trapped in her own mind's Mad wanderings. The thought choked her.

She turned to face her mother, brother, and two companions, resolve in her heart. Nadia was right—she had work to do. And she'd never know how her and Osaze's story would end until she faced him. Despite her uncertainty at his response, her heart stuttered, and she drew in a deep breath of anticipation.

"Let's go home."

96

THE FALL

Shouts and jeers from the onlooking crowd of men reverberated around the Great Hall of Margaret House, but Osaze barely heard them over the blood rushing through his ears. He kept his hands raised and his attention on the sweaty sailor across from him. His opponent moved with surprising nimbleness and speed, considering his size, and his eyes sparkled with malice beneath bushy strawberry-blond eyebrows. Osaze took a swing, which the man ducked with a gleeful laugh.

"Is that all ye've got?" Cogger tossed back, his face red with effort.

Cogger's meaty fists bore none of the grace of a man trained in *Tropos Hydor Zon*, but that didn't affect the man's fighting ability as much as Osaze had expected it would—as his bruised ribs could attest. Still, Osaze grinned, blood pumping through his veins. This was exactly what he'd hoped for.

Osaze had barely slept a wink last night, especially after the strange darkness paralysis came and went. Instead, he'd paced the floors of Margaret House, tormented by his guilt and grief. This morning when he'd come upon the guard posted outside one of the sleeping cells and learned about the belligerent sailor with a hatred for Africans within, a savage yearning Osaze couldn't explain had come over him. He'd marched to the dining table where Rhea sat and convinced her to let him try training Cogger, telling her that maybe the man only needed something constructive to do with his time, much like the other men had. Rhea had looked at him askance, but, distracted by a messenger calling her to the commstone tower for a report from the team who'd gone to heal the Heartstone, she had agreed, much to Osaze's satisfaction.

800

It had been less than ten minutes into sparring practice when Osaze's hunch had paid off. Cogger had started giving his partner—a young African man who'd been harvested from the *Atlanta* along with him—a severe beating. And Osaze had easily convinced the sailor to turn his fists on him instead.

Osaze's shin connected with Cogger's side, and the sailor let out a grunt, but barely shifted his footing. A follow-up kick to the kidney had more effect, and Cogger staggered forward.

"Go, Osaze!" shouted a young voice—Alexander, watching from the sidelines, his face alight.

Osaze didn't turn, but every blow he landed energized him. He'd show this arrogant son of a goat where he stood. Spotting his opportunity, he swung his leg toward the man's knees, knocking Cogger to the floor. The big man grunted, then scrambled to his feet.

"Ye think ye can best me, darkie?" he snarled. He spoke English, but Osaze understood him well enough—along with the man's irrational hate-filled intent. But Osaze was feeling a little irrational himself—he was tired of being rational and measured. What good had that done him? What good had it done Calandra?

Why couldn't he have just told her he forgave her?

Cogger swung a fist toward Osaze's face and Osaze stepped to the side, simultaneously grabbing the man's wrist with his near hand and slamming his own palm into the man's upper arm with his off hand, forcing Cogger to his knees. The man grunted but Osaze didn't stop. He grabbed the sailor's head with both hands and threw him to the ground, to the resounding shouts of the watching men. Young Jason and Alexander stood at the front of the crowd, their excitement at a fever pitch. Alexander's high-pitched voice rose above the others.

"C'mon, Osaze, you show him!"

Cogger had lost, and he knew it, looking up at Osaze from the pavement with no attempt to stand.

"Get up," Osaze barked in English.

Cogger looked at him warily.

"I said get up!" Osaze shouted and landed a swift kick in the man's thick abdomen.

Cogger let out his breath in a *whoof* of air, curling around himself. Wheezing, he looked up at Osaze with disdain. "Ye can beat me to death, but that won't change what ye are."

With a roar that sounded like a wounded animal, all the rage Osaze had been holding in since he'd found out Calandra was dead—no, since Zoe had left him on that beach in Barbados—exploded out of him. Abandoning the graceful defensive moves of the *Tropos Hydor Zon*, he unleashed his fury on the hapless sailor, kicking and punching. With every blow, he poured out his fury and powerlessness at the cruel twists of his own fate—for Bayowa and Bussa and Ifeoluwa, whom he'd had to abandon; for the cruelty of Middleton, Eric, and David; and, most of all, for Calandra's death.

I wasn't there.

Punch.

I told her I'd protect her, and I wasn't there.

Kick.

I couldn't have helped her if I'd tried.

Punch.

It took Ewelike and three other men to pull him off the bruised, bleeding man, but his pumping adrenaline had not been spent, and he fought to be released so he could continue the punishment.

"Osaze!"

His mother's single word held more sadness, more disappointment, and more shock than he'd known a word could contain. He stopped struggling, his arms going limp at his sides, finally seeing the damage he'd done—Cogger's lip was already swelling around a bleeding crack, as was his eye, and he lay moaning, curled in on himself. Osaze's knuckles were covered with blood—Cogger's blood. He turned slowly to face his mother, dreading the disappointment on her face. But when he looked up, he crumpled to the pavement.

Urbi stood in front of a small group of people—Xeni, Rhea, Hammad, Judith, Gerrick, Bunmi, and a dark-haired middle-aged undine woman he'd never seen before, among several others—all of them with expressions of shock and horror on their faces—but it wasn't their faces that had floored him. Zale stood with them holding hands with a young undine girl, and next to him, her expression as horrified and confused as the rest, stood—

"C—Calandra?" His eyes blurred with tears. "Are you real? Are you really here?"

Her hair was dishevelled, her swimming skirt torn, and she had several bruises, but she was still the most beautiful woman he'd ever seen.

She gazed at him in open-mouthed shock, then rushed toward Cogger, pressing her fingers under his jaw to check for a pulse. "He's alive."

Xeni gave Osaze a look of consternation as she made her way toward the injured man. Catching sight of her son and Alexander, she shooed them away. "Boys, go help in the kitchens. I'll talk to you later."

"But . . ." Alexander began.

"No buts," said Kynthia, stepping forward from the group of new arrivals with her hands on her hips. "You do as you're told."

"Yes, Mama," Alexander said, his shoulders slumping as he turned to leave. Begrudgingly, Jason followed suit, and they disappeared into the crowd of men.

"Let me," Xeni said quietly to Calandra.

Calandra gave a tight nod, then stood to face Osaze.

Osaze got warily to his feet. "Calandra, I . . ."

She cut him off with a shake of the head. She glanced at Cogger again, then gave Osaze a hard stare.

"Why did you do this?" she asked at last.

Gerrick came to stand at the edge of his line of vision, his hands clasped in front of him. He appeared to want an answer as much as anyone else.

But Osaze didn't have an answer. Not a good one, anyway. If those men hadn't pulled him off of Cogger, he would have kept going until the man was dead, and maybe not stopped even then. How could he have done such a thing? Shame burned hot inside him.

"I'm sorry, Calandra," he said. He turned to Cogger, who glared at him from the floor even while Xeni repaired his wounds. "I'm sorry. I shouldn't have. I lost my temper, is all. I . . ."

Calandra gave him a long, unreadable look. Then, with a sharp shake of her head, she pushed past the crowd of people and ran out the front door of the hall into the outer cavern beyond.

Osaze watched her go, then turned to face the uncomfortable expressions of the men he'd been training. His mother looked up at him with sad, compassionate eyes.

"Osaze . . ." She laid a hand on his arm.

With a jerk, he shrugged off her touch and fled toward the tower steps and the door that would lead him to the top of the falls—opposite the direction Calandra had taken. This time, the self-flagellation was not about failing to keep Calandra alive, but for losing control and letting a part of himself he didn't know existed take over. He wouldn't blame Calandra if she never spoke to him again—not after she'd seen him become the exact monster she'd been raised to fear.

Calandra was alive. But their love was probably dead. And this time, he had no one to blame but himself.

EPILOGUE: LOST AND FOUND

By the time Robert climbed the back steps to his room at the Port House Inn after his flight from Huntley Hall, the sun was high in the sky and the mosquitoes were gathering in swarms in the humid late morning air. He went into the room he'd shared with Berian and locked the door, then he took off his boots and stretched out on the bed. The maid had made up the bed since Osaze had slept here last, and the wool blanket was scratchy against his skin.

He'd stuffed a piece of linen he'd torn from his shirt hem into the wound on his side. He knew he should get it cleaned, but he was just so tired. He hadn't slept in over a day, and the exhaustion, coupled with his shame and sorrow, dragged him into the depths of slumber. Someone knocked at his door, but he ignored them and they eventually left. He sunk deeper into his fevered sleep—a troubled dream filled with hellfire and witches and black-eyed demons dragging him down to hell.

Like a breath of spring, Miss Bethel came to him, a lovely angel of light with feathered golden wings, her soft curls pulled away from her face by a golden hairband.

"I thought you were dead," he said to her, holding her in his arms.

"I can't die," she said. "And it's time you learn to live." She tilted her head up and kissed him.

He woke up, the taste of her soft lips on his, to the drab plaster walls of his room. A tray of food sat on the table—courtesy of Mr. Varley, no doubt. Sighing, he got up, ignoring the stale roll and the bowl of cold soup. He didn't know how long he'd slept, but the soft morning light outside indicated it had been at least a day.

He took off his jacket and waistcoat in preparation to clean his wound, laying them on the bed. As he did, he placed Berian's heartstone bracelet on the desk, then removed the watch Gryffyn had given him from his waistcoat pocket and placed it next to the heartstone. In the upper corner of the desk lay the letter Gryffyn had sent him, the one that had started him on this whole mad quest.

He stared at it. He'd wanted so badly to gain his brother's respect and earn his place among the great men of his country that he'd sacrificed the life of the woman he loved.

Well, not her life exactly. She wasn't dead, but she may as well be. She was as far from him as the dead, and just as inaccessible.

He picked up his watch and opened the ornate golden case. Releasing the clasp on the glass cover, he swung it away from the odd clock, with its slim silver hands that weren't attached to the stone face yet always kept impeccable time. It was almost noon. He rubbed his thumb on the smooth stone next to the upright hands.

An image of Abela flashed into his mind. She looked as she had in his dream—golden-winged, surrounded by light, and wearing a long white robe. She was standing in a place that reminded him of a courtroom, but everything was vibrant and colourful and shone with an unnatural glow. She looked like she was giving testimony about something.

A tear ran down his cheek, and the vision faded. Where had it come from? He frowned at the watch. Once before while touching the watch, he'd had a vision of Gryffyn on a ship on the way here to Barbados. He wondered where his brother actually was. Probably having tea with Amelia and her family again, as Mayor Albright often had business to discuss with his son-in-law. A thought struck him—had Mr. Albright been on the list of men on Middleton's desk? He hadn't had time to look through them all.

The image of his brother sitting at a desk, writing, appeared before Robert's eyes. The small desk sat next to a narrow bunk fixed to the wall—a ship's desk in one of the nicer cabins. Robert watched as though standing behind his brother as Gryffyn stood, stretched, and left his berth. Then he followed as Gryffyn made his way abovedeck and peered at the seas around them.

The seas were covered in sailing ships, flying flags of every nation. Every one of them was outfitted for war, floating on the turquoise waters of the tropics.

Robert dropped the watch and staggered backward as the vision cleared, sitting once more on the bed.

These visions—they felt real. But why would Gryffyn be on a warship in the middle of an armada? Where were the ships going?

He thought of all he'd overheard ever since he'd met Miss Abela Bethel, her mission and purpose and why she'd even come in flesh form.

It had always been about Zale. Zale and the undines of Sirenia. He didn't know why, but there was something vitally important about that island—important enough for Gryffyn and an armada of warships to be on their way there, he was sure of it, though he couldn't explain how he knew.

He wondered if the undines were prepared. Would Berian retrieve Zale from Hades only to land him in the middle of an all-out war? And, since Berian's heartstone was sitting on Robert's desk, would he even be able to return to this plane at all?

Robert looked helplessly at the two items on his desk. Abela had returned to wherever she was from, Berian was in Hades rescuing Zale and Mrs. Teague, and Gryffyn was part of an armada of warships that was mostly likely part of the Order of the Ascension's plans to take over the world. And now they even had Abela's heart, which was apparently so instrumental to their schemes.

He wanted to do something to make up for his many mistakes. But what could he do that wouldn't make it worse? He'd proved over and over again that his natural tendency was to make the wrong choice. *Choose the Light*, Miss Bethel had said. How was he supposed to do that when every choice he made only led to deeper darkness?

Help me, God. I keep trying to do what's right, but it only leads to more wrong. Let Abela's death not be in vain. Show me what to do next.

Under sudden inspiration, his gaze fell on the watch once more. Picking it up, he pressed his finger to the stone and pictured Romero.

An hour later, in a clean set of clothes, his wound bandaged, and after consuming a hot bowl of soup from the Port House Inn's kitchen, he made his way up the steps of a small red plastered-brick building, feeling completely out of place. He'd worn a hat but, standing on the front step and staring out over the stone graves in the cemetery next to the elegant square building, took it off, uncertain what the protocols were for a synagogue. Nervously, he knocked on the dark wooden door.

It swung open to reveal a wizened man with long grizzled hair and a full iron-grey beard, wearing a round black cap that made his ears seem to protrude slightly. His shoulders hunched into a permanent stoop beneath his long robe. He looked at Robert with guarded curiosity.

"Yes? May I help you?"

Robert cleared his throat. "Er, you don't happen to have a gentleman by the name of Eduardo Romero here, do you?"

The man frowned. "No, I don't . . ."

"He's a Spaniard about this tall, ridiculously handsome, has golden eyes?"

At the mention of the golden eyes, the man's eyes brightened. "Oh, you must mean Mr. Castillo. Yes, come in, come in."

Robert followed the man into a breathtakingly beautiful room. Pale plaster walls regularly punctuated by elegant arched windows along the upper galleries and main floor were an elegant backdrop to the glass chandeliers hanging from the ceiling, the calming tile beneath his shoes, and the finely crafted furnishings fashioned from dark mahogany, the likes of which he'd never seen. At one end of the room above a tall wooden cabinet were mounted two rounded plaques inscribed with five lines of Hebrew each. They reminded Robert of nothing more than the stone tablets in a woodcut he'd once seen of Moses with the Ten Commandments. On one of the long benches facing the centre of the room sat a man with his back to Robert, regarding the plaques. Under his top hat, wavy black curls fell to the shoulders of his finely cut navy blue coat.

"Someone to see you, Mr. Castillo," said the old rabbi, then shuffled up the steps of a low platform enclosed with a wooden rail at one end of the small hall. Bending over a book that lay open on the desk, he soon gave the impression of being unaware of his surroundings, muttering softly to himself as he read.

The man on the bench stood and turned, and Robert blinked in surprise. There were subtle differences from the last time Robert had seen Romero—longer hair, more conservative clothing style, and none of the swagger that had been present even when Romero had been sitting—but it was definitely him. Romero didn't say anything, just crossed his arms across his chest and regarded Robert with a steady golden stare.

Robert shifted his weight. "I suppose you know about Miss Bethel . . . ?"

Romero nodded once, his lips firm.

Robert cleared his throat, looking at the floor. "I . . . I know I've had more chances than I deserve. And I know I'm most likely the last person you want to see right now. But I want . . . I want to help. I've made so many mistakes, but I want to do the right thing, finally. I . . ." He met Romero's gaze. "I want to enter the service of Elyon, if he'll have me." He stepped forward and held out his hand palm-up, revealing the heartstone. "Here. I believe Mr. Berian—er, Rumiel, was it?—is going to need this."

Romero took the bracelet and looked it over, then crossed his arms once more. Slowly, his lips spread into a smile.

"It's about time," said Romero. "Your first task is to save Miss Josefine Chapman."

Save Miss Chapman? That would mean facing her father again. And probably Middleton and Hayward.

His throat closed, but then he took a deep breath. After facing a dragon made of fire, mere mortal men seemed much less intimidating. Despite himself, Robert found a small, hopeful smile on his lips.

"Where should I start?"

*

NARCISSA woke up to something poking her in the side. She sat up in the dim light, brushing straw out of her hair and looking around at the dimly lit dungeon cell in which she found herself. Green feldspar encircled her wrists—her captors must not have wanted to take the chance she no longer had any powers. Standing, she went and banged on the door.

"What is the meaning of this?" When she received no answer, she banged again, harder. "Let me out!"

The round brown face of a siren singer appeared through the barred window in the door. What was her name again?

"Good morning, your highness. Comfy?" The woman smirked.

"Carly—no, Calliope. Open this door this instant, or you'll be sorry."

Calliope kor'Renata put her fists on her hips. "No can do. We don't let murderers wander around free in this city."

Fear tightened Narcissa's chest, but she tamped it down. "That . . . that wasn't me, it was Semyaza, remember? You were there. You saw Calandra take him away."

"I was there, and I did." She leaned closer to the bars. "But unless you can explain how the dragon could be fighting with Princess Calandra and Prince Zale in the Mother's Heart and possessing you in the Garden of the Mother's Delight at the same time, you've got a problem."

Narcissa swallowed, trying to work moisture into her dry mouth. "That wasn't me," she said, but her voice lacked conviction. "I'd never hurt anyone. Not like that."

A *tapeinos* named Anthony stepped into her field of vision, but there was something wrong with him. Instead of the blank expression of a *doulos*, his brown face was set in hard lines, and he was looking right at her. Cold sweat erupted on her forehead. He'd been one of her favourite pets when she'd wanted to sate her lust for inflicting pain. And now he was Free and guarding her cell.

"Hello, your highness," he said, his voice like iron. "You were saying?"

She took a trembling step back, leaning against the marble wall and sinking to the floor. If Anthony had been Released, did that mean all her other toys from over the years would also be free to tell the world what she had done to them?

For those crimes alone, she could spend years in this cell. But for murder, the penalty was death.

Anthony gave a derisive snort, then she heard the two guards walk away.

She lay a hand on her belly, thinking of the small life that grew within. She wouldn't let her daughter grow up without a mother, whether because Narcissa were imprisoned or dead.

But who had told everyone that she'd killed her mother and Thea in the first place? Whoever it was, they must pay.

As soon as she could figure out a way to escape. But unless someone were to help her, she knew full well how difficult it would be to break out of this prison. And she knew how likely it was she'd find anyone sympathetic to her plight, especially now that Semyaza had been dragging her name through the muck for weeks. Whether they believed it was him or not, that kind of stench tended to linger.

Her thoughts went in fruitless circles for hours. She'd started to doze when a movement in the corner of her cell startled her awake.

Squatting in the shadows was the unsettling man with the ivory skin and the eyes like shiny dark holes. Squeaking, she scrambled backwards, trying to force herself into the stone.

"Hello, Highness," Dagiel said. "Remember me?"

Her heart hammered against her ribs. Should she call for the guard? What could they do against a man who could disappear before she'd taken a breath?

"Looks like you've got yourself a bit of a problem here." Dagiel gestured with an exaggerated sweep of the cell. "Nice place."

"What do you want?" Her voice didn't sound nearly as firm as she would have liked.

"I think we can help each other. You could use a way out of here, am I right?"

No chains, numbskull. Narcissa bit her tongue to keep her caustic comment contained. She had no doubt this man could help her escape, if he chose. And she had no other real options.

"For what price?"

Dagiel reached into his jacket and pulled out a familiar oval red gemstone on a gold chain. Narcissa froze, staring into its sparkling depths. How did he get that? Wouldn't Calandra have taken it back to the Underworld with her?

"You see, my master used your blood to bind the Heart of Chaos to himself. Unfortunately, he wasn't planning to get trapped in it. Now it seems you're the only one who can release him."

Fear wrapped around Narcissa's chest in taut ropes. "No. Go away."

"Not so hasty." Dagiel stood and came nearer, squatting right in front of her so she could smell his foul breath. "He's willing to make a deal with you."

Despite herself, Narcissa looked up at the man's terrifying eyes. "What kind of deal?"

Dagiel grinned. "The kind you can't refuse."

He leaned closer and she pulled away, opening her mouth to scream. The guards may not be able to fight him, but maybe he'd disappear and she could buy herself some time.

But before she'd made more than a squeak, he slammed his clammy hand over her mouth.

"What are you on about, eh? Don't you want to hear the deal?"

Seeing little other choice, she nodded as best she could while he had her head immobilized.

"Promise to listen quietly?"

She nodded again. He smiled and released her, leaning back on his haunches.

"I won't share my body with him again," she said as firmly as she could manage—which wasn't very.

"You won't need to. Not for long, anyway. The Master says you're too much trouble, and he's made other plans. Besides, you're no longer in a position to be of use to him—other than this."

Narcissa narrowed her eyes. "What kind of plans? I know he needs a body if he wants to stay here. How does he mean to get one?"

Maybe Semyaza finally intended to use the heartstone to create a body of his own, like he'd claimed all along. But the thought of him in his own form with the limitless power the Heart of Chaos would give him made her blood run almost as cold as the idea of letting him possess her again.

Dagiel studied her as though deciding if she planned to scream again, then shrugged. "I suppose there's no harm in telling you. He needs to lie low for a while, so he intends to inhabit a human for the time being, even though he'll have almost no powers while he does. He'll cause you no trouble, he says. All he needs is for you to release him from the heartstone and then he'll use his powers to get you both out of here before he buggers off."

"I trust his word about as much as I'd trust a hungry orca not to chase blood. I need a guarantee that he'll leave me alone as soon as we've gotten to safety."

Dagiel cocked his head in interest. "What kind of guarantee?"

What kind, indeed? She could think of nothing Semyaza or Dagiel could offer her that would cost them anything.

Dagiel laughed softly. "That's what I thought. Be realistic, Highness. You've got very little to lose and everything to gain from taking the deal. Or, I suppose you could wait here and let the council decide your fate . . ."

Narcissa closed her eyes, pressing her fingers to her temples. She knew how likely the council was to be lenient on her. Even assuming they believed Semyaza had been responsible for the terrorism of the past few weeks, there were still her own crimes to account for, and they appeared to have enough evidence to execute her. If Calandra had already seized power, she might believe her. Her cousin had always been a gullible sap, and she'd been playing awfully fast and loose with the law lately.

But even if Calandra did pardon her, did Narcissa really want to spend the rest of her life indebted to her arrogant cousin? Bad enough that Calandra had been the one to free her from Hades and get rid of Semyaza when she could not. But to play Calandra's faithful liege, doing her bidding, for as long as she lived?

The thought ran down her spine like a bucket of cold water. She wanted to live . . . but not that way.

If Semyaza was true to his word—if he wasn't lying about this one thing—then she might have a chance to make a new life. No, she would never be on the throne of Sirenia. But, for the first time, she could live life on her terms, with no impossible expectations to fulfill.

She and her daughter could be free.

"Okay, fine. What do I have to do?"

Dagiel blinked in surprise. "That was easier than I thought. All right, simple, really. Take the stone. The master will guide you from there."

Dagiel held up the chain, and the stone swung in wild circles. Narcissa regarded the gem, shrinking in terror. *This is my best chance.*

"Tell him that I got rid of him once, I can do it again," she said.

Dagiel chuckled. "He can hear you, and I'm sure he's shaking in his shackles."

Narcissa's gaze snapped to Dagiel's dark sockets, noting the tension at the corners of his cocky grin. Semyaza was in chains, and only she could release him. She wondered if she held more power here than Dagiel was letting on.

Hesitantly, she grasped the gold chain. Immediately, Semyaza's familiar voice filled her head.

Wise choice, my beauty. Now all you need to do is hold the stone and accept my control. As Dagiel said, it will be temporary, I assure you.

She looked at the stone, which had been cleansed from the black smears that had previously marred its beauty. The gem practically vibrated with untapped power.

Semyaza had said this heartstone was a conduit to channel spirit, and required only a will to shape it. Narcissa had minimal skill with spirit . . . but she had some. Maybe she would have enough.

After all, there was a spirit with much more power already in the stone. Perhaps she could channel his power.

She wrapped her hand around the stone, but the moment she felt Semyaza try to press his darkness into her mind, she rebelled. Using everything she'd learned while trapped in her own mind, she put up a block.

"No."

Dagiel blinked at her. "No? Master, is that you?"

Smiling, she looked up at him, her fear gone. "You and Semyaza forgot to mention something, Dagey," she said.

She held out her free hand with the palm up, and a ball of fire—actual flames, not the illusions Semyaza had used for so long—flared to life above it. She stood, and Dagiel backed away, the white-hot light reflecting in his dark orbs.

"Now that I hold the heartstone, I hold the power," she said. "And I don't need Semyaza's permission to use it."

The trapped voice in her mind screamed obscenities. Without warning, Dagiel lunged at the chain, but she stopped him by jamming her fiery hand into his nose. Howling with pain and rage and holding his face, he skittered away. She prepared another fiery globe, daring Dagiel to attack again with her eyes. Glaring daggers at her, he disappeared.

Grinning, she released the flames and slipped the heartstone necklace over her head, pulling her dishevelled hair free. Semyaza's voice grew louder and more persistent, and she turned her thoughts inward.

"That's enough."

She hemmed him into a dark cell inside the stone. His voice quieted like a door had been closed. Shaking out her shoulders, she turned to her own cell door, new purpose in her voice as she called her guards.

It was time to take control of her life. And now, no one would be able to stop her.

*

Two weeks later

GIOVANNI Chapman swung in a hammock on the lower deck of the *Lady Anne* and turned another page in the journal. He wasn't shirking his duties, exactly, but he'd discovered he could often steal at least a half hour at a time to himself before some exasperated seaman kicked him out of the hammock—sometimes quite literally. The bruises on his hindquarters were worth the momentary freedom from scrubbing decks or whatever other menial task he'd been assigned that day to help pay for passage.

Today, however, he had no need to fear such repercussions. Two weeks ago, the captain had declared they were nearly at their destination, and, travelling under full sail, they would arrive the following morning. But then they'd hit the interminable fog and their boat had come to a complete standstill. The captain had had them break out the oars, but when that proved fruitless, Mr. Cox, the owner, had called a cease and desist while he consulted with his comrades on the other vessels. As the days had turned into weeks with little to do, the sailors took breaks more frequently than usual—his wasn't the only swinging hammock today.

Reaching the page he'd been looking for, Gio paused, studying the sketch depicting a bracelet made to look like a snake swallowing its own tail. He'd seen the actual bracelet once, on the arm of the *shuvani* Marin Stanley. Recognizing it as the same one from the journal, he'd dared to ask about it, but she'd handed him a tongue-lashing with a side of ear-twisting in reply. Later, he'd asked his younger sister Sylvie to press her mentor for answers, and she'd been equally scornful. He could have made her, he supposed.

Who was he kidding? No one had been able to *make* Sylvie do any-thing since she was four years old. At thirteen, she'd had plenty of time to hone her stubbornness to perfection.

If only he could read more than the few letters Zale had taught him, the words on the page around the sketch might satisfy his curiosity. Since he couldn't, he studied every detail of the image itself for the hundredth time. It was quite a detailed sketch, right down to the shine and gloss of the black jet of the wristband. But what intrigued him most were the beams of light that shone from the bejewelled eyes. What kind of stone could shine like that?

At shouts and the sound of sudden activity above, he tucked the journal safely into his satchel and hopped out of the hammock. After stashing the satchel in his cubbyhole, he skittered up the ladder, swerving around sailors to stand next to his sister at the rail. Beside Sylvie, Marin stood peering into the fog bank, the skin around her eyes so wrinkled they barely looked open, her tiny frame swathed in a thick wool shawl against the damp. She glanced at him, then went back to scanning the fog as though she expected the ship to break through it any moment.

Sylvie brushed a lock of her thick black hair from her eyes and squinted at him while she tucked it beneath her headscarf. "Where've you been?"

He shrugged. "Nowhere. What's happening?"

She turned and leaned against the rail facing the deck, watching the sailors trim sails and scramble over the rigging. Up on the quarterdeck, Mr. Gryffyn Cox stood with his arms crossed next to the helm, his gaze fixed on the fog ahead of them with purpose on his handsome face.

"We're moving," Sylvie said. "I don't know why. Maybe someone found a way to get past the barrier."

"Yes," said Marin absently, as though she were talking more to herself than them, "it won't be long now."

Gio peered over the side of the ship. Sure enough, what water could be seen before being lost in the thick fog streamed against the hull.

Excitement boiled in his belly. *Finally!* He patted the pocket of his breeches and felt the small, hard lump of stone concealed there, a gift Zale had given him long ago. Grinning, he gripped the rail and whooped.

"We're coming for you, Zale!" he shouted into the grey morass beyond.

But among the shouts of sailors from the hundreds of ships dotting the waters about them, his voice was completely lost.

Thank you for reading *The Sphinx's Heart* (Rise of the Grigori Book 2). If you'd like to be notified about when the next book will be released, I invite you to join my newsletter community. You'll also get a free downloadable, printable colour map of Sirenia. New subscribers will also get Zale's origin story, *The Waterboy*, as a free eBook novella as a welcome gift.

Join my newsletter and download the map at www.talenawinters.com/shfreebie.

DEAR READER,

I am beyond thrilled you've continued on this adventure with me.

Writing this book did not go *at all* like I expected. But that can be said for most things that spanned the March 2020 barrier in history, am I right? While my characters were literally going through hell, the world was, too, and I sometimes struggled to remember that the exhaustion and grief I was feeling couldn't be *all* my characters experienced.

But here's the beauty of a transitional chthonic experience—when you've been baptized with death, you can no longer remain the same. Going forward, Calandra and Zale will be forever changed. And so will we who have joined them on this journey.

So, dear reader, until we reunite during the next volume of their story, hang onto hope, joy, and the people you care about. For in the end, love is all that matters.

Can you do me a favour? If you read a free or pirated copy of this book and you enjoyed it, please consider purchasing a copy or, at the least, leaving a review. As an independent author, I pour vast amounts of time, love, and money into producing a quality product meant to bless and inspire my readers. The income I receive from this work allows me to help feed my family and produce even more work for you to enjoy. Thank you for being an important part of the free market for published works.

Word-of-mouth is an indie author's bread and butter, so please remember to review this book on the selling platform of your choice. (Just a single sentence makes a difference!)

Do you want to extend the story experience? There are bonuses meant to accompany *The Sphinx's Heart* on my website, including a curated soundtrack playlist inspired by the story. Check it out at www.talenawinters. com/sphinxs-heart.

I love hearing from my readers! Drop me a note at www.talenawinters.com/contact. Also, find me on Instagram, Facebook, or Twitter. I'd love to get to know you!

Until next time,

Talena Winters

GLOSSARY

Abyss: a place of eternal confinement for undines and lumasi where their powers are negated.

Adonia kor'Helena: (uh-DOE-nee-uh) queen of Sirenia; Calandra's guardian.

Aikaterini: (eh-kat-uh-REE-nee) the first undine woman.

Airlea kor'Phile: (AIR-lee kor FEE-lee) a siren singer from Tanni's pod who joined the cause of the Free Will Society.

Amaltheia kor'Herafili: (uh-muhl-THEY-uh kor HEER-uh-FEEL-ee) the Stone Healer House head at the Royal Academy.

anthropos: human man or woman.

Archon: (ARK-un) a leader, either of a community or an elected councillor that represents a community in the Royal Council of Archons.

Archpiper: (ARK-pie-pur) the third rank of siren officer. Usually oversees a city or several country precincts.

Atargatis: (ah-ter-GAY-tis) the goddess worshipped by the Sirenians; the first mermaid.

Atargasian: (ah-ter-GAY-zhen) an undine of the same race and form as Atargatis; undines that worship Atargatis as the First Mother.

Atlantis: an island in the Atlantic ocean destroyed by Nadia, queen of the Atargasian undines, when the Madness took her three thousand years ago; sister island to Sirenia.

Berian, Jowan: (BEH-ree-in, JOW-in) lumasi undercover as a Methodist minister. True name is Rumiel.

Bethel, Abela: (uh-BAY-luh) lumasi woman guarding Zale. True name is Guriel of Bethiyel.

Bezaziel: an unimprisoned Grigori working with Tamiel.

bondmistress: a woman who holds the *sklavia* (Redemption) bond of at least one man. See also *KYRIA; MISTRESS OF BONDS.*

Bryce kor'Dreama: Polyxo kor'Theano's lady-in-waiting.

Cain, Miguel: a former *doulos* and Adonia's lover at the time of her death.

Calandra kor'Delphine: (cuh-LAN-druh kor del-FEEN) a panacea and the niece of Adonia, the late queen of Sirenia.

Calliope kor'Renata: (cuh-LIE-uh-pee kor ren-AH-tah) a siren singer of the Opal Palace Guard.

chalkydri: (khal-KID-rie) a water-borne flying dragon spirit race. Singular **chalkydra.**

chariot: a lumasi gyroscope device used for teleportation.

Charis: stone healer apprentice at the Royal Academy; member of the Student FWS.

Chazdiel: a guardian seraph; Gatekeeper of the Fifth Legion.

cherubim: (chair-uh-BEEM) see *LUMASI.* Singular **cherub.**

Cleo kor'Olympias: the *despoina* (Mistress of Sirens) of the Sirenian military; second in authority only to the queen and the Royal Council of Archons.

Cogger, Jaydee: a sailor from the *Atlanta.*

Cox, Amelia: Gryffyn Cox's wife; daughter of Mr. Albright, Mayor of Bristol, England.

Cox, Gryffyn: second son of James, Lord Alverton I. Part of the Order of the Ascension of the Grigori.

Cox, Robert: third son of James, Lord Alverton I. Childhood playmate of Zale Teague.

Crow: former first mate of the *Atlanta.*

Dagiel: a demon loyal to Semyaza.

Damaris kor'Dione: undine siren cadet that befriends Zale. Sister of Zoe and Eudora.

Damon: name of the Grigori dragon spirit who appeared to Calandra in her dreams. See *SEMYAZA.*

Danai kor'Panora: (duh-NIGH kor puh-NOR-uh) a siren rhapsodist in Tanni's pod.

daskala: (DAH-skuh-luh) teacher. Masculine *daskalos.*

datastone: a crystal used to store information, usually shaped like a teardrop and called a Tear. Sometimes called a memory stone. See *TEAR.*

David: slave foreman at Huntley Hall; son of Ifeoluwa and Lord Middleton.

deiktis: (DEEK-teez) the staff weapon used by siren soldiers. Plural *deiktes* (DEEK-tez).

Delphine kor'Helena: (del-FEEN kor hee-LEHN-uh) Calandra and

Zale's mother; Adonia's sister; fled Sirenia when Calandra was only one year old.

despoina: (DEZ-pee-nah) head of the military; answers only to the queen and Royal Council of Archons; highest rank of siren.

Dione kor'Eirene: (dee-OH-nee kor eye-REE-ne) noblewoman; mother of Zoe, Eudora, Damaris, Sabina, and Lily. Matriarch of Steadfast House. City Councillor/Archon for Sireniapolis.

doulos: (DOO-lohs) a man who has been Redeemed with the *sklavia* bond. Plural **douloi** (DOO-loy).

EK: the undine calendar, short for "étos *kataclysmos*," or "years since the deluge."

Elpida: (AYL-pee-duh) The name of Calandra's family property.

Elyon: (el-YON) the Creator.

Erel: see *ROMERO, EDUARDO*.

erelim: (air-uh-LEEM) air-born guardians. Singular **erel**.

Eric Chapman: Romani man who took Zale in as a child.

Eudora kor'Dione: (yoo-DOR-uh kor dee-OH-nee) second daughter of Dione kor'Eirene and matron of Steadfast House; sister of Zoe and Damaris.

Evadne: (ee-VAHD-nee) head of the Physic House of the Royal Academy and the royal physician.

Ewelike: (eh-way-LEE-kay) Eudora's consort.

Ezekiel bet'Ignatia: Ignatia's son. Goes by Zeke.

Fedra: household guard at Steadfast House.

Free Will Society (FWS): name of the rebel society created to honour Delphine kor'Helena's legacy.

gallu: a gargoyle-like class of Underworld demon. Singular **galla**.

Geronimi: sixth-year physic apprentice at the Academy. Part of the Student FWS.

Gerrick: Thea's consort. Freeman for nearly their entire marriage.

Giovanni (Gio) Chapman: Zale's best friend among the Roma. Eric's nephew.

Grigori: the Watchers; erelim who rebelled against Elyon long ago, most of whom were imprisoned for their crimes.

Guriel: see *BETHEL, ABELA*.

Haven: the small city on the northeast tip of Sirenia that houses the trade academy; centre of arts and trades.

Hayward, Colonel Fitzwilliam: a colonel in the British navy who is a friend of Middleton's.

healer: an undine capable of working with one or more elements to repair stones, plants, and/or animals.

Heartstone: the quartz-encased fire opal that powers the barrier protecting Sirenia.

Hebe kor'Adonia: (HEE-bee) Adonia's younger daughter; Narcissa's younger sister.

Holy Triquetra: a triquetra with a circle joining the three pisces shapes in an outer ring. Usually depicted with a single point on the top and two other points as the "feet". The undines use the symbol to represent Atargatis, the elements, their two states, the three spheres (land, sea, sky), and more.

Hypatia kor'Fotini: (high-PAY-shee-uh kor foh-TEE-nee) Royal Council member for Trinity, a small fishing and mining community on Sirenia's northwest side.

ichthys **state:** (IK-thiss) the undine form that has a scaled, fish-like tail and gills.

Ifeoluwa: (ih-FAY-oh-LOO-wa) an enslaved woman at Huntley Hall; mother of David and Olubunmi.

Ignatia kor'Eudoxia: (ig-NAY-shee-uh kor yoo-DOCKS-ee-uh) Rhea's sister. Resident of Elpida.

Iris kor'Lucilla: Royal Council member for Fire Lake.

Jacob: Ignatia's husband.

Josefine Chapman: Eric's adult daughter and right-hand woman.

Judith kor'Ignatia: a rebel of the Free Will Society who briefly worked as Calandra's lady's maid. Her parents are Ignatia and Jacob, and her brother is Ezekiel: (Zeke).

Kassiel Ophiuchus: (off-ee-UH-kus) a griffin cherub with a reputation as a dragon slayer; guardian of the Forest of Forgetfulness.

kedoshim: (kee-doh-SHEEM) the servants of Elyon. Singular **kedosh**.

Kelaino kor'Clymene: (keh-LEN-oh kor KLIH-mih-nee) a servant girl in the house of Dione; discordant.

Kenver Teague: Zale's and Calandra's father; Delphine kor'Helena's consort/husband.

Kofi: (KHOH-fee) an enslaved sailor on the *Atlanta* who later becomes a Freeman with the FWS. Also known as Ebenezer Smith.

kyrios: (KEE-ree-ohs) master.

kyria: (KEE-ree-uh) 1. mistress; 2. woman who owns or traffics human men. 3. a correct form of address from a *doulos* to his mistress. See also *BONDMISTRESS; MISTRESS OF BONDS.*

Kynthia kor Amphitrite: (KIN-thee-uh kor AM-fih-TRY-tee) a woman of the FWS.

Lamia: princess of the shedim; a shapeshifting djinn.

Larissa kor'Damiani: Councillor/archon for Sirenia; matriarch of Summerside Court.

Letitia: the Opal Palace steward; a human.

Lida: head of the Siren House of the Royal Academy; in charge of student discipline.

lumasi: (loo-MAH-see) a race of spirits that can take the form of humans or winged animals; guardians of people and holy places. Also known as cherubim. Singular **lamassu, lamma**.

lyrista: (lee-REE-stuh) the fourth rank of siren officer. In charge of a county. There are three lyristas on Sirenia.

Madness: the insanity that eventually infects all powerful healers and sirens who misuse the *sklavia* bonds.

malakim: (mah-luh-KEEM) messenger-class spirits. Singular **malak**.

Mari kor'Ana: (MAA-ree kor-AAN-uh) siren cadet; Narcissa's friend and lover.

Matthew bet'Elizabeth: a man from Elpida whom Calandra healed from deafness right before Adonia killed his mother.

Megara kor'Sibylle: stone healer acolyte; Thea's great-niece.

Melany: novice at the Royal Academy.

Meredith, Captain William: captain of the ship *Atlanta*.

Middleton, Lord John: an English baron with landholdings in Barbados named Huntley Hall.

Mistress of Bonds: 1. a woman in charge of holding the Redemption Bonds of unmarried men in a given community or organization. 2. A woman who deals in trafficking human men. See also *BONDMISTRESS; KYRIA*.

mindover: a lumasi medical device.

Nadia kor'Hera: (NAH-dee-uh kor HEE-ruh) a queen of the Atargasians that ruled three thousand years ago; an extremely powerful healer, the first panacea to go insane, which resulted in the sinking of Atlantis.

Narcissa kor'Adonia: (nar-SISS-uh) princess of Sirenia; Adonia's oldest daughter.

Néa Selini: new moon. Marks the first day of the month.

Nicandra kor'Nyx: (nick-AN-druh kor NIX) salvager and submersible skipper in the FWS; Penelope's sister. Goes by Nick.

Olubunmi: (oh-LOO-boon-mee) an enslaved girl raised at Huntley Hall;

daughter of Ifeoluwa. Goes by Bunmi.

Opal Palace: home of the government and royal family of Sirenia; also houses the Royal Academy. Located in Sireniapolis.

Osaze: (ow-SAA-zeh) Yoruba man raised in the Opal Palace; Urbi's son.

panacea: (PAH-nuh-SEE-uh) a healer in all three disciplines of stone healing, plant healing, and physic.

panselinos: (pan-SAY-lee-nohs) full moon.

Panselinos: (pan-SAY-lee-nohs) the monthly festival celebrating the full moon.

Paradise Valley: the large, south-facing valley on Sirenia that is the location of Sireniapolis, the island's capital.

Penelope kor'Nyx: (Pen-EL-uh-pee kor NIX) a woman of the FWS; Nicandra's sister. Goes by Nelly.

physic: an undine healer able to repair animal tissue.

piper: the second rank of siren officer. Usually in charge of a division of a city or one precinct. In villages, this may be the highest local military authority or law enforcer.

pisti **bond:** (PEE-stee) the loyalty bond; does not fade over time; creates an empathic connection between the parties involved.

plant healer: an undine healer able to repair and assist plant growth.

podia **state:** (POH-dee-uh) the undine form with human legs.

Polyxo kor'Theano: (puh-LIX-oh kor thee-AH-no) a noblewoman's daughter from Haven; volunteers for the FWS.

quaternaria: (kwat-ur-NAHR-ee-uh) the symbol formed at the centre of four overlapping circles: four conjoined pisces, or *ichthys* fish, joined by a fifth circle woven between the other lines.

rhapsodist: the lowest rank of siren officer; usually oversees a group of twelve singers.

Rhea kor'Eudoxia: (REE-uh kor yoo-DOCKS-ee-uh) the steward of Calandra's family property, Elpida.

Romero, Eduardo: an undercover lumasi malak who appears as a roguish Spaniard. True name: Erel.

Royal Academy: the school for undines that show talent with Song and the elements. *Tsirakis* enter at age six and specialize to novice or cadet at age 12, and usually graduate as a siren or a healer at age 17 or 18; located in the Opal Palace in Sireniapolis.

Royal Council of Archons: the civil council that serves as advisers to the queen, elected from among the people.

Rumiel: see *BERIAN, JOWAN*.

Semyaza: true name of Damon, the dragon spirit who oppressed Calandra; one of the Grigori.

seraphim: (sair-uh-FEEM) a race of fiery spirit dragons. Singular **seraph**.

Shinara: High Priestess of Atargatis; serves in the temple in Sireniapolis.

Shriniel: Captain of the Fourth Chthonic Guard of the erelim.

singer: the lowest rank of undine soldier.

siren: an undine soldier; the general name of the Sirenian military members; must be strong in the spirit element, but often have little ability with the other elements.

Sirenia: an island somewhere in the Bermuda Triangle; home of the Atargasian undines.

Sireniapolis: the capital city of Sirenia.

sirensong: the type of undine Song used to stun men to subdue them. The effect wears off as soon as the Song stops being sung.

***sklavia* bond:** the slave-bond known as *Redemption* which undine females are able to impose on any male.

Stamatia kor'Zylina: (stah-MAY-shya kor zy-LEE-nuh) a siren rhapsodist and *daskala* at the Royal Academy.

Stella kor'Panorea: granddaughter of Iris kor'Lucilla, archon of Fire Lake, and member of the FWS council.

stone healer: an undine healer able to repair and write datastones and crystals.

***syzagos* bond:** the consort bond.

Tafrara Baya: a human of the Amazigh whose family has been on Sirenia for hundreds of years.

Talia: fifth-year siren cadet; part of the student FWS.

Tamiel: one of the Grigori who participated in the Rebellion with Semyaza.

Tanni kor'Zelia: (TAH-nee kor ZEEL-yuh) a siren rhapsodist and Calandra's best friend growing up.

tapeinos*:** (tah-pay-NOS) the lowest rank of law enforcement, used for humans trained as guards. Plural ***tapeinoi. Slang term ***tap*** or ***taps***.

Tear: can be used to refer to any number of different types of stones and crystals used for storing data or communicating; shaped like a teardrop; often made from opal, aquamarine, or beryl. See *DATASTONE*.

The Grotto: the nickname for the Garden of the Mother's Delight, the garden housing the statue of Atargatis in the public-access portion of the Opal Palace.

The Mother's Heart: the chamber of the Royal Palace housing the Heartstone.

Thea kor'Aglaia: (THEE-uh kor uh-GLIGH-uh) head of the Healing House of the Royal Academy and also the Academy's headmistress until she was killed; Calandra's mentor and foster mother. Consort: Gerrick.

Tropos Hydor Zon: (TROH-pos HEE-dor TZOHN) the Way of Living Water, the name of the martial art practised by the undines.

tsiraki: (tsee-RAH-kee) student.

Trinity: a fishing and mining town on the northwest side of Sirenia.

triquetra: (trigh-KET-ruh) the symbol formed at the centre of three overlapping circles. The shape, if drawn with a single line, looks like three conjoined pisces, or *ichthys* fish. See also *HOLY TRIQUETRA*.

undine: (UN-deen or un-DEEN) an elemental water being, of which there are several races, such as Atargasians (merfolk), tritons, nixies, naiads, silkies, and more.

Urbi: (UR-bee) Yoruba governess at the Royal Palace of Sirenia; Osaze's mother.

Valac: a child-like chthonic entity.

Varley, Felix: innkeeper at the Port House Inn in Bridgetown, Barbados. Father of Mildred.

Wilhelmina: the human housekeeper of Steadfast House.

Xeni kor'Rhea: Rhea's adult daughter; a physic who lives at Elpida.

Zale Teague/Zale bet'Delphine: an undine raised in England; Calandra's brother.

Zoe kor'Dione: (ZOH-ee kor dee-OH-nee) a siren singer working with the FWS; sister of Eudora and Damaris.

ACKNOWLEDGEMENTS

My eternal gratitude to my Lord and Saviour Jesus Christ, who wrote my redemption story.

To my husband, Jason, and sons, Jude, Noah, and Jabin, who endured me talking about my characters as though they were real people and provided constant encouragement and inspiration to keep going, even when it was hard. Jason, thank you for helping me get my characters through some particularly tricky plot points. You're my best brainstorming partner. More than that, I couldn't ask for a better life partner. Thank you for believing that my words are worth putting into the world and for enabling me to do so.

To my mother, Laurel Easton, whose belief and encouragement in me and my writing has never flagged. You inspire me each and every day. Thank you for all you are.

To Tormaigh and Jenelle Van Slyke, owners and editors of *Move Up* magazine, who poured into me and my writing and gave me the opportunity to develop the confidence I needed to do this for a living. Thank you for the opportunity to work with you for four and a half years. You are both amazing.

To those who supported me on Patreon, especially Richard Lawry, Laurel Easton, and Stephanie Atkins, thank you.

Thank you to my fans, whose notes of encouragement often came at just the right time when I needed a little pick-me-up. Thank you for the reminders of why I do this.

And, of course, thank you to the amazing team that worked on this book—Denise Willson for your insightful and thoughtful analysis of my story, Ellen Forget for helping me polish it to a shine, Viveca Shearin for letting me know what I didn't know, and Patrick Knowles for another gorgeous cover. And to anyone who answered a tweet or a direct message that began, "This might sound like a weird question, but . . ."—you're the best.

Thank you to the amazing community of indie authors and mentors who provide so much inspiration and encouragement every day. You all rock. I would like to make special mention of Jessica Renwick, Jennifer E. Lindsay, Brenna Davies, Joshua Pantalleresco, Melissa Keaster, Mark Leslie Lefebvre, Becca Syme, and Angela Ackerman. Your encouragement, friendship, mentorship, and help has been so treasured.

Lastly, thank you, dear reader. I may have already mentioned you, but whether I have or not, to quote one of my recent favourite movies, *Late Night*, "I dearly hope I have earned the privilege of your time." If this work has brought you joy or blessed your life in any way, it has been worth mine.

ALSO BY TALENA WINTERS

Rise of the Grigori Series:
The Waterboy (prequel)
The Undine's Tear (Book 1)

Romantic Suspense:
Finding Heaven

Inspirational Romance:
The Friday Night Date Dress

Short fiction:
Cryptozoological thriller - *Up in Smoke*
Feel-good drama - *All I Want for Christmas*

TALENA WINTERS IS ADDICTED TO stories, tea, chocolate, yarn, and silver linings. She writes page-turning fiction for teens and adults in multiple genres, coaches other writers, has written several award-winning songs, and designs knitting patterns under her label *My Secret Wish*. Master of the ironic GIF response. She currently resides on an acreage in the Peace Country of northern Alberta, Canada, with her husband, three surviving boys, two dogs, and an assortment of farm cats. She would love to be a mermaid when she grows up.

You can find her on the web at www.talenawinters.com.